last man standing

David Baldacci is the fifteen-time *New York Times* bestselling author of *Absolute Power, Total Control, The Winner, The Simple Truth, Saving Faith, Wish You Well, The Christmas Train, Split Second, Hour Game, The Camel Club, The Collectors, Simple Genius, Stone Cold* and *The Whole Truth*. His latest novel, *Divine Justice,* was published in 2008. He lives in his native state of Virginia.

For more information visit his official website at www.david-baldacci.com

DAVID BALDACCI

last man standing

PAN BOOKS

First published 2001 by Warner Books, USA

First published in Great Britain 2002 by Simon & Schuster UK Ltd

This edition published 2003 by Pan Books
an imprint of Pan Macmillan Ltd
Pan Macmillan, 20 New Wharf Road, London N1 9RR
Basingstoke and Oxford
Associated companies throughout the world
www.panmacmillan.com

ISBN 978-0-330-41970-3

A CIP catalogue record for this book is available from
the British Library.

Printed and bound in the UK by
CPI Mackays, Chatham ME5 8TD

Visit **www.panmacmillan.com** to read more about all our books and to buy
them. You will also find features, author interviews and news of any author
events, and you can sign up for e-newsletters so that you're always first to hear
about our new releases.

"A wrongly accused man is always vilified
by the ignorant masses.
Such a man should fire at will,
he is bound to hit something."
—Anonymous

_____

"Speed, surprise and violence of action."
—Hostage Rescue motto

last man standing

1

Web London held a semiautomatic SR75 rifle custom built for him by a legendary gunsmith. The SR didn't stop at merely wounding flesh and bone; it disintegrated them. Web would never leave home without this high chieftain of muscle guns, for he was a man steeped in violence. He was always prepared to kill, to do so efficiently and without error. Lord, if he ever took a life by mistake he might as well have eaten the bullet himself, for all the misery it would cause him. Web just had that complex way of earning his daily bread. He couldn't say he loved his job, but he did excel at it.

Despite having a gun welded to his hand virtually every waking moment of his life, Web was not one to coddle his weapons. While he never called a pistol his friend or gave it a slick name, weapons were still an important part of Web's life, though like wild animals guns were not things easily tamed. Even trained lawmen missed their targets and everything else eight out of ten times. To Web, not only was that unacceptable, it was also suicidal. He had many peculiar qualities, but a death wish was not one of them. Web had plenty of people looking to kill him as it was, and once they had nearly gotten their man.

About five years prior he had come within a liter or two of spilled blood of checking out on the floor of a school gymnasium strewn with other men already dead or dying. After he had triumphed over his wounds and stunned the doctors tending him, Web started carrying the SR instead of the submachine gun his comrades-in-arms toted. It resembled an M16, chambered a big .308 bullet, and was an excellent choice if intimidation was your goal. The SR made everyone want to be your friend.

Through the smoked-out window of the Suburban, Web eyed each fluid knot of people along the corners and suspicious clumps of humanity lurking in darkened alleys. As they moved farther into hostile territory, Web's gaze returned to the street, where he knew every vehicle could be a gun cruiser in disguise. He was looking for any drifting eye, nod of head or fingers slyly tapping on cell phones in an attempt to do serious harm to old Web.

The Suburban turned the corner and stopped. Web glanced at the six other men huddled with him. He knew they were contemplating the same things he was: Get out fast and clean, move to cover positions, maintain fields of fire. Fear did not really enter into the equation; nerves, however, were another matter. High-octane adrenaline was not his friend; in fact, it could very easily get him killed.

Web took a deep, calming breath. He needed his pulse rate to be between sixty and seventy. At eighty-five beats your gun would tremble against your torso; at ninety ticks you couldn't work the trigger, as blood occlusion in veins and constricted nerves in shoulders and arms combined to guarantee that you would fail to perform at an acceptable level. At over one hundred pops a minute you lost your fine motor skills entirely and wouldn't be able to hit an elephant with a damn cannon at three feet; you might as well slap a sign on your forehead that read KILL ME QUICK, because that undoubtedly would be your fate.

Web pushed out the juice, drew in the peace and for him there was calm to be distilled from brewing chaos.

The Suburban started moving, turned one more corner and stopped. For the last time, Web knew. Radio squelch was broken when Teddy Riner spoke into his bone microphone or "mic." Riner said, "Charlie to TOC, request compromise authority and permission to move to yellow."

Through Web's mic he heard TOC's, or Tactical Operations Center's, terse response, "Copy, Charlie One, stand by." In Web's Crayola world, "yellow" was the last position of concealment and cover. Green was the crisis site, the moment of truth: the breach. Navigating the hallowed piece of earth that stretched between the relative safety and comfort of yellow and the moment of truth green could be quite eventful. "Compromise authority"—Web said the words to himself. It was just a way of asking for the okay to gun down people if necessary and making it sound like you were merely getting permission from your boss to cut a few bucks off the price of a used car. Radio squelch was broken again as TOC said, "TOC to all units: You have compromise authority and permission to move to yellow."

Thank you so very much, TOC. Web edged closer to the cargo doors of the Suburban. He was point and Roger McCallam had the rear. Tim Davies was the breecher and Riner was the team leader. Big Cal Plummer and the other two assaulters, Lou Patterson and Danny Garcia, stood ready with MP-5 machine guns and flash bangs and .45-caliber pistols, and their calm demeanors. As soon as the doors opened, they would fan out into a rolling mass looking for threats from all directions. They would move toes first, then heels, knees bent to absorb recoil in case they had to fire. Web's face mask shrunk his field of vision to a modest viewing area: his miniature Broadway for the coming real-life mayhem, no expensive ticket or fancy suit required. Hand signals would suffice from now on. When bullets were flying at you, you tended to get a bit of cotton mouth anyway. Web never talked much at work.

He watched as Danny Garcia crossed himself, just like he did every time. And Web said what he always said when Garcia crossed himself before the Chevy doors popped open. "God's too smart to come 'round here, Danny boy. We're on our own." Web always said this in a jesting way, but he was not joking.

Five seconds later the cargo doors burst open and the team piled out too far away from ground zero. Normally they liked to drive right up to their final destination and go knock-knock-boom with their two-by-four explosive, yet the logistics here were a little tricky. Abandoned cars, tossed refrigerators and other bulky objects conveniently blocked the road to the target.

Radio squelch broke again as snipers from X-Ray Team called in. There were men in the alley up ahead, X-Ray reported, but not part of the group Web was hunting. At least the snipers didn't think so.

As one, Web and his Charlie Team rose and hurtled down the alley. The seven members of their Hotel Team counterparts had been dropped off by another Suburban on the far side of the block to attack the target from the left rear side. The grand plan had Charlie and Hotel meeting somewhere in the middle of this combat zone masquerading as a neighborhood.

Web and company were heading east now, an approaching storm right on their butts. Lightning, thunder, wind and horizontal rain tended to screw up ground communications, tactical positioning and men's nerves, usually at the critical time when all of them needed to operate perfectly. With all their technological wizardry, the only available response to Mother Nature's temper and the poor ground logistics was simply to run faster. They chugged down the alley, a narrow strip of potholed, trash-littered asphalt. There were buildings close on either side of them, the brick veneer blistered by decades of gun battles. Some had been between good and bad, but most involved young men taking out their brethren over drug turf, women or just because. Here, a gun made you a man, though you might really only be a child, running outside after watching your Saturday morning cartoons, convinced that if you blew a large hole in someone, he might actually get back up and keep playing with you.

They came upon the group the snipers had identified: clusters of blacks, Latinos and Asians wheeling and dealing drugs. Apparently, potent highs and the promise of an uncomplicated cash-and-carry business cut through all troublesome issues of race, creed, color or political affiliation. To Web most of these folks looked a single snort, needle nick or popped pill from the grave. He marveled that this pathetic assemblage of veteran paint hackers even had the energy or clarity of thought to consummate the simple transaction of cash for little bags of brain inferno barely disguised as feel-good potion, and only then the first time you drove the poison into your body.

In the face of Charlie's intimidating wall of guns and Kevlar, all but one of the druggies dropped to their knees and begged not to be killed or indicted. Web focused on the one young man who remained standing. His head was swathed in a red do-rag symboliz-

ing some gang allegiance. The kid had a toothpick waist and barbell shoulders; ratty gym shorts hung down past his butt crack and
a tank shirt rode lopsided across his muscular torso. He also had an
attitude several miles long riding on his features, the kind that
said, *I'm smarter, tougher and will outlive you.* Web had to admit,
though, the guy carried the rag-look well.

It took all of thirty seconds to determine that all but Bandanna
Boy were looped out of their minds and that none of the druggies
were carrying guns—or cell phones that could be used to call up
the target and warn them. Bandanna Boy did have a knife, yet
knives had no chance against Kevlar and submachine guns. The
team let him keep it. But as Charlie Team moved on, Cal Plummer
ran with them backward, his MP-5 trained on the young back-
alley entrepreneur, just in case.

Bandanna Boy did call after Web, something about admiring
Web's rifle and wanting to buy it. He'd give him a sweet deal, he
yelled after Web, and then said he'd shoot Web and everyone else
dead with it. HA-HA! Web glanced to the rooftops, where he knew
members of Whiskey Team and X-Ray were in their forward firing
positions with rounds seated and lethal beads drawn on the brain
stems of this gaggle of losers. The snipers were Web's best friends.
He understood exactly how they approached their work, because
for years he had been one of them.

For months at a time Web had lain in steamy swamps with
pissed-off water moccasins crawling over him. Or else been
wedged into wind-gusted clefts of frigid mountains with the custom-built rifle stock's leather cheek pad next to his own as he
sighted through his scope and provided cover and intelligence for
the assault teams. As a sniper he had developed many important
skills, such as learning how to very quietly pee into a jug. Other lessons included packing his food in precise clusters so he could
carbo-load by touch in pitch-darkness, and arranging his bullets
for optimal reloading, working off a strict military model that had
proved its worth time and time again. Not that he could easily
transfer any of these unique talents to the private sector, but Web
didn't see that happening anyway.

The life of a sniper lurched from one numbing extreme to another. Your job was to achieve the best firing position with the least amount of personal exposure and oftentimes those twin goals were simply incompatible. You just did the best you could. Hours, days, weeks, even months of nothing except tedium that tended to erode morale and core skills would be sliced wide open by moments of gut-wrenching fury that usually came at you in a rush of gunfire and mass confusion. And your decision to shoot meant someone would die, and you were never clear whether your own death would be included in the equation or not.

Web could always conjure up these images in a flash, so vivid were they in his memory. A quintuplet of match-grade hollow points would be lined up in a spring-loaded magazine waiting to rip into an adversary at twice the speed of sound once Web's finger pulled the jeweled trigger, which would break ever so sweetly at precisely two-point-five pounds of pressure. As soon as someone stepped into his kill zone, Web would fire and a human being would suddenly become a corpse crumbling to the earth. Yet the most important shots Web handled as a sniper were the ones he *hadn't* taken. It was just that kind of a gig. It was not for the faint-hearted, the stupid or even those of average intelligence.

Web said a silent thank-you to the snipers overhead and raced on down the alley.

They next came upon a child, maybe all of nine, sitting shirtless on a hunk of concrete, and not an adult in sight. The approaching storm had knocked at least twenty degrees off the thermometer and the mercury was still falling. And still the boy had no shirt on. Had he ever had a shirt on? Web wondered. He had seen many examples of impoverished children. While Web didn't consider himself a cynic, he was a realist. He felt sorry for these kids, but there wasn't much he could do to help them. And yet threats could come from anywhere these days, so his gaze automatically went from the boy's head to his feet, looking for weapons. Fortunately, he saw none; Web had no desire to fire upon a child.

The boy looked directly at him. Under the illuminated arc of the one flickering alley lamp that somehow had not been shot out, the child's features were outlined vividly. Web noted the too-lean body and the muscles in shoulders and arms already hard and clustering around the protrusion of ribs, as a tree grows bark cords over a wound. A knife slash ran across the boy's forehead. A puckered, blistered hole on the child's left cheek was the unmistakable tag of a bullet, Web knew.

"Damn to hell," said the child in a weary voice, and then he laughed or, more accurately, cackled. The boy's words and that laugh rang like cymbals in Web's head, and he had no idea why; his skin was actually tingling. He had seen hopeless kids like this before, they were everywhere around here, and yet something was going on in Web's head that he couldn't quite figure. Maybe he'd been doing this too long, and wasn't it a hell of a time to start thinking that?

Web's finger hovered near his rifle's trigger, and he moved farther in front with graceful strides even as he tried to rid himself of the boy's image. Though very lean himself and lacking showy muscles, Web had enormous leverage in his long arms, and strong fingers, and there was deceptive power in his naturally broad shoulders. And he was by far the fastest man on the team and also possessed great endurance. Web could run six-mile relays all day. He would take speed, quickness and stamina over bulging muscles any day. Bullets tore through muscle as easily as they did fat. Yet the lead couldn't hurt you if it couldn't hit you.

Most people would describe Web London, with his broad shoulders and standing six-foot-two, as a big man. Usually, though, people focused on the condition of the left side of his face, or what remained of it. Web had to grudgingly admit that it was amazing, the reconstruction they could do these days with destroyed flesh and bone. In just the right light, meaning hardly any at all, one almost wouldn't notice the old crater, the new rise of cheek and the delicate grafting of transplanted bone and skin. Truly remarkable, all had said. All except Web, that is.

At the end of the alley they stopped once more, all crouching low. At Web's elbow was Teddy Riner. Through his wireless Motorola bone mic, Riner communicated with TOC, telling them that Charlie was at yellow and asking permission to move to green—the "crisis site" of the target, which here was simply a fancy term for the front door. Web held the SR75 with one hand and felt for his custom-built .45-caliber pistol in the low-slung tactical holster riding on his right leg. He had an identical pistol hanging on the ceramic trauma plate that covered his chest, and he touched that one too in his pre-attack ritual of sorts.

Web closed his eyes and envisioned how the next minute would play out. They would race to the door. Davies would be front and center laying his charge. Assaulters would hold their flash bang grenades loosely in their weak hand. Subgun safeties would be off, and steady fingers would stay off triggers until it was time to kill. Davies would remove the mechanical safeties on the control box and check the detonator cord attached to the breaching charge, looking for problems and hoping to find none. Riner would com-municate to TOC the immortal words, "Charlie at green." TOC would answer, as it always did, with, "Stand by, I have control." That line always rankled Web, because who the hell really had con-trol doing what they did?

During his entire career Web had never heard TOC reach the end of the countdown. After the count of two, the snipers would en-gage targets and fire, and a bevy of .308s firing simultaneously was a tad noisy. Then the breach charge would blow before TOC said "one" and that high-decibel hurricane would drown out even your own thoughts. In fact, if you ever heard TOC finish the countdown you were in deep trouble, because that meant the breach charge had failed to go off. And that was truly a lousy way to start the workday.

When the explosive blew the door, Web and his team would in-vade the target and throw their flash bangs. The device was aptly named, since the "flash" would blind anyone watching, and the "bang" would rupture the unprotected eardrum. If they ran into any more locked doors, these would yield quickly either to the im-polite knock-knock of Davies's shotgun or to a slap charge that looked like a strip of tire rubber but carried a C4 explosive kicker that virtually no door could withstand. They'd follow their rote patterns, keying on hands and weapons, shooting with precision, thinking in chess maneuvers. Communication would be via touch commands. Hit the hot spots, locate any hostages, and take them out fast and alive. What you never really thought about was dying.

That took too much time and energy away from the details of the mission, and away from the bedrock instincts and disciplines honed from doing this sort of thing over and over until it became a part of what made you, *you*.

According to reliable sources, the building they were going to hit contained the entire financial guts of a major drug operation head-quartered in the capital city. Included in the potential haul tonight were accountants and bean counters, valuable witnesses for the government if Web and his men could get them out alive. That way the Feds could go after top guys criminally and civilly from a number of fronts. Even drug lords feared an IRS full frontal assault, because seldom did kingpins pay taxes to Uncle Sam. That was why Web's team had been called up. They specialized in killing folks who needed it, but they also were damn good at keeping people alive. At least until these folks put their hands on the Bible, testified and sent some greater evil away for a very long time.

When TOC came back on, the countdown would begin: "Five, four, three, two . . ."

Web opened his eyes, collected himself. He was ready. Pulse at sixty-four; Web just knew. *Okay, boys, pay dirt's dead ahead. Let's go take it.* TOC came through his headset once more and gave the okay to move to the front door.

And that's precisely when Web London froze. His team burst out from the cover heading for green, the crisis site, and Web didn't. It was as though his arms and legs were no longer part of his body, the sensation of when you've fallen asleep with a limb under your body and wake up to find all the circulation has vacated that extremity. It didn't seem to be fear or runaway nerves; Web had been doing this too long. And yet he could only watch as Charlie Team raced on. The courtyard had been identified as the last major danger zone prior to the crisis site, and the team picked up its pace even more, looking everywhere for the slightest hint of coming resistance. Not a single one of the men seemed to notice that Web was not with them. With sweat pouring off him, every muscle straining against whatever was holding him down, Web managed slowly to rise and take a few faltering steps forward. His feet and arms seemingly encased in lead, his body on fire and his head bursting, he staggered onward a bit more, reached the courtyard, and then he dropped flat on his face as his team pulled away from him.

He glanced up in time to see Charlie Team running hard, the target in their sights, seemingly just begging them to come take a piece of it. The team was five seconds from impact. Those next few seconds would change Web London's life forever.

2

Teddy Riner went down first. Of the two seconds it took him to fall, the man had been dead for one of them. On the other side Cal Plummer fell to the ground like he'd been pole-axed by a giant. As Web watched helplessly, up and down the compact lines heavy ordnance impacted with Kevlar and then flesh, and then there was nothing else. It didn't seem right for good men to die so quietly.

Before the guns started firing, Web had fallen on his rifle and it was wedged under him. He could barely breathe; his Kevlar and weapons seemed crushed against his diaphragm. There was stuff on his mask. He couldn't know, but it was part of Teddy Riner, throw-off from the monster round that had blown a hole the size of a man's palm through his body armor and sent part of Riner flying back to where Web lay, dead last of Charlie Team and, ironically enough, the only one still living.

Web still felt paralyzed, none of his limbs responding to pleas from his brain to move. Had he suffered a stroke at age thirty-seven? Then suddenly the sounds of gunfire seemed to clear his head, the feeling finally returned to his arms and legs and he managed to rip off his mask and roll on his back. He exhaled a gush of foul air and screamed in relief. Now Web was staring straight up at the sky. He saw spears of lightning, though he couldn't hear even the belly rumbles of the thunder over the gunfire.

He had a powerful if insane urge to lift up his hand into the maelstrom above him, perhaps to confirm the presence of the bullets racing past, as though he were a youngster told not to touch a hot stove and who would then, of course, think of nothing else. Instead he reached down to his belt, undid the latch on a side pouch and pulled out his thermal imager. On the blackest night the TI would pick up an entire world invisible to the unaided eye, zeroing in on the core heat signature that burned in just about everything.

Though he was unable to see them even with the TI, Web could easily sense the vapor trails thrown off by the net of bullets zipping across above him. Web also observed that the dense gunfire was coming from two separate directions: the tenement building dead ahead and a dilapidated structure to the immediate right. He looked through his TI at the latter building and saw nothing but jagged glass. And then Web observed something that made his body tense even more. The muzzle flashes were erupting at the same time at each of the shattered windows. They moved across the apertures, stopped for a few seconds, and then moved back across, as the gun barrels he could not see yet knew were there completed their controlled firing arc.

As the gunfire began anew, Web rolled over on his belly and stared at the original target building through his imager. Here too there was a line of windows in the lower level of the target. And the same muzzle flashes were occurring with the exact same synchronized arc of movement. Web could now make out the long barrels of the machine guns. Through the TI the silhouettes of the guns were brick-red, the metal molten hot from the amount of ammo they were spraying. No human outline, though, came up on his thermal, and if any man had been in the vicinity, Web's imager would have nailed him. He was for sure looking at some kind of remote-controlled firing post. He now knew that his team had been set up, ambushed, without the enemy putting a single man at risk.

The slugs ricocheted off the brick walls behind and to the right of him, and Web felt bits of shrapnel hitting all around, like hardened raindrops. At least a dozen times the deflections had skimmed his Kevlar, but most of their speed and lethality had already been depleted. He kept his unarmored legs and arms tight to the asphalt. However, not even his Kevlar could withstand a direct hit, for the machine guns were almost certainly doling out .50-caliber ordnance, with each round as long as a butter knife and probably armor-piercing too. Web could gauge all this from the supersonic cracking sound made by the guns and the signature muzzle flash. And the vapor trail of a .50-caliber was also something pretty damn unforgettable. In fact you *felt* the snap before you even heard the round. It raised every hair on your body, as lightning did right before its fatal blow.

Web screamed out the names of his teammates one by one. No answer. No movement. No moans, no body twitches to show that life was still out there somewhere. And still Web yelled out their names again and again, like some insane roll call. Everywhere around him garbage cans exploded, glass burst, walls of brick were being eroded as if bludgeoning rivers were carving canyons. This was Normandy Beach, or more aptly Pickett's Charge, and Web had just lost his entire army. Alley vermin fled the slaughter. That courtyard was as clean of such rodents as it ever had been. No city inspector had ever done as good a job as rhythmic .50-caliber ordnance did that night.

Web didn't want to die, but every time he looked at what was left of his team, a part of him wanted to join them. The family fought and died together. It held some appeal for Web. He actually felt his legs tense for such a leap to eternity, yet something stronger took hold and he stayed hunkered down. To die was to lose. To give up was to let everyone perish in vain.

Where the hell were X-Ray and Whiskey? Why weren't they fast-roping to the rescue? The snipers on the buildings overlooking the courtyard couldn't come down without getting ripped apart, though, yet there were other snipers on the roofs of the buildings along the alley Charlie had come through. They could rope down. But would TOC give them the green light? Maybe not, if TOC didn't know what was going on, and how could they? Web didn't even know what the hell was going on, and he was right in the middle of it. Yet he couldn't exactly hang around waiting for TOC to make up their mind until a stray round made it a clean sweep of Web's team.

He felt a thin layer of panic settle over him despite years of train-ing designed specifically to banish that weakness from his psyche. Action, he needed to be doing something. His bone mic lost, Web snared his portable Motorola from its shoulder Velcro patch. He pushed the button, yelled into it. "HR fourteen to TOC, HR four-teen to TOC." No response. He changed to the backup frequency and then to a general purpose one. Still nothing. He looked at the radio and his spirits sank. The front was smashed from where he had fallen on it. Web slithered forward until he reached Cal Plum-mer's body. When he tried to grab Plummer's two-way radio, something hit Web's hand and he pulled it back. A ricochet only; a direct hit would've taken his hand off. Web counted five fingers still there, and the intense pain made him want to fight, to live. If for no other reason than to destroy whoever had done this, al-though Web's bag of tricks was almost empty. And for the first time in his career Web wondered if the opposition he now faced was actually better than he was.

Web knew that if he stopped thinking he still might leap up, fir-ing at nothing that could be killed. So he focused on the tactical scenario. He was in a carefully confined death zone, automatic fir-ing arcs on two sides, forming a ninety-degree angle of destruction and providing no human agent that could be stopped. Okay, that was the field situation. Now what the hell was he supposed to do about it? What chapter was that in the manual? The one that read, "You're screwed"? God, the sounds were deafening. He couldn't even hear his heart pounding. His breath came in short gasps. Where the hell were Whiskey and X-Ray? And Hotel? They couldn't run any faster? And yet what really could they do? They were trained to gun down human targets at both long and close range. He screamed out, "There's nothing for you to shoot!"

Chin tucked hard to his chest, Web started in surprise as he saw the little boy, the shirtless one from the chunk of concrete. Hands over his ears, the kid was crouched at the edge of the corner, along the alleyway Web and company had come from. If he moved out into the courtyard, Web knew the boy's body would be going into a morgue bag—probably two morgue bags, because the .50 rounds could actually cut the kid's skinny body in half.

The boy took a step forward, nearing the end of the brick wall and almost at the courtyard. Maybe he was intending to come help. Maybe he was waiting for the gunfire to stop so he could strip the bodies of any valuables, snagging their weapons for later resale on the streets. Maybe he was just flat-out curious. Web didn't know or really care.

The guns stopped firing, and just like that there was quiet. The boy took another step forward. Web screamed at him. He froze, obviously not expecting the dead to yell at the living. Web inched up his hand, called to him to keep back, but the gunfire started again and drowned out the end of his warning. Web slithered on his belly under the hail of fire, shouting at the boy with every twist and thrust of his pelvis. "Stay back! Get back!"

The kid didn't flinch. Web kept his gaze on him, which was difficult when you were double-timing on your gut, afraid that if you raised your head another centimeter you would no longer have a head. The boy finally did what Web thought he would do: He started to fall back. Web crawled faster. The kid turned to run and Web yelled at him to stop. Shockingly, he did.

Web was almost to the edge of the alley. He was going to try and time this just right, for there was now a new element of danger for the child. During the last pause in the firing Web had heard synchronized footsteps and shouts in the distance. They were coming. Web thought it must be everybody: Hotel and the snipers, and the reserve unit that TOC always kept back for emergencies. Well, if this didn't qualify as an emergency, nothing ever would. Yes, they were hustling to the rescue, or so they thought. What they were really doing though was running blind with no reliable intelligence.

The problem was the kid heard them coming too. Web could tell the boy knew exactly what and who they were, like a scout sniffing the earth and deducing from that the location of great buffalo herds. The boy was feeling trapped, and for good reason. Web knew that for the alley kid to be seen around people like Web was a death sentence here. The powers that be would just assume he was a traitor and deposit his body in the woods as his reward.

The child twitched, looked behind him even as Web picked up his pace. Web lost half his equipment whipping along the rough asphalt like that, a two-hundred-pound serpent on speed. Web could feel the blood coming from a dozen scratches on his legs, hands and face. His left hand stung like a couple thousand wasps were partying there. The body armor was so damn heavy now, his body ached with each thrust of his arms and legs. Web could have dropped his rifle, but he still had use for it. No, he would never let go of the damn SR75.

Web knew what the kid was going to do. Retreat cut off, he was going to go for it, race across the courtyard and then disappear into one of the buildings on the far side. The boy could hear the bullets as well as Web could. Yet he could not *see* the lines of fire. He could not dodge them. And yet Web knew the boy was about to try.

The child jumped out of the blocks, and Web leapt off his belly at the last possible second so that the two met right at the fringe of safety in a collision Web would win ten times out of ten. The child kicked at Web; his knotty fists struck him about the face and chest as Web's long arms wrapped around him. Web went back farther into the alley, carrying the kid. Kevlar was not easy on the hands, and the boy finally stopped punching and looked at Web. "I ain't do nothing. Let me go!"

"You run out there, you die!" Web yelled over the gunfire. He held up his bloody hand. "I'm wearing body armor and I can't survive out there. Those bullets will cut you in half."

The boy calmed as he studied Web's injury. Web carried the kid farther away from the courtyard and the guns. Now they could at least talk without shouting. From some odd impulse, Web touched the bullet wound on the boy's cheek. "You've been lucky before," Web said. The boy snarled and jerked away from him, breaking free of Web's grip. He was up, ferretlike, before Web could blink and had turned to run back down the alley. "If you go at them in the dark," Web said, "your luck runs out. They'll blow you away."

The kid stopped and turned back. For the first time his eyes truly seemed to focus on Web. Then he peered beyond to the courtyard.

"They dead?" he asked.

In answer Web slipped the big rifle from his shoulder. The boy took a step back at the sight of the intimidating weapon.

"Damn, mister, whatcha gonna do with that?"

"Stay here and keep down," Web said. He turned back to the

courtyard. Sirens were everywhere now. The cavalry was coming, too late, as the cavalry always did. The smartest thing to do would be nothing. Yet that just wasn't going to cut it. Web had a job to finish. He ripped a piece of paper from the notebook he carried on his belt and scribbled a quick note. He then pulled off the cap he wore under his helmet "Here," he said to the kid. "Walk, don't run, back down the alley. Hold up this cap and give this note to the men coming this way." The boy took the items, his long fingers curled around the cloth of the cap and the folded paper. Web pulled his flare gun from its pouch and loaded in a flare. "When I fire, you go. Walk!" Web said again. "Don't run."

The boy looked down at the note. Web had no idea if he could even read. Around here you didn't assume that children received the fundamentals of education that other kids took for granted. "What's your name?" Web asked. The boy needed to be calm now. Nervous people made mistakes. And Web knew the charging men would cremate anyone who came rushing at them.

"Kevin," the boy answered. As he said his own name, he suddenly looked like the frightened little kid that he was, and Web felt even guiltier about what he was asking the boy to do.

"Okay, Kevin, I'm Web. You do what I say and you'll be okay. You can trust me," he said, and then felt guiltier still. Web pointed the flare gun to the sky, looked at Kevin, nodded reassuringly and then fired. The flare would be their first warning. The note carried by Kevin would be their second. The boy moved off, walking, but walking fast. "Don't run," Web yelled. He turned back to the courtyard and slid his thermal imager onto the rifle's Picatinny rail and locked it into place.

The red-colored flare bloodied the sky and in his mind Web saw the assaulters and snipers stop and consider this development. That would give the boy time to reach them. Kevin would not die, not tonight anyway. When the next pause in the wave of fire came, Web burst out from the alley, rolled and brought the rifle up as he assumed a prone firing position and flipped down the rifle's bipod, pressing the weapon's butt flush against his shoulder. The three windows dead ahead were his first targets. He could see the muzzle flashes with his own eyes easily enough, but the thermal allowed him to draw a bead on the heated outlines of the machine guns. That's what he wanted to hit. The SR75 roared and one machine gun nest after another exploded. Web rammed in another twenty-round mag, aimed the rifle and pulled the trigger, and four more machine guns were finally silenced. The last gun nest was still firing when Web crawled forward and lobbed a concussion grenade into its throat. And then there was silence until Web emptied both of his .45s at the now-silent window openings, ejected cartridges tumbling out of the weapons like parachutists from a plane's belly. When the last shot was fired, Web doubled over, sucking in precious air. He was so hot he thought he might spontaneously combust. Then the clouds opened and the rain came down hard. He looked over and saw an armor-coated assaulter cautiously edge into the courtyard. Web tried to wave to him, but his arm wouldn't follow through; it just hung limply by his side.

Web surveyed the shattered bodies of his team, his friends spread over the slick pavement. Then he sank to his knees. He was alive and he didn't really want to be. The last thing Web London remembered from that night was watching drops of his sweat fall into the blood-tinted pools of rain.

3

Randall Cove was a very big man endowed with great physical strength and also remarkable street instincts that he had further honed over many years of working them. He was an FBI undercover agent and had been one for nearly seventeen years. He had infiltrated Latino drug gangs in LA, Hispanic crews on the Tex-Mex border and heavyweight Europeans in south Florida. Most of his missions had been startling and, at times, nail-biting successes. He was currently armed with a .40 semiautomatic chambering hollow points that would collapse to small pancakes when they entered a body, wreaking internal havoc and probably death. He also had a sheathed knife with a serrated edge that he could use to slash vital arteries in a blur. He always prided himself on being professional and reliable in his work. Right now some ignorant people would condemn him as a vicious criminal who should be locked up for life or, better yet, executed for his terrible sins. Cove knew he was in serious trouble and he also realized he was the only one who could get himself out of it.

Cove crouched low in the car and watched as the group of men climbed in their vehicles and headed out. As soon as they passed, Cove rose, waited a bit and then followed them. He pulled his ski cap tighter over his newly shorn head, the dreadlocks all gone, and about time too, he had decided. The cars stopped up ahead and Cove did too. When he saw the group of men emerge from the vehicles, Cove pulled a camera from his backpack and clicked away. He put away the Nikon, pulled out a pair of night binoculars and adjusted the distance magnifier. Cove nodded to himself as he tallied the men one by one.

He inhaled and let go of one last deep breath and took a fast-forward reel on his life thus far as the group disappeared into a building. In college Cove had been a bigger, faster version of Walter Payton; a consensus All-American from Oklahoma, every NFL team was throwing bales of cash and other perks at him. They were, that is, until a ruptured ACL in both knees during a freakish spill at the scouting combine had reduced him from a supernatural guaranteed number-one pick to a man with merely normal abilities who no longer excited NFL coaches. Millions of potential dollars had disappeared instantly and the only way of life he had ever known had vanished along with them. He had moped for a couple of years, looking for excuses and pity, and his life had spiraled downward until it had nowhere else to go, and then he had found her. His wife had been a divine intervention, he had always believed, saving his miserable, self-pitying carcass from oblivion. With her help, he had straightened himself out and fulfilled a secret dream of his to be a real-life G-man.

He had bounced here and there in the Bureau. It was a time when opportunities for black men were still severely limited. Cove had found himself pushed toward drug undercover work, because his superiors had bluntly informed him that most of the "bad dudes" were people of his color. You can walk the walk and talk the talk and you look the part too, they had said. And he couldn't argue with that, really. The work was dangerous enough to never be boring. Randall Cove had never easily tolerated being bored. And he put away more crooks in a month than most agents put away in their entire careers, and these were big fish, the planners, the true moneymakers, not the nickel-and-dime streetwalkers one bad snort from a pauper's grave. He and his wife had had two beautiful children and he was thinking seriously of calling it a career when the bottom had dropped out of his world and he no longer had a wife or kids.

He snapped back as the men came out, climbed in the cars, drove off and Cove once more followed. Cove had lost something else that he could never get back. Six men had died because he had messed up badly, been snookered like the most green agent there was. His pride was hurt and his anger was molten. And the seventh member of the shattered team deeply intrigued Cove. The man had survived when he should have been dead too and apparently nobody knew why, though it was early in the game yet. Cove wanted to look the man in the eye and say, *How come you're still breathing?* He didn't have Web London's file and he didn't see himself getting it anytime soon. Yeah, Cove was FBI, but yeah, everyone was no doubt thinking he had turned traitor. Undercover agents were supposed to live right next to the edge, weren't they? They were supposedly all head cases, right? What a thankless job he'd been doing all these years, but that was okay because he had done it for himself, nobody else.

The cars pulled into the long drive and Cove stopped, took some more pictures and then turned around. That was apparently it for tonight. He headed back to the only place he could be safe right now, and it wasn't home. As he rounded a curve and sped up, a pair of headlights seemed to appear out of nowhere and settled in behind him. That wasn't good, not on a road like this. Attention from his fellow man was not something Cove ever sought or encouraged. He turned; so did the car. Okay, this was serious. He sped up again. So did the tail. Cove reached down to his belt holster, pulled out his pistol and made sure the safety was off.

He glanced in the rearview mirror to see if he could tell how many folks he was dealing with. It was too dark for that, no streetlights out this way. The first bullet blew out his right rear tire, the second bullet his left rear. As he fought to keep control of the car, a truck pulled out from a side road and hit him broadside. If his window had been up, Cove's head would have gone right through it. The truck had a snowplow on its front end, though it was not wintertime. The truck accelerated and Cove's car was pushed in front of it. He felt his car about to roll and then the truck pushed his sedan over a guardrail that had been placed there principally to protect vehicles from plummeting down the steep slope that the curve of road was built around. The car's side smashed into the dirt and then rolled, both doors popping open as the sedan continued its cartwheeling, finally landing in a heap at the rocky bottom of the slope and bursting into flames.

The car that had tailed Cove stopped and one man got out, ran to the twisted guardrail and looked down. He saw the fire, witnessed the explosion as fuel vapor met flames and then ran back to his car. The two vehicles kicked up gravel leaving the scene.

As they did, Randall Cove slowly rose from the spot where he'd been thrown when the driver's door had been ripped open by the first impact with the ground. He had lost his gun and it felt like a couple of ribs were cracked, but he was alive. He looked down at what was left of his car and then back up at where the men who had tried to kill him had raced off. Cove stood on shaky legs and started slowly making his way back up.

Web clutched his wounded hand even as his head seemed primed to explode. It was like he had taken three quick slugs of straight tequila and was about to reflux them. The hospital room was empty. There was an armed man outside, to make sure nothing happened to Web—nothing *else* anyway.

Web had been lying here all day and into the night thinking about what had happened, and he was no closer to any answers than when they first brought him here. Web's commander had already been in, along with several members of Hotel and some of the snipers from Whiskey and X-Ray. They had said little, all of them reeling in their personal agony, their disbelief that something like this could have happened to them. And in their eyes Web could sense their suspicions, the issue of what had happened to him out there.

"I'm sorry, Debbie," Web said to the image of Teddy Riner's widow. He said the same to Cynde Plummer, Cal's wife and also now a widow. He went down the list: six women in all, all friends of his. Their men were his partners, his comrades; Web felt as bereaved as any of the ladies.

He let go of his injured hand and touched the metal side of the bed with it. What a sorry wound to bring back with him. He hadn't taken one round directly. "Not one damn shot did I get off in time," he said to the wall. "Not one! Do you realize how unbelievable that is?" he called out to the IV stand, before falling silent again.

"We're going to get them, Web."

The voice startled Web, for he had heard no one enter the room. But of course a voice came with a body. Web inched up on his bed until he saw the outline of the man there. Percy Bates sat down in a chair next to Web. The man studied the linoleum floor as though it were a map that would guide him to a place that held all the answers.

It was said that Percy Bates had not changed a jot in twenty-five years. The man hadn't gained or lost a pound on his trim five-ten frame. His hair was charcoal-black without a creep of white and was combed the same way as when he first walked into the FBI fresh from the Academy. It was as though he had been flash-frozen, and this was remarkable in a line of work that tended to age people well ahead of their time. He had become a legend of sorts at the Bureau. He had wreaked havoc on drug operations at the Tex-Mex border and then gone on to raise hell on the West Coast in the LA Field Office. He had risen through the ranks quickly and was currently one of the top people at the Washington Field Office, or "WFO," as it was called. He had experience in all the major Bureau divisions and the man knew how all the pieces fit together.

Bates, who went by Perce, was usually soft-spoken. Yet the man could crumple a subordinate with a look that made one feel unworthy to be occupying a square foot of space. He could either be your best ally or your worst enemy. Maybe that's how a man turned out after growing up with a name like Percy.

Web had been on the end of some of the classic Bates tirades before, when he had been under the man's direct command in his previous professional life at the Bureau. A good deal of the abuse had been deserved, as Web had made mistakes as he learned to be a good agent. Yet Bates did play favorites from time to time and, like everyone else, sometimes went searching for scapegoats to pin blame upon when things went to hell. Thus, Web did not accept the man's statements right now at face value. Nor did he accept the subdued tone as a token of peace and good-will. Yet the night Web had lost half his face in the fury of combat, Bates had been one of the first people by his bedside, and

Web had never forgotten that. No, Percy Bates was not a simple equation, not that any of them were. He and Bates would never be drinking buddies, yet Web had never believed one had to do shooters with a guy to respect him.

"I know you've given us the prelims, but we'll need your full statement as soon as you're able," said Bates. "But don't rush it. Take your time, get your strength back."

The message was clear. What had happened had crushed them all. There would be no outbursts from Bates. At least not right now.

"More scratches than anything," Web mumbled in response.

"They said a gunshot wound to your hand. Cuts and bruises all over your body. The docs said it looked like somebody had taken a baseball bat to you."

"Nothing," Web replied, and then felt exhausted by saying the word.

"You still need to rest. And then we'll get your statement." Bates rose. "And if you're up to it, and I know it'll be hard, it would help if you could go back down there and run us through exactly what happened."

And how I managed to survive? Web nodded. "I'll be ready sooner than later."

"Don't rush it," Bates said again. "This one ain't gonna be easy. But we'll get it done." He patted Web on the shoulder and turned to the door.

Web stirred, trying to sit up. "Perce?" In the darkness the whites of Bates's eyes were really the only things visible of him. To Web they were like a pair of dice hanging, showing deuces somehow. "They're all dead, aren't they?"

"All of them," Bates confirmed. "You're the only one left, Web."

"I did all I could."

The door opened and then closed, and Web was alone.

Outside in the hallway, Bates conferred with a group of men dressed exactly as he was: nondescript blue suit, button-down shirt, muted tie, rubber-soled black shoes and big pistols in small clip holsters.

"This will be a media nightmare, you know that," said one of them. "It already is, in fact."

Bates stuck a piece of gum in his mouth, substitute for the Winstons he had given up for the fifth time now and counting. "The needs of suck-wad journalists are not high on my priority list," he said.

"You have to keep them informed, Perce. If you don't, they'll assume the worst and start making it up. There's already been stuff on the Internet you wouldn't believe, that this massacre is tied to either the apocalyptic return of Jesus or something to do with a Chinese trade conspiracy. I mean, where do they get this crap? It's driving the media relations people nuts."

"I can't believe anybody would have the guts to do this to *us*," said another man, who had grown gray and plump in the service of his country. Bates knew this particular agent had not seen anything other than the top of his government desk in more than a decade but liked to act as though he had. "Not the Colombians, the Chinese or even the Russians could have the guts to attack *us* like that."

Bates glanced at the man. "It's 'us' against 'them.' Remember? We try to cram it down their throats all the time. You think they don't want to return the favor?"

"But my God, Perce, think about it. They just slaughtered a squad of our men. On our home turf," the old fellow blustered indignantly.

Perce looked at him and saw an elephant without tusks, just about ready to drop and die and become dinner for the jungle carnivores. "I didn't realize we had laid claim to that part of D.C.," said Bates. He had last slept the day before yesterday and was now really starting to feel it. "In fact, I was under the impression that that was *their* home turf and we were the visiting team."

"You know what I mean. What could have prompted this sort of attack?"

"Shit, I don't know, maybe because we try so damn hard to pull the plug on their billion-dollars-a-day drug pipeline and it's starting to really piss them off, you idiot!" As he said this, Bates backed the man into a corner and then decided the guy was far too harmless to be worth a suspension.

"How's he doing?" asked another man, with blond hair and a nose red from the flu.

Bates leaned against the wall, chewed his gum and then shrugged. "I think it's messed more with his mind than anything else. But that's to be expected."

"One lucky guy is all I can say," commented Red Nose. "How he survived it is anyone's guess."

It took barely a second for Bates to get in this man's face. He was obviously taking no prisoners tonight. "You call it luck to watch six of your team get ripped right in front of you? Is that what the hell you're saying, you dumb son of a bitch?"

"Geez, I didn't mean it like that, Perce. You know I didn't." Red Nose coughed a good one, as though to let Bates know he was sick and in no shape to fight.

Bates moved away from Red Nose, thoroughly disgusted with them all. "Right now I don't know anything. No, I take that back. I know that Web single-handedly took out eight machine gun nests and saved another squad and some ghetto kid in the process. That I do know."

"The preliminary report says Web froze." This came from another man who had joined their ranks, yet he was one who clearly stood above them all. Two stone-faced gents were in lockstep behind the intruder. "And actually, Perce, what we know is only what Web has told us," said the man. Though this person was obviously Percy Bates's superior in official rank, it was equally apparent that Bates wanted to bite his head off yet didn't dare.

The man continued. "London's got a hell of a lot of explaining to do. And we're going into this investigation with our eyes *wide* open, a lot more wide open than last night. Last night was a disgrace. Last night will never, ever happen again. Not on my watch." He stared hard at Bates and then said with sarcasm driven home with a sledgehammer, "Give London my best." With that, Buck Winters, head of the FBI's Washington Field Office, stalked off, followed by his two robotic escorts.

Bates gazed with loathing at the man's back. Buck Winters had been one of the principal frontline supervisors at Waco and had, in Bates's opinion, contributed to the eventual carnage with his ineptness. Then, in the funny way of big organizations, Winters had received promotion after promotion for his incompetence until he had reached the top of WFO. Maybe the Bureau was just unwilling to admit it had messed up and believed that promoting from the ranks of the leadership of the Waco fiasco was a strong message to the world that the Bureau considered itself blameless. Eventually, many heads had rolled because of the flameout of David Koresh in Texas, but Buck Winters's head was still firmly attached to his shoulders. For Percy Bates, Buck Winters represented much that was wrong with the FBI.

Bates leaned against the wall, crossed his arms and chewed his Wrigley's so hard his teeth hurt. He was certain that old Buck would be running off to confer with the FBI director, the attorney general, probably even the President. Well, let him, so long as they all kept out of Percy Bates's way.

The group of men slithered away singly and in pairs until just Bates and the uniformed guard remained. Finally Bates moved off too, hands in his pockets, gaze fixed on nothing. On the way out he spit his gum into the trash can. "Assholes and idiots," he said. "Assholes and idiots."

4

Web, dressed in a set of blue surgery scrubs, carried a bag with his personal belongings and stared at the sunlit sky that filled the window of his hospital room. The layers of gauze around his wounded hand were irritating; he felt like he was wearing a boxing glove.

He was about to open the door to leave when it opened all by itself. At least that's what Web thought until the man appeared there.

"What are you doing here, Romano?" said Web in surprise.

The man didn't acknowledge Web right away. He was just under six feet tall, about one-eighty, very powerful-looking in a wiry way. He had dark wavy hair and wore an old leather jacket, a Yankees baseball cap and jeans. His FBI shield was pinned to his belt; the grip of a pistol poked out from its clip holster.

Romano looked Web up and down until his gaze came to rest on the man's bandaged hand. He pointed at it. "Is that it? Is that your damn *wound*?"

Web looked at his hand and then back at Romano. "Would it make you happier if the hole was in my head?"

Paul Romano was an assaulter assigned to Hotel Team. He was one very intimidating guy among many such folks and you always knew where you stood with the man, which was usually nowhere good. He and Web had never been close—principally, Web thought, because Web had been shot up more than he had, and Romano strongly resented the perception that Web was more heroic or tougher.

"I'm only going to ask you this once, Web, and I want it straight, man. You bullshit me and I'll pop you myself."

Web looked down at the guy and stepped a bit closer so that his height advantage was even more evident. He knew this ticked off Romano too. "Gee, Paulie, did you bring me some candy and flowers too?"

"Just give it to me straight, Web." He paused and then asked, "Did you wimp out?"

"Yeah, Paulie, those guns somehow shot themselves all up."

"I know about that. I meant before that. When Charlie Team went down. You weren't with them. Why?"

Web felt his face growing warm and he hated himself for it. Romano usually couldn't get to him. Yet the truth was, Web didn't know what to tell the man.

"Something happened, Paulie, in my head. I don't know exactly what. But I didn't have anything to do with the ambush, in case you suddenly lost your mind and were thinking that."

Romano shook his head. "I wasn't thinking you turned traitor, Web, just that you turned chickenshit."

"If that's all you came to tell me, then you can go on and get the hell out now."

Romano looked him up and down again and Web felt like less and less of a man with each pronounced glare. Without a word, Romano turned and left. Web would have preferred the man had exited on the heel of another insult rather than silence.

Web waited another few minutes and then opened the door.

"What are you doing up?" asked the surprised guard.

"Docs discharged me, didn't they tell you?"

"Nobody told me anything like that."

Web held up his bandaged hand. "Government isn't paying for another night on account of a scratched hand. And damn if I'm paying the difference on my paycheck." Web didn't know the guard, but he seemed like the type to be sympathetic to such a commonsense plea. Web didn't wait to get an answer but just walked off. He knew the guard had no grounds to stop him. All he would do was communicate this development to his superiors, which he was assuredly doing right now.

Web ducked out a side exit, found a phone, called a buddy and an hour later he was inside his split-level thirty-year-old rancher in a quiet Woodbridge, Virginia, suburb. He changed into jeans, loafers and a navy blue sweatshirt, ripped off the gauze and replaced it with a single Band-Aid of blazing symbolism. He wanted no pity from anyone, not with six of his closest friends right now lying in the morgue.

He checked his messages. There weren't any of importance, yet he knew that would change. He unlocked a firebox, pulled out his spare nine-millimeter and thrust it into his belt holster. Although he had not technically shot anyone, this was still an SRB—or Shooting Review Board—matter now, since Web had most definitely fired his weapons. They had confiscated his guns, which was akin to taking his hands. Next, they had advised him of his rights and he had given them a statement. It was all standard, by-the-books practice and yet it still made him feel like a criminal. Well, he wasn't about to walk around without hardware. He was paranoid by nature, and the massacre of his team had made him a walking schizoid, capable of seeing real threats in babies and bunnies.

He went out to the garage, cranked up his 1978 coal-black Ford Mach One and headed out.

Web had two vehicles: the Mach, and an ancient and iron-gutted Suburban that had carried him and his Charlie Team to many Redskin football games, to the beaches in Virginia and Maryland, to beer-drinking outings and on assorted other manly campaigns up and down the East Coast. Each guy had had his own assigned seat in the Suburban, based on seniority and ability, which was the way everything was divvied up where Web worked. What outstanding times they had had in the big machine. Now Web wondered how much cash he could get for the Suburban, because he didn't see himself driving the beast anymore.

He jumped on Interstate 95, headed north and fought through the obstacle course that was the Springfield Interchange, which apparently had been designed by a highway engineer strung out on cocaine. Now that it was undergoing a major overhaul scheduled to last at least ten years, the driver navigating it each day had the option of laughing or crying as years of his life slipped by while the traffic's progress was measured in inches. Web sailed over the Fourteenth Street Bridge, cleared the Northwest quadrant where all the major monuments and tourist dollars were kept and was quickly in a not-so-nice part of town.

Web was an FBI special agent, but he did not see himself as such. First and foremost he was a Hostage Rescue Team (HRT) operator, the Bureau's elite crisis response group. He didn't dress in suits. He didn't spend much time with fellow agents outside HRT. He didn't arrive on the crime scene after all the bullets had stopped flying. He was usually there from the get-go, running, dodging, firing, wounding and occasionally killing. There were only fifty HRT operators, because the selection process was so grueling. The average time at HRT was five years. Web had bucked that trend and was going on his eighth year of duty. It seemed that HRT was being called upon a lot more often these days and to hot spots all over the world, with HRT's unwritten policy of being wheels up in four hours from Andrews Air Force Base. Well, the curtain had fallen on his part of that show. Web was teamless now.

It had never occurred to Web that he would be the sole survivor of anything. It just didn't seem in his nature. They all had joked about it, even had morbid betting pools on who would die one moonless night. Web had almost always been first on the list, because he always seemed to be first in the line of fire. Now it was torturing Web, though, not knowing what had gotten between him and the seventh coffin. And the only thing worse than the guilt was the shame.

He pulled the Mach to the curb and got out at the barricade. He showed his ID to the men posted there, who were all stunned to see him. Web ducked down the alley before the army of reporters could glom on to him. They had been reporting live here since the massacre from their tall-mast satellite broadcast trucks. Web had caught some of the news from the hospital. They were feeding the public the same facts over and over, using their little charts and pictures, and sporting their little dour expressions, and saying things like, "That's all we know right now. But stay with us, I'm certain we'll have more later, even if we have to make the shit up. Back to you, Sue." Web jogged down the alley.

Last night's storm had long since blown itself into the Atlantic. The air pushing behind it was cooler than the city had had in a while. Built on a swamp, Washington, D.C., handled heat and humidity better than cold and snow. When the snow fell, the only street likely to be cleared was the one in your dreams.

He ran into Bates halfway down the alley.

"What in the hell are you doing here?" Bates said.

"You said you wanted my take on things, so I'm here to give it to you." Bates glanced at Web's hand. "Let's get going, Perce. Every minute counts."

From the exact spot where the Chevy had dropped them off, Web retraced the steps of his squad. With every stride Web took toward the target, he could feel both his anger and his fear swell. The bodies were gone; the blood was not. Even the hard rain apparently was incapable of clearing it all away. In his mind, Web blitzed through every move he had made, every emotion he had felt.

The ruined machine gun nests were being dismantled and examined by a team of people who consistently pulled legal convictions out of microscopic scraps. Others walked the square courtyard kneeling, stooping, tagging things, probing and basically looking for answers from objects that did not appear willing to give any. Watching them, Web was not confident. It was highly unlikely that crystal-clear tented arches and plain whorls were just waiting around on the guns to be plucked by the fingerprint techs. Whoever had planned this intricate ambush wouldn't be that careless. He stepped between the bloodstains like he was tiptoeing around a graveyard, and wasn't he really?

"Windows were painted black so the guns couldn't be spotted until they started firing. No light reflections off barrels, no nothing," said Bates.

"Nice to know we were done in by professionals," replied Web bitterly.

"You did a number on the fifties." Bates pointed to one of the ruined weapons.

"An SR75 will do that for you."

"They're mini-guns, military design. Six-barrel Gatling style, tripod-mounted with the pods bolted to the floor so the firing position wouldn't deviate. There were feeder box and conveyor belt attachments and four thousand linked rounds per gun. Firing rates were set at four hundred a minute, though its maximum setting is eight thousand."

"Four hundred was plenty. And there were eight guns. That's thirty-two hundred slugs flying at you every sixty seconds. I know because all except one ricochet missed me by a few inches."

"With that low firing rate those guns could shoot a long time."

"They did."

"Power drive was electric, and they were chambering armor-piercing rounds."

Web just shook his head. "Did you find what tripped them?"

Bates led him over to a brick wall on the side farthest from the alley Web had come down. It was part of the building perpendicularly placed to the targeted abandoned tenement house and the source of one-half of the firing arc that had wiped out Charlie, save Web. What was invisible in the dark was only a bit more apparent in the daylight.

Web knelt down and looked at what he recognized as a laser device. A small hole had been punched in the brick and the laser point and power pack inserted into it. The hole was deeper than the power pack so that once inside the hole, it was pretty much invisible. The snipers wouldn't have been able to ID it from where they had their posts set up, even if they had been looking for such a thing, and their intelligence had given them no indication of it, as far as Web knew. The path of the laser was knee height and the invisible light stream no doubt had run across the courtyard when activated.

"Beam breaks, firing starts and doesn't stop except for a few seconds' pause after each cycle until the ammo's gone." He looked around in bewilderment. "What if a dog or cat or somebody just strolling by here tripped the laser before we got there?"

From Bates's expression, it was clear he had already considered this possibility. "I'm thinking people were discreetly warned to stay away. Animals are another issue. So I'm thinking the laser was armed via remote."

Web rose. "So they waited until we were just about there before activating the laser. That means the person would have to be reasonably close by."

"Well, he hears you guys coming, or he gets intelligence to that effect. He waits until you've maybe turned the corner and he hits the remote and runs."

"We didn't see a damn soul in the courtyard, and my thermal didn't pick up a ninety-eight-point-six temp anywhere."

"They could've been in the building—hell, any one of these buildings. They point the device out one of the windows, hit the button and they're long gone."

"And the snipers and Hotel saw nothing?"

Bates shook his head. "Hotel's story is they saw zip until the kid brought them your note."

At the mention of Hotel, Web thought of Paul Romano and his spirits sank even more. Romano was probably at Quantico right now telling everyone that Web had turned coward and let his team die and was trying to blame it on a mental lapse. "Whiskey? X-Ray? They had to see something," Web said, referring to the snipers on the rooftops.

"They saw some things, but I'm not prepared to discuss it quite yet."

Web's instincts told him to let that one alone. What would the snipers say? That they saw Web freeze, let his team charge on without him and then drop to the ground while his comrades-in-arms got obliterated? "How about the DEA? They were with Hotel, and there was a crew of them in reserve too."

Bates and Web looked at each other and Bates shook his head.

The FBI and DEA weren't the best of friends. The DEA, Web had always thought, was like a little brother kicking at his older sibling's shins until big brother hit back, and then the little punk ran off and tattled.

"Well, I guess we have to accept that until something makes us not," commented Web.

"Guess so. Were any of you wearing night-vision equipment?"

Web immediately understood the logic of the question. NV goggles would have picked up on the laser, transforming it into a long, unmistakable band of light.

"No. I pulled my thermal after the shooting started, but assaulters don't wear NVs. You get any source of ambient light while you're wearing them, then you are basically blind if you have to take them off and start shooting. And the snipers probably wouldn't have been using them during the assault; they screw up depth perception too much."

Bates nodded toward the gutted buildings where the guns had been set up. "The techs examined the guns. Each had a signal link box. They're thinking that there was a delay of a few seconds between when Charlie Team tripped the laser and when the guns were activated in order to make sure the team was squarely in the kill zone. The courtyard and firing lanes were large enough to allow for that.

Web suddenly felt dizzy and put his hand against the wall. It was as though he were reexperiencing the paralysis he had suffered during the doomed attack.

"You should've given yourself some more time to recover," said Bates as he slid an arm under Web's to help support him.

"I've had paper cuts worse than this."

"I'm not talking about your hand."

"My head's fine too, thanks for your concern," Web snapped, and then relaxed. "Right now I just want to do, not think."

For the next half hour Web pointed out the locations and descriptions of all the persons they had passed that night, and everything else he could recall from the time Charlie left the final staging area to the moment the last bullet was fired in the courtyard.

"You think any one of them could have been working with the target?" said Bates, referring to the people Web and company had passed in the alley.

"Down here anything's possible," replied Web. "There was obviously a leak. And it could have come anywhere along the line."

"There's a lot of possibilities there," Bates said. "Let's go over some."

Web shrugged. "This wasn't a triple-eight-beep scenario," he said, a reference to the three number eights that appeared on his pager representing a command for all HRT operators to haul butt to Quantico. "Last night was selected as the target date in advance, so everybody met at HRT to get our gear and team configurations ready and then we moved out in the Suburbans. We did the prelim staging at Buzzard Point and then drove to the last staging area. We had a U.S. attorney available in case we needed some additional warrants issued. The snipers were already in place. They went in early posing as HVAC rehab workers doing a job on roof units on two of the buildings along the strike path. Assaulters did our down-and-dirty with the local police just like always. After we left the last point of concealment, Teddy Riner requested and received compromise authority because of the unfriendly logistics. We wanted to be able to shoot on the fly if we had to. We knew that hitting the place from the front and exposing ourselves to fire in the courtyard was risky, but we also thought they wouldn't expect it. Plus the way the building was situated and configured, there weren't a lot of options. We got the green light to move to crisis site and then we were going to execute on TOC's countdown. We had one primary exterior breach point. The assault plan was to split once we were inside and hit from two points while Hotel and DEA blew in from the rear, with a unit in reserve and the snipers as backup firepower and cover. Hard and fast, just like always."

The two men sat on a pair of trash cans. Bates tossed his pack of gum in the trash, pulled out his cigarettes and offered one to Web, who declined.

"The local police knew the target, didn't they?" Bates asked.

Web nodded. "The approximate physical location. So they can keep a presence, help quadrant off the area and keep people on the outside of the perimeter out of the way, look for associates of the target tipping them off, that sort of thing."

"How much advance time you figure the locals had in case there was a leak from there?"

"Hour."

"Well, nobody set up that death trap in an hour."

"Who was the undercover on this one?"

"Goes without saying that you take this name to the grave with you." Bates paused, presumably for emphasis, and then said, "His name is Randall Cove. A real vet. Working the target from deep inside. I mean deep, like down-in-the-sewer deep. African-American, built like a truck and could do the street stuff with the best of them. He's done a million of these gigs."

"So what's his story?"

"I haven't asked him."

"Why not?"

"I can't find him." Bates paused and then added, "Do you know for certain if Cove was aware when the hit was happening?"

Web was surprised by this question. "Your end would know that better than mine. I can tell you for a fact that we were not briefed that the undercover or any snitches would be at the target. If they were supposed to be there, they'd tell us in the pre-op. That way we'd know who they were, what they looked like and we'd cuff 'em and get 'em out just like everybody else, so the real target wouldn't get a heads-up and kill them."

"How much did you know about the target?"

"Druggies' financial ops, with bean counters present. Heavy security. They wanted the money guys as potential witnesses that we were to treat as hostages. Bag 'em fast and get them out before anyone figured out what we were doing and popped them so they couldn't rat. Our strike plan was approved, ops orders written; we got blueprints of the target and built a copy of it at Quantico. Practiced our butts off until we knew every inch. Got our rules of engagement, nothing out of the ordinary, suited up and climbed in the Suburban. End of story."

"You guys do your own surveillance, snipers on glass," Bates said, referring to snipers observing the target through binoculars and spotting scopes. "Anything pop on that?"

"Nothing special or else we would've been told in our briefing. Except for the possible witness angle, to me it was just a glorified dope house raid. Hell, we cut our teeth on those."

"If it was just a dope house, they wouldn't have needed you guys to crack it, Web. WFO could've used its SWAT team."

"Well, we were told the logistics were really tricky, and they were. And we knew the targets were supposed to be real nasty and were packing some ordnance SWAT didn't think they could handle. And then you had the issue of the potential witnesses. That was enough to make it our gig. But none of us were expecting eight remote-controlled mini-guns."

"Obviously it was all bullshit. Fed to us like mother's milk. Except for the guns, the place was empty. Ambush all the way. There were no bean counters, no records, no nothing."

Web rubbed his hand against the bullet gouges on the brick. Many were so deep Web could see the concrete block underneath—armor-piercing, for sure. The only good thing was death for his team would have been instantaneous. "The snipers had to see something." He was hoping they had seen whatever had made Web freeze. Yet how could they?

"I haven't finished talking to them," was all Bates would offer on that point, and again Web chose not to press it.

"Where's the kid?" Web hesitated, trying to remember. "Kevin."

Bates also hesitated for a second. "Disappeared."

Web stiffened. "How? He's a kid."

"I'm not saying he did it on his own."

"We know who he is?"

"Kevin Westbrook. Age ten. Got some family around, but most are guests of the state. Has an older brother, street name of Big F, the *F* standing for what you think it does. Head street ganger as big as a tree, and smart as a Harvard MBA. Deals in meth, Jamaican sinsemilla, the really cool stuff, though we've never been able to build a case against him. This area is sort of his turf."

Web stretched the fingers of his injured hand. The Band-Aid wasn't doing the trick right now, and he felt guilty for even thinking about it. "That's a pretty big coincidence that the little brother of the guy who runs this area was sitting out in the alley when we came by." Even as he talked about the boy, Web could feel a change come over his body, as though his very soul were sliding out and moving on. He actually thought he might pass out. Web was starting to wonder if he needed a doctor or an exorcist.

"Well, he does live around here. And from what we found out, his home life isn't all that great. He probably avoided it if he could."

"This big brother missing too?" Web asked as his balance began to return.

"Not that he actually lives at a normal address. When you're in the kind of business he is, you keep moving. We don't have any direct evidence tying him to even a misdemeanor, but we're looking for him real hard right now." He stared at Web. "You sure you're okay?"

Web waved off this comment. "How exactly did you lose the kid?"

"That's not real clear right now. We'll know more after we finish going through the neighborhood. Somebody had to see those weapons coming in and that machine gun nest being put up. Even around here that qualifies as a little unusual."

"You really think anybody here's going to talk to you?"

"We have to try, Web. We only need one pair of eyes."

The men fell silent for a while. Bates finally looked up, his expression uncomfortable.

"Web, what really happened?"

"Say what you really mean. How come it wasn't a perfect seven-for-seven?"

"I *am* saying it."

Web gazed across the courtyard at the exact spot where he had hit the asphalt. "I came out of the alley late. It was like I couldn't move. I thought I'd had a stroke. Then I went down right before the shooting started. I don't know why." Web's mind suddenly went blank and then came back, like he was a television and there had been a lightning strike nearby. "It was over in a second, Perce. A second was all it took. The worst timing in the history of the world." He looked at Bates to gauge his reaction to this. The narrowed eyes of the man told Web all he needed to know.

"Hell, don't feel bad. I don't believe it either," said Web. Bates remained silent, and Web decided to get to the other reason he had come here. "Where's the flag?" he asked. Bates looked surprised. "The HRT flag. I have to bring it back to Quantico."

On every mission HRT undertook, the senior member was given the HRT flag to carry with him in his gear. When the mission was completed, the flag was to be returned to the HRT commander by the senior member of the team. Well, now that happened to be Web.

"Follow me," said Bates.

An FBI van was parked at the curb. Bates popped open one of

the back doors, reached in and pulled out a flag folded military style. He handed it to Web.

Web held the flag in both hands, staring down at the colors for a moment, every detail of the slaughter once more working through his head.

"It's got a few holes in it," Bates observed.

"Don't we all," said Web.

5

The following day Web headed down to Quantico to the HRT facility. He drove along Marine Corps Route 4 past the campus-style FBI Academy that was home to both FBI and DEA grunts. Web had spent thirteen very intense and stressful weeks of his life at the Academy learning how to be an FBI agent. In return Web was paid peanuts and lived in a dorm room with a shared bath and he even had to bring his own towels! And Web had loved it and had devoted every waking moment to becoming the best FBI agent he could because he felt he had been born for the job.

Web had walked out of the Academy as a newly minted and sworn agent of the FBI with his Smith & Wesson .357 wheel gun, which required a staggering nine pounds of pull to fire. Rarely did one shoot oneself in the foot with the weapon. Recruits now carried .40 Glock semiautomatics with fourteen-round magazines with a much easier trigger pull, but Web still had fond memories of his Smith & Wesson with the three-inch bull barrel. Fancier didn't necessarily mean better. He had spent the next six years learning how to be an FBI agent in the field. He had sweated through the infamous FBI paperwork mountain, ferreted out leads, drummed up informants, answered criminal complaints, kept his butt on wiretaps, undertaken all-night surveillances, built up cases and arrested people who badly needed to be. Web had gotten to the point where he could concoct a battle plan in five minutes while he was driving a Bureau car—or Bucar, as it was always called—a hundred and ten miles an hour down the highway steering with his knees and shoving shells into his shotgun. He had learned how to interrogate suspects, establishing baselines and then asking them tough questions designed to knock them for a loop, to later gauge when they were lying. He had also learned how to testify without being cracked by slick defense lawyers whose only goal was to not discover the truth and instead to bury it.

His superiors, including Percy Bates (when Web had been transferred to the Washington Field Office after several years in the Midwest), had filled his personnel file with commendation after commendation, impressed with his dedication, his physical and mental skills and his ability to think on his feet. He had worked outside the rules at certain points, yet most of the really good agents did, he thought, because some of the Bureau rules were just plain stupid. That was also something Percy Bates had taught him.

Web parked, got out of the car and headed into HRT's building, which would never be termed beautiful by anyone who could actually see. He was welcomed with open arms, and tough, hardened men, who had seen more death and danger than the average citizen could possibly imagine, broke down with him in private rooms. HRT was not a place where anyone rushed to show his vulnerabilities and emotions. No man wanted to be firing guns and risking his life next to the shy, sensitive type. You left your warm fuzzy aura at the door and just brought your alpha male kick-ass side to work. Everything here was based on seniority and ability; those two attributes usually, though not always, paralleled each other.

Web returned the flag to his commander. Web's chief, a lean, muscular man with salt-and-pepper hair and a former HRT operator who could still outwork most of his men, accepted the flag with dignity and a handshake that dissolved into an embrace in the privacy of the man's office. Well, thought Web, at least they didn't hate his guts.

The HRT's admin building had been built to hold fifty personnel, yet now a hundred people called it their home away from home. There was a two-holer for all those folks, so the pee lines were long even for elite crime-busting Feds. There were small offices behind the reception area for the commander, who was at the rank of an

ASAC, or assistant special agent-in-charge, and his down-the-line chain of command that consisted of one supervisor for assaulters, and one for snipers. The HRT operators had honeycomb cubicle areas across the hallway from each other, split between snipers and assaulters. There was only one classroom in the building, which also doubled as a conference and briefing room in the space-challenged complex. There was a line of coffee mugs on a shelf on the rear wall of the room. Whenever the choppers landed here, the force of the blades would make the mugs vibrate. Somehow that sound had always been very soothing to Web. Team members coming home safe, he supposed.

He stopped by to see Ann Lyle, who worked in the office. Ann was sixty, much older than the other women who worked in administration, and could be truly termed the matriarch and unofficial mother hen of the hardcore lads who called HRT home. The unwritten rule was that you did not curse around Ann or use any other sort of uncouth language or gestures. Both rookie and veteran operators who ran afoul of this policy quickly found themselves the target of retribution ranging from glue in their helmets to taking a particularly hard shot during a training drill, the kind that left you wondering if one of your lungs had fallen out. Ann had been with HRT almost since its inception after working at the WFO for many years and had become a widow during that time. Childless, she let her entire life revolve around her work, and she listened to the young, single agents and their problems and doled out sensible advice. She also served as HRT's unofficial marriage counselor and had on more than one occasion prevented a divorce. She had come to Web's hospital room every day while he was waiting to get his face back, far more often than his own mother had bothered to. Ann regularly brought home-baked goodies to the office. And she was known as the primary information source for all things having to do with the Bureau and HRT. She was also a whiz at navigating the Bureau's requisition morass, and if HRT needed something, no matter how big or small, Ann Lyle made sure they got it.

He found Ann in her office, closed the door and sat across from her. Ann's hair had been white for several years now, and her body had lost its shape, but her eyes were still youthful-looking and her smile was truly beautiful.

Ann rose from her desk and gave Web a much-needed hug. Her cheeks were wet from tears. She had been especially close to the members of Charlie Team, who took great pains to show her their affection for all she did for them.

"You don't look good, Web."

"I've had better days."

"I wouldn't wish this on anybody, not even my worst enemy," she said, "but you're the last person in the world this should have happened to, Web. Right now, all I want to do is scream and never stop."

"I appreciate that, Ann," said Web. "I still don't know what happened, really. I've never frozen like that before."

"Web, honey, you've spent the last eight years of your life getting shot at. Don't you think that adds up? You're only human."

"That's just it, Ann, I'm supposed to be more than that. That's why I'm at HRT."

"What you need is a good long rest. When's the last time you took a vacation? Do you even remember?"

"What I need is some information and I need you to help me get it."

Ann accepted this change in subject without comment. "I'll do what I can, you know that."

"An undercover named Randall Cove. He's MIA."

"That name sounds familiar. I think I knew a Cove when I worked at WFO. You say he's gone missing?"

"He was the inside guy on the HRT hit. Guess he was either in on it or else got his cover blown. I need whatever you can find on him. Addresses, aliases, known contacts, the works."

"If he was working in D.C., his home won't be around there," said Ann. "There's an unofficial twenty-five-mile rule for UCs. You don't want to run into one of your neighbors while you're working your shift. For big-time assignments they might even bring the agent in from another part of the country."

"Understood. But twenty-five miles out still leaves a lot of possibilities. Maybe we can get a record of phone logs, communications with WFO, that sort of thing. I don't know how you manage it, but I really need whatever you can get."

"UCs mostly use disposable phone cards with low amounts on them to call in with. Buy them at convenience stores, use them up, chuck them and buy another. No record of anything that way."

Web's hopes dimmed. "So there's no way to trace?" He had never had to track down an undercover agent before.

Ann smiled her beautiful smile. "Oh, Web, there's always a way. You just let me dig around a little."

He looked at his hands. "I'm feeling kind of like a guy at the Alamo that the Mexicans somehow missed."

Ann nodded in understanding. "There's some fresh coffee in the kitchen and a chocolate walnut cake I brought in. Go help yourself, Web, you've always been too skinny." Her next words made Web look up into that wonderfully reassuring face. "And I'm watching your back here, honey, don't think that I'm not. I know what's what, Web. I hear everything, uptown or down. And nobody, and I mean nobody, is going to pull anything on you while I'm sitting here."

As he walked out, Web wondered if Ann Lyle would ever consider adopting him.

Web found an empty computer terminal and logged on to HRT's database. It had occurred to him, as he was sure it had to others, that his team's annihilation might have been a simple case of revenge. He spent considerable time going through past cases where HRT had been called up. Memories came flooding back to him of chest-thudding victories and heart-wrenching failures. The problem was that if you added up all the people who had been affected by an HRT mission and factored in family and friends, along with fringe crazies chasing any cause they could get their demented hands around, the numbers ran into the thousands. Web would have to leave that to somebody else to run down. He was certain the Bureau computers were crunching that data right now.

Web passed down the main hallway and lingered in front of the photo displays of past HRT operations. Here there were visual images of many stunning successes. The credo of hostage rescue was, "Speed, surprise and violence of action," and HRT put big-time action to those words. Web looked at a photo of a terrorist on the most-wanted list who had been plucked from international waters ("grabs," they called them) like an unsuspecting crab taken from a sand hole and whisked away to stand trial with a lifelong prison term to follow. There were photos of a joint international task force operation on a drug farm in a Latin American country. And finally there was a picture of a very tense hostage situation in a high-rise government building in Chicago. The result was all hostages were saved, with three of the five hostage-takers dead. Unfortunately, it didn't always work that way.

He walked outside the admin building and observed the lone tree there. It was a species of the state tree of Kansas, planted there in memory of the HRT operator who had been killed in a training accident and who had hailed from there. Each time Web had passed that tree he had said a silent prayer that it would be the only one they would ever have to plant. So much for answered prayers. Soon they'd have a damn forest here.

Web really needed to be doing something, anything that would make him not feel like a total failure. He went to the equipment cage, snagged a .308 snipe rifle and some ammo and headed back out. He needed to calm down and, ironically, firing guns did that for him, as it required a precision and focus that would block out all other thoughts, however troubling.

He passed the HRT's original headquarters building, which was narrow and tall and looked like a glorified grain silo instead of home for an elite law enforcement unit. Then he stood and looked out at the sheered-off hillside where one of the shooting ranges was situated. There was a new thousand-yard rifle range, and work crews were in the process of leveling an adjacent forest in order to add to the HRT's ever-growing complex, which also included a new indoor shooting range facility. Behind the outdoor shooting range, the trees were leafy green. It had always seemed an odd juxtaposition to Web: nature's beautiful colors serving as a backdrop to where he had stood for so many years learning better ways to kill. Yet he was the good guy, and that made it all right. At least that's what the bill of goods that came with the badge had very strongly implied.

He set up his targets. Web was going to play a game of sniper's poker. The cards were slightly fanned out across the target holder such that only the tiniest portion of each card, other than the front card, was visible. The goal was to build a winning hand. The trick was you could only count a card that you hit cleanly. If your round even nicked another card, you couldn't claim the card you were shooting at. And you only got five shots. The margin of error was impossibly tiny. It was just the sort of nerve-wracking task to relax a person, if that person happened to be an HRT grunt.

Web set himself up a hundred yards away from the targets. Lying flat on the ground, he placed a small beanbag under the .308's stock to support his upper body weight as he settled in. He aligned his body with the recoil path to minimize muzzle jump; his hips were flat against the ground, his knees spread shoulder-width and ankles flat to the ground to shrink his target profile in case someone was aiming at him. Web dialed the proper settings on the scope's calibration wheel and figured in wind too. The humidity was high, so he added an extra half-minute click. As a sniper, every shot he had ever fired during a mission had been recorded in his log. It was a very valuable record of environmental effects on bullets fired and also might explain why a sniper had missed a target, which was the only time anybody gave a damn. When you hit your target you were just doing your job, you didn't get a key to the city. There was no detail too small when it concerned killing at long range. A hint of a shadow across your objective lens could easily make the less-than-vigilant shooter wipe out a hostage rather than the person holding him.

Web lightly squeezed the pebbled pistol grip. He pulled the stock to his shoulder, pressed his cheek to the stock, set the proper eye relief and gripped the butt pad with his weak hand to steady the .308's bipod. He sucked in a breath, eased it out. No muscle could come between Web and his sniping. Muscle was erratic; he needed bone on bone because bone didn't flinch. Web had always used the ambush technique when sniping. This entailed the shooter waiting until the target entered a predetermined kill zone. The sniper would plant his crosshairs just ahead of the target and then count the mil-dots in the reticle to calculate distance to target, angle of incidence and speed. You also had to judge elevation, wind and humidity and then you waited to kill, like the proverbial spider in the web. You always shot into the skull for a very simple reason. Targets shot in the head never fired back.

Bone on bone. Pulse at sixty-four. Web let out one last breath; his finger slid to the trigger and he fired five shots with the precise motion of a man who had done this very thing well over fifty thousand times. He repeated the process four more times, three times at a hundred yards, and the last hand of poker was played out at two hundred yards, which was the outer reaches of distance for sniper's poker.

When he checked the targets Web had to smile. He had a royal flush in spades on two hands, aces with king high on two others and a full house on the hand at two hundred yards; and not one mark on any other card. And not one round thrown either, which in Bureau parlance meant not a shot missed. This allowed him to feel good about himself for about ten seconds and then the depression came roaring back.

He returned the weapon to the equipment cage and continued his stroll. Over at the adjacent Marine Corps facility was the Yellow Brick Road, which was a hellish seven-and-one-half-mile obstacle course with fifteen-foot rope drops, bear pits with barbed wire just waiting for a slip and fall and also sheer rock cliffs. During his HRT qualification days, Web had run that course so many times he had memorized every single disgusting inch of it. Team events had involved fifteen-mile runs, loaded with upward of fifty pounds of gear and precious objects carried, such as bricks that must not touch the ground lest your team lose. There were also swims through icy, filthy water, and fifty-foot long ladders pointed straight to God. That had been followed by a trek up "heartbreak hotel," a mere four-story jaunt, and the optional (yeah!) leap off the gunwale of an old ship into the James River. Since Web's joining HRT, heartbreak hotel had been tamed somewhat, with guide wires, railings and nets. It was undoubtedly safer but, in his opinion, a lot less fun. Still, those with a fear of heights most definitely need not apply. Rappelling from choppers into thick forest really separated the men from the boys, where if you missed your brake point a hundred-foot oak got to know your insides far too well.

And along the way to graduation each recruit had to navigate the hothouse, which was a three-story concrete tower with steel shutters over the windows, welded shut. The interior configuration, with its mesh floors, allowed a fire at the bottom to shoot smoke all the way to the top in seconds. The luckless recruit got thrown into the third floor and had to use his sense of touch, guts and instincts to find his way to the bottom and out to safety. Your reward for surviving that was a bucket of water in the eyes to clear out the smoke there, and the chance to do it again a few minutes later with a hundred-and-fifty-pound dummy on your back.

Crammed in between all that was tens of thousands of rounds fired, classroom drills that would have perplexed and confounded Einstein, fitness grinders that would have left many an Olympian heaving from exhaustion, plus enough paralyzing split-second decision-making scenarios to make a man give up booze and women, crawl in a padded room and start talking to himself. And every step of the way were the real HRT operators grading your sorry butt on every mistake and every triumph, and you just hoped you ended up with far more of the latter, but you never really could tell, because the HRTs never talked to you. To them you were scum, busting-your-ass scum, but still scum. And you knew they wouldn't even acknowledge your presence until and if you graduated. Hell, they probably wouldn't even attend your funeral if the tryout managed to kill you.

Web had somehow survived it all, and upon graduation from the New Operators Training School, or NOTS, as it was known, he had been "drafted" as a sniper and spent two more months at the Scout Sniper School of the Marine Corps, where he had learned from the very best the skills of field craft, observation, camouflage and killing with rifle and scope. After that Web had spent over seven years as first a sniper and later an assaulter either being bored to death at long standoffs, often in miserable conditions, or else shooting or being shot at all over the world by some of its most deranged inhabitants. In return he got all the guns and ammo he wanted and a pay scale equivalent to what a sixteen-year-old could earn programming computers during his lunch hour. All in all it had been really cool.

Web walked by the hangar facility, which housed the team's big Bell 412 helicopters, and the much smaller MD530s, which they all referred to as the Little Birds, because they were fast and agile and could carry four men on the inside and four more on the skids at a speed of 120 knots. Web had ridden the Little Birds into some hellish situations and the 530s had always brought him back out, a couple of times dangling upside down from a rope hooked to the chopper's swing arm, yet Web had never been picky about exactly how he survived a mission.

The motor pool was behind a chain-link fence. Web stopped and zipped up his jacket against a chilly wind. The sky was quickly becoming overcast as a storm system swept into the area, something it routinely did this time of day at this time of year. He went inside the fence and sat atop the team's sole armored personnel carrier, a hand-me-down gift from the Army. His gaze swept across the row of parked Suburbans. The vehicles had been reconfigured with ladder packages such that they could drive right up to a building and extend the ladder and go knock-knock-surprise! on the fifth floor of some criminal's lair. There were mount-out trucks that carried their gear, Jet Skis, food service trucks and a rigid-hull boat with inflatable gunnels that had been designed by Navy SEALs. The thing had twin Chrysler V-8s whose effect Web could only equate to being inside a building while it was being demolished via wrecking ball. He had ridden in it on numerous occasions—or more aptly had survived it.

They had it all here, from equipment for jungle assaults to arctic expeditions. They trained for every contingency, put everything they had into the work. And yet they could still be beaten by coincidence, by the blundering luck of inferior opponents or by the skillful planning and insider knowledge of a traitor.

It started to rain, so Web ducked inside the training facility, which was a large warehouse-style building with long corridors to simulate hallways in hotels and moveable, rubber-coated walls. It was very much like a Hollywood studio back lot. If they were lucky enough to get the blueprints of a target, HRT would reconstruct it on-site here and train within exact parameters. The last set they had built here was for the operation where Charlie had ceased to be. As Web studied this configuration, it hadn't occurred to him that he would never see the insides of the actual target for real. They had never even gotten to the front door. He hoped they would tear out the guts of this place soon, get it ready for the next operation. The result couldn't be any worse, could it?

The rubber-coated walls here absorbed the slugs, for HRT often practiced with live fire. Stairways were made of wood that would not allow ricochets; however, the team had discovered, fortunately without serious injury, that the nails in the wood could catch a bullet and send it on to unintended places. He passed by the aircraft fuselage mockup that had been constructed so they could practice on skyjacking scenarios. It hung from the rafters and could be raised or lowered for training purposes.

How many imaginary terrorists had he shot down in here? The training had paid off, for he had done it for real when an American airliner had been stormed in Rome. The terrorists had ordered the plane flown to Turkey and then on to Manila. Web and crew had gone wheels up at Andrews Air Force base within two hours of learning of the skyjacking. They had followed the hijacked plane's movements from their airborne perch in an USAF C141. On the ground at Manila where the jetliner was being refueled, the terrorists had tossed out two dead hostages, both Americans, one of them a four-year-old girl. A political statement, they proudly announced. It was the last one they would ever make.

The hijacked plane's takeoff had been delayed first by weather and then by mechanical failure. At around midnight local time, Web and his Charlie Team had boarded the plane disguised as mechanics. Three minutes after they got on the plane, there were five dead terrorists and no more slain hostages. Web had shot one of them with his .45 directly through the diet Coke can the guy had been holding up to his mouth. To this day he still couldn't drink the stuff. Yet he never regretted pulling the trigger. The image of an innocent little girl's body on the tarmac—American, Iranian,

Japanese, it didn't matter to Web—was all the motivation he would ever need to keep pulling the trigger at rank evil. These guys could claim all the geopolitical oppression in the world, call upon all the grand and omniscient deities in their religious warehouses, make every half-assed justification they wanted to, so they could detonate their bombs and fire their weapons, and none of it meant a damn thing to Web when they started killing innocent people, and in particular kids. And he would fight them for as long as they wanted to perform their perverted little dance of sin and mayhem across the globe, for wherever they could go, so could he.

Web moved through small rubber-walled rooms where posters of bad guys pointing guns at him hung on support poles. He instinctively drew a bead with his finger and blew them away. With an armed person you always keyed on hands, not the eyes, because no one in history had ever been killed by a pair of eyes. As he lowered his "gun," Web had to smile. It was all so easy when no one was actually firing at you. In other rooms were the heads and upper torsos of dummies on poles, their "skin" and bulk replicating that of a real human. Web threw side kicks to their heads followed by a series of paralyzing kidney punches and then moved on.

From inside one room he heard some movement and looked in. The man there had on a tank shirt and cammie pants and was wiping the sweat from his muscular neck, shoulders and arms. Long ropes dangled from the ceiling. This was one of the rooms where the men practiced their fast-roping skills. Web watched as the man went up and down three times with graceful, fluid motions, cords of muscles in his arms and shoulders tensing and then relaxing.

When the man finished, Web stepped inside and said, "Hey, Ken, don't you ever take a day off?"

Ken McCarthy looked over at Web and his gaze was not exactly what Web would have called friendly. McCarthy was one of the snipers who had been overhead along the alley the night Charlie Team had disappeared under the wave of .50s. McCarthy was black, thirty-four years of age, a Texan by birth as well as an Army brat who had seen the world on Uncle Sam's dime. He was a former SEAL yet did not exude the flagrant cockiness that most SEALs tended to. Only five-ten, he could bench-press a truck and held advanced multidegree black belts in three different martial arts. He was the most skilled water operator HRT had, and he could also place a bullet between a person's eyes at a thousand yards in the dead of night while straddling a tree limb. A three-year veteran of HRT, he was quiet, kept mostly to himself and lacked the ghoulish sense of humor that most operators had. Web had taught him things McCarthy hadn't known or was having trouble picking up, and in return McCarthy had shared some of his remarkable skills with Web. To Web's knowledge McCarthy had never had a problem with him, yet the man's look right now possibly heralded an end to that streak. Maybe Romano had turned everyone against him.

"What're you doing here, Web? Figured you'd still be in the hospital nursing your injuries."

Web took another step toward the man. He didn't like McCarthy's tone or words, yet he could understand where they were coming from. Web could also understand where Romano was coming from too; it was just that sort of a place. You were expected to do your job, perfectly. Perfection was all they asked for here. Web hadn't come close. Sure he had knocked out the guns, after the fact. That counted for zip with these men.

"I take it you saw it all."

McCarthy slipped off a pair of workout gloves and rubbed his thick, heavily callused fingers. "Would've fast-roped down to the alley, but TOC told us to sit tight."

"There was nothing you could do, Ken."

McCarthy was still looking at his feet. "Finally got the go-ahead. Took too long. Hooked up with Hotel. Took damn way too long," he said again. "We kept stopping, trying to raise you guys on the mic. TOC didn't know what the hell was going on. Our chain of command sort of broke down. Guess you knew that."

"We were prepared for everything except what went down."

McCarthy sat on the rubber mat floor and drew his knees up. He glanced up at Web. "Heard you were a little late coming out of the alley and that you kind of fell down or something."

Or something. He sat down next to McCarthy. "The guns were triggered by a laser, but the laser was probably activated by a remote so the fifties wouldn't kick on prematurely and hit the wrong target. Somebody had to be around there to do that." Web let that last statement hang as his gaze remained on McCarthy.

"I've already talked to WFO."

"I'm sure."

"It's an ongoing AFO, Web," he said. An AFO was an investigation of an assault on a federal officer, actually lots of them in this case.

"I know all that too, Ken. Look, I'm not sure what happened to me. I didn't plan it that way. I did all I could." Web drew a long breath. "And if I could take it all back right now, I would. And I've got to live with that every day of my life, Ken. I hope you can understand that."

McCarthy lifted his head and his hostile look faded.

"There was nothing to shoot, Web. There wasn't a damn thing for the snipers to blow away; all that training and no party to show it off at. We had three guys on the buildings overlooking the courtyard and not one of them could get even a decent bead on the mini-guns. Hell, they were afraid to fire because they thought one of their ricochets might nail you."

"How about the kid? Did you see the kid?"

"The little black kid? Yeah, when he came down the alley, with your cap and the note."

"We passed him going in too."

"You guys must have blocked our view. And the light in that alley really reflected weird up where we were."

"Okay, how about the other guys? The dudes doing the drugs?"

"We had a sniper on them the whole time. They never left where they were until the firing started, then they took off running. Jeffries said they seemed as surprised as anybody. When TOC gave us the green light, we took off."

"What happened then?"

"Hooked up with Hotel, like I said. We saw the flare, stopped, fanned out. Then the kid came to us. We got the note, your warning. Everett and Palmer went forward as scouts. Too damn late." McCarthy paused here, and Web saw a single tear slide down the man's youthful, handsome features; normal features like what Web had once possessed.

"I never heard gunfire like that in my life, Web. I've never felt helpless like that in my whole life."

"You did your job, Ken, and that's all you can do." Web paused and then said, "They can't seem to find the kid. Know anything about that?"

McCarthy shook his head. "Couple guys from Hotel took charge of him. Romano and Cortez, I think."

Romano again. Shit, that meant Web had to go talk to the man. "What'd you do?"

"I went into the courtyard with some of the others. We saw you, but you were out of it." He looked down again. "And we saw the rest of Charlie." He glanced at Web. "A couple of the snipers told me how you went back out there, Web. They saw what you did and still can't believe you did it. Said you must have the luck of the Irish somewhere in your back pocket to have gone back out there. I don't think I could have."

"Yes you would, Ken. And you would've done it better than me."

McCarthy seemed startled at this praise.

"After you came back out of the courtyard, did you see the kid?"

McCarthy thought about this. "I remember him sitting on a trash can. By that time, everybody was showing up."

"Did you see any suits take custody of the kid?"

McCarthy thought again. "No, I sort of recall Romano talking to somebody, but that's all."

"Did you recognize any of them?"

"You know we don't interface with the regulars that much."

"How about DEA?"

"That's all I can tell you, Web."

"You been talking to Romano?"

"A little."

"Don't believe everything you hear, Ken. It's not healthy."

"Including from you?" McCarthy asked pointedly.

"Including from me."

As Web drove away from Quantico, he realized he had a lot of ground to cover. This was officially not his investigation, yet in some ways it was more his than anyone else's. But he had to take care of something else first, something even more important than finding out who had set up his team. And finding out what had happened to a little boy with a bullet hole on his cheek and no shirt to his name.

6

Six funerals. Web attended six funerals over three days. By the fourth one, he couldn't muster a single tear. He walked into the church or the funeral home and listened to people he mostly didn't know talk about fallen men he knew better than he understood himself in some ways. It was as though all of his nerves had been boiled away, along with part of his soul. In a way he felt incapable of reacting as he was supposed to. He was terrified he would start laughing when he should be mourning.

At the services half the caskets were open, the rest not. Some of the dead men had fared better with the size and placement of the wounds that had killed them and thus had open caskets. However, staring at pale, collapsed faces and rigid, shrunken bodies in metal boxes, inhaling flower fragrance and hearing the sobs of all those around him made Web wish he could just lie down in a box too and be put away in the ground to hide forever. The funeral of a hero; there were far worse ways to be remembered.

He had wrapped his hand back up in the layers of gauze because he felt guilty walking among the bereaved without a trace of a wound. It was a pathetic thing to be concerned with, he knew, yet he felt like a walking slap in the face to the survivors. All they really knew was that Web London had somehow gotten off with barely a scratch. Had he run? Had he left his comrades to die? He could see those questions in some of the people's faces. Was that always the fate of the sole survivor?

The funeral processions had passed between endless lines of

men and women in uniform and hundreds of others dressed in the neat suits and sensible shoes of the FBI. Motorcycles led the way, citizens lined the streets and flags everywhere flew at half mast. The President and most of his Cabinet came, along with many other VIPs. For a few days, the entire world talked of nothing else except the slaughter of six good men in an alley. Not much was said about the seventh man, and for that Web was mostly grateful. Still, he wondered how long that moratorium could possibly last for him.

The city of Washington was deeply stricken. And it was not entirely over the fate of the slain men, for the broader implications were troubling. Had criminals really become so brazen? Was society coming apart at the seams? Were the police not keeping pace? Was American law enforcement's crown jewel, the FBI, losing its luster? The Middle Eastern and Chinese news services were having a particularly delicious time reporting yet another example of Western mayhem that would one day bring arrogant America to its soft knees. Cheers were no doubt racing up and down the streets of Baghdad, Teheran, Pyongyang and Beijing at the thought of the old USA falling apart one miserable media-fueled crisis at a time. The pundits on American soil were spouting so many absurd scenarios that Web no longer even opened a newspaper or turned on a TV or radio. If anyone had asked him, though, he would have said that the whole world, and not just the United States, had been screwed up for a long time.

There had been some relief from this crossfire, though its catalyst was another appalling tragedy. A Japanese commercial jetliner had crashed off the Pacific Coast, so the newsmongers had chased after that story and left the alley and its dead behind for now. A single news truck was still there, but scraps of three hundred bodies floating in the ocean was a far bigger draw than a days-old story about a team of dead FBI agents. And for that Web was also grateful. *Leave us alone to grieve in peace.*

He had been debriefed "uptown" at the Hoover Building and at the WFO on three different occasions, by several teams of investigators. They had their pads and pencils, their recorders and some of the younger agents even had laptops. They had asked Web many more questions than he had answers for. However, when he told each group that he didn't know why he had frozen and then fallen, the pencils had stopped scribbling on paper, fingers had stopped clacking on keyboards.

"When you say you froze, did you see something? Hear something to make you do that?" The man spoke in a monotone, which, to Web, was one imperceptible inflection short of incredulity or, worse, outright disbelief.

"I don't really know."

"You really don't know? You're not sure if you froze?"

"I'm not sure. I mean, I did. I couldn't move. It was like I was paralyzed."

"But you moved after your team was killed?"

"Yes," Web conceded.

"What had changed to allow you to do that?"

"I don't know."

"And when you got to the courtyard, you fell?"

"That's right."

"Right before the guns opened fire," said another investigator.

Web could barely hear his own answer. "Yes."

The silence that followed these meager responses came close to dissolving Web's already bludgeoned insides.

During each debriefing, Web had kept his hands on top of the table, his gaze steady on each questioner's face, his posture in a slight forward lean. These men were all professional, seasoned inquisitors. Web knew that if he looked away, sat back, rubbed his head the wrong way or, worse yet, crossed his arms, they would instantly conclude he was a lying sack of shit. Web wasn't being untruthful, but he wasn't telling all of the truth either. Yet if Web started talking about how the vision of a little boy had had a weird effect on him, perhaps inexplicably caused him to freeze, thus saving his life—or about then feeling weighed down as though encased in concrete and then seconds later being able to freely move—he would be finished at the Bureau. The higher-ups tended to frown on field agents making insane comments. Yet he had one thing going for him. Those machine gun nests didn't disintegrate by themselves. And his rifle rounds were embedded in all of them. And the snipers had seen everything, and he had warned Hotel Team and saved the boy on top of it. Web made sure he said that. He made sure all of them knew that. *You can kick me while I'm down, friends, just not too hard. I'm a damn hero after all.*

"I'll be all right," Web had told them. "I just need a little time. I'll be all right." And for one awful moment Web thought that might be the first actual lie he had told all day.

They would call him back in as needed, they told him. For now, they just wanted him to do nothing. He was to take plenty of time to get himself together. The Bureau had offered the assistance of a counselor, a mental health professional, in fact they had insisted on it, and Web said he would go, although there was still a stigma at the Bureau for those seeking such help. When things looked okay, Web was told, he would be assigned to another assaulter or sniper team, if he so desired, until Charlie could be rebuilt. If not, he could take another position within the Bureau. There was even talk of allowing him to burn an "office of preference" transfer that would allow him to proceed directly to "Go" in the form of an office he would retire from. That sort of treatment was usually reserved for senior-level agents and symbolized that the Bureau was really unsure of what to do with him. Officially, Web was in the middle of an administrative inquiry that might well blossom into a full investigation, depending on how things shook out. Well, no one had given Web his Miranda rights, which was both good and bad. Good because Web getting his Miranda warning would mean he was under arrest, bad in that anything he said during the inquiry could be used against him in civil or criminal proceedings. The only thing he had done wrong, apparently, was having survived. And yet that was a source of guilt far stronger than anything the Bureau could charge him with.

No, really, whatever he wanted, Web was told, he could have. They were all his friends. He had their full support.

Web asked how the investigation was going and didn't get an answer in return. So much for their full support, Web thought.

"Get better," another man had told him. "That's *all* you need to focus on."

As he was leaving from his last debriefing, he got one final question. "How's the hand?" the man asked. Web didn't know the guy, and although the question seemed innocent enough, there was something in the fellow's eyes that made Web want to deck him. Instead, Web said it was just fine, thanked them all and left.

On the way out from the last session he had passed the FBI's Wall of Honor, where hung plaques for each of the FBI personnel killed in the line of duty. There would be a major addition coming to the wall, the largest single one in the history of the Bureau, in fact. Web had sometimes wondered if he would ever end up on there, with his professional life compacted into a chunk of wood and brass hanging on a wall. He left Hoover and drove home, besieged by many more questions than he wanted to confront.

FBI also officially stood for Fidelity, Bravery and Integrity, and right now Web didn't feel he possessed any of these qualities.

7

Francis Westbrook was a giant of a man, with the height and girth of a NFL starting left tackle. Regardless of the weather or season, his clothes of choice were silk tropical short-sleeved shirts, matching slacks and suede loafers with no socks. His head was bald, his large ears were covered with diamond studs and his enormous fingers were festooned with gold rings. He wasn't a dandy of any sort, but there simply weren't that many things he could spend his drug earnings on without the law or, even worse, the IRS sniffing around. And he also liked to look good. Right now Westbrook was riding in the backseat of a large Mercedes sedan with black-tinted windows. To the left of him was his first lieutenant, Antoine Peebles. Driving was a tall, well-built young man named Toona, and in the passenger seat was his chief of security, Clyde Macy, the only white guy in Westbrook's entire crew, and it was easy to see that the man carried that distinction with great pride. Peebles had a neatly trimmed beard and Afro, was short and heavyset, but he wore his Armani and his designer shades well. He looked more like a Hollywood exec than a high-level drug entrepreneur. Macy looked like a breathing skeleton, preferred his clothes black and professional-looking and with his shaved head could easily have been mistaken for a neo-Nazi.

This represented the inner circle of Westbrook's small empire and the leader of that empire held a nine-millimeter pistol in his right hand and seemed to be looking for someone to use it on. "You want to tell me one more time how you lost Kevin?" He looked at

Peebles and clutched the pistol even tighter. Its safety was in the grip and Westbrook had just released it. Peebles seemed to recognize this and yet didn't hesitate in responding. "If you let us keep somebody on him twenty-four and seven, then we'd never lose him. He goes out sometimes at night. He went out that night and didn't come back."

Westbrook slapped his enormous thigh. "He was in that alley. The Feds had him and now they don't. He's mixed up with this shit somehow and it happened in my damn backyard." He smacked the gun against the door and roared, "I want Kevin back!"

Peebles looked at him nervously, while Macy showed no reaction.

Westbrook put a hand on the driver's shoulder. "Toona, you get some of the boys together and you gonna hit every part of this damn town, you hear me? I know you already done it once, but you do it again. I want that boy back nice and safe, you hear me? Nice and safe and don't come back till you done it. Damn it, you hear me, Toona?"

Toona glanced in the rearview mirror. "I hear you, I hear you."

"Set up," said Peebles. "All around. To put the blame on you."

"You think I ain't know that? You think 'cause you went to college that you smart and I'm stupid? I know the Feds coming after my ass on this. I know the word on the street. Somebody's trying to get all the crews together, almost like a damn union, but they know I ain't joining shit and it's messing up their plan." Westbrook's eyes were red. He hadn't slept much in the last forty-eight hours. That was just his life; surviving the night was usually the big project of the day. And all he could think about was a little boy out there somewhere. He was getting close to the edge; he could feel it. He had known this day might come, and still, he was not prepared for it.

"Whoever got Kevin, they gonna let me know it. They want something. They want me to jump my crew in, that's what they want."

"And you'll give it to them?"

"Anything I got they can have. So long as I get Kevin back." He paused and looked out the window, at the corners and alleys and cheap bars they were passing, where his drug tentacles slithered.

He did a brisk business in the suburbs too, where the real money was. "Yeah, that's right. I get Kevin back and then I kill every one of the mothers. I do it myself." He pointed the pistol at an imaginary foe. "Start with the knees and work my way up."

Peebles looked warily at Macy, who still showed no sign of any reaction; it was as though he were made of stone. "Well, nobody's contacted us so far," said Peebles.

"They will. They didn't take Kevin 'cause they want to shoot hoops with him. They want me. Well, I'm right here, they just got to come to the party. I'm ready to party, bring it the fuck on." Westbrook spoke more calmly. "Word is one of them dudes didn't eat it in that courtyard. That right?"

Peebles nodded. "Web London."

"They say machine guns, fifty-caliber shit. How's a dude slip that?" Peebles shrugged his shoulders and Westbrook looked at Macy. "What you hear on that, Mace?"

"Nobody's saying for sure right now, but what I hear is the man didn't go in that courtyard. He got scared, freaked or something."

"Freaked or something," said Westbrook. "Okay, you get some shit on this man and you let me see it. Man walk away from something like that, man got something to tell me. Like maybe where Kevin is." He looked at his men. "Whoever shot them Feds up got Kevin. You can count on that."

"Well, like I said, we could've had him on round-the-clock," commented Peebles.

"What the hell kind of life is that?" said Westbrook. "He ain't got to live that way, not because of me. But the Feds come after my ass, then I'll just point them boys in another direction. But we got to know which way that is. With six damn Feds dead, they ain't gonna be looking to cut no deals. They'll want some serious ass to fry and it ain't gonna be mine."

"Whoever took Kevin, there's no guarantee they'll let him go," said Peebles. "I know you don't want to hear this, but we have no way of knowing if Kevin's even alive."

Westbrook lay back against the seat. "Oh, he's alive, all right. Ain't nothing wrong with Kevin. Not right now anyway."

"How can you be sure?"

"I just know and that's all you need to know. You just get me something on this Fed mother."

"Web London."

"Web London. And if he ain't got what I need, then he'll wish he died with his crew. Hit it, Toona. We got bizness."

The car sped on into the night.

8

It took Web a couple of days to make an appointment with a psychiatrist whom the Bureau used on an independent contractor basis. The FBI had trained people on staff, but Web had opted for someone on the outside. He wasn't sure why, yet spilling his guts to anyone on the inside right now didn't seem like a good idea. Rightly or not, tell the Feds' shrink, you're telling the Feds, was Web's thinking, to hell with patient confidentiality.

The Bureau was still pretty much in the Dark Ages when it came to the mental health of their people, and that probably was as much the fault of the individual agents as the organization. Until several years ago, if you worked at the FBI and were feeling stressed or were having problems with alcohol or substance abuse, you pretty much kept it to yourself and dealt with it in your own way. The old school agents would have given no more thought to seeking counseling than they would about leaving home without their gun. If an agent was seeking professional help, no one knew about it, and certainly no one talked about it. You were, in a sense, tainted goods if you did, and the indoctrination process of being a member of the Bureau seemed to instill both a stoicism and stubborn independence that were difficult to overcome.

Then the powers that be had finally decided that the stress of working for the FBI, reflected in rising rates of alcohol and drug abuse and the high incidence of divorce, needed to be addressed. An Employee Assistance Program, or EAP, was instituted. Each FBI division was assigned an EAP coordinator and counselor. If the in-house counselor couldn't handle the situation, he or she would refer the patient to an approved outside source, as Web had opted to have done. The EAP wasn't widely known at the Bureau and Web had never gotten any written materials on its existence. It was just sort of whispered ear to ear. The old stigma, despite the Bureau's efforts, was still there.

The psychiatric offices were in a high-rise building in Fairfax County near Tyson's Corner. Web had seen Dr. O'Bannon, one of the psychiatrists who worked here, before. The first time was years ago when HRT had been called up to rescue some students at a private school in Richmond, Virginia. A bunch of paramilitary types belonging to a group calling themselves the Free Society, who apparently were seeking to create an Aryan culture by means of their own version of ethnic cleansing, had burst into the school and immediately killed two teachers. The standoff had lasted almost twenty-four hours. HRT had finally gone in when it appeared imminent that the men were going to start killing again. Things were going perfectly until something had alerted the Frees right before HRT was ready to pounce. The resulting shootout had left five of the Frees dead and two HRT personnel injured, Web critically so. The only other hostage to die was a ten-year-old boy named David Canfield.

Web had been almost close enough to the child to pull him to safety when things went to hell. The dead boy's face had intruded into his dreams so often that Web had voluntarily sought counseling. At that time there was no EAP, so after he had recovered from his injuries Web had discreetly gotten O'Bannon's name from another agent whom O'Bannon was seeing. It had been one of the hardest things Web had ever done, because, in effect, he was admitting that he couldn't handle his problems. He never talked about it with other HRT members and he would have cut out his tongue before he would reveal that he was seeing a shrink. His colleagues would have only seen that as a weakness, and at HRT there was no room for that.

The operators at HRT had had a previous encounter with mental health counseling, and it had not gone well: After Waco, the

Bureau had brought in some counselors who had met directly with the stricken men as a group instead of individually. The result would have been comical if it hadn't been so pathetically sad. That was the last time the Bureau had tried that sort of thing with HRT.

The most recent time Web had seen O'Bannon was right after Web's mother had died. After quite a few sessions with O'Bannon, Web concluded that things were never going to be right on that score and he had lied and told O'Bannon that he was just fine. He didn't blame O'Bannon, for no doc could make that mess right, he knew. It would have taken a miracle.

O'Bannon was short and heavyset and often wore a black turtleneck that made his multiple chins even more pronounced. Web remembered that O'Bannon's handshake was limp, his manner pleasant enough, and yet Web had felt like running for the door the first time the two had met. Instead, he had followed O'Bannon back to his office and plunged into some dangerous waters.

"We'll be able to help you, Web. It'll just take time. I'm sorry we have to meet under such difficult circumstances, but people don't come to me because things are wonderful; it's my lot in life, I suppose."

Web said that was good and yet his spirits sank. O'Bannon clearly had no magic that would make Web's world normal again.

They had sat in O'Bannon's office. There was no couch but rather a small love seat not nearly long enough to lie down upon. O'Bannon had explained it as, "The greatest of all misperceptions in our field. Not every psychiatrist has a couch."

O'Bannon's office was sterile, with white walls, industrial furnishings and very few items of a personal nature. It all made Web feel about as comfortable as sitting on death row waiting to do a last dance with Mr. Sparky. They made small talk, presumably to ease Web into opening up. There was a pad and pen next to O'Bannon, but he never picked them up.

"I'll do that later," O'Bannon had said when Web asked him about his lack of note-taking. "For now, let's just talk." He had a darting gaze that had been unsettling to Web, though the psychiatrist's voice was soft and relatively soothing. After an hour the session was up, and Web could see nothing much that had been accomplished. He knew more about O'Bannon than the man knew about Web. He had not gotten around to any of the issues disturbing him.

"These things take time, Web," O'Bannon had said as he led Web out. "It'll come, don't you worry. It just takes time. Rome wasn't built in a day."

Web wanted to ask him exactly how long it would take to build Rome in this case, but he said nothing except good-bye. At first Web had believed that he would never go back to see the short, pudgy man with the blank office. And yet he had. And O'Bannon had worked through the issues with him session after session, getting him to deal with things. But Web had never forgotten the little boy who had been gunned down in cold blood with Web mere feet away and unable to save him. That would have been unhealthy, to ever forget something like that.

O'Bannon had told Web that he and others at his psychiatric practice had catered to the needs of Bureau personnel for many years and had helped agents and administrative staff through lots of crises. Web had been surprised at that because he assumed he was one of the few who had ever sought professional counseling. O'Bannon had looked at him in a very knowing way and said, "Just because people don't talk about it doesn't mean they don't want to address their issues or don't want to get better. I can, of course, reveal no names, but trust me, you are definitely not alone in coming to me from the FBI. Agents who hide their heads in the sand are just ticking bombs waiting to explode."

Now Web wondered if he was a ticking bomb. He went inside and over to the elevators, each step heavier than the previous one.

With his mind clearly elsewhere, Web nearly collided with a woman coming from the other direction. He apologized and pushed the elevator button. The car came and they both got on. Web punched the button for his floor and stepped back. As they headed up, Web glanced over at the woman. She was average height, slender and very attractive. He put her age at late thirties. She wore a gray pantsuit, the collar of a white blouse topping it. Her hair was a wavy black and cut short, and she had on small clip earrings. She carried a briefcase. Her long fingers curled around the handle, pressing tightly, noted Web, whose whole professional life was spent obsessing over the small details, because the little things almost always determined his future, or lack of one.

The car stopped at Web's floor and he was a little surprised when the woman got off too. But then he recalled she had not pushed another floor button. Well, so much for always observing the little details. He followed her to the office he was going to. She glanced back at him.

"Can I help you?"

Her voice was low, precise and somehow inviting, comforting to him. The unusually deep blue of her eyes caught Web's attention. The eyes were also big, sad and peering. They held you, those eyes did.

"I'm here to see Dr. O'Bannon."

"Did you have an appointment?"

She seemed wary, Web thought. Yet he also knew women had every right to be suspicious when confronted with strange men. He had seen the ugly results of many such encounters and those images never left you.

"Yes, for nine o'clock, Wednesday morning. I'm a little early."

She gave him a sympathetic look. "Actually, today is Tuesday."

Web muttered, "Shit," and shook his head wearily. "Guess I'm getting my days sort of mixed up. Sorry to bother you." He turned to leave and he was reasonably sure he would never come back.

"I'm sorry, but you look very familiar to me," the woman said. Web turned slowly back. "I apologize," she added. "I'm not usually that forward, but I know I've seen you before."

"Well, if you work here, you probably did. I've been to see O'Bannon before."

"No, it wasn't here. I believe it was on TV." Realization finally swept across her features. "You're Web London, the FBI agent, aren't you?"

He couldn't decide what to say for a few moments and she simply looked at him, apparently awaiting confirmation of her observation. "Yes." Web glanced past her. "Do you work here?"

"I have an office here."

"So you're a shrink too?"

She put out her hand. "We prefer psychiatrist. I'm Claire Daniels."

Web shook her hand and then they stood there awkwardly.

"I'm going to put some coffee on if you'd like a cup," she finally said.

"Don't go to any trouble."

She turned and unlocked the door. Web followed her inside.

They sat in the small reception room and drank the coffee. Web glanced around the empty space.

"Office closed today?"

"No, most people don't get in before nine."

"It always surprised me that you don't have a receptionist here."

"Well, we want to make it as comfortable for people as possible. And announcing yourself to a stranger because you're here to receive treatment can be very intimidating. We know when we have appointments and the doorbell lets us know when someone has arrived, and we come right out. We have this common waiting area because that's unavoidable, but, as a rule, we don't like to make patients sit out here with one another. That can be awkward too."

"Sort of like people sitting around playing 'Guess My Psychosis'?"

She smiled. "Something like that. Dr. O'Bannon started this practice many years ago and he cares quite deeply about the comfort zone of the people who come here for help. The last thing you want to do is to increase the anxiety level of already anxious people."

"So you know O'Bannon well?"

"Yes. I actually used to work for him. Then he simplified his life a while back and we're all on our own now, but we still share this office space. We've come to prefer it that way. He's very good. He'll be able to help you."

"You think so?" Web said without a trace of hope.

"I guess like the rest of the country I've been following what happened. I'm very sorry about your colleagues."

Web drank his coffee in silence.

Claire said, "If you were thinking of waiting, Dr. O'Bannon is teaching at George Washington University. He won't be in at all today."

"No big deal. My mistake. Thanks for the coffee." He rose.

"Mr. London, would you like me to tell him you were here?"

"It's Web. And no, I don't think I'll be back on Wednesday."

Claire stood too. "Is there something I can do to help you?"

He held up his cup. "You already made the java." Web took a breath. It was time to get out of here. "What are you doing for the next hour?" he asked instead, and then was stunned to hear his own words.

"Just paperwork," she said quickly, her gaze downcast, her face slightly red as though he had just asked her out to the prom and instead of saying no to his advance she was deciding, for some unknown reason, to encourage it.

"How would you like to talk to me instead?"

"Professionally? That's not possible. You're Dr. O'Bannon's patient."

"How about human to human?" Web had absolutely no idea where any of these words were coming from.

She hesitated for a moment and then told him to wait. She went into an office and then came back out a few minutes later. "I tried reaching Dr. O'Bannon at the university, but they couldn't track him down. Without talking to him, I really can't counsel you. You have to understand, it's a touchy thing ethically, Web. I'm not into poaching patients."

Web abruptly sat down. "Wouldn't it ever be justified?"

She mulled this over for a few moments. "I suppose if your regular doctor wasn't available and you were in crisis, it would be."

"He's not available and I'm in an honest-to-God crisis." Web was being absolutely truthful, for it was like he was back in that courtyard, unable to move, unable to do a damn thing to help, useless. If she still refused him, Web wasn't sure he could even manage to get up and leave.

Instead she led him down the hallway to her office and closed the door behind them. Web looked around. There could not have been a greater difference between Claire Daniels's digs and those of O'Bannon. The walls were a muted gray instead of stark white, and cozy with femininely floral curtains instead of industrial shades. There were pictures hung everywhere, mostly of people, presumably family. The degrees on the wall evidenced Claire Daniels's impressive academic accomplishments: degrees from Brown and

Columbia Universities and her medical sheepskin from Stanford. On one table was a glass container that had a label reading, "Therapy in a Jar." There were unlit candles on tables and cactus lamps in two corners. On shelves and on the floor were dozens of stuffed animals. There was a leather chair against one wall. And by God, Claire Daniels had a couch!

"You want me to sit there?" He pointed to it, trying desperately to keep his nerves in check. He suddenly wished he wasn't armed, because he was starting to feel a little out of control.

"Actually, if you don't mind, I prefer the couch."

He collapsed in the chair and then watched as she switched her flats for slippers that were lying next to the couch. The momentary sight of her bare feet had prompted an unexpected reaction from Web. There was nothing sexual about it; it made Web think of the bloodied skin in the courtyard, the remains of Charlie Team. Claire sat down on the couch, pulled a pad and pen off the side table and uncapped the pen. Web took a series of small breaths to arrest his nerves.

"O'Bannon doesn't take notes during the session," he commented.

"I know," she said with a wry smile. "I don't think my memory is as good as his. Sorry."

"I didn't even ask if you're on the Bureau's approved list of outside contractors. I know O'Bannon is."

"I am too. And this session will have to be revealed to your supervisor. Bureau policy."

"But not the content of the session."

"No, of course not. Just that we met. The same *basic* rules of confidentiality apply here as they would in a normal psychiatrist and patient relationship."

"Basic rules?"

"There are modifications, Web, because of the unique job you have."

"O'Bannon explained that to me when I was seeing him, but I guess I was never really clear on it."

"Well, I'm under an obligation to inform your supervisor if during a session anything is revealed that poses a threat to yourself or others."

"I guess that's fair."

"You think so? Well, from my point of view, it gives me a great deal of discretion, because where one hears something benign, another hears genuine threats. So I'm not so sure that policy is very fair to you. But just so you know, I have never had occasion to use that discretion and I've been working with people from the FBI, DEA and other law enforcement agencies for a long time."

"What else has to be revealed?"

"The other major one is drug use or specific therapies."

"Right. The Bureau is a stickler for that, I know," said Web. "Even over-the-counter stuff you have to report that you're taking. It can actually get to be quite a pain in the ass." He looked around. "Your place is a lot more comfortable. O'Bannon's office reminds me of an operating room."

"Everybody approaches their work differently." She stopped and stared at his waist.

Web glanced down and saw that his windbreaker had fallen open there, and the grip of his pistol was visible. He zipped up the jacket, as Claire looked down at her pad.

"Sorry, Web, it's not like it's the first time I've seen an agent with a gun. Though I suppose when you don't see them every day—"

"They can be scary as hell," he finished her thought.

He eyed the array of furry toys.

"What's with all the stuffed animals?"

"I have a lot of children as patients," she said, adding, "unfortunately. The animals make them feel more at ease. To tell the truth, they make me feel more at ease too."

"It's hard to believe kids would need a psychiatrist."

"Most of them have eating disorders, bulimia, anorexia. Usually centered on issues of control between them and their parents. So you have to treat the child *and* the parent. It's not an easy world for children."

"It's not all that great for adults either."

She gave him a look that Web interpreted as a quick appraisal. "You've been through a lot in your life."

"More than some, less than others. You're not going to make me take an inkblot test, are you?" He said this as a joke, but he was actually serious.

"Psychologists perform Rorschach, MMPI, MMCI and neuro-testing, I'm just a humble psychiatrist."

"I had to take the MMPI when I joined Hostage Rescue."

"The Minnesota Multiphasic Personality Inventory, I'm familiar with it."

"It's designed to ferret out the crazies."

"In a manner of speaking, yes. Did it?"

"Some of the guys failed it. Me, I figured out what the test was for, and just lied my way through it."

Claire Daniels's eyebrows lifted slightly and her gaze once more went to where his gun was. "That's comforting."

"I guess I'm not real clear on the difference. Between psychologists and psychiatrists, that is."

"A psychiatrist has to take the MCATs, then do four years of medical school. After that you have to serve three years of residency in psychiatry at a hospital. I also did a fourth-year residency in forensic psychiatry. I've been in private practice ever since. As medical doctors, psychiatrists can also prescribe medication, whereas psychologists generally can't."

Web clasped and unclasped his hands nervously.

Claire, who was studying him closely, said, "Why don't I tell you how I go about my work? Then, if you're comfortable with that, we can continue. Fair enough?" Web nodded in agreement and she settled back into the cushions. "As a psychiatrist, I rely on understanding patterns of normal human behavior, so that I can recognize when certain behavior falls outside the norm. An obvious example is one you're no doubt familiar with: serial killers. In the vast majority of cases such people have suffered consistent, terrible abuse as children. They, in turn, exhibit clear patterns of rage when young, like torturing small animals and birds as they single-mindedly transfer the pain and cruelty foisted upon them onto living things less powerful than themselves. They move on to larger animals and other targets as they grow older, stronger and bolder, and eventually progress to human beings when they reach adulthood. It's actually a fairly predictable evolution of events.

"You also have to listen with a third ear of sorts. I take what someone tells me at face value, but I'm also looking for cues underlying those statements. Humans are always layering their statements with other messages. A psychiatrist wears many hats, often at the same time. The key is to listen, I mean really listen to what you're being told, in words, body language, that sort of thing."

"Okay, how would you like to start with me?"

"I usually have a patient fill out a background questionnaire, but I think I'll skip that with you. Human to human," she added with a very warm smile.

Web finally felt the heat in his belly start to ease.

"But let's talk a little about your background, all the typical information. Then we can move on from there."

Web let out a deep breath. "I'll be thirty-eight next March. I did the college route and then somehow got into the University of Virginia law school and actually managed to graduate. After that I worked in the commonwealth attorney's office for about six months in Alexandria until I realized that life wasn't for me. I decided to apply to the Bureau along with a buddy of mine. It was really on a whim, to see if we could do it. I made the cut, he didn't. I survived the Academy and I've been with the FBI for a lucky thirteen years. I started out as a special agent, cutting my teeth on this and that in a string of field offices across the country. A little over eight years ago, I applied to HRT. That stands for Hostage Rescue Team. It's part of CIRG, Critical Incident Response Group, now, though that's a fairly recent development. They kill your ass in the selection process and ninety percent of the applicants don't make the cut. They sleep-deprive you first, break you physically and then force you to make snap decisions of life and death. They make you work and sacrifice as a team but still compete against one another, because there aren't many slots available. It was a real walk in the park. I saw former Navy SEALs, Special Forces guys, Deltas even, break down, cry, pass out, hallucinate, threaten suicide, mass murders, anything to make their tormentors stop. By a miracle, I somehow got through and then spent another five months at the New Operators Training School, or NOTS. In case you couldn't tell, the Bureau is big on acronyms. We're based at Quantico. I'm an assaulter right now." Claire looked confused. "HRT has Blue and Gold Units, with four teams in each. They mirror each other, so we can handle two crises in two different places simultaneously. Half the teams are made up of assaulters or the main attack force, the other half are snipers. Snipers train at the Marine Corps Scout Sniper School. We switch off periodically, cross-train. I started out as a sniper. They used to really get the short end of the stick, though after HRT was reorganized in 1995 it's gotten a lot better. Still, you lie in the mud and rain and snow for weeks, spying on the target, learning the weaknesses of your opponents that will help you kill them later. Or maybe even save their lives, because watching them, you may spot something that will tell you that they won't shoot back in certain situations. You wait to take your shots of opportunity, never knowing if the shot you take will trigger some damn firestorm."

"You sound like you've experienced something like that."

"One of my very first assignments was Waco."

"I see."

"Right now I'm assigned to Charlie Team in the Blue Unit." *Was,* Web mentally corrected himself. There was no more Charlie Team.

"So you're not an FBI agent per se?"

"No, we all are. You have to have at least three years at the Bureau and a superior performance rating to even apply to HRT. We carry the same shields, the same credentials. But we HRT guys keep to ourselves. Separate facilities, no other duties outside HRT. We train together. Core skills, knots, CQB."

"What are those things?"

"Knots covers combat and firearm training. CQB stands for close-quarters battle training. Firearms and CQB are the most perishable skills, so you're constantly working them."

"Sounds very military."

"It is. And we are very military. We're split into active duty and training. If you're on duty and a mission comes up, you go. Any downtime for active duty operators is spent on special projects and special skills like rope climbing, chopper rappelling, SEAL training, first aid. And also field craft, what we call snooping and pooping in the woods. The days go quickly, believe me."

"I'm sure," said Claire.

Web studied his shoes and they sat there quietly for a while. "Fifty alpha males together is sometimes not a good thing." He smiled. "We're always trying to one-up each other. You know those Taser guns that shoot out electrified darts and paralyze people?"

"Yes, I've seen them."

"Well, we had a contest one time to see who could recover the fastest after getting hit by one of those."

"Good God," exclaimed Claire.

"I know, crazy." He added, "I didn't win. I went down like I'd been hit by an NFL lineman. But that's sort of the mentality. Ultracompetitive." He became more serious. "But we're good at our jobs. And our jobs aren't easy. What nobody else wants to do, we do. Our official motto is, 'To save lives.' And we mostly succeed. We try to think of every contingency, but there's not a lot of room for error. And whether we succeed or not could come down to a chain on a door you weren't expecting when you're doing a dynamic entry, or turning left instead of right, or not firing instead of firing your weapon. And these days if the target gets a little nick while he's trying to blow our heads off, everybody starts screaming and suing and FBI agents start falling like flies. Maybe if I'd checked out after Waco, my life would really be different."

"Why didn't you?"

"Because I have a lot of special skills that I can use to protect honest citizens. To protect the interests of this country from people who would do it and them harm."

"Sounds very patriotic. Some cynics might take you to task over that philosophy, though."

Web stared at her for several seconds before answering. "How many TV pundits have ever had a sawed-off shotgun stuffed up their noses while some deranged lowlife freaked on meth has his finger on the trigger deciding whether to end their lives? Or waited out in the middle of nowhere USA, while some pseudo-Jesus psycho, who finds it in his holy book somewhere that it's all right to screw his disciples' kids, messes with the psyche of the whole country and then ends his fifteen minutes of fame in a fireball that takes every abused child with him? If the cynics have a problem with my motivation or methods, then they can get out there and do it. They'd last all of two seconds. They expect perfection from the good guys in a world where that just is never going to happen. And the bad guys could've ripped the heads off a thousand babies, and you're still going to get their lawyers screaming holy hell if you give them a hangnail while you're trying to arrest them. Now, the higher-ups at the Bureau do make mistakes when issuing orders and some of them shouldn't be holding the jobs they have because they're incompetent. I wasn't at Ruby Ridge, but that was a disaster from minute one and the Feds were more to blame than anybody else for innocent people dying. But it's ultimately guys like me, following those orders, who get their nuts cut off because they had the *audacity* to risk their lives to do what they believe is the right thing and get paid jack-shit for the privilege. That's my world, Dr. Daniels. Welcome the hell to it."

Web took a deep breath, started trembling and looked over at Claire, who looked as stunned as he felt. "Sorry," he finally said, "I'm kind of a *patriotic* jerk when it comes to all of that."

When Claire spoke, she sounded contrite. "I think I should apologize. I'm sure you find your job thankless at times."

"I'm kind of finding it that way right now."

"Tell me about your family," she said after a few more moments of awkward silence.

Web sat back and put his hands behind his head, as he once more took several small breaths. *Sixty-four beats a minute, Web, that's all you need, man. Sixty-four smacks a minute. How hard can it be?* He leaned forward. "Sure. No problem. I'm an only child. I was born in Georgia. We moved to Virginia when I was around six."

"So who is the *we* here? Your mother and father?"

Web shook his head. "No, just me and my mother."

"And your father?"

"He didn't come. The state wanted to keep him awhile longer."

"Was he employed with the government?"

"You could say that. He was in prison."

"What happened to him?"

"Don't know."

"Weren't you curious?"

"If I had been, I would have satisfied that curiosity."

"All right. And so you came to Virginia. What then?"

"My mother remarried."

"And your relationship with your stepfather?"

"Fine."

Claire said nothing, apparently waiting for him to continue. When he didn't, she said, "Tell me about your relationship with your mother."

"She's been dead nine months now, so we don't have a relationship."

"What was her cause of death?" She added, "If you don't mind my asking."

"The Big B."

Claire looked confused. "You mean the Big C? Cancer?"

"No, I mean the Big B, booze."

"You said you joined the FBI on a whim. Do you think it could have been more than that?"

Web shot her a quick glance. "You mean, did I become a cop because my real father was a crook?"

Claire smiled. "You're good at this."

"I don't know why I'm still alive, Claire," Web said quietly. "By all rights I should be dead along with my team. It's driving me crazy. I didn't want to be the sole survivor."

Claire's smile quickly faded. "That sounds important. Let's talk about that."

Web's hands ground against each other. Then he stood and looked out the window. "This is all confidential, right?"

"Yes," Claire said. "Absolutely."

He sat back down. "I went into the alley. I'm hauling butt with my team, we're almost at the breach point and then . . . and then—" He stopped.

"And then I, shit, I froze. I couldn't move. I don't know what the hell happened. My team went out into that courtyard and I couldn't. Then I finally get going and it feels like I weigh a thousand pounds, like my feet were in concrete blocks. And I dropped, because I couldn't keep myself up. I just went down. And then—" He stopped, a hand went to his face, not the damaged side, and he pushed hard there, as though keeping things that wanted to come out from doing so. "And then the guns started. And I lived. I lived, and none of my team did."

The pen sat idle in Claire's hand as she looked at him.

"It's okay, Web, you need to get this out."

"That's it! What in the hell can I add to that? I freaked out. I'm a damn coward!"

She spoke very calmly and precisely. "Web, I understand that this is extremely difficult to discuss, but I'd like you to go over the exact events leading up to you 'freezing,' as you referred to it. As accurately as you can remember. That might be very important."

Web went through the details with her, starting from the moment the Chevy doors popped open to the point where he couldn't do his job, where he had watched his friends die. When he had finished he felt totally numb, as though he had given away his soul as well as his pitiful story.

"It must have felt paralyzing," she said. "I'm wondering whether you felt any earlier symptoms before it hit you so completely. Something like a drastic pulse change, rapid breathing, a feeling of dread, cold sweats, dry mouth?"

Web thought about this for a bit as he again went over in his mind every step he had taken. He started to shake his head in answering no, but then he said, "There was a kid in the alley." He wasn't about to reveal to Claire Daniels the importance that Kevin Westbrook was taking in the investigation; however, there was something that he could tell her. "When we passed him he said something. Something really odd. I remembered his voice sounded like an old man's in some ways. You could tell from his appearance that life had not been exactly kind to him."

"You don't remember what he said?"

Web shook his head. "I'm drawing a blank on that, but it was something weird."

"But *what* he said made you feel something, something beyond the usual pity or sympathy?"

"Look, Dr. Daniels—"

"Please, call me Claire."

"Okay, Claire, I'm not looking to make myself out to be a saint. With my job I go into some real hellholes. I try not to think about all the other things, like the kids."

"It sounds as though if you thought that way you wouldn't be able to do your work."

Web shot a glance at her. "Is that what you think might have happened to me? I see the kid and it snapped something in my brain?"

"It's possible, Web. Shell shock, post-traumatic stress syndrome that induces physical paralysis along with a whole host of other physical debilitations. It happens more often than people think. The stress of combat is unique."

"But nothing had happened yet. Not one shot fired."

"You've been doing this for many years, Web; it can all accumulate inside you and the *effect* of that accumulation can manifest itself at the most inopportune moments and in the most unfortunate ways. You aren't the first person to go into battle of sorts and have that kind of reaction."

"Well, it's the first time it's happened to me," Web said with an edge to his voice. "And my team had been through just as much as me, and none of them locked up."

"Even though this was the first time it's happened to you, Web, you have to understand that we're all different. You can't compare yourself to anyone else. It's not fair to you."

He pointed a finger at her. "Let me tell you what's fair. What's fair is me maybe making a difference that night. Maybe I could have done something, seen something that would have warned my guys, and maybe they'd still be living and I wouldn't be sitting here talking to you about why they're not."

"I understand that you're angry and that life is often not fair. You've doubtless seen hundreds of examples of that. The point is how best for you to deal with what happened."

"How exactly do you deal with something like this? It doesn't get any worse than this."

"I know it may seem hopeless, but it would be worse if you can't work through your issues and move on with your life."

"Life? Oh, yeah, that's right, I guess I have something of a life left. You want to switch with me? I'll give you a real deal."

"Do you want to go back to HRT?" she asked flatly.

"Yes," he said immediately.

"You're sure?"

"I'm absolutely sure."

"Then that's a goal that we both can work toward."

Web ran a hand up his thigh and stopped at the bulge of his pistol. "Do you really think that's possible? I mean, at HRT if you can't cut it mentally or physically, well, then you're gone." Gone, he thought, from really the only place he had ever fit in.

"We can try, Web, that's all we can do. But I'm pretty good at my job too. And I promise that I'll do all I can to help you. I just need your cooperation."

He looked squarely at her. "Okay, you've got it."

"Is there anything particularly troubling in your life right now? Any especially stressful issues out of the usual?"

"Not really."

"You mentioned that your mother had died recently."

"Yes."

"Tell me about your relationship with her."

"I would've done anything for her."

"So I take that as you were very close to her?" Web hesitated for so long that Claire finally said, "Web, right now the absolute truth is important."

"She had her problems. Her drinking, for one. And she hated what I do for a living."

Claire's gaze drifted again to where Web's gun rested under his jacket. "Not so unusual for a mother. What you do is very dangerous." She glanced at his face and then quickly looked down. Web, though, had noted it.

"It can be," he said evenly, and turned the damaged side away from her; it was a movement he had grown so adept at he usually didn't notice he was even doing it.

"I'm curious about something. What did you inherit from her? Did she leave you anything that means something to you?"

"She left me the house. I mean, she didn't leave it to me, she didn't have a will. Under the law it went to me."

"Do you plan to live there?"

"Never!"

Claire jumped at his tone.

He said quickly but in a calmer tone, "I mean, I've got my own house. I don't need hers."

"I see." Claire made a note and then seemed to consciously shift gears. "By the way, have you ever been married?"

Web shook his head. "Well, at least not in the conventional way."

"What do you mean?"

"The other guys on my team all had families. I felt like I had a bunch of wives and kids through them."

"So you were very close to your colleagues?"

"In our line of work, you tended to hang together. The better you knew each other, the better you worked together, and down the road that could save your life. Plus, they were just great guys. I liked being with them." As soon as he finished saying this, the fire in his belly returned. Web jumped up and headed to the door.

"Where are you going?" an astonished Claire called after him. "We've just started. We have a lot more to talk about."

Web paused at the door. "I've talked enough for now."

He closed the door behind him, and Claire made no move to follow. She put her pad and pen down and stared after him.

9

At Arlington National Cemetery, Percy Bates walked from the visitors' center up the paved road that led to the Custis-Lee House. After Robert E. Lee had chosen his native state of Virginia and leadership of the Confederate forces over a similar offer from the Stars and Stripes at the outset of the Civil War, the federal government had responded to this rebuff by confiscating Lee's home. Anecdotal history stated that the Lincoln Administration had offered the property back to the Confederate general during the war. All he had to do was come and pay the back taxes. In person. Lee, of course, had not taken Lincoln up on the offer and his estate had been turned into what was now the country's most prestigious national cemetery. That bit of history had always made the Michigan-born Bates smile, although the mansion was now a memorial of sorts to Lee and was popularly known as Arlington House.

Bates reached the front of Arlington House and looked out over what many considered the finest view in all of Washington and perhaps the country. From here, the entire capital city lay at your feet. Bates wondered if old Bobby Lee ever thought this as he got up each morning and looked out.

The cemetery covered over six hundred acres of grounds and was dominated by simple, uniform white headstones. There were also some very elaborate memorials to the dead, erected by survivors or other grateful parties; however, the sea of white headstones, which at the right angle created the illusion of snow-covered ground even in summer, was what most people remembered from their visit here. Arlington National was the final resting place for American soldiers killed while fighting for their country, five-star generals, an assassinated President, seven Supreme Court justices, explorers, famed minorities and many others who qualified to be interred at this national shrine. There were well over 200,000 dead buried here and that number increased at the rate of eighteen bodies every weekday.

Bates had come here numerous times. On several occasions he had attended funerals of friends and colleagues. Other times he had come as a tour guide of sorts when his family had company in town. A favorite thing to do was watch the changing of the guard by members of the U.S. Third Infantry, who maintained around-the-clock vigil over the Tombs of the Unknowns. Bates checked his watch. He would be just in time if he hurried.

As he arrived at the tombs area, Bates could see that the crowd was already gathering, mostly out-of-towners with their cameras and kids. The guard on duty was performing his excruciatingly precise routine of marching twenty-one steps, pausing for twenty-one seconds, switching his rifle to his other shoulder and then marching back along the same narrow path.

Bates had often wondered if the rifle the guards carried was even loaded. However, Bates believed that if anyone ever tried to pillage or defile one of the tombs, he would be met with a swift and painful response. If there was sacred ground for the military in this country, this was it. Arlington Cemetery ranked right up there with Pearl Harbor.

As the changing of the guard started and the crowd grew and moved in for their photo opportunities, Bates glanced across to his left and then started working his way through the rows of tourists and down the steps. The changing of the guard was an elaborate ceremony and would take some time to fully complete. The spectacle drew just about everyone in the cemetery, but not Percy Bates.

He walked around the large Memorial Amphitheater that was situated adjacent to the tombs area. Bates continued strolling, crossed over Memorial Drive and walked around the *Challenger*

Space Shuttle Memorial. Then he turned back and entered the amphitheater. He walked down to the stage area with its large columns, pediments and balustrades; moved over to a wall there and pulled out a map of the cemetery, held it up and studied it.

The man was hidden from Bates's or anyone else's view. He had a pistol in a belt holster and one hand rested on its grip even as he drew nearer to where Bates was standing. He had shadowed Bates around most of the cemetery, making certain that the FBI agent was alone. He moved closer.

"Didn't think you were going to show until you gave me the high sign back there," said Bates. The map completely hid his face from whoever might be watching.

"Had to make sure conditions were right," said Randall Cove. He remained in hiding behind a section of wall.

"I made sure I wasn't followed."

"Whatever any of us can do, somebody out there can do better."

"Can't exactly argue with that. How come you always like to meet in a cemetery?"

"I like the peace and quiet. I rarely get it anywhere else." Cove paused and then said, "I got set up."

"I figured as much. But I've got six men dead and the seventh one is a question mark right now. Did your cover get blown from the inside? Instead of killing you, did they feed you bad stuff to set up HRT? I need details here, Randy."

"I was in that damn building myself. Went in as a potential player with those folks and wanted to check out their operation. I saw desks, files, computers, geeks running around spouting numbers, cash, product, the whole nine yards. With my own eyes I saw it. I don't call up you guys on something like that unless I've seen it for myself. I'm no rookie."

"I know that. But that building had zip in it when we got there. Other than eight trashed machine guns."

"Right. Trashed. Talk to me about London. You trust him?"

"As much as I trust anybody."

"What's his story? Why is he still kicking?"

"I don't think he knows. He says he froze."

"Damn good timing on that."

"He shot those guns up. Saved a little kid in the process."

"That's a real special little kid. Kevin Westbrook."

"So I know."

"Look, we went into this thing hunting the elder Westbrook 'cause the higher-ups thought it was about time to bring him down so they could toot their own horn. But the more I got into it, the more I realized he's small fish, Perce. He makes a good living but not a great one. He doesn't shoot up neighborhoods, keeps a low profile."

"But if not him, who?"

"There're about eight main street sellers in this town and Westbrook is just one of them. Collectively they sell a ton of the shit. Now, you multiply that action by every major metropolitan area from here to New York and south to Atlanta, and you got yourself a real heavyweight."

"What, are you saying one group controls all that flow? That's impossible."

"No, what I'm saying is that I think one group is controlling the flow of Oxycontin from rural areas to metropolitan areas up and down the East Coast."

"Oxycontin, the prescription drug?"

"Right. They're calling it hillbilly heroin, because the illegal trafficking started in rural areas. But now it's moving to the cities. See, that's where the real money is. The hicks in the mountains don't have the kind of cash the city folks do. It's synthetic morphine, for chronic pain or for the terminally ill. Abusers crush it, snort it, smoke it or inject it, and they get popped like something close to heroin."

"Yeah, except it's time-released, so you do a whole pill like that, bypassing the time release, you could kill yourself."

"A hundred deaths and counting so far. It's not as potent as heroin, but it's got double the kick of morphine and it's a legal drug, and that makes some people believe it's safe even if abused. You even got old people selling one pill on the street to cover the cost of the rest of their prescription because their insurance doesn't. Or else you get docs to write up bogus prescriptions or you burglarize pharmacies or homes of patients using it."

"It's bad," agreed Bates.

"That's why the Bureau and DEA ran their joint task force. And it's not just Oxy, you got the older stuff like Percocet and Percodan too. Now you can get 'Perks' on the street for ten to fifteen bucks a pop. But they don't pack the wallop of Oxy. You'd have to take sixteen tablets of Percocet to get the same high as one eighty-milligram Oxy pill."

During this discussion Bates had looked around casually several times, to see if anyone was observing him, yet there was no one. Cove had picked a good place to meet, actually, Bates concluded, since no one could see him, and the way Bates was facing the wall and holding the map up, he appeared simply to be a tourist in need of directions.

Bates said, "Well, the government watches dispensation of controlled narcotics, of course, and you get a doc and a pharmacy dispensing tens of thousands of the same pills, it raises red flags, but you also don't have to worry about getting it over the border."

"Right."

"How come I didn't know this Oxy angle, Randy?"

"'Cause I just figured that part of it out. I didn't know I was dealing with an Oxy pipeline when I first stumbled into this. I just thought it was your run-of-the-mill coke and heroin. But then I started seeing and hearing stuff. Most of the drug seems to be coming in from little pockets up and down Appalachia. For the longest time it just used to be little mom-and-pop operations, mostly by people hooked on the drugs themselves. But I'm sensing a single force out there that's putting all this together and shipping it to the big cities. See, that's the next step. This could be the mother of all gravy trains and somebody's figured it out, at least around here. Bringing it up to the standards of a real drug operation but with profit margins triple what the cartels or anybody else is doing and with a lot lower risk. That's the people we want. That's actually who I thought was operating out of the building HRT hit. I thought we could crack this thing wide open if we got to the bean counters. And it'd make sense to hide your money clearinghouse in a big city."

"Because in the rural areas that sort of thing would stick out," Bates completed his thought.

"You got it. And they have plenty of incentive. Say you work up to moving a million pills a week with a street value of a hundred mil; well, you get my point."

"But whoever's driving the product, they'd have no incentive to waste an HRT unit. That'll bring them grief they just don't need. Why would they do that?"

"All I can tell you is the operation I saw in that building was *not* Westbrook's. It was huge. Lots of activity, way more than his business could generate. If I thought it was just Westbrook, I would have said no-go on the HRT hit. We would've gotten a little fish, but the big one would've just floated away. With that said, I think Westbrook is distributing the product in D.C. and so are the other crews. But hard proof of that I don't have. The guy's real smart and he's seen it all."

"Yeah, but you got to someone in his crew. That's valuable."

"Right, but snitch today, dead tomorrow in my line of work."

"So somebody really put on a damned Broadway production for us by loading up that warehouse to make it look like a big-time drug operation. Any thoughts on that?"

"Nope. After I passed along the intel to you guys and the hit was set, whoever snookered me didn't need old Randall Cove anymore. I'm figuring I'm lucky to be alive, Perce. In fact, I'm wondering why I am alive."

"So is Web London. I guess after a massacre there's always a lot of that going around."

"No, I mean somebody tried to waste me after the HRT hit. Cost me my Bucar and a couple of cracked ribs."

"Jesus, why didn't you let us know? You have to come in, Randy. Get fully debriefed, so we can figure this out."

Bates looked around once more. This was taking too long. He would have to move on soon. He could only look at the cemetery map for so long without arousing suspicion. But he didn't want to leave without Randall Cove.

"No way in hell am I doing that, Perce," replied Cove in a tone that made Bates lower his map. "I'm not doing that because this shit hits way too close to the bone."

"Meaning exactly what?" said Bates with an edge to his voice.

"Meaning that this shit stinks from the *inside* and I'm not putting my life in somebody's hands unless I know they're going to play fair with me."

"This is the FBI, Randy, not the KGB."

"Maybe to you it is. You've always been an insider, Perce. Me, I'm about as outside as somebody can get. I come in now, without knowing what happened, then all of a sudden they might not ever find me again. I know a lot of folks uptown think I was behind what happened to HRT."

"That's crazy."

"Crazy as six dudes getting wiped? How'd they manage that without inside info?"

"That crap happens in our line of work."

"Okay, you telling me you haven't noticed stuff falling down everywhere? Blown assignments, two undercover agents getting killed in the last year, Bureau strike teams showing up to do their thing and finding nobody home to play, major drug busts going down the tubes because folks got tipped off. I think there's some big, stinking rat right in the Bureau selling a lot of folks down the river, including me!"

"Don't go conspiracy theorist on me, Randy."

Cove's voice grew calmer. "I wanted to let you know I wasn't in on it. You got my word because that's all I got to give right now. I hope to have more later."

"So you're on to something?" said Bates quickly. "Look, Randy, I believe you, okay, but I've got people I've got to answer to. I understand your concerns, a lot of bad things have been happening, and we're trying to find the source, but you've got to understand my concerns too." He paused. "Damn it, come on, I'll give you every assurance that if you come in now, I will watch over you like it's my father on his deathbed, okay? I hope you feel that you can trust me, after all we've been through together. I've gone to bat for you before." There was no answer from Cove. "Look, Randy, tell me what you need to come in and I'll see what I can do." There was still no answer. Bates swore under his breath and darted behind the wall. Across the space he saw the door leading out from the other side. He went to it, but it was locked. He ran back around the amphitheater and out into the open. The guard ceremony was breaking up and large crowds had spilled out onto paved walkways and cemetery ground. As Bates looked everywhere, he knew he had already lost him. Despite his large physical size, Cove had spent many years learning how to blend in with any surroundings. For all Bates knew, he was dressed as a groundskeeper or possibly a tourist. Bates threw his map in the trash and trudged off.

10

The neighborhood Web was driving in was identical to most others in the area. Modest postwar homes with boxy shapes, gravel driveways and metal awnings. The front yards were tiny, but there were big back spaces where detached garages lurked and grills sat in protected areas and split-trunk apple trees gave comforting shade. This was the land of working-class families who still took pride in their homes and never took it for granted that their children would go to college. Today men fussed with old cars in the coolness of their garages, women gathered on front porch stoops to drink coffee, smoke cigarettes and exchange gossip under a sun that was very hot for this time of year and skies that were finally clear of the last storm. Kids in shorts and tennis shoes raced up and down the street on scooters that actually required one to use his legs to make it go.

As he pulled up in front of Paul Romano's house, Web could see Paulie, as everyone called him, laboring under the hood of a vintage Corvette Stingray that was his absolute pride and joy, his wife and kids rating a little farther down on the love and gush meter. Originally from Brooklyn, Paul Romano was a "get your fingers dirty" kind of guy and fit in a neighborhood like this, with its mechanics, power linemen, truck drivers and the like. The only difference was Romano could kill you in a hundred different ways if he wanted to and damn if there was anything you could do about it. Paul Romano was one of the ones who talked to his guns, gave them names like you would a pet. His MP-5 was Freddy, as in Freddy from *Nightmare on Elm Street,* and his twin .45s were Cuff and Link, named after the turtles in the movie *Rocky.* Yes, as hard as it was to believe, Paul Romano from Brooklyn was a big Sly Stallone fan—although he was forever complaining that that "damn Rambo character was one wimpy ass."

Romano looked up in surprise as Web walked over and peered into the guts of the Nassau-blue 'Vette with a white convertible soft top. Web knew the car was a model year 1966, which was the first production year of the famous 427-cubic-inch block engine that carried 450 horses inside, because Romano had told him and all the other HRT guys this about a thousand times. "Four-speed manual close ratio. Top speed of about one sixty-five. Blow anything off the street," he had said until Web was sick of hearing it. "Police cruisers, morphed street shit-cans, hell, half the damn stock cars racing at the smaller tracks."

Web had often wondered what it would have felt like to be a kid pulling wrenches and tearing apart cars in the driveway with your old man. Learning stuff about carburetors, sports, women, all the things that made life worth living. *Like, hey, Pop, you know how she's next to you and you're wondering, should I slip my arm around her, and maybe take a chance placing my hand* there? *Yeah, there, Pop, help me out, you were young once, weren't you? Don't tell me you never thought about stuff like that, because I'm standing here, aren't I? And when should I go in for the kiss? What signs should I be looking for? Pop, you won't believe this, but I can't figure these crazy women out. Does it get easier when they get older?* And the old man would wink, smile knowingly, take a swig of beer, a long drag on a Marlboro and sit down, wipe off his greasy hands on a rag and say, *Okay, listen up, Junior, this is how you work it. Let me lay it out for you here, and you better write this down 'cause this is the gospel, son.* Staring into the Corvette's chest cavity, Web wondered what that exchange would feel like.

Romano eyed Web and didn't mention the 450 HP Big Block that could blow away morphed street shit-cans. All he said was, "Beer's in the cooler. Buck a can. And *don't* make yourself comfortable."

Web reached inside the small Coleman at his feet and popped open a Budweiser without, however, leaving a dollar bill in payment. "You know, Paulie, Bud's not all there is. Got some wicked South American brews you should try."

"Right, on my salary?"

"We make the same money."

"I got a wife and kids, you got shit."

Romano gave the socket wrench a few more pulls and then stepped past Web and fired up the engine. It sounded powerful enough to burst through the thin metal keeping it all together.

"Purring like a kitten," said Web as he sipped his beer.

"Hell, like a tiger."

"Can we talk? Got some questions."

"You and everybody else. Sure, come on. Got all the time in the world. What the hell am I supposed to do on my day off, enjoy myself? So what do you need? Some ballet tights? I'll check with my wife."

"You know I'd appreciate you not ragging my ass to everybody at Quantico."

"And I'd appreciate you not ordering me around. And while we're at it, get the hell off my property. I got standards on people I hang with."

"Let's just talk, Paulie. You owe me that."

Romano pointed the wrench at him. "I owe you nothing, London."

"After eight years doing this crap, I think we *both* owe each other more than we'll ever be able to cover."

The two men stared at each other until Romano finally put down the wrench, wiped off his hands, turned the tiger off and headed toward the backyard. Web took this as an invitation to follow. Yet, part of Web was thinking that maybe Romano simply was going to the garage to get a bigger wrench to hit him with.

In the backyard the grass was cut short, the trees pruned, a fat rosebush billowed out from one side of the garage. The temperature must have been near eighty in the sun, and it felt good after all the rain. They pulled up a couple of lawn chairs and settled down. Web watched as Romano's wife, Angie, hung clothes on the line to dry. She was from Mississippi originally. The Romanos had two kids, both boys. Angie was petite and still curvy with big blond hair, bewitching green eyes and a "let me eat you up, darlin'" look. She was always flirting, always touching your arm or grazing your leg with her foot, saying that you were cute, but it was all innocent stuff. It drove Romano nuts sometimes, yet Web could tell he really loved that other guys were attracted to his wife. That was just part of what made Romano tick. And yet when Angie Romano got pissed off, you had better look out. Web had seen that side of her too at some HRT get-togethers; the little woman could be a hellcat on speed—she had made intensely confident guys who shot big guns for a living dive for cover when she was on the warpath.

Paul Romano was a Hotel Team assaulter now, but he and Web had come to HRT in the same class and been paired as snipers for about three years. Romano had been with the Deltas before joining the FBI. Though Romano was built like Web, lacking big muscles, the muscle he did have was like cable. You couldn't break it, and the guy's motor never quit. No matter what you threw at him, he never stopped. Once, during a night raid on a drug boss's Caribbean stronghold, the assault boat had dropped Romano off too far from shore, and the guy, carrying sixty pounds of gear, had plunged into fifteen feet of water. Instead of drowning like everybody else would have, he hit the bottom, stood, somehow got his bearings, held his breath for a mere four minutes, walked to shore and participated in the attack. Because there had been a snafu in communications and the target wasn't exactly where he was supposed to be, Romano had actually ended up nailing the drug lord himself after killing two of his bodyguards. And the only thing Romano had bitched about afterward was getting his hair wet and losing the pistol named Cuff.

Romano had tattoos over most of his body, dragons, knives and snakes, and a cute little ANGIE in a heart on his left biceps. Web had run into Romano on the very first day of the HRT selection class for that year, when most of the applicants had stood naked and scared, awaiting the terror they all knew was ahead of them. Web had been checking out all the other guys, looking for scars on knees or shoulders that evidenced physical weakness or expressions on faces that demonstrated mental paralysis. This was both free enterprise and Darwinism at their full, feverish pitch, and Web had been looking for anything to get an edge over the competition. Web knew that only half of them would survive the first cut that would take place in two weeks, and only one in ten of those would get an offer to come back and really kill himself.

Romano had come from the FBI's New York City SWAT team, where he had the reputation of being extremely intimidating among a group of intimidating folks. He hadn't looked scared standing in a room with seventy stripped males that first day of HRT qualifying. To Web, he had looked like a guy who loved pain, who was just itching for HRT to start clobbering his butt with it. And the guy could dole out the hurt too. Back then Web hadn't known himself if he would make the cut for the HRT slots, yet he had known from day one that Paul Romano would. The two had always been supercompetitive and the guy regularly made Web mad, but Web had to admire the man's ability and courage.

"You wanted to talk, talk," said Romano.

"Kevin Westbrook. The kid from the alley."

Romano nodded at his beer. "Okay."

"He's missing."

"The hell you say!"

"You know Bates? Percy Bates?"

"No. Should I?"

"He's heading up WFO's investigation. Ken McCarthy said you and Mickey Cortez were with Kevin. What can you tell me?"

"Not much."

"What'd the kid say?"

"Nothing."

"So who'd you pass him off to?"

"Couple of suits."

"Get their names?"

Shake of the head.

"Hey, Paulie, you know the difference between talking to you and talking to a wall?"

"What?"

"Not a damn thing."

"What do you want me to say, Web? I saw the kid, I watched the kid and then the kid was gone."

"Are you telling me he didn't say one thing to you?"

"He was pretty tight-lipped. He told us his name and gave us his address. We noted that down. Mickey tried to talk to him some more but got nothing. Hell, Cortez doesn't even talk to his own kids. See, we weren't all that sure what the boy's role in all this was. I mean, we're hauling ass to the courtyard, see your flare and stop. Then this kid comes out of the dark with your cap and a note. I wasn't sure if he was on our side or not. I didn't want to screw up legally by ask-ing him stuff I shouldn't."

"Okay, that was actually smart of you. But you passed him off to the suits without a word? How the hell does that compute?"

"They flashed their creds, said they were there for the kid and that was that. It's not like we had the authority to say no. HRT doesn't do investigations, Web, we just bang 'em and hang 'em. The suits do the snooping. And I had other things on my mind. You know me and Teddy Riner were in Delta together."

"I know, Paulie, I know. So about what time was that, when the suits showed up?"

Romano thought about this. "We weren't there that long. It was still dark. Say, two-thirty or so."

"Pretty efficient for WFO to get its act in order and send guys for the kid that quickly."

"So what'd you want me to say to them? Hey, guys, you can't have the kid, you're way too efficient, and the FBI just doesn't work that way? Boy, that'd do wonders for my career. I could kiss my GS fourteen salad days good-bye with that one."

"The suits, can you give me a description?"

Romano thought this over. "I already told the agents."

"A bunch of other suits. So tell me. It won't kill you. Trust me."

"Right. If I was that stupid you wouldn't have to stop at the bridge because you could sell me Brooklyn too."

"Come on, Paulie, assaulter to assaulter. Hotel Team to what's left of Charlie."

Romano thought about this for a bit and then cleared his throat. "One of them was a white guy. A little shorter than me, thin but wiry. Satisfied?"

"No. Hair?"

"Short and blond—he's a Fed, what else is it going to be? You think J. Edgar walked around with a ponytail?"

"Some folks claim he did. That and a dress. Young, old, in be-tween?"

"Thirties. Had on your standard-issue Fed suit, maybe a little nicer than that, actually. A lot nicer than anything you have in your closet, London."

"Eyes?"

"He had on shades."

"At two-thirty in the morning?"

"Well, they might have been tinted prescription glasses. I wasn't exactly gonna interrogate the guy on his choice of eyewear."

"You remember all that and you can't remember the guy's name?"

"He flashed his creds and I zoned out. I'm in the middle of a crime scene with people running everywhere and six of our guys with their heads blown off. He came for the kid and he took the kid. He walked the walk and talked the talk. Hell, he probably outranked my ass."

"What about his partner?"

"What?"

"His partner, the other suit, you said there were two of them."

"Right." Romano didn't look so certain now. He rubbed at his eyes and sipped his beer. "Well, see, that guy didn't actually come over. The one suit pointed at him, said it was his partner and that was that. That other guy was talking to some cops, so he never actually came over."

Web looked at him skeptically. "Paulie, that means you don't know for sure if the guy you talked to was even with that other guy. He could've been working all alone and just been blowing smoke up your butt. Did you tell the *real* honest-to-God FBI all this?"

"Look, Web, you were an honest-to-God Fibbie. You're used to investigating this kind of crap. I was a Delta. I only joined the FBI so I could jump to SWAT and then onto HRT. It's been a long time and I've forgotten how to play detective. I just bang 'em and hang 'em. Just bang 'em and hang 'em, man."

"Well, you might just have hung a little boy."

Romano stared at him angrily for a few seconds and then slouched down and looked off. Web figured Romano was thinking about his own two sons. Web wanted the guy to feel guilty, so this blunder would never happen again. "That kid's probably in some landfill right now. He has a brother. Some badass named Big F."

"Don't they all," growled Romano.

"Kid hasn't had much of a life. You saw the bullet hole on his cheek. At all of ten years old."

Romano took a slug of beer and wiped his mouth. "Yeah, well, six of our guys are dead and they shouldn't be and I'm still wondering why it wasn't seven." He shot Web a nasty look as he said this.

"If it makes you feel any better, I'm getting some professional help now trying to figure that out." This was a huge admission for Web to make, particularly to Romano, and he immediately regretted it.

"Oh, yeah, that makes me feel so good I'm gonna run through the streets yelling 'Web's seeing a shrink, the world is safe.'"

"Give me a break here, Paulie, you think I wanted to freeze out there? Do you think I wanted to see my team get shot up? *Do* you?"

"I guess you're the only one who can answer that," Romano fired back.

"Look, I know this all looks bad, but why are you giving me such a hard time?"

"You want to know why? You really want to know why?"

"Yeah."

"Okay, I did talk to that kid, or let me put it better. The kid talked to me. You wanta know what that kid said?"

"I'm sitting here, Paulie."

"He said you were so scared you were bawling like a baby. He said you begged him to please don't tell anybody. You were the biggest piece of chickenshit he'd ever seen. He said you even tried to give him your gun because you were scared to use it."

Talk about your ungrateful kid. "And you believed that crap?"

Romano took a swig of his beer. "Well, not the part about the gun. You ain't giving that damn SR75 to nobody."

"Thanks a lot, Romano."

"But the kid must have seen something to make him say stuff like that. I mean, why would he lie about everything?"

"Oh, I don't know, Paulie, maybe because I'm a cop and he's just not big into law enforcement types. Why don't you go ask some of the snipers about it? They can tell you if I was crying or shooting. Or maybe you wouldn't believe them either."

Romano ignored this. "I guess people turn chickenshit all the time, course I wouldn't really know about that."

"You know, you're a real bastard."

Romano put down his beer and half rose out of his chair. "You want to find out how much of a bastard I really am?"

The two looked to be working up to blows when Angie came over and said hello to Web and gave him a comforting hug along with some soothing words.

"Paulie," she said, "maybe Web would like to stay for dinner. I'm making pork chops."

"Maybe I don't want Web to stay for damn pork chops, okay?" growled Romano.

Angie bent down and grabbed Romano's shirt, jerking him up. "Excuse us for a sec, Web," she said.

Web watched as Angie dragged her husband over to the side of the garage and gave him what Web could only describe as a dressing down of intimidating proportion. She tapped her bare foot and waggled her hand in his face and did a very fine impersonation of a drill sergeant taking a serious bite out of an enlisted man's ass. And Paul Romano, who could kill just about anything that lived, just stood there, head down, and quietly took it from his "little woman." Angie finally led him back over to Web.

"Go ahead, Paulie, ask him."

"Angie," said Web, "don't make him—"

"Shut up, Web," snapped Angie, and Web shut up. Angie smacked the still-silent Romano on the back of the head. "Either ask him or else you'll be sleeping in the garage with that stupid car of yours."

"Do you want to stay for dinner, Web?" asked Romano as he stared at his lawn, arms folded across his chest.

"A pork chop dinner," prompted Angie, "and why don't you try saying it like you actually mean it, Paulie?"

"Would you like to stay for a pork chop dinner, Web?" asked Romano in the meekest little voice Web had ever heard, and damn if he didn't even look Web in the eye when he said it. That Angie was a miracle worker. With all Romano's suffering, how could Web say no, although the truth was, he was really tempted to decline the invitation just to tick the guy off.

"Sure, Paulie, I'll stay, thanks for thinking of me."

As Angie went in to start dinner, the men worked on their beers and stared at the sky.

"If it makes you feel any better, Angie scares the crap out of me too, Paulie."

Romano looked over and for the first time, at least in Web's recent memory, he actually smiled.

Web looked down at his beer. "I guess you told uptown what the kid said."

"Nope."

Web glanced up, surprised. Romano just stared straight ahead. "Why not?"

"Because it wasn't true."

"I appreciate that."

"I know when kids are lying their asses off, my own boys do it enough. I guess I was just pulling your chain. Guess that's gotten to be a habit."

"But I really can't believe the kid said all that, Paulie. I saved his butt. Hell, he got lucky twice. It's only thanks to me he didn't have another bullet hole in his head.

Romano looked at him, puzzled. "That kid didn't have a bullet wound."

"Sure he did, on his left cheek. And he had a knife slash on his forehead too, long as my pinky."

Romano shook his head. "Look, Web, I was with the kid and maybe I wasn't paying all that much attention to him, but I wouldn't have missed something like that. I know what a bullet wound looks like because I got one of my own. And I sure as hell have popped enough guys to know what they look like."

Web sat up very straight. "What was his skin color?"

"What the hell are you talking about, what was his skin color? He was black!"

"Damn it, I know that, Paulie! I mean light-skinned? Dark?"

"Light-skinned. Smooth as a baby's ass, and not a mark on him. From my lips to the Pope, I swear."

Web smacked the arm of the chair. "Damn!" Kevin Westbrook, at least the one Web had run into, had chocolate brown skin.

After dinner with the Romanos, Web visited Mickey Cortez and got the same story. He'd heard no other statements from the kid. No ID on the suit who had taken him away, but corroboration on the time. And no bullet wound on the boy's cheek.

So who had made the kid-switch? And why?

11

Fred Watkins climbed out of his car after another long day for the U.S. attorney. It took him an hour and a half to drive into Washington each day from his northern Virginia suburb and about the same coming home. Ninety minutes to drive barely ten miles— he shook his head at the thought of it. His work wasn't over either. Despite having risen at four A.M. and having labored ten hours already today, he had at least another three hours awaiting him in the small study he used as an office in his house. A little dinner and some brief quality time with his wife and teenage kids and he would burn the midnight oil. Watkins specialized in high-profile racketeering cases at the Department of Justice in Washington after a long stint as a humble commonwealth's attorney in Richmond prosecuting whatever miscreants came his way. He enjoyed the work and felt he was doing a real service for his country. He was reasonably well compensated for doing so, and though the hours were sometimes long, his life had turned out all right, he believed. His oldest would be going off to college in the fall, and in another two years so would his youngest child. He and his wife had plans for traveling then, seeing parts of the world they had only viewed in travel magazines. Watkins also had visions of taking an early retirement and teaching as an adjunct professor of law at the University of Virginia, where he had received his degree. He and his wife were thinking of maybe even moving to Charlottesville someday permanently and escaping forever the traffic dungeon that northern Virginia had become.

He rubbed his neck and breathed in the fresh air of a nice, cool evening. A good plan overall; at least he and his wife had a plan. Some of his colleagues patently refused to think beyond tomorrow, much less years from now. But Watkins had always been a practical, commonsensical man. That's how he had always approached his law practice and that's how he dealt with life.

He closed the car door and headed up the sidewalk to his house. On the way he waved to a neighbor pulling out of her driveway. Another neighbor was grilling next door, and the smell of cooking meat filled his nostrils. He might just fire up the barbecue tonight too.

Like most people in the Washington area, Watkins had read about the ambush of the Hostage Rescue Team unit with great interest and sinking despair. He had worked with some of those folks on a case once and had nothing but good things to say about their bravery and professionalism. Those guys were the best, at least in his book, and they did a job that virtually no one else would be willing to do. Watkins had thought he had had it tough until he saw what those fellows went through. He felt especially sorry for their families and was even thinking about inquiring if a fund had been established to help them. If there wasn't such a fund, Watkins was thinking about starting one. Just another item to add to the old to-do list, but that's just how life worked, he guessed.

He never saw it until it rose from the bushes and charged right at him. Watkins yelled out and then ducked. The bird missed him by inches; it was the same damn blue jay. The thing seemed to lie in wait for him most nights, as though trying its best to scare him into a premature coronary. "Not this time," said Watkins to the fleeing creature. "Not ever. I'll get you before you get me." He chuckled and walked up to the front porch. As he opened the front door, his cell phone rang. *Now what?* he thought. Few people had this number. His wife, but she wouldn't be calling him because she had no doubt seen him pull in the driveway. It had to be the office. And if it was the office, that meant something had happened that would probably take up the remainder of his evening and perhaps even require him to turn around and drive back into town.

He pulled out his phone, saw that caller ID was unavailable and thought about not answering it. But that just wasn't how Fred

Watkins did things. It might be important, yet maybe it was just a wrong number. No, no barbecuing tonight, he thought as he punched the talk button, ready to confront whatever it was.

They found what remained of Fred Watkins in the neighbor's bushes across the street where the blast that disintegrated his house had delivered him. The instant he'd hit the talk button a tiny spark from his phone ignited the gas that had filled his house, gas that Watkins had little chance of detecting when he opened the door because of the smells of grilling meat next door. Somehow his briefcase had survived, still clamped in a hand that was now virtually all bone. The precious papers were intact and ready for another attorney to take over from the deceased lawyer. The bodies of his wife and children were found in the wreckage. Autopsies would show that all of them had already died from asphyxiation. It took four hours to extinguish the fire, and two other homes were engulfed before the conflagration was put out. Thankfully no other people were seriously injured. Only the Watkins family had ceased to exist. The question of how he and his wife would spend their retirement years after a lifetime of hard work was laid to rest with them. They had no problem finding Watkins's phone, because it had melted to his hand.

At about the time Fred Watkins's life was ending, ninety miles south in Richmond, Judge Louis Leadbetter was climbing into the back of a government car under the watchful eye of a United States marshal. Leadbetter was a federal trial judge, a position he had held for two years after being elevated from being chief judge of the Richmond Circuit Court. Because of his relative youth—he was only forty-six—and his exceptional legal ability, many folks in powerful places had their eye on Leadbetter as eventually a candidate for the Fourth Circuit Court of Appeals, and perhaps even one day taking his seat on the Supreme Court of the United States. As a judge in the legal trenches Leadbetter had overseen many trials of varying complexity, emotion and potential volcanic eruption. Several men that he had sentenced to prison had threatened his life. Once he had almost fallen prey to a letter bomb sent by a white supremacist organization that hadn't cared for Leadbetter's stead-fast belief that all persons, regardless of creed, color or ethnicity, were equal under the eyes of God and the law. These circumstances dictated that Leadbetter receive additional security, and there had been a recent development that had further increased concerns for his safety.

There had been a daring prison escape by a man who had sworn revenge on Leadbetter. The prison where the man had been held was very far away and the threats were from several years ago, yet the authorities were wisely taking no chances with the good judge. For his part Leadbetter simply wanted to live his life as he always had and the beefed-up security was not particularly appealing to him. However, having barely escaped death once, he was practical enough to realize that the concern was probably legitimate. And he didn't want to die violently at the hands of some piece of filth who should be rotting away in prison; Judge Leadbetter wouldn't want to give the man the satisfaction.

"Any news on Free?" he asked the U.S. marshal.

That the man who had escaped from prison was named Free had always rankled Leadbetter. Ernest B. Free. The middle initial and surname weren't his real ones, of course. He had had his name legally changed when he had joined a paramilitary neo-conservative group whose members all had taken that name as symbolism of the perceived threats to their liberty. In fact, the group called themselves the Free Society, ironic since they were violent and intolerant of anyone who didn't look like them or who disagreed with their hate-filled beliefs. They were the type of organization that America could certainly do without and yet they were also an example of the vastly unpopular types of groups that the First Amendment to the United States Constitution was constructed to afford protection to. But not when such groups killed. No, not when they killed. No bit of paper, no matter how cherished, could protect you from the consequences of that.

Free and other members of his group had broken into a school, shot two teachers to death and taken numerous children and teachers hostage. Local authorities had surrounded the school, and a SWAT team had been called up, but Free and his men were heavily armed with automatic weapons and body armor. Thus, federal lawmen specializing in hostage rescue had been called up from Quantico. At first things looked like they would end peacefully, but shooting had erupted from inside the school and eventually the Hostage Rescue Team had gone in. A horrific gun battle had ensued. Leadbetter could still vividly recall the heartbreaking sight of a young boy lying dead on the pavement, along with two teachers. A wounded Ernest B. Free had finally given up when his accomplices had been gunned down.

There had been some question as to whether Free would be tried in federal or state courts. While it was believed that the school was targeted because it was a cutting-edge magnet school for integration and enhancement of race relations, and Free's racist views were well known, it still would have been hard to prove, Leadbetter recognized. To start with, the three people killed—the two teachers and the young boy—were white, and thus prosecuting Free under a federal hate crime statute looked relatively weak. And while technically Free could have been charged with assaults on federal officers, it seemed the best shot was to make things simple and try him in state court and seek the death penalty for the multiple murders. The result was not one any of them had intended.

"No, Judge," replied the marshal, snapping Leadbetter out of his reminiscing. The marshal had been looking out for Leadbetter for a while now and they had quickly established a good rapport. "If you ask me, that man's plan is to head to Mexico and then on to South America. Hook up with some Nazis, people of his own kind."

"Well, I hope they get him and put him right back where he belongs," said Leadbetter.

"Oh, they probably will. Feds are on it and they sure got the resources."

"I wanted that bastard to get the death penalty. That's what he deserved." It was one of the few regrets that Leadbetter had as a circuit court judge. But Free's defense counsel had, of course, raised the issue of insanity and even tiptoed along the fringe of alleging a claim of brainwashing by the "cult," as he had described the organization Free belonged to. The attorney was just doing his job, and in the minds of the prosecution, it apparently had raised just enough doubt about the odds of a solid conviction that they had struck a deal with Free's counsel before the jury had come back in. Instead of a potential death penalty, Free had gotten twenty to life with the possibility, however slight, that he might someday be paroled. Leadbetter hadn't agreed with the deal, yet he really had no choice but to sign off on it. The media had taken an informal poll of the jury later. Free had the real last laugh then. All jury members would have voted for conviction and all would have recommended the death penalty. The press had had a field day with that one. Everyone had ended up with egg on his face. Free had been transferred, for a variety of reasons, to a maximum security prison in the Midwest. That was the place he had escaped from.

Leadbetter looked over at his briefcase. Folded neatly inside was a copy of his beloved *New York Times*. Leadbetter had been born and attended school in New York City before heading south and settling in Richmond. The transplanted Yankee loved his new home, but each evening when he got home, exactly one hour was spent reading the *Times*. It had been his habit for all his years on the bench and his copy was specially delivered to the courthouse before he left each day. It was one of the few acts of relaxation the man was able to enjoy anymore.

As the marshal drove out of the court's garage, his phone rang and the answered it. "What's that? Yes, sir, Judge. Yes, sir, I'll tell him." He put the phone down and said, "That was Judge Mackey. He said to tell you to look at the last inside page of the front section of the *Times* if you want to see something really amazing."

"Did he say what it was?"

"No, sir, just that you were to look and then to call him right back."

Leadbetter glanced at the paper, his curiosity running high. Mackey was a good friend and his intellectual interests ran similar to Leadbetter's. If Mackey thought something fascinating, probably so would he. They were stopped at a light now. That was good because Leadbetter couldn't read in a moving car without getting violently ill. He pulled the paper out, but it was too dark to see in the car. He reached over and turned on the reading light switch and opened the paper.

The annoyed marshal looked back and said, "Judge, I told you not to be turning that light on. It makes you a durn sitting duck—"

The tinkle of glass stopped the marshal cold, that and the sight of Judge Louis Leadbetter toppling facedown onto his precious *New York Times*, its pages now soiled with his blood.

12

Kevin Westbrook's mother, Web learned, was probably dead, though no one could tell him for sure. She had disappeared years before. A meth and crack addict, she had most likely ended her life with the prick of a dirty needle or snort of impure powder. The identity of Kevin's father was unknown. Apparently these were not unusual gaps in personal history in the world where Kevin Westbrook dwelled. Web drove down to a section of Anacostia even the cops avoided, to a crummy, falling-down duplex amid others just like it where Kevin reportedly lived with a hodgepodge of second cousins, great-aunts, distant, kind of, sort of uncles or step brother-in-laws. Web wasn't really clear on the boy's living situation and, apparently, neither was anyone else. It was the new and improved American nuclear family. The area looked like a reactor had been hemorrhaging nearby for a few decades. Apparently, no flowers or trees could grow here; the grass in the small yards was a sickly yellow; even the dogs and cats in the street looked ready to keel over. Every person, place and thing looked totally used up.

Inside, the duplex was a dump. From outdoors the stench of rotting garbage was overpowering, and indoors there were offensive odors heightened even more by the close quarters. This lethal combination hit Web so hard when he walked through the doorway, he thought he might end up kissing the floor. Lord, he'd take tear gas over this homemade toxin any day.

The people who sat across from him didn't look unduly worried that Kevin was not among them. Maybe the child routinely disappeared after a shootout of staggering proportions. A sulky young man sat on the couch. "We already talked to the cops," he said, more spitting the words at Web than saying them.

"Just following up," said Web, who didn't want to think about what Bates would do to him if he found out Web was nosing around on his own. Well, he owed it to Riner and the other guys, to hell with official Bureau policy. Still, the butterflies were numerous and reproducing freely in his belly.

"Shut your mouth, Jerome," said the grandma-type who sat next to Jerome. She had silver hair, big glasses, an enormous bosom and a no-bullshit attitude. She had not given Web her name and he had not pushed it; it was in the FBI file no doubt, but he had tracked it down from other sources. She was as large as a small car and looked like she could take Jerome, no problem. Hell, it looked like she could take *Web*, no problem. She had asked to see Web's badge and credentials twice before unchaining the door. "I don't like letting people I don't know into my house," she explained. "Police or otherwise. This area ain't been safe for as long as I can remember. And that's from *both* sides of the table." She said this with raised eyebrows and a knowing look that penetrated right to Web's federal law enforcement soul.

I really don't want to be here, Web wanted to tell her, *particularly since I'm holding my breath so I won't puke.* When Web sat down he could see between the wide cracks in the floorboards all the way down to the hard clay the house was built on. This place must be toasty warm in the winter, he thought. It was about sixty-five outside right now and it felt like thirty inside. There was no comforting sound of a furnace going and no smells of good food simmering in Grandma's nice kitchen. In one corner of the room was a pile of diet Pepsi cans. Somebody was watching her weight. Yet next to that was a mound of McDonald's trash. Probably Jerome's, thought Web. He looked like a Big Mac and fries kind of guy. "I can understand that," said Web. "Have you lived here long?"

Jerome simply snorted while Granny looked down at her clasped hands. She said, "Three months. Other place we were in, we'd been there a long time. Had it fixed up nice."

"But then they decided we made too much money to be living in such a nice place, and they kicked us out," added Jerome angrily. "Just kicked us out."

"Nobody said life was fair, Jerome," she told him. She looked around the filthy place and drew in a heavy breath that seemed to drain all of Web's hope away. "We gonna fix this place up too. It'll be fine." She didn't sound too sure, Web noted.

"Have the police made any progress on Kevin's disappearance?"

"Why don't you go ask them?" asked Grandma. "Because they ain't telling us nothing 'bout poor Kevin."

"*They* lost his ass," said Jerome as he slid farther down into the mound of sagging, heavily stained cushions that passed for a couch. Web couldn't even tell if there was a frame left. The ceiling was split open in three different spots that Web could see and it sagged down so far you almost didn't need stairs to get to the second floor, you could just reach and pull yourself up. The walls had black mold growing over them, and there was probably lead paint in there as well. And no doubt asbestos clung around the pipes. There was rodent excrement everywhere, and Web would have bet a thousand bucks that termites had eaten most of the wood in the place, which was probably why it had that little lean to the left he had observed as he had come up the front sidewalk. The building inspectors must have just written off this whole area, or else they were drinking coffee somewhere and laughing their butts off.

"Do you have a picture of Kevin?"

"Course we do, gave one to the police," said Grandma.

"Got another?"

"Hey, we ain't got to keep giving you stuff," snarled Jerome.

Web leaned forward and let the grip of his pistol show very prominently. "Yes, Jerome, you do. And if you don't lose the attitude, I'll just haul your ass downtown and we can go over your record for any outstanding warrants that'll put your little butt away for a while, unless you want to try and bullshit me and claim you've never been arrested, slick."

Jerome looked away and muttered, "Shit."

"Shut up, Jerome," said Grandma. "You just shut your damn mouth."

There you go, Granny, Web thought.

She pulled out a little wallet and lifted out a photo. She handed it across to Web, and when she did, her fingers started to tremble a little and her voice caught in her throat, but then she straightened everything out. "That's my last picture of Kevin. Please don't lose it."

"I'll take good care of it. You'll get it back."

Web glanced down at the photo. It was Kevin. At least the Kevin Web had saved in the alley. So the kid Cortez and Romano had babysat was somebody else who had lied and said he was Kevin Westbrook. That took some planning, but it also would have to have been on the fly. And yet for what purpose?

"You said you gave the police a photo of Kevin?"

Grandma nodded. "He's a good boy. He goes to school, you know, most every day he does. A special school because he's a real special little boy," she added proudly.

Down here, Web knew, going to school was an accomplishment to tout, perhaps second only to surviving the night.

"I'm sure he is a good boy." He looked over at wild-eyed, felony-in-waiting Jerome. *You were a good boy too once, weren't you, Jerome?* "Were they uniformed police?"

Jerome stood. "What, you think that we're stupid? They was FBI, man, just like you."

"Sit down, Jerome," said Web.

"Sit down, Jerome," said Grandma, and Jerome sat.

Web thought rapidly. So if the Bureau had a photo of Kevin, then they had to know that they'd had the wrong boy, however briefly, in custody. Or did they? Romano had been clueless about there being two boys. He had just described him as a black kid. What if that was the entire official report? If the fake Kevin Westbrook had disappeared before Bates and the others got on the scene, then all they'd know was a black kid around ten years old named Kevin Westbrook who lived at such-and-such address near the alley was missing. They'd come here and talk to the family, get a picture, like they had done, and go about their investigation. It's not like they'd for sure go ask Romano and Cortez for a positive ID, especially if they had no reason to suspect a switch. And Ken McCarthy had said the snipers hadn't gotten a look at the real

Kevin when Charlie Team had passed him on the way in. Perhaps only Web knew about the deception.

Web looked around, and for the sake of the grandmother, or whatever her relation to Kevin was, he tried hard not to show his disgust. "Did Kevin actually live here?" Bates had said Kevin's home life was miserable and that he probably avoided it when he could, which would explain why he'd been out alone in the middle of the night instead of here in bed. The physical surroundings truly were awful, but probably no worse than many of the other homes down here. Poverty and crime were everywhere and the marks they left were in no way pretty. Yet Granny seemed solid as a rock. A good person, and it seemed like she genuinely cared for Kevin. Why would he avoid her?

Granny and Jerome exchanged a glance. "Most of the time," said Granny.

"Where would he live other times?"

Neither of them said a word. He watched as Granny looked at her very substantial lap and Jerome closed his eyes and swayed his head, apparently to some bitchin' music in his head.

"I understand Kevin has a brother. Does Kevin live with him *sometimes*?"

Jerome's eyes popped open and Granny stopped looking at her lap. In fact, from the expressions on their faces it was as though Web were pointing a gun at them and had just told the pair to kiss their respective butts good-bye.

"Don't know him, never seen him," said Grandma quickly as she sat there rocking back and forth like something suddenly was hurting her. She didn't look like she could take anybody right now. She looked like an old woman scared out of her wits.

When Web looked over at Jerome he jumped up and was gone before Web could even rise. Web heard the front door open and then slam shut and then came the sound of feet running away.

Web looked back at Granny.

"Jerome don't know him neither," said Grandma.

13

The morning came for the official memorial service, and Web rose early, showered, shaved and dressed in his nicest suit. The time to formally honor and mourn all of his friends had come, and all Web wanted to do was run like hell.

Web had not spoken with Bates about what he'd learned from Romano and Cortez, nor about his visit to Kevin's home. Web wasn't exactly sure why he hadn't, only that he wasn't feeling in a real trusting mood, and because Bates would no doubt chew him out for interfering in the investigation. To Web, Bates had identified the kid as Kevin Westbrook, which meant either the boy had told him that was his name or Bates had gotten it from Romano and Cortez if the boy had disappeared before Bates had arrived on the scene. Web would have to confirm which it was. If Bates had seen the other kid, then when he had taken Kevin's photo from the grandmother, he'd have known there were two different kids involved.

So Web had given a kid with a bullet wound on his cheek a note to take to his HRT guys. That kid had told Web his name was Kevin. The note had been delivered, but apparently not by the same kid Web had given the note to. That meant that between him giving the kid calling himself Kevin the note and the note being delivered, the boy had been switched with another kid. That could only have taken place in the alley between where Web was and the charging HRT unit. That wasn't a whole bunch of space, yet it had been enough to pull the switch, which meant other people had been lurking somewhere in that alley, waiting for this to happen, maybe waiting for a lot to happen.

Was Kevin's coming down that alley planned? Was he working for his brother, Big F? Was he supposed to check for survivors, and had he not expected to find any? And when he did find Web alive, had that thrown a monkey wrench in somebody's plan? And what the hell could that plan have been? And why pull one kid out and put another one in? And why did the fake Kevin lie and say Web was a coward? And who was the suit who had taken the replacement kid? Bates had been pretty tight-lipped about losing the kid. Was the suit Romano had talked to even an FBI agent? If not, how could one imposter have walked right in with creds and bravado impressive enough to fool Romano and Cortez and waltz off with *another* imposter? It was bewildering, and Web was so full of doubt that turning to Bates for answers and information sharing was not real high on his list of action items.

He parked the Mach One as close to the church as he could. There were many cars already there, and the parking spaces relatively few. The church was a somber-faced stone monolith built in the latter part of the nineteenth century when the architectural commandment had been, "Thou house of worship shalt have more turrets, balustrades, Ionic columns, broken pediments, arches, gables, doors, windows and cool masonry curlicues than thy neighbor."

It was at this holy temple that Presidents, Supreme Court justices, members of Congress, ambassadors and other, lesser dignitaries of varying degrees did their praying, singing and, very occasionally, confessing. Political leaders were often photographed or filmed going up or down its broad steps, Bible in hand and God-fearing looks on their features. Despite the separation of church and state in America, Web had always believed that voters liked to see a little piety in their elected officials. No HRT members had attended this church, yet the politicos had to have a grand stage to say their words of consolation. And the little backwoods house of religion near Quantico, where some of the members of Charlie Team had actually done their worshiping, apparently didn't cut it.

The sky was clear, the sun warming and the slight breeze refreshing. It was too fine an afternoon for such a depressing thing as a memorial service, it seemed to Web. Yet he went up the church steps, each click of his polished shoes on the stone simulating the ding of a wheel gun's cylinder being turned, one chamber, one bullet, one potentially spent life at a time. Such violent analogies were Web's lot in life, he supposed. Where others saw hope, he only witnessed the raw sores of a festering, degenerating humanity. God, with that attitude, it was no wonder he was never invited to parties.

Secret Service agents were everywhere, with their shoulder holsters, poker expressions and curly ear cords. Web had to go through a metal detector before entering the church. He showed his gun and his FBI creds, which told the Secret Service the only way Web and his gun would be parted was if he was dead.

As soon as he opened the door, Web almost bumped into the rear of the mass of people that had somehow squeezed itself into the space. He took the rather uncouth tactic of flashing his FBI shield, and the seas parted and he was allowed to move through. Over in one corner a camera crew had set up and was broadcasting the entire spectacle. What idiot had authorized that? Web wondered. And exactly whose idea was it to invite the whole frigging world to what should have been a private ceremony? This was how the survivors were to remember their dead, at a circus?

With the help of some fellow agents Web managed to wedge himself into one of the pews and then looked around. The families were in the front two rows, which had been roped off. Web bowed his head in prayer, saying one for each of the men, lingering the longest on Teddy Riner, who had been a mentor to Web, a crackerjack agent, a wonderful father, a good man all around. Web dropped a couple of tears as he realized how much he had really lost in those few seconds of hell. Yet when he looked up front to where the families sat, he knew he had not lost as much as those folks had.

The truth was beginning to set in with the younger kids, for Web could hear their wails at Daddy being gone forever. And the sobbing and screaming continued through all the tired speeches, from the get-tough-on-crime bullcrap from the politicians to the preachers who had never met any of the men they were eulogizing.

They fought the good fight, Web wanted to stand up and quietly say.

They died protecting all of us. Never forget them, for they were all unforget-
table in their own way. End of eulogy. Amen. Let's hit the bars.

The memorial service finally was over, and the congregation
heaved a collective sigh of relief. On his way out, Web spoke with
Debbie Riner and offered some words of comfort to Cynde Plummer and Carol Garcia and exchanged hugs and snatches of more
words with some of the others. He squatted down and talked to the
little kids, held small trembling bodies in his arms and Web just
didn't want to let go. This simple physical giving threatened to
make Web start bawling. Tears had never come easily to him, and
yet he had shed more of them in the last week or so than he had in
his entire life. But the kids were just killing him.

Someone tapped him on the shoulder. As he rose and turned,
Web thought he would be comforting one more bereaved person.
However, the woman staring back at him did not appear to need or
want his sympathy.

Julie Patterson was the widow of Lou Patterson. She had four
kids and had been expecting a fifth but had miscarried it three
hours after learning she had become a widow and single mother. A
look at her glassy eyes told Web that the woman was heavily
drugged with what he hoped were doctor-ordered prescriptions.
And Web could smell the liquor. Pills and booze was not a good
combo to serve oneself on a day like today. Of all the wives, Julie
had been least close to Web, because Lou Patterson loved Web like
a brother and Web had easily sensed that Julie was jealous of that
relationship.

"You really think you should be here, Web?" said Julie. She tot-
tered in her black heels, her eyes not entirely able to focus on him.
Her words were slurry, her tongue moving on to form others before
they had completed the last. She was puffy, her skin pale yet
blotched red in spots. She had not carried the baby long enough for
her belly to swell, and this lost opportunity seemed to have deep-
ened the woman's hurt. She should be home in bed and Web wondered why she wasn't. "Julie, let's go outside and you can get some
air. Come on, let me help you."

"Get the hell away from me!" Julie shouted in a voice loud
enough to make those within twenty feet of them stop and stare.

The TV crew saw this exchange too, and both the cameraman and reporter apparently simultaneously saw potential gold. The camera swung in Web's direction and the reporter headed over.

"Julie, let's go outside," Web said again quietly. He put his hand lightly on her shoulder.

"I'm not going anywhere with you, you bastard!" She ripped Web's hand off and he grunted in pain, cupping his wounded hand near his body. Her fingernails had bitten right into the hole there, ripping out the stitches; it started to bleed.

"Wasamatter, your little hand hurting, you gutless sonovabitch? You with the Frankenstein face! How'd your mother stand looking at you? You freak, you!"

Cynde and Debbie tried to talk to her, console her, but Julie pushed them away and got close to Web again. "You froze up before the shooting started, only you don't know why? And then you fell down? You 'spect us to buy that bullshit!" Her liquor breath was so intense Web had to close his eyes for a moment, and that only magnified his sense of faltering balance.

"You coward. You let them die! How much did you get? How much did Lou's blood get you, you asshole?"

"Ms. Patterson." This came from Percy Bates, who had swept up next to them. "Julie," he said very calmly, "let's get you to your car before the traffic gets really bad. I've got your kids right over here."

Julie's lips trembled at the mention of her children. "How many are there?" Bates looked confused. "How many kids?" Julie asked again. One hand slid to her empty belly and stayed there, and wet spots from tears marked the front of her black dress. Julie focused once more on Web, her lips curling back in a snarl. "I was supposed to have five of them. I had five kids and a husband. Now I got four kids and no Lou. My Lou's gone. And my baby's gone, damn you! Damn you!" Her voice edged upward again, her hand was making crazy circles on her belly, as though she were rubbing a magic lamp, perhaps making a wish for the baby and husband to come back. The camera was eating up all of this. The reporter was scribbling furiously.

"I'm sorry, Julie. I did all I could," said Web.

Julie stopped rubbing her belly and spit in his face. "That's for

Lou." She spit again. "That's for my baby. Go to hell. You go to hell, Web London." She slapped his face, hitting him right on his ruined cheek, and she almost fell over with the effort. "And that's for me, you bastard! You . . . you freak!"

Julie's energy was spent and Bates had to grab the woman before she collapsed to the floor. They got her outside and the nervous crowd started to drift away into small pockets of discussion; many of them cast angry backward glances at Web.

Web did not move. He had not even wiped away Julie's spit. His face was red from where she had hit him. He had just been proclaimed a freakish monster and a coward and a traitor. Julie Patterson might as well have cut off his head and took that with her too. Web would've beaten to death any man who had said those things to him. But coming from a bereaved widow and mother, her insults had to be accepted; he felt like taking his own life instead. None of what she said was true, yet how could Web deny her any of it?

"Sir, it's Web, right? Web London?" said the reporter at his shoulder. "Look, I know this is probably a really awkward time, but the news sometimes can't wait. Would you be willing to talk to us?" Web didn't answer. "Come on," said the reporter. "It'll only take a minute. Just a few questions."

"No," said Web, and started to leave. He wasn't sure until right then that he actually could even walk.

"Look, we're going to talk to the lady too. And you don't want the public to have only her side of things. I'm giving you a shot to tell your story here. Fair is fair."

Web turned back and grabbed the man by the arm. "There are no 'sides.' And you let that woman alone. She's had enough for the rest of her life. You let her alone. Stay away from her! You understand me?"

"Just doing my job." The man carefully edged Web's hand off his arm. He looked at the cameraman. *Excellent,* was the unspoken thought that seemed to travel between the two men.

Web walked out the door and quickly left behind the church of the famous and well heeled. He climbed in the Mach, fired it up and headed off. He stripped off his tie, checked his wallet to make sure he had some cash, stopped at a liquor store in the District and bought two bottles of cheap Chianti and a six-pack of Negra Modelo.

He drove home, locked all the doors and pulled the shades on all the windows. He went into the bathroom, turned on the light and looked at himself in the mirror. The skin on the right side of his face was slightly tanned, relatively smooth, a few odd whiskers in spots he had missed with his razor. A nice side of skin, not bad at all. "Side of skin." That was how he had to analyze it now. The days were long gone when anyone could remark on his handsome face. Julie Patterson had had no trouble commenting on his mug, though. *But Frankenstein? That was a new one, Julie.* Given time to think about it, he wasn't feeling quite so understanding towards the woman right now. *You would've lost Lou a long time ago if Frankenstein hadn't done what he'd done that cost him half his damn face. Did you forget that? I haven't, Julie. I see it every day.*

He turned slightly to fully reveal the left side of his face. No whiskers sprouted there. And the skin never really did tan. The doctors had said that this might happen. And there didn't seem to be enough of it, the skin was stretched so tight. Sometimes, when he wanted to laugh or smile really wide, he couldn't because that side of his face just wouldn't cooperate, as though it were telling him to kiss off, buddy, look what you did to me! And the damage had reached to the edge of his eye such that the socket was pulled more to the temple than normal. Before the operations, it had given him quite an unbalanced appearance. Now the look was better, but the two sides of his face would forever be misaligned.

Under the transplanted skin were lumps of plastic and metal that had replaced destroyed bone. The titanium in his face set off the airport detectors just about every damn time. *Don't worry, guys, it's just the AK-47 I've got stashed up my butt.*

Web had endured numerous operations to bring his face back to this point. The docs had done a good job, though he would always be considered disfigured. At last the surgeons had told him they had reached the end of their professional skills and even their medical miracles, and they'd wished him well. It had been a more difficult adjustment than he had thought, and to this day he couldn't say he was actually through it. It wasn't the sort of thing you ever really got over, he supposed, since it stared back at you in the mirror every day.

He cocked his head a little more, inched down his shirt collar and the old bullet wound on the base of his neck was fully revealed. It had come in above his armor line, and how it missed all vital arteries and his spine was nothing short of miraculous. The wound resembled a cigar burn, a big-ass cigar burn on his skin, he had joked when lying in the hospital bed with one side of his face missing and two large holes in him. And all the guys had laughed with him, though he had sensed the nervousness amid all the chuckling. They were reasonably sure he was going to make it, and so was he. Yet none of them knew what physical and emotional nightmare lay under those bandages. The plastic surgeons had offered to cover up the bullet wounds. But Web had said no. He had had enough with doctors stealing skin from places on his body and gluing it to others. This was as good as old Web was going to get.

He touched his chest where the other "cigar burn" was in full, blooming glory. It had entered his body and exited at the back of his shoulder, somehow skirting his Kevlar on both ends, and still had enough kick left to erase the head of a guy behind him who was about to cleave Web's skull with a machete. And who said he wasn't lucky? Web smiled at himself in the mirror. "Lucky is as lucky does," he said to his reflection.

HRT had always held Web in the highest possible regard for the heroism he had shown that night. It had been the school hostage situation in Richmond, Virginia, executed by the Free Society. Web had recently switched from sniper to assaulter and was still feeling his way a bit, eager to show his mettle in the front lines. The explosion had occurred from a homemade concoction thrown by one of the Frees. It would have hit Lou Patterson if Web hadn't leapt and knocked him out of the way. The fireball caught Web dead on the left side of his face, knocking him down and melting his shield against his skin. He had ripped the shield off along with a good part of his face and kept fighting, the adrenaline that always came with battle the only thing blocking out the horrible pain.

The Frees had opened fire and Web had taken a bullet through his torso, and the second round had tagged his neck. Many innocent men would have died but for what Web had done *after* receiving these injuries. Instead of weakening him, the shots seemed to have energized him, for how he had fought, how he had killed men trying to kill him and his team! He had dragged injured comrades to safety, including the late Louis Patterson, who had taken a round through the arm a minute after Web had saved him from the flames. The acts Web performed that night had far surpassed what he had done in that courtyard; for he had been so badly wounded at the time, no mere hand scratch that time, no simple Band-Aid that day. To both veteran and new operators at HRT, Web was a legend. And at the highly competitive alpha male agency, there was no better way to elevate oneself on the pecking order than bravery and skill shown in the heat of battle. And all it had cost him were a few vanity points and most of the blood in his body.

Web didn't even remember the pain. But when the last bullet had been fired and the last man had fallen, he too had slumped to the ground. He had touched the open wound on his face and felt the blood pouring out of him from the two wounds, and Web knew it was finally his time to die. He had gone into shock in the ambulance and by the time the doctors at the Medical College of Virginia got to him he was almost flat-line. How he had come back that night was anyone's guess, Web certainly didn't have an answer. Never a religious man, he had started to wonder about things like God.

The recovery had been the most painful thing Web had ever done. Though he was a hero, it was no guarantee that Web would be able to rejoin HRT. If he couldn't carry his full weight, they wouldn't want him, hero or not—it was just the way things were. And Web would never have wanted the terms to be anything else. How many weights lifted, how many miles run, walls climbed, choppers rappelled from, rounds fired? Fortunately, the wounds to his face had not affected his eyesight or aim. Without perfection there, you were gone from HRT. The psychological battering of his recovery, however, had been even worse than the physical cramming. Could he fire when called up? Would he freeze in a crisis and place his team in jeopardy? Well, no, he never had, at least not until that damn courtyard came along. He had come back, all the way back. It had taken almost a year, but no one could say he didn't deserve to return on his own, with no corners cut. Now what would people say? Would he make it back this time? The trouble wasn't physical this time; it was all in his head and thus was a hundred times more terrifying.

Web made a fist and put it right through the mirror, cracking the drywall behind it. "I didn't let them die, Julie," he said to the shattered glass. He looked at his hand. It wasn't even bleeding. His luck was holding, wasn't it?

He opened the smashed medicine cabinet and took out the bottle of mismatched pills. He had collected them over time from a variety of sources, some official, some unofficial. He used them to help him sleep occasionally. He was careful, though, because he'd almost become addicted to the painkillers while they were rebuilding his face.

Web flicked off the light and Frankenstein was gone. Hell, everybody knew monsters were more comfortable in the dark.

He went downstairs and carefully laid out all his bottles of booze and sat in the middle of them, like a general with his aides going over a battle plan. Yet he didn't open a single bottle. The phone rang every few minutes, but Web never answered it. There were knocks on the door; he let them go. Web sat there and stared at a wall until it grew quite late. He rummaged through the mismatched pills and took out a capsule, looked at it and then put it back. He leaned back against a chair and closed his eyes. At four A.M. he fell asleep on the floor of the basement. Web still had not bothered to wash his face.

14

Seven in the morning. Web knew this because the mantel clock was chiming when he lifted himself groggily off the basement floor. He rubbed at his back and neck; as he sat up, his foot hit one of the bottles of wine and it fell over and cracked slightly and Chianti leaked across the floor. Web threw the bottle away, grabbed some paper towels and cleaned up the spill. The wine stained his hands red, and for a dazed moment his sluggish mind told him he'd been shot in his sleep.

The noise outside the rear lower window made him race up the stairs and grab his pistol. Web went to the front door with the intent of circling around back and getting the drop on whoever was out there. Maybe it was just a stray dog or squirrel, but Web didn't think so. Human feet trying their best to keep quiet just had a certain sound to them if you knew how to listen, and Web knew how to.

When he opened the door, the surge of people toward him almost caused Web to pull his gun and fire. The reporters were waving microphones and pens and sheets of paper and calling out questions so fast, they cumulatively appeared to be speaking Mandarin. They were screaming for him to look this way or that way so they could take his picture, film his video, as though he were some celebrity or, perhaps more apt, an animal in the zoo. Web looked past them to the street, where the media ships with their tall electronic masts now were docked outside his modest rancher. The two FBI agents assigned to watch over his house seemed to be attempting to hold back the masses but were clearly losing the battle.

"What the hell do you people want?" Web cried out.

One woman wearing a beige linen suit, her blond hair sculpted, pushed forward and planted her high-heeled feet on the brick stoop bare inches from Web. Her heavy perfume made Web's empty stomach turn queasy. She said, "Is it true you're claiming that you fell down right before the rest of your squad was killed but can't explain why? And *that's* why you survived?" The hike of her eyebrows signaled exactly what the woman thought of that preposterous story.

"I—"

Another reporter, a man, shoved his microphone near Web's mouth. "There have been reports that you didn't actually fire your weapon, that the gunfire stopped on its own somehow and that you were actually never in any danger. How do you respond to that?"

The questions kept coming as the bodies pressed closer. "Is it true that when you were at the Washington Field Office you were put on probation for a shooting infraction that resulted in the wounding of a suspect?"

Web said, "What the hell does that—"

Another woman elbowed him from the side. "I have it on good authority that the boy you 'allegedly' saved was actually an accomplice to this whole thing."

Web stared at her. "An accomplice to what? To who?"

The woman gave him a penetrating look. "I was hoping you could answer that."

Web slammed the door, raced to the kitchen, grabbed the keys for the Suburban and headed back out. He pushed through the crowd and looked at his fellow agents for help. They came forward, yanked and pulled on a few people, yet to Web it seemed their hearts clearly were not in it, and they refused to meet his gaze. *So that's how it's going to be,* Web thought.

The crowd suddenly surged closer, sealing off the path to his truck.

"Get out of my way," Web yelled. He looked around. The entire neighborhood was out watching this. Men, women and children who were his friends or at least his acquaintances were staring at this spectacle with wide eyes, open mouths.

"Are you going to respond to Mrs. Patterson's charges?"

Web stopped and looked at this questioner. It was the same reporter from the memorial service.

"Are you?" the man said grimly.

"I didn't know Julie Patterson had the authority to bring charges," said Web.

"She made it abundantly clear that you either acted with cowardice or were somehow involved. Paid off."

"She didn't know what she was saying. She's just lost her husband and unborn child."

"So you're saying the charges are false?" the man persisted and pushed the microphone closer. Somebody jostled him from behind and his arm jerked forward and the microphone hit Web in the mouth, drawing blood. Before he knew it, Web's fist had shot out and the man was lying on the ground holding his nose. He didn't appear to be all that upset. In fact, he was screaming to his camera unit, "Did you get that? Did you get that?"

They all pressed forward more, and Web, being in the middle of this circle, was pushed around by the sheer weight of the crowd. Cameras were snapping in his face, blinding him. Fat video machines were feeding away, dozens of voices were jabbering at once. As the knot of people and machines jostled him around, Web's feet got tangled in a cable and he went down. The crowd moved in, but he pushed his way back up. This was far past being out of control. Web felt a bony fist hit him in the back. When he turned, he recognized the attacker as a man who lived down the street and who had never cared much for Web as a neighbor or human being. Before Web could defend himself, the man ran off. As Web looked around, it was clear that the crowd was not filled just with reporters ravenous for a Pulitzer. This was a mob.

"Get the hell away from me," Web screamed. He yelled at the two agents, "Are you guys going to help or not?"

"Somebody call the cops," said the perfumed blonde, pointing at Web. "He just assaulted that poor man, we all saw it." She bent down to help up her fellow reporter while a slew of cell phones appeared from out of pockets.

Web looked around at a level of chaos he had never before experienced, and he had seen more than most. But he had had enough of this. Web pulled his pistol. The FBI agents saw this and were suddenly interested once more. Web pointed the pistol straight up and fired four shots into the air. On all sides of him the mob now was in full retreat. Some dropped to the ground, crying out, pleading for him not to shoot them, that they were just doing their job, miserable though it might be. The perfumed blonde let her dear reporter friend drop back to the muddy earth and turned and ran for her life. Her heels sank in the soft grass and she ran right out of them. Her fleshy bottom made a nice target if Web had been so inclined. The reporter with the bloody nose was crawling on his belly shouting, "Are you getting this? Damn it, Seymour, are you getting this?" Neighbors swooped up their kids and fled to their homes. Web put his pistol away and walked to his Suburban. When the federal agents moved toward him, all he said was, "Don't even think about it." He climbed in the truck and started it up. He rolled down the window. "Thanks for the assist," he told the two men, and then drove off.

15

"A re you out of your mind?" Buck Winters stared over at Web, who stood by the door of the small conference room at the Washington Field Office. Percy Bates was next to Web. "Pulling and firing your gun, in front of a bunch of reporters, no less, and them taping the whole damned thing. Have you lost your mind?" he said again.

"Maybe!" Web shot back. "I want to know who leaked information to Julie Patterson. I thought the Charlie Team inquiry was supposed to be confidential. How the hell did she know what I said to the investigators?"

Winters looked at Bates in disgust. "Bates, you were this guy's mentor. How the hell did you foul it up so bad?" He looked back at Web. "There are a bunch of different guys looking into this thing. Don't act like a virgin and be surprised when something slips, particularly to a wife who wants to know what the hell happened to her husband. You lost your head, Web, and you screwed up, and it's not like it's the first time."

"Look, I walk out my door and get mobbed, and my own guys not lifting a hand to help me. People were punching me, screaming accusations in my face. I did what anybody would've done."

"Show him what he's done, Bates." Bates quietly went over to a TV sitting in the corner. He picked up the remote and punched some buttons. "Compliments of the media department," Winters added. The tape started to run and Web was looking at the inside of the church during the memorial service. Specifically, he was watching Julie Patterson rubbing her childless belly, screaming at him, spitting in his face, slapping him with all her strength. And him just standing there silently taking it. His statement about having done all he could was mysteriously absent, or at least couldn't be heard. On the tape all he said to Julie was, "I'm sorry." It made Web look like he had pulled the trigger on Lou Patterson himself.

"And that's not the best part," said Winters, who rose and snatched the remote from Bates. He hit the device and Web watched as the scene outside his house ran across the TV. It had been craftily edited such that the atmosphere of the mob scene was gone, the edges of the camera shots crisp and narrow. The individual reporters were depicted as being tough—pushy, even—but polite, professional in every way. The one fellow Web had slugged looked particularly heroic, not even bothering to hide his bloodied nose but going on about his business of introducing the madness the viewer was about to see. And then there was Web looking like a rabid animal. He was screaming, cursing and then he raised his gun. The film speed made him almost appear to pull the gun in slow motion so that it seemed deliberate, controlled and not a man fighting for his life. There were some chilling cinematographic moments too of neighbors running with their children, escaping from this mad fiend. And then there was Web standing alone. Cold, hard, as he put the gun away and walked calmly from the chaos *he* had caused.

Web had never seen anything so slick outside a Hollywood movie. He looked sadistic, evil, the man with the Frankenstein face. The camera had gotten several close-ups of the damaged skin, yet with no mention of how he had come by such injuries.

Web shook his head and looked at Winters and said, "Damn it, that's not how it happened. I'm not Charlie Manson."

Winters bristled. "Who cares if it's the truth or not! Perception is everything. Now that's running on every TV station in town. And it's hit the national pipe too. Congratulations, you're a breaking news story. The director flew back from a high-level meeting in Denver when he was briefed on this. Your ass is in the fire, London, in the fire."

Web slumped in a chair and said nothing. Bates sat across from him and tapped a pen against the table.

Winters stood in front of him, his hands clasped behind his back. To Web, it seemed the guy was really enjoying this.

"Now, you know that the Bureau's SOP in responding to something like this is to do nothing We've followed the ostrich-head-in-the-sand before. Sometimes it works and sometimes it doesn't, but the higher-ups like the passive tactic. The less said, the better."

"Bully for them. I'm not asking the Bureau to do jack-shit on my behalf, Buck."

Bates picked up the conversation. "No, Web, we're not taking this lying down. Not this time." Bates ticked the points off on his fingers. "First, the media relations guys are putting together a highlight film of our own. The world right now thinks you're some sort of psycho. They're going to find out you're one of the most decorated agents we have. We're issuing press releases detailing all of that. Second, although he wants to strangle you right now, Buck here is holding a televised press conference at noon tomorrow to clearly state what an outstanding agent you are, and we're going to run our highlight film in all its glory. And we're going to release some details of what happened in that alley that will damn sure demonstrate that you didn't turn and run but managed single-handedly to take out enough fire-power to wipe out an Army battalion."

Web said, "You can't do that while the investigation is still going on. You could blow some leads."

"We're willing to take the risk."

Web looked over at Winters. "I don't give a damn what these people say about me! I know what I did. And what I don't want is to do anything to jeopardize finding who wiped out my team!"

Winters placed his face a couple of inches from Web's. "If I had my way, your ass would already be gone. But to some in the Bureau you're kind of a hero, and the decision has been made that we're going to bat for you. Believe me, I argued against it, because from a PR point of view it doesn't really help the Bureau, it's just to make you look good." He glanced at Bates. "But your friend here won that battle."

Web looked in surprise at Bates.

Winters continued, "But not the war. And I'm not looking to

make you some damn martyr." Winters glanced at Web's damaged face. "A disfigured martyr. Now Perce is going to take you through the Bureau's little dog-and-pony show that we're doing to clean up your mess. I'm not going to stay for that, because it would make me nauseous. But listen up, London, and you listen really good. You're hanging by a thread right now, and I'd love nothing better than to cut that string. I'll be watching you so close I'll be able to count every one of your breaths. And when you screw up, and you will, then the hammer comes down and you are gone for good, and I'll smoke me the biggest damn cigar I can find. Is that clear?"

"Yeah, a lot clearer than your orders at Waco were."

Winters straightened up and the two men stared intently at each other.

Web said, "I always wondered, Buck, how come you were the only one in the chain of command—excuse me, the chain of *chaos*—that didn't get his career path cut off for that mess. You know, while I was sitting out there on sniper duty a couple of times I actually thought you were working for the Branch Davidians because of all the dumb-shit decisions you made."

Bates said sharply, "Web, shut your damn mouth." He looked anxiously at Winters. "I've got it from here, Buck."

Winters stared at Web for several more seconds and then headed to the door, but he looked back. "If I had my way, there wouldn't be an HRT, and I'm going to have my way yet. And guess who'll be the first son of a bitch to go? How's that for chain of command!"

Winters shut the door and Web let out a big breath he wasn't even aware he'd been holding. And then Bates got right in his face. "I put my neck out for you, called in every chit I've ever earned at the Bureau and you almost screwed it up, taking on Winters like that. Are you really that big a damn idiot?"

"I guess I must be," Web answered defiantly. "But I didn't ask for any of this. The press can strip me clean, but nothing, nothing is going to mess up the investigation."

"You're going to give me a coronary, you really are." Bates finally calmed down. "Okay, here are your marching orders. You're going to lay low for a while. Don't go home. We'll get you a car from the motor pool. Head out somewhere and stay there awhile. The Bureau will foot the bills. We'll communicate via your secure cell phone. Check in regularly. As bad as you looked on the tube right now, you'll look just as good when we tell our side. And if I find you anywhere near Buck Winters during the next thirty years, I will personally shoot you myself. Now get out of here!" Bates went to the door, but Web remained sitting.

"Perce, why are you doing all this? You're taking a big risk standing up for me."

Bates studied the floor for a few moments. "This is gonna sound sappy, and maybe it should, but anyway it's the truth. I'm doing this because the Web London I know has risked his life for this agency more times than I can remember. Because I've watched you lying in a hospital room for three months not sure if you were going to make it. You could've retired then with full pay, gone out on top. Gone fishing or whatever the hell it is retired FBI do. But you came back and got in the line of fire again. I don't know many guys that have ever done that." He drew a long breath. "And because I know what you did in that alley even if the rest of the world doesn't. But they're going to damn sure know it, Web. There aren't many heroes left anymore. But you're one of them. That's all I'm going to say about it. And don't you ever, ever ask me again."

The man walked out and left Web to contemplate another side of Percy Bates.

It was almost midnight and Web was on the move. He was climbing over fences and sneaking through neighbors' yards. The goal tonight was a simple if absurd one. He had to break into his *own* home through a rear window because the media were still moored out front waiting to board him. And then sink him. Two uniformed Bureau security officers were there too, backed up by a Virginia state police cruiser, its blue waggle lights slicing through the darkness. Web hoped there would be no more mobs, no more riots. So long as no one spotted him climbing in his own bathroom window, that is. Then all bets were off.

Web quietly packed a duffel in the dark, threw in some extra rounds of ammo, some other pieces of equipment that he thought might come in handy, then crawled back out. He cleared the fence and slipped back into his neighbor's yard and then stopped. He opened the duffel, pulled out a battery-operated ambient light monocular that made the dark look as clear as day, albeit with a greenish tint, and looked through it. He surveyed the army camped outside his house and focused the magnifier for a better look. All those people whose sole purpose in life right now was to get any possible dirt and damn the truth made Web decide that paybacks, however small, should be taken when the opportunity arose. And right now he could use a generous fix. Web pulled out a flare gun, loaded in a cartridge, aimed the weapon to the sky at a spot right over the top of this fine group of people and fired. The flare sailed upward, exploded and lit the heavens a brilliant yellow. Web watched through his monocular as the pack of fine, exemplary people looked up with fearful eyes and then ran screaming for their lives. It truly was the little things that made life so sweet: long walks, rain showers, puppies, scaring the crap out of a bunch of sanctimonious reporters.

He jogged back to the Crown Vic that Bates had arranged for him and drove off. Web stayed that night at a dump motel off Route One in south Alexandria where he could pay in cash, no one bothered him and the only room service was the McDonald's bag you brought with you or the soda and snack machine chained to a graffiti-stained support column outside his room. He watched TV and ate his cheeseburger and fries. The he pulled out from his duffel his bottle of pills and swallowed two of them. He fell into a deep sleep and for once nightmares didn't rouse him from it.

16

Early on a Saturday morning, Scott Wingo navigated his wheelchair up the ramp and unlocked the door to a four-story nineteenth-century brick building that housed his law office. Divorced, with grown children, Wingo had a thriving criminal defense practice in Richmond, the city of his birth, where he had remained his whole life. Saturdays were a time for him to go into the office and not be bothered by pealing phones, clacking keyboards, harassed associates and demanding clients. Those pleasantries were left for during the week. He went inside, made a pot of coffee, spiked it with his favorite Gentleman Jim bourbon and rolled his way to his office. Scott Wingo and Associates, Counselors at Law, had been a Richmond institution for almost thirty years. During that time Wingo had gone from being a sole practitioner working out of an office the size of a closet, basically defending anyone with enough cash to pay him, to head of a firm with six associates, a full-time PI and a support staff of eight. As the sole shareholder of the firm Wingo pulled down seven figures in a good year, and even mid-six money in bad times. His clients had also grown more substantial. For years he had resisted taking on the drug people, but the cash flow was undeniable and Wingo had wearied of seeing far inferior attorneys drawing down those dollars. He comforted himself with the knowledge that anyone, regardless of what heinous thing he had done, deserved a competent—even inspired—defense.

Wingo had considerable skills as a courtroom lawyer, and his presence before a jury had not been diminished one iota by his confinement two years ago to a wheelchair because of ongoing diabetes and kidney and liver ailments. In some ways, he felt his ability to reach out to a jury had been enhanced by his physical predicament. And many a member of the state bar envied Wingo's string of victories. He was also loathed by those who felt he was simply a means for rich criminals to avoid the rightful consequences of their terrible misdeeds. Wingo naturally didn't see it that way, but he had long ago stopped trying to win that argument because it was one of the very few issues he had ever come upon that didn't seem worth arguing about.

He lived in a substantial home in Windsor Farms, a very affluent and coveted area of Richmond; drove a specially configured Jag sedan to accommodate his disability; took luxurious trips overseas when he wanted to; was good to his children and generous and on good terms with his ex-wife, who still lived in their old home. But mostly he worked. At age fifty-nine Wingo had outlived many predictions of his premature death. Those had come either because of his various medical conditions or because of threats from disgruntled clients or folks on the other side of a crime who felt justice had not been served largely through Wingo doing what he did best, which was finding reasonable doubt in twelve peers of the defendant. Yet he knew that his time was running out. He could feel it in his tired organs, in his poor circulation, his general fatigue. He figured he would work until he died; it wouldn't be such a bad way to go.

He took a sip of coffee and Gentleman Jim and picked up the phone. He liked to work the phones, even on the weekends, particularly in calling back people he didn't want to talk with. Rarely would they be in on Saturday morning and he'd leave a polite message telling them he was sorry to have missed them. He did ten of these and felt like he was being very productive. His mouth was growing very dry, probably from all the talking, and he took another shot of the whiskey coffee. He turned to a brief he was working on that would, if granted, suppress evidence in a burglary ring matter he was involved in. Most people didn't realize that trials were often won before anyone stepped foot inside a courtroom. In this case if the motion were granted there would be no trial because the prosecution would have no case.

After several hours of work and more phone calls, he took off his glasses and rubbed his eyes. The damn diabetes was wreaking havoc with just about every part of him and he had found out last week that he had glaucoma. Maybe the Lord was getting him back for the work he was doing here on earth.

He thought he heard a door open somewhere and figured one of his overpaid associates might have wandered in to actually perform some weekend labor. The young folks these days, they just didn't have the same work ethic of Wingo's generation, even though they made outrageous sums. When had he *not* worked a weekend for the first fifteen years of his practice? The kids today grumbled about working past six. Damn if his eyes weren't killing him. He finished the cup of coffee, but his thirst returned just as bad. He popped open a desk drawer and drank from the bottle of water he kept there. Now his head was throbbing. And his back was aching. He put a finger on his wrist and counted. Well, hell, his pulse was out of whack too; yet that happened just about every day. He had already taken his insulin and wouldn't need another shot for a while; still, he wondered about speeding up the schedule. Maybe his blood sugar had plummeted somehow. He was always adjusting his insulin, because he could never get the damn right dosage. His doctor had told him to stop drinking, but that was just not going to happen, Wingo knew. For him, bourbon was a necessity, not a luxury.

He was sure he heard the door that time. "Hello," he called out. "Is that you, Missy?" Missy, he thought, Missy was his damn dog that had died ten years ago. Where the hell had that come from? He tried to focus on the brief, but his vision was now so badly blurred and his body was doing such funny things that Wingo finally started to get scared. Hell, maybe he was having a coronary, though he felt no pain in his chest, no dull throb in his left shoulder and arm.

He looked at the clock but couldn't make out the time. Okay, he needed to do something here. "Hello," he called out again. "I need some help here." He thought he heard approaching footsteps, but then no one ever came. *Okay, damn it,* he thought. "Sons of bitches," he yelled. He picked up the phone and managed to guide his hand to the nine and then twice on the one. He waited, but no one came on the line. That was our tax dollars at work. You dial 911 and get jack. "I need some help here," he called into the phone. And then he noted there was no dial tone. He hung up and lifted the receiver again. No dial tone. Well, shit. He slammed the phone down and missed the cradle and the receiver fell to the floor. He pulled at his shirt collar because it was getting hard to breathe. He'd been meaning to get one of those cell phones but never had gotten around to it. "Is anybody out there, damn it?" Now he could hear the footsteps. His breathing was becoming impossible, like something was wedged down his gullet. Sweat was pouring off him. He looked up at the doorway. Through his clouded vision he could see the door opening. The person came in.

"Mother?" Damn if it wasn't his mother, and she would be dead twenty years this November. "Mother, I need some help, I'm not feeling too good."

There was no one there, of course. Wingo was just hallucinating.

Wingo slid to the floor now, because he couldn't keep himself up in the chair any longer. He crawled along the floor to her, gasping and wheezing as he did so. "Mother," he said hoarsely to the vision he was experiencing. "You got to help your boy, he ain't doing too good." He got to her and then she just disappeared on him, just like that, right when he needed her. Wingo put his head on the floor and slowly closed his eyes.

"Anybody out there? I need help," he said one last time.

17

Francis Westbrook was feeling seriously hampered. His usual haunts, his normal places of conducting business were not available to him. The Feds, he knew, were looking for him, and whoever had set him up was no doubt trying to get the jump on him too. Westbrook couldn't assume anything else. In his line of work extreme paranoia was really the only thing keeping him alive. Thus he was hanging out, at least for the next hour, in the back of a meat warehouse in Southeast D.C. Ten minutes' drive from where he was sitting and freezing his ass off was the Capitol and other great national buildings. Westbrook had lived his whole life in Washington and had never been to a single monument. These grand edifices to a great nation meant absolutely nothing to him. He didn't consider himself an American, a Washingtonian or a citizen of anything. He was just another brother looking to get by. His goal when he was ten was to live to fifteen. Then his objective was to make it to twenty before he was killed. Then twenty-five. When he hit thirty a couple of years ago he had given himself a party worthy of a person achieving octogenarian status, because in his world, he had. Everything was relative, maybe more so in the eyes of Francis Westbrook than other people.

What was occupying most of his thinking now was how he had screwed up with Kevin. His desire to let the boy have a somewhat normal life had led him to be careless about Kevin's safety. He had once had Kevin with him all the time, but then a crew dispute had erupted into a full-fledged battle and Kevin had been shot in the face and almost died. Francis hadn't even been able to take him to the hospital because he probably would've been arrested. After that, he let Kevin live with some quasi-family, an old lady and her grandson. He kept close watch on Kevin and visited him as often as he could; however, he let the boy have his freedom because every child needed that.

And the fact was Kevin was not going to grow up like Francis. He was going to have a real life, away from guns and drugs and the quick drive to the medical examiner's office with a tag on your toe. Being around Francis too much, being witness to such a life, any young man might be tempted to stick his toes in the water. And once you did, you were caught for life, because that sweet-looking pond was pure quicksand and filled with water moccasins all claiming to be your friend until you weren't looking and one of them sunk his fangs in your neck. That was not going to happen to Kevin, Francis had pledged when Kevin had been born, and yet maybe it already had. It would be truly ironic if Kevin did not outlive him.

While Westbrook headed up one of the more lucrative drug operations in the D.C. metro area, he had never been arrested for anything, not even a misdemeanor, though he was going on his twenty-third year in the "bizness," having started very young and never looked back, because there was nothing to look back to. He was proud of that clean record, despite his felonious ways. It was not all luck; in fact, most of it was due to his carefully crafted survival plans, the way he gave information when it was needed to the right people, who in return then let him carry on his thing peacefully. That was key, don't rock the boat, don't be causing trouble on the street, don't be shooting nobody or nothing if you can help it. Don't give the Feds a hard time, because they got the manpower and money to make your life hell and who needed that shit. His life was complicated enough as it was. And yet without Kevin his life was nothing.

He looked over at Macy and Peebles, his twin shadows. He trusted them as much as he trusted anyone, which was not all that much. He always carried a gun and had needed it on more than one occasion to save his life. You only had to learn that lesson once. He glanced toward the door where big Toona had just come in.

"Toona, you got me some news, ain't you? Some good news 'bout Kevin."

"Nothing yet, boss."

"Then get your sorry ass back out there till you do."

A sour-looking Toona immediately left and Westbrook looked at Peebles.

"Talk to me, Twan."

Antoine "Twan" Peebles looked chagrined and carefully adjusted his expensive reading glasses. The man's eyesight was excellent, Westbrook knew, he just thought wearing spectacles helped him to look the part of an executive, trying to be something he never would be, legitimate. Westbrook had made his peace with that issue a long time ago. Really the choice had been made for him the moment he had been born in the backseat of a Cadillac up on cinder blocks, his mother snorting coke even as Francis had slipped out between her legs into the arms of her man of the moment, who had promptly set the child aside, cut the cord with a dirty knife and forced the new mother to perform oral sex on him. His mother had told him about this later, in graphic detail, as though it were the funniest story she had ever heard.

"It's not good news," said Peebles. "Our main distributor said until the heat died down on you, he wasn't sure he could provide us with any more product. And our inventory levels are pretty low as it is."

"Damn, now ain't *that* a shock," said Westbrook. He sat back. Westbrook had to put on a strong front before Peebles and Macy and his people, yet the fact was he had a real problem. Like any reseller of sorts, Westbrook had obligations to folks down the line. And if they couldn't get what they needed from him, they would get it from somebody else. His survival time would not be long. And once you disappointed folks, they almost never did business with you again. "Okay, I'll deal with that later. This Web London dude, what you got?"

Peebles opened a file he had pulled from a leather briefcase and adjusted his reading glasses once more. Using his monogrammed handkerchief, Peebles had carefully wiped off the seat he was sitting on and had made it clear that holding a meeting inside a meat warehouse was far beneath his dignity. Peebles liked rolls of cash in his pockets and nice clothes and nice restaurants and the nice ladies doing whatever he wanted for him or to him. He didn't carry a gun, and for all Westbrook knew, Peebles didn't even know how to shoot one. He had come up at a time when drug operations had been far less violent and run in a more orderly way, with accountants and computers and business files, and taking dirty money and making it clean, and having stock portfolios and even vacation homes that one traveled to in one's private jet.

Ten years older than Peebles, Westbrook had come up purely on the streets. He had run crack for pennies a bag, slept in rat holes, gone hungry more often than not, dodged bullets and fired them into others when he had to. Peebles was good at what he did; he made sure that Westbrook's operation ran smoothly and that product came in when it was supposed to and went out to the people that it was intended for. And he also ensured that accounts receivable—Westbrook had belly laughed when Peebles had first used that term with him—that accounts receivable were promptly paid. Money was efficiently laundered, excess cash flow prudently invested, innovations in the industry kept abreast of, the latest technology utilized, all under the watchful eyes of Antoine Peebles. And still Westbrook couldn't bring himself to respect the man.

When personnel issues arose, though, which basically meant that somebody was trying screw them, Antoine Peebles quickly stepped aside. He had no stomach for that part of the business. That's when Westbrook took over and handled things. And that's where Clyde Macy really earned all the dollars that he was paid.

Westbrook looked over at his little white boy. He had thought it a joke when Macy had come to him for work. "You on the wrong side of town, boy," he had told Macy. "Whitey-town's up Northwest way. You go get your ass to where it belongs." He had figured that would be the end of that until Macy had popped two gents trying to mess with Westbrook and, as Macy had explained at the time, he'd done it on a *pro bono* basis, just to prove his value. And the little skinhead had never failed his boss. Who would have thought it, big black Francis Westbrook being an equal opportunity employer?

"Web London," said Peebles, who stopped and coughed and then blew his nose, "has been with the FBI for over thirteen years and with Hostage Rescue for about eight. He's highly thought of. Got lots of commendations and things like that in his file. He was badly injured and almost died during one mission. Militiamen thing."

"Militiamen," said Westbrook. "Right, that's white people with guns think the government's fucked *them* over. They ought come see us black folk, see how good they really got it."

Peebles continued, "There's an investigation currently going on into the shooting in the courtyard."

"Twan, tell me something I don't know, 'cause I'm freezing my ass off and I see you are too."

"London's going to a psychiatrist. Not one at the Bureau, an outside firm."

"We know who?"

"It's a group at Tyson's Corner. Not sure yet of the psychiatrist seeing him."

"Well, let's get that nailed down. He'll talk to the shrink about things he ain't talk to anybody else about. And then maybe we have a talk with the shrink."

"Right," said Peebles as he made a note.

"And Twan, can you tell me what the hell they were going after that night? Don't you think that might be important shit?"

Peebles bristled at this. "I was just about to get to that." He rustled through some more papers while Macy meticulously cleaned his pistol, wiping away from the barrel dust motes that apparently only he could see.

Peebles found what he was looking for and glanced up at his boss. "You're really not going to like this."

"There's a lot of shit I really don't like. Tell me."

"Word is that they were going after you. That building was supposed to house our entire financial operations. Bean counters, computers, files, the whole deal." Peebles shook his head and looked offended, as though his personal honor had been impugned. "Like we'd be stupid enough to have that centralized. They sent HRT in because they wanted to bring the money guys out alive, to testify against you."

Westbrook was so stunned by this that he didn't even take Peebles to task for saying "our" financial operations. They were Westbrook's, clear and simple. "And why the hell they think that? We ain't never even used that building. I ain't never even been in the damn place." A thought suddenly seized Westbrook, but he decided to keep it to himself. When you wanted to deal, you needed to bring something to the party, and maybe he had something, something to do with that building. When Westbrook was just starting out on the streets, he had actually known that place real well. It was part of government-funded tenement housing built in the 1950s and designed to give poor families the subsidies they needed to get back on their feet. What it ended up being twenty years or so later was one of the worst drug areas in the city, with killings nightly. White kids in the suburbs watched TV at night while Westbrook had watched homicides in his own backyard. But there was something about that building and others like it that maybe the Feds didn't know. Yeah, that one went in his "deal-making" file. He started feeling a little better, but just a little.

Peebles perched his glasses on the end of his nose as he eyed Westbrook. "Well, I'm assuming the Bureau had some undercover working this thing and that agent must have told them otherwise."

"Who's the damn agent?" asked Westbrook.

"That we don't know."

"Well, that's shit I *got* to know. People going around lying about me, I want to know who it is." Something very cold had suddenly seized in Westbrook's chest even as he tried to put on a strong front. Now he was not feeling so good. If a Bureau agent had targeted what he thought was Westbrook's operations center, then this meant the FBI had turned its attention to him. Why the hell had they done that? He wasn't that big an operation and he sure wasn't the only game in town. A bunch of crews did things a lot worse than he did. Now, nobody walked over him and nobody touched his turf, but he had played it low and cool for years, causing nobody trouble.

Peebles said, "Well, whoever tipped the Bureau off knew what strings to pull. They don't call up HRT unless they got something very serious to go on. They hit that building because it was supposed to be filled with evidence to be used against you. At least that's what our sources say."

"And what'd they find there, except the guns?"

"Nothing, place was empty."

"So the undercover was full of shit?"

"Or else *his* sources were."

"Or else they set him up, to set me up," said Westbrook. "See, Twan, the cops ain't going to care what's *not* there. They still gonna think my ass was behind it 'cause it's on my turf. So whoever did this was taking no risk. They stacked the deck against me right from the go. Ain't no way I could win that. Am I right, Twan, or you see it different?"

Westbrook studied Peebles closely. The man's body language had very subtly shifted. Westbrook, who had made the noticing of such things an instinct, an instinct that had saved his life numerous times, definitely picked up on it. And he knew its source. Despite his college education and his skill at managing the business, Peebles was just not as quick as Westbrook was at sizing up a situation and coming to the right conclusion. His street instincts paled in comparison to his boss's. And there was a simple reason for that: Westbrook had spent years surviving on those instincts and all the while honing them to an even sharper precision. Peebles had never had to do that.

"You're probably right."

"Yeah, probably," said Westbrook. He stared grimly at Peebles until the man finally looked down at his papers.

"So the thing is, as I *probably* see it, is we know jack-shit about London, only that he's seeing a shrink 'cause he froze up. He could be in on it and just faking everybody out and saying it's all in his head."

"I'm certain he is in on it," commented Peebles.

Westbrook sat back and smiled. "No, he ain't in on it, Twan, I was just seeing if you could finally show me some street mind. You ain't there yet, bro. Not by a long shot."

Peebles looked up in surprise. "But you said—"

"Yeah, yeah, I know what I said, Twan, I can hear myself talk, okay?" He hunched forward. "I been seeing the TV and newspapers, catching up on this dude Web London, Twan. Like you say, man's a damn hero, got his ass shot up and all."

"I've been following it too," said Peebles. "And I didn't see any-thing that convinced me London's not in on the setup. In fact, the widow of one of his own men thinks he was in on it. And did you see what happened outside his house? The guy pulled his gun and fired on a bunch of reporters. He's crazy."

"No, he fired in the air. Man like that, if he had wanted to kill any-body, they'd be dead. That man, he knows guns, that's easy to see."

Peebles wasn't backing down. "I think the reason he didn't go out in that courtyard was because he *knew* the guns were there. He went down right before the guns started shooting. He *had* to know."

"Is that right, Twan? He had to know?"

Peebles nodded. "You wanted my informed opinion, that's it."

"Well, let me inform your damn opinion some more. You ever been shot at?"

Peebles looked over at Macy and then back at Westbrook. "No. Thankfully."

"Yeah, that's a hell of a lot to be thankful for. Well, see, I have. You too, right, Mace?"

Macy nodded and put his pistol away as he followed this dis-cussion.

"See, folks don't like to get shot at, Twan. It just ain't natural to like something like getting your head blown off. Now, if London was in on it he coulda done lots of shit to stay away from that hit. He coulda shot himself in the foot during training, ate some bad food and put himself in the hospital, run into a wall and broke his arm, all sorts of shit so his ass not even been anywhere near that place. But he was, he hauling butt with all the rest of his crew. Then he can't haul no more and his team gets shot up. Now, a man on the take, what's he gonna do if he is stupid enough to go on the gig? He gonna sit back, maybe fire a few rounds in there and then go see the shrink saying his mind's messed up. But what a guilty man ain't gonna do is go out in that courtyard and mess with those machine guns. He gonna stay nice and safe and collect his money for setting everybody up. Now, this man, he went out there and did something even I ain't got the balls to do." He paused. "And he done something else just as crazy."

"What's that?"

Westbrook shook his head and decided it was really fortunate for

Peebles that he was so good at the business end because he was surely lacking everywhere else. "Unless the whole world's lying their asses off, that man saved Kevin. Ain't no way a guilty man gonna bother with that shit."

Peebles sat back, looking thoroughly whipped. "But if you are right and he's not involved, then he won't know where Kevin is."

"That's right. He ain't. In fact, I ain't know nothing, do I, except shit that don't matter?" He said the last with a hard stare right at Peebles. "And I ain't no closer to getting Kevin back than I was a week ago, am I? You happy about that, Twan? 'Cause I ain't."

"So what do we do?" asked Peebles.

"We keep a line on London and find out what shrink he's seeing. And we wait. Them folks took Kevin didn't do it for nothing. They'll come to us, and then we see what happens. But let me tell you this: I find out somebody sold me and Kevin out, baby, they could run to the South Pole and I'd find 'em and feed 'em to the polar bears limb by limb, and folks think I'm shitting, they better hope they never find out."

Despite the severe chill in the room, a bead of sweat crept down Peebles's brow as Westbrook adjourned the meeting.

18

The air here was not fresh, the smells noxious at times, yet at least it was warm. They fed him all the food he wanted and it was good. And he had books to read, though the light was fairly poor, but they had apologized for that. And they had even given him sketchpads and some charcoal pencils when he had asked for them. That had made his imprisonment easier. When things were going badly in his life, he could always turn to his drawings for a measure of solace. And yet despite everyone's kindness, every time someone came to the room he was convinced that it would be the moment of his death, because why else would they have brought him here but to kill him?

Kevin Westbrook looked around at a room that was far bigger than the one he had at home, yet it seemed close all around him, as though it were shrinking or he was growing larger. He had no idea how long he had been here. Without the rise and fall of the sun, telling time was not possible, he had found. He never thought about calling out anymore. He had tried that once and the man had come and told Kevin not to do that. He said it very politely and in a nonthreatening way, as though Kevin had merely walked across a prized flower bed. Yet Kevin could sense that this man would kill him if he yelled out again. It was always the soft-talking ones who were the most dangerous.

The clanking sound was always there, that and the hissing and the sound of running water nearby. Collectively it would probably cover any noises he could make, but it was very irritating, and interrupted his sleep. They apologized for that too. They were much more polite than captors probably should be, thought Kevin.

He had looked for ways to escape, yet there was only one door to the room, and it was locked. So he read his books and drew his pictures. He ate and he drank and he waited for the time when somebody would come and kill him.

While he was sketching another drawing decipherable only to him, Kevin flinched when he heard the footsteps. As he listened to the door being unlocked, he wondered if that time had come.

The man was the same one who had told him not to yell. Kevin had seen him before but didn't know his name.

He wanted to know if Kevin was comfortable, if he needed anything else.

"Nope. You treating me real good. But my grandma be worried about me. Maybe I ought be getting on home now."

"Not right now," was all the man said. He perched on the large table in the middle of the room and eyed the small bed in the corner. "You sleeping well?"

"Okay."

Then the man wanted to know, one more time, exactly what happened between Kevin and the man in the alley, the one that had grabbed Kevin, given him the note, sent him on his way.

"I didn't tell him nothing, because I ain't had nothing to tell him." Kevin's tone was more defiant than he would have liked, but the man had asked him these questions before and he had told him the same answers and he was growing weary of it.

"Think," said the man calmly. "He's a trained investigator, he may have picked up on something you said, though it didn't seem important when you said it. You're a smart boy, you'll be able to remember."

Kevin held the piece of charcoal pencil in his hand, squeezing it until his joints cracked. "I went down the alley like you told me to. I done what you told me to, and that's all. And you say he ain't gonna be moving or nothing. All messed up and stuff. Well, that ain't happen. He scared the crap out of me. See, you were wrong about that."

The man put out a hand and Kevin flinched, but the man merely rubbed him gently on the shoulder. "We didn't tell you to go near that courtyard, did we? We said to just sit tight and we'd come get you. See, we had everything timed out perfectly." The man laughed. "You really made us jump through some hoops, son."

Kevin felt the hand tighten on his shoulder and despite the man's laughing he could tell the fellow was upset so he decided to change the subject. "Why you have that other boy with you?"

"Just something for him to do, just like you did. He made some nice money, just like you did. In fact, you weren't supposed to see him, but we had to change things, see, because you weren't where you were supposed to be. Cut it pretty darn tight." The hand tightened some more.

"So you already let him go?"

"Go ahead with your story, Kevin, that boy's no concern of yours. Tell me why you did what you did."

How did Kevin explain this? He had had no idea what would happen when he had done what they told him to. Then the guns started firing and he was scared, terrified, but it had been a terror rife with curiosity. It had been a curious dread, actually, to see what he had wrought; as though, say, you'd dropped a rock from a bridge onto a highway with no purpose other than to scare some motorists, only to see your handiwork result in a fifty-car pile-up and numerous deaths. And so when he should have run like hell, Kevin had gone farther down the alley to see what he had done. And the guns, instead of making him flee, had somehow drawn him closer, like both the horror and allure of a dead body. "And then that man yelled at me," he now told his captor. Lord, how that had scared him. Rising up from all those bodies, that voice telling him to get back, stay back, warning him!

Kevin looked at the man after describing all this. He had done what they had told him for one of the oldest reasons in the world, money, enough to help his grandma and Jerome get into a nicer place. Money enough to allow Kevin to believe he was helping out, taking care of others, rather than always being taken care of. His grandma and Jerome had warned him about accepting offers of fast money from people who trolled his neighborhood looking for folks to do things they shouldn't. Many of Kevin's friends had been so taken in, now dead, crippled, imprisoned or disillusioned for life. And now he had been added to that miserable pile, at all of ten years old.

"And then you heard the others coming from down the alley," prompted the man smoothly.

Kevin nodded as he thought back to that moment. He had been so scared. Guns in front of him, men with more guns cutting off his only avenue of escape. Except across that courtyard. At least he had thought so. That man had stopped him from doing that; had saved his life. Didn't even know him and he had helped him. That was a new experience for Kevin. "What was the man's name again?" he asked.

"Web London," the man said. "He's the guy you talked to. He's the one I'm really interested in."

"I told him I ain't done nothing," Kevin said again, hoping that the same answer once more would make this man leave and let him get back to his drawing. "He told me if I went out there I'd get killed too. He showed me his hand, where he been shot. I started to run the other way and he say if I do that, they kill me too. That's when he give me the hat and the note. He shot that flare off and told me to go on. And that's what I did."

"Good thing we had another boy lined up to take your place. You'd been through a lot."

Somehow Kevin didn't think it was such a good thing for the other kid.

"And London actually went back into the courtyard?"

Kevin nodded. "I looked back once. He had that big-ass gun. He went back in there and I heard that gun go off. I was walking fast." Yes, he had walked fast. Walked fast until some men had appeared out of a doorway and snatched him clean. Kevin had caught a glimpse of the other boy, roughly his age and size, yet who was a stranger to Kevin. He looked just as scared as Kevin. One of the men had quickly read the note, asked Kevin what had happened. And then the other boy had been given the cap and note and sent off to deliver it in Kevin's stead.

"Why you bring that other boy?" Kevin asked again, but the

man didn't answer. "How come you sent him with the note and not me?"

The man ignored the question. "Did London seem at all out of it to you? Like he wasn't thinking clearly?"

"He tell me what to do. He thinking pretty good from where I be standing."

The man took a deep breath and shook his head, obviously pondering this. Then he smiled at Kevin. "You'll never realize how extraordinary that is, Kevin. Web London must be truly special to have done that."

"You ain't tell me all what was gonna happen."

The man continued to smile. "That's because you didn't need to know, Kevin."

"Where's the other boy? Why you bring him?" he asked again.

"You think of every contingency, then most times things turn out okay."

"Is that other boy dead?"

The man rose. "Let us know if you need anything else. We'll try and take care of you."

Kevin decided to toss out a threat of his own. "My brother be looking for me." He hadn't said this before, but he had been thinking it, every minute he had. Everybody knew Kevin's brother. Just about everybody he knew feared his brother. Kevin prayed that this man feared him too. Kevin's spirits sank when he could clearly tell from the man's face that he didn't. Maybe this man wasn't afraid of anything.

"You just rest up, Kevin." The man looked at some of his drawings. "You know, you've got a lot of talent. Who knows, maybe you could've ended up *not* like your brother." The man closed and locked the door behind him.

Kevin tried to stop them, but the tears just came in a rush down his cheeks, dripped onto his blanket. He rubbed them away, but more took their place. Kevin sank into a corner and wept so hard he kept losing his breath. Then he pulled a blanket over his head and sat there in the darkness.

19

Web drove the Crown Vic down the street his mother used to live on. It was a neighborhood on its last legs, its potential never realized and its vitality long since exhausted. Yet the location, thirty years ago considered rural, was now smack in the middle of prime suburbia, what with the continued sprawl of the metropolitan area, where commuters rose from their beds at four to get to the office by eight. In five years' time, a developer would probably buy up all the dilapidated properties, bulldoze them under and new homes costing too much would arise from the dust of old ones sacrificed for too little.

Web got out of the Crown Vic and looked around. Charlotte London had been one of the older people living here, and her house, despite Web's efforts, was about as run-down as the rest. The chain-link fence was a few rusting strands from collapse. The house's metal awnings sagged with water and carried grime that could no longer be cleaned away. The lone maple in front was dead, with brown leaves on it from the year before scraping a sad tune in the breeze. The grass had not been cut for a while because Web had not been around to push the mower. He had fought a valiant effort over the years to keep it as it had once been but had finally given up because his mother had taken little interest in maintaining her home and yard. Now that she was dead, Web figured he would be selling the place at some point; he just didn't want to deal with it right now, maybe never.

Web went inside and looked around. Right after her death he

had come here. The place had been a mess, exactly as his mother had left it. He had spent an entire day cleaning the house and ended up carrying ten thirty-gallon bags of trash to the curb. Then Web had kept the electricity, water and sewer going after his mother's death. It wasn't that he ever envisioned himself living here, but something just wouldn't let him go. Now he surveyed the rooms, clean except for dust and the occasional cobweb. He settled down, checked his watch and flipped on the TV just as a soap opera was interrupted for a special news event. This was the promised FBI news conference. Web scooted forward and adjusted the picture and sound.

Web gaped as Percy Bates appeared at the podium. Where the hell was Buck Winters? Web thought. He listened as Bates ran through Web's distinguished career at the FBI and some feel-good film was shown of Web accepting various awards, medals and citations from the Bureau heads and one from the President himself. Bates spoke of the horror in the courtyard and Web's bravery and grit in doing what he had done when confronted with such an overwhelming foe.

One shot was of Web in the hospital with half his face bandaged. This made Web reach up and touch the old wound. He felt proud and cheap at the same time. He suddenly wished Bates had not done this. This "promo" wasn't going to change anyone's mind. It just made him seem defensive. The journalists would crucify him, probably accuse the Bureau of covering their ass by shielding one of their own. And maybe, in a way, they were. He let out a low moan. He didn't think it could get any worse, yet it just had. He turned off the TV, sat there and closed his eyes. In his mind he felt a hand on his shoulder, but there was no one there. This seemed to always happen to him when he came here; his mother's presence was everywhere.

Charlotte London had kept until her death the shoulder-length hair that had over the years turned from glorious, sexy blond to elegant, luxurious silver. Her skin had been unwrinkled because she was allergic to the sun and had covered herself from it all her life. And her neck had been long and smooth with tight muscles set at the base. Web wondered how many men had been seduced by that delicate but overpowering curve. When he was a teenager Web had had dreams about his young, sexy mother that to this day he still felt shame for.

Despite the drinking and less-than-healthy eating habits, his mother had not gained an ounce in forty years and the weight had remained pretty much in its original locations. When she really put herself together, she had been a knockout at age fifty-nine. It was too bad that her liver had given out. The rest of her could have kept going for a while longer.

As beautiful as she had been, it was her intellect that attracted most people. Yet the conversations between mother and son had been downright bizarre. His mother did not watch TV. "They call it an idiot box for good reason," she had often said. "I'd rather read Camus. Or Goethe. Or Jean Genet. Genet makes me laugh and cry at the same time, and I don't really know why, for there is arguably nothing humorous about Genet. His subject matter was vile. Depraved. So much suffering. Mostly autobiographical."

"Right. Sure, Genet, Goethe," Web had told her several years before. "G-men, like me, sort of." His mother had never gotten the joke.

"But they can be wonderfully compelling—erotic, even," she had said.

"What can?" he had asked.

"Vileness and depravity."

Web had taken a deep breath. He had wanted to tell her that he'd seen some vileness and depravity in his time that would have made old Jean Genet barf up his lunch. He had wanted to unequivocally inform his mother that these evils were nothing to joke about, because one day somebody filled to the brim with vileness and depravity might appear on her doorstep and violently end her life. Instead he had remained silent. His mother had often had that effect on him.

Charlotte London had been a child prodigy, astounding folks with her broad-ranging intellect. She had entered college at age fourteen and earned a degree in American literature from Amherst, graduating near the top of her class. She had spoken four foreign languages fluently. After college Charlotte had trav-

eled the world alone for almost a year, Web knew, because he had
seen the photos and read her journals. And that was back in the
days when young women didn't do that sort of thing. She had
even written a book chronicling her adventures, and the book
was still selling to this day. Its title was *London Times*; London had
been her maiden name, and she had changed it back after her
second husband had died. She had had Web's surname legally
changed from Sullivan after she had divorced her first husband.
Web had never carried his stepfather's name. His mother would
not allow it. It was just how she was. And to this day he never
knew why he had been given such an odd name as Web with only
the one *b*. He had gone up and down his maternal family tree and
the answer wasn't there. His mother had steadfastly refused even
to tell Web who had named him.

When he had been little, his mother had shared with Web much
of what she had seen and done on her teenage travels, and he had
thought hers the most wonderful stories he had ever heard. And
he had wanted to go on trips with her just like that and write in his
journal and take photos of his beautiful, adventurous mother
against the backdrop of pristine water in Italy or on a snowcapped
mountain in Switzerland or at an outdoor café in Paris. The beautiful mother and the dashing son taking the world by storm had
dominated his boyhood thoughts. But then she had married Web's
stepfather and those dreams went away.

Web opened his eyes and rose. He went to the basement first.
Thick dust covered every surface, and Web found nothing remotely close to what he was looking for. He went back upstairs
and into the rear of the house where the kitchen was. He opened
the back door and looked outside at the small garage that housed,
among other things, his mother's ancient Plymouth Duster. Web
could hear the cries of children at play nearby. He closed his eyes
and rested his face against the mesh as those sounds sank in. In
his mind Web could almost see the football being thrown, the
coltish legs hustling after it, a very young Web thinking that if he
didn't catch that ball, his life would end. He sniffed the air, the
smell of wood smoke mingling with the sweet aroma of freshly
cut fall grass. There was nothing better, it seemed, and yet it was

only a scent, never lasting for very long. And then you were pretty much right back in the shit of life. The shit, he had discovered, was never temporary.

In his vision, the young Web ran harder and harder. It was growing dark and he knew his mother would be calling him in soon. Not to eat, but to run over to the neighbors to bum cigarettes for his stepfather. Or to hustle down to the neighborhood Foodway with a couple dollars and a sad tale for Old Man Stein, who ran the place with a bigger heart than he should have. Always hustling down to the Foodway was young Web. Always singing the sad Irish song, his mother coaching him on the lyrics. Where had she learned it, the sad song? Web had asked her. As with the origin of his given name, she had never answered him.

Web could vividly remember Mr. Stein squatting down with his big glasses, old cardigan and neat white apron and graciously accepting the crumpled dollar bills from "Webbie" London, as he liked to call Web. Then he would help Web pick out food for supper and maybe even breakfast. These groceries, of course, always cost far more than two dollars, and yet Stein had never said a word about the cost. Yet he had not been so reserved about other things.

"You tell your mother not to drink so much," he had called after Web as he had run off home carrying two bulging bags of groceries. "And you tell that devil of a husband of hers that God will strike him down for what he has done, if a man's hand does not do so sooner. And if only God would allow me that honor. I pray for it every night, Webbie. You tell her that. And *him* too!" Old Man Stein was in love with Web's mother, as were just about all the men in the neighborhood, married or not. In fact, the only man who didn't seem to be in love with Charlotte London was the man she was married to.

He went upstairs and stared at the attic pull-down stairs in the middle of the hallway. This was where he should have started his search, of course, but he did not want to go up there. He finally grabbed the rope pull, hauled down the stairs and climbed up. He clicked on the light, his gaze darting to every darkened corner as soon as he did so. Web took another deep breath and told himself that simpering cowards rarely accomplished anything with their lives, that he was a big, brave HRT assaulter with a loaded nine-millimeter in his holster. He moved into the attic and spent an hour compulsively going through more elements of his history than he really cared to.

The school yearbooks were here with the awkward pictures of boys and girls trying to look older than they were, when only a few short years would pass before they would desperately be trying to do the opposite. He also spent time deciphering the yearbook scribbles from classmates outlining lavish plans for their futures, which had not come true for any of them that Web knew of, including himself. His old varsity jacket and his football helmet were there in a box. There was a time when he could remember where every scratch on the helmet came from. Now he couldn't even remember the jersey number he had worn. There were old and useless schoolbooks, journals that had nothing in them but stupid pictures drawn by bored hands. *His* bored hands.

In one corner was a clothes rack with garments from the last four decades gathering dust, mold and moth holes. There were also old records warped in the heat and cold. There were boxes of baseball and football trading cards that might now be worth a tidy fortune if Web hadn't used them as targets for dart games and BB shooting. There were pieces of a bicycle Web vaguely remembered owning, along with a half dozen burned-out flashlights. There was also a clay figurine his mother had sculpted, and quite well; but it had been bashed around so much by his stepfather that the figure was now not only blind but also lacking ears and a nose.

It was all a sad memorial to a quite ordinary family that actually had been anything but ordinary in certain ways.

Web was thinking of giving up when he found it.

The box was under a collection of his mother's college books, the works of long-dead philosophers and writers and thinkers. Web quickly looked through the box's contents. It was enough to start with. He would be one poor investigator if he couldn't follow it up to something. He was surprised he had never noticed it before while growing up in this house. But he had never been looking for it back then.

He jerked around and stared at the farthest corner from him. It was dark, shadowy and he could almost swear something had moved there. His hand eased to his gun. He hated this attic. Hated it! And yet he didn't really know why. It was just a damn attic.

He carried the box to his car and on the way back to his motel Web used his cell phone to call Percy Bates. "Nice job, Perce. What a difference a day makes. But what happened to old Bucky?"

"Winters backed out at the last minute."

"Right. In case I go crashing down. And so he left you to do it for him."

"I actually volunteered when he waffled on it."

"You're a good guy, Perce, but you'll never rise higher in the Bureau if you keep doing the right thing."

"Like I give a crap about that."

"Any breaks?"

"We traced the guns. Stolen from a military facility in Virginia. Two years ago. Big help. But we'll chase it down every path until it dies on us."

"Any sign of Kevin Westbrook?"

"None. And no other witnesses have come forward. Apparently everyone down that way was struck deaf and dumb."

"I guess you've talked to the people Kevin lived with. Anything come out of that?"

"Not much. They haven't seen him. Like I said, he avoided that place anyway."

Web chose his next words carefully. "So nobody to love the kid? No old lady or grandmother lying around?"

"There is an old woman. And we think she's Kevin's mother's stepmother or something like that. She wasn't real clear on the relation either. You'd think it'd be pretty simple to say one way or another, but talk about your extended families. Dads in prisons, moms gone, brothers dead, sisters hookers, you got babies dropped off everywhere with anybody who looks halfway respectable, and that's usually the older folks. She seemed genuinely worried about the boy, but she's scared too. They're all scared down there."

"Perce, did you ever actually see Kevin before he went missing?"

"Why?"

"I'm trying to put together a time line between when I last saw him and when he disappeared."

"A time line. Damn, wish I'd thought of that," Bates said sarcastically.

"Come on, Perce, I'm not trying to step on anybody's toes, but I saved that boy's life and I'd kind of like him to keep it."

"Web, you know the likelihood of the kid turning up alive is pretty damn slim. Whoever took him wasn't planning a surprise party at Chuck E. Cheese's for the boy. We've searched every place we can think of. Got APBs out in all the surrounding states, and even on the Canadian and Mexican borders. It's not like they'd hang around the city with the kid."

"But if he was working for his brother, he might be safe. I mean, I understand this Big F is one mean bastard, but popping your little brother? Come on."

"I've seen worse and so have you."

"But did you see Kevin?"

"No, no, I didn't personally see the kid. He was gone before I got there. There, you satisfied?"

"I spoke with the HRT guys who were babysitting him. They said they turned him over to a couple of FBI suits." Web had decided not to mention Romano's statement that actually only *one* man had been definitively involved, because he wanted to hear Bates's take on it.

"You'll be no doubt stunned that I talked to them too and found out the same thing."

"They couldn't tell me the names of the agents. Any luck there?"

"It's a little early in the game."

Web now gave up any pretense of congeniality. "No, it's really not, Perce. I spent a lot of years doing what you do. I know how these cases go down. If you can't tell me by now who the suits were, that means they weren't FBI. That means a couple of impostors got inside an FBI crime scene, *your* crime scene, and made off with a key witness. Maybe I can help."

"That's your theory. And I don't want or need your help."

"Are you telling me I'm wrong?"

"What I'm going to tell you is to keep the hell out of my investigation. And I mean what I say."

"It was my damn team!"

"I understand that, but if I find out you're doing anything, ask-

ing one question, following up one lead on your own, then your ass
is mine. I hope I'm making myself clear."

"I'll call you when I crack the case."

Web clicked off and quietly berated himself for blowing his last
asset at the Bureau. He had been as subtle as a dump truck, but
Bates just seemed to bring out the bulldog in folks. And to think
he had originally called merely to thank the guy for the press conference!

20

Claire stretched her arms and stifled a yawn. She had been up too early and had worked too late the night before; such had become her life's routine. Married at nineteen to her high-school sweetheart, she had been a mother at twenty and divorced at twenty-two. The sacrifices she had made over the next ten years while she pursued her medical and psychiatric degrees were too numerous for her to recall. Yet she had no regrets about her daughter, now a freshman in college. Maggie Daniels was healthy, bright and well adjusted. Her father had wanted no part in his daughter's upbringing and he would be given no role in her adulthood either. Actually, that was up to Maggie, Claire knew, but she had never asked much about her dad and had taken single parenting in stride. Claire had never really gotten back into the social circles and she had finally come to the conclusion that her career would be her life.

She opened her file and studied the notes she had made there. Web London was a fascinating subject for any student of human psychology. From the little Claire had gathered before his very abrupt departure from her office, the man was a walking billboard of personal problems. From the obvious issues in his childhood to his disfigurement as an adult to the sort of dangerous work that he did and seemed to derive so much from, a person could devote her professional life to such a patient. The knock on her door interrupted her thoughts.

"Yes?"

The door opened and one of Claire's colleagues stood there. "You might want to come and see this."

"What is it, Wayne? I'm kind of busy."

"FBI press conference. Web London. I saw him leaving here the other day. You counseled him, right?"

She frowned at his question and didn't answer it. But she got up and followed him out to the reception area, where there was a little TV set up. Several other of the psychiatrists and psychologists who had offices here, including Ed O'Bannon, were already assembled and watching the screen. It was lunchtime and none of them appeared to have patients. Several of them held parts of their meals in their hands.

For the next ten minutes or so, Claire Daniels got a much more in-depth look at the life and career of Web London. She found herself putting her hand up to her mouth when she saw Web in the hospital, most of his face and torso bandaged. The man had been through a lot, more than someone should have to go through. And Claire was feeling an incredibly strong urge to help him, despite how dramatically he had ended their session. When the press conference was over and people started to filter back to their offices, Claire stopped O'Bannon.

"Ed, you remember I told you about seeing Web London when you weren't available?"

"Sure, Claire. I appreciate you doing that, actually." He lowered his voice. "Unlike some of the others around here, I know I can trust you not to pilfer my patients."

"Well, I appreciate that, Ed. But the truth is I've taken a particular interest in Web. And he and I really hit it off at our session." She added very firmly: "And I want to take over his counseling."

O'Bannon looked stunned and shook his head. "No, Claire. I've seen London before, and he's a bit of a tough nut. He and I never really finished exploring it, but he seems to have serious mother-son issues."

"I understand all that, but I really want to work on his case."

"And I appreciate that, but he's my patient and there is something to be said for continuity of treatment, starting with keeping the same doctor."

Claire took a deep breath and said, "Can we let Web decide?"

"Excuse me?"

"Can you call him and let Web decide on which of us he'd prefer?"

O'Bannon looked very annoyed. "I hardly think that's necessary."

"We really seemed to click, Ed, and I think that perhaps another pair of eyes on his case might be beneficial."

"I'm not liking what you're insinuating, Claire. My credentials are impeccable. In case you didn't know, I served in Vietnam, where I dealt with combat syndrome cases, shell shock, prisoners of war who'd been brainwashed, and I was very successful."

"Web is not in the military."

"HRT is about as military as you can get for a civilian agency. I know the breed and I speak their language. I think my experience is uniquely suited to his case."

"I'm not implying anything to the contrary. But Web did tell me that he wasn't completely comfortable with you. And I know you would agree that the best interests of the patient are paramount."

"I don't need you to lecture me on professional ethics." He paused for a moment. "But he said that—that he wasn't completely comfortable with me?"

"Yes, but I think that's more a reflection on the fact that you're right, he is a tough nut. For all I know, he may not like me once we get going in treatment." She touched O'Bannon on the shoulder. "So you'll call him? Today?"

O'Bannon grudgingly said, "I'll call him."

Web was driving when his phone rang. He checked the readout on the screen. It was a number in Virginia he didn't recognize.

"Hello?" he answered cautiously.

"Web?"

The voice seemed very familiar, but nothing clicked.

"It's Dr. O'Bannon."

Web blinked. "How did you get this number?"

"You gave it to me. During our most recent session."

"Look, I've been thinking that—"

"Web, I talked to Claire Daniels."

Web felt his face growing warm. "Did she tell you we talked?"

"She did. But she didn't tell me what you had talked about, of course. I understand that you were in a bit of crisis and Claire tried to get hold of me before talking to you. That's really why I'm calling."

"I'm not exactly following this."

"Well, Claire said that you two really seemed to hit it off. She seemed to think that maybe you would be more comfortable with her. Since you're my patient, you and I need to consent to such an arrangement."

"Look, Dr. O'Bannon—"

"Web, I want you to know that we were successful in the past in dealing with your issues and I think we can be again. Claire probably was just embellishing somewhat on your uncertainty about me. But just so you know, Claire does not have the experience I do. I've been seeing FBI agents for longer than she has. I don't like to say this, but between you and me, Claire would be out of her league with you." He paused, apparently awaiting Web's answer. "So, we're good, you'll continue to see me?"

"I'll go with Claire."

"Web, come on!"

"I want Claire."

O'Bannon was silent for a bit. "Are you sure?" he finally said curtly.

"I'm sure."

"Then I'll have Claire get in contact with you. I hope you two click," he added brusquely.

The line went dead and Web continued driving. Two minutes passed and the phone rang again. It was Claire Daniels.

"I guess you feel like quite the pursued man," she said in a disarming tone.

"It's nice to be popular."

"I like to finish what I start, Web, even if it means upsetting a colleague."

"Claire, I appreciate everything, and I know I told O'Bannon it was okay, but—"

"Please, Web, I think I can help you. At least I'd like to try."

He thought about this for a bit as he stared over at the cardboard box. What treasures did it hold? "Can I reach you at this number?"

"I'll be here until five."

"After that?"

He pulled into a gas station and wrote down Claire's cell and home phone. He said he'd call her back later and clicked off. Web punched the numbers into his phone's memory, pulled back onto the road and tried to think all this through. What he didn't like was that she was trying really hard, maybe too hard.

Web drove back to the motel room. He checked his messages at home. A few people who had seen the press conference had called to wish him well. And an equal number of voices he didn't recognize were basically telling him that they wanted to punch him in his cowardly, messed-up face. Once Web thought he heard Julie Patterson's voice and kids bawling in the background, but he couldn't be sure. He wouldn't exactly be at the top of the woman's phone list.

He sat on the floor with his back to the wall and suddenly felt so sorry for Julie he started to shake. Sure, things were going rough for him right now, but that would blow over. She had the rest of her life to work through, with the weight of a lost husband and child forever around her neck and four young kids to raise on her own. She was a survivor, like Web. And survivors hurt the most of all, for they had to pick up the pieces somehow and go right on living.

He dialed the number and a child answered. It was the oldest, Lou, Jr., all of eleven years old and the man of the house now.

"Louie, is your mom in? It's Web."

There was a long pause. "Did you get our dad killed, Web?"

"No, I didn't, Louie. You know better than that. But we're going to find out who did it. Go get your mom, son," he added firmly.

Web heard the boy plunk down the phone and walk off. While he waited, Web felt himself start trembling once more, for he had absolutely no idea what he would say to the woman. His nervousness grew as he heard footsteps approaching the phone and then it was picked up, but the person said nothing.

"Julie?" he finally said.

"What do you want, Web?" Her voice was tired. Ironically, the weary tone was more painful to Web than her angry screams at the church.

"I wanted to see if there was anything I could do to help."

"There's nothing you or anybody else can do."

"You should have somebody with you. It's not good to be alone right now."

"My sister and mother came down from Newark."

Web took a breath. Well, that was good. Julie at least sounded calm, rational. "We're going to find who did this, Julie. If it takes the rest of my life. I just want you to know that. Lou and the others meant everything to me."

"You do what you need to do, but that won't bring them back, Web."

"Did you see the press conference on TV today?"

"No. And please don't call again." She hung up.

Web sat there while he absorbed this. It wasn't that he had actually expected her to say she was sorry about trashing him the other day. That was far too much to expect. What bothered Web was that he felt dismissed by her. *Please don't call again?* Maybe the other wives felt the same way. Neither Debbie nor Cynde nor any of the others had contacted him to see how he was doing. Then again, he reminded himself, their loss was much greater than his. They had lost their husbands. He had just lost his friends. He supposed there was an enormous difference. It was just in his case there didn't seem to be.

He ran across the street to a 7-Eleven and bought a cup of coffee. It had started to drizzle and the temperature had dropped. What had started as a beautiful warm day now was gray and wet, so common for this area, and so reinforcing for his suicidal spirits.

Web returned to his room, sat on the floor and opened the cardboard box. The documents were musty, some mildewed, the few photos yellowed and torn. And yet he was enthralled by it all, for he had never seen these things before. Partly it was because he had never known his mother had kept these items from her first marriage. And he had also never searched the house for them before either. Why not, he wasn't sure. Perhaps his relationship with his stepfather had smothered all interest Web had in dads.

He arranged the photos fanlike on the floor and then examined them. His father, Harry Sullivan, had been a handsome man. Very

tall and broad-shouldered, he had wavy dark hair worn in a
greased pompadour and possessed a confident look as he stared
out from the photo. He looked like a 1940s-era film star, young and
commanding, with a mischievous gleam in his blue eyes. Web
could see how Harry Sullivan could be attractive to a young
woman who was naive perhaps despite her intelligence and her
world travels. Web wondered what his father would look like now,
after years in prison, after decades of what he assumed was a fast
life to nowhere.

In another photo, Sullivan had his arm around Charlotte's tiny
waist. The man's arm was so long it curled around her torso and
his fingers were placed just under her breasts, maybe even touching them. They looked very happy. Indeed, Charlotte London in
her pleated skirt and flip hairstyle looked more beautiful, more
enchanting and more excited to be alive than Web had ever seen
her. Yet that was part of youth, he supposed. They hadn't experienced the hard times yet. Web touched his cheek. No, the hard
times weren't great, and they didn't necessarily always make you
stronger. Looking at her so full of life, Web had a hard time believing that the woman was actually dead.

As the rain started to pour harder outside, Web sat in his motel
room and sipped his coffee and looked at some of the other items.
He fingered the Sullivans' marriage certificate. Web was surprised
his mom had kept that. Then again, it *was* her first marriage, however awry it might have gone. His father's signature was surprisingly small for such a big, confident-looking man. And the letters
were badly formed, as though old Harry were embarrassed by the
exercise of signing his name, unsure of how to make out the letters. An uneducated man, Web concluded.

He laid down the certificate and picked up another slip of paper.
A letter. At the top was the heading of a correctional facility in
Georgia. The date of the letter was a year after mother and son had
fled the convict that the husband and father had become. The letter was typewritten, but Harry Sullivan's signature appeared at the
bottom. And this signature was written bolder, the letters larger
and more exactly formed, as though the man had been really
working at it. But then, he had had a lot of "free" time in prison.

The contents of the letter were brief. It took the form of an apology to Charlotte and Web. When he got out, he would be a changed man, he claimed. He would do right by them. Well, actually, the letter said that Harry Sullivan would *try* hard to fulfill all these promises. Web had to concede that it was perhaps brutal honesty on Sullivan's part, not an easy thing for a man rotting slowly in prison. Web had conducted enough interrogations to know that steel bars and big locks and no future as a free person tended to make people lie shamelessly if they thought it would help their cause. He wondered if the divorce papers had reached his father soon after he had sent the letter. What did that do to a man in prison? His freedom taken and then his wife and son gone too? It certainly didn't leave a person with much. Web had never faulted his mother for doing what she did, and he didn't fault her now. Yet these little snippets of his family history made him feel a little sorry for Harry Sullivan, wherever he might be, dead or alive.

Web put the letter aside and spent the next couple of hours going through the other contents. Most were items completely useless to him in tracking down his father, yet Web spent time over them all, if just to get a better feel for the man. His hand closed around two objects that promised a lead. One was an expired driver's license that had his father's photo on it, and the other, more importantly, was his Social Security card. These opened up all sorts of possibilities. Web also had another angle to work.

He swallowed his pride, called Percy Bates and apologized to an almost embarrassing degree. Then he told him Harry Sullivan's name, Social Security number and a guesstimate of the dates of Sullivan's incarceration in the Georgia prison. Web had thought about calling Ann Lyle with this request but he didn't want to go to that well too often. Ann had enough to do, and HRT really needed her full attention right now. Besides, she hadn't gotten back to Web yet on Cove, and he didn't want her to feel pressured.

"Who is this guy?" Bates wanted to know.

When Web had applied to join the Bureau, he had had to put down his real father's name, and the investigators had wanted further particulars. He had asked his mother back then to supply more information on the man, but she had absolutely refused to discuss it. Web had told the investigators he didn't know the whereabouts of his father and had no information to help them track him down. As far as he knew, that had been the end of it. He had passed the background check and was off and running in his FBI career. His last contact with his father had been at age six, and the Bureau couldn't exactly hold it against Web that his father was a con.

"Just some guy I need to find," Web told Bates. Web knew that the Bureau was very thorough in its background checks and could very well have information about Web's father. Web had just never felt inclined to check the file over the years. And yet Bates might know that Harry Sullivan was Web's father. If so, he was lying very well.

"Any connection to the investigation?"

"No, like you said, that's off-limits, but I'd really appreciate the favor."

Bates said he'd see what he could do and then hung up.

Web packed the box away and slid it into a corner. He pulled out his cell phone and dialed his voice mail again. He had been obsessive about it since the courtyard and not really sure why. When he heard the voice, he was glad he was so diligent. Debbie Riner wanted to know if Web could come to dinner tonight. He immediately called her back and said he would. She had seen the piece on TV. "I never had any doubts, Web," she said. He let out a long breath. Life seemed a lot better right now.

He brought up the number he wanted on the phone screen. It was after five, so Claire Daniels wouldn't be at her office. His finger hesitated over the button. And then he called her. She was in her car heading home, she told him. "I can see you first thing in the morning. Nine A.M.,"she said.

"So, you've got all my problems solved?"

"I'm efficient, but I'm not that quick." He found himself smiling at this remark. "I appreciate you letting me counsel you. I know change is hard."

"Change I can handle, Claire. It's the going crazy part that's bothering me. I'll see you at nine."

21

The dinner with Debbie Riner and her children did not go nearly as well as Web had hoped. Carol Garcia was there too, with one of her kids. They sat around the dining room table, made small talk and mostly avoided matters having to do with the total destruction of their lives. When the Garcias made the sign of the cross on their chests, Web thought about what he told Danny Garcia before every mission. Web had been right, for God had not been with them that night. Yet all Web said was, "Would you pass the potatoes, please?"

HRT operators didn't really encourage support groups among their wives. In some cases it was because they didn't want their spouses to gossip among themselves about their husbands. Operators showed many sides of themselves at training and during missions, and not all good ones. An inadvertent slip by one of them to his wife could spread like wildfire among the women if they seriously networked. In other cases it was to discourage the wives from collectively worrying themselves to death, swapping incorrect information, speculation and outright falsehoods generated by fear of where their husbands were, how long they would be gone, whether they were dead.

The kids poked at their food, slouched in their seats and clearly did not want to be there. They treated Web, who had been their bosom friend, playing and joking and watching them grow up, like they had no idea who he even was. Everyone, even Debbie Riner's seven-year-old daughter, who had loved Web from almost the day she was born, looked relieved when he said his good-byes.

"Keep in touch," Debbie said, pecking him on the cheek. Carol merely waved to him from a safe distance, while she clutched her glassy-eyed son to her wide hips.

"You bet, sure thing," Web said. "Take care. Thanks for dinner. You need anything, just let me know." He drove off in the Vic, knowing he would most likely never see them again. Time to move on, that was clearly the message of the dinner.

At nine sharp the next morning Web stepped into Claire Daniels's world. Ironically, the first person he saw was Dr. O'Bannon.

"Web, good to see you. Would you like some coffee?"

"I know where it is. I'll get it, thanks."

"You know, Web, I was in Vietnam. Never under fire, I was a psychiatrist back then too. But I saw a lot of guys who were. Things happen in combat, things you never think will. But you know what, you'll probably be stronger for it. And I worked with POWs who'd been tortured by the damn Viet Cong. It's terrible what they were put through, classic physical and mental manipulation, ostracizing troublemakers, robbing them of every scrap of moral and physical support. Controlling their lives down to the position of their sleep, turning each individual against the other in the name of the group, as it was defined by their captors. Now, of course it's not ethical for one psychiatrist to poach patients off the other, although, frankly, I was a little surprised about what happened with Claire. But I think Claire would agree that the paramount issue here is your best interest, Web. So if you ever change your mind about working with Claire, I'm here for you." He slapped Web on the back, gave what Web assumed was intended to be an encouraging look and walked off.

Claire came out of her office a few moments later, saw him and they made their coffees together. They watched as a uniformed repairman with a box of tools came out of the closet housing the office's electrical and phone lines and left.

"Problems?" asked Web.

"I don't know, I just came in," answered Claire.

As they were making their coffees Web checked the woman out. Claire was wearing a blouse and knee-length skirt that showed off nice tanned calves and ankles, but her hair, though short, was in a bit of disarray. She seemed to note Web's observation and swiped at the errant strands.

"I've been fast-walking around the building in the mornings to get a little exercise. Wind and humidity aren't really good for hair." She took a sip of her coffee and added some more sugar. "You ready?"

"As ready as I'll ever be."

Once in her office Claire perused two files for a bit while Web stared over at a pair of sneakers in the corner. Probably what she fast-walked in. He looked over at her nervously.

"First of all, Web, I want to thank you for having enough confidence in me to let me take over your treatment."

"I'm not really sure why I did," he said candidly.

"Well, whatever the reason, I'm going to work hard to make sure your decision was a good one. Dr. O'Bannon wasn't very happy about it, but the primary concern is you." She held up a small file. "This is the file Dr. O'Bannon gave me when I took over your case."

Web attempted a weak smile. "I would've thought it would have been thicker."

"Actually, I was thinking the same thing," was Claire's surprising reply. "It shows the notes from a number of standard sessions; he prescribed various medications, antidepressants, again nothing out of the ordinary."

"So? Is that good or bad?"

"Good, if it helped you, and I'm assuming it did, since you returned to a productive life."

"But?"

"But maybe your case deserves a little more digging. I have to tell you that I am surprised that he didn't hypnotize you. He's very skilled at that, and that is usually part of his course of treatment. In fact, O'Bannon teaches a course at GW, where every third or fourth year he hypnotizes a student and does things like making them block out a letter from the alphabet so they'll look at the word 'cat' on the blackboard and pronounce it 'at.' Or make them believe a gnat is flying around their ear, things like that. We do that as part of a routine to demonstrate visual- and auditory-induced hallucinations."

"I remember we talked about it the first time I saw him years ago. I didn't want to do it, so we didn't," he said flatly.

"I see." She held up a much thicker folder. "Your official Bureau file, or at least part of it," she said in response to his inquisitive look.

"So I gathered. I thought they kept that confidential."

"You signed a release when you agreed to counseling. The file is routinely given to the therapist for help in treatment minus any top-secret or other sensitive information, of course. Dr. O'Bannon transferred the file to me when you became my patient. I've been going over it thoroughly."

"Good for you." Web cracked his knuckles and looked at her expectantly.

"You didn't mention in our initial interview that your stepfather, Raymond Stockton, died from a fall in the house when you were fifteen."

"Didn't I? Huh, I thought I did. But you didn't take notes, so you have no way of checking, do you?"

"Trust me, Web, I would've remembered that. You also told me you got along with your stepfather, didn't you?" She looked down at the papers.

Web felt his heart rate accelerate and his ears burn. Her interrogation technique was classic. She had baselined him and had just now jerked his chain using a five-hundred-pound gorilla for added leverage. "We had some differences, who doesn't?"

"There are page after page of assault claims in here. Some filed by neighbors, some by you. All against Raymond Stockton. Is that what you refer to as 'some differences'?" He flushed angrily and she quickly added, "I'm not being sarcastic, I just want to try and understand your relationship with the man."

"There's nothing to understand because we didn't have a relationship."

Claire consulted her notes again, flipping back and forth, and Web watched every movement with growing anxiety.

"Is the house that your mother left you the same one where Stockton died?" Web didn't say anything. "Web? Is it the same—"

"I heard you!" he snapped. "Yeah, it's the same one, so what?"

"I was just asking. So, do you think you're going to sell it?"

"Why do you care? Do you do real estate on the side?"

"I'm just getting a sense that you seem to have issues about the house."

"It wasn't a real nice place to have a childhood."

"I understand that completely, but often to get better and move on you must confront your fears head-on."

"There's nothing in that house I need to confront."

"Why don't we talk about it some more?"

"Look, Claire, this is getting pretty far afield, isn't it? I came to you because my team got blown away and it's messed me up. Let's stick to that! Forget the past. Forget the house and let's just forget fathers. They've got nothing to do with me or who I am."

"On the contrary, they have a great deal to do with who you are. Without understanding your past I can't help with your present or your future. It's that simple."

"Why don't you give me some damn pills and we'll call it a day, okay? That way the Bureau's satisfied that I did my little mind massage and you did your job."

Claire shook her head. "I don't work that way, Web. I want to help you. I think I can help you. But you have to work with me. I can't compromise on that."

"I thought you said I had combat syndrome or something. What does that have to do with my stepfather?"

"We merely talked about that being one possibility for what happened to you in that alley. I didn't say that it was the only possibility. We need to thoroughly explore all angles if we're to really address your issues."

"Issues—you make it sound so simple. Like I'm moping about having acne."

"We can use another term if you prefer, but it really won't affect how we approach the problems."

Web covered his face with his hands and then spoke through this shield. "What the hell exactly do you want from me?"

"Honesty, to the extent you can give it. And I think you can, if you really try. You have to trust me, Web."

Web removed his hands. "Okay, here's the truth. Stockton was a creep. Pills and a boozer. He never got past the sixties, apparently. He held some low-level office job where he got to wear a suit to work and fancied himself another Dylan Thomas on his off-hours."

"So what you're telling me is he was some sort of frustrated dreamer, perhaps even a phony?"

"He wanted to be more of an intellectual and more talented than my mother, and he wasn't, not by miles. His poetry was for shit; he never got anything published. The only thing he had in common with old Dylan was the fact that he drank too much. I guess he thought the bottle would inspire him."

"So he beat your mother?" She tapped the file.

"Is that what it says in the file?"

"Actually, what it doesn't say in the file is even more interesting. Your mother never filed charges against Stockton."

"Well, I guess we have to believe the record, then."

"Did he beat your mother?" she asked again, and once more Web didn't answer. "Or did he just beat you?" Web slowly lifted his gaze to her, yet still said nothing. "So just you? And your mother let this occur?"

"Charlotte wasn't around a lot. She'd made a mistake in marrying this guy. She knew it, so she avoided it."

"I see. I guess divorce wasn't an option."

"She'd done that once. I don't think she felt like bothering with it again. It was easier just to drive off into the night."

"And she left you with a man who she knew abused you? And how did that make you feel?"

Web said nothing.

"Did you ever talk to her about it? To let her know how it made you feel?"

"Wouldn't have done any good. To her, the guy never existed."

"Meaning she repressed the memory?"

"Meaning whatever the hell you want it to mean. We never talked about it."

"Were you home when your stepfather died?"

"Maybe, I don't really remember. I've sort of repressed it too."

"The file just said your stepfather fell. How did he fall?"

"From the top of the attic stairs. He kept his secret stash of mind goodies up in the attic. He was wigged out, missed a step, cracked his head on the edge of the opening going down and broke his neck when he hit the floor. The police investigated and it was ruled an accidental death."

"Was your mother home when it happened, or had she gone out on one of her *drives*?"

"What, are you pretending you're an FBI agent now?"

"Just trying to understand the situation."

"Charlotte was home. She was the one who called the ambulance. But like I said, he was already dead."

"Have you always called your mother by her first name?"

"Seems appropriate."

"I imagine you had to feel relief at Stockton's death."

"Let's put it this way, I didn't cry at the funeral."

Claire leaned forward and spoke in a very low voice. "Web, this next question is going to be very difficult, and if you don't want to answer it now, fine. But in instances of parental abuse, I have to address it."

Web held up both hands. "He never touched my private parts, and he never made me touch his private parts, okay? Nothing like that. They asked back then and I told the truth back then. The guy wasn't a molester. He was just a cruel, sadistic asshole who made up for a lifetime of insecurities and disappointments by beating the shit out of a boy. If he had messed with me like that, I would've found a way to kill him myself." Web realized what he had just said and hastily added, "But the guy saved everybody the trouble by taking his tumble."

Claire sat back and put aside the file. This small measure relieved Web's anxiety somewhat and he sat up. She said, "You obviously remember your time with your stepfather and loathed it for good reason. Have you thought more about any memories with your natural father?"

"Fathers are fathers."

"Meaning what, you lump your real father and Raymond Stockton together?"

"Saves the trouble of thinking about it too much, doesn't it?"

"The easy way out usually solves nothing."

"I wouldn't know where to begin, Claire, I really wouldn't."

"All right, let's go back to the courtyard for a bit. I know it'll be painful, but let's go through it again."

Web did so and it was painful.

"All right, the first group of people you met, you don't remember that having any sort of effect on you?"

"Nothing other than wondering if one of them would try to kill us or tip somebody off, but I knew the snipers had them covered. So other than the potential of instant death, everything was cool."

If she was put off by his sarcasm, the woman didn't show it. That actually impressed Web.

"All right, in your mind's eye, picture the little boy. Do you remember any better exactly what he said?"

"Is that really important?"

"At this stage we really don't know what's important and what's not."

Web sighed heavily and said, "Okay. I saw the kid. He looked at us. He said . . ." Web stopped here because he could see Kevin clearly in his mind. The bullet hole in his cheek, the slash across his forehead, he was a little wreck of a kid who had obviously already lived a long, crappy life. "He said . . . he said, 'Damn to hell,' that's what he said." He looked at her excitedly. "That's it. Oh, and then he laughed. I mean, this really weird laugh, like a cackle, really."

"At which part did you feel affected?"

Web thought about this. "I'd have to say when he first spoke. I mean, it was like this fog pushed into my brain." Web added, "'Damn to hell,' that's exactly what he said. It's happening again, I can feel my fingers tingling. This is nuts."

Claire wrote some notes down and then looked at him. "That's pretty unusual for a young boy to use that phraseology, especially from the inner city. Certainly 'damn' and 'hell' would be used, but 'damn to hell'? I mean, it sounds sort of archaic, like from another era. Maybe Puritanical, fire and brimstone. What do you think about that?"

"To me it sounds like from the Civil War or around that time, actually," said Web.

"It's all very strange."

"Trust me, Claire, the whole night was strange."

"Did you feel anything else?"

Web thought hard. "We were waiting for final orders to hit the target. Then we got them." He shook his head. "As soon as I heard the orders in my earpiece, I froze. It was immediate. You remember I was telling you about the Taser guns we messed around with at HRT?" She nodded. "Well, it was like I'd been hit with one of those electrified darts. I couldn't move."

"Could someone have actually shot you with a Taser gun in the alley? Could that be why you froze?"

"Impossible. No one was that close, and the dart wouldn't have penetrated my Kevlar. And last but not least, the thing would've still been sticking in me, right?"

"Right." Claire made more notes and said, "Now, you stated before that even though you froze, you were able to actually get up and move into the courtyard."

"It was the hardest thing I've ever done in my life, Claire. It was like I weighed two thousand pounds, nothing on me was working right. And it finally won and I just fell and stayed there. And then the guns started up."

"When did you start to recover?"

Web thought about this. "It felt like years where I couldn't move. But it wasn't all that long. Right when the guns started firing, I felt everything start to come back. I could move my arms and legs, and they were burning like hell, like when your arm or leg falls asleep and the circulation starts going again? That's what my limbs felt like. And it wasn't like I needed them at that point, I pretty much had nowhere to go."

"So it just came back on its own? You don't remember doing something that might have paralyzed you? Maybe a back problem suffered in training? Have you ever had any nerve damage? That could immobilize you too."

"Nothing like that. If you're not in top-notch condition, you don't go on an operation."

"So you heard the guns firing and the feeling started to come back to your body?"

"Yes."

"Anything else?"

"The kid, I'd seen a million just like him. And yet he seemed different. I couldn't get him out of my head. It wasn't just that he'd been shot, I've seen kids like that too. I don't know. While the guns were firing I saw him again. He was crouched down next to the alley. Another step and he'd have been cut in half. I screamed for him to get back. I belly-crawled over to him. I could tell he was scared to death. He heard Hotel Team coming from one end, me from the other, these damn guns firing. And I could tell he was going to run for it, across the courtyard, and that'd be it. I just couldn't let that happen, Claire. So many people had already died that night. He jumped and I jumped and I caught him, got him calmed down because he was yelling that he hadn't done anything, and of course when a kid says that you know he's hiding something.

"Like I said, I got him calmed down. He asked if my team was dead and I told him yes. I gave him the note and my cap and shot the flare. I knew that was the only way Hotel wouldn't kill him coming at them in the dark. I just didn't want him to die, Claire."

"It must have been an awful night for you, but, Web, you should feel good about saving him."

"Should I? What did I save him for? To go back to the streets? See, this is a special little kid. He's got a brother named Big F who runs one of the local drug ops. He's bad news."

"So maybe all this could involve some of this Big F person's enemies?"

"Maybe." He paused and decided whether to reveal this or not. "Somebody switched kids. In the alley."

"Switched kids? What do you mean?"

"I mean the Kevin Westbrook that I saved in that alley was not the boy that delivered the note to Hotel Team. And the little boy that disappeared from the crime scene was not the Kevin Westbrook I saved."

"Why would somebody do that?"

"That's the sixty-four-thousand-dollar question, and it's driving me nuts. What I do know is I saved Kevin Westbrook's butt in that courtyard and the kid he was switched for told Hotel Team that I was this big coward. Why would he do that?"

"Sounds like he was almost trying to intentionally discredit you."

"A kid I didn't even know?" Web shook his head. "Somebody *was* trying to make me look bad, that's for sure, and must have told the kid just what to say. And then they waltzed right in and waltzed out with the fake kid. He's probably dead. Hell, Kevin's probably dead."

"Sounds like somebody put a lot of planning into this," said Claire.

"And I'd love to know why."

"We can only try, Web. I can help you with some of it, but the investigation part is way out of my bailiwick."

"It actually may be out of my league too. I haven't really been doing much detecting over the last eight years." He played with a ring on his finger. "O'Bannon gave me a little pep talk on combat syndrome when I came into the office this morning."

Claire hiked her eyebrows. "Oh, did he? His Vietnam angle?" She seemed to be trying hard not to smile.

"I didn't think it was the first time he'd used that line. But is that what you think it is—I mean, despite this other stuff with the kid?"

"I can't tell you that, Web, not yet."

"See, I know soldiers get that way. Folks shooting at them and they freak. Everybody can understand that."

She eyed him closely. "But?"

He started talking very quickly. "But most soldiers get a little boot camp and then they're thrown into the firestorm. They know *nothing* about killing somebody. They know nothing about what it's like to be in the line of fire for real. Me, I've trained most of my adult life to do this job. I've had stuff coming at me that you wouldn't believe, Claire. From machine gun fire to frigging mortar rounds that if they hit me there'd be nothing left of me. I've managed to kill men with most of the blood in my body pooling on the floor. And never once, not one damn time, did I ever lose it like I did that night. And there hadn't even been one damn shot fired at that point. Tell me, how the hell is that possible?"

"Web, I know that you're looking for answers. We have to keep plugging. But I can tell you that when we're dealing with the mind, anything is possible."

He stared at her, shaking his head and wondering where the hell he could get off whatever road he was on. "Well, Doc, that's not a whole lot of help, is it? How much is the Bureau paying you to tell me nothing?" He abruptly got up and left.

Once again Claire didn't try and stop him, not that she could have. She had had patients walk out on her before, although never during their first two sessions. Claire settled back in her chair and started going over notes and then picked up a recorder and started dictating.

Unknown to Claire, hidden in the smoke detector attached to the ceiling was a sophisticated listening device that ran off the building's electrical current and also had a battery backup. Every psychiatrist and psychologist who worked here had a similar listening device secretly housed in his office. The phone closet in the office housed additional electronic taps, one of which had broken down, prompting the "repairman's" visit that morning.

These prying ears had swept up enormous amounts of intelligence on every patient who had come through the doors. Over the last year over one hundred FBI agents from all divisions, including undercover, Public Corruption, WFO, uptown and HRT, and over twenty spouses of those personnel, had come here expecting the utmost confidentiality as they revealed their secrets and problems. They had received anything but that.

As soon as Web stormed out of the office, Ed O'Bannon slipped out as well, rode the elevator down to the garage, climbed in his brand-new Audi coupe and drove off. He picked up his cell phone and punched in a number. It took a few rings, but the phone was finally answered.

"Is this a good time?" he asked anxiously.

The party on the other end answered that it was as good as any if the conversation was short and to the point.

"London came here today."

"So I heard," said the voice. "My guy was there to repair a glitch. So how's it going with old Web?"

O'Bannon swallowed nervously. "He's seeing another psychiatrist." He quickly added, "I tried my best to stop it, but no go."

O'Bannon had to hold the phone away from his ear, so loud and angry was the response from the other person.

"Listen, it's not what I intended," said O'Bannon. "I couldn't believe he would actually see another psychiatrist. It came out of the blue. . . . What? Her name is Claire Daniels. She used to work for me. She's been here for years, very competent. Under other circumstances there wouldn't be a problem. I couldn't make too much of a stink without them getting suspicious."

The other person made a suggestion that caused O'Bannon to tremble. He pulled the car off the road. "No, killing her would only arouse suspicion. I know London. Too well, maybe. He's smart. If anything happens to Claire, he'll latch on to that and never let it go. That's just how he is. Trust me, I've worked with the man a long time. Remember, that's why you hired me."

"But that's not the only reason why," said the other person. "And we pay you well, Ed. Real well. And I don't like it one bit that he's seeing this Daniels chick."

"I've got it under control. If I know London, he'll come a few times and then blow the rest of it off. But if anything else comes of it, we'll know it. I'll keep on top of it."

"You better," said the other. "And the second you no longer have it under control is the time we step in." The line went dead and O'Bannon, looking very distraught, pulled back on the road and drove off.

22

Web had spent considerable time in the Vic cruising the streets near where the slaughter had taken place. He was on unpaid leave and not part of the official investigation. Thus he could request no backup, should he need it, nor did he have a clear idea of what he was looking for. The darkness of the streets was broken by the uniform glare of traffic lights. There were cameras at many of these intersections ostensibly to photograph drivers who ran red lights. However, Web thought they actually might be serving the dual purpose of surveillance devices in these high crime areas. He had to appreciate the ingenuity of the local criminals, though, because many of the cameras had been knocked out of their viewing lanes. Some pointed to the sky, others to the earth, a few at buildings, still others had been smashed. Well, so much for Big Brother.

Web kept checking messages at home. No more wives had called. Cynde and Debbie had probably worked the grapevine, informed the others that they had done the dirty work of getting him clear of all their lives. Web could almost hear the ladies' collective sigh.

Web had finally made another appointment to see Claire. She did not mention his parting insult and second abrupt exit from her office. She merely noted the time and said that she would see him then. The woman must have a really thick skin, he thought.

There were several other people in the waiting room when Web got there. None of them made eye contact and Web attempted none. He supposed that's the way it was in a shrink's waiting room. Who wanted strangers to see you attending to your insanity?

Claire came out and got him with a reassuring smile and handed him a fresh cup of coffee, the cream and sugar already in it, just like he liked it. They settled in her office.

Web slid a hand through his hair. "Look, Claire, I'm sorry about last time. I'm not usually that big a jerk. I know you're just trying to help and I know none of this is easy to figure out."

"Don't apologize for doing exactly what you should be doing, Web, which is getting all these thoughts and feelings out in the open so that you can deal with them."

He gave her a weak smile and said, "So where to today, Doc? Mars or Venus?"

"To start off with let's explore post-traumatic stress disorder and really see if it applies to your case."

Web inwardly smiled. Now, this he could handle. "Like shell shock?"

"That term is very often misused, and I want to get a little more precise. Now, clinically speaking, you have probably suffered traumatic stress with the events that transpired in that courtyard."

"I'd probably agree with that."

"Well, let's test that conclusion. If that is the diagnosis, then there are several proven methods of coping with it, including stress management techniques, proper nutrition and sleep patterns, relaxation drills, cognitive reframing and prescription anxiolytic medications."

"Damn, sounds simple," he said sarcastically.

She looked at him in what Web thought was a strange way.

"Sometimes it is simple." She looked down at her papers. "All right, have you noticed any changes in yourself physically? Chills, dizziness, chest pain, elevated blood pressure, difficulty breathing, fatigue, nausea, anything like that?"

"The first time I went back to the courtyard and went over what happened, I felt a little dizzy."

"Anything since then?"

"No."

"All right, have you been excessively excitable since then?"

Web didn't have to think long. "No, not really."

"Any type of substance abuse to help you cope?"

"Nothing! I've been drinking less, actually."

"Flashbacks of the event?"

Web shook his head.

"Do you feel numb, wanting to avoid life, people?"

"No, I want to find out what happened. I want to be proactive."

"Are you more angry, irritable or hostile than normal with people?" She looked at him and smiled. "Present company excluded."

Web returned the smile briefly. "Not really, Claire. I think I've been relatively calm, actually."

"Persistent depression, panic attacks, heightened anxiety or phobia formations?"

"Nothing like that."

"Okay, do you have repetitive memories of the event that intrude suddenly on your thoughts? Traumatic dreams or nightmares, in other words?"

Web spoke slowly as he picked his way through this mental minefield. "The night in the hospital, after it happened, I had some bad dreams. They had me drugged up, but I remember I kept apologizing over and over to all the guys' wives."

"Perfectly natural under the circumstances. Anything since then along those lines?"

Web shook his head. "I've been really busy with the investigation," he said by way of defense. "But I think about it all the time. I mean, what happened in that courtyard, it crushed me. Like a pile driver. I've never experienced anything like it."

"But in your line of work you have experienced death before?"

"Yes, but never to any of my team."

"Do you find you've blocked part of what happened out of your mind, something we refer to as memory dysfunction or amnesiac syndrome?"

"No, I pretty much remember every damn detail," Web replied wearily.

While Claire looked down at her notes, Web blurted out, "I didn't want them to die, Claire. I'm sorry that they did. I would do anything to have them back."

She looked up at him and put aside her notes. "Web, listen to me very carefully. Just because you don't have the symptoms of post-traumatic stress disorder does not mean you don't care what happened to your friends. It doesn't mean you're not suffering. You have to understand that. What I see in you is a man who is suffering all the normal symptoms of having gone through an ordeal that would have left most people unable to function, at least for quite a long time."

"But not me."

"You have unique skills, years of training and a psychological makeup that aided you considerably in being selected for HRT in the first place. I've learned a lot more about HRT since you came to me. I know that the physical pounding and stress they put you through is extraordinary, but the ordeal they put you through mentally is even more daunting. Because of *both* your physical and psychological makeup, you can deal with more than just about anyone, Web. You survived that courtyard, obviously not just with your life but also with your mind intact."

"So I don't have post-traumatic stress disorder?"

"No, I don't think that you do."

He looked down at his hands. "Does this mean we're done?"

"No. Just because you're not traumatized over what happened in that courtyard doesn't mean you don't have some issues that need working through. Perhaps some issues that have been with you since long before you joined HRT."

He sat back, instantly suspicious; he couldn't seem to help himself. "Like what?"

"That's what we're here to talk about. You mentioned that you felt a part of your colleagues' families. I'm wondering if you ever wanted a family of your own."

Web thought about this for a while before answering. "I always thought I'd have a big family, you know, lots of sons to play ball with and lots of daughters to spoil, let them wrap old dad around their pretty little fingers, and me smiling all the way."

Claire picked up her pad and pen. "And why didn't you?"

"Years got away from me."

"Is that all?"

"Isn't that enough?"

She looked at his face, both the good and the bad. Web turned away just like he had last time.

"Do you always do that?"

"Do what?"

"Turn the injured side of your face away when someone looks at it."

"I don't know, I don't really think about it."

"It seems to me, Web, that you think very carefully about everything you do."

"Maybe you'd be surprised."

"We haven't talked about personal relationships. Are you dating anyone?"

"My job doesn't leave a lot of time for that."

"Yet the other men on your team were all married."

"Maybe they were just better at it than me," he said curtly.

"Tell me, when did you receive the injuries to your face?"

"Do we really have to go there?"

"It seems as though you're uncomfortable with this. We can go on to something else."

"No, what the hell, I'm not uncomfortable about it." He stood, took off his jacket, and while Claire watched in growing amazement, Web undid the top button on his shirt to reveal the bullet wound on his neck. "I got the *injuries* to my face right before I got this *injury*." He pointed to the wound on the base of his neck. "Some white supremacists called the Free Society took over a school in Richmond. While my face was on fire, one of them got me with a .357 Magnum round. Nice clean wound, went right through me. Another millimeter to the left, I'm either dead or a quad. Now, I got another one, but I won't show you the hole. It's right here." He touched the wound near his armpit. "That bullet was what we in the business call a Chunneler round. You know, like the tunnel under the English Channel and those monster drills that dug it? It is damn wicked ordnance, Claire, steel-jacketed. It spirals into you at about Mach Three. And if anything gets in its way, it's pulverized. It went right through me and then killed the guy behind me who was looking to pop my head open with a machete. If it had been a dum-dum round instead of steel-jacketed, the bullet would still be in me and I'd be dead from a machete sticking in my skull." He smiled. "I mean, can you believe the timing on that one?"

Claire looked down, remaining silent.

"Hey, Doc, don't look away, you haven't seen the best yet." She glanced up as he cupped his chin with his hand and angled the damaged side of his face so it was fully on display for her. "Now, this beauty came from a flame gusher that almost took out my good buddy Lou Patterson—you know, the late husband of the woman who dissed me to the whole world? I'm sure you saw that on TV, right? Damn shield melted right to my face. They tell me a doctor and a nurse fainted when they saw me at the hospital in Richmond. The whole side was a raw, open wound. Somebody said I looked like I had already decomposed. Five operations, Claire, and the pain, well, let me tell you the pain just doesn't come any better. They had to strap me down more than a few times. And when I saw what was left of my face, all I wanted to do was put a gun in my mouth and chew on a round, and in fact I almost did. And after finally getting past all of that and checking out of the hospital, it was really fun to see how the women ran screaming when they saw old Web coming their way. My little black book just went right down the old toilet. So, no, I really don't date that often, and marriage just seemed to take a backseat to important things like taking out the garbage and cutting the grass." He sat back down and buttoned his shirt. "Anything else you want to know?" he asked amiably.

"I actually saw the Bureau press conference where they revealed a lot about how you received your injuries. What you did was incredibly heroic. Yet it seems like your view of yourself is someone who is unattractive and unacceptable to women." Then she added, "And I'm also wondering if you think you would have made a good father."

Damn the woman, she just didn't quit. "I'd like to think so," he said evenly, trying very, very hard to keep his temper in check.

"No, I'm asking you if you *do* think so."

"What the hell kind of question is that?" he said angrily.

"Do you think if you had children, you would have ever abused them?"

Web came halfway out of his chair. "Claire, I'm about two seconds from walking out of here! And not coming back."

She stared him down. "Remember, when we first started therapy, I said you had to trust me. Now, therapy is not easy, Web, particularly if you have issues you don't want to address. All I'm trying to do is help, but you need to deal straight with me. If you want to waste time with histrionics, that's your call. I'd prefer to be more productive."

Psychiatrist and lawman stared at each other for a very long moment. Web finally was the one to blink and he sat back down. He had just achieved a much better appreciation for Romano's plight with Angie. "I wouldn't have beaten my kids. Why would I, after what Stockton did to me?"

"What you say seems perfectly logical. However, the reality is that most parents who abuse their children were also abused as children. It's not as easy as learning from our parents' mistakes because our emotional psyche doesn't work that efficiently. And children aren't equipped to think that way. They are powerless to resist the abuse and thus they repress the hatred and anger and feelings of helplessness often over many years. It doesn't just go away by itself, this boiling pot of confusion, feelings of betrayal or the low self-esteem that accompanies the abused child—Daddy or Mommy can't love me because they hit me and it must be my fault, because Daddy and Mommy can do no wrong. Abused children grow up and have children, and sometimes they work through their problems and become outstanding parents. Other times, the anger and hatred that has lain dormant for so long comes out and is directed at their own children, just as it was done to them."

"I would never raise my hand to a child, Claire. I know what I do for a living might make me seem that way, but I'm not like that."

"I believe you, Web. I really do. But more to the point, do *you* believe you?"

His face flushed again. "You are really throwing me here, lady."

"Let me phrase it more directly, then. Do you think it just possible that your decision not to marry and have children may have come from the fact that you were abused and you feared you may abuse your own children? It's not unheard of, Web; it's really not. Some might claim it's the ultimate sacrifice, in fact."

"Or the ultimate running away from your problems."

"Some might claim that too."

"What do you think?"

"It could very well be you're both. But if that is the reason you've held back from marriage and a family, we can work through it, Web. And while I can understand how the injuries to your face might make it difficult for *some* women to be attracted to you, don't think all women are like that, because they're not."

He shook his head and then stopped, glanced up at her, held her gaze. "When I was sitting out in the middle of Montana during yet another standoff with yet another group pissed off at the government, I'd spend my morning watch drawing beads on the guys with my sniper rifle as they passed by the window. I spent several hours every day just waiting for the moment when I'd have to kill one of them. That sort of thing just wears you down, Claire, the waiting-to-kill part. So when I was off watch, sitting under the stars in the evenings out there in the middle of nowhere Montana, I used to write letters home."

"To whom?"

Web looked a little embarrassed and took a few moments to get going, for he had never revealed this before to anyone. "I pretended I had kids." He shook his head and couldn't even look at her now. "I even made up names like Web Junior, Lacey. My youngest was Brooke, with red hair and teeth missing. And I'd write them all letters. I actually sent them to my house, so they'd be waiting there when I got home. In the middle of waiting to kill a bunch of losers in Montana who were so outgunned it wasn't even funny, I'm writing to Brooke Louise and telling her Daddy will be home soon. I actually started believing I had a family back home. It's really the only thing that got me through, because I finally did have to pull that trigger and the population of Montana dropped by a couple." He stopped and wiped his mouth, swallowed what seemed to Web like a mountain of belly bile and stared at the carpet. "When I got home, there were all those letters waiting for me. But I didn't even read them. I already knew what they said. The house was empty. No Brooke Louise."

He finally looked up. "That's pretty crazy, isn't it?" he said. "Writing letters to kids you don't even have?"

Without trying to, Web could see that he had finally gotten to Claire Daniels.

When Web left Claire's office and saw the two people conversing in low voices in the waiting area, he blanked for a second, because the context was wrong. O'Bannon was standing there, and that fit, for the man worked here, after all. The woman he was there with, though, she shouldn't be here. When she glanced over and saw Web standing there, Debbie Riner actually gasped.

O'Bannon saw Web too and came over to him, his hand extended.

"Web, I didn't know you were going to be in today. I guess there was no way I would know, Claire and I don't exactly share calendars, bit of an ethical nightmare if we did."

Web didn't take the doctor's hand; he kept staring at Debbie, who seemed frozen, like she had just been caught in a tryst with O'Bannon.

O'Bannon looked between them. "Do you two know each other?" Then he smacked his forehead and answered his own question. "HRT."

Web moved over to Debbie, who was pulling a tissue out of her purse.

"Deb? You're seeing O'Bannon?"

"Web," O'Bannon said, "that's really confidential."

Web waved the little man off. "Yeah, I know, top secret."

"I never liked this common waiting area—it's not good for patient privacy, but there's no other configuration possible," O'Bannon said, though the two were clearly not listening to his complaint. Finally, he said, "See you, Debbie." To Web he said, "Take it easy, Web. I'm sure Claire's doing wonders for you." He looked at Web inquiringly.

She is, Doc, Web wanted to say. *The woman's doing such wonders for me, she's driving me nuts.*

Web held the door for Debbie and they walked to the elevators. She wouldn't look at him and Web felt himself growing red in the face, with anger, embarrassment, he wasn't quite sure what.

He finally said, "I'm seeing a shrink to help me through what happened. I guess you are too."

She blew her nose and finally looked at him. "I've been seeing Dr. O'Bannon for well over a year, Web."

Again he stared blankly at her, and didn't even hear the elevator doors open.

"Are you going down?" Debbie wanted to know.

They got out on the street and were about to go off in different directions when Web swallowed his confusion and said, "You got time for a cup of coffee, Deb?" He was absolutely certain that she wouldn't have any time at all for the likes of him.

"There's a Starbucks around the corner. I know the lay of the land quite well around here."

They sat with their Grande cups in a lonely corner while shiny machines whirred, slurped and sputtered for their thirsty customers.

"Over a year, you say? You've been seeing a shrink all that time?"

Debbie stirred sprinkles of cinnamon deep into her cup. "Some people are in therapy their whole lives, Web."

"Yeah, other people. Not people like you."

She looked at him in a way she never had before. "Let me tell you about people like me, Web. When Teddy and me were first married he was regular military. I knew what I was in store for, assignments overseas where no one spoke your language, or else in swampy backwater USA where you had to drive a hundred miles to go to the movies. But I loved Teddy and I went, eyes wide open. Then he went Delta. And the kids started coming, and while we mostly stayed in one place, Teddy never was in that place. Half the time I didn't know where he was. Dead or alive. I'd read about it in the newspaper or see it on CNN like everybody else. But we got through that. Then he joins HRT, and I thought it might actually be better. My God, nobody told me HRT was even crazier than Delta, Web, or that my husband would be gone more than he ever was before. I could take it when I was twenty with no kids. I'm not twenty anymore, Web. And I've got three kids that I raised pretty much on my own, on Teddy's paycheck, which, after all those years of serving his damn country, was about what a cashier at Kmart earns. I was there every day for my children and all my youngest wants to know is, why did Daddy have to go away? Why can't Daddy come home? And I have absolutely no answer to give her."

"He died fighting the good fight, Deb. He died for his country."

Her fist came down so hard on the table, the slurping customers all turned and stared. "That's a bunch of bullshit and you know it." With a monumental effort, she gathered herself.

To Web, the woman seemed like an erupting volcano desperately trying to recall its lava.

She said, "He made his choice. He wanted to be with his buddies and his guns and his adventures." Her voice grew calmer, sadder. "He loved you guys. He loved *you*, Web. God, you have no idea how much he did. Far more than he cared about me, or even his own kids, because he didn't know them half as well as he knew you. You guys fought together, you saved each other's lives, each day you walked in harm's way and were good enough and trained hard enough to make it through. As a team. The greatest damn team there ever was. He talked to you about things he never would with me. He had this whole other life I could never be a part of. And it was more exciting, more of a rush than anything else he had." She spread her arms wide. "How can a mere wife and family compete with all that? Teddy would only tell me things here and there about what he was doing, just little tidbits to keep peace in the family." She shook her head. "There were so many days I hated all of you for taking him away from us." She put a tissue to her eyes to catch the tears.

Web wanted to put his hand out and touch her, but he didn't know if that would be welcome. He felt guilty of grand and awful crimes, and he never realized he'd even been indicted.

"Did Teddy go to therapy too?" he asked quietly.

Debbie wiped her eyes clear and took a sip of her coffee. "No. He said if anyone at HRT found out he was seeing a shrink they'd throw him off the team, that there was no room for guys with weaknesses on HRT. And, besides, he said, he had no reason to go to a shrink. There wasn't anything wrong with *him*, even if I had some crazy problem. He didn't want me to go, but I put my foot down for once in my life. I had to, Web, I had to talk to somebody. And I'm not the only HRT wife who's seeing a psychiatrist. There are others, like Angie Romano."

Angie Romano! Web wondered if she came to talk about Paulie. Maybe he beat her. No, more likely *she* beat Paulie. "I'm sorry you weren't happy, Deb. You deserve to be." At his house Web had a hundred pictures of himself and his Charlie buddies doing fun things together. And not one wife appeared in any of those photos because they had never been invited to come. Web had judged others without walking in their shoes. It was not a mistake he cared ever to repeat, for the exposure of one's ignorance could be so devastating and complete.

She looked at him, reached out and touched his hand, even attempted a smile. "So, now that I've unloaded on you like a ton of bricks, how's your therapy going?"

Web shrugged. "It's going. I'm not sure where. I know it doesn't come close to what you lost, but it suddenly occurred to me that those guys were all I had in my life. And they're gone and I'm still here and I'm not sure why. I don't think I'll ever be sure why."

"I'm sorry what Julie Patterson did to you. She's totally screwed up. She was never that stable to begin with. She resented you guys, I think, most of all."

"Julie could do it to me again and I'd take it again," he said flatly.

"You should get out now, Web. You've paid your dues. You've damn well served your country. You've given enough. They can't ask for any more of you."

"I figure after about thirty years of psychobabble, I'll be as good as new."

"It does work, Web. O'Bannon's even hypnotized me; got me to think about things I never thought I could. I guess they were hidden really deep inside." Debbie gripped his hand more tightly. "I know the dinner at my house was awful. We didn't know what to say to you. We wanted to make you feel comfortable, but I know we didn't. I'm surprised you didn't run out screaming before dessert."

"It wasn't your job to make me feel comfortable."

"You've been so good with everybody's kids over the years. I want you to know how much we all appreciated that. And there's not one of us who isn't glad you survived. We all know how you've risked your life over the years to keep our husbands alive." She reached across and touched the damaged side of his face, sliding her soft fingers up and down the rough, jerry-rigged surface and Web did not pull away.

"We all know the price you've paid, Web."

"Right now it seems worth it."

23

Toona popped back into the driver's seat and closed and locked the door. He stretched out a long arm and handed the envelope back to Francis, who was sitting in the rear section of seats in the jet-black Lincoln Navigator. Macy sat in the middle section, a pair of sunglasses on, though the vehicle's glass was tinted. He wore an ear radio and a holstered gun. Peebles was not with them.

Francis looked at the envelope but didn't take it. "Where'd you get this, Toona? Don't be handing me shit you ain't know where it comes from. I taught you better'n that."

"It's clean. They already checked it out, boss. Don't know where it come from, but it ain't no letter bomb or nuthin'."

Francis snatched the letter away and told Toona to drive on. As soon as his hand touched the object in the envelope, Francis knew what the letter was. He opened it and took out the ring. It was small and gold and wouldn't have even fit over his pinky, but it had fit Kevin's middle finger just fine when Francis had bought it for him. On the inside of the ring was engraved the names Kevin and Francis. Actually, it read, FRANCIS AND KEVIN. FOR LIFE.

Francis felt his hands begin to shake and he quickly glanced up and saw Toona staring at him the rearview mirror. "Drive the damn car, Toona, or you're gonna find your sorry ass in a Dumpster with my whole pistol mag in your damn head."

The Navigator pulled away from the curb and sped up.

Francis looked down at the envelope and carefully slipped the letter out. It was all block print, something you might see in some mystery show. Whoever had Kevin was asking—no, telling Francis to do something if he wanted to see the boy alive again. What they were telling him to do was odd. Francis would have expected a demand for money or for him to give up all or part of his territory and he would have done it, gotten Kevin back and then tracked down his abductors and killed all of them, probably with his bare hands. But there was no such demands, and thus Francis was confused and suddenly more afraid for Kevin than he already had been, because he had no clue as to what these people were up to. He had seen first-hand the motivations that made people do everything from taking someone's money to taking someone's life. He thought he'd seen it all. And from the contents of the letter these people were obviously aware of something that Francis was too, something special about the location of the building where all the Feds had gotten shot up.

"Where'd this letter come from, Toona?"

Toona's gaze in the rearview mirror caught his. "Twan said it was at the downtown place. Somebody slipped it under the door."

The downtown place was a condo that was one of the few places that Francis used more than a couple times. It was held in the name of a corporation whose sole purpose was to allow Francis the drug lord to actually own something legally without the police knocking his door down. He had fixed it up nicely, with original artwork of some ghetto brothers he admired and who were trying to do almost the impossible and live life straight. That's right, Francis Westbrook was a patron of the arts of sorts. And the condo was also filled with custom-made furniture that was big enough and sturdy enough to allow him to lounge on it without breaking it. The address of the condo had been one of his most jealously guarded secrets and it was the one place where he could actually relax. Now someone had discovered the location, had violated the place, and Francis knew he could never go back there.

He folded up the letter and put it away in his pocket, but he held the tiny ring in his big hand and looked at it. Then he slipped the photo out of his shirt pocket and looked at it. It had been taken on Kevin's ninth birthday. Francis had the boy on his shoulders. They had gone to a Redskins game and had on matching jerseys. Francis was so big that most people at the stadium thought he was a Redskin. That's right, big and black, must be good for nothing except playing ball for outrageous bucks. He remembered, though, that Kevin had thought that very cool. Better than your old man being a drug dealer, he supposed.

And what did his son really think of him, the man he believed was his big brother yet who was really his daddy? What did he think when he got caught in a cross-fire intended to kill Francis? Francis remembered holding Kevin with one arm, shielding him from more harm, while his other hand held a gun and he was firing at the sons of bitches who had turned a birthday party into a kill zone. Couldn't even take him to the damn hospital, had to give him to Jerome. And Kevin screaming that he wanted his brother and Francis not being able to do anything about that, because the cops were all over D.C. General after the shootout. They were just waiting for men with bullets in them to show up, and on would go the cuffs. The cops had been looking for a long time for some excuse to put his butt away. And Francis would've left on a nice lengthy visit to some super-max prison for the benign act of dropping his wounded son off so doctors could save his life.

He felt tears welling up in his eyes and he tried hard to push them away. He could only recall crying twice in his life. When Kevin was born, and when Kevin had been shot and almost killed. His plan had always been to make enough money to last him two lifetimes, his and Kevin's. Because when Francis retired from the "bizness" and left for his little island somewhere, his son was coming with him, away from the drugs and the guns and the premature deaths happening all around them. Maybe he would even summon the courage to tell Kevin the truth: that he was his father. He wasn't really sure why he had created this lie about being his big brother. Was he afraid of fatherhood? Or were lies just an essential part of Francis Westbrook's life?

His cell phone rang, just like the letter said it would. They must be watching him. He slowly held it up to his ear.

"Kevin?"

Toona turned his head around when he heard the name. Macy sat impassively.

"You all right, little man? They treating you okay?" Francis said into the phone. He nodded at the answer he heard. They spoke for about a minute and then the line went dead. Francis put down the phone.

"Mace?" he said.

Macy instantly turned and looked at him.

"Mace, we got to get to this Web London dude. Things have changed."

"You talking killing or information exchange? You want him to come to us, or us go to him? Be better if he found us, if you're talking info. You want him dead, though, I'll go to him and it's done."

Macy was always logical like that. He read your mind, thought for himself, reviewed the possibilities and took the pressure off his boss from having to do all the analysis, making all the tough decisions. Francis knew that Toona would never be like that, and even Peebles was limited in that capacity. Damn ironic that a little white boy with a vicious streak would become his number one kind of guy, his soul mate of sorts as much as black and white could be.

"Info, for now. So he comes to us. How long you reckon?"

"He's been seen nosing around in that Bucar of his probably looking for clues. I'd say it wouldn't take all that long. He comes our way, we got a nice carrot to dangle in front of him."

"Let's do it. Oh, and Mace, nice call on that other thing." Francis glanced at Toona.

"Just doing my job," replied Macy.

Kevin looked up at the man as he put the phone away.

"You did real good, Kevin."

"I want to see my brother."

"One step at a time. You just talked to him. See, we're not bad people. Hell, we're into family stuff, see." He laughed in a way that made Kevin think he wasn't into family at all. He rubbed his finger where his ring had been.

"Why you let me talk to him?"

"Well, it's important that he knows you're okay."

"So he do what you tell him to do."

"Damn, you really are one smart kid. You want a job?" He laughed again, turned and left, locking the door behind him.

"What I want," Kevin called after him, "is out of here."

24

Web had not read a paper in several days. He finally bought a copy of the *Washington Post* and went through it over coffee at a table near the large fountain at the Reston Town Center. He had been making slow circles of the Washington metropolitan area and racking up some serious motel bills for the Bureau. Web occasionally looked up and smiled at the kids climbing up on the ledge and throwing pennies into the fountains while their mothers held on to their shirttails so they wouldn't go plunging into the water.

He had gone through Sports, Metro, Style, working his way backward to the front section. On page A6 his nonchalant attitude disappeared. He reread the article three times and looked closely at the accompanying photos. When he sat back and digested it all, he found himself coming to conclusions that didn't seem possible, so far-fetched were they. He touched the damaged side of his face and then pressed a finger against the spot of each bullet hole. After all this time was he going to have to confront it again?

He punched his speed dial. Bates wasn't in. Web had him paged. The guy called back a few minutes later. Web told him about the article.

"Louis Leadbetter. He was the judge down in Richmond who tried the Free Society case. Gunned down. Watkins was the prosecuting attorney in the case. He goes in his house and it implodes. All on the same day. And then you got Charlie Team. We were the team that responded to the Richmond Field Office's request. I killed two of the Freebies myself before I got my face toasted and two holes in me. And then you have Ernest B. Free himself. Busted out of prison, what, three months ago? One of the guards was paid off, got him out in a transfer van and ended up with his throat slit for his trouble."

Bates's reply was surprising. "We know all that, Web. We've had our computers crunching that stuff, and then those two deaths, murders, happened. And there's something else."

"What?"

"You better come on down."

When Web arrived at the WFO, he was escorted to the strategic operations room that had all the bells and whistles one would expect at the deep-pocketed crime-busting federal behemoth, including the standard-issue copper-coated walls, sophisticated interior security system, white noise at all vulnerable portals, retinal and palm scanners, stacks of high-powered computers, video equipment and, most important, fresh coffee in high quantities and a mound of hot Krispy Kreme doughnuts.

Web poured himself a cup and said hello to some of the folks scurrying around the large room. He looked at computer-generated diagrams of the courtyard and its environs that had been tacked to large boards and mounted on the walls. There were pins at various places on the diagrams that represented, Web knew, significant points of evidence or clues. The bustle of feet, the nonstop clack of computer keys, the ringing of phones, the rustle of paper and the ballooning body-heat index told Web that something was up. He had been part of these war room operations before.

"Oklahoma City set the standard way too high," said Bates with an ironic smile as Web sat down across from him. "Now everybody expects us to examine a few hunks of metal, check a few videotapes, run a few plates, hit some computer keys and bingo, we have our man hours later." He dropped his legal pad on the table. "But it almost never works that way. Like everything else, you need some breaks. Well, we just got a bunch telegraphed to us. Somebody definitely wants us to know he's out there."

"I'll take a lead however it comes in, Perce. Whoever it is can't control how it's followed up."

"You know I really hated it when you left WFO to go climb ropes and shoot big guns. If you'd stuck with me, you might have made a decent FBI agent one day."

"You make your bed, you lie and die in it. You said there was something else?"

Bates nodded and slid a news clipping over to Web, who looked down at it.

"Scott Wingo . . . that name rings a bell."

"Yeah, he defended our friend Ernest B. Free. I wasn't at the trial, of course. I was still recuperating. But the guys who were there talked about Wingo."

"Slick and smart. He cut his guy a sweetheart deal. And now he's dead."

"Murdered?"

"Atropine was applied to his telephone receiver. You pick up the phone, you naturally press it against your skin, near your nostrils and such. Atropine is absorbed through the membranes much faster than via the bloodstream. Causes your pulse to go into overdrive, breathing constricted, can make you hallucinatory, all within an hour or so. If you have bad kidneys or other circulatory problems so the body can't quickly rid itself of the stuff, that would speed up the poison's effect. Wingo was diabetic, had heart problems and was confined to a wheelchair, so atropine was the perfect choice. He went in alone on Saturdays, so nobody would be around to help when he started feeling the atropine hit him. And on weekends he was known to return a lot of calls, or so the folks in Richmond tell us."

"So whoever killed him knew both his medical history and his work routine?"

Bates nodded. "Leadbetter got shot when he turned on the light to read an article another judge supposedly told him about. The marshal who took the call said it was a Judge Mackey. Of course, it wasn't."

"The phone again."

"That's not all. Watkins's neighbor was pulling out of his driveway at the time Watkins was walking up to his house. He told police that he saw Watkins reach into his pocket and pull out his phone. The guy couldn't hear the phone ringing, but he said it looked like Watkins was answering a call. Gas in the house, he hits the talk button. Boom."

Web said, "Wait a minute. A cell phone isn't like a light switch. It doesn't have the right type and amount of electrical spark to ignite gas."

"We examined the phone, or what was left of it. The forensic folks actually had to scrape it off Watkins's hand. Someone had planted a solenoid inside the phone that would cause the exact type of spark necessary to ignite that gas."

"So somebody had to snatch his phone, probably while he was asleep or away from it for any length of time, plant the solenoid and then they had to be watching him when it happened to get the timing that exact."

"Yep. We checked the logs for Watkins's and the marshal's phones. Both calls were made with disposable calling cards you buy with cash and then discard. No record."

"Like undercover agents use. I take it yours hasn't surfaced yet?"

"Forget our undercover."

"No, I'll just come back to him later. So what's the latest on Free?"

"Nothing. It's like the guy's gone to another planet."

"Is the organization still active?"

"Unfortunately, yes. You probably remember they disavowed being part of the hit on the school in Richmond and Ernie wouldn't rat on his soul mates, said he'd planned the job himself without their knowledge, so there went that case. The other gunmen were dead, two of them thanks to you. We couldn't crack any of the other members and get them to testify, so the Free Society was never even charged with anything. They laid low for a while because of all the negative publicity, but word is they're coming back with fresh blood."

"Where are they now?"

"Southern Virginia, near Danville. You better believe we've got that place covered. We figured old Ernie would head there after his escape. But so far, nothing."

"After all this, can't we get a search warrant for their headquarters?"

"What, we go to the magistrate and say we've got three murders, six if you count Watkins's family, and we think this Free Society might be behind them, but we've got absolutely no evidence linking them to the hit on HRT or anybody else? Wouldn't the ACLU just love to hit that one out of the park?" Bates paused. "It all makes sense though. Prosecutor, judge, perfect motive for revenge."

"But why the defense lawyer? He saved Ernie from lethal injection. Why take him out?"

"That's true, but you're not talking about rational people, Web. For all we know, they're pissed because their fellow madman served one day in prison. Or maybe Ernie had a falling out with the guy and when he got out he decided to take them all out."

"Well, at least that should end the killings. There's nobody left."

Bates reached in a file and pulled out another slip of paper and a photograph. "Not quite. You remember there were two teachers gunned down at the school too."

Web took a deep breath as the painful memories came flooding back. "And the boy, David Canfield."

"Right. Well, one of the slain teachers was married. And guess what? Her husband was killed three days ago in western Maryland while driving home late one night from work."

"Homicide?"

"Not sure. It was a car crash. Police are still investigating. Looks like a hit and run."

"Telephone involved?"

"There was one in the car. After we contacted them, the police said they would check the phone logs to see if he received a call right before the crash."

"How about the other teacher's family?"

"The husband and kids moved to Oregon. We've contacted them and they're under twenty-four-hour surveillance right now. And we're not stopping there. You remember David Canfield's parents? Bill and Gwen?"

Web nodded. "I was in the hospital at MCV for a while. Billy Canfield came to visit me a couple of times. He's a good guy. He took the loss of his son really hard, who wouldn't? I never met his wife, and I haven't seen Billy since."

"They moved. Live up in Fauquier County now, run a horse farm."

"Anything strange happen to them?"

"We contacted them as soon as we made the connection. They said nothing out of the ordinary had occurred. They knew about Free's escape. And to quote Bill Canfield, he said he doesn't want our help and he hoped the bastard came after him because he'd just love to blow his head off with a shotgun."

"Billy Canfield is no shrinking violet. I could tell that when he came to the hospital to see me; rough, tough and opinionated. Some of my team who testified at the trial told me he was a pretty loud presence there too. Came close to contempt citations a couple of times."

"He ran his own trucking firm and then sold it after his kid died."

"If the Frees are behind the killings in Richmond, Fauquier County is a lot closer than Oregon. The Canfields really could be in danger."

"I know. I've been thinking of taking a ride out there and trying to talk some sense into him."

"I'll go with you."

"You sure about that? I know that what happened at that school in Richmond is something you'd be better off not revisiting."

Web shook his head. "That's not something you ever put behind you, Perce, I don't care how much time goes by. The two teachers died before we got there. I couldn't do anything about that, but David Canfield was killed on my watch."

"You did more than anybody could have, including almost getting killed. And you got a permanent badge from it right there on your face. You have nothing to feel guilty about."

"Then you really don't know me."

Bates studied Web closely. "Okay, but let's not forget about you, Web. If wiping out Charlie Team was the Frees' goal, they haven't accomplished it yet. You're the last man standing."

Barely, thought Web. "Don't worry, I look both ways before crossing the street."

"I'm serious, Web. If they tried once, they'll try again. These people are fanatics."

"Yeah, I know. Remember, I got the 'permanent badge.'"

"And another thing. At the trial Wingo filed that countersuit against HRT and the Bureau for wrongful death."

"That was bullshit all the way."

"Right. But it allowed them to make some discovery on HRT. The Free Society probably learned some things about your methods, procedures and such. It could have helped them in setting up the ambush."

Web hadn't considered this yet. It actually made a lot of sense.

"I promise if I get any weird-ass phone calls, you'll be the first to know. And I'll check my receiver for atropine. Now tell me about this undercover. Maybe the Frees are involved, but they had to have some inside help. Now, I know he's black and it's hard for me to believe the Frees would work with a man of color, but we can't afford to discount anything right now. You told me Cove was a loner. What else do you know about him?" Web hadn't heard back from Ann Lyle on his inquiries into Cove, so he had decided to go right to the source.

"Oh, lots of stuff. It's right in that file over there, marked 'FBI Undercover Agents, All You Ever Wanted to Know.'"

"Perce, this guy could be the key."

"He's not! Take my word for it."

"All I'm saying is I worked these kind of cases. And contrary to what you think, I didn't forget how to be an FBI agent when I joined HRT. I had a great teacher, and don't let that swell your head. And another pair of eyes is another pair of eyes. Isn't that what you always beat into me?"

"That's not how it works, Web, sorry. Rules are rules."

"I seem to remember you telling me differently way back when."

"Times change, people change."

Web sat back and pondered whether he should play his trump card. "Okay, what would you say if I told you something you don't know but that could be important?"

"I'd say why the hell didn't you tell me before?"

"I just figured it out."

"Yeah, right."

"Do you want to hear it or not?"

"And what's in it for you?"

"I give you info on the case, you do the same for me."

"How about I make you tell me for nothing?"

"Come on, for old times' sake."

Bates tapped the file in front of him. "How do I know it's really something I can use?"

"If it's not, then you owe me nothing. I'll trust your judgment."

Bates eyed him for a few more moments. "Go."

Web told him about the switch with Kevin Westbrook. As he went on, Bates's face grew more florid and Web could tell the man's pulse was nowhere near sixty-four and had probably left double digits far behind.

"When *exactly* did you figure this out? And I want it to the minute."

"When I was having a beer with Romano and I mentioned that the Kevin Westbrook I saw had a hole in his cheek from a bullet wound. The kid he had, he said, didn't. Cortez corroborated that. And don't go after those guys. I told them I'd fill you in ASAP."

"Sure you did. Who would switch the kids and why?"

"Not even a good guess. But I'm telling you the kid I saved in the alley and the kid Romano turned over to the 'alleged' FBI agent were two different boys." He tapped the table. "So what's your judgment? Worth it or not?"

In answer Bates opened a file, although he recited the facts from memory. "Randall Cove. Age forty-four. Been with the Bureau his whole career. He was an All-American tailback from Oklahoma but blew out his knees before the NFL draft. Here's a recent photo." Bates slid it across and Web looked at the face. The guy had a short beard, dreadlocks and eyes that could only be described as piercing. The vitals said he was a big man, about six-three, two-forty. He looked powerful enough to take on a grizzly and maybe win. Web hunched forward and while he pretended to study the picture in greater depth he was actually reading as much as he could from the file Bates had open. His years as an FBI agent had left him with many tricks to help his short-term memory retention until he could write things down. And he had also become very proficient at reading upside down.

Bates said, "He could take care of himself, knew the street better than most kingpins. And cool under pressure."

"Yeah, Princeton white-breads named William and Jeffrey just never seem to fit in with Drug Town, USA, I wonder why," said

Web. "You mentioned before that he didn't have a wife or kids. So he never married?"

"No, his wife's dead."

"And they didn't have kids?"

"He did."

"What happened to them?"

Bates shifted uncomfortably in his seat. "It happened a while back."

"I'm all attention."

Bates let out a long breath and didn't seem like he was going to start talking.

"I lost my whole team, Perce, I'd kind of appreciate full disclosure here."

Bates sat forward and clasped his hands in front of him. "He was working an assignment in California. Heavy cover because it involved the Russian mob, and those guys will fire a missile up your ass for coughing around them. They make the Mafia look like preschoolers." Bates stopped there.

"And?"

"And his cover got blown. They traced his family."

"And killed them?"

"Slaughtered would be more like it." Bates cleared his throat. "I saw the photos."

"Where was Cove?"

"They had intentionally diverted him away so they'd have a free hand."

"And they didn't go after him too?"

"They tried, later. They waited until he buried his family, nice guys that they were. And Cove was waiting for them when they came."

"And he killed *them*?"

Bates started blinking rapidly and Web noted a sudden tic over the man's left eye.

"Slaughtered. I saw those photos too."

"And the Bureau just let this guy keep working? What, they don't believe in early retirement for agents with butchered families?"

Bates spread his hands in resignation. "The Bureau tried, but he wouldn't go. He wanted to work. And to tell you the truth, after what happened to his family, the guy worked longer and harder than any UC we ever had. They transferred him to WFO to get him out of California. Let me tell you, he got into places we were never able to get into before. We got convictions on serious large-scale operators all across the board because of Randall Cove."

"Sounds like a hero."

Bates finally smoothed out his tic. "He's unorthodox, goes his own way a lot, and the higher-ups can only take so much of that, even from the undercover dudes, slaughtered family or not. But none of it really stuck to Cove. I can't say it hasn't hurt his career, I mean, it's not like the Bureau has a place for a guy like this outside of undercover, and I'm sure he knew that too. But he plays the Bureau games. Always covered his back. You take the dirt with the good and the guy always delivered. Until now."

"And the trace on his family by the Russians—would that have been in any way the Bureau's screw-up?"

Bates shrugged. "Cove didn't seem to think so. He's been plugging away ever since."

"You know what they say about revenge, Perce, it's the only dish best eaten really cold."

Bates shrugged again. "Possibly."

Web was just starting to get worked up. "You know, it just gives me the warm fuzzies that a guy like that was able to stay in the Bureau and maybe lead my team down the primrose path to Armageddon to avenge his wife and kids. Don't you guys have some kind of quality control over this shit?"

"Earth to Web, undercover agents are a different breed. They live a lie all the time and sometimes they get in too deep and get turned or just go nuts all on their own. That's why the Bureau switches people in and out, changes assignments and lets them recharge their batteries."

"And they did all that with Cove? Switched him out, let him recharge his dreadlocks? Gave him crisis counseling after he buried his family?" Bates was silent on this. "Or was he so good at his job that they just let him keep rocking along until he finally erupted all over *my* team?"

"I'm not going to discuss that with you. I *can't* discuss that with you."

"What if I told you that was unacceptable bullshit?"

"What if I told you, you were getting way too close to the line?"

The men glared at one another until the fires died down.

"And his snitches? Were they all-pro too?" asked Web.

"Cove always played it close. He had access to them only, not anybody else. That's not exactly Bureau procedure, but like I said, you couldn't argue with the guy's results. Those were his rules."

"So we know any more about this target? You said it was the financial guts of some drug op. Whose?"

"Well, there's some difference of opinion about that."

"Oh, swell, Perce. I love a puzzle at both ends."

"This stuff is not an exact science, Web. The area where your mission went down is controlled pretty much by one crew, Big F's—I told you that."

"So it was his operation we were hitting in that building."

"Cove didn't think so."

"He didn't know for sure"

"What, you think the bad guys carry union cards or ID reading, 'I'm a member of X crew'?"

"So what was Cove's opinion?"

"That the money operation was that of a much bigger player. Maybe the ring supplying a drug called Oxycontin to the D.C. area. You heard of it?"

Web nodded. "DEA guys talk about it all the time down at Quantico. You don't have to drug-lab the stuff or worry about sneaking it past customs. All you have to do is get your hands on it, which you can a dozen different ways, and then start printing money."

"A criminal's Nirvana," added Bates dryly. "It's one of the most potent and frequently prescribed painkillers on the market right now. It blocks pain signals from the nerves to the brain and gives you a feeling of euphoria. Normally, it works on a twelve-hour time release, but if you crush it or smoke it you get a brain rush that some say is almost equal to heroin. It also can throw the abuser into respiratory arrest, which it has frequently."

"Nice little side effect. Are you telling me you have no idea who his inside guy might have been?"

Bates tapped the file in front of him. "We have some ideas. Now, this is totally unofficial."

"At this point, I'll take rumors and lies."

"For Cove to get in as deep as he was, we figure the snitch has to be in the inner circle, pretty tight. He was working the Westbrook angle when he stumbled into the Oxy piece. But I have to presume that whomever he was using to infiltrate Westbrook's operation is the person who helped him get on to this new development. Antoine Peebles is Westbrook's COO, for want of a better term. He runs a damn tight ship and it's largely because of him that we haven't been able to lay a finger on Westbrook. Here's Westbrook, and the other one is Peebles." He slid across two photos.

Web looked at them. Westbrook was a monster, far bigger even than Cove. He looked like he'd been through a war, his eyes, even staring out from the paper two-dimensionally, had the keenness that you always saw in survivors. Peebles was an altogether different picture.

"Westbrook is a warhorse. Peebles looks like he should be graduating from Stanford."

"Right. He's young and we figure Peebles is the new breed of drug entrepreneurs, not as violent, more businesslike and ambitious as hell. Word on the street is that someone's looking to band all the local distributors together, to make them more efficient, enhanced bargaining power up the line, economies of scale, a real business approach to it."

"Sounds like old Antoine may want to be CEO instead of just COO."

"Maybe. Now, Westbrook came up through the streets. He's seen and done it all, but we've heard that he may be looking for an exit from the drug business."

"Well, Peebles may have a different agenda if he's the one behind the organization of the local crews. But giving away valuable stuff to Cove doesn't exactly figure with being the heir apparent. If you bust the operation, what does Peebles have left to run?"

"That's a problem," conceded Bates.

"Who else is in the picture?"

"Westbrook's main muscle. Clyde Macy."

Bates handed him the photo of Macy, who, to put it kindly, looked like he should be taking up space on death row somewhere. Macy was so white he looked anemic; a skinhead with the sort of calm yet merciless eyes that Web associated with the worst serial killers of his experience.

"If Jesus saw this guy coming at him, he'd scream for a cop."

"Apparently Westbrook only works with the best," commented Bates.

"How did Macy fit in with all the brothers? He looks like a white supremacist."

"Nope. Apparently just doesn't like hair. We don't know much about him before he came to D.C. Though we could never prove it, he was believed to be a foot soldier for a couple kingpins who got sent to federal Shangri-La in Joliet. After that he came to D.C. and joined Westbrook. He has a well-deserved rep on the street for loyalty and extreme violence. A real crazy-ass, but professional in his own way."

"Just as any good criminal should be."

"His first big act of malice was putting a meat cleaver in his grandma's head because, he claimed, she was shortchanging him at dinnertime."

"How come he's walking around free after a murder rap like that?"

"He was only eleven, so he did time at a juvie detention center. Since then, the only crime the guy's committed is three speeding tickets."

"Nice guy. Mind if I keep these photos?"

"Help yourself. But if you run into Macy in a dark alley or a well-lit street, my advice to you would be to run."

"I'm HRT, Perce. I eat guys like him for breakfast."

"Right. Keep telling yourself that."

"If Cove's really as good as you say, then he didn't just walk into an ambush. Something else is going on."

"Maybe, but everybody makes mistakes."

"Did you confirm that Cove didn't know when we were coming?"

"I did. Cove was not told the date of the hit."

"How come he didn't know?"

"They didn't want any leaks, and he wasn't going to be there anyway, so he didn't qualify as a need-to-know."

"That's great, you didn't trust your own undercover. That doesn't mean he couldn't have gotten the information from another source. Like WFO?"

"Or like HRT?" Bates shot back.

"And the potential witnesses being there, was that intel from Cove?" Bates nodded. "You know, Perce, it would have been nice to know all this up front."

"Need-to-know, Web. And you didn't need to know that to do your job."

"How the hell can you say that when you don't have a damn clue how I do my job?"

"You're getting close to that line again, my friend. Don't push it!"

"Does anybody give a damn that six men were killed in the process?"

"In the grand scheme of things, Web, no. Only people like you and me care."

"So, anything else I *don't* need to know?"

From his large stack of documents Bates pulled out a very thick expandable file, slid out one of the manila folders and opened it. "Why didn't you tell me Harry Sullivan was your old man?"

Web immediately rose and poured himself another cup of coffee. He didn't really need the extra caffeine, but it gave him time to think of a response or a lie. When he sat back down Bates was still looking over the file. When he glanced at Web, it was clear Bates wanted an answer to that question before he would give up the material.

"I never really thought of him as my father. We parted company when I was barely six. To me, he's just a guy." After a moment, he asked, "When did you find out he was my father?"

Bates ran his finger down one of the pages. "Not until I pulled your entire background-check file. Frankly, looking at this arrest and conviction record, I'm surprised he had time to get your mother pregnant. Lotta stuff in here," he added enticingly.

Web wanted to snatch the file out of Bates's hands and run from the room. However, he just sat there, staring at the upside-down pages, waiting. The bustle of the room had receded for him now. It was just him, Bates and, on those pages, his father.

"So why are you suddenly so interested in, as you say, 'just a guy'?" asked Bates.

"I guess you get to a certain age, things like that start to matter."

Bates put the folder back and slid the entire file across to Web. "Happy reading."

25

The first thing Web noticed when he got back to the motel was that there was a fresh oil patch in the parking space he had been using. Nothing unusual, really, for another guest could have used that spot, though it was directly in front of Web's unit. Before he unlocked the door, he checked out the doorknob while pretending to fumble for his room key. Unfortunately, even Web could not tell if the lock had been picked or not. It hadn't been forced, but somebody who knew what he was doing could pop the simple lock in the time it took to sneeze and leave not a trace.

Web opened the door, his other hand on the butt of his gun. It took him about ten seconds to discover that no one was in the tiny room. Nothing was out of place, and even the box he had taken from his mother's attic was there, each piece of paper exactly where he had left it. However, Web had five different types of tiny booby traps set up throughout his room and three of them had been tripped. Over the years, Web had developed this system whenever he was on the road. Well, whoever had searched his room was good but not perfect. That was comforting, like knowing the four-hundred-pound brute you were about to rumble with had a glass chin and occasionally wet his bed.

Ironic, that while he'd been meeting with Bates, someone had searched his room. Web had never been naive about life, because he had seen the worst of it, as both a child and an adult. Yet the one thing he had always thought he could count on was the Bureau and all the people who gave it life beyond the technical forms and guns. For the first time in his career, that faith had been shaken.

He packed his few belongings and was on the road within five minutes. He went to a restaurant near Old Town Alexandria, parked where he could see his car through the restaurant's window, ate his lunch and made his way through Harry Sullivan's life.

Bates had not been joking. Web's old man had been a guest of some of the finest correctional facilities the country had to offer, most of them in the South, where Web knew they grew some exceptionally fine human cages. His father's offenses were myriad yet had a common theme: They were typically low-level financial crimes, business scams, embezzlement and fraud. From some of the old court transcripts and arrest records in the file, Web could see his old man's main weapon had been a smooth tongue and more chutzpah than any one human being should be toting around.

There were various photos of his father in the file, from the front, right and left sides, with the little line of prisoner identification numbers running underneath. Web had seen many mug shots of arrested people, and they all looked remarkably the same: stricken, terrified, ready to slice wrist or blow out temple. Yet in all his mug shots Harry Sullivan was smiling. The bastard was grinning, like he had put one over on the cops, even though he was the one busted. But his father had not aged well. He was no longer the handsome man he had been in the photos in the attic box. The last series of shots showed a very old man, though he was still smiling, albeit with fewer teeth. Web had no reason to care about him, yet it was difficult for him to witness the man's decline in all its impersonal Kodak glory.

As Web read some of the trial testimony of his father, he couldn't help but laugh in places. One slick operator emerged from the lines of dialogue as the cagey con battled with prosecutors determined to put him away.

"Mr. Sullivan," asked one D.A., "is it not true that on the night in question you were—"

"Begging your pardon, lad, but what night would that be again? Me memory's not what it was."

Web could almost see the lawyer rolling his eyes as he answered, "The twenty-sixth of June, sir."

"Ah, that's right. Go on, now, lad, you're doing fine. I'm sure ye mum's proud of yer."

In the transcript the court reporter had typed parenthetically, "Laughter in courtroom."

"Mr. Sullivan, I am *not* your lad," replied the lawyer.

"Well, forgive me, son, for I'm not quite experienced in such matters, and I surely meant nothing by it. Truth is, I don't know what to be calling you. Though in the ride over from the jail to this fine courthouse I heard others call you names I wouldn't be saying to me dearest enemy in the world. Words that woulda made me poor God-fearing mum roll over in her good Catholic grave. Attacking your honesty and integrity, and what man can be standing for mucha that?"

"I could care less what criminals say about me, sir."

"Begging your pardon, son, but the worst of it be coming from the guards."

"Laughter again," the stenographer had typed. Huge thunders of laughter, Web concluded, judging from the regiment of exclamation points tacked on the end.

"Can we continue, Mr. Sullivan?" said the lawyer.

"Ah, now, you be calling me Harry. It's been me name since me Irish arse came into this world."

"Mr. Sullivan!" This came from the judge, Web read, and in those two words he seemed to sense a long laugh, though Web was probably wrong. But the judge's last name *was* O'Malley, and perhaps he and Harry Sullivan shared a hatred of the English, if nothing else.

"I certainly won't be calling you Harry," said the lawyer, and Web could almost see the righteous indignation on the man's features for having to carry on such a conversation with a common criminal and getting the worst of it.

"Well, now, lad, I know it's your job to put me old, withered self into a cold, dark cell where men treat other men with no dignity atall. And all over a wee misunderstanding that might amount to nothing more than bad judgment, or perhaps a pint or two more than I should have had. But even so, you call me Harry, for though you've got to see this terrible deed through, there's no reason we can't be friends."

As Web finished the file on that particular chapter in his father's life, he had to note, with some satisfaction, that the jury had acquitted Harry Sullivan on all counts.

The last crime his father had been sent to prison for had gotten him twenty years, by far his longest sentence. So far he had punched fourteen years of the time in a prison in South Carolina that Web knew to be a sweat-hole one short step from hell, and he had six more years to go unless he got paroled or, more likely, died behind bars.

Web took the final bite of his pastrami and the last swallow of his Dominion Ale. There was one more file to check. It did not take long to read and left Web stunned and even more confused.

The Bureau was good; they left no stone unturned. When they checked somebody's background out, damn it, man, you were checked out. If you were applying to work at the Bureau in any capacity, they talked to everybody you had any contact with in your entire life. Your first-grade schoolteacher, your paper route manager, even the pretty girl you had taken to the prom and subsequently slept with. And they had no doubt also spoken with her father, to whom you had to explain your miserable conduct afterward when the secret got out, even though it was his innocent little girl who had ripped off your pants and brought the extra-lubricated condoms. Your Boy Scout troop leader, your in-laws, the bank manager who had turned down your first car loan, the woman who cut your hair—nothing, absolutely nothing was sacred when the FBI was on the case. And damn if they hadn't managed to track down old Harry Sullivan.

He had been newly ensconced in his little South Carolina retirement cell, and he had given the background-checking agents his two cents on Web London, his son. "My son." It was a phrase Harry Sullivan had used thirty-four times during the meeting because Web took the time to count them.

Harry Sullivan gave "my son" the best damn recommendation anyone could give another person, though he had only known "my son" for the first six years of his life. But according to Harry Sullivan, a proper Irishman could tell if "my son" had what it took from nearly the day the diapers came off. And his son had what it took to be the finest FBI agent there ever was or ever would be and they could quote him on that. And if they wanted him to come up to Washington to tell the powers-that-be that very thing, he gladly would, though it would be with leg and arm shackles he'd be trooping in, yet his heart would still be bursting with pride. There was nothing on earth that was too good for "my son."

Web continued reading and his head dropped lower and lower as he did so, and then finally it almost hit the table with Harry Sullivan's last written statement: "And would the good agents, the fine agents," he'd begun, mind telling "my son" that his father has thought about him every day over all these years, never once letting him out of his heart, and though it was not likely that they would ever hook up again, that Harry Sullivan wanted "my son" to know that he loved him and wanted the best for him? And to not think too badly of the old man for how things had turned out? Would the good agents mind telling "my son" that, for he'd be much in their debt if they did. And he would be proud to buy them each a pint or two if the opportunity ever arose, though the prospects did not look at all promising for that, given his current living arrangements, though one just never knew.

Well, they never had told Web anything. Web had never seen this report until right this minute. Damn the Bureau! Was there never any room to bend the rules? Did everything have to be lockstep, their way or the highway? And yet Web could have discovered this information years before if he had really wanted to. He just hadn't wanted to.

The next thought that hit Web made his features turn grim. If the Bureau had sent Claire Daniels Web's file, was she already privy to some or all of this information regarding Harry Sullivan? If so, why hadn't she bothered to tell him that?

Web packed the file up, paid his bill and walked back to the Vic. He drove to one of the Bureau's motor pools, switched vehicles and drove a late-model Grand Marquis out another gate not visible from the street he had come in on. The Bureau wasn't exactly rolling in available Bucars, but the Grand had come in for a ten-thousand-miler, and Web had persuaded the supervisor that he deserved a nicer set of wheels than the twenty-year vet uptown at HQ the car was assigned to. If anyone had a problem with that, Web had added, go talk to Buck Winters, he's my best friend.

26

Bates was still in the strategic ops room when the man entered. Bates looked up and did his best to keep the dismay off his face.

Buck Winters sat down across from him. The crease on his suit was Bureau letter-perfect, the shine on his wing tips equally regulation. The insertion of his pocket handkerchief looked like it had been done with a ruler. The man was tall, broad-shouldered, with confident, intelligent features, a walking poster boy for the FBI. Maybe that's how he had risen so far.

"I saw London leaving the building earlier."

"Just checking in per his orders."

"Oh, I'm sure he is." Winters laid his palms flat on the table and seemed to study every feature on Bates's face. "Why the hell do you care so much about that guy?"

"He's a good agent. And like you said, I was sort of his mentor."

"That's not something I'd lay claim to, frankly."

"He's almost gotten himself killed for this place a lot more than you or me."

"He's a hothead. All those HRT guys are. They're not part of us. They go their own way and thumb their noses at the rest of us, like they're somehow better. What they really are is a bunch of alphas with big guns just itching to use them."

"We're all on the same team, Buck. They're a specialized unit that takes care of stuff nobody else can. Yeah, sure, they're cocky, who wouldn't be? But we're all FBI agents; we're all working toward the same goal."

Winters shook his head. "You really believe that?"

"Yeah, I really do. If I didn't, I wouldn't be here."

"They've also been the cause of some of the Bureau's worst moments."

Bates dropped his file. "That's where you're dead wrong. The Bureau throws them into the fire on a moment's notice and when something pops, usually because of knuckleheaded orders from the top that any guy on the front lines expected to execute said orders could tell you in a heartbeat won't work, they take all the heat. I'm actually surprised they haven't ask to be split off from *us*."

"You've never played the games you need to, to move up here, Perce. You're at the glass ceiling or, in your case, the steel ceiling. There's no getting through it."

"Well, I like right where I am."

"Piece of advice: When you stop rising here, you eventually start falling."

"Thanks for the career advice," Bates said curtly.

"I've been getting your memos on the investigation. Frankly, they're pretty sparse."

"So are the results of the investigation."

"Cove, what's the status? You were sort of vague on that."

"Not much to report."

"I trust you're working under the assumption that any Bureau undercover who hasn't shown after all this time is either dead, or if he isn't dead, he's been turned and the way we should be looking for him is through an APB."

"Cove hasn't turned."

"So you've talked to him? Funny, I didn't see that in any of your reports."

"I'm still feeling my way. But I did receive information from Cove."

"And what did our illustrious undercover say about this mess?"

"That he thinks he was set up."

"Gee, that's stunning," said Winters sarcastically.

"That he doesn't want to come in because he thinks the rat is somewhere in the Bureau." Bates stared hard at Winters when he said this, though he wasn't really sure why. It wasn't like Winters would be leaking secrets, would he? "He knows all about the leaks happening and the blown missions. He thinks what happened to HRT was another one of those."

"Interesting theory, but I'm assuming he has no proof of that."

That question struck Bates as odd. "None that he cared to share with me," he answered. "I've got it under control, Buck. I know how busy you are, and I don't want to clutter your legendary vision with small details. You have my word that if anything big is going down, you'll know beforehand. That way you can do the media circus. You're really good at that."

Winters could hardly have missed the sarcasm yet apparently chose to ignore it. "If I remember correctly, you and Cove were really tight at one time. California, right?"

"We worked together."

"About the time his family got hit."

"That's right."

"A disaster for the Bureau."

"Actually, I always thought it was a disaster for the Cove family."

"What's got me puzzled is how all this went down. As I understand it, Cove had discovered a drug crew's financial operations in that building."

"And HRT was called up to hit it," said Bates. "There were potential witnesses in there. HRT specializes in getting those kind of folks out alive."

"Boy, they really did a bang-up job of that. They couldn't keep themselves alive."

"They were set up."

"Agreed. But how? If not Cove, how?"

Bates thought back to his meeting with Randall Cove at the cemetery. Cove believed there was a leak inside the Bureau that accounted for all the things going wrong. Bates studied Winters for a moment. "Well, in order to accomplish something like that I would suppose that somebody would have to have inside information of the highest order."

Winters sat back. "Of the highest order. From inside the Bureau, you're saying?"

"Inside is inside."

"That's a very serious allegation, Bates."

"I'm not alleging anything. I'm just pointing out one possibility."

"It would be a hell of a lot easier to turn one undercover agent."

"You don't know Randall Cove."

"And maybe you know him too well. So well, you can't see the forest for the trees."

Winters rose. "No surprises, Bates. Nothing substantial goes down unless I know about it ahead of time. Clear?"

As Winters left, Bates muttered under his breath, "Waco clear, Buck."

Web was in his car when Ann Lyle called.

"Sorry it took me so long, but I wanted to get something solid for you."

"That's okay. I just got some stuff on Cove from the Bureau; understandably it was like pulling teeth."

"Well, I got you some*one*."

"Who? Cove?"

"I'm good, but I'm not that good, Web. I've drummed up a D.C. police sergeant who was a regular contact of Cove's when he worked the WFO beat years ago."

"A local cop as a contact for an FBI undercover? How's that?"

"It's not unusual for UCs to use a cop they trust to act as a go-between, Web. Cove had one of those during his first stint here, and the guy's willing to talk to you."

He pulled the car over, grabbed pen and paper and wrote down the name Sonny Venables, who was still a uniform in D.C.'s First District. Ann also gave him the man's number.

"Ann, anybody else got hold of the Venables angle?"

"Not that Sonny said, and I think he would've mentioned it. He was Cove's informal contact on his first tour through D.C., and that was a long time ago. Some folks might not make the connection. Though Sonny Venables tends to stand out," she added.

"You sound like you know him."

"Web, honey, when you've been around as long as I have, you tend to know everybody. I worked a lot with the D.C. cops."

"And Venable's willing to talk to me? Why?"

"The only thing he said was he had heard of you. And I threw my two cents in, for what it was worth."

"But we still don't know his take on things?"

"I guess that's up to you to find out." Ann clicked off.

Web called the number. Venables wasn't in, and Web left his name and cell number. Venables called him back twenty minutes later and the two arranged to meet later that afternoon. Web also asked him another question and Venables said he would see what he could do. If the guy could give Web a handle on Cove, then Web might be able to follow it up. However, something was bothering Web about Bates, namely that he had never told Web that Cove had worked at WFO before his stint in California. Not that it really mattered. He had given Web a look at the guy's file, and Web would have picked it up on his own, he supposed. He just hadn't had enough time to go through the man's entire history. But why not tell Web?

Venables had asked Web to meet him in the early afternoon at a bar around the area of his beat, nothing unusual about that. Web knew that that way you could quench your thirst and maybe over-hear some info that might help you crack a case later. Cops were nothing if not efficient with their time.

Sonny Venables was white, mid-forties and a veteran of almost twenty years on the force, he told Web as they were buying their beers. He was over six feet tall and beefy, the kind of body mass one got from pumping lots of weights; the man looked like he could military-press a semi. He wore a baseball cap that read ALL FISHER-MEN GO TO HEAVEN and wore a leather jacket with the NASCAR logo on the back. His neck was almost as thick as his very wide head. His voice had a twangy commonsense southern charm to it, and Web noted the circular outline of a can of tobacco chew in the back pocket of his jeans as they walked to a booth in the bar. They found a quiet corner and settled down with their beers.

Venables worked the night shift, he told Web. He liked it, more excitement. "Be hanging it up soon, though, right at twenty years. Go off and fish, drink beer and watch fast cars go around a little track the rest of my time, like most good cops do." He smiled at his own words and took a long pull of his Red Dog beer. From the jukebox Eric Clapton was going on and on about Layla. Web looked around. Two guys were playing pool in the back room, a stack of twenty-dollar bills and a couple of Bud Lights siting on the edge of the table. They occasionally glanced over at the booth, but if they recognized either Venables or Web, they made no sign of it.

Venables eyed Web over the rim of his beer mug. The man's face held enough wrinkles to be considered experienced and craggy. A man who had seen a lot in life, mostly bad, Web judged, just like him.

"Always wondered about you HRT guys."

"What's to wonder? We're just cops with a few more toys at our disposal."

Venables laughed. "Hey, give yourself some credit. I got a few FBI buddies who tried out for HRT and came back with their tails between their legs. Said they'd rather deliver a damn baby with just a stick between their teeth for the pain than go through that again."

"From the picture I saw of Randall Cove, he looked like he could've cut it at HRT."

Venables studied the head on his beer for a bit. "You're probably wondering what Randy Cove had in common with the likes of a redneck-looking gent like myself?"

"It crossed my mind."

"We grew up together in a backwater of Mississippi so small it never really did have a name. We played sports together all the way through because there wasn't much else to do around there. And our little backwater was state football champs two years in a row. We also played together at Oklahoma." Venables shook his head. "Randy was the greatest running back I ever saw, and the Sooners have turned out more than their share of those. I was fullback. First string, three years running, just like him. Blocked for Randy on every play. Threw my body in there like a damn runaway train and loved every minute of it, though I'm really starting to feel the effects of it now. See, you just needed to get Cove a little bit of daylight and that boy was gone. I'd look up from a pile of bodies and he'd already be in the end zone, usually with a couple of guys hanging on him. We were national champs our senior year and he was the reason. Oklahoma didn't believe in the forward pass back then. We just handed the damn ball off to Randy Cove and let him do his thing."

"Sounds like a friendship that would endure."

"It did. I never had the talent to play pro ball, but Randy sure as hell did. Everybody, and I mean everybody, wanted him." Venables stopped there and ran his fingers along the top of the table. Web decided to just wait the man out.

"I was with him at the combine when he blew out his knees. We both knew it, as soon as it happened. It wasn't like it is today. Just go in and clean it up and then you're back on the field the next year pretty much good as new. His career was over. Just like that. And football, man, football was all he had. We sat on that damn field and cried together for nearly an hour. I never even did that at my own mama's funeral. But I loved Randy. He was a good man."

"Was?"

Venables played with the pepper shaker and then sat back, tilted his cap farther up on his head and Web saw a lock of curly gray hair spring out.

"I take it you know what happened to his family," said Venables.

"I heard about some of it. Why don't you tell me what you know."

"What's to tell? Bureau screwed up and it cost Randy his wife and kids."

"You saw him back then?"

Venables looked like he wanted to throw his beer in Web's face. "I was a damn pallbearer at the funerals. You ever carry a four-year-old's casket?" Web shook his head. "Well, let me tell you, that's something you don't ever forget."

"Is that what Cove told you, that it was the Bureau's fault?"

"Didn't really have to tell me. I was a cop. I know how those things shake down. Ended up in D.C. because my wife's from here. Randy started out with the Feds here too. I guess you know that. Used me as a go-between because he knew he could trust me, and that's a rare thing in his line of work."

"It seems to be a rare thing in a lot of lines of work."

The two men shared a knowing look that seemed to come at a good time, perhaps strengthening a fledgling bond.

"Then Randy got transferred out to California and that's where his family got hit."

"I understand he took out his revenge."

Venables laid a cold gaze on Web, a look that clearly said the man had far more secrets than he would ever care to part with. "Wouldn't you have?"

"I guess maybe I would. Cove must really be something. The Russians are no lightweights."

"Try growing up the wrong color in shit-poor Mississippi." Venables leaned forward, putting his elbows on the table. "I heard about you. From the papers, some from Ann Lyle." He stopped and seemed to be checking Web out. Then Web realized Venables was staring at the messed-up side of Web's face.

"In almost twenty years on the force, I've pulled my gun maybe a dozen times, and fired it on six occasions. Four times I missed what I was shooting at, and twice I didn't. I've never been hurt on the job, not even a hangnail, and that's something to brag about in this town, especially these days. Now I'm in the First District, which isn't lily white and rich Northwest, but it's not exactly the Sixth and Seventh Districts in Anacostia, where your team got shot up. And I have great respect for guys on the thin blue line who've taken it and gotten back up. You seem like a damn walking ad for that."

"I never asked to be."

"Point is I respect you or else I wouldn't be sitting talking to you. But the thing is you'll never get me to believe that Randy has done anything wrong. I know undercover work screws with your mind and Randy's got no reason to feel good about the Bureau, but what happened to your team is not something he'd ever be a party to, I want you to understand that."

"And I want you to understand that while you seem sincere as hell and I wouldn't mind sharing another beer with you some other time, I can't accept a statement like that at face value."

Venables nodded in understanding. "Well, you'd be a real dumbshit, I guess, if you did."

"He could've walked away. I checked on that. Bureau offered him a new life, full pension. Why do you think he didn't take it?"

"And, what, spend the next forty years mowing his grass in a cookie-cutter suburb in the Midwest? That's not Randy. What else was he going to do except keep on plugging? It may sound funny, but he took pride in his work. He thought he was doing good."

"So do I. That's why I'm here. I'm going to find out the truth. If Cove was part of it, I may take out my revenge just like he did. I can't promise you I won't, friend of his or not. But if he had nothing to do with it, I'll be his best buddy. And believe me, Sonny, most folks would rather have me as a friend than an enemy."

Venables sat back and seemed to be considering this. Then he apparently made up his mind and hunched forward, eyed the pool players chalking their cues, smoking their cigs and sipping their beers, and started talking in a very low voice. "I have no idea where Randy is. Haven't heard from him since before this all went down. Way before, in fact."

"So he never talked to you about what he was working on?"

"You got to understand, I was his contact on his first gig through D.C. Now, I've seen him on his latest tour through here, but not for business, so to speak. I knew he was working on something pretty big, but he never told me what."

"So you two weren't that close anymore?"

"As close as you can be to somebody like Randy. After what happened to his family, well, I don't think he could really be close to anybody again. Not even to old Sonny Venables from Mississippi and all those damn blocks I threw for him."

"He ever mention another contact he might have been using on the force?"

"No, if he was using anybody, it would've been me."

"When's the last time you saw him?"

"Little over two months ago."

"How'd he seem?"

"Tight-lipped, mind somewhere else. Not looking too good, actually."

"He hasn't been back to his place in a while. The Bureau checked that out."

"I never knew where that was; we always met on neutral ground because of his work. We'd just talk about old times, really. Just somebody to talk to is what he wanted, I think. If he needed me to pass something on, I did."

"How'd he get in touch with you when he wanted to meet?"

"He'd never call me at home. Called at the precinct. Used a different name every time. And each time we met he'd tell me the new name he'd be using next when he called, so I'd know it was him."

"And he hasn't called?" Web eyed him closely. Venables appeared to be dealing straight with him, but one never really could be sure.

"No. Not one word. I started to worry something happened to him. In his occupation, that's a legitimate concern."

Web sat back. "So I guess you can't really help me track him down."

Venables finished his beer. "Let's take a walk."

They went outside and strolled down a street that was pretty empty. The workday wasn't over yet and most folks were probably still in their offices, counting the minutes until they could bolt, Web figured.

"On his first tour through WFO there was a place that Randy would use as a drop spot if he wanted to leave me a message. He told me he'd also use it to change clothes, as a safe house of sorts."

"The Bureau know about it?"

"No. Even back then I don't think he trusted the higher-ups at the Bureau all that much. That's why he used me, I guess."

"Probably a smart move. Have you been there lately?"

Venables shook his head. "Guess I'm a little afraid of what I might find, not really sure why. Don't even know if Randy uses it anymore. It could have been demolished, for all I know."

"Care to give me that address?"

"You smoke, don't you?"

"No, I don't."

"You do now." Venables pulled a pack of Winstons out of his coat pocket and handed it to Web, who took it. "Better light up, in case anybody's watching." Venables handed him a book of matches.

Web lit up and tried not to gag and then slipped the pack into his pocket. "I appreciate the help. But if Cove was involved . . ." He let his voice trail off.

"If Randy did something like that, I don't think he'd want to go on living."

As Sonny Venables walked off, Web went back to his car, ripped open the Winstons and clutched the rolled-up piece of paper inside. He looked at the address written on it. Also inside the pack of cigarettes were three small photos folded over. Web had asked Venables about any light-skinned black kids about Kevin Westbrook's age who had been reported missing in the city in the last month, and this obviously was what he had found. Web looked at the three photos; they were all slightly different versions of Kevin, he decided. All hopes of a decent life, their expressions told him, had already been torn from them. He drove off.

Twenty minutes later Web stared out the car window, his spirits hovering near an all-time low. Venable's offhand remark had proved to be right on target. Where once stood Randall Cove's old safe house there was an open construction pit; a tall crane rose in the middle of this hole, and a group of construction workers were just now walking off the job after what looked to Web to be a hard day's work. Judging from the degree of work already performed there, Web had to assume that Cove had not been using his old digs in the recent past. It was a total dead end. Web crumpled up the piece of paper with the address written on it and threw it on the floorboard. But he still had one more angle to take on Randall Cove.

He called Romano from the car. "You up for a little snooping around?"

He picked up Romano and they headed south toward Fredericksburg.

Romano looked around the car's interior. "What a piece-of-shit car."

"It's a Grand Marquis, the director is probably driven around in one of these."

"Still a piece of shit."

"I'll try to do better for you next time." He glanced at Romano and wondered what Angie told her shrink about him. With Romano as a significant other, she probably had a lot to talk about to a mental health professional.

"How're things at HRT?"

"Same old, same old. We haven't been called up for anything. Just training. I'm getting bored with that, man."

"Hang in there, Paulie, you'll be getting to fire your guns pretty soon."

"Maybe I should go join the French Foreign Legion or something like that."

"You just won't admit when you have it good."

"The guys been talking about you some, Web."

He should have been expecting this change in the conversation, but it still surprised Web. "So, what's the word?"

"Pretty even split for and against."

"Gee, I thought I was more popular than that."

"It's not that. Nobody thinks you're a coward, Web. You've done too much crazy stuff over the years. Almost as crazy as me."

"But . . ."

"But some of the guys think if you freeze once, you'll freeze again. What happened to you wouldn't have made a difference in what happened to Charlie Team, but next time it might."

Web stared straight ahead. "I guess I can't argue with that logic. Maybe *I* should go join the French. You armed?"

"Do politicians lie?"

R andall Cove lived on the outskirts of Fredericksburg, Virginia, roughly fifty miles south from Washington, D.C., and Cove's work arena, which roughly doubled Ann Lyle's twenty-five-mile rule of thumb on the minimum distance undercover agents should keep between their abode and their beat. Cove's home address was one of the pieces of information Web had surreptitiously read from Bates's file.

Just missing the brunt of rush-hour traffic, forty minutes later they pulled down the quiet suburban street where Randall Cove lived. It was a line of carbon-copy townhouses, many with rental signs out front. There were no moms or kids outside, though the weather was pleasant, and there were very few cars parked on the street. The community actually looked abandoned, and Web knew it would be until the commuters started arriving from D.C. and northern Virginia. This place had bedroom community written all over it, no doubt with mostly single people or childless couples living here until their salaries or expanded family demands prompted them to move. He could understand why Cove would pick such a place to live. No curious neighbors, people keeping to themselves and no one around during the day when he was probably at home. Most undercover agents in the drug arena did their hunting at night, he knew.

There was a government-plated Bucar parked in front of the house. "Fed babysitter," commented Romano. Web nodded and pondered how best to handle it. He drove up to the Bucar and he and Romano got out.

The agent rolled down his window, glanced at Web's and Romano's FBI identifications and then at Web.

"You're famous now, don't even need to show your creds," said the agent, whom Web didn't know. He was a young guy, full of vigor and promise, and Web figured he was probably hating life right now, watching a house no one expected Randall Cove to ever come near again. He got out of the car and extended his hand to the pair.

"Chris Miller, out of the Richmond Field Office." He flashed his own credentials, which he pulled from his right breast pocket so that he could shake with his strong hand, which was how the FBI trained you to do it. If the Bureau did nothing else, it enforced upon its agents a stark commonality of how they performed the smallest details. Without looking, Web knew that Miller had an extra layer of lining in his jacket so the gun he carried there wouldn't wear a hole in it. He also knew that when he had pulled in behind Miller and approached the car, Miller's gaze had been on the rearview mirror and then locked on Web's eyes, for eyes always told a person's intent.

The men shook hands and Web glanced at the quiet and dark townhouse. "You guys pulling round-the-clocks here?"

"Eight, eight and eight," said Miller wearily. He checked his watch. "And I've got three more hours on my shift."

Web leaned against the sedan. "So I take it not very exciting."

"Not unless you count a cat fight I watched about two hours ago." He paused, eyed Web closely and then blurted out, "You know, I've been thinking about trying out for HRT."

"Well, we can always use a few good men." *Six of them, in fact*, Web thought, *to rebuild Charlie Team*.

"I hear the tryouts are hellacious."

Romano almost snorted. "Take everything you've heard and raise it by a factor of ten, and then you're getting close to the truth."

From his skeptical look Miller obviously didn't buy that, Web could tell. Yet he was young and overconfident in his abilities, as the young always were.

"Were you at Waco?" Miller asked. Web and Romano nodded. "You get any shots off?"

"I've actually tried to banish it from my subconscious," said Web. *Wouldn't Claire Daniels be proud?*

"I could see that," said Miller in a doubtful manner that made Web feel sure the young agent actually did not get the point.

"How long you been with the Bureau?" asked Romano.

"Almost two years."

"Well, when you get the big three under your belt you can try out for HRT. Give me a buzz sometime. If you're serious about HRT, I can show you around." Romano handed him his card.

As Miller tucked the card away in his pocket, Romano and Web exchanged amused glances.

"Man, that would be great," said Miller. "I hear you guys have some awesome firepower."

The initial draw for many, Web knew, was the guns. Several men he knew had joined the Bureau solely for the opportunity to carry and fire fancy weapons. "That we do. And we'll show you exactly why it's always best if you *don't* have to use them."

"Right." Miller looked disappointed, but he would get over it, Web knew. There was an awkward silence, and then Miller asked, "Uh, can I help you guys with anything?"

"We just drove out here because I wanted to see the place. You know anything about the guy?"

"Not all that much. I know he's involved in what happened to you guys. Makes you wonder how somebody can turn like that, on their own kind, I mean."

"Yeah, it sure does." Web looked around the row of townhouses. They backed up to woods. "Hope you got somebody covering the rear."

Miller grinned. "*Something,* anyway. K-9s in the backyard. It's fenced in. Somebody tries to go in that way, they got a surprise. Cheaper than posting two agents out here, I guess."

"I guess." Web checked his watch. "Getting close to dinnertime. You eaten?"

Miller shook his head. "I brought some crackers and stuff along. And a bottle of water. Went through that. And like I said, I got three more hours before my relief shows up. Worst part is having no place to use the john."

"Tell me about it. Worked a bunch of surveillance details in the Midwest. Covered thousand-acre farms that were suspected drug distribution facilities and some trailer parks looking for good old boys that thought decent work included robbing banks and shooting people with sawed-off shotguns. Had to either hold it, pee in a bottle or just stand out in the fields and let it go."

"Yeah," said Romano. "And when I was a Delta we used to squat together in rows in whatever piece-of-shit place we were in and take our dumps. You get to know guys real well when you're crapping next to them. I had to shoot a guy once right when I was taking a shit. Man, let me tell you that was awkward."

Miller didn't look like any of those avenues of relief held sway with him. He was dressed very sharply, Web noted, and no doubt peeing in a bottle or taking the chance of exposing himself wasn't part of the young agent's image.

"There's a Denny's up the road. You want to take a dinner, we'll stay put until you get back."

Miller looked uncertain about abandoning his post.

"Offers like that don't come along every day, Chris." Web partially opened his jacket so Miller could see he was armed. "And yeah, I got some shots off at Waco. Go have yourself a good meal."

"You sure it'll be okay?"

Romano answered in his most intimidating voice. "If anybody comes along who shouldn't, they'll wish they got the dog over us."

At that, Agent Miller quickly got in his car and drove off.

Web waited until he was out of sight before he went to his trunk, pulled out a small device along with a flashlight, looked around and then walked with Romano up to the front door of Cove's house.

"Damn, that dude would last all of two minutes at HRT," said Romano.

"You never know, Paulie. You made it, didn't you?"

"You really gonna pop this place?"

"Yeah, I'm really gonna. You have a problem with that, go sit in the car."

"There's not much in life I have a problem with."

The pick gun made fast work of the simple front door lock and Web and Romano were inside in a few seconds. Web closed the door and turned on his flashlight. He saw the alarm panel next to the front door, but it was not armed. Presumably only Cove would have known the pass code. They walked down the short hallway and entered the living room. Web hit all corners with the light. Both men's hands were on their pistol grips. The place was very sparsely furnished. Cove probably didn't spend much time in here anyway, Web assumed. They did a quick search of the main floor and found nothing of interest, which didn't surprise Web. Cove was a veteran, and vets didn't exactly leave detailed records of what they were doing lying around for folks to find.

The basement was unfinished. There were a few boxes down there. Romano and Web quickly went through them. The only item Web lingered over was a framed photograph of Cove, his wife and their children. Web shone the light at an angle so it wouldn't reflect off the glass. Cove was in a suit, no dreadlocks in sight, his features handsome and confident. His smile was contagious. From simply looking at the photo, Web felt the corners of his mouth curl. One big arm was around his wife and the other enveloped both his children. His wife was remarkably beautiful, with shoulder-length hair, a big smile of her own and eyes that could have reduced any man to the quivers. The boy and girl favored their mother. They would have grown up into beautiful people, no doubt, at the same time their mother and father grew old together. That was how life was supposed to work out anyway, and rarely did, at least for people who did what Cove and Web did for a living. The photograph captured the other side of

Randall Cove, focusing on the man as husband and father. Web envisioned the former All-American tailback tossing a football to his son in the backyard; maybe the boy had inherited his old man's athletic skills. Perhaps he could've had the professional career that had been denied his father. In a Hollywood movie that might happen, but it rarely did in the unfairness of real life.

"Nice family," commented Romano.

"Not anymore." Web didn't bother to explain.

He put the photo back in the box and they headed upstairs. As his light glanced off the rear sliding door, something flung itself against the glass. In unison Web and Romano pulled their guns until they heard the barking and realized it was the K-9 doing its job.

Well, at least a dog would never rat on you; maybe that was the real reason they were man's best friends, thought Web. They kept your secrets to the grave.

They hustled to the upstairs level, wanting to be done long before Miller got back. Web didn't like conning a fellow agent, but he definitely didn't want to be caught conducting an unauthorized search of a major suspect's home. Bates would throw away the key on that one and Web probably couldn't blame him. There were two rooms up here connected by a bathroom. The front room that overlooked the street was Cove's bedroom. The bed was made and the closet held few clothes. Web lifted a shirt out and held it up to himself. Web could have almost fit his leg into one of the arms of the shirt. Web wouldn't have wanted to play defense against the man; one might as well try and tackle a van.

The room that was on the rear side of the house was empty. It was set up as a bedroom but apparently had never been used as one. The inside of the small closet had no hanger scratches on the walls, and the carpet held no imprints of furniture having been there. Web and Romano were about to leave when Web noticed something. He looked at the windows in this back room and then went through the connecting bath and into the front bedroom and looked at the windows there. They had miniblinds for privacy; logical, since this room overlooked the street. Web went back through the bathroom and into the other room. There were shades on these windows too but not miniblinds, noted Web; these were old-fashioned roll-up shades. The back bedroom overlooked dense woods, so privacy wasn't really an issue. Web looked out the window and saw where the sun was falling. The back room faced to the north, so it would get no afternoon light that required shades to block. And since the room wasn't being used, why have shades at all? And if one did elect some sort of window treatment, why not the same throughout the house? At least with miniblinds one could allow some light in and still have a reasonable degree of privacy. With shades it was all or nothing, and with little light back here as it was and no overhead light built in, this room would stay in perpetual darkness. It didn't make a lot of sense, but perhaps Cove had inherited this arrangement from a previous owner and had no interest in changing it.

"What's got your antenna up?" asked Romano.

"The man's choice in shades."

"You going feminine on me?"

Web ignored Romano and stepped to the window. The shades were fully pulled up. Web took the rope and jerked. The shade did its thing and came down, nothing out of the ordinary there. He stepped to the other window and did the same thing. The rope was stuck, and the shade did not come down. For an instant Web was about to just call it quits and leave. But then he shone his light up at the trip mechanism on the shade and saw that it had been bent such that the rope pull wouldn't work anymore. He bent the trip back into place and pulled on the rope. Down came the shade, and Romano gaped as the envelope that had been secreted in the rolled-up shade literally dropped into his hands.

Romano stared at him. "Damn, you are good at this."

"Let's go, Paulie." Web pulled the shade back up and they jogged down the stairs. Romano checked to make sure the coast was clear and then they slipped out. Web pulled the front door closed behind him.

Web and Romano got in their car and Web turned on the overhead light and settled down to review what they had found.

He opened the envelope and pulled out the yellowed news clipping. It was from the *Los Angeles Times,* and it was reporting on the deaths of an undercover agent's family at the hands of the Russian mafia. The official speaking on behalf of the Bureau gave a stinging attack on the criminals and vowed that they would be brought to justice. The official was identified as someone very close to the investigation. He was actually the case supervisor of the under-cover agent, whom they refused to identify even though the names of the slain family members had been made public. Web could only shake his head at the name of the Bureau official.

Percy Bates.

Miller drove up a few minutes later, got out and walked over to the car. He patted his belly. "Thanks for the assist, guys."

"No problem," said Romano. "We been there, done that."

"Anything come up while I was gone?"

"Nope, all clear."

"Hey, I'm off duty in about two hours. You guys interested in having a beer?"

"We—" Web glanced past Miller because the failing sunlight had just glanced off some reflective object in the distance.

"Web, look out," Romano cried out, because he obviously had seen the same thing.

Web reached across to Miller, grabbed his tie and tried to pull him down. The shot hit Miller dead center of the back and came through his chest, zipped right in front of Web and shattered the glass on the passenger side. Romano was already out of the car and behind one of the wheels. He poked the gun over the hood but didn't fire.

"Web, get the hell out of there."

For a split second Web held on to Miller's tie even as the young agent slid down the side of the car. The last thing Web saw was the dead man's eyes staring at him and then Miller hit the ground.

"Web, get your ass out of that car or I'll shoot you myself."

Wed ducked down as another shot shattered the rear side win-dow of the Bucar. Web slid out and took up position behind the rear wheel. At the Academy you were taught that squatting behind car wheels was the place to be because there were few weapons that could penetrate all that metal.

"You see anything?" asked Romano.

"Just that first reflection. Off a scope. A damn good thousand yards away, in the woods, between those two sections of town-houses. Miller's dead."

"No shit. I'm figuring something like a .308 chambering steel-jackets with a Litton ten-powerscope."

"Great, the same stuff we use," replied Web. "Just keep your damn head down."

"Oh, thanks for telling me, Web. I was just about to jump up screaming for my mommy."

"We can't fire back; our pistols don't have that range."

"Why don't you tell me something I don't know? You got any goodies in your trunk?"

"I would if it were my car."

Another shot hit the sedan and both men ducked. Yet another shot came and the left front wheel blew. Another and steam rose from the radiator.

"Don't you think somebody might try calling the cops?" complained Romano. "What, you got snipers in the suburbs every day?"

"My phone's in the car."

"Well, don't try and get it. Whoever's out there knows what he's doing."

They waited another five minutes and no more shots hit; then they could finally hear sirens in the distance. Web edged his head up over the side and looked through the car's windows. He didn't see any more reflections from the woods.

The police finally showed and Web and Romano held up their creds and motioned for the cops to get down. After another few minutes Web crawled over to the squad car and explained the situation. No more shots came and then apparently all the county cops showed up, along with a half dozen state troopers. The woods were combed without finding anyone, although a dirt road leading out to the main one on the other side of the subdivision Cove lived in had fresh tire tracks. And they also found a number of spent rifle shells. Romano had been right: steel-jacketed .308s.

Chris Miller was officially pronounced dead and the ambulance came and took him away. Web noted the wedding band on his finger before they zipped the body bag shut. Well, Mrs. Miller was going to get the dreaded visit from the Bureau tonight. He shook his head and looked over at Romano.

"I'm really getting sick of this life."

27

Web and Romano had given their statements about three times each. And Bates had come down and had taken a bite out of Web's butt for conducting an unauthorized investigation.

"I told you they'd be gunning for you, Web. But you stubborn son of a bitch, you just won't listen," ranted Bates.

"Hey, take it easy," said Romano.

"Do I know you?" said Bates, as he got right in Romano's face.

"Paul Romano, Hotel Team assaulter." He put out his hand.

Bates ignored the gesture and turned back to Web. "Do you realize that Buck Winters is looking for any excuse to squash you?" He glanced at Romano. "To officially cremate all of HRT? And you're playing right into his hands."

"All I'm trying to do is find out what happened to my guys," rejoined Web. "And you'd be doing the same thing if you were me."

"Don't you throw that bullshit in my face." Bates stopped cold because Web was holding up the newspaper clipping.

"I found this in the house."

Bates slowly reached out and took the clipping.

"You want to talk about it?" asked Web.

Bates led them away from the crime scene and over to a quiet slice of ground. He glanced at Romano and then at Web.

"He's okay," said Web. "Cleared for all sorts of top-secret stuff."

"Even did joint VIP protection on Arafat once," said Romano. "Now, you talk about a target, lots of people after that man."

"You didn't mention you were working with Cove when his family was killed," said Web.

"I don't owe you my life story," snapped Bates.

"Maybe you just owe me an explanation."

Bates folded the clipping up and put it in his pocket. "It was really nobody's fault. Cove didn't mess up and we didn't either. It was a fluke and the Russians got lucky. I wish I could take it back, but nobody can. Randy Cove is a hell of an agent."

"So Cove has no reason to be seeking payback?"

"No. I've talked to him. He almost got popped not that long after Charlie Team. He said he saw that building filled to the brim with everything that was supposed to be there."

"So his story is he got set up to feed us bad intel. Out went the files and in came the guns?" said Web.

"Something like that. It was a short time fuse. Cove said he was in the building shortly before you guys hit it. He thought he'd infiltrated a big-time drug op."

"Perce, I'm not looking to tell you how to do your job, but the smart thing may be to bring him in. With his cover blown, he sounds like he needs protection."

"Cove can take care of himself. And he can do more on the outside. In fact, he might be getting close to a big-time drug supplier."

"That I don't care about. All I want are the guys who set us up."

"That's just it, Web, they might be one and the same."

"Well, that doesn't make a lot of sense. Why would a drug supplier want to have the Bureau coming after them loaded for bear?"

"There could be any number of reasons. Paybacks, to keep distributors in line. Even to set up a rival to take the heat and reduce the competition."

"You let me have a crack at those guys," said Romano, "and I'll reduce something, like their life span."

"So I take it he's not reporting in regularly," said Web.

"How'd you know that?" said Bates.

"If he's really that good, he'll know that everybody thinks he's in on it. So he lies low, doesn't trust anybody and goes about his own investigation, trying to get to the truth before somebody gets him."

"That's a pretty good deduction."

Web said, "Actually, I'm just speaking from experience."

"Speaking of experience, I finally got a call back from Bill Canfield. I've got an appointment to meet him tomorrow at his farm. Care to join me?"

"I said I would. You want to come too, Paulie?"

Bates stared at him. "Are you the same Paul Romano that was with Delta Force and then New York SWAT?"

"There's only one Paul Romano," said Romano without a trace of conceit.

"Arafat, huh?"

"Hey, when you want to send the very best . . ."

"Good, consider yourself temporarily reassigned. I'll talk to your commander."

Romano looked stunned. "Reassigned doing what?"

"Doing what I tell you to do. See you two tomorrow."

Web dropped off Romano at home.

Before he got out, Romano said, "Hey, Web, you think this new gig pays more? Angie's been talking about getting a new washer-dryer and maybe finishing the basement."

"If I were you, I wouldn't mention anything like that to Angie. You'll be lucky if it doesn't pay less."

Romano shook his head as he got out. "Story of my life."

Web pulled away and drove aimlessly. He felt miserable about Chris Miller and didn't envy the people who would have to tell his wife. He hoped Miller didn't have any kids, but he looked like the kind who would. Damn, there was just too much misery in the world. Finally he decided he needed another dose of old-fashioned police work.

Web took the outer loop of the Capital Beltway around to Interstate 395, headed north and steered the Mercury Bates had gotten for him across the dilapidated Fourteenth Street Bridge that an airplane taking off from National Airport in a snowstorm had actually fallen on years ago. He pointed the car toward an area of town where few law-abiding citizens, other than those who were lost or those who carried a gun and a badge, ever dared venture, especially at this hour.

The scene was a familiar one to Web. It was the same route his squad had followed their last night on earth. Web knew the car and its government plates just screamed "Fed Man," but he really didn't care. For an hour he cruised up and down every dead-end street, every alley, every hole in the wall that looked promising. Several times he passed patrol cars that were nosing around looking for trouble, which here was akin to being a cat in an aviary: What you wanted was damn near everywhere.

He was just about to give it up when his gaze caught on the flash of red under a streetlight. He slowed the car, grabbed his trusty binoculars from the bag and got a better look. It was probably nothing, for many wore the do-rag here and many of them were red. Red for blood; even people down here had a sense of purpose and also humor about their work. A few seconds later Web's pulse kicked to a higher gear. The gent was even wearing the same clothes. A tank shirt over barbell shoulders and shorts below the butt crack. It was his good old neighborhood purveyor of fine crack cocaine and other illegal drugs from the alley where Charlie Team had run its last lap.

Web cut the car's engine, let the car drift to a stop and quietly got out. He thought about taking his shotgun but then decided his pistol would be enough. It was hard to pounce holding a shotgun. He gripped his pistol and slowly made his way down the street, keeping to the shadows. There was a streetlight under which he had to pass on his way to the kid. Just when he stepped into its pool of light, there came a scream from somewhere. The kid looked up, saw him. Web swore under his breath and took off running.

"Still want to deal on my rifle?" Web called out to him as he hustled forward.

The kid bolted down the alley. Web knew he shouldn't do it, not even armed, and he stopped. Going down that alley without any backup, he might as well phone in his casket order. It was still a tough decision because Web wanted Bandanna Boy in the worst sort of way. In Web's connect-the-dots manner of thinking, maybe Bandanna was the one who hit the remote that had activated the laser that had tripped the machine guns that had sent Web's dearest friends into oblivion. He finally made up his mind.

Another night, my friend. And next time I won't stop until my hands are around your damn neck.

Web turned to go back to his car. That's when he saw them coming. They seemed in no hurry. There were maybe a dozen of them Along with their elongated shadows against the brick he saw the array of weapons they were carrying. Cut off from his car, Web ducked down the alley and started running hard. He heard the group behind him do the same.

"Shit," he said to himself. Could anybody say setup?

The light from the street lamp was quickly left behind and Web could only rely on the presence of some dregs of ambient light from the sky and the sounds of running feet ahead and behind him. Unfortunately, in this high-walled labyrinth the echoes were not reliable guides. Web made lefts and rights until he was hopelessly lost. He turned one last corner and stopped. He imagined half the group had probably headed around to block his escape, though for all he knew he was running in circles. He thought he could still hear them coming, but he couldn't tell from where. He ducked down another alley and stopped. Listened. Quiet. Quiet he didn't like. Quiet meant stealth. He looked left, right and then up. Up. Up sounded good. He climbed a nearby fire escape and then froze. The footsteps were close. He soon saw why. Two of them came around the corner. They were tall, lean, with shaved heads and dressed in leather and baggy low-riding prison shuffle jeans and big jailhouse shoes with thick heels they were no doubt just itching to grind into Web's face.

They halted and looked around. They were directly underneath him. Just like Web had done, they looked left and then right. He figured it would only be a matter of seconds before—as he had done—they looked up. So he swung down and each foot collided with one head and both men slammed into the brick wall. Web landed a little awkwardly, his ankle twisting under him. Since each husky fellow was groaning and attempting to get up, he landed the butt of his pistol against the backs of their necks, and they went down for a long winter's nap. He grabbed their guns, threw them all into a Dumpster standing nearby and then sprinted off.

He could still hear running feet and also an occasional gunshot.

Web didn't know if it was his pursuers or simply your run-of-the-mill gangbanger dispute that happened around here every night. He rounded another corner and was hit low and hard. The impact knocked him off his feet, and he lost his weapon as he sprawled on the asphalt. He rolled and came up, fists cocked.

Bandanna Boy was standing there, a knife almost as big as he was in hand. He was grinning the same shit-eating grin that he'd had in the alley on the night that Charlie Team had disappeared.

Web noted he held the weapon with some skill. The kid probably had fought a hundred knife fights. He was shorter than Web, yet more muscular, probably quicker. This was to be a classic test of youth against experience. "Well, come on and eat some experience, young man," muttered Web as he prepared to defend himself.

The kid lunged at Web, whipping the knife blade around so fast Web could hardly follow. Yet he didn't really have to, because Web executed a loop kick that clipped Bandanna's legs out from under him and he went down hard. The kid was up quickly, but only in time to take one of Web's size twelves to the head. With the kid stunned, Web was all over him. He locked down the arm holding the knife and proceeded to break Bandanna's grip on both the knife and his forearm. With his security of the blade gone and a jagged shaft of his forearm staring him in the face, the kid fled, his cries of pain sweeping the alley with him, and his shit-eating attitude lying next to the knife on the bloody ground. Web shook his own fuzzy head clear and started to stumble over to retrieve his gun. He never made it.

Web could only watch silently as the group of men appeared from all corners, blocking the path to his weapon. They carried sawed-off shotguns and pistols. Web could sense they were all so very happy to see him here, outnumbered as he was ten to one. Web figured he had nothing to lose by taking an aggressive posture. He held out his FBI shield. "I could bust every one of you on weapons charges. But I tell you what, I'm feeling generous and not up to all the paperwork, so you just pack up and go about your business, and we'll forget about it. For now. But don't be pulling this shit again."

Their response was to move forward. Web's response to that was to move back until he felt the wall behind him, and further retreat and ultimate escape would have to be confined to his imagination. Then two of the crew directly in front of him were tossed to the side so violently it was like gravity had been suspended from underneath them. In this gap Web found himself staring up at the largest man he had ever seen outside a professional football game. The giant was six-foot-six or -seven and if he carried less than four hundred pounds on his frame, Web didn't know how. He realized that this new antagonist must be the legendary Big F.

The man was dressed in a short-sleeved burgundy-colored silk shirt that was so large Web could have used it for a blanket. Beige linen pants covered long legs that actually looked short, so thick and massive were they. He had on no socks, his bare feet were in suede loafers and his shirt was open to the navel, even though it was only about fifty degrees with a sneaky little breeze that quickly got under one's skin. His skull had a shadow of fuzz covering it. His facial features matched his great size, with a heavy blob of nose and conical ears, each pierced with about a dozen diamond studs that gleamed impressively even in the poor light.

He wasted no time and strode right up to Web. When Big F reached out to grab a fistful of him, Web delivered a vicious blow to the man's gut that would have dropped a heavyweight boxer. All he got from Big F was a grunt. Then he lifted Web off the ground, reared back like he was preparing to hurl a shotput and threw the two-hundred-pound Web a good ten feet down the alley. The rest of the gang hooted, cursed and otherwise had themselves a little federal agent ass-kicking party, high-fiving, exchanging growls and knuckle-banging each other with animalistic glee.

Web had not even gotten to his feet before the man was on him again. This time he hooked Web by his belt, lifted him up and sent him sailing into a line of garbage cans. Web came up fast, gagging for air and nauseous with the pounding he was taking. Before Big F could get to him, Web shot forward, lowered his shoulder and laid his very solid frame directly into the man's gut. Web might as well have slammed himself into a pickup truck, for all the good it did. He dropped to the asphalt without having budged Big F one damned inch. His shoulder felt dislocated. Web got to his feet, feigned being seriously hurt and then exploded with a leaping kick that caught Big F flush on the side of the head. Splotches of blood appeared at the corner of Big F's ear, and Web noted with satisfaction that he had relieved the man of some of his diamond studs, leaving jagged bits of earlobe in their bloody wake.

Yet Big F was still standing, like one of the brick buildings surrounding them. Web had knocked hundred-pound body bags right off their supports with that kick. How could this be? Well, he had no time really to think about how it could be because Big F, moving faster than a man his size should ever have been able to, delivered a forearm the size of a six-by-six to the side of Web's head that came one dizzying star from knocking him out. A few seconds later, Big F was half carrying and half dragging Web down the alley, his shoes and jacket lost somewhere along the way. His pants were ripped and his legs and arms were bleeding from being dragged over the pavement.

Apparently just for fun, since Web was putting up no further resistance, Big F tossed him headfirst against a Dumpster. This did knock out Web, and he stayed that way until he felt himself being thrown onto something soft. He opened his eyes; it was the interior of the Mercury. He flinched when he saw Big F slam the door and walk away. The guy hadn't said one word, and Web had never been more humbled in his life. No wonder Granny and Jerome had acted the way they had. Hell, Jerome was probably still running.

Web sat up slowly and felt around for broken bones. When he opened his right hand a paper fluttered out of it. Web saw the numbers and words scribbled on it, looked over in amazement at where Big F had been but was no longer. He put the slip of paper in his pocket, pulled out his keys, revved up the Mercury and burned rubber off the rear wheels getting the hell out of there, leaving behind his jacket, his shoes, his pistol and a big chunk of his confidence.

28

It was early in the morning and Web was soaking in the tub in another crummy motel. Every part of him ached. The long scrapes on his arms and legs burned like there was a branding iron pressed to them. He had a knot on his forehead from where his noggin had met Dumpster and a gash along the good side of his face that probably still had some grains of asphalt inside. Boy, he was aging really well. He should try out for male modeling when he left the Bureau.

The phone rang and Web swung his hand out and snagged it. It was Bates.

"I'll pick you and your buddy up in an hour at Romano's house."

Web groaned.

"What's wrong?" asked Bates.

"Late night. Got a bitch of a hangover."

"Oh, I'm so sorry, Web. One hour. Be there or find another planet to live on." Bates hung up.

Exactly one hour later Bates picked up Web and Romano and they headed to Virginia horse country.

Bates looked at Web's fresh injuries. "What the hell happened to you?" asked Bates. "You better not have trashed another car, because after the Mercury you're riding a bicycle." Bates glanced over at Web's car parked at the curb.

"I slipped getting out of the bathtub."

"You did all that getting out of the tub?" Bates clearly did not believe this.

"You know what they say, Perce, most accidents happen at home."

Bates stared at him for a long moment before deciding not to pursue it. He had a lot of other items on his to-do list.

After an hour's drive they got off the highway and drove for miles along twisting roads and hairpin curves bracketed by thick woods. They missed a turn somewhere because they ended up on a dirt road barely wide enough for their car. Web looked over at a sagging metal gate and the sign next to it that read, EAST WINDS FARM NO HUNTING, FISHING OR TRESPASSING. VIOLATORS PROSECUTED TO THE FULLEST EXTENT OF THE LAW.

East Winds, they knew, was the name of the Canfield farm. They must have come in on the rear side, Web concluded. He smiled as he read the sign. Well, damn, these people meant business; he was shaking with fear. He glanced at Romano, who was looking at the sign and smiling too because he was probably thinking the same thing. The fencing here was low, rail board on post. The place was in the middle of nowhere. "Somebody who knew what they were doing could hop that fence in a second, go to the main house, kill the Canfields and everyone else there, have a drink, watch some TV and no one would probably know until the spring thaw," opined Romano knowledgeably.

"Yeah, and since murder isn't one of the offenses listed on the sign," added Web, "I guess he'd be free from prosecution."

"Keep that crap to yourself," growled Bates. However, Web could tell the guy was worried. This place was vulnerable.

They finally found the correct turn and reached the front entrance to East Winds. The gates reminded Web of the ones in front of the White House. And yet with all the exposed property, the big gates were a joke from a security perspective. Above the entrance was an arch of metal scrollwork with the name of the farm written large. And to top it all off, the gates were open! There was a call box, however, and Bates hit the button. They waited and someone finally came on.

"Special Agent Bates with the FBI."

"Come on up," said the voice. "Follow the main road and take the first right up to the main house."

As Bates pulled forward, Web pointed out, "No closed-circuit TV. We could be Charlie Manson and company, for all they know."

They headed straight. The rolling green land stretched as far as they could see, much of it enclosed by horizontal rail fencing. Large rolls of hay lay in the fields. Off to one side was a small pond. The main road was asphalt and ran straight for a while and then curved right around a swath of towering oak and hickory, with scrub pines wedged between. Through the trees to the right they caught glimpses of an enormous structure.

They finally came to a large two-story stone house with high Palladian windows and broad sliding doors below and topped with a large tin-sheathed cupola patinaed by the elements, with a weather vane of a horse and rider mounted on top. To Web it looked like a color Martha Stewart might try to copyright and then sell to the masses as something far more chic than simple weather rot.

They turned right, away from the carriage house, and passed down a long paved drive. Some of the largest maple trees Web had ever seen were situated in rows on each side of the drive, forming a natural roof of limbs and leaves.

Web looked up ahead and his eyes widened. It was the largest house he had ever seen and it was constructed all from stone, with an enormous front portico supported by six massive columns.

"Damn," said Romano, "that looks to be about the size of the Hoover Building."

Bates parked the car in front and started to get out. "It's a house, Romano, and put your tongue back in your mouth and try not to embarrass the Bureau."

The massive door opened and a man stood there.

Billy Canfield had not aged well, thought Web.

He was still tall and trim, but the broad shoulders and deep chest—which Web remembered from the man's visits to Web in the hospital—had fallen in. His hair was now thinner and almost fully gray and the face had grown even craggier. As Canfield walked out to see them, Web noted the limp in the man's gait and he saw where one knee turned inward more than normal. Canfield, he figured, would be in his early sixties now. Fifteen years ago he had married for the second time, to Gwen, a woman much younger than he was. He had grown children from his first marriage, and he and Gwen had also had their own boy, the ten-year-old who had been killed by members of the Free Society at the school in Richmond. Web still

saw David Canfield's face often in his dreams. The guilt had not lessened over the years; if anything, it had grown more intense.

Canfield eyed each of them fiercely from under thick tufts of
eyebrows. Bates put out his strong hand and held up his credentials with the other, just like the Bureau taught you, observed Web.

"I'm Agent Bates with the FBI's Washington Field Office, Mr.
Canfield. Thanks for letting us come out."

Canfield ignored Bates and instead looked over at Web. "I know
you, don't I?"

"Web London, Mr. Canfield. I'm with Hostage Rescue. I was down
in Richmond that day," he added diplomatically. "You visited me in
the hospital. That meant a lot to me. I want you to know that."

Canfield nodded slowly and then put out his hand to Web, who
shook it. "Well I appreciate what y'all tried to do then. You did all
you could, risked your life and all for my boy." He stopped and
looked over at Bates. "But I told you on the phone that nothing's
happened out here and if that son of a bitch comes my way he'll
end up dead and not the other way round."

"I understand that, Mr. Canfield."

"Billy."

"Thank you, Billy, but you have to understand that three people
with a connection to what happened at that school in Richmond,
and possibly a fourth person, have already been killed. If the Free
Society is behind it, and I have to tell you that as yet we have no direct proof that they are, but if they are, you could be a target. That's
why we're here."

Canfield looked at his watch. "And what, you want to put me
under lock and key? I got a damn horse farm to run, and let me tell
you it don't run on autopilot."

"I understand that, but there are unobtrusive steps we can
take—"

"Y'all want to keep talking, you got to come on with me. I got
things to do."

Bates exchanged glances with Web and Romano and then
shrugged. They followed Canfield over to a jet-black Land Rover
and climbed in.

Canfield didn't wait for seat belts to be put on. He hit the gas and they sped off. Web was in the front seat next to him. As they drove along, he surveyed the farm.

"Last I heard, you owned a trucking company in Richmond. How'd you end up on a horse farm in Fauquier County?"

Canfield slipped a cigarette out of his shirt pocket and lit up, cracked the window and blew smoke out. "Gwen doesn't let me smoke in the house. Take my shots when I can," he explained. "Now, that's a damn good question, Web, from trucking to horses. I ask myself that sometimes and sometimes I wish I was back in trucking. I was born and bred in Richmond and like it there. That city creeps into your bones for better or worse, and I've seen both sides of that coin.

"But Gwen's always loved horses; she grew up on a farm in Kentucky. I guess it gets in your blood too. All it's done for me is make my blood *pressure* go through the roof. Anyway, we decided to make a go of it. Jury's still out on how we're doing. Sunk every damn dime I have into this place, so at least we have the incentive to make it work."

"What exactly do you do on a horse farm?" asked Romano as he leaned forward. "See, the only horses I've seen are the ones that pull the carriages around Central Park. I grew up in the Big Apple."

"Sorry to hear that, Yank," said Canfield. He looked around at Romano. "Didn't catch your name."

"Romano, Paul Romano. Friends call me Paulie."

"Well, we're not friends, so I'll just call you Paul. Now, the main thing you do on a horse farm is bleed money, Paul. Bleed it like it's ice in a damn hailstorm. You pay out your ass for a property like this and all the people to help run it. You get you some horses and they eat you out of house and home. You pay outrageous stud fees so some son-of-a-bitching horny stallion with a few track victories to its name will impregnate your mares. And then nature delivers you some foals that proceed to chip away at what little money you got left. As the foals grow into yearlings, you spend enough on the little sons of bitches to send a dozen kids to Harvard. And then you hope and pray that maybe one of 'em shows some promise and you can sell it to some poor sucker and maybe get a five percent return on your money for working your ass off sixteen hours a day. And if you don't, then the bank that you've sold your life to comes and takes every single thing you've ever owned in your whole life and you die dirt poor without a roof over your head, a stitch of clothes on your back or a single person you could call a friend." He looked back at Romano. "That's about it, *Paul*. You got any other questions?"

"Nope, that about covers it," said Romano as he sat back.

They reached a compound consisting of barns, stables and other buildings, and Canfield drove underneath a pediment wooden arch that Canfield said was based upon the one at George Washington's Mount Vernon; only that it cost more.

"This is the equestrian center. Horse stalls, big hay barn, manager's office, trainers work center, wash stalls, riding rings and the like. God's Little Acre if ever there were one," said Canfield, and he laughed as he climbed out of the Rover. The FBI agents followed him.

Canfield called out to a man who was talking to a number of what looked to Web to be farmhands. "Hey, Nemo, come on over here for a sec."

The man walked over. He was about Web's height, yet burly, with the powerful physique of someone who worked with his body for a living. He had short, wiry black hair, slightly graying at the temples, and strong, handsome features. His clothes were clearly ranch: loose-fitting jeans and a faded denim shirt. Pointed-toe boots were on his feet. They weren't fancy, no alligator or kangaroo skin and no silver toe clips. They were dusty and creased from hard use and worn away where Web figured stirrups met the leather. Muddy canvas gloves stuck out from his back pocket. He took off his sweat-stained Stetson as he walked over and wiped his brow with a rag.

"Nemo Strait here is my farm manager. Nemo, this is a bunch of folks from the FBI. They've come here to tell me I'm in danger because they let the asshole that killed my son break out of jail and he might be gunning for me."

Strait gave them all a terrifically unfriendly stare.

Web put out his hand. "I'm Agent Web London."

Strait shook his hand, and Web felt the extra force the man gave to the grip. Nemo Strait was a very strong gent and obviously wanted to let Web know it. Web caught the man checking out his damaged mug. For most it evoked sympathy, which Web loathed. Nemo, though, came away just looking a little surlier, as though he had suffered far greater wounds on a good day. Web instantly liked the man.

Canfield pointed at Web. "Now, this fellow here actually tried to save my boy, which is more than I can say for some others involved in the process."

"Well, in my opinion the government's not good for much 'cept messing up folks' lives," said Nemo, looking at Web. His voice was pure country, with little dips in between each syllable, mimicking the bobbing of his prodigious Adam's apple. For some reason, Web envisioned big Nemo performing country and western karaoke and being just a stitch at it.

Web looked over at Bates, who said, "What we're trying to do here is help you, Billy. If somebody tries something with you, we want to be here to stop it."

Canfield surveyed his property and then stared at Bates. "I got ten men full-time on my farm and every one of them is pretty good with a gun."

Bates shook his head. "We waltzed right in here and you didn't even know who we were. You came out the front door unarmed and alone. If we were looking to kill you, you'd already be dead."

Canfield smiled. "What if I told you I had some of my boys watching you from the time you stepped on the property? And that they were pointing something at you that wasn't their fingers?"

Web and Romano glanced around without seeming to do so. Web had a sixth sense about people aiming guns his way and he was wondering why it hadn't kicked in.

"Then I'd tell you your *boys* probably would end up shooting some innocent people," said Bates.

"Well, hell, that's what I got insurance for, I guess," Canfield shot back.

"I checked the records, Billy. During the trial you received death threats from Ernest Free among others. The Bureau put you under protection then."

Canfield's features grew very grim. "That's right, every time I turned around there was some suit with a gun staring at me and reminding me that my little boy was dead and buried. So, no of-fense, but I've had enough of you folks to last the rest of my life. That's about as clear as I can make it."

Bates squared his shoulders and got closer to Canfield. "The Bu-reau is offering you protection again. And until Ernest Free is caught and we're sure that you're not in danger, I'm kind of insist-ing on it," added Bates.

Canfield folded his arms across his chest. "Well, then we got us a problem, because this is the United States of America and a per-son has the right to choose who comes on his property and who doesn't and I'm asking you to get the hell off my land right now." Strait moved closer to his boss and Web saw some of the other farmhands also draw nearer. He also noted that Romano's hand had eased to his pistol grip.

One big fellow made the truly enormous mistake of putting his hand on Romano's shoulder. In an instant the man was facedown on the ground, Romano's knee against the base of his spine, one .45 in the guy's ear, and another .45, which Romano had pulled from the second holster he wore on the back of his waistband, pointed at Canfield's other men.

"Okay," said Romano, "any of you other buckaroos want to bring it on?"

Web quickly stepped forward before Romano killed them all. "Look, Billy, I shot two of the Frees, and if I had gotten the chance I would have blown Ernest away too. But the bastard got lucky and took a round through his shoulder instead, and I walked out with half a face and missing most of my blood. Now, I really believe that we all want the same thing here; we're just differing a bit on how to get there. What if Romano and I came to stay with you on the farm? No suits, just jeans and boots. We'll even help with the work. But in exchange you have to cooperate with us. You'll have to lis-ten to us when we tell you there might be a problem, and if we tell you to get your butt down, you get down. It looks like the Frees have already taken out several people and they did it in ways that were pretty damn ingenious. So while I'm sure your men are really good at what they do, it might not be enough if these people really want to take you out. I can see that you're not the sort of guy who likes other people to tell you what to do, but I also don't believe you want to give the Frees the satisfaction of killing you. You and your wife have already been through that hell with your son. I don't believe you want her to have to grieve again over you."

Canfield looked at Web a long moment. And for that entire time Web wasn't sure if the man was going to jump him or maybe order his men to open fire. Finally, Canfield looked down and kicked the dirt. "Let's go on back to the house and talk about this." He motioned for Strait and his men to go back to work. Romano helped the man up and even dusted him off.

"Nothing personal, slick, I would've done that to anybody who touched me. Get the message?"

The man grabbed his hat and hustled off. From the look of fear in the man's eyes, Web didn't think he'd be "touching" Romano ever again.

Canfield and the agents climbed in the Rover. As they were driving back, Canfield looked over at Web.

"Okay, I'm not disputing that what you say makes a lot of sense, but I'm not looking forward to revisiting that part of my life. And I'm kind of hating it that these assholes are pulling me back into that shit hole."

"I understand that, but—" Web was interrupted by the ringing of a cell phone. He checked his phone, but it wasn't his. Bates and Romano did the same thing. Canfield pulled a phone out of a storage panel in the Rover and looked at it. It wasn't ringing. He glanced at the floorboard and reached down and picked up the phone that was lying there.

"Somebody must have left their phone in here, although it's not Gwen's and I don't know who the hell else drives this truck. Probably somebody wanting to sell me something." He was about to punch the talk button when Web grabbed the phone out of his hand, hit the window button on his door and threw the phone out.

Canfield looked at him. "What in the hell do you think you're doing?"

They watched as the phone flew through the air and then hit the ground in the middle of an empty dirt field. Nothing happened. Canfield pulled the Rover to a stop. "You get your ass out there and go get that damn phone—"

The explosion was powerful enough to rock the Land Rover and send a cloud of black smoke and flames a hundred feet in the air.

All the men stared at this fiery spectacle for several seconds. Finally a shaken Canfield looked over at Web. "When do you boys wanta start?"

29

Web drove down the street to his mother's home. He still didn't know what the hell to do with it. To sell it would require him to fix it up and he would have to do that himself, since his bank account wouldn't allow the convenience of hiring professionals to do it. And yet he had no desire to tighten one hinge or replace one shingle on the place.

Web was here because it had occurred to him that if he was going to be staying out at the farm for a while he would need some clothes. He didn't want to go back to his own home right now. The reporters were probably still staking it out. However, he kept some clothes at his mom's house too. He also wanted to return the box containing much of Harry Sullivan's life to the attic. Being constantly on the move now, Web didn't want to chance losing it. He also wasn't sure what to do about his father. Should he call the main prison? Was that the place to get reacquainted with his old man? Yet chances were, at his age, Harry Sullivan was going to die in prison. This might be Web's only shot. It was funny how almost being blown to bits by a bomb in a phone made you reorder your priorities.

His musings about his father stopped when his phone rang. It was Claire, and she sounded nervous yet determined.

"I've been giving our sessions a lot of thought, Web. I think we need to change tactics somewhat. I'm curious about a few things and I think they can be better addressed in a different sort of way."

"Well, that's incredibly vague, Claire. What exactly are you talking about?"

"From our discussions so far, Web, it seems to me that many of your issues stem from your relationship with your mother and stepfather. During our last session you told me that you had grown up in your mother's house and that you had recently inherited it from her."

"So?"

"And you also mentioned that you would never consider living there. Also that your stepfather died there."

"Again, so what?"

"I think there might be something else there. You remember I said I listen for cues from my patients? Well, I'm getting a big one from you here."

"What does an old house have to do with my *issues*?"

"It's not the house, Web, it's what might have happened in the house."

He persisted. "What might have happened in the house other than my stepfather kicking the bucket that has anything to do with me?"

"Only you know that."

"And I'm telling you that's all I know. And I really don't see how my freezing in an alley has anything to do with my growing up in that house. That was a long time ago."

"You'd be amazed, Web, at how long the mind can keep something under wraps until it erupts one day. Your encounter with the little boy in the alley could have triggered something from your past."

"Well, I'm telling you I don't know what that is."

"If I'm right, you do know, Web, only your conscious mind doesn't realize it."

He rolled his eyes. "What kind of psychobabble crap is that?"

In response Claire said, "Web, I'd like to hypnotize you."

He was stunned. "No."

"It really could help us get somewhere."

"How can making me bark like a dog while I'm unconscious help?"

"Being in a hypnotic state is a form of *enhanced* consciousness, Web. You'll be aware of everything going on around you. You will be in complete control. I can't make you do anything you don't want to."

"It won't help."

"You can't know that. It can allow you to address some issues you ordinarily would be inhibited from doing."

"There are some things in my head maybe I don't want to figure out."

"You never know, Web, until you try. Please think about it. Please."

"Look, Claire, I'm sure you've got lots of crazy people to help. Why don't you think about them for a while." He clicked off.

Web pulled his car into the driveway, went inside, packed a duffel of clothes and then hesitated at the bottom of the attic stairs, holding the Harry Sullivan box under one arm. This really shouldn't be so hard, he told himself. An attic was an attic. Though he had told Claire otherwise, there was something about this house that had rattled him somewhere deep in his soul. Yet he reached up, gripped the cord and pulled down the stairs.

When he got to the attic, he put the box down and reached for the light cord but then drew his hand back. He looked to the various corners, seeking out threats, an endeavor that was now more instinct than habit. He drew his gaze across the plywood floor and then to all the blackened shapes of his family's bleak history, in the form of clothes racks, piles of books, heaps of junk left to rot. The stack of burgundy-colored rug remnants near the stairway held his attention. They were tightly rolled and bound with tape. He picked one up. It was heavy and very hard, stiff as it was with both cold and age. The remnants matched the rug on the floor below and Web wondered why his mother had kept them.

Off to the side there once had been a large pile of clothes. Now the space was empty. Web had sometimes come up here, pulled the attic door closed after him and hidden under the clothes pile during his stepfather's many rampages. His stepfather had also kept his stash of drugs and special liquor up here too, because he feared his wife getting her hands on them. He would stumble up here in the middle of the night, already wasted, and seek out additional means to do his mind further damage. It was the early seventies, the country still digging itself out from Vietnam, and people like his stepfather, who had never taken up arms for his country or for any other cause, used the general angst and indif-

ference of the times as an excuse to live life on a perpetual high.
Part of the attic floor was also over the ceiling of Web's bedroom.
When he was young and in bed, Web would hear his stepfather's
footsteps overhead as the man sought out his mood-altering substances. Young Web would be terrified that Stockton might come
crashing down through the ceiling, to land on top of him, and
beat the hell out of him. A cobra in your bed, kill or be killed.
When Stockton did beat him Web would have gone to his mother,
but most of the time she was not there to console him. She often
took long drives at night and came home in the morning, hours
after Web had dressed and fed himself and rushed off to school so
he wouldn't have to confront the old man across the breakfast
table. The creak of steps still bothered him to this day. He closed
his eyes and breathed in the chilly air, and in his mind that old,
vanished pile of clothes rose high into the air. And then right on
cue there was a slash of red and then sounds flooded him that
made Web open his eyes and rush back down the stairs and close
the attic door. He had had this vision a thousand times and could
never figure it out. He had gotten to the point where he didn't
want to decipher it, but for now, for some reason, he felt like he
was closer to its true meaning than ever before.

He sat in the Mercury and pulled out his cell phone and the piece
of paper Big F had given him the night before. He checked his
watch. It was right at the time the paper said to call. He punched in
the numbers and the phone was immediately answered. He was
given a set of instructions and then the line went dead. At least they
were an efficient bunch. Well, he was going to have a busy night.

As he drove off, he paraphrased the immortal words of TOC:

"Web London to the rest of the human race, *nobody* has control."

30

Web drove to Romano's house and picked him up. Angie was standing in the doorway when Romano came out with his bags and she didn't look very happy. At least, Web deduced this when he waved to Angie and got the finger in return for his troubles. Romano loaded two sniper rifles, an MP-5, a set of Kevlar and four semiautomatic pistols along with ammo clips for each into the trunk.

"Christ, we're not going after Saddam, Paulie."

"You do it your way and I'll do it mine. The guy who blew away Chris Miller is still out there and if he's getting off thousand-yard shots at yours truly, then I want to be able to shoot the son of a bitch back. Capeesh?" He turned and waved to Angie. "Bye-bye, sweetie-pie."

Angie flipped him the bird too before slamming the door behind her.

"I take it she's upset," said Web.

"I had some leave time. We were supposed to go see her mother in bayou country. Slidell, Louisiana, to be exact."

"I'm sorry, Paulie."

Romano looked at him and smiled, before pulling his Yankees cap over his eyes and settling back in his seat. "I'm not."

They drove to East Winds, where they were met at the gate by a pair of FBI agents. They showed their creds and were allowed in. The Bureau presence was here in its full glory after the attempted murder of Billy Canfield via exploding cell phone. The Bureau's bomb squad van passed them going out, no doubt with every bit of evidence they could scrounge from the debris. Web felt sure that Bureau agents were interviewing everyone on the farm who might be remotely connected with where that phone might have come from. Web was also sure Billy Canfield would be less than thrilled with all that activity. Yet at least he had saved the man's life. That had gotten them entry into the farm.

He had just finished this thought when a horse and rider came into view. It was a big, glossy Thoroughbred with a perfect blending of shimmering muscle, tendon and bone, all moving in a delicate synchronicity that made it seem more machine than animal. Web had ridden a few times but had never really gotten into it, and yet he had to admit, the sight was really something to behold. The rider was dressed in brown riding britches, high, polished black boots and a light-blue cotton sweater. The hands were gloved. The black riding helmet failed to fully cover the long blond hair.

He rolled his window down as the woman rode the horse over to the car.

"I'm Gwen Canfield. You must be Web."

"I am. This is Paul Romano. Did your husband tell you the arrangement?"

"Yes. He asked me to show you to where you'll be staying," said Gwen.

She took off her helmet, pulled back her blond hair and it fell across her shoulders.

Web looked at the horse and said, "She's a beauty."

"It's a he."

"Sorry, didn't check the equipment. Didn't want to embarrass anybody."

She patted the horse's neck. "Baron doesn't mind, do you? Secure in your masculinity, aren't you?"

"We should all be so lucky."

Gwen eased a bit back on the small English-style riding saddle, one hand firmly holding on to the double loop of reins, and looked around. "Billy told me what happened in the Rover. I want to thank you for what you did. Billy probably forgot to."

"Just doing my job." Though he had never met Gwen, other HRT members at the trial in Richmond had described her as high strung and emotional. This woman was very calm, almost detached in a way; despite her words of gratitude her tone was subdued. Maybe she had just used up all the emotions she had back then.

Web had seen pictures of Gwen Canfield taken by the media at the trial. Unlike her husband, Gwen had aged very well. She was, he figured, in her mid- to late thirties. Her blond hair was still long. Her figure was that of a woman ten years younger, with curves where men enjoyed seeing them and a bosom that would never fail to draw stares. Her features were lovely, with high cheekbones and full lips. If she had been an actress, the camera would have fallen in love with her. She was also tall and carried herself very erect. The horse rider's posture, Web assumed.

"We're going to the carriage house. It's right down this road."

Gwen turned Baron around, punched the horse in the sides with her boots, gave a loud call that sounded indecipherable to Web yet in horse language must have meant gallop like holy hell, because that's exactly what old Baron did. Horse and rider flew down the road. Then Gwen leaned forward, actually blending in with the horse's torso as Baron lifted off the ground, clearing the three-foot slanted jump-in fence line—a breach in the fence designed to allow horse and rider to pass through—landing in one of the paddocks and galloping on without missing a step. Or hoof. Web honked his horn in applause, and Gwen waved without looking back.

The carriage house, as it turned out, was the place with the big Palladian windows and patinaed weather vane Web had seen earlier. Gwen dismounted from Baron and tethered him to a post. As they were unloading their stuff from the car, Web gave Romano a sign not to unpack his weapons in front of the woman.

Web looked at the location of the carriage house and its relation to the main house, which he could barely see down the long, tree-lined road. He turned to Gwen. "I don't mean to sound ungrateful, but would it be possible for us to stay in the main house? If anything goes down, it might take us a little too long to get to you."

"Billy said the carriage house. If you have a problem with that, you'll have to take it up with him."

Well, I guess I will, Web told himself. To her he said, "I'm sorry about all this, Mrs. Canfield. You shouldn't have to go through this again."

"I never assume the world is fair anymore." She looked at him closely. "I'm sorry, Billy said that we know you, but I don't remember from where."

"I was part of the Hostage Rescue Team that was at the school that day."

She looked down for a moment. "I see. And now that man is loose again. The one who killed David."

"Unfortunately, yes. But hopefully not for long."

"He should have been put to death."

"I'm not arguing with you, Mrs. Canfield."

"Just make it Gwen. We're not too formal out here."

"Okay, Gwen. And you can make it Web and Paulie. But we're here to make sure that you and your husband are safe."

She glanced at him. "I haven't felt safe in years, Web. I don't think things are going to change now."

She led them inside. The ground floor of the carriage house was filled with restored antique cars. Web looked at car-happy Romano and thought his partner was going to have a coronary.

Gwen explained, "Billy collects them. His little private car museum, I guess."

"Geez," exclaimed Romano, "that's a right-hand-drive Stutz Bearcat." He walked around the space in wonder, like a boy at the Baseball Hall of Fame. "And that's a 1939 Lincoln LeBaron. Only nine of them were ever made. And omigod." He rushed over to the far corner of the room and stopped dead. "Web, this, this is a 1936 Duesenberg SSJ Speedster." He looked at Gwen. "Am I wrong, or were there only two of these ever built, one for Clark Gable and the other for Gary Cooper? Please tell me I'm not wrong."

Gwen nodded. "You know your cars. That's Coop's."

Romano looked to Web like he was going to faint.

"This is beautiful," said Romano. He turned to the woman. "I want you to know, Gwen, that I am truly honored to be under the same roof with these legendary machines."

Web thought he was going to be sick to his stomach.

Gwen looked at Web and shook her head, a tiny smile clutching at the corners of her mouth. "Men and their toys. Do you have any toys, Web?"

"Not really. Didn't have any as a kid either."

She gave him a penetrating stare and then said, "Upstairs are two bedrooms, each with its own bath and a fully stocked kitchen and living area. This used to be the estate's carriage house back in Colonial times. It's a very historical property. In the 1940s the owner set it up as the firehouse. Billy reconfigured it as guest quarters when he bought the place, although with twenty bedrooms in the main house, I always thought a guest house was a bit superfluous."

"Twenty bedrooms!" said Romano.

"I know," said Gwen. "I grew up on a farm outside of Louisville. We had two bedrooms for seven people."

"Billy didn't come from money either that I remember," said Web. "Trucking is not an easy business, but he did it."

"He was complaining that this farm is sucking every cent of his down the drain," commented Romano. "But those cars don't come cheap."

Gwen really smiled for the first time and Web felt himself smiling at her. "You'll soon learn that Billy Canfield likes to complain. About everything. But especially about money. I'm sure he told you we sank every cent we had into this place, and we did. But what he probably didn't tell you is that the first colt we ever sold won the Kentucky Derby and was third in the Preakness."

"What was that horse's name?"

"King David," Gwen answered quietly. "Now, we didn't get any of that purse, of course, but it put us on the map, and we have the brood mare here that had the King. The stallion that we had her studded with wasn't all that great, which means that our mare's bloodlines got a lot of the credit for the King's prowess."

"Seems sort of right, though, considering the female does all the real work," said Web.

Gwen shot him a glance. "I like your way of thinking. So with the King to our credit, everybody in this country who knows anything about horse racing knows about East Winds and our horses generally fetch a nice premium. Now, we do have some race winners here and the stud fees are impressive. On top of that we've got a good crop of yearlings the past two years and we run a tight ship. Don't get me wrong, it is amazingly expensive to run a breeding farm. But as much as Billy complains, I think we'll be okay."

"That's good to know," said Web. "I guess you came up here soon after the trial."

She said curtly, "If you need anything, just call the house and we'll take care of it. The number's on the wall next to the phone upstairs." She left before they could even thank her.

They went upstairs and looked around. The furnishings were all antique, the appointments refined and elegant and Web was sure that Gwen Canfield's touches had been felt heavily here. Billy Canfield just didn't seem the interior decorator type.

"Man, this is some place," said Romano.

"Yeah, some place that's a long way from the people we're supposed to be protecting, and that I don't like."

"So call Bates and have him call Canfield and they can yell at each other. We're just the foot soldiers, we do what we're told."

"So what do you make of Gwen Canfield?"

"Seems nice enough. She's a real looker too. A lady. Canfield's a lucky guy."

"Don't get any ideas, Paulie."

"Yeah, like Angie would let me live to enjoy it."

"Unpack your stuff and let's make rounds. I want to hook up with Canfield. If we're going to protect him, we need to at least be near the guy. And we're probably going to have to go in shifts, Paulie, so we'll alternate sleep."

"Hey, just like the good old sniper days."

"Yeah, just like the good old sniper days, except you snore like a damn freight train."

"Not anymore; Angie had me fixed."

"How'd she do that?"

"I really don't want to get into it, Web."

They went outside and immediately ran into Percy Bates.

"Any luck on the bomb?" asked Web.

"It was a pretty sophisticated device, from what the techs told me. We're talking to everybody who might know something, but so far nothing. But that phone didn't get in there by itself."

"So maybe we have an inside job. A Free Society member on the premises, maybe?" added Web.

Bates nodded and he looked very worried. "They recruit people from areas just like this. Rural white guys who like guns and land and the old ways and have a big chip on their shoulder because they see the world changing fast and they're no longer on top of it."

"Anything happening with the Frees in southern Virginia?"

"We've got people watching them but nothing so far. Now they might just be lying low after all this activity. That would be the smart thing to do. And they're not dumb. They have to know they're suspected in this and that we're watching. All we need is one link and we can go after them."

"Where's Canfield? I sort of like to keep track of the man I'm supposed to be protecting."

Bates said, "And Gwen too. She received the same death threats that her husband did."

Web thought about this. "Well, Paulie and I can split up, but it'd be nice to have more men on this. East Winds looks to be a pretty big place."

"Two thousand acres and sixty-eight buildings, actually. I talked to Canfield about that and he said if I wanted to bring more guys out here, he'd see me in court and then see me in hell, and I'm taking the guy at face value. It's up to you two, but listen, Web, we're not going to be very far away."

"I'm counting on that, Perce."

"Oh, and Web?"

"Yeah?"

"Thanks for saving my life."

They found Billy Canfield down at the equestrian center examining the foreleg of a stallion while Nemo Strait and two young men dressed in riding clothes looked on.

Canfield said to one of the young men, "Better call the vet; might only be a sprain, but maybe a fracture. Hope to hell it's not." As the man walked off, Canfield called after him, "And tell that damn farrier that unless he comes up with a better shoe, I'm changing shops. We got some stock with soft hooves and the glue-ons are pretty damn good for that and he doesn't even carry 'em."

"Yes, sir."

Canfield patted the horse's flank, wiped off his hands and walked over to the HRT men.

"Farrier?" asked Romano.

"The horseshoer man," answered Canfield. "A glorified black-smith. In the old days horse farms would keep one on full-time. Now they come around once a week in their truck with a forge in the bed and their anvil and hammer and prestamped shoes and do their work. They're not cheap, but who'd want to do that kind of work? It's hard, hot and dangerous, what with crazy horses trying to kick your brains out."

"What are those glue-ons you mentioned?" Web wanted to know.

Strait answered, "Sometimes a horse's hoof walls get too thin for the nails and they break up, especially horses imported from Europe, because of the climate and soil differences; their hooves get brittle. A soft shoe doesn't require any nails, it's like a little bag over the hooves. It lasts a couple of months if done right. And the glue-ons are just what they sound like. Shoes glued on, no nails."

"Sound like a lot to learn about this business."

"Well, I've always been a quick learner," said Billy with a glance at Strait. Next he stared over at Bates. "You guys done talking to my boys? I've got a farm to run."

"We'll be out of here pretty soon."

Canfield looked at Web then pointed at Bates. "He told me about the phone killings and all. But that was still pretty quick thinking on your part."

"I'm a fast learner too," said Web.

Canfield studied him curiously. "Well, what's the next thing you'd like to learn about?"

"East Winds. I'd like to go over every inch of it."

"Have to get Gwen to do that. I've got things requiring my attention."

Web looked at Romano. "Paulie here will go with you."

Canfield looked like he was going to erupt but then seemed to pull it back in. "All right." He looked at Romano. "Paul, how are you on a horse?"

Romano jerked, blinked and looked at Web and then at Canfield. "I've never been on one."

Canfield put an arm around the HRT man and smiled. "Well, I hope you're as fast a learner as your partner."

31

Gwen was at the equestrian center with Baron when her husband asked her to show Web around the place. She led Web to the horse stalls.

"The best way to see the farm is on horseback. Do you ride?" she asked.

"A little. I'm certainly not in your league."

"Then I've got just the horse for you."

Boo, Gwen told him, was a Trakehner, a German breed, a warm-blooded horse bred to be superior warhorses and a cross between a hot-blooded, high-spirited and temperamental Arabian and a cold-blooded, calm and hardworking draft. The horse weighed about seventeen hundred pounds, stood almost eighteen hands high and looked at Web like he wanted to take a bite out of his skull as they stood next to Boo in the stall.

"Boo was a great dressage horse, but now his work is done and he doesn't really like to move all that much. He's gotten fat and happy. We call him 'old grump' because that's what he pretty much is. But deep down he's a sweetheart, and he's very flexible too. You can ride him English or western saddle."

"Yeah, I'm sure," said Web as he stared up at the beast. Boo didn't look the least bit happy that Web was in his personal space.

Gwen put the square saddle pad over the horse's back and next had Web help her place the heavy Western-style saddle over the pad. "Now watch while I cinch the saddle, he'll hold his breath and push out his belly." Web watched in fascination as the horse did exactly that.

"When you think it's tight, he'll let out his breath and it loosens. Then you try and climb on and the saddle slides over his withers. The horse gets a good laugh and the rider gets a few bruises."

"Good to know dumb animals are that smart," said Web.

Gwen showed Web how to transfer from the halter to the bridle and how to slip the latter over Boo's head, seat it correctly and then buckle it. They led Boo outside and over to a stone mounting block.

Web adjusted the chaps Gwen had given him to prevent the saddle from chafing his legs and to allow Web to get a better grip, stepped onto the block and climbed aboard, while Boo just stood there patiently.

"So what do you think?" asked Gwen.

"It's a long way down."

She noted the pistol in his holster. "Do you have to bring the gun?"

"Yes," Web said firmly.

They went to the riding ring and Gwen led horse and rider around the ring. Next Gwen showed Web neck-reining to brake, turn and back the horse up, and sounds and leg pressure to make the animal go and stop. "Boo's been all over the farm, so if you let him, he'll go where he's supposed to. Nice and easy."

Hired help had brought Baron around while they were working with Boo. Gwen mounted up on her horse. "Now, Boo is the patriarch of this place and he and Baron have never ridden together before. So Boo may try and establish his dominance over Baron to show him who's boss."

"Sort of like guys with too much testosterone," opined Web.

Gwen looked at him in a strange way. "Boo's a gelding, Web." He looked at her blankly, not getting it. "If he were a man, we'd call him a eunuch."

"Poor Boo."

The two horses seemed to establish a grudging truce, and Web watched as Gwen slipped a Motorola walkie-talkie radio out of her back pocket and turned it on. "Just in case there's a problem," she said.

"Smart to keep in communication," said Web. "I've got my cell phone too."

"After what happened today with Billy, I'm not sure I'll ever use one again," she said.

Web looked down at his phone and started having some doubts.

They started off, trailed by a golden retriever named Opie, and another compact but strongly built canine Gwen called Tuff. "Strait has a dog running around here too," she said. "Calls him Old Cuss, and it's an apt description because he's nothing but trouble." The sky was clear, and as they went up and down the small hills on the property, it seemed to Web that he could see almost all the way to Charlottesville. Boo was content to follow Baron and kept up a sedate pace that didn't tax Web.

Gwen reined Baron to a halt. Web eased Boo next to her.

"As I said, East Winds has been around a very long time. The King of England gave Lord Culpeper a land grant consisting of millions of acres in the 1600s. A descendant of Lord Culpeper's gave a thousand acres of this land grant to his eldest daughter upon her marriage to a man named Adam Rolfe. The central part of the house was started in 1765 and completed in 1781 by Rolfe, who was an expert builder and also a merchant. You've seen the outside of the main house?" Web nodded. "Well, it was constructed in the Georgian style. And the millwork, particularly the dentil moldings, are some of the best I have ever seen."

"Georgian, that's what I would have guessed." Web was lying; he wouldn't have known a Georgian style if it leapt up and bit him in his dentil moldings.

"The estate remained in the Rolfe family until the early 1900s. During that time it was a true working plantation and crops were raised here: tobacco, soybeans, hemp, that sort of thing."

"And slaves to work it, I guess," said Web. "At least until the end of the Civil War."

"Actually, no, the plantation was close enough to Washington that its owners were Northern sympathizers. In fact, East Winds was part of the Underground Railroad.

"In 1910," Gwen continued, "the estate was sold out of the family. It passed through a series of hands until Walter Sennick bought it at the end of World War II. He was an inventor and made a huge fortune selling his ideas to the automobile manufacturers. He made East Winds into a small self-contained town, and at its peak he had over three hundred full-time employees here. There was also a company store, phone exchange, firehouse, those sorts of things."

"Nothing like never having to leave home." The whole time Gwen was talking, Web had been surveying the grounds, judging where possible attacks might come from and how best to defend against them. Yet if there was a rat on the inside, that sort of strategy might be futile. A Trojan horse worked as well now as it had thousands of years ago.

Gwen nodded. "Now there are sixty-eight buildings in total with twenty-seven miles of board fencing. Nineteen paddocks. Fifteen full-time employees. And we still farm here—corn, mostly— although our main interest is breeding Thoroughbreds. Next year we have twenty-two foals due. And we've got a great crop of yearlings going to sale very soon. It's all very exciting."

They rode on and soon came to a high-banked water crossing, where Gwen instructed Web on how to let the horse choose its own footing when going down into the mud. She had Web lean back very far, so that his head was almost resting on Boo's rump when the horse was going down the bank. Then she had Web meld his body into the horse's neck and grasp Boo's mane when the horse was heading up the bank on the other side. Web successfully navigated the stream and earned high praise from Gwen.

They passed an old stone and wood building that Gwen told him was an old Civil War–era hospital that they were thinking of turning into a museum. "We've rehabbed it, put in central air and heat, it's got a kitchen, bedroom, so the curator could live in there," Gwen told him. "An operating table and surgical instruments from the time period are there as well."

"From what I know of that, a Civil War soldier would've taken a minié ball any day over a trip to the hospital."

They rode by a two-hundred-year-old bank barn, so named because it was two stories and built on such a steep grade that it had two entrances on separate levels. There was also a riding ring where horse and rider practiced their dressage. Dressage, Gwen explained, consisted of specialized steps and movements of a horse and rider, akin to a figure skater's routine. They passed a tall wooden tower with a stone foundation that Gwen told him had been used for both observation of wildfires and also for the horse races that had been held here a century ago.

Web studied the place and the surrounding countryside. As a

former sniper constantly on the lookout for the best ground, Web concluded that the tower would definitely be a good observation post, yet he didn't have the manpower to utilize it properly.

They rode past a two-story frame building that Gwen identified as the farm manager's house.

"Nemo Strait seems to do a good job for you."

"He's experienced and knows what he's doing, and he brought a full handpicked crew with him, so that was a plus," Gwen said with what Web perceived as little interest.

They examined entry and exit points in the rear grounds and Web made mental notes of each. Once, a deer broke clear of the tree line and Opie and Tuff took off after it. Neither horse reacted to this clamor, although Web was so startled by the deer flashing in front of him that he had almost fallen off Boo.

Next she led him into a little tree-shaded glen. Web could hear water running nearby and he was not prepared, as they rounded a short curve, to see a small, open building, painted white and with a cedar shake roof, that looked like a gazebo until Web saw the cross on top and the small altar inside with a kneeling pad and a small statue of Jesus on the cross.

He looked over at Gwen for an explanation. She was staring at the small temple as though in a trance and then she glanced over at him.

"This is my chapel, I guess you'd call it. I'm Catholic. My father was a Eucharistic minister, and two of my uncles are priests. Religion runs pretty deep in my life."

"So you had this built?"

"Yes, for my son. I come out here and pray for him just about every day, rain or cold. Do you mind?"

"Please."

"Are you a religious person?"

"In my own way, I guess," Web answered vaguely.

"I used to be a lot more than I am now, actually. I've tried to understand why what happened could happen to someone so innocent. I've never been able to find an answer."

She dismounted and went inside the chapel, crossed herself, took out her rosary from her pocket and then knelt down and started to pray while Web watched her in silence.

After a few minutes she rose and rejoined him.

They rode on and finally came to a large building that had clearly been abandoned for some time.

"The old Monkey House," said Gwen. "Sennick built it and kept all sorts of chimps, baboons, even gorillas there. Why, I don't know. Legend has it that when some of the animals would escape from their cages they'd be chased through the trees by beer-drinking local yokels with shotguns, who didn't want the monkeys around anyway. For that reason they called the forest around here the monkey jungle. The thought of those poor animals being gunned down by a pack of drunken morons makes me sick."

They dismounted and went into the building. Web could see through the roof where large holes had been worn in by time and the elements. The old cages, rusted and broken, were still lined up against the walls, and there were trenches presumably for catching animal waste and other disgusting things. Trash and old broken machinery littered the concrete floor, along with tree branches and rotted leaves. Tree roots clung to the outside walls and there was what looked to be a loading dock. Web tried to imagine what an inventor of auto accessories would want with a pack of monkeys. None of his theories were pleasant ones. All Web could think of was animals strapped to gurneys, electrical lines capturing the power of lightning bolts and old man Sennick in surgical garb ready to do his dirty work on the terrified simians. The place had a distinct feeling of melancholy, of hopelessness, of death, even, and Web was glad to leave it.

They continued their ride and Gwen dutifully pointed out all the buildings and their associated history until Web was having a hard time keeping track of everything. He was very surprised to look at his watch and see that three hours had passed.

"We should probably head back," said Gwen. "For your first ride, three hours is plenty. You're going to find yourself a little sore."

"I'm good," said Web. "I really enjoyed it." The ride had been peaceful, tranquil, relaxing, everything he hadn't been experiencing for practically all of his life. However, when they got back to the equestrian center and Web climbed off Boo, he was surprised to find that his legs and back were so stiff he could barely walk upright once his feet hit the ground. Gwen noted this and smiled wryly. "Tomorrow it'll be another part of your body that hurts."

Web was already rubbing his buttocks. "I *feel* what you mean."

A couple of hired help came out and took the horses from them. Gwen told Web that they would take off the gear and scrub and wash down the horses. That was usually the job of the person riding the horse, Gwen said. It helped you bond with the animal. "You take care of the horse, and the horse takes care of you," she said.

"Kind of like having a partner."

"Exactly like having a partner." Gwen looked over at the complex's small office and said, "I'll be back in a minute, Web, I want to check on a few things."

As she walked off, Web started taking off his chaps.

"First time on a horse in a while?" Web looked up and saw Nemo Strait heading his way. A couple of other guys in baseball caps were sitting in the cab of a pickup truck that had large hay bales in the back. They were watching Web closely.

"Damn, how could you tell?"

Strait came up next to Web and leaned against the stone mounting block. He looked off in the direction where Gwen had gone.

"She's a good rider."

"I'd say she is too. But then, what do I know?"

"She pushes the horses sometimes further than she should, though."

Web looked at him curiously. "She seems to really love them."

"You can love something and still hurt it, now, can't you?"

Web had not anticipated this sort of mental process from Strait. He thought he had the big, dumb Neanderthal figured out, and here the guy was being thoughtful and maybe even sensitive. "I take it you've been around horses a long time."

"All my life. Folks think they can figure them out. You can't. You just have to go with the flow and never make the mistake of thinking you have them pegged. That's when you get yourself hurt."

"Sounds like a good formula for people too." Strait almost smiled, Web noted. *Almost.*

Strait glanced over at the truck where his men still were watching the two closely. "You really think Mr. Canfield might be in danger?"

"I can't be a hundred percent sure, but I'd rather be safe than sorry."

"He's a tough old cuss, but we all respect him. He didn't inherit his money like most folks around here; man earned it with his sweat. Got to respect that."

"Yes, you do. You have any ideas on how that phone might have got into his truck?"

"Been thinking about that. See, thing is, nobody drives that car 'cept him and Mrs. Canfield. We all got our own vehicles."

"When he got in it, it was unlocked. And do they keep their vehicles in the garage at night?"

"They got lots of cars and trucks, and the garage at the house is only two bays, and one of them is filled with supplies."

"So somebody, particularly at night, could have accessed the Rover, left the phone and probably nobody would have seen him."

Strait scratched the back of his neck. "I guess so. You got to understand, out here lots of folks don't even bother to lock the doors to their homes."

"Well, until this is over, tell everybody to lock everything they can. You have to understand that threat can come from everywhere, inside and out."

Strait stared at him for a long moment. "This Free Society thing, I've heard of it."

"You know anybody who might be a member or a former member?"

"No, but I could ask around."

"Well, if you do, keep it low-key. We don't want to spook anybody."

"We all got a good gig here, don't want to see nothing happen to the Canfields."

"Good. Anything else you think I need to know?"

"Look, if somebody here is in on this, you got to understand that a farm can be a real dangerous place. Big tractors, sharp tools, propane gas tanks, welding equipment, horses that'll kick your brains out if you let down your guard, snakes, steep slopes. Lot of ways to get killed and make it look like an accident."

"That's real good to know too. Thanks, Nemo." Actually, Web didn't know if that was advice or a threat.

Strait spit on the ground. "Hey, you keep up that riding, you'll be Roy Rogers in no time."

Gwen rejoined Web and showed him through the equestrian center. There were eleven buildings in total.

The foaling stalls were their first stop and Gwen showed Web how they were equipped with closed-circuit television to monitor the expectant mares. The floors were rubber-matted and had a covering of straw to keep the dust down.

"We have really high hopes for some of the foals coming next year. We had several mares bred out in Kentucky by stallions with remarkable bloodlines."

"How much does that stuff run?"

"It can run six figures a pop."

"That's expensive sex."

"There are a lot of conditions attached to that payment, of course, the most important being that the foal is actually born alive and can also stand and nurse. But a great-looking yearling sired by a successful racehorse can bring enormous amounts of money. It's a very picky business, though. You have to think of every contingency, and yet simple bad luck can still ruin your chances."

Web thought that sounded very much like being an HRT man. "Yeah, the way Billy described it to us, it doesn't sound like a business for the faint of heart."

"Well, the money is nice, Web, but that's not why I do it. It's the rush you get from seeing a horse you raised, nurtured and trained thundering around that track; the most beautiful, the most perfect racing machine every created. And seeing the finish line, watching this truly noble animal prance into the winner's circle, knowing that for at least a few minutes everything in your life is absolutely perfect. Well, there's no other feeling quite like that."

Web wondered if the nurturing of horses had replaced the lost son. If it had, he was glad that Gwen Canfield had found something in her life she could feel good about.

"I guess you probably feel the same way about your work."

"Maybe I used to," he replied.

"I didn't put two and two together before," she said. "I didn't know you were part of what happened to those men in Washington. I'm very sorry."

"Thanks. It's a pretty sorry situation all around, actually."

"I never really understood how men could do that sort of job."

"Well, I guess the easiest way to look at it, Gwen, is that we do that job because there are people in the world who make us do it."

"People like Ernest Free?"

"People just like him."

As they finished at the center, Gwen asked him what Strait had wanted.

"Just some friendly neighborly advice. By the way, did he come with the farm or did you hire him?"

"Billy did. He and his crew came with good references." She looked around. "So what now?"

"How about the main house?"

As they drove up to the mansion in an open Jeep, Web heard a roaring overhead and looked up. A small chopper was coming in low and fast. It flew past and disappeared over the treetops.

Web looked over Gwen. "Where is that going?"

She frowned. "The neighboring farm. Southern Belle. In addition to the chopper pad, they also have an airstrip. When their jet comes over, it scares the horses to death. Billy's talked to them about it, but they go their own way."

"Who are they?"

"*What* are they is more like it—a company of some sort. They run a horse farm too but a pretty strange one."

"What do you mean?"

"I mean they don't have all that many horses, and the men they have working for them don't look to me to know the difference between a colt and a filly. But they must be doing something right. The house at Southern Belle is even bigger than ours."

"I guess they have a lot of buildings, like you."

"Yes, although the ones we have came with the spread. They've built a bunch of new ones there, massive ones, almost like warehouses, though I don't know what they'd be storing in that sort of quantity. They only came here about two and a half years ago."

"So you've been over there?"

"Twice. Once to be neighborly and they weren't. The second time to complain about their low-flying aircraft. We weren't thrown off the place, but it was pretty awkward, even for Billy, and he's usually the one making people feel uncomfortable."

Web sat back and thought about all this even as he glanced in the direction where the chopper had disappeared.

It took them a while, but they covered the stone mansion from top to bottom. The lower level held a billiard room, a wine cellar and a dressing area to change into swimsuits. The pool itself was thirty by sixty feet and made entirely of steel from a World War II–era battleship that had been decommissioned, she said. There was a lower kitchen with a Vulcan stove that had a big chrome hood dating from 1912, working dumbwaiters and a laundry room. In the boiler room Web got to see big McLain units kicking out radiant steam heat, and there was a room containing nothing except wooden bins for storing firewood. Each woodbin was labeled for a particular room.

The main-level dining room had the heads of English stags on the walls and an antler chandelier. The kitchen was impressively large, with delft wall tile and a genuine silver closet. There were three ballrooms, assorted studies, parlors and living rooms and an exercise room. On the upper floors there were seventeen bathrooms, twenty bedrooms, a library that seemed to have no end and numerous other spaces. The place was truly enormous, and Web knew he was incapable of making it totally secure.

As they ended the tour, Gwen looked around with a wistful air. "I've really come to love this place. I know it's too big and grandiose in parts, but it's also very healing, you know?"

"I guess I can see that. How many staff do you have in the house?"

"Well, we have three women who come and clean and do laundry and look after things and then they leave, unless we're having a lot of guests of dinner and then they'll stay and help. They're all local folks."

"Who does the cooking?"

"I do. It's something else I enjoy. We have a handyman of sorts. He looks like he's a million years old, but he's just lived life really hard. He comes most days. Nemo and his men run the rest of the farm. Racehorses have to be exercised every day, so we also have riders, three young women and one man. All of them live at the equestrian center."

"And there is a security system. I noted the alarm pad as we came in."

"We never use it."

"You will now."

Gwen said nothing to this. She showed Web into the last room.

The master bedroom was vast but curiously sparsely furnished. Web also noticed the anteroom off the master bedroom that also had a bed.

"Billy works late a lot and doesn't want to disturb me when he comes to bed," explained Gwen. "He's always considerate that way."

The way she looked when she said this made Web think Billy wasn't all that considerate.

She continued, "Most people only see the hard side of Billy, and I guess there were more than a few people that were a little skeptical of our getting married. I guess half of them thought I was marrying Billy for money and the other half thought he was robbing the cradle. But the fact is, we just clicked. We enjoy each other's company. My mother was in the last stages of lung cancer when we started dating, and Billy came to the hospice every day for four months. And he didn't just sit there and stare at my mother dying. He brought her things, talked with her, argued with her about politics and sports and made her feel like she was still living, I suppose. It made it a lot easier for all of us and I'll never forget that. He's had a rough life and he's rough around the edges because of it. But he's been everything in a husband that a woman could ask for. He left Richmond, a place he loved, and gave up the only business he's ever known to start over on a horse farm because I asked him to. And I think he knew we had to get away from it all, too many bad memories.

"And he was a wonderful father to David, did everything with him. He didn't spoil him because he thought that would make David weak, but he loved that boy with every ounce of his being. If anything, I think losing him destroyed Billy more than it did me because, while he had children from his first marriage, David was his only son. But if he considers you a friend, there is absolutely nothing he wouldn't do for you. He'd spend his last nickel to help you. There aren't many people like that left."

Web noted the photos on the wall and on a built-in cabinet. There were many pictures of David. He was a handsome boy who had taken after his mother more than his father. Web turned and found Gwen at his shoulder looking at her son.

"It's been a long time now," she said.

"I know. I guess time really doesn't stop for anyone or anything."

"Time's also supposed to help. But it doesn't."

"He was your only child?"

She nodded. "Billy has grown kids from his first marriage, but David was my only one. Funny, when I was a little girl I was certain I'd have a big family. I was one of five. Hard to believe my little boy would be in high school now." She suddenly turned away and Web saw a hand go up to her face.

"I think that's enough for now, Gwen. I really appreciate your taking the time."

She turned back to him and he could see her damp cheeks. "Billy wanted me to invite you and your friend up for drinks and dinner tonight."

"You don't have to do that."

"Well, we want to. You saved his life, after all, and if we're going to be spending time together, we probably should get to know each other a little better. Say five-thirty?"

"Only if you're sure."

"I'm sure, Web, but thanks for asking."

"Just so you know, we didn't bring any fancy clothes."

"We're not fancy people."

32

Claire was walking to her car in the underground garage of her office building when a well-built man in a suit approached her. "Dr. Daniels?"

She looked at him cautiously. "Yes."

He held out his identification. "I'm Agent Phillips with the FBI. We'd like to talk to you—right now, if that's convenient."

Claire looked bewildered. "*Who* wants to talk to me?"

Agent Phillips turned and pointed past the garage gate, where a black limousine with tinted windows was waiting, its engine running.

"It'll all be explained, ma'am." He gently put a hand on her elbow. "Just right this way, Doctor, it won't take long at all and we'll bring you right back here."

Claire allowed herself to be led out of the garage. Phillips held the door for her and then climbed in the front passenger seat. Before Claire was even settled against the cushion, the limo sped off.

Claire was startled when the man sitting across from her in the rear-facing seats leaned forward.

"Thank you for agreeing to talk to us, Dr. Daniels."

"I didn't agree to talk with anyone. I don't even know why I'm here."

She noted that a glass partition that separated the back of the car from the front had been raised. "Who are you?"

"My name is John Winters. I'm head of the FBI's Washington Field Office."

"Well, Mr. Winters—" Claire began.

"My friends call me Buck."

"Well, Mr. Winters, I don't know why you'd want to talk to me."

Winters sat back. "Oh, I think you have an idea. You're a very smart woman." He tapped a large file next to him. "Quite an impressive C.V."

Claire stared at the file. "I'm not sure whether I should be flattered or deeply annoyed that you've been investigating me."

Winters smiled. "For now, we'll just assume you're flattered. But you also have to realize that in your position you see quite a few members of the Bureau, their spouses, support people."

"All my security clearances are up to date. And it's not like I'm exposed to anything that's top secret. All files are thoroughly censored before they get to me."

"But how do you censor the human mind, Dr. Daniels?"

"What my patients tell me is absolutely confidential."

"Oh, I'm sure it is. And I'm also certain that stressed-out people, folks with serious mental and emotional issues, probably pour out their hearts to you."

"Some more than others. Exactly where is this going, Mr. Winters?"

"The fact is, Dr. Daniels, you are in a position to hear some pretty important information given to you by some very vulnerable people."

"I am well aware of that. And it goes no farther than my office."

Winters leaned forward again. "One of your current patients is Web London. Is that right?"

"I can't answer that."

Winters smiled. "Come on, Doctor."

"When I said that I do not reveal confidences, I meant it. That includes whether someone is a patient of mine."

"Well, just so you're aware, as head of WFO, I'm privy to who at the Bureau is seeing a shrink, okay?"

"We prefer 'psychiatrist,' or at least 'mental health professional.'"

"So I know that Web London is seeing you," Winters said. "And I know that he's seen another psychiatrist there several times in the past. An Ed O'Bannon." Again Claire said nothing. "So one thing I want to know is why the switch to you?"

"And again, I can't answer those—"

She watched as Winters pulled a slip of paper out of the file next to him. He handed it to her. She looked down at it. It was a release form signed by Web London and notarized. It stated, among other things, that anyone providing psychiatric care to Web London could discuss the parameters of the diagnosis and treatment with one John Winters, director of WFO. Claire had never seen a form like this before, but it was an original document on official Bureau stationery.

"Now we can dispense with the reluctance."

"Where did this document come from and why haven't I seen it before?"

"It's a new policy. In fact, Web's case is the first time we've used it. My idea."

"It's an invasion of doctor-and-patient confidentiality."

"Not if the patient has waived it."

Claire read the document very carefully—so carefully, in fact, and she took such a long time doing it, that Winters finally started to fume. She handed it back to him.

"Okay, let me see some ID," she said.

"Excuse me?"

"It says I can reveal certain information to John Winters, head of WFO. All I know about you is you drive around in a limo and say you're John Winters."

"I thought my aide identified himself."

"He did. But *you* haven't."

Winters smiled, pulled out his creds and showed them to Claire. She spent longer than necessary going over them, just to put the man on notice that she didn't like this one bit and that she was not going to make this easy.

He sat back. "Now, about Web London."

"He selected me because Dr. O'Bannon wasn't available. We had a good session and he decided to stay with me."

"What's his diagnosis?"

"I'm not sure I've made one yet."

"Have you suggested any treatment to him?"

"That would be a little premature," she said dryly, "since I haven't made a diagnosis yet. That would sort of be like operating on someone before you've even done a physical."

"Sorry, but most shrinks—excuse me—psychiatrists I know just prescribe some pills."

"Well, I guess I'm not like any psychiatrists you know, then."

"Can you tell me what happened to him in that courtyard?"

"No, I cannot."

"Can't or won't?" He held up the release form. "We can make this smooth for you or extremely difficult."

"That form also states that I may withhold any information told to me in confidence by a patient and also any conclusions of mine based on such information, if, using my professional discretion, such disclosure would do harm to the patient."

Winters moved across and sat next to Claire. "Dr. Daniels, are you aware of what happened in that courtyard?"

"Yes. I've read the papers, and I've talked to Web about it."

"You see, it goes beyond the murder of six agents, horrific as that is. It strikes right at the fundamental integrity of the Bureau. And without that, you have nothing."

"I'm not sure how someone ambushing a team of FBI agents diminishes the integrity of the FBI. If anything, it should evoke sympathy."

"Unfortunately, that's not the world we work in. Let me tell you what this ambush has done. First, by taking out our elite strike force, criminal elements now believe we are vulnerable at all levels. Second, the press has blown this unfortunate incident to such extraordinary heights, using such incendiary language, that the public confidence in us has been badly shaken and even the lawmakers on Capitol Hill who should know better are doubting us. And lastly, the morale of the Bureau as a whole is at an all-time low over this. It really is a triple whammy."

"I guess I can see that," Claire said cautiously.

"So the sooner the matter is resolved, the sooner we understand how it happened in the first place, the sooner we can make matters right again. I'm sure you don't want the criminals in this country thinking they can run roughshod over honest citizens."

"I'm certain that won't happen."

"Are you?" He stared hard at her. "Well, I'm right in the middle of it, and I'm not nearly so certain as you seem to be."

Claire felt a chill go up her back at the man's words.

He patted her on the shoulder. "Now, what can you tell me about Web without, *in your discretion*, violating any professional standards?"

Claire began slowly, the whole process loathsome to her. "He has some issues. I believe they go back to his childhood, as such issues often do. He froze in that alley. I'm sure he's told the investigators at the FBI that." She looked at him for affirmation of this, but Winters didn't take the bait.

"Go on," he said simply.

Claire went through the details of what Web had seen and heard in the alley, including the words spoken to him by Kevin West-brook, how they affected him, his subsequent feelings of paralysis and how he had fought against them and ultimately won.

"Yes, he won," said Winters. "He dropped right before the guns fired and he managed to walk away alive."

"I can tell you that he feels enormous guilt for having been the sole survivor."

"And so he should."

"He didn't suddenly turn coward, if that's what you were wondering. He's one of the bravest men I've ever met. In fact, he might be too brave, too much of a risk-taker."

"I wasn't thinking he had become a coward; not even his own worst enemy could say that Web London was a coward."

She looked at him curiously. "What, then?"

"There are worse things than being a coward." He paused. "Like being a traitor."

"My professional opinion is that that is not the case. His freezing in that alley represents deep-rooted problems stemming from a very challenging childhood that Web is trying to cope with."

"I see. So perhaps he shouldn't be with HRT, then. Perhaps not in the Bureau at all."

Now Claire could feel herself freeze. *What had she just done?*

"That's not what I said."

"No, Doctor, that's what *I* said."

As promised, they dropped her back off at the garage. As she was getting out, Buck Winters leaned forward and gripped her arm. Claire felt herself instinctively drawing back.

"I certainly can't stop you from telling Web about our meeting,

Doctor, but I'm asking you not to. This is an ongoing FBI investigation and the results, whatever they happen to be, will rock the
Bureau more than it's ever been. So I'm asking you, as a good citizen, to keep all this on the QT for now."

"I can't guarantee you that. And I trust Web."

"I'm sure you do. There's a lot about him to trust. Do you know
how many men he's killed in his career?"

"No, is that important to know?"

"I'm sure the relatives of those people would think it important."

"You're making it sound like he's the criminal. I'm assuming
that if he's killed people, it was part of his job, the job you expect
him to do."

"Well, I guess that's always open to interpretation, isn't it?" He
let go of her arm and added a parting shot. "I'm sure we'll be seeing each other again."

When Romano and Web left for dinner at the mansion, Romano
was walking a little funny. He told Web that Billy had gotten him
on a horse and Romano had immediately fallen off.

"I don't know why the hell I can't follow the guy in a truck.
Horses just ain't my thing."

"Well, I rode over most of the property today and a lot of it you
can't get to even by truck."

"Did you fall off too?"

"Yeah, twice," Web said. Why tell the truth and get Romano's
hair up again? he figured.

"So who'd you ride with?" asked Romano.

"Gwen. Had a nice time. How about you? Have any fun?"

"Yeah, I never knew how much fun mucking a stall could be. You
should try it sometime."

Billy met Web and Romano at the front door of the stone house.
He was wearing an old corduroy jacket with patched elbows, a pair
of khaki pants, a wrinkled white button-down shirt and loafers
without socks. And he already had a drink in hand. He led them
through the front hall and down a curving staircase of walnut that
looked old enough to have arrived in the Colonies as a gift from a
long-dead king or queen. Though he'd been through the place ear-

lier, Web still caught himself occasionally ogling the large rooms, elaborate millwork, heavy draperies and enormous artwork that looked museum-quality and probably was, and then they arrived at the lower level. Romano looked around and kept muttering, "Holy shit," under his breath.

Web again noted Billy's limp. "You have an accident?" he asked, pointing to the man's leg.

"Yeah, a one-ton draft horse decided to take a roll while I was on the sumbitch."

The floor in the lower level was flagstone, the exposed walls stone and twelve-by-twelve beams had the task of holding up the ceiling. There were large leather couches and chairs placed precisely, probably to encourage several conversation groups, or perhaps even conspiratorial factions, for this definitely looked like that sort of place to Web, though the Canfields didn't seem the type. If they didn't like you, they probably weren't bashful about showing it, especially Billy. The walls were festooned with the racks of yet more English stags along with numerous mounted heads of deer, a cheetah, a lion, a rhino, a moose and mounted full bodies of a large variety of birds and fish. Mounted on another wall was a very large walleyed pike. There was also a full-sized grizzly in a charging pose and an enormous swordfish in perpetual soar. On one display table was a coiled diamondback rattler and a king cobra, with eyes seemingly ablaze and fangs showing and ready to do some serious damage. Web gave both stuffed reptiles a wide berth. He had never cared much for snakes after almost being bitten by an enraged water moccasin on a mission in Alabama.

There was a well-stocked gun cabinet against one wall. Web and Romano enviously checked out the array of Churchill, Rizzini and Piotti firearms, weapons that would easily set you back five figures. You really couldn't be a member of HRT and not be an aficionado of showpieces like these, though most FBI agents lacked the financial wherewithal to do more than press their noses to the glass. Web wondered if the weapons were for show only or whether anybody here ever actually used them. Billy looked like he would be comfortable around guns, maybe even Gwen too. If the man had killed all these animals, he would damn well have to be handy with firearms.

A full bar of dark cherry sat against another wall. It looked like it had been yanked straight from a London pub. Web's strong impression when he had first seen this room was that it had the feel of an English club spiked with a bit of the Wild West.

Gwen was sitting on a couch that looked substantial enough to sail in across the Atlantic. She rose when they entered the room. She was wearing a beige sundress that went down to her ankles and that had a scooped neckline showing a good portion of cleavage. A bit of her white bra strap showed from under the sundress's thin shoulder straps. Her bare arms were browned by the sun and were tight and firm. Probably from horse-reining, Web assumed, since his arms were aching a little from doing just that for three hours. Black leather flats were on her feet. Still, she was only a couple inches shorter than Romano. As she sat back down and crossed her legs, the sundress slipped back an inch or so and Web was a little surprised to see that she wore a gold ankle chain, because it seemed a bit out of sync with her refined bearing. Her face was nicely tanned too and the contrast of the blond hair was striking. Billy Canfield was indeed a fortunate man, thought Web, though he wondered how much of the life in their marriage had died with their son.

Web was surprised to see Nemo Strait sitting in one of the chairs. The farm manager had cleaned up and was wearing a Polo shirt that showed off his muscular physique, with chino pants and loafers. He was a striking man, Web had to admit.

Strait raised his glass to Web and Romano.

"Welcome to Casa Canfield," he said with a big grin.

Web looked at the numerous animal trophies. "They come with the house?" he asked Billy.

"Hell, no," said the man. "About four years ago I had me a calling, I guess you'd say, to go off and shoot things. Became a big-game hunter and a deep-sea fisherman. Was even on TV a few times on some sporting shows. Went round the world bagging stuff like that." He pointed to the tusked head of a wild boar on one wall and then over at the grizzly, which stood at least nine feet tall on a specially built display unit, its fangs bared and its long claws looking ready to shred somebody.

He went over and rubbed the thick neck of the enormous bear. "Now, this thing did its best to kill me, twice. Second time it almost did, but I got it." He pointed over at the rhino. "Those damn things look slow and heavy-footed. That is, they do until they're coming at you about thirty miles an hour with nothing between you and your Maker but your nerves, good aim and a steady trigger finger. You aim for the brain. Now, if you miss and hit the rhino's horn, you're a dead man."

"Poor animals," said Gwen.

"Hell, the damn things cost me a fortune," replied her husband dryly. He looked at one of the stags and then nodded at Web. "You know, the stag is the old symbol of virility, wisdom and life. And there it is hanging on my wall, dead as a doornail. I kind of like the irony in that. Now, I do all my own stuffing. Got to be a pretty damn good taxidermist, if I do say so myself."

Web was wondering about the timing of Billy's desire to kill. It must have occurred soon after the trial had ended in Ernest Free's plea bargain that had most certainly let him live.

Billy continued, "Here, let me show you. You want to come, Nemo?"

"No way. I've already seen your little operation and I ain't had my dinner yet."

Billy led them down a hallway and unlocked a door there. Gwen did not accompany them either. They went inside and Web looked around. The place was large and crammed with worktables and shelves and on the these surfaces were cans of liquids and pastes and sharp knives and scalpels, dozens of other tools, large vises, ropes and complicated pulley systems hanging from the ceiling. In one corner was the skin of an elk partially stretched over a form, and in another corner stood a wild turkey in all its dead glory. In other corners were stuffed birds and fish and some large and small animals Web couldn't even recognize. Web had smelled rotted corpses and it wasn't that bad in here, but, all the same, Web wouldn't want to breathe it every day.

"You killed all these?" asked Romano.

"Every one," said Billy with delight. "I only stuff what I kill. I don't do nobody any favors on that score." He picked up a rag and squirted some liquid on it and started rubbing on one of the tools. "Other folks golf for relaxation, I kill and stuff."

"I guess it's all relative," opined Web.

"It's therapeutic, I've found. But Gwen don't see it that way. She's never come in here and I suspect she never will. Now, taxidermy has come a long way. You don't have to build your forms anymore, you can buy real good ones made out of compressed cork, laminated paper and such, and then fit it to what you're mounting. It's still quite a process, a lot of planning and measuring and you got to have a bit of both the butcher and the artist in you. The basic steps are you gut the body and then prep the skin. A lot of folks use borax, but the purists like myself still poison the skin with arsenic. You get your best longevity there. And I even do some of my own tanning."

"You keep arsenic around here?" asked Romano.

"Tons of it." Billy eyed the man. "Don't worry, I always wash my hands after working down here, and I don't do none of the cooking." He laughed and Romano joined him, albeit a little nervously.

"Then you prep the skull, assemble your wires and such and then do your filling and final assembling."

Web eyed the room's equipment. It seemed one bare step removed from a slaughterhouse. "Lots of stuff in here."

"Well, you need a lot of stuff to do the job right." He pointed out various pieces. "Like I said, you got your anatomically correct urethane forms for the animals, but I still make some of my own using plaster of paris, modeling clay, cord-wrapped excelsior and the like. Ain't got to have everything handed to you, right?"

"Right," said Romano.

"Then you got your chemicals, poisons and salt, lots of salt to preserve the skin. Then you need your measurite and calipers for linear measurements and achieving symmetry. Scalpels for the obvious reason; I use what's called a perfect knife, German-made, those damn Germans know how to make the knives. It's for skinning and caping—you know, severing the neck from the body hide, for example—the detail work around the eyes and mouth and the like. You got your skinning knives, paring knives, bone saw, shavers, skifes for leather, even a fleshing machine. Now, that is a damn fine invention."

Under his breath Web said, "Lucky, lucky world."

"Got me Kevlar fleshing gloves so I don't chop off one of my fingers. Scissors, hide pullers, lip tuckers, nippers, forceps, probes and surgical needles. Sounds like a cross between a mortician and a plastic surgeon, don't it?" He pointed to mixing bowls, paintbrushes, an air compressor and a number of tins.

"That's the artistic part of the business. The finishing touches to do justice to the animal."

"Funny thing," said Web, "thinking about doing justice to something you've killed."

"I guess that separates folks like me from sons of bitches that kill and keep on walking," Billy shot back.

"I guess so," said Web.

Billy walked over to a deerskin that was drying on a large table. "You know what's the first thing you cut off when you're gutting a deer?" he asked looking directly at Web.

"What's that?"

"Its penis."

"Good to know," said Web dryly.

"Deer die like people," continued Billy. "With their eyes open. Glazing takes place almost immediately. If the eyes are closed or blinking, you better shoot 'em again." He looked at Web again. "I suppose you run across that a lot in your line of work."

"Sometimes that's not an option with human beings."

"I guess not, though I'd take any one of the animals I got on display here over the human scum you got to deal with." He took a sip of his drink. "I think that's one of the reasons I like this place so much," said Billy. "Damn contradictions, since I seem to be a living breathing one myself. Born dirt poor, barely finished ninth grade, made a lot of money in the unglamorous business of hauling cigarettes and other junk up and down the highways of this fine country and married me a beautiful, intelligent young woman with a college degree. And now here I am, the master of an estate smack in the middle of fancy-ass Virginia hunt country stuffing animals. One lucky man. Makes me want to get drunk, so let's go do something about that."

He led them back and they rejoined Gwen. She gave Web a weak smile as if to say, *I know and I'm sorry.*

Bill went behind the bar and pointed at his wife. "Scotch, honey?" She nodded. "I'll join you in another," he said. "Boys? And don't hand me that bullshit that you're on duty. If you don't drink with me, I'm throwing your butts out of here."

"Beer, if you have it."

"We have everything here, Web."

Web made a mental note that the man said it like he damn well meant it.

"Same for me," said Romano.

"I'll have one too, Billy," said Strait. He walked over and took a bottle of beer from his boss and then joined Web and Romano.

"I'm a lot more used to beer than I am fancy mixed drinks."

"Country boy?" asked Romano.

"Yes, sir, I grew up at the foothills of the Blue Ridge on a horse farm," said Strait. "But I wanted to see the world." He rolled up his sleeve and showed them his Marine Corps insignia. "Well, I did, on Uncle Sam's dime. Actually, I only saw a little slice of it called Southeast Asia, and it's hard to enjoy something like that when people are shooting at you."

"You don't look old enough to have been in Vietnam," commented Web.

Strait smiled broadly. "All my clean living, I guess." He added, "Truth is, I got drafted right near the end, only eighteen years old and change. First year in the jungle, I just kept my head down and tried my best to keep it on my shoulders. Then I got my ass caught and spent three months as a POW. Damn Viet Cong were into some sick stuff, messing with your mind, trying to turn you traitor."

"I didn't know that about you, Strait," said Billy.

"Well, it's not something I put on my résumé." He laughed. "But I finally escaped and an Army shrink helped me to straighten out myself. That and a lot of booze and other stuff I can't mention," he added, grinning. "Got discharged, came back to the States and pulled a little duty as a guard at a juvenile detention center. Now, let me tell you, some of the kids I was guarding, they'd make the damn Viet Cong look like a bunch of wimps. Then I got married, but my ex didn't like my pay scale of six bucks an hour, so I got me a desk job for a while, but that just wasn't me. Like I said, I grew up in the outdoors, around horses all my life. It's in your blood." He looked over at Billy. "It better be, because it ain't in your bank account."

They all laughed at that one, except Gwen. She looked annoyed that the cowpoke was even in her home, thought Web, who was watching her closely.

"So anyway," Strait continued, "I went back to horses and my wife walked out on me and took my boy and girl."

"You see them much?" asked Web.

"Used to, not anymore." He grinned. "Thought my son would follow in his old man's footsteps and be either a military grunt or maybe even get into the horses." He slapped his thigh. "Hell, you know what?"

"What's that?" asked Romano.

"Found out he was allergic to the damn things. Life sure is funny sometimes."

As Web studied the man, it didn't seem to him that Strait thought life was humorous at all. He had initially pegged Strait as a slow-witted fellow who did what he was told. He was going to have to re-think that.

"Then Billy come along, and now I'm helping him"—he glanced at Gwen—"and Ms. Canfield build their little empire right here."

Billy raised his beer to the man. "And doing a fine job of it, Strait."

On that, Web noted, Gwen looked away, and despite Billy's words of praise it seemed that he was not all that enamored of his foreman. Web decided to change the flow of conversation.

"Lower levels are usually cold," Web said to Billy. "Especially with all this stone. And yet it feels warmer down here than it did upstairs."

"We have the best heat in the world here," replied Billy, who worked the bar like he had been born to it. "Radiant steam. Gwen said she showed you around. Well, those three Weil McLain boilers you saw heat the water to two-twelve and turn it into steam, of course. The steam flows through the pipes and into the cast-iron Gurney radiators that are in each room in the house. Then the steam cools back to water, runs through the system again, is turned into steam once more and on it goes. And you have not only warmth, but a built-in humidifier." He handed Web his beer. "A lot of the steam pipes run under this floor, that's why it's so nice down here. I love it. And this time of year, it can get to be eighty-five in the day and forty at night. But McLain boilers is why Gwen can go bare-armed down here and still feel nice and toasty, ain't that right, honey?"

"Actually, I've felt hot all day."

Web rubbed his hand against the bar. "Nice setup with this thing."

"Dates from 1910," said Billy. "The owner back then put a lot of work into the place. It needed it, though. Unfortunately, it needed a lot more by the time we got to it. Story of my life." He carried the drinks over on a serving platter and handed them out. They all sat down.

"Gwen tells me you've got some promising yearlings."

"Yeah, maybe a Triple Crown winner in there," said Billy. "Now, that would be nice. Pay at least a month's worth of bills on this damn place."

Gwen and Web exchanged smiles at this comment.

"We can always hope," said Gwen. "But being one step from the poorhouse all the time at least is exciting."

"Well, we do okay here," said Strait, looking at her.

Web thought the choice of pronouns interesting. He was starting to wonder who actually owned the place.

Billy took a pull on his scotch. "Yeah, this ain't such a bad place. Even got fox hunting around here."

Gwen looked repulsed. "That's disgusting."

"Well, this *is* fox-hunting country, and in Virginia you got to do like the snooty Virginians do." Billy smiled at Web. "Actually, our damn neighbors can be kind of a pain in the ass. They got ticked at me because I wouldn't let them ride across my land while they were chasing that damn fox. I told them they didn't fox-hunt down Richmond way and it seemed like the deck was stacked against the little feller anyway and I've always tended to root for the underdog. Well, those pricks took me to court. And won. There were some old covenant in my chain of title that said fox hunting apparently runs with the land."

Romano looked disgusted. "Now, that's a bitch. Talk about your unfree country."

"Well, they don't come across East Winds anymore," said Strait.

"Why's that?" asked Web.

"Billy shot one of their dogs—excuse me, hounds." He slapped his leg and laughed.

Billy was nodding as though remembering a pleasant memory. "He took after one of my horses. That particular horse was worth about three hundred thousand dollars. Damn hound dog's a dime a dozen. So damn right I shot him."

"Did they take you to court again?" asked Web.

"They did, and this time I kicked their ass." He smiled, took another drink and looked at Web. "So did you enjoy the fifty-cent tour Gwen gave you?"

"She'd make a great tour guide, actually. I was interested in the farm being a stop on the Underground Railroad during the Civil War."

Billy pointed to the gun cabinet. "And that stop's right over there."

Web looked at the gun cabinet and said, "I'm not getting it."

"Go ahead and show him, Billy," said Strait.

Billy motioned for Web and Romano to follow him. He went over and pushed down on what Web figured must be a lever concealed in the cabinet's frame. Web heard a click and the cabinet swung toward him, revealing a small opening.

"There's no electricity or windows in there, just a couple of rough bunks, but when you're running for your freedom, you can't be too picky," said Billy. He picked up a flashlight that was hanging on a wall peg and handed it to Web. "Have a look."

Web took the flashlight, poked his head inside and swung the light around. He almost dropped the flashlight when the light caught on a man sitting there in a bentwood rocker. As his eyes adjusted to the poor light, he saw it was actually a mannequin dressed as a male slave, with a hat and muttonchop whiskers, the whites of its eyes in unsettling contrast to the painted black skin.

Billy laughed and said, "You've got some damn strong nerves. Most people scream."

"Billy put that in there, not me, Web," said Gwen quickly, with a trace of disgust in her voice.

"It's one of my sick little jokes," added Billy. "But hell, if you can't laugh at life, what are you gonna laugh at?"

On that they finished their drinks and went in to dinner.

They didn't eat in the formal dining room. As Billy explained it, the room was so big that when you wanted to talk to one another you had to scream to be heard and he was a little hard of hearing as it was. They ate in a small room off the kitchen. Gwen gave the blessing and made the sign of the cross, as did Romano. Strait, Web, and Billy just looked on.

Gwen had made a Caesar salad, sirloin tips, fresh asparagus in a cream sauce and what smelled and tasted like homemade rolls. Cherry pie and coffee finished off the meal, and Romano sat back, rubbing his flat, hard stomach.

"A lot better than MREs," he said, referring to the U.S. military's meals-ready-to-eat.

"Thanks, Gwen, it was great," said Web.

"We used to entertain quite a bit in Richmond," she said. "We don't do a lot of that anymore." She shot a quick glance at her husband as she said this.

"Lots of things we don't do anymore," said Billy Canfield. "But it was a fine meal and my toast to the chef." He went over to the sideboard and brought back a decanter of brandy and four cut-crystal glasses. "Now, I'm partial to my Jim Beam, like any good southern gentleman, but a proper toast requires a proper libation." He poured out the brandy and filled his glass with Beam, and they toasted Gwen.

She smiled and raised her glass to them. "Well, it's nice to be so popular with so many men."

As they took their leave, Web drew Billy aside.

"I just want to get the ground rules clear. Be sure to set the alarm when we leave, and set it every night before you go to bed. There are so many ways in and out of this place, I want you and Gwen to come and go the same way. That way you won't inadvertently leave a door unlocked. If you're thinking of going out, even if it's just a stroll, you call us first and we go with you. If anything spooks you or Gwen, you call us. Nothing is too small, okay? Here's my cell phone number. It'll be on twenty-four hours a day. And I want you to strongly consider letting Romano and me stay in the house. If something goes down, seconds do count."

Billy looked at the slip of paper with Web's number on it. "Pris-

oners in our own home, I guess it's come to that. Those bastards."
He shook his head wearily.

"Those guns in your cabinet, they just for show or you use them
in your hunting?"

"Most of them are shotguns. Couldn't use them on game you
want to mount because shotgun ammo ruins the skin and takes off
heads. I keep my big-game weapons in a locked cabinet upstairs.
I've also got me a twelve-gauge and a .357 Magnum too. Both
loaded. They're for two-legged sumbitches trespassing on my land.
Gwen's a damn fine shot too. Probably better'n me."

"Good, just remember to shoot only the bad guys. Now, you got
any travel plans coming up?"

"Just a shipment of horses we're taking up to Kentucky in a few
days. I'm going with Strait and some of the boys."

"Talk to Bates, he may see it differently."

"Listen to Web," said Nemo, who walked over after overhearing
their conversation. "Somebody's looking to get to you, Billy. Stay
put so the Feds can protect you."

"Going soft on me, Nemo?" asked Billy.

"Hell no. Something happens to you, I'm out of a job."

"Any visitors you expecting out of the ordinary?" Web asked.

Billy shook his head. "Most of our friends in Richmond aren't
our friends anymore. Maybe it's mostly our fault. We keep to ourselves here."

"These neighbors of yours, at the Southern Belle, what do you
know about them?"

"Only that they're ruder than me." He laughed. "To tell you the
truth, I don't know much about them. They don't join in much local stuff, not that I do either. I've only seen what I guess was the
foreman."

"How about that chopper and their plane?"

Billy made a face. "That is damn aggravating. Scares the horses."

"How often do you see the plane and the chopper go out?"

Billy considered this. "A lot."

"What's a lot? Nightly, weekly?"

"Not nightly, but more often than weekly."

"Same direction each time or different?"

"Different." He looked at Web warily. "What're you thinking?"

Web gave a tight smile. "I'm thinking we'll just keep an eye on that airline next door."

When Romano and Web got back to the carriage house, Web filled him in on the talk he had had with Billy.

"You think something's going down on the property next door?" said Romano.

"No, I think something going's *up*."

"Well, that was an interesting evening. I gotta tell you, that hobby of Canfield's is kind of spooky."

"Yeah, it's not exactly like building model planes. And what's your take on Nemo Strait?"

"Seems like a regular enough fellow."

"I was sort of surprised he was invited to the big house for dinner with the boss."

"Well, look at where Billy came from. He's probably more comfortable around people like Strait than a bunch of rich fat cats fox hunting."

"You're probably right. Gwen didn't seem to care for him, though."

"She's more of a lady. And he's kind of crude." He added with a smile, "Like me. I didn't know she was Catholic."

"Yeah, she's got a little chapel in the woods where she goes to pray every day for her son, the one I let die."

"You didn't let the kid die, Web. Hell, if the negotiators had let you guys do your thing from the get-go, the boy probably would be alive."

"Look, Paulie, I got an appointment tonight, so you're going to have to go it alone. I don't have to leave for a while, so you can get some shut-eye. Bates is keeping agents at the rear and front gates for the next couple of days, though, so you're not really all by your lonesome."

"Appointment, what kind of appointment?"

"I'll tell you all about it when I get back."

"This have something to do with what happened to Charlie Team?"

"Maybe."

"Well, damn, Web, I'd like to be in on that."

And I'd like you to be covering my back. "Can't desert the old post. I should be back before morning. Now, if I were you, I'd patrol around a little bit. I wouldn't be surprised if Canfield started off by testing us and so he might slip out. Although I think almost dying this morning put the fear of God in him, but we can't take that chance."

"Not to worry, I'll do some snooping."

"If you see that plane or chopper go over, log it in. And I brought a bunch of night optics, help yourself."

"Those damn things always give me a headache and they screw with your depth perception too much."

"Yeah, well, you remember those 'damn things' saved our necks in Kosovo."

"Okay, okay. I'm gonna hit the sack."

"And Paulie?"

"Yeah?"

"Just because there aren't a bunch of guys with big guns surrounding us doesn't mean it's not dangerous. Be extra careful. I don't want to lose anybody else, okay?"

"Hey, Web, remember who you're talking to."

"You and me have had our differences over the years, but we've also been to hell and back together. I kind of like having you around. You hear me?"

"Gee, Web, you really do care."

"You're a real prick, Romano, you know that?"

33

When Web had called the number on the slip of paper Big F had given him, the voice that had answered was a man's. Web didn't know if it belonged to Big F, since his initial encounter with the giant had involved concussions rather than words. Web had hoped it was Big F on the line because the voice was high and shrill. What a wonderful joke for God to play on the man by giving him a squeaky set of pipes. Yet a silly voice wasn't going to lessen the fear of doing the two-step with the walking oak again. Big F didn't hit with his tonsils.

The man had told Web to be driving north across the Woodrow Wilson Bridge at exactly eleven o'clock that night. Web would receive additional instructions at that time; by cell phone, Web figured. His number was unlisted, but it seemed nothing was sacred these days.

Web, of course, had sensibly questioned why he should even go.

"If you want to know what happened to your buddies, you'll be there," the man had said. "And if you want to keep on living," he added. Appropriately enough, the phone line had gone dead after that.

Web thought about running down to Quantico and snagging a Barrett .50 rifle and a couple thousand rounds of ammo from the equipment cage. One of the great things about HRT was that it purchased for its operators the very latest weapons and then let them do with them what they wanted. It was like a giant candy store for the violence-minded. Yet he finally decided that even at gun-happy HRT, it might raise some eyebrows—his checking out a .50 and enough ammo to shoot up a good-sized city. He did briefly think about calling in Bates as backup but then realized that might hold disastrous consequences. Big F hadn't survived on the streets this long by being stupid or impossibly lucky. He would smell the Bureau boys for sure, and wouldn't that just royally piss off the big guy. But if he had information about who had set up his team, Web had to find out what it was.

He had driven past the entrance to the Southern Belle farm. The opening was not as ornate at East Winds. And Web noted that the gates were closed and locked. He thought he could see a man patrolling near the entrance, but he wasn't certain of that or whether the man was armed. An interesting place. Even as he was thinking this, he heard the chopper coming overhead. He looked up, saw it passing by and then it disappeared from his sight. Maybe it was landing at Southern Belle. Maybe terrorists had landed in America. Web was only half kidding.

He had stopped to fill the car with gas. He thought about calling Claire but then decided against it. What would he say? *Maybe I'll see you tomorrow, and maybe I won't.*

The Woodrow Wilson Bridge had long been the single worst traffic bottleneck in the United States interstate highway system. To most local drivers, mentioning the name of the twenty-eighth President of the United States sent them into fits of rage. What a legacy, Web thought, for a life of selfless public service. Better to have your name attached to a rest stop. At least then people would think of you in connection with badly needed bodily relief.

He rolled onto the aging bridge and checked his watch. Thirty seconds to eleven. The Potomac was calm tonight, with no boat traffic apparent. The thick line of trees on the Maryland side contrasted sharply with the bright lights of Old Town Alexandria on the Virginia side and the Capitol dome and national monuments to the north. He passed the halfway point on the bridge. Traffic was relatively light and flowing well. A Virginia state police car passed Web heading in the opposite direction. Web felt like yelling after him, *Hey, wanta be my friend tonight? Got an appointment with Doctor Death.*

Web left the bridge and kept driving. He looked around. Nothing. So much for exact timing. Then a chilling thought hit him. Was he being set up to take a hit? Was there a sniper out there somewhere drawing a bead on him right now with his scope? Was the guy dialing in the drop compensation right now, seating the shell, settling his finger on the trigger, exhaling one last breath before he fired? Was Web London the world's biggest idiot?

"Take the next right. NOW! NOW!"

The voice seemed to come from everywhere and nowhere and startled Web so badly he almost pulled the Mercury into a one-eighty.

"Shit!" Web cried out even as he shot the car across three lanes of traffic while horns blared at him and cars dodged around him. He cut it so close the sedan skimmed the guardrail.

Web was now on the entry ramp onto Interstate 295.

"Take it to D.C.," the voice said in a calmer tone.

"Damn it, give me a little more notice next time," Web shot back, and then wondered if the guy could even hear him. He also wondered how they had managed to plant a communications device in his car without anyone seeing them. Web pointed the car north to D.C. He took deep breaths to calm himself. Right now he wished to never again hear another voice without a face to go with it.

"Keep going," the voice said. "I'll tell you where to turn."

Well, so much for what one wished for. It wasn't Squeaky Voice. Maybe this was Big F. It seemed to be a Big F voice, thought Web, for it was deep, blunt, threatening. Figured.

Web was very familiar with the area he was now in. The low-down on this stretch of lonely, woods-bracketed highway was that if one's car broke down, it would not be there when the owner came back for it. And if the owner stayed with his broken-down car, he wouldn't be coming back either. The boys that hunted here were the AAA of felony. Also down this way was St. Elizabeth's, the mental hospital for celebrity maniacs like John Hinckley and for those who kept trying to go over the fence at the White House, among many others.

The voice said, "Take the next exit. Turn left at the light, go one-point-one miles and take a right."

"Should I be writing this down or can you fax it to me?" asked Web, because he just felt like it.

"Shut the hell up!"

Well, at least they could hear him. And *see* him. He looked in his rearview mirror, but there were quite a few headlights back there. And yet if there was one thing Web couldn't stand, it was a criminal who lacked a good sense of humor. He slipped that one away in his payback file. He followed the directions and soon was smack in the middle of the death zones of Northeast and Southeast D.C. that bordered the Anacostia River and where over a thousand people had been murdered in the last seven years. By comparison, across the river and seemingly several universes away the affluent Northwest area had suffered a little over twenty homicides in the same time span. However, there was some sense of perverse balance because the Northwest quadrant had far more larcenies and thefts committed, for a very simple reason: the poor rarely had things criminals wanted to steal while the wealthy, of course, had an abundance of them. The Frederick Douglas National Historical Site was along where Web was traveling, and Web figured that the Martin Luther King, Jr., of his time would not be at all pleased with how things had turned out.

Web was given another set of directions and soon was pulling down a dirt road winding between nothing but trees and dense foliage. Web had been around here before. It was a favorite dumping ground for those in the more violent stretches of the city who didn't like to mess up their neighborhoods with body parts. HRT had done a couple of ops down here, in fact. One had gone textbook, without one shot fired. The other had left three men dead. All bad guys who just couldn't accept the fact that they were so outclassed and thus had stupidly pulled guns instead of putting up their hands. Maybe they thought there would be warning shots fired. Well, there was no chapter in the HRT manual on warning shots. Whenever Web had pulled his trigger, somebody ended up dead.

"Stop the car," said the voice, "and get out. Lay your gun on the front seat."

"How do you know I have a gun?"

"If you don't, you got horseshit for brains."

"And if I give my gun up, what exactly do I have for brains?"

"If you don't, you ain't gonna have no brains left."

Web placed the pistol on the front seat and slowly got out of the car and looked around. He saw nothing except trees and a moonless sky. He could smell the river water, and it was hardly comforting. The few movements he heard were assuredly not Big F–like, most likely squirrels, foxes or minor-grade criminals trolling for their supper. Right now the only thing Web wished he had done was stash Romano in the trunk. *Well, now you think of that.*

He stiffened slightly when he heard them coming. As they appeared from the cover of trees, Web could make out three large men in a row. They were all taller than Web, and they all had some serious hardware pointed at him. Web wasn't really focusing on them, though, for the far larger man was right behind them. Web had felt sure he was going to see the giant tonight, and yet the sight of Big F was still a little unnerving. He had on different clothes, but the same Club Med style. The shirt, though, wasn't open this time. All of Web's wounds inflicted by the giant criminal seemed to tingle in the man's presence as though some chemical interaction had just been triggered. Next to Big F was a white guy, which surprised Web until he recognized Clyde Macy in the flesh. He resembled a skeleton more in person than he did in the photo. Web recalled his talk with Bates when they had speculated who Cove's inside person might be. Macy? Peebles? Macy didn't look like a snitch, but who really knew? As Web kept his gaze on the man, he noted that the suit Macy wore and the ear radio made him look like Secret Service. Maybe he'd had aspirations to join the Service once, until he realized he liked killing people more. Peebles was nowhere in sight. The new breed of criminal entrepreneurs apparently didn't like to get their fingernails dirty.

The three underlings circled Web while Big F stood there and watched. Macy hung off to the side. He looked alert and relaxed at the same time. But it was easy to tell the man took his work very seriously. To Web, the other men looked a little bored, as though they were the varsity called in to scrimmage with the JV. Well, that was a real confidence booster. One man drew a short object from his coat pocket that looked like a microphone. He ran it up and

down Web's body while another man checked Web for additional
weapons. He found none but did confiscate Web's cell phone. Another of the men, with what Web knew now was an electronic
wand designed to ferret out nosey surveillance devices, did the
once-over on Web's car. The wand only sounded once, near the
rear seat, but the man seemed unconcerned by this. He turned
and nodded at Big F. Web understood this silent exchange: The
man had detected the electronic device they had planted in Web's
car. The men stepped back and Big F came forward and leaned his
bulk on the hood of Web's car. Web thought he could hear the car
groaning, and who could blame it?

"How's the face?"

The man's voice was neither squeaky high nor brutally deep. It
was middle-of-the-road, calm, nonthreatening. It wasn't the face-
less voice inside Web's car. Web could be talking to his stockbroker—if he had a stockbroker, that is.

"Only thing hurt was my pride. I take it you're Big F."

The man smiled at that and then slapped his thigh. To Web it
sounded like the ominous smack of thunder. Everything this guy
did was big. The other men laughed too, obviously cueing off
their boss.

"Shit. Big F. Damn right I'm Big F. That's good. Ain't that good,
boys?"

They all nodded and said it was good. Damn good. Macy didn't
even crack a smile. He just stood there and stared at Web like he
was trying to will him to die.

"Because if there was somebody bigger than you coming down
the pike, then I don't think I want to make his acquaintance." Web
knew it was always good to get on the bad guy's good side, show
you weren't afraid. Violent criminals just loved fear. And they just
loved to cut the throats of fearful people.

Big F laughed again. Yet when he stopped and looked serious, so
did everybody else. Instantly, Web noted.

"I got me a problem."

"I'm here to help." Web eased forward just a notch. Now he
could take out two of the guys with kicks. Big F was something
else altogether, sort of like punching Mount Rushmore, but you
went with the point of least resistance first.

"Somebody's setting me up to take a fall for something I ain't done."

"You know what happened to my team?"

"I don't need that shit, you understand me?" He stood, towering over them all, and the look in his eyes made Web's heart race. "How old you think I am?"

Web gave him the once-over. "Twenty-two."

"Thirty-two," Big F said proudly. "Now, that in black years." He turned to Macy. "What that be in tidy whitey time?"

"A hundred and twenty," said Macy in a learned tone, as though he were the Ph.D. of this illustrious group.

Big F looked back at Web. "I'm a hundred and twenty. I'm an old man in a young man's bizness. I don't need this shit. You go tell your crew that. Don't come hunting my ass down, 'cause I ain't done it."

Web nodded. "Then I need to know whose business it is. Without that, I can guarantee you squat."

Big F eased himself back down on the car and slid out a Beretta nine-millimeter, with a muzzle suppressor attached, Web noted. Things were definitely not looking good.

"Messengers a dime a dozen," said Big F, eyeing Web calmly.

"It'll mean a lot more coming from me. I've got a lot invested in this one." Web took one tiny step forward as he pretended to be merely shifting his weight. Now he could tag Big F with a spin kick right on the cerebellum. If the man could shake that off, then crown him king of the world. "And maybe you figure you owe me one for saving Kevin. Him being your little brother and all."

"He ain't my brother."

Web tried hard not to show his surprise. "Is that right?"

"He my son." Big F rubbed his nose, coughed and then spit. "Course, we got the same mama."

Web started for a moment and then looked at the other men. They obviously already knew this and seemed to accept it as mainstream, at least their version of mainstream. Yet why shouldn't they? Web thought. What was a little incest among family? You couldn't exactly do it with strangers. Grandma had said Kevin was a little slow. Well, with that twisted family tree, Web could see why.

"Well, I hope Kevin's okay," said Web.

"The boy's got nothing to do with you," Big F said sharply.

Okay, thought Web, so Kevin did mean something to the man. That was valuable intelligence. "Who took out my team? Tell me, and we go our separate ways. No hard feelings."

"Ain't that easy."

"Sure it is," Web prompted. "Names. That's all I want."

Big F studied his pistol. "You know what my biggest problem is?"

Web eyed the Beretta and wondered if *he* was Big F's biggest problem. He prepared to launch himself.

"Economy's too hot. I can't keep good people." He looked over at his men. "Toona-man, front and center."

Web watched as one of the men stepped forward. He was six-foot-four and broad-shouldered and wore what looked to Web to be a very expensive suit and enough gold and silver on his neck, wrists and fingers to start his own precious metals exchange.

"You think you can take this little dude with just your hands, Toona?"

Toona smirked. "Ain't be needing both hands for that boy."

"Don't know 'bout that," said Big F. "Way this boy kicked me, I felt that shit. Well, if you think you can, lay your gun down and get to it."

Toona slipped his gun out of his waistband and placed it on the ground. He was at least fifteen years younger than Web and much larger. And yet he moved so gracefully that Web was certain the man was as nimble as he was strong. And when Toona assumed a classic martial arts stance, Web knew he was in for something serious, and he hadn't even recovered from last night.

Web held up his hand. "Look, we don't have to do this. You think you can kick my ass, I think I can kick yours. Let's just call it a draw."

Big F shook his head. "Uh-uh, little dude. Either fight or take the bullet."

Web stared at the man and his gun, sighed, then put up his fists.

The two men circled each other for a few moments. Web sized his opponent up and saw few weaknesses, yet he did see something else that might be helpful. He tried a kick and Toona easily caught Web's leg and held on to it for a moment before twisting the limb and throwing Web down. Web quickly rose and took a side kick on the forearm. It stung like hell, but better his arm than his head. The two feinted and parried a few times more before

Toona caught Web with a flying spinner and he went down again, but he bounced right back up.

"Is that all the shit you got, Toona?" taunted Web. "Man, you got me by fifty pounds and fifteen years. If I was you, your ass would be out for the count by now."

Toona dropped his smirk and hit Web with an old-fashioned right jab but ate a hard left cross to the head in return. Toona didn't seem to like his face getting marked, something Web was quick to pick up on.

"Hey, Toona, a screwed-up face isn't the end of the world. With no ladies eating up your paycheck, you can probably really put some bucks away for retirement."

"You going down, man," said Toona. "And you staying down."

"Not from some pussy like you, I'm not."

An enraged Toona lunged at Web and caught him with a sharp punch right to the kidney. Web almost went down from the blow, but he wrapped his arms around Toona's middle and started to squeeze. Toona hit him with two more shots to the head, but Web held on. Like a constrictor, each time Toona took a breath, Web would squeeze a little bit more, not letting the man's diaphragm return to its original position.

More head shots and more squeezes and Web could start to feel the bigger man wavering, his gasps of breath so pleasant to hear. And then Web loosened his grip just a little, and it was enough for Toona to get his own clench on Web, which was what Web had intended. The two men swung each other around, panting heavily, their rivulets of sweat meeting each time their bodies did.

Toona tried to throw Web off, but Web held on, because he had other plans. Finally, Toona swung Web around and Web's grip was broken and he went sprawling. Actually, he did a controlled forward roll, grabbed Toona's pistol where he had left it on the ground, came upright, lunged forward, put a neck lock on the stunned Toona and placed the gun to his head, all in a blur of motion.

"You have to get yourself some better security," Web said to Big F. "Ain't that right, Toona?"

Big F raised his pistol and fired. His shot hit Toona dead center in the forehead. The man dropped and died without making one sound. Most gunshots to the head had that effect, Web knew, the ability of the victim to speak gone before the brain could dial up the scream. Bullets and flesh were like ex-wives. They just never mixed that well.

Web stared as Big F casually slipped the gun back in his waistband as though he had just disposed of an irksome mole in a vegetable garden. Big F's men looked as stunned as Web. Toona's demise had obviously been on only Big F's agenda. Macy, however, just stood there, his gun trained on Web; the sudden violent death of a colleague didn't seem to interest him at all. He was all cool and professional, standing there in a classic Weaver firing stance, his gaze riveted on the gun in Web's hand. Web wondered where the guy had received his training. Probably some paramilitary outfit staffed by ex-good-guys who, for some reason or other, had slid to the dark side.

With his hostage gone and multiple guns pointing at him, Web dropped the pistol.

"Good help," said Big F to Web, "I can't find it. I give my crew cash, clothes, cars and bitches. Show 'em the ropes, teach 'em the bizness, 'cause I ain't be doing this shit all my life. Cash in my chips, lose myself till I kick living. And you think that makes 'em loyal? Shit, no. They just keep biting the hand that feeds 'em. Toona making his own action on the side and think I ain't know it. Skimming dollars and dope off all the time. And he thinking I stupid and don't check that shit. But that ain't the dumbest thing he done. Dumbest thing the boy done is he be using the products. You put that shit in you, you talk to anybody 'bout anything. He be high on that shit and he be mouthing off to a whole crew a DEA and his ass not even know it. Sell us all down the river. Well, I ain't going down no river. I ain't being no drug kingpin working my bizness from the inside with no chance in hell of ever getting on the outside again. Uh-uh. No way, baby. No way. That ain't how it ending for me. I eat me some bullets before I go to mighty whitey's house."

He glanced sharply at his men. "You just gonna leave Toona there or what? Show some *damn* respect for the dead."

"What the hell you want us to do with him?" said one of them, his arms spread wide, his features angry, though Web easily sensed the fear he held for his boss. Web was certain Big F could smell that fear too. He no doubt counted on it in running his "bizness." If he wanted to teach his people loyalty, they had one very compelling reason lying right there in a growing red pond. And taking out Toona had probably been meant as a warning to Web too. Well, he felt incredibly warned.

Big F shook his head in obvious disgust. "I got to tell you every damn thing to do like you a little baby or something? I smell me water and so can you. Throw his ass in the river. And tie something to it, so it ain't come up!"

The men gingerly picked up their fallen comrade, bitching the whole time about getting blood and other Toona bits on their fine Versace. Macy stood in exactly the same spot. Apparently, Web thought, he was inner circle and thus was allowed to stay for extra innings.

When the others had disappeared down the trail, Big F eyed Web. "See what I mean 'bout good help? Can't get none. Everybody wants to get rich overnight. Nobody wants to work for a damn thing no more. Start at the top. They all wanta start at the top. I started at eight years old running dollar bags of white rock. Worked my ass off for over twenty years and these brothers today be thinking they deserve every dime I got 'cause they be doing this shit for a coupla months. New economy, my ass!"

If Big F had been sitting in a maximum-security prison cell wearing Hannibal Lecter ready-to-wear and Web was safely on the other side of the bars, Web might have started laughing his guts out at this capitalistic tirade. Yet right now all he was wondering was when Big F would finally focus on the fact that Web was an eyewitness to murder.

"Now, Toona, he must've killed five or six people. So I just saved you the trouble of frying his ass. Ain't gotta thank me."

Web didn't. In fact, he said nothing. He probably could have made some smart remark, but witnessing the cold-blooded murder of another human being, no matter how much he might have deserved it, was not a great lead-in to humor for Web.

"I guess everybody got trouble." Big F wiped at one of his eyes. "But the Lord done showered me with some extra helpings. I got me family coming out my ass and every one of them looking for cash. Got me a ninety-year-old great-aunt I ain't even know I had coming round talking like this." His voice rose higher. "'Now, Francis, can't you take care of my eyes? Got me the cataracts, honey, can't see to play the Bingo no mo'. Do something about it for me, will you, honey? Used to bounce you on my knee. Used to change your shitty diaper.' And I peel off some cash and there you go. And she back a week later 'bout her damn cat what got female problems." He looked at Web incredulously. "A fucking cat with female problems. 'And it only be a thousand dollars, Francis,' she says, 'that all it be, honey, and remember I wiped your shitty diaper while your mama was down the river or else shooting herself up with that little needle of hers.' And you know what I do? I peel off ten hundreds and give it to her and her cat."

"The *F* stands for Francis?"

Big F grinned. And it seemed to Web that he saw for the first time signs of little Kevin in this hulking, murderous adult.

"Yeah, what'd you think it stood for?"

Web shook his head. "No clue."

Big F took out a small box, unwrapped a pill and put it in his mouth. He offered one to Web, who declined.

"Tagamet, Pepcid AC, Zantac," said Big F. "I eat 'em like peanuts. Had me an upper GI done. Damn belly looks like a mole's been through it. This shit's getting to me, ain't no lie."

"So why don't you retire?"

"Easy to say, not so easy to do. Ain't like they give me a going-away lunch and a gold watch in my line a work."

"Sorry to tell you, but the cops never stop looking."

"The cops I can deal with. It's some folks in the bizness what giving me the pain in the ass. They think if you want to quit working you gonna rat 'em out. They can't understand why'd you walk away from a life like mine. Money out the ass, 'cept you got to keep hiding it, and you got to keep moving around, and you're still always wondering when somebody, like maybe your bitch or your brother or your cat-loving great-aunt, is gonna put a hole in your head while you sleeping." He grinned. "Now, don't you worry 'bout me. I be fine." He popped another pill and then closely eyed Web. "You one of them guys from HRT?"

"I am."

"I hear you dudes are some serious shit. When you hit me the other night, boy, that hurt. That's rare, little man, let me tell you, that's rare. You guys must be some bad shit."

"We're actually really lovable when you get to know us."

Big F didn't crack a smile at Web's remark. "So how come you ain't dead?"

"Guardian angel."

Now Big F smiled broadly. "Right, that's good shit. Tell me where I can get me one."

Big F shifted his bulk along with the direction of the conversation. "You want to know how them guns got in that building?"

Web stiffened. "You willing to testify to it?"

"Yeah. I come on down to the courthouse. You go on ahead and wait for me."

"Okay, how'd they get the guns in there?"

"You know how old them buildings are?"

Web's eyes narrowed. "Old? No. Why?"

"The 1950s. I ain't old 'nough to remember, but my mama was. She told me."

"Was?"

"Too much coke. Not the soda pop. Yeah, 1950s. Think, HRT. Think."

"I'm not getting it."

He shook his head and looked over at Macy and then back at Web. "I thought you damn Feds all went to college."

"Some colleges are better than others."

"If you can't fly the shit in through the roof and you can't take it in the front door, what you got left?"

Web thought for a moment before it hit him. "Under. The 1950s. Cold War. Underground bomb shelters. Tunnels?"

"Damn, you smart after all. There you go."

"That's still not much to go on."

"That's your problem. I gave you something, now you tell your folks to back off my ass. I ain't got no reason in the world to waste a buncha Feds. You go back and make sure they understand that." He paused and rubbed some pine needles with his huge foot, and then he looked directly at Web. "You guys ain't playing games on me and got Kevin but ain't saying, are you?"

Web considered how best to answer that. Ironically, given his present company, he decided that the truth was the best approach. "We don't have Kevin."

"See, local cops I don't trust as far as I can throw 'em. Too many brothers end up dead when the local cops get to 'em. Now, Feds ain't worth too much in my book neither, but you guys ain't killing people for no reason."

"Thanks."

"So other things being equal, see, if you guys got Kevin, then I know he be all right. And maybe you boys just hold on to him for a while till this shit blows over."

The way the man was half looking at him, Web could tell Big F really wanted Kevin to be in the custody of the FBI, where he would be reasonably safe.

"I wish we did have him, but we don't. I'm playing it straight with you." Then he added, "But I think Kevin might have been involved somehow."

"Bullshit," roared Big F. "He a kid. He ain't done nothing. He ain't going to no jail, no way is he. Not Kevin."

"I didn't say he knew what he was doing. You're right: He's just a kid, a scared kid. But whoever took him is behind what happened. At least that's what I think. I don't know why Kevin was in that alley, but his being there wasn't a coincidence. I want him just as bad as you do. And I want him safe too. I saved him once in that alley, I don't want it to be for naught."

"Right, so he can testify and then spend the rest of his life in witness protection. Some life."

"At least it's a life," Web shot back.

Big F and he had a prolonged stare-down until the big man finally looked away.

"I'm going to do everything I can to get Kevin back safe and sound, Francis. I promise you that. But if he knows something, he's going to have to tell us. We'll protect him."

"Yeah, sure you will. Done a real good job of that so far, ain't you?"

They heard the other men returning. "A name would be nice to go with the tunnels," said Web, but Big F was already shaking his head.

"Ain't got none to give."

When the two men came into sight, Big F motioned to one of them. "Make sure the two-way in the car ain't working."

The man nodded, slid into the front seat of Web's car and fired two bullets into the government-issued radio and then ripped out the hand-held microphone. He also popped the ammo clip out of Web's gun, fired the round that was chambered into the dirt and handed it back to him. The other man pulled out Web's cell phone from his pocket, ceremoniously smashed it against a tree and then handed it back to Web with a broad smile. "Ain't making 'em like they used to."

"We got to be going now," said Big F. "And in case you thinking 'bout coming after my ass for pulling the trigger on Toona, think 'bout this." He paused and stared grimly at Web. "Anytime I want you dead, you dead. Anytime I want any of your friends dead, they dead. You got a pet and I want it dead, it dead."

Web eyed the man steadily. "You don't want to go down that road, Francis. You really don't."

"What? You gonna kick my ass? You gonna hurt me bad? You gonna kill me?" He unbuttoned his shirt and stepped closer to Web. Web had seen a lot in his line of work, yet he had never seen anything quite like this.

The man's chest and belly were covered with knife wounds, bullets holes, thick, angry-looking scars, burn marks and what looked to be tunnels of ripped flesh badly healed. To Web it seemed a painting collectively produced by an insane world.

"One hundred and twenty in nice little tidy-whitey years," Big F said quietly. He closed the shirt and his face held, to Web's thinking, a look of obvious pride at surviving all that those scars represented. And right now, Web couldn't deny the man that.

Big F said, "You come after me, you better bring something to do the job right. And I'll still cut off your dick and stuff it down your throat."

Big F turned away and it was all Web could do not to leap on the man's back. Now was not Web's time to settle this, yet he couldn't just leave it like this.

He called after Big F. "So I guess you're grooming Kevin to inherit your empire. Your brother-son. I'm sure he's real proud of you."

Big F turned back. "I said Kevin's not your bizness."

"We shared a lot back in that alley. He told me lots of stuff." It was all a bluff, but a calculated one, if Web was reading the signals right. Whoever had switched Kevin out might be Big F's enemy. If that was the case, then playing one against the other might not be such a bad idea. Web was thinking that Big F was not above lying about not being involved, but that didn't mean the street capitalist hadn't done a joint venture with somebody else to knock off Charlie Team. If so, Web wanted everybody. Everybody.

Big F walked up to Web and looked him over, as though gauging either his guts or his stupidity.

"If you want Kevin back, I expect some cooperation," said Web. He hadn't mentioned what Big F had told him. He figured Big F wanted to keep the information about the tunnels under the target building between him and Web, which was why Big F had sent the two men off to give Toona a burial in the river.

"Expect this," said Big F.

Web managed to partially block the blow with his forearm, but the impact of Big F's bowling-ball fist and his own arm against his jaw still knocked him on top of the hood of the car, where his head smacked against the windshield, cracking it.

Web woke up a half hour later, slowly slid off the car hood and staggered around holding his arm and rubbing his jaw and head and cursing. Calming down, he discovered that his jaw, arm and head did not appear broken and he wondered how that was possible. He also wondered how many more concussions he could endure before his brain fell out of his head.

And then Web whirled and pointed his gun at the man who had just emerged from behind a stand of trees. The man was pointing his own gun at Web.

"Nice try," said the man, "but your gun doesn't have any bullets." He stepped forward and Web got a better look at him.

"Cove?"

Randall Cove put his gun away and leaned up against the car. He said, "That dude is one seriously dangerous person. Him blowing away his own guy like that, that was a new one even for me." He looked at Web's face. "You're gonna have some good bruises tomorrow, but it's better than a visit with the coroner."

Web put his empty gun away and rubbed the back of his head. "I take it you had a ringside seat. Thanks for the assist."

Cove looked at him grimly. "Look, man, I'm a fellow agent, undercover or not. Carry the same creds, took the same oath, work through the same bullshit you do at the Bureau. If they'd tried to take you out, you would have known my presence. But they didn't and so I didn't. If it makes you feel any better, while you were unconscious, I shooed away some brothers who came sniffing around your carcass."

"Thanks, because I'm not done with this carcass yet."

"We need to talk, but not here. Some of Big F's boys might still be hanging around. And this place ain't safe, not even for armed lawmen."

Web looked around. "Where, then? They knocked your old office down."

Cove smiled. "You been talking to Sonny, I know. I guess if old Sonny Venables thinks you're all right, you're all right. Boy's got a nose for bad meat like the best hound dog I ever had me in Mississippi."

"There's a lot of shit going on. You been in touch with Bates lately?"

"We talk, but neither one of us is telling the other everything, and that's cool. I know where Perce is coming from and he knows where I'm standing." He handed Web a slip of paper. "Meet me here in thirty minutes."

Web looked at his watch. "I'm on special assignment. I've got to get back."

"Don't worry, it won't take long. Oh, one more thing." He climbed inside Web's car and searched for a few moments before coming back out holding something.

"Satellite-based tracking device. Good as the stuff we use," said Cove.

"They've got a satellite," said Web. "That's comforting."

"It's got a wireless communicator too."

So Web had been correct in deducing how they had relayed the directions to him after crossing over the Wilson Bridge.

Cove switched the device off and pocketed it. "Evidence is evidence. Surprised they didn't take it," he added before disappearing into the woods.

Sufficiently recovered to keep both eyes open at the same time and seeing only double instead of in gauzy triplicate, Web put the car in gear and headed out. He met Cove at the Mall downtown, at a bench near the Smithsonian Castle. When Web sat down there, he heard a voice but didn't react. All that had been on the paper. Web reasoned that Cove was behind a set of bushes near the bench.

"So Bates said he filled you in on me."

"He did. I'm sorry what happened to your family."

"Yeah," was all Cove said to that.

"I found the news clipping at your house, about you and Bates."

"You are good. That hiding place has worked for years."

"Why hide it?"

"Red herring. Somebody searching your house, it gives them something to find that really means nothing. Anything really important I keep in my head."

"So the clipping was just a dodge? Nothing important?"

Cove didn't respond, so Web said, "Bates said you were on the butts of some big-time dealers, that they might have set up my team."

"That's right. But this story is a long way from over. And I heard Westbrook tell you about the tunnels. I never figured that one. Good way to get the computers out and the guns in."

"I'm going to fill in Bates on that one ASAP and we'll go take a look. You want in?"

Cove didn't answer and it took a second for Web to figure out why. Across the street a man was walking by. He was dressed like a homeless person, was staggering slightly as though he were drunk and he could very well have been both. However, Web couldn't take any chances and obviously neither could Cove. Web reached for his gun and realized again that it was empty. He had a spare mag in the trunk of the car, but that was parked a good hundred feet away and he had forgotten to get the ammo out, idiot that he was. As though in answer to his thoughts, Web felt something slide next to him through the back support of the bench. He gripped the pistol that Cove had just handed him, whispered a thank-you and sat there, the gun held at his side, its muzzle following each move of the man across the street until he moved off.

"You just never know what riffraff's going to come on by," Cove said.

"Bates said that you might have been working through one of Westbrook's guys, maybe Peebles or Macy, and that they might've set you up."

"Macy and Peebles weren't my inside connection. I think my guy was dealing straight with me, at least mostly, but I think *he* was set up."

"So if the guy was shooting straight with you, any chance we can use him to get to the truth?"

"Not anymore."

"How come?"

"Because my inside guy was Toona."

"You're kidding me."

"Big F's guys skim all the time. That was just bullshit he was feeding you. He killed Toona for the ultimate sin, working with the cops."

"Did Toona think there were others involved besides Westbrook?"

"Toona was basically muscle, but he had some brains. I've been working with him for about six months. We nailed him on some small stuff, but he'd already done four years in prison early on in his career and didn't want to do any more. He told me about this new group coming in that was handling some of the local crew's distribution and even cleaning up their dirty money through some legit operations. The service didn't come cheap, but most of the crews apparently signed on—except Westbrook. He doesn't trust anybody that much. But even drug crews get tired of shooting each other up. And consolidation of operations and cost-cutting works just as well in illegal businesses as it does legitimate ones. I'd been digging deep on this group but couldn't crack it. My undercover identity was as a point man for a drug crew looking to relocate from Arizona to rural Virginia. We'd heard about this group and I got myself invited to look over their operation. At first I thought it was connected to Westbrook's piece. But when I saw what was there, I knew it was big-time stuff."

"Bates mentioned the Oxycontin piece."

"That's what makes this one special. I think the product this group was principally supplying the locals with were prescription drugs like Oxy, Percocet and the like. Low risk and huge profit margins. Now, Toona wasn't in the ops side of the business, but he seemed to think that too. It'd be a whole new paradigm in the District's drug trade. And this new group wasn't stopping at D.C. I believe they're moving the stuff up and down the East Coast."

"Oxy started out rural."

"Yeah, you heard of Rocky Mountain high? Well this is Appalachian high. But the Appalachian Mountains touch on about twenty states, from Alabama all the way up to the Canadian border. And there's lots of room there to carve out a new homegrown drug empire on the backs of legitimate drugs. That's why I called in WFO as soon as I realized the operation in that warehouse was a lot bigger than Westbrook. Now, I could have kept digging and maybe got some more stuff, but I ran the risk of them pulling out. I figured if we could get the bean counters to testify, we could bring this whole Oxy crew down. Man, I look back at it now, and you know what I think?"

"That it was too good to be true?"

"You got it." Cove stopped talking for a moment. "Look, Web, I'm sorry what happened to your guys. I never in a million years smelled the setup. But I'll take the responsibility because it was my screwup. And I'll sacrifice everything I got left, even my life, to make it right."

"What you do for a living, I never could. I don't know how you guys do it."

"Funny, I was thinking the same thing about you. Now you go to those tunnels and figure out how they got that stuff in and out. And maybe you'll see something that'll tell you who. And I'm not thinking that it's Westbrook. There's somebody else out there, having a nice laugh at our expense."

"You got any firmer thoughts on that?"

"I'm still feeling my way. Whoever it is, they are wired in tight somewhere important, because they seem to be able to keep one step ahead of everybody."

"Wired tight to who, somebody at the Bureau?"

"You said it, I didn't."

"You got proof of that?"

"My gut. You listen to yours?"

"All the time. I take it you feel like the odd man out."

"What, you mean everybody and their brother thinking I turned traitor and helped burn a bunch of my own? Yeah, it has occupied my thoughts of late."

"You're not alone there, Cove."

"Hey, Web, we're blood brothers in a way. Branded traitors for something we didn't do, and some people just don't want to hear it."

"Is that why you're not coming in?"

"See, the bottom line is, I got taken, snookered, suckered, whatever you want to call it. I'm no traitor, but I messed up, that's almost as bad as jumping sides in my line of work."

"We are blood brothers, then, because I did the same damn thing."

"Well, maybe we'll both be standing at the end of this dance, what do you say?"

"I say I'll give it my best shot."

"Keep your head down, London, these mothers shoot low."

"Hey, Cove?"

"Yeah?"

"Apology accepted."

Web drove to DuPont Circle. He grabbed a spare mag for his pistol from the trunk and put the gun Cove had given him in the rear of his waistband and then took a cab to the WFO. Bates had long since gone home and Web decided he would wait until morning to contact him. The guy could probably use a good night's sleep and those tunnels weren't going anywhere. Instead of checking out another set of Bucar wheels, Web decided to do something really crazy. He was going to go get his very own car.

The press army wasn't parked outside his house anymore, yet Web still did not take any chances. He entered the house from the rear, slipped inside the Mach, opened the garage doors and eased the car out, its lights off. He waited until he was down the street before he turned on the lights, then he stepped on the gas, all the while looking in his rearview mirror. Nothing. He headed back to East Winds.

34

When Web got back to the carriage house, Romano wasn't there; Web even checked the antique cars downstairs in case his partner had crawled into one to admire it and had fallen asleep. It was almost four o'clock in the morning and his partner was probably prowling around outside. As a sniper, Romano had been restless with too much natural energy despite all their training to take things slow and methodically unless drastic circumstances dictated otherwise. Yet when it was time for action, just about everybody took a backseat to Paul Romano. Since Web's cell phone was out of operation, he used the phone in the house to call Romano and breathed a sigh of relief when the man answered.

"So how'd your appointment go?" asked Romano.

"Boring. I'll fill you in later. Where are you?"

"Everything was secure, so I've been poking around the place. There's an old watchtower on the west side. See for miles in every direction."

"I know; I've been there."

"Well, I'm there right now. Felt like a little jog."

"That's a bit of a hike, Paulie."

"Walk in the park. You might want to come out here and bring out a pair of NVs."

"What are you spying on?"

"You'll see."

Web left the carriage house from the rear, slipped on his head-gear, attached his ambient light source night-vision binoculars to it, powered up and fixed the relief to his eyes. The world instantly became an ethereal, fluid green. You couldn't use the contraption for very long because the goggles were heavy enough that you would get a piercing pain in your neck, followed by a headache that would make you forget the neck ache. Web always kept one eye closed when scanning through the goggles even though this distorted your depth perception even more; if you didn't keep one eye closed, when you stopped looking through the goggles all you'd see would be a brilliant orange ball in each eye. And at that point a ninety-year-old in a wheelchair could get the drop on you.

As a sniper, one had to use various pieces of equipment to get the job done, from high-tech to the lowest tech of all: camouflage. Web coveted his Ghillie suit, a concoction of burlap and cordura material that he had patiently covered with animal excrement and other foul substances to allow it to blend into a rugged forest or jungle environment. Each HRT sniper gave his Ghillie his own personal stamp and Web had spent years improving on his by defiling it even more. The Ghillie had been originally designed by the Scots over four hundred years ago in the course of waging countless guerrilla wars against those seeking to conquer them. It worked just as well now as it had then. Web had lain under his Ghillie in the middle of a jungle in Central America with dope dealers toting submachine guns walking all around him, and they never knew Web was there until he stuck his gun in their backs and read them their rights.

He moved forward again and pushed and then clicked the NV to IR status, which caused an internal light source to come on and vastly intensified the field of vision. Web wanted to make sure the equipment worked, for NV goggles batteries were notorious for failing right when you needed them to work. He didn't like to use the IR for very long, because it had one major drawback. For anyone watching *him* with night-vision goggles, the IR magnifier gave off a light beacon, like a large flashlight in one's face. Web would be a sitting duck. He clicked off the IR and put the headgear away in his backpack. He would rely on merely his eyes from now on, something he had done with every shot he had ever taken. Sometimes you couldn't improve on nature.

The air was crisp and the sounds of the farm and surrounding woods many and varied. Web set a good pace and he covered the ground to the watchtower in enviable time. It was good to know he was still in decent shape. After eight years of relentless training you didn't lose it all in a short period of time, he reasoned. He liked the forest in the darkness; it felt as comfortable to him as a La-Z-Boy and a big-screen TV would to the average American male.

He sighted the watchtower and stopped. Since he didn't have a cell phone, Web put his hands up to his face, formed a rude bugle of sorts and let out a call, the same signal he and Romano had used when they were sniping. It could either be a gust of wind or a bird commonly found just about anywhere. Web was sure Romano would remember, and a few seconds later he heard the answering message. All clear.

Web broke from the tree line and hustled to the watchtower, gripped the wooden rungs and climbed silently up. Romano greeted him at the little hinged door in the floor of the observation space. Web knew Romano couldn't see Web's fresh injuries courtesy of Toona and Big F, and that was just as well, because he didn't want to waste breath right now explaining them. And of course Romano would give him a hard time about it. He could just hear the words *Shit, you let them do that to you?* passing through the man's lips.

Web looked at Romano as he pulled out a ten-power Litton scope that was normally attached to a .308 sniper rifle.

"Anything good on?" asked Web.

"Check this out, right through that break in the trees to the northwest."

Web looked through the scope. "I take it I'm looking at the Southern Belle."

"Interesting stuff going on, for a horse farm."

Web adjusted the scope to his eye and sighted through it. There was indeed a nice break in the trees, which revealed a fine view of the neighboring spread.

There were two sizable buildings that looked relatively new. Large trucks were parked next to them and Web watched as men with walkie-talkies raced in different directions. A door opened on the side of one of the buildings and Web saw that whatever was going on inside required a lot of light. A tractor-trailer was backed up to a warehouse-type roll-up door and men were bringing large boxes out on hand trucks and rolling them up inside the truck's trailer.

"Something big is going on," said Web. "Auto chop shop, drugs, stolen aviation parts, spies, technology pirates or lots of other things. Damn."

"Fascinating neighborhood. And here I was, thinking Virginia horse country was just a bunch of old duffers riding around drunk chasing little foxes while the little women had tea in the afternoon. Boy, have I got a lot to learn." He looked at Web. "So what do you think?"

"I think with all we got going on, the Southern Belle will have to keep. But if something pops at least we'll be right here to do something about it."

Romano grinned, obviously happy with the thought of coming action and possible mayhem. "Now you're talking my language."

35

Kevin Westbrook had filled up all his sketchbooks and was now sitting and staring at the walls. He wondered if he would ever stand under sunlight again. He had grown used to the sounds of the machinery and the water running. It no longer affected his sleep, though he regretted growing used to this condition of his imprisonment, as though it were an omen that those conditions would become permanent.

The footsteps reached his ears over the other sounds and he retreated to his bed like an animal in a zoo cage as visitors approached.

The door opened and the same man who'd visited him earlier came in. Kevin didn't know who he was and the man had never bothered to tell Kevin his name.

"How you doing, Kevin?"

"Got a headache."

The man reached in his pocket and pulled out a bottle of Tylenol. "In my line of work, I always got some of this handy." He gave two pills to the boy and poured him out a glass of water from the bottle on the table.

"Probably lack of sunlight," added Kevin.

The man smiled at this. "Well, we'll see if we can do something about that soon."

"That mean I be getting out of here soon?"

"It might mean just that. Things are rolling along."

"So you won't be needing me no more." As soon as Kevin said this he regretted it. That statement could certainly cut both ways.

The man stared at him. "You did a pretty good job, Kev. Real good, considering you're just a kid. We'll remember that."

"Can I go home soon?"

"Not up to me, actually."

"I ain't say nothing to nobody."

"Nobody like Francis?"

"Nobody means nobody."

"Well, it won't matter, really."

Kevin instantly looked suspicious. "You ain't hurting my brother."

The man held up his hands in mock surrender. "I didn't say we were. In fact, if things go okay, only people who need to get hurt are going to get hurt, okay?"

"You hurt all them men in that courtyard. You hurt them dead."

The fellow perched on the table and crossed his arms over his chest. Though the man's movements weren't threatening, Kevin drew back a bit.

"Like I said, the people who deserve to be hurt are the ones who get hurt. It's not always that way, you know that, lots of innocent people get hurt all the time. I had me enough lessons on that, and looks like you have too." He eyed the wounds on the boy's face.

Kevin had nothing to say to this. The man opened one of the sketchbooks and looked at some of the drawings.

"This the Last Supper?" he asked.

"Yep. Jesus. Before they crucified him. He's the one in the middle," said Kevin.

"I went to Sunday school," the man said with another big smile. "I know all about Jesus, son."

Kevin had drawn the painting from memory. He had done it for two reasons: to pass the time and for the sheer comfort of having the Son of God close right now. Maybe the Lord would get the message and send some guardian angels down to help one Kevin Westbrook, who desperately needed some type of intervention, divine or otherwise.

"This is good stuff, Kevin. You're real talented."

He looked at another picture and held it up. "What's this of?"

"My brother reading to me."

His pistol on the nightstand, his men outside the room with their own guns, his brother Francis would put a big arm around Kevin and draw him close to his massive chest and they would sit and read far into the night, until Kevin would fall asleep. He would awake in the morning and all the men would be gone and so would his brother. But the place they had stopped in the book would be marked; it was a sure sign that his brother intended to come back and finish reading it to him.

The man looked surprised. "He'd read to you?"

Kevin nodded. "Yeah, why not? Ain't nobody ever read to you when you was little?"

"No," he replied. He put the sketchbook back on the table. "How old are you, Kevin?"

"Ten."

"That's a good age, your whole life ahead of you. Wish I had me that."

"You ever gonna let me go?" asked Kevin.

The man's look managed to cut Kevin's hopes right to nothing.

"I like you, Kevin. You kind of remind me of me when I was little. I didn't really have any family to speak of neither."

"I got my brother!"

"I know you do. But I'm talking about a normal life, you know, Mommy and Daddy and sisters and brothers living in the same place."

"What's normal for some folks ain't normal for everybody."

The man grinned and shook his head. "You got a lot of wisdom in that little head. I guess nothing about life is normal when you get down to it."

"You know my brother. He ain't somebody you fool around with."

"I don't know him personally, but me and him do some business together. And I'm sure he ain't somebody you want to fool around with, and thank you for the advice. But the thing is, we're working together right now, sort of. I asked him real nicely to do something for me having to do with that Web London fellow, and he did it."

"I bet he done it 'cause you told him you had me. He doing it 'cause he don't want nothing to happen to me."

"I'm sure he did, Kevin. But just so you know, we're going to return the favor. Some folks real close to your brother want to cut in on his business. We're going to help him out there."

"Why you gonna help him?" Kevin asked suspiciously. "What's in it for you?"

He laughed. "Man, if you were just a little bit older, I'd make you my partner. Well, let's just put it this way, it's a win-win for everybody."

"So you ain't answered my question. You gonna let me go?"

The man rose and went over to the door. "You just hang in there, Kev. Good things tend to happen to patient folks."

36

When he got back to the carriage house, Web called Bates at home, waking him up, and told him about his violent encounter with Big F. He also told him about his meeting with Cove. He rendezvoused with Bates and a team of agents at the courtyard in southeast D.C. an hour later. The sun was just starting its rise and Web could only shake his head. He hadn't even been to sleep yet and it was time to start a new workday. Bates gave him another phone to replace the one Westbrook's guy had smashed; same phone number, so that was convenient.

Web thanked Bates, who didn't comment on the fresh injuries to Web's face, though Bates clearly was not in a good mood.

"You keep going through government equipment like that, it's coming out of your damn paycheck. And I left you messages on your old phone that you never returned."

"Well, damn, Perce. I get voice-mail messages popping up on my screen sometimes a day after I get them."

"I never had a problem."

"Well, that really helps me, doesn't it?"

They had left one agent to watch their cars. In this neighborhood, nothing was safe or sacred, least of all Uncle Sam's property. In fact, some enterprising young fellows would like nothing better than to chop-shop a Bucar and make a tidy profit in the bargain.

As they walked, Bates's temper seemed to grow. "You're lucky you're alive, Web," he snapped, not seeming happy at all that Web had been so lucky. "That's what you get for going off on your own.

I can't believe you went into that with no backup. You disobeyed my orders. I could have your ass, all of it."

"But you won't because I'm giving you what you need. A break."

Bates finally calmed down and shook his head. "Did he really blow the guy away right in front of you for being a snitch?"

"That's not something one tends to get wrong."

"Jesus, the balls the guy must have."

"Bowling balls, if they fit the rest of him."

They all went inside the target building and down to the basement level. It was dark and damp, and it stank. Going from a stone mansion in Virginia horse country to a dungeon in Anacostia made Web want to laugh. Yet he really had to concede that he was more of a dungeon guy.

"Tunnels, the man said," commented Bates, looking around. There were no working lights down here, so each agent had brought a searchlight. "See, the thing is, we checked for things like that, Web."

"Well, we need to check again, because he seemed to know what he was talking about, and there's really no other way those guns could have been brought in with no one seeing anything. Don't they have plans down at the Department of Public Works that would show the location of the tunnels?"

"This is D.C., okay? If you want to go and try and find anything at a city agency, be my guest. Stuff from yesterday is hard enough to track down, much less from half a century ago."

They searched everywhere until Web came to a large collection of fifty-gallon oil drums in a far corner. They were ten abreast and ten deep. "What's with all this?"

"Furnace system was oil-based. Supply just got left when the place was shut down. Too costly to move it."

"Anybody check under them?"

In answer, one of the agents went over to the pile and pushed against one of the drums. It didn't budge. "Nothing's under here, Web. You wouldn't park a million tons of oil on top of a tunnel you had to get in and out of."

"Is that right?" Web eyed the drum the man had tried to move. He put his foot against it and it was indeed full. Web pushed the one next to it and the one next to that. Then he pushed against drums in the second row. All full.

"Okay, are you convinced?" asked Bates.

"Humor me."

As Bates and the other agents watched, Web climbed on top of the drums and started stepping from one to another. With each one he would stop and rock his weight back and forth. When he reached the middle of the cluster of oil drums, he rocked on top of one can and almost fell over. "This one's empty." He stepped over to the drum next to it. "This one too." He marched out a four-drum-by-four-drum grid. "These are all empty. Give me a hand."

The other agents scampered up to help and very quickly they had cleared away the empty drums and their lights shone on a door in the floor.

Bates stared at it and then looked at Web. "Son of a bitch. How'd you figure that one out?"

"I did a case when I worked in the Kansas City Field Office. Guy scammed a bunch of bankers by filling up a warehouse with drums that were supposed to contain heating oil the guy was using for collateral for this huge loan. The bankers sent their inspectors out and sure enough, they opened a few drums and they were all filled with heating oil. But they only checked the front fringes because guys in suits don't like to climb over dirty oil drums. Turns out ninety percent of the drums were empty. I know because I checked every damn one after we were called in when the guy skipped town."

Bates looked chagrined. "I owe you one, Web."

"And believe me I'll hold you to that."

Guns drawn, they opened the door, climbed down into the tunnel and followed its straight and then sharply angled path.

Web flashed his light on the floor. "Somebody's been through here recently. Look at all those tracks."

The tunnel ended in a stairwell. They headed quietly up, every man alert and ready to fire. They eased the unlocked door open and found themselves in another building much like the one they had just left. The area they were in had a lot of abandoned property. They moved stealthily upstairs. The room they found there was large and empty. They moved back downstairs, exited the building and looked around.

"I figure we went west about two blocks," said one of the agents, and Web agreed with that. They all looked at the building where the tunnel had led. Faded lettering on one wall identified it as once having been a food distribution company, and it came complete with a loading dock where trucks could deliver bananas. Or machine guns. At the loading dock were a couple of abandoned trucks, tires gone, doors missing.

"In the middle of the night you pull up with a truck and squeeze it right between these two, off-load your crates, take 'em through the tunnel and that's it," said Web. His gaze swept the area. "And there are no residences around here, no one to see anything, that's probably why they used it."

"Okay, but we got Big F on murder one. With your testimony he goes away forever."

"You have to find him first, and from what I've seen he's pretty good at what he does."

"We're going to need to put you in protective custody."

"No, you don't. I'm good on that."

"What the hell do you mean, you're good on that? This guy has every incentive to blow you away."

"If he had wanted to do that, he would've done it last night. I was just a tad helpless then. Besides, I've got a job to do—protect Billy and Gwen Canfield—and I'm going to finish that job."

"That's what I don't get. He murders a guy right in front of you and lets you walk."

"So I could deliver the message about the tunnels."

"What, he's never heard of a damn phone? I'm not kidding, Web, I want you in protection."

"You said you owed me, I'm calling in my chit."

"What the hell is more important than staying alive?"

"I don't know, Perce, in my line of work I've never really thought about it very much. And I'm not going in."

"I'm your superior, I can make you."

"Yeah, I guess you can," said Web, looking at the man evenly.

"Aw, shit, you're more trouble than you're worth, London."

"Figured you learned that a long time ago."

Bates looked around the loading dock. "The thing is, there's nothing tying the Frees to this warehouse or those guns. Without something to go on, we can't hit them. Right now they're being little angels, giving us no excuse to pay a visit."

"Nothing has turned up with the killings in Richmond to connect them to the Frees? That's a lot of tracks to cover."

"From the angle of the shot on Judge Leadbetter we traced it to a building across the street that's under construction. Hundreds of people work there all the time, laborers who come and go."

"What about the phone call he got?"

"Pay phone in southside Richmond. No trace."

"But the judge was downtown. So at least two people were involved and they had communication links so the timing of the call was right."

"That's right. I never thought we were dealing with amateurs here."

"What about Watkins and Wingo?"

"All the people in Wingo's office have been checked out."

"Cleaning people? One of them could have applied the atropine to the phone receiver."

"Again, we checked. Those people come and go, but we found no leads."

"Watkins?"

"Gas leak. It was an old house."

"Come on, he gets a phone call right as he walks in. Again, it's split-second timing. And by somebody who knew all three men's routines. And he just happened to have a solenoid in his phone that would make the spark necessary to blow him to heaven?"

"I know, Web, but these guys also had lots of other people with incentives to kill them. One or two of the murders might be related, but maybe all of them aren't. At least right now all we have to link them are the phones and the Ernest Free case."

"They're connected, Perce, trust me."

"Right, but we have to convince a jury, and that's getting almost impossible to do these days."

"Anything on the bomb out at East Winds?"

"Very sophisticated C4 device. We've checked the backgrounds of all the people working out there. Most of the farmhands came with Strait when the place they were working at closed down. They're all pretty much clean. A few had misdemeanors, mostly for drunk and disorderly, stuff you'd expect from a bunch of rednecks."

"What about Nemo Strait?"

"Like he told you. Grew up on a small horse farm that his father managed. That's how he learned the business. He fought in Vietnam and was a superb soldier. Lots of medals and lots of hard fighting. He spent three months as a POW."

"One tough dude, to be able to survive that. The Cong weren't known for their hospitality."

"He did some odd jobs when he got back to the States, prison guard, computer sales. Along the way he married, had some kids, started working again with horses and got divorced. He came to the Canfields just about the time they bought East Winds."

"What about old Ernest B. Free?"

"Not one damn sighting, and that's got me amazed, frankly. Usually we have thousands of phone calls, ninety-nine percent of them wrong, but usually we get one or two legit leads. This time, nothing."

A very frustrated Web looked around. His gaze went past the device and then came back to it and was riveted. "Damn," he said.

"What? What is it, Web?" said Bates.

Web pointed. "I think maybe we've got another eyewitness of sorts."

Bates looked over at the traffic signal at the corner diagonal from the warehouse loading dock. Like other signals in the area, on top of it was mounted a surveillance camera. And like the other cameras Web had seen in the area on his last trip through, this one had been pointed in another direction, presumably by mischievous hands, and that direction happened to be right at the loading dock.

"Damn," echoed Bates. "You thinking what I'm thinking?"

"Yeah," said Web. "That looks like one of the older models on video loops that run twenty-four hours a day. The newer ones only activate when they're triggered by the speed of a car and take a still photo of the rear license plate."

"Well, let's hope the District police haven't taped over a certain segment."

Bates signaled for one of his men to make that call immediately.

Web said, "I've got to get back to the farm. Romano's probably starting to feel lonely."

"I really don't like this, Web. What if you end up dead between now and then?"

"You got Cove. He saw it too."

"What if *he* ends up dead too? That's just as likely, with everything that's been going down."

"Got a pen and some paper?"

Web wrote out the entire account of Toona's murder. Toona's real name was Charles Towson, Web had found out from Bates, and no one knew where the nickname had come from, yet everyone working the streets seemed to have one. Well, whoever pulled Charlie Towson's body out of the river, if anyone ever did, was going to lose whatever was in his stomach. Web positively identified the killer as Francis "Big F" Westbrook. He signed it with a flourish and two other agents witnessed his signature.

"Are you kidding me? A defense attorney will tear that apart," raged Bates.

"It's the best I can do right now." Web walked away.

37

When he returned to East Winds, Web checked in with Romano and then went to the carriage house and eased into a hot bath. A catnap while he was soaking and he'd be as good as new, he figured. He'd gotten by on a lot less sleep over the years.

Romano had seen Web's fresh wounds and his comment had been predictable.

"You let somebody beat the crap out of you *again*? You're giving HRT a bad name, Web."

Web had told him that next time he'd make sure he was beaten in places that didn't show.

For the next several days, his and Romano's routine was just that—routine. When Gwen and Billy had seen his injuries from the encounter with Big F, Gwen exclaimed, "My God, are you all right?"

"Looks like old Boo kicked you in the face," commented Billy as he sucked on an unlit cigarette.

"Actually, I would have preferred Boo," replied Web.

Gwen had insisted on putting some medicine on Web's cuts. Her fingers felt very nice against his skin. As she tended to him, Billy had said, "Never a dull moment for you federal types, I guess."

"I guess," replied Web.

He and Romano got to know the Canfields better and saw how much work it took to run a farm. As promised, they both pitched in, although Romano bitched and complained every evening to Web about it. East Winds was vast and wondrous, and Web actually started to feel that maybe he should try something else for a living. He figured those feelings would disappear as soon as he left

East Winds permanently. Gwen Canfield was an interesting woman, fascinating in many ways and as intelligent and reserved as she was beautiful and mannered. She and Billy were like the proverbial fire and ice.

Web had ridden with her every day, as much to protect her as to understand the lay of the land better. And, he had to admit, there were far worse ways to spend one's time than riding around a beautiful place with a beautiful woman. She had stopped and prayed at the chapel each day and Web had sat on Boo and watched her. She never invited him to join her and he never suggested that he should. The fact that David Canfield had died on his watch was enough reason for him to keep his distance around the woman.

Each evening the FBI agents had gone to the large house and spent time with them. Billy had led a fascinating life and loved to share stories from it. Each time Nemo Strait had attended and Web found he had more in common with the ex-Marine than he would have thought. Strait had done a lot in his life, everything from soldiering to bronco busting.

"Live by my brains and my brawn, though I seem to have less of both as time goes by."

"We're sort of in the same boat," said Web. "You see yourself doing the horse thing until you drop?"

"Well, I have to say I think about the day I walk away from all the manure and ornery animals." He glanced at the Canfields, lowered his voice and added, grinning, "I'm talking about the two- *and* four-legged varieties." In a normal tone he said, "But like I said, it gets in your blood. Some days I see myself getting my own little spread and running it right."

"Nice dream," said Romano. "Some days I want to have my own NASCAR team."

Web looked at his partner. "I didn't know that, Paulie."

"Hey, a guy's got to have some secrets."

"You got that right," said Strait. "My ex told me once that she never knew what I was thinking. You know what I told her? I told her that was the difference between men and women. Women tell you exactly what they think of you. Men just hold it in." He glanced over at Billy Canfield, who was across the large room examining his stuffed grizzly and downing his third beer in the last half hour. Gwen had gone upstairs to check on dinner. "Although sometimes the reverse is true, you know," said Strait.

Web looked at Canfield and then back at Strait. "Is that right?"

What was becoming more apparent also was that Gwen and Billy spent a lot of time apart. Web never directly asked Gwen about this, but her occasional comments made it seem as though that was more Billy's choice than Gwen's. The blame game over David, perhaps, thought Web.

And despite what Gwen had suggested earlier, it was also clear that Nemo Strait was an integral part of the operation at East Winds. Several times Web had seen Billy turn to the foreman for a definitive answer on matters related to the horses or the running of the farm.

"Been doing this since I was a baby," Strait told Web once. "Ain't much I haven't seen when it comes to horses and farms and such. But Billy, he's picking it up fast."

"And Gwen?"

"She knows more than Billy, but she's sort of set in her ways too. Been trying to put a soft shoe on Baron because that animal has got some brittle hooves, but she won't have no part of it. 'I know my horse,' she tells me. Stubborn. Probably one of the reasons Billy married her."

"*One* of them, anyway," said Web.

Strait sighed. "You got that right, she's a looker. But you know what, lookers make a man's life miserable. Know why? 'Cause some other guy's always trying to take her away. My ex wouldn't of won no beauty contests on her best day, but hell, I didn't sit around worrying about some other fox in the chicken coop either."

"Billy doesn't seem worried about that."

"Fellow's hard to read sometimes. But he's a thinker, all right. A lot going on in that old head of his."

"That one I agree with," replied Web.

Web had been in contact with Bates every day, but nothing, as yet, had come through on the surveillance tape.

Early one morning, Web had just got out of the shower when his phone rang. He reached over and snagged it off the toilet. It was Claire Daniels.

"Have you thought any more about the hypnosis?"

"Look, Claire, I'm on a job."

"Web, if you really want to make some progress, then I feel hypnosis is the key."

"Nobody is looking around in my head."

She persisted. "We can start and if you're uncomfortable in any way, we'll stop. Fair enough?"

"Claire, I'm busy. I can't deal with this right now."

"Web, you came to me for help. I'm doing my best to help you, but I need your cooperation. Trust me, you've been through a lot worse than anything hypnosis will throw at you."

"Right. Sorry, no sell."

She paused and then said, "Listen, Web, I met with someone that you might want to know about."

He didn't answer.

"Buck Winters? Name ring a bell?"

"What did he want?"

"You signed a release that allowed him to ask me about your treatment. Do you remember doing that?"

"I guess. I signed a lot of papers around that time."

"I'm sure. They really took advantage of you."

"What did he want and what did you tell him?"

"Well, there was a big difference between the two. He tried to make a convincing case for why I should tell him everything, but the release form gave me enough wiggle room to stall him. I'll probably hear about it later, but that's just the way it goes."

He thought about this for a few seconds. "You stuck out your neck for me, Claire. I appreciate that."

"But that's one of the reasons I'm calling you. Winters seemed dead set on nailing you to the wall on what happened. He even used the word 'traitor.'"

"That's actually not such a big surprise. Buck and I haven't really seen eye to eye since Waco."

"But if we can get to the root of your issues, Web, and show him and everyone else very clearly that you're not a traitor, well, I can't see how that would be a bad thing. Can you?"

Web sighed. He didn't want to waive on this, but Web also didn't want people to have doubts about him forever. *He* didn't want to have doubts about his ability to do his job at HRT. "Do you really think the hypnosis will help?"

"We won't know, Web, until we try. But I've had great success with hypnosis in other patients."

He finally said, "Okay, maybe we can talk about this some more. Face to face."

"Here at my office?"

"I'm on an assignment."

"Can I come to where you are?"

Web thought about this. Did he really want to do this? The smart thing would be to tell Claire Daniels to go to hell and get on with his life. The problem with that was, he had never really gotten the help he was now coming to believe he actually needed. At some point he would have to pay the piper. And he was coming to understand that Claire really did want to help him. "I'll send somebody for you."

"Who?"

"His name's Romano, Paul Romano. He's HRT. Don't tell him anything, okay, because sometimes he's got a big mouth."

"Fine, Web. Where are you?"

"You'll see, Doc. You'll see."

"I'm free in about an hour. Do you need more time?"

"That's plenty of time."

Web dried off, dressed, found Romano and told him what he wanted him to do.

"Who is the woman?" he asked suspiciously. "Is this your shrink?"

"They like to be called psychiatrists."

"I'm not your chauffeur. I'm on a job, Web."

"Paulie, come on. I want to check in with Billy and Gwen. And you've been carrying the full load out here, let me take it for a while. If you leave now, she'll be ready to go by the time you get there."

"And what if something goes down while I'm gone?"

"Then I'll handle it."

"And what if you get popped?"

"What, you worrying about me all of a sudden?"

"No, I don't want to get my butt in a ringer over it. I got a family to think of."

"You mean Angie will kill you."

"That's exactly what I mean."

"Look, just do it and I swear to you I'll be grafted to the Canfields' souls until you get back."

Romano didn't look happy about it, but he finally agreed and got Claire's name and address from Web. "But listen up: The real reason I'm doing this is so I can go get my own wheels."

"You mean the 'Vette?"

"Yeah, I mean the 'Vette. I bet Billy would love to see it, him and me being automotive aficionados."

"Just go, Paulie, before I throw up."

Romano had told him that the Canfields were at the main house, so Web jogged up there and knocked on the door. An older woman dressed in jeans and a T-shirt and wearing a brightly colored bandanna answered the door and escorted him back to the small sunlit breakfast area off the kitchen where Gwen and Billy were eating.

Gwen rose and said, "Would you like some coffee or something to eat?"

Web accepted some coffee, eggs and toast. "Romano and I were patrolling the place the other night and saw some interesting activity going on next door," he said.

Gwen and Billy exchanged glances and Billy said, "At the Southern Belle? Damn right it's interesting."

"So you've seen some things too?"

"Billy," said Gwen, "you have no proof."

"Proof of what?" asked Web quickly.

"Maybe I ain't got any proof, but I got my common sense," said Billy, "and the goings-on over there make about as much sense with running a horse farm as me running a convent."

"So what have you seen?"

"You tell me first."

Web did so and Billy acknowledged that all of it jived with what he had seen. "See, what gets me," said Billy, "are the semis. Now, I was in trucking for twenty years, and you only use those over-the-road rigs to haul some serious cargo long distances."

"Have any of the other neighbors complained?" asked Web.

He shook his head. "I'm by far the closest one they got. The place on the other side, the owners are at their home in Naples or their other one in Nantucket. They just bought the farm so they can ride when they want to. Can you imagine that, shell out eight million dollars for nine hundred acres just so you can ride twice a year? What, the dumb shits never heard of a stable?" He shook his head and continued, "And the trucks only come and go at night. A little tricky, driving those beasts in the dark on these narrow windy roads. It's not like we have streetlights out here. And there's something else."

Web perked up. "What's that?"

"Remember I told you that a company had bought the place?"

"Right."

"Well, a while back, after all the planes and choppers and such, I went over to the courthouse and did a little digging. The company—it's an LLC, by the way, a limited liability company—is owned by two gents from California. Harvey and Giles Ransome, I guess they're brothers, or maybe they're married, you know, being from California and all." He shook his head.

"You know anything about them?"

"Nope. But you're the detective, figured you could dig something up fast if you wanted to."

"I'll look into it."

"I invited them over once I found out their names. Walked right over there and everything."

"What happened?"

"This time their *people* thanked me real polite-like but said they weren't in. Said they'd pass along the invite. Yeah, right! And I'm a Chinaman."

Gwen poured herself another cup of coffee. She had on jeans, a light brown pullover sweater and low-heeled boots. Before returning to her seat, she pinned up her hair and revealed a very long neck that for a few moments Web found he couldn't take his eyes off of. She sat back down and looked anxiously back and forth at the two men before coming to rest her gaze on Web.

"What do you think it might be, Web?"

"I've got my suspicions, but that's all they are."

Billy eyed him keenly as he took a last bite of toast and wiped his mouth with his napkin. "You're thinking it's maybe the mafioso running stolen goods or something. Believe me, that crap went on in the trucking business. If I had a dollar for every I-talian come through my door with a suitcase full of money in exchange for hauling their stuff in my trucks, well, I wouldn't need to be working my ass off on this farm."

"God," said Gwen, as she pounded the table with her hand, "we leave Richmond to get away from murderous white supremacists and move next door to a bunch of criminals." She stood, went over to the sink and stared out the window.

Billy said, "Look here, Gwen, whoever is next to us, it don't matter in our lives, okay? They do their thing and we do ours. If they got something illegal, it's not our problem, 'cause Web is gonna bust 'em, okay? We're running a horse farm, just like you wanted. Okay?"

She turned and looked at him anxiously. "But not what you wanted?"

He grinned. "Oh, sure. Hell, I even kind of like mucking the stalls." He glanced at Web for a moment. "Pushing manure is sort of therapeutic." To Web, the man didn't look like he meant it. Billy looked away and said, "Well, look what the cat dragged in."

Web glanced over at the doorway and saw Nemo Strait standing there, his Stetson in his hands. He was staring at Billy and his features were a little unkind, it seemed to Web.

Billy said, "Y'all ready to go?"

"Yes, sir, just come up to let you know before we hit the road."

They all went outside and down to the main road, where Web saw a caravan of ten horse trailers, some bumper-pulled, others fifth wheels hooked to heavy-duty trucks, and each emblazoned with the East Winds logo.

"Most of those are brand-new trailers," said Billy. "Cost a damn fortune 'cause we had to customize some, but I guess you got to look good, at least that's what folks keep telling me. Ain't that right, Nemo?"

"If you say so, Billy."

Billy pointed to the trailers. "Now, those three are custom fab three-horse slant loads." He continued pointing. "Then we got two Sundowner Pro Stock MPs, a straight-load gooseneck with horse dressing room, a ten-foot Townsmand bumper pull with young Bobby Lee all by his lonesome inside, two Sunlite 760s and that big-ass one over there." He pointed to the last trailer, an elaborate-looking contraption that resembled more of a people coach than one for horses. "Now, that's the little jewel in this group, though it sure ain't little. That's a Classic Coach Silverado. Living compartment for the boys in front, tack space and other equipment and such in the middle and then space for two horses in the back. It's a beaut. All self-contained."

"Where are they heading?" asked Web.

"Kentucky," answered Gwen. "They have a big yearling sale up there." She pointed to the trailers. "These are our best yearlings, nineteen of them in all."

She sounded a little sad, thought Web. Maybe for her it was like more children going away.

Billy said, "This is what separates the men from the boys. This sale goes well, we have a good year. I normally go too, but the FBI has persuaded me otherwise." He shot a glance at Web. "So if the sales aren't like they should be, I guess you guys can make up the difference."

"That's not my call," said Web.

Billy shook his head. "Yeah, I bet. Those bastard buyers pick the horses apart and lowball us, then we're selling pencils on the sidewalk. Now, these yearlings are some of our best ever. But those folks will hem and haw and find every little flaw they can, and then try to buy 'em for pennies on a dollar, and next thing you know, they got the next Secretariat. Well, that's not going to happen. I been down that road before. You haul their asses back here, Strait, if they don't fetch the reserves I gave you. Screw 'em."

Nemo nodded. "Yes, sir."

Web watched as Gwen went over to one of the smaller trailers and looked inside it.

"That's Bobby Lee," said Billy, pointing to the horse inside the trailer Gwen was looking at. "Now, if things go right, that horse will bring us a nice little bundle. He's special, so he doesn't have to share his ride with another horse. Damn, wish I had me a deal like that. That's my problem, too many people around."

Web wondered whom, if anyone, the man was referring to. "How come you don't keep the horses and race them yourself?" asked Web.

"It takes mountains of money to raise and maintain Thoroughbreds for racing, that's why the most successful farms are run by corporations and syndicates primarily. They have lots of capital behind them, so they can weather bad times. We can't compete with that. East Winds is a breeding farm and that's all we really want to be. Believe me, that's a big enough pain in the ass. Ain't that right, Gwen?"

She said nothing and moved away when Web went over to Bobby Lee and looked inside the Townsmand ten-foot trailer. The rear windows of the trailer were open and Web could see the horse inside, starting with the top of his bushy tail. Strait came over and stood next to him.

"Hate to see Bobby Lee go, he's a good horse. Fifteen hands already, beautiful chestnut coat, glossy, damn impressive musculature, look at that chest, and he's got a lot of growing left to do."

"He is a nice-looking animal." Web looked at the heavy-duty equipment boxes welded on the interior walls of the horse trailer. "What are those for?"

Strait opened the trailer and went inside, coaxing Bobby Lee over to the side. He opened one of the boxes. "Horses are worse than women when it comes to traveling." He grinned and stepped aside. Inside the box Web saw halters and bridles and blankets and every other piece of equipment a horse might need.

Strait ran his hand along the soft rubber that lined the outside of the boxes. "We pad the sides so the horse doesn't hurt itself against the edges."

"Not a lot of room for error," Web said as Strait closed up the box.

"There's a lot of little details that might not seem so obvious to nonhorse folks. For example, you riding with a single horse in a two-staller, you got to keep the animal on the driver's side so the extra weight don't keep pulling you to the side of the road. These trailers are real versatile. All the dividers swing out and you can reconfigure them. Keep a mare in the back and the foal up front, for example." He tapped the walls. "Galvaneal metal, and that lasts a lot longer than people." He pointed to the long, open space directly in front of the horse. "And up here is their feeding and water trough. And over there"—he pointed to the door on the side—"is the escape hatch if you got to get the horse out fast and don't want to get kicked in the process."

"Where's the TV?"

Strait laughed. "Tell me about it. I wished I traveled half as good as these animals, although I tell you, with the Silverado over there, we're going to be living in style now. Even got its own toilet and kitchen, so no more Porta Potties and fast food for yours truly. Billy really outdid himself with that one, and me and the boys sure appreciate it."

Web looked at the roof of the trailer. Bobby Lee's head was close to it.

Strait was watching him and smiled. "Bobby Lee is a big yearling and we can't make the roof any higher."

"How come?"

"Give horses enough room, they'll take advantage of it. Hell, I watched one horse that didn't like to be trailered do a backward somersault, if you can believe it, and jump out the rear onto the highway, where he got hit by a truck. It wasn't a pretty sight and almost cost me my job. That's why horses are situated facing the front of the trailer, or else they'll try and jump right out. And we got a side access door and side ramp on all the trailers so you can take the horses out frontways if there's an emergency. It's faster, and you try taking a frightened horse out from the back on a highway, you might just get your head handed to you if it decides to kick. See what I mean?"

"Gotcha."

"Yep, they're complicated machines. Sort of like my ex-wife." Strait laughed again.

Web fanned the air in front of his nose. "Boy, these trailers get pretty ripe."

"Huh," said Strait as he patted Bobby Lee's neck, came back out and secured the trailer latch, "just wait until that horse has been in there a few hours, then you'll really smell something. Now, dogs love the smell of horse manure, but humans don't. I guess that's why we're called civilized. That's why we replaced the aluminum floors with wooden ones, they drain better; and also why we spread the sawdust on the floors. You just sweep it clean, manure and all. Better than the straw."

They left Bobby Lee and went back over to Billy.

"Now, you got all the trailer stickers for state inspection and the horse papers?" asked Billy.

"Yes, sir." Strait looked at Web. "You cross state lines with a bunch of animals, the police stop you at random, and they ain't gonna let you go one step farther until they check your commercial license and the horse's vet certificates and such. They're worried about spreading equine diseases and such."

"And who can blame them?" said Gwen as she rejoined them.

"No, ma'am," said Strait. He tipped his hat. "Well, here's to making East Winds some big bucks."

Strait climbed in one of the trucks and Web and the Canfields watched as the caravan of trailers started up and passed down the main road and out of East Winds. Web glanced over at Gwen, who looked very upset. Billy walked back up to the house.

"You okay?" he asked her.

"I'm as okay as I'm ever going to be, Web." She crossed her arms over her chest and walked off, away from the house.

Web just stood there, looking at husband and wife going their separate ways.

38

Romano picked up Claire and was driving her back to East Winds, taking great care that they weren't followed.

Claire glanced at the man's hand and said, "When did you graduate from Columbia?"

Romano looked at her in surprise and then saw that she was staring at the ring on his finger. "Good eye. I graduated longer ago than I'd like to admit."

"I went there too. Pretty nice, going to college in New York."

"Nothing like it," agreed Romano.

"What was your major?"

"Who cares? I barely got in and I barely graduated."

"Actually, Paul Amadeo Romano, Junior, you entered Columbia at the age of seventeen and graduated in three years near the top of your class with a degree in political science. Your senior thesis was titled 'The Derivative Political Philosophies of Plato, Hobbes, John Stuart Mills and Francis Bacon.' And you were accepted into the Kennedy School of Government at Harvard but didn't attend."

Romano's gaze was chilling. "I don't appreciate people checking me out."

"Part of a therapist's job is not only to understand the patient but also to become familiar with significant people in his life. Web must trust you and think highly of you for him to send you to bring me back here. So I did a few mouse clicks and looked you up. Nothing classified, of course."

Romano still looked at her suspiciously.

"Not many people would have turned down Harvard."

"Well, nobody ever accused me of being most people."

"You were awarded a scholarship, so it wasn't money."

"I didn't go because I'd had enough of school."

"And you joined the military."

"Lots of people do."

"Lots of people out of high school do, but not those near the top of their class at Columbia with a free ticket to Harvard."

"Look, I'm from a big Italian family, okay, we got priorities. Traditions." He added quietly, "Sometimes people get around to them a little too late. That's all."

"So you're the oldest son?"

He shot her another suspicious glance. "Another mouse click? Damn, I hate computers."

"No, but you are a junior, and that normally goes to the oldest son. And your father's deceased and he wasn't a college man?"

Romano almost pulled the car over. "You're freaking me, lady, and you better knock it off."

"I'm not a magician, Mr. Romano, just a humble psychiatrist. You mentioned large Italian family, traditions and priorities. But you didn't mention expectations. The oldest sons in such families usually face expectations they have to live up to. You said people get around to these traditions sometimes too late. So I'm thinking that you went to college against your father's wishes, he died, and you left academia to pursue the occupation your father envisioned for you. And yet you still wear your college ring. That's probably your way of showing you didn't totally capitulate to living out your father's plans for you. It's just observation and deduction, Mr. Romano, just the sorts of tools law enforcement people use every day."

"That don't make it any easier to take."

She studied him. "Do you realize that you talk like an uneducated man at times?"

"You're pushing my buttons all the wrong way."

"I'm sorry. But you're extremely interesting. In fact, you and Web are both interesting. I suppose it comes with the territory. What you do for a living takes a very, very special sort of person."

"Don't try and brown-nose your way out of this, Doc."

"I guess innate curiosity about my fellow human beings comes with what I do for a living. I meant no offense."

They drove in silence for a while.

"My old man," said Romano, "wanted only one thing in life. He wanted to be one of New York's finest."

"NYPD?"

Romano nodded. "Only he never finished high school and he had a bad ticker. He spent his life on the docks hauling crates of fish and hating every second of it. But he wanted that uniform, man, like nothing else in life."

"And because he couldn't, he wanted you to wear it for him?"

Romano looked over at her and nodded. "Only my ma didn't see it that way. She didn't want me working on the docks and she sure as hell didn't want me strapping on a gun for a living. I was a smart student, aced the college boards, got into Columbia, did great there and had my sights on maybe even teaching."

"And then your father died?"

"Ticker finally quit on him. I made it to the hospital right before he died." Romano stopped and looked out the window. "He said I'd shamed him. He said I'd shamed him and then he died."

"And with him died your dreams of teaching?"

"I never could bring myself to go out for NYPD. I could've made it, easy. I hooked on to the military, made Delta, jumped to FBI and then on to HRT. None of it was too much for me. The harder they tried to hurt me, the more I thrived."

"So you eventually did become a policeman of sorts."

He stared at her. "But I did it my way." He paused. "I loved my old man, don't get me wrong. But I never shamed him. And every day I think about that being his dying thought. And it either makes me want to start bawling or killing somebody."

"I can understand that."

"Can you? I sure as hell never could."

"You're not my patient, obviously, but just a friendly piece of advice: At some point you have to live your life the way you want to. Otherwise the building up of resentment and other negative factors can do great damage psychologically. You'll find that not only will you hurt yourself, but those you love."

He looked at her with a level of sadness that touched her deeply.

"I think it might be a little too late for that." Then he added, "But you're right about the ring."

S‍o, talk to me about this hypnosis," said Web.

Romano had dropped Claire off at the carriage house and gone on to watch over the Canfields. Claire and Web were sitting in the living room staring at each other.

"I know that you didn't agree to do it with him, but didn't O'Bannon explain it to you when he offered to hypnotize you?"

"I guess I forgot."

"Just relax and go with the flow, Web. You know, seat-of-the-pants kind of guy. You're one of those types."

"Oh, you think so?"

She smiled at him over the rim of the cup of tea he had made for her. "I don't have to be a psychiatrist, Web, to see that." She looked out the window. "This is some place."

"Yes, it is."

"I suppose you can't tell me what you're doing out here?"

"I'm probably breaking every rule in the book just by having you out here, but I figured Romano would know if anyone was following him." And it's not like whoever was behind the killings didn't know where the Canfields lived, thought Web, because they had gotten the phone bomb in here.

"Romano would make an interesting case study. I identified about five major psychoses, classic passive-aggressive posturing and an unhealthy appetite for pain and violence just in the car ride here."

"Really? I would have guessed more."

"And he's also intelligent, sensitive, deeply emotional, incredibly independent but amazingly loyal. Quite a smorgasbord."

"If you need somebody to cover your back, there's nobody better than Paulie. He's got this rough outside, but the guy has a big heart. But man, if he doesn't like you, watch out. His wife Angie is even more of a piece of work, though. I found out recently that she's seeing O'Bannon. So are some of the other wives. I even saw Deb Riner there. She's the widow of Teddy Riner—he was our team leader."

"We have a large number of FBI and other law enforcement clientele. Years ago Dr. O'Bannon worked in-house at the Bureau.

When he went into private practice, he brought quite a few patients with him. It is a specialty practice because law enforcement people have unique jobs and the stress and personal issues associated with that occupation can be devastating if left untreated. I personally find it all fascinating. And I admire what all of you do very much. I hope you know that."

Web looked over at her, his expression searching and pained.

"Is there something else bothering you?" she asked quietly.

"My Bureau file you were given. Did it by chance have the background interview with Harry Sullivan in it?"

She took a moment to answer. "Yes. I thought about telling you, but I thought it better for you to find out for yourself. I take it you did."

"Yeah," he said in a tight voice. "About fourteen years too late."

"Your father had no reason to say anything good about you. He was going to be in prison for the next twenty years. He hadn't seen you in forever. And yet—"

"And yet he said I'd make the best damn FBI agent there ever was or ever would be and you could quote him on that."

"Yes," she said quietly.

"Maybe some day he and I should meet," said Web.

Claire met his gaze. "I think, Web, that that might be traumatic, but I also think it might be a good idea."

"A voice out of the past?"

"Something like that."

"Speaking of voices, I was thinking about what Kevin Westbrook said to me in that alley."

Claire sat up straighter. "'Damn to hell'?"

"What do you know about voodoo?"

"Not much. You think Kevin put a curse on you?"

"No, the people behind him. I don't know, I'm just thinking out loud."

Claire looked doubtful. "I guess it's possible, Web, though I wouldn't count on that being the answer."

Web cracked his knuckles. "You're probably right. Okay, Doc, pull out your watch and start swinging."

"I use a blue pen, if you don't mind. However, first I want you to sit in the recliner over there and lean back. You don't undergo hypnosis while standing at attention, Web. You need to relax and I'm going to help you do that."

Web sat in the recliner and Claire positioned herself across from him on an ottoman.

"Now, the first thing we need to address are the myths surrounding hypnosis. As I told you, it's not a state of unconsciousness, it's an altered state of *consciousness*. Your brain, in fact, will experience the same brain wave activity it would in a relaxed state, which is alpha rhythm. While in the trance you'll be incredibly relaxed, but it's also a heightened state of awareness and of suggestibility and you are in complete control of what goes on. All hypnosis, in fact, is self-hypnosis, and I'm merely here to help guide you to the point where you are relaxed enough to reach that state. No one can hypnotize anyone who doesn't really want to be hypnotized, and you can't be forced to do something you really don't want to do. So you are completely safe. No barking dogs need apply." She smiled reassuringly. "Are you with me?"

Web nodded.

She held up the pen. "Would you believe this is a pen that Freud himself used?"

"No, I wouldn't."

She smiled again. "Good, because he didn't. We use an object like this when hypnotizing patients. Now I want you to become totally focused with your eyes on the tip of this pen." She held it about six inches from Web's face and above his natural line of sight. Web raised his head to look at it. "No, Web, you can only use your eyes." She placed a hand on top of his head to keep it level. Now Web had to direct his gaze nearly straight up to see the tip.

"That's very good, Web, very good. Most people get tired very quickly, but I'm sure you won't. I know you're very strong and very determined, just keep staring, staring at the tip of the pen." Without seeming to, Claire's voice had dropped to an even level without being a monotone, her words coming steadily and always in the same soothing manner as she offered him encouragement.

A minute passed. Then, as Web continued to stare at the tip of the pen, Claire said, "And blink." And Web blinked. Claire could see that his eyes were becoming strained staring from that very uncomfortable angle, and then they started to water. And he had actually blinked first and then she had instantly said, "And blink." But he wouldn't be sure of the sequence of events. He was too busy concentrating on the pen's tip, on keeping his eyes open. But it made him believe something had happened, that she was slowly assuming control over him. Even if he'd been through it before he would still be wondering whether this hypnosis thing actually worked. First came eye fatigue, and next came mind confusion. All to get him relaxed enough to open up.

"You are doing so well, Web," she said, "better than just about anyone. You're getting more and more relaxed. Just keep staring at that tip." And she could tell he was so determined to keep staring, to keep getting that encouragement. He was a classic overachiever, she easily deduced; he was eager to please and receive praise. He needed attention and love because he obviously had not gotten much of either as a child.

"And blink." And he did so again and she knew it felt so good to him, relieved the strain. She knew the tip of the pen was starting to grow larger and larger for him, and that he was beginning not to want to look at it anymore.

"And it seems you really want to close your eyes," Claire said. "And your eyelids are getting heavier and heavier. It's hard to keep them open and it seems you really want to close them. Close your eyes." And Web did, but he immediately reopened them. That almost always happened, Claire knew. "Keep staring at the pen, Web, just keep staring at the tip, you're doing really well. Outstanding. Just let your eyes close naturally when they're ready to close."

Web's eyes slowly drifted closed and stayed that way.

"I want you to say out loud the word 'ten' ten times fast. Go ahead and do that."

Web did so and then Claire asked. "What are aluminum cans made from?"

"Tin," Web said in a proud voice, and smiled.

"Aluminum."

His smile faded.

Claire continued in her soothing voice, "You know what a strop is? It's a rough leather strap that men used to use in the Old West to sharpen their razors. I want you to say the word 'strop' ten times very fast. Go ahead and do it."

Obviously very wary now, Web said the word ten times.

"What do you do at a green light?"

"STOP!" he said loudly.

"Actually, at a green light, you go." Web's shoulders collapsed in obvious frustration, but Claire was quick to praise him.

"You're doing really well. Almost nobody gets those answers right. But you look so relaxed. Now I want you to count out loud backward from three hundred by threes."

Web started to do so. He had counted back to 279 when she told him to start counting backward by fives. He did so until she had him do it by sevens and then by nines.

Claire interrupted and told him, "Stop counting and just relax. Now you're at the top of the escalator, and that point represents more relaxation. And the bottom of the escalator is the deepest relaxation there is. You're going to take the escalator down, okay? You're going to be more relaxed than you've ever been. Okay?" Web nodded. Claire's voice was as welcome and as gentle as a wispy summer breeze.

"You're going slowly down the escalator. You're gliding down, as if on air. Deeper into relaxation." Claire started counting backward from ten and offered soothing words as she did so. At the count of one she said, "You appear to be very relaxed."

Claire studied Web's features and his skin color. His body had gone from tense to loose. His face was red, evidencing enhanced blood flow there. His eyelids were closed yet fluttering. She told him that she was going to pick up one of his hands—before she did so, to avoid startling him. She gently took it. The hand was limp. She let it go.

"You're near the bottom of the escalator. You're just about to get off. Deepest relaxation, like nothing you've ever felt. It's perfect."

She once more picked up his hand after warning him first that she was going to do so. "What's your favorite color?"

"Green," Web said softly.

"Green, a nice soothing color. Like grass. I'm putting a balloon, a green balloon, in your hand. I'm doing that right now. Do you feel that?" Web nodded. "Now I'm going to pump it up with helium. As you know, helium is lighter than air. I'm pumping up the green balloon. It's getting more full. It's beginning to rise. It's getting fuller."

Claire watched as Web's hand rose from the arm of the recliner as if buoyed by the imaginary balloon.

"Now, on the count of three, your hand will drop back to the chair." She counted to three and Web's hand returned to the chair. She waited about thirty seconds and then said, "Your hand is now getting cold, very cold, I think I see frostbite."

She watched as Web's hand curled and shook. "All right, it's gone now, all normal, all warm." The hand relaxed.

Typically, Claire would not have been as elaborate in putting Web through these paces, the deepening of relaxation techniques. Normally she would have stopped with the balloon. However, she had been curious about something, and that curiosity had been answered because Claire concluded that Web was probably a somnambule. Most people in the field would agree that between five and ten percent of the general population was highly susceptible to hypnosis, with the same percentage highly resistant to it. Somnambules went a step further. They were so susceptible to hypnosis that they could be compelled to experience physical sensations hypnotically, as Web had just done. They could also be expected to reliably execute posthypnotic suggestions. And, surprisingly, very intelligent people often were the easiest to hypnotize.

"Web, can you hear me?" He nodded. "Web, listen very carefully to my voice. Focus on my voice. The balloon is now gone. Just keep on relaxing. Now you're holding a video camera in your hand. You're the cameraman. What you see through your lens is all that you and I can see, do you understand, Mr. Cameraman?" Another nod. "Okay, my only role is to point you around in time, but you control everything else. Through the camera you'll be looking in on other people, to see what they're up to. The camera has a microphone, so we'll be able to hear too. All right?" He nodded. "You're doing so well, Mr. Cameraman. I'm so proud of you."

Claire sat back and thought for a moment. As a therapist who had studied Web's background, she knew exactly the area she should be focusing on in his past to help him. His most severe psychological problems did not stem from the death of his HRT colleagues. They came directly from the triangular relationship between his mother, stepfather and himself. And yet her first stop in Web London's past would be earlier.

"I want you to go back to March eighth, 1969, Mr. Cameraman. Can you get me back there?"

Web didn't respond for a bit. Then he said, "Yes."

"Tell me what you see, Mr. Cameraman." She knew that his birthday was March 8. In 1969, Web would be turning six years old. That was probably the last year he would have been with Harry Sullivan. She wanted to establish a baseline for Web with the man, a pleasant memory, and a birthday party for a little boy would set that tone perfectly. "The relaxed Mr. Cameraman will focus and swing his camera around. Whom do you see?" she prompted again.

"I see a house. I see a room, a room with no one in it."

"Concentrate and focus, swing your camera around. Don't you see anyone? March eighth, 1969." She suddenly feared that there had been no party for Web.

"Wait a minute," said Web. "Wait a minute, I see something."

"What do you see?"

"A man—no, a woman. She's pretty, very pretty. She has a hat on, a funny hat, and she's carrying a cake with candles."

"Sounds like somebody must be having a party. Is it a boy or a girl, Mr. Cameraman?"

"A boy's. Yes, and now there are other people coming out, like they were hiding. They're yelling something, they're yelling, 'Happy birthday.'"

"That's great, Web, a little boy's having a birthday party. What does he look like?"

"He has dark hair, sort of tall. He's blowing out the candles on the cake. Everybody's singing happy birthday."

"Does this boy hear a daddy singing? How about daddy, Mr. Cameraman?"

"I see him. I see him." Web's face was turning red and his breathing had accelerated. Claire watched his physical signs closely. She would not put Web at risk physically or emotionally. She would not go that far.

"What does he look like?"

"He's big, really big, bigger than anybody else there. A giant."

"And what is happening between the boy and his giant daddy, Mr. Cameraman?"

"The boy is running to him. And the man's lifting him up on his shoulders, like he doesn't weigh anything."

"Oh, a strong daddy."

"He's kissing the boy, they're dancing around the room and they're singing some song."

"Listen carefully, Mr. Cameraman, turn up the sound control on the microphone. Can you hear any of the words?"

Web first shook his head and then nodded. "Eyes, shining eyes."

Claire searched her memory and then it hit her: Harry Sullivan, the Irishman. "Irish eyes. Irish eyes are smiling?"

"That's it! But no, he's made up his own words to the song, and they're funny, everyone's laughing. And now the man's giving the boy something."

"A present? Is it a birthday present?"

Web's face contorted and he lurched forward. Claire looked alarmed and she sat forward too. "Relax, Mr. Cameraman. It's just a picture you're looking at, that's all. Just a picture. What do you see?"

"I see men. Men have come in the house."

"What men? What do they look like?"

"They're in brown, dressed in brown with cowboy hats. They have guns."

Now Claire's heart skipped a beat. Should she pull the plug on this? She studied Web closely. He appeared to be calming down. "What are the men doing, Mr. Cameraman? What do they want?"

"They're taking him, they're taking the man away. He's yelling. He's screaming, they're all screaming. The cowboys are putting shiny things on the man's hands. The mommy is screaming, she's grabbed the little boy."

Web covered his ears with his hands and was rocking back and forth so violently he was close to tipping the recliner over. "They're yelling, they're yelling. The little boy's yelling, 'Daddy! Daddy!'" Web was now screaming himself.

Oh, shit, Claire thought. *Shiny things on his hands?* The police had come to arrest Harry Sullivan right in the middle of Web's sixth birthday party. Good God!

Claire looked back at Web. "Okay, Mr. Cameraman," she said in her smoothest, most comforting voice, "just relax, we're going somewhere else. Take your camera and turn it off for right now until we decide where to go. Okay, your camera is going dark now, relaxed Mr. Cameraman. You see nothing. You're relaxed and seeing nothing at all. Everyone is gone. There's no one left yelling. All gone. All dark."

Web slowly calmed and put his hands down and leaned back.

Claire sat back and tried to relax as well. She had been through some intense hypnosis sessions before and discovered some surprising things about patients' pasts, but each time was still new, still emotional. For a minute or more Claire wavered. Should she move forward? There was the very real possibility she would never get Web in a hypnotic state again.

"Okay, Mr. Cameraman, we're moving forward." She glanced at the notes she had pulled from the file she had placed under a couch pillow. She had waited until Web was under hypnosis before taking them out. She had noted from their previous sessions that the use of files bothered him. That wasn't unusual, for who would want their life set forth on paper for all to see and scrutinize? And she remembered how she had felt when Buck Winters had pulled the same tactic on her. The pages had dates scribbled on them. She had gotten them from Web's file and discussions with him. "We're moving on to . . ." She hesitated. Could he handle this? Could *she* handle this? She made up her mind and told Web the new date to move on to. It was the date his stepfather had died. "What do you see, Mr. Cameraman?"

"Nothing."

"Nothing?" Claire remembered. "Turn your camera back on. Now what do you see?"

"Still nothing. It's dark, totally black."

That was odd, thought Claire. "Is it nighttime? Turn on the light on your video recorder, Mr. Cameraman."

"No, there are no lights. I don't want a light."

Claire leaned forward, as Web was now referring to himself. This was tricky. This now placed the patient right in the bull's-eye of his very own unconscious. Still, she decided to press forward.

"Why doesn't the Cameraman want a light?"

"Because I'm scared."

"Why is the *little boy* scared?" She had to keep the objectivity here even as Web continued to wander to the cliff of subjectivity. It could be a long way down, Claire well knew.

"Because he's out there."

"Who, Raymond Stockton?"

"Raymond Stockton," Web repeated.

"Where is the little boy's mother?"

Web's chest started to heave again. He was gripping the sides of the recliner so tightly his fingers were shaking.

"Where is your mother?"

Web's voice was high, like a boy still a ways from puberty. "Gone. No, she's back. Fighting. Always fighting."

"Your mother and father are fighting?"

"Always. Shhh!" Web hissed. "He's coming. He's coming."

"How do you know, what do you see?"

"The door's coming down. It always squeaks. Always. Just like that. He's coming up the steps. He keeps it up here. His drugs. I've seen him. I've seen him."

"Relax, Web, it's all right. It's all right." Claire didn't want to touch him, for fear she would startle him, but she was so close to Web there was practically no discernible space between them. She watched over Web as she would have over her mother if it were the woman's last minute on earth. Claire prepared herself to end this before it got out of control, yet if they could just get a little further. Just a little further.

"He's up at the top of the stairs. I hear him. I hear my mother. She's down there. Waiting."

"But you can't see. You're still in darkness."

"I can see." The tone of voice took Claire by surprise, for it was deep and menacing, no longer the cry of a terribly frightened boy.

"How can you see, Mr. Cameraman? What do you see?"

Web screamed the next words out so suddenly that Claire nearly fell to the floor.

"Damn it, you already know this."

For a split second she was sure he was talking directly to her. That had never happened before in a hypnotic session. What did he mean? That she already knew this information? But then he calmed and continued.

"I lifted up the pile of clothes a little. I'm under the pile of clothes. Hiding."

"From the little boy's stepfather?"

"I don't want him to see me."

"Because the little boy is scared?"

"No, I'm not scared. I don't want him to see me. He can't see me, not yet."

"Why, what do you mean?"

"He's right in front of me, but his back is to me. His stash is right over there. He's bending down to get it."

Web's voice was growing deeper, as though he were growing from a boy to a man right in front of her.

"I'm coming out of hiding, I don't have to hide anymore. The clothes are rising up with me. They're my mother's clothes. She put this pile up here for me."

"She did? Why?"

"To hide under, for when he came. I'm up. I'm standing up. I'm taller than he is. I'm bigger than he is."

There was a tone to Web's voice now that made Claire very nervous. She realized that her own breath was coming in gasps even as Web had calmed. She had a cold dread of where this was going. She should pull him out. Every professional instinct she had told her to stop this, and yet she just couldn't.

"The carpet rolls. Hard as iron," Web said in his deep-man voice. "I've got one, had it under the clothes. I'm up now, bigger than he is. He's a little man. So little."

"Web," began Claire. She dropped all pretense of the cameraman. This was getting out of hand.

"I've got it in my hand. Like a bat. I'm a great baseball player. Can hit it a mile. Swing harder than anyone. I'm big and strong. Like my dad. My *real* dad."

"Web, please."

"He's not even looking. Doesn't know I'm there. Batter up."

She changed tactics again. "Mr. Cameraman, I want you to turn off your camera."

"Pitch is coming. Fastball. I see it. Easy. I'm getting ready."

"Mr. Cameraman, I want you—"

"It's almost here. He's turning. I want him to. I want him to see this. See me."

"Web! Turn it off."

"He sees me. He sees me. I'm swinging for the fences."

"Turn off the camera. Stop, you don't see this. Stop!"

"I'm swinging. He sees me, he knows how hard I can hit. He's scared now. He's scared! He's scared, I'm not! No more! No more!"

Claire watched helplessly as he gripped an imaginary bat and swung for the fences.

"It's a hit. It's a hit. Slash of red, slash of red. The ball's going down. It's going down. It's a home run, a country mile. It's outta here. Outta here. Good-bye, good-bye, mister asshole." He grew quiet for a long moment while Claire studied him carefully.

"He's getting up. He's getting back up." He paused. "Yes, Mom," he said. "Here's the bat, Mom." He reached out his hand as though handing off something. Claire almost reached out her hand to take it before she caught herself.

"Mom's hitting him. In the head. Lots of blood. He's not moving anymore. He's not. It's over."

He became silent and slumped back in the recliner. Claire slumped down too, her heart beating so hard she put a hand over her chest as though to prevent it from bursting through. All she could envision was Raymond Stockton plunging down the attic stairs after being hit by a hard roll of carpet and hitting his head on the way down and then being finished off by his wife with the same roll of carpet.

"I want you to completely relax, Web. I want you to sleep, to sleep, that's all."

She watched as his body dissolved even farther into the chair. As Claire looked up, she received another shock. Romano was standing there, staring at her, his hand near his gun.

"What the hell's going on?" he demanded.

"He's under hypnosis, Mr. Romano. He's all right."

"How do I know that?"

"I guess you'll just have to trust me." She was still too stricken to argue with the man. "How much did you hear?"

"I was coming back here to check on him when I heard Web screaming."

"He's reliving some very delicate memories of the past. I'm not sure what it all means yet, but it was a big step to get to this point."

Claire's experiences in forensics had prompted several theories to consider. It had obviously been planned that the blows had been struck with the rolled-up carpet. Stockton presumably would have had carpet fibers in his head wound when he hit the floor. And if the carpet on the floor were the same carpet as the remnant in the attic, then the police would just assume that the fibers became embedded in his head wound when he hit the floor. They would not suspect that someone had slugged him with a rolled-up remnant in the attic. After all the complaints of abuse against the man, everyone, including the police, had probably been grateful he was finally dead. Finished with the stepfather, Claire moved on to the mother.

Web had said Charlotte London had placed the pile of clothes there. Had she also supplied the rolled-up carpet? Had she coached her tall, strong teenage son on how to do away with the abusive husband? Was that how the woman had decided to handle it? And then stepped in to finish the job, leaving Web to later pick up the pieces, allowing him to repress guilt so deep he couldn't even remember the event except under hypnosis? But such an extraordinary repressed memory would taint every aspect of his being and of his future. It would manifest itself in many ways, none of them positive. Claire could now clearly understand why Web was like he was. He had become a lawman not to make up for Harry Sullivan's felonious ways but because of his own guilt. A boy helping to kill his stepfather at the instruction of his natural mother; from a mental health perspective it didn't get more screwed up than that.

Claire looked over at Web, who just sat there so peacefully, with his eyes closed, awaiting her next instruction. She also now understood his somnambulism. Children from homes of terrible abuse often withdrew into fantasy worlds as protection from the horrors of reality. Such children created imaginary friends to combat loneliness and also invented wonderful lives and adventures to ward off feelings of insecurity and depression. Claire had treated somnambules who could control their higher brain functions to such an extent that they could either embellish or completely wipe out whole sections of their memories, just as Web had done. Though a dynamic, independent, self-reliant sort on the outside, Web London, she concluded, was obedient and relied upon others on the inside; hence, his dependence on his HRT team and his exceptional ability to carry out orders. He was eager to please, to be accepted.

She shook her head. The man was a mess inside. And yet he had withstood the psychological battering of both the Bureau and HRT. Web had said he had figured out the MMPI test and had managed to lie his way right through it. He did not know how right he was about that.

She looked at Romano as something new occurred to her. She would have to craft the question delicately because she couldn't reveal any patient confidences. Web had told her previously that he wasn't taking any medications, and she had accepted his word on that. With what she had just learned, though, she wondered if he were taking something that would help combat the internal traumas that were clearly eating away at him. She motioned Romano over to a far corner, out of Web's hearing. "Do you know anything about any medications Web might be taking?"

"Did Web say he was taking any pills?"

"I was just wondering. It's sort of standard operating procedure for shrinks to ask," she answered evasively.

"Lots of people take pills to help them sleep," Romano said defensively.

She hadn't said they were sleeping pills. So Romano did know about them, thought Claire. "I'm not saying it's wrong, I was just wondering if he ever mentioned to you if he took anything, and if so, what he took."

"You think he might be addicted, is that it? Well, I'm telling you you're nuts."

"I'm not implying that at all. It's just important that I know in case I want to prescribe something for him. I don't want any dangerous drug interactions."

Romano still was not buying it. "So why don't you ask him?"

"Well, I'm sure you're well aware that people don't always tell their doctors the truth, particularly the kind of doctor I am. I just want to make sure there are no problems."

Romano looked over at Web, apparently to make sure he was still out. He looked back at Claire and seemed to be having trouble getting the words out. "I saw him holding what looked like a prescription bottle the other day. But look, he's hurting right now and he's probably a little screwed up about things and maybe needs a little help pill wise, but the Bureau's real stiff on that crap. They throw you overboard and let you sink or swim on your own. Well, guys have to look out for each other, then." Romano stopped, looked over at Web and said a little wistfully, "He's the best HRT's ever had."

"You know he thinks very highly of you too."

"I guess I did know."

Romano left the room. Claire went to the window and watched as he crossed the road and was soon out of sight. It would have been very hard for him to reveal a confidence like that about his friend, and he probably felt himself a traitor for doing it. But in the end it would help Web far more than hurt him.

She sat across from Web, leaned forward and spoke slowly so that he wouldn't miss a word. Ordinarily hypnosis was used to pare away the inhibitions and layers covering repressed memories that prevented patients from really talking about their troubles. Typically the patient was brought out of hypnosis fully remembering everything that had happened while he was under. Here, Claire could not do that. It would be too traumatic. Instead, she gave Web a posthypnotic suggestion. It instructed him that when he came out of the hypnotic state he would remember only enough to allow him to deal adequately with the situation. What would control what, if anything, he remembered would be his unconscious. Under the circumstances, Claire felt certain he would remember almost nothing. He was not prepared to deal with this, so buried was it within his unconscious. She slowly brought him up the escalator, step by step. Before he came fully out of it, she finished composing herself, prepared herself to face him.

When he finally opened his eyes, he looked around the room and then at her. He smiled. "Anything good?"

"First I need to ask you a question, Web." She paused to collect herself again before saying, "Are you taking any medication?"

His eyes narrowed. "Didn't you already ask me that?"

"I'm asking you now."

"Why?"

"You mentioned voodoo as an explanation for why you froze. Let me offer another one: negative drug interaction."

"I wasn't taking any medication before we went into that alley, Claire. I would never do that."

"Drug interactions are funny," replied Claire. "Depending on what you're taking, the effects can materialize some time after you've stopped taking them." She paused once again and added, "It's important for you to be entirely truthful on this point, Web. It really is, if you want to get to the truth."

They stared at each other for a long moment, and then Web rose and went into his bathroom. A minute later he came back and handed her a small vial with pills in it. He sat back down as she examined the contents.

"Since you have them with you, should I assume you've been taking them recently?"

"I'm on a job, Claire. No pills. So I deal with the insomnia and the pain you sometimes get with two big holes in you and half a face."

"So why do you have them?"

"Security blanket. You're a psychiatrist—you understand that and thumb-sucking, don't you?"

Claire took out the pills and examined them one by one. They were all different. Most she recognized, some she didn't. She held up one of the pills. "Do you know where you got this?"

"Why?" he asked suspiciously. "Is there something wrong with it?"

"Perhaps. Did you get these pills from O'Bannon?" she said doubtfully.

"It's possible, I guess. Although I thought I finished his prescription a long time ago."

"Well, if not O'Bannon, who, then?"

Web became defensive. "Look, I had to get off the painkillers they were giving me for my *injuries,* because I was growing dependent on them. And then I couldn't sleep, for like a year. Some HRT guys have the same problem. It's not like we're doing illegal drugs or crap like that, but you can only go so long without sleep, even at HRT. Some of the guys have given me pills over the years. I just collect them in a bottle and take them when I need them. That pill might have come from one of them. What's the big deal?"

"I'm not blaming you for taking medication to help you sleep, Web. But it's stupid and dangerous for you to take an oddball assortment of pills, even from friends, when you have no idea what drug interactions might occur from their use. You're very lucky something serious hasn't happened to you. And maybe it did. In the alley. Maybe this odd method of pill taking is the reason you froze." Claire was also thinking that the traumatic events surrounding Raymond Stockton's death might have bubbled to the surface at the worst possible time—when Web was in that alley. Perhaps, as she had thought earlier, seeing Kevin Westbrook had triggered something in Web, disabling him.

Web covered his face with his hands. "Shit! This is unbelievable. Unbelievable!"

"I can't say for sure that's the case, Web." She looked at him sympathetically, but there was something else she needed to know. "Have you reported the medication you've been taking to your supervisor?"

He uncovered his face but didn't look at her.

"Okay," she said slowly.

"Are you going to say anything?"

"Are you still taking them?"

"No. As best I can recall, the last time I took one prior to the mission in the alley was a week before. That's it."

"Then I have nothing to report." She held up the same pill again. "I don't recognize this medication, and as a psychiatrist I've seen just about all of them. I'd like to get it analyzed. It'll be on the QT," she quickly added, as he looked alarmed. "I have a friend. Your name will never come up."

"Do you really think it was the pills, Claire?"

She stared at the pill before pocketing the vial and looking back at him. "Web, I'm afraid we'll never know for certain."

"So was the hypnosis a bust?" Web asked finally, though Claire could tell his mind was clearly on the pills and their possible implication in what had happened to Charlie Team.

"No, it wasn't. I learned a lot."

"Like what?"

"Like Harry Sullivan was arrested during your sixth-year birthday party. Do you remember talking about that?" She was reasonably certain he might recall that from the hypnosis session. But *not* the event with Stockton.

Web slowly nodded. "Actually, I do. Some of it, anyway."

"For what it's worth, before the arrest, you and Harry were having a great time. He clearly loved you very much."

"That's good to know," Web said, without enthusiasm.

"Often situations that are traumatic are repressed, Web, sort of a safety valve. Your psyche can't handle it, that level of confrontation, and you basically bury it so you don't need to face it."

"But that's like burying toxic waste," he said in a low voice.

"That's right. And it sometimes seeps out and does considerable damage."

"Anything else?" he asked.

"Do you recall anything else?"

He shook his head.

Claire looked away for a moment. Web, she knew, was in no shape to hear the truth about his stepfather's death. She looked back at him and managed a tiny smile. "Well, I think that's enough."

She looked at her watch. "And I need to get back."

"So my dad and me were really getting along?"

"You were singing songs, he was carrying you on his shoulders. Yes, you were having a great time."

"It's starting to come back to me. So there's still hope for me, right?" Web smiled, perhaps to show he was partly kidding.

"There's always hope, Web," Claire replied.

39

Sonny Venables was off duty and out of uniform as he sat in an unmarked car and surveyed the area. There was stirring in the backseat as the big man who was lying on the floorboard stretched out his long legs.

"Don't get antsy, Randy," said Venables. "We got some time to go yet."

"Trust me, I've waited dudes out a lot longer than this, and from places a lot shittier than the backseat of a car."

Venables nudged out a cigarette from the pack in his pocket, lit it, cracked his window and blew smoke out.

"So you were telling me about your meeting with London."

"I covered his backside even though he didn't know it at the time. Good thing too, though I don't think Westbrook would have really killed him."

"I heard about that guy, but I've never run into him."

"Lucky you. But let me tell you there's a lot worse than him out there. At least Westbrook's got a little code of honor. Most dudes out there are just flat-out nuts. Kill you just to kill you and brag about it. Westbrook does everything for a real good reason."

"Like maybe take out HRT?"

"Don't think so. But he delivered a message to London about the tunnels under the building that was HRT's target. That's apparently how the guns came in. London checked it out with Bates. And I heard that he was right."

"From what you've told me about Westbrook, he doesn't sound like a message boy."

"He is if the person he delivered the message for has somebody he cares about, like his son."

"Gotcha. So *that* person was behind what happened to HRT?"

"That's my thinking."

"So where's the Oxy come into to all this?"

"That's the op I saw in the building that night. They even had some of the product there. No coke bricks, just bags of pills. And I saw computerized records that laid it all out. Millions of bucks in business. And in two days it was cleared out."

"Why all that trouble to set you up? Why wipe out HRT? That just brings the Bureau down on them like a ton of bricks."

"It doesn't make a lot of sense," Cove agreed, "but that seems to be what happened."

Venables stiffened and flicked his cigarette out the window. "Show time, Randy."

Venables watched as a man left the building they'd been watching, walked along the street, turned right and headed down an alley. Venables started the car and it moved slowly forward.

"Is it the guy you were expecting?" asked Cove.

"Yep. You want some info on new drugs coming to town, this boy will know it. Name's Tyrone Walker, but he goes by T. Real imaginative. Belonged to three or four different crews over the years. Time in jail, time in the hospital, time in drug rehab. He's about twenty-six and looks ten years older than me and *I* don't look all that good for my age."

"Funny I never ran across T before."

"Hey, you don't have a monopoly on information in this town. I might just be a lowly street cop, but I get around."

"Good thing, Sonny, because I'm tainted goods right now. Nobody will talk to me."

"Well, old T will, with the right persuasion."

Venables pulled around the corner, hit the gas, then turned right onto a street that ran parallel to the one where they had been parked. As soon as they turned the corner, T emerged from the alley, which cut through to this street.

Venables looked around. "Coast looks clear. You want to do your thing?"

Cove was already out of the car. Before he knew what was happening, T had been searched expertly and was lying facedown in the backseat of Venables's car, with one of Cove's big hands on the back of his neck, keeping him there. Venables drove off while T loudly cursed them. By the time he calmed, they were two miles away and in a better part of town. Cove pulled T to a sitting position. The man looked first at Cove and then at Venables.

"Hey, T," said Venables. "You looking good. Been taking care of yourself?"

Cove could sense T was about to make a lunge out the other door, so he clamped his arm around T's shoulders. "Hey, we just want to talk to you, T. Just talk."

"What if I don't wanta talk?"

"Then you can just get out of the car," said Cove.

"Is that right? Okay, stop the car and I'm getting out."

"Whoa, there, T, he didn't say anything about me stopping the car *before* you got out." Venables cut the wheel, entered an on-ramp, and they pulled onto Interstate 395, crossed the Fourteenth Street Bridge and they were in Virginia. Venables pushed the accelerator to sixty.

T stared out the window at the traffic streaming by and then sat back, his arms folded across his chest.

"Now, my friend here—" began Venables.

"Your damn friend got a name?"

Cove tightened his grip on T's shoulders. "Yeah, I got a name. You call me T-Rex. Tell him why, Sonny."

"'Cause he eats little T's for breakfast, lunch and dinner," said Sonny.

"And I just want some information about some new product in town. Crews buying it up and stuff like that. No problems. Just a couple of names and we let you off right where we picked you up."

"And trust me, T, you don't want to piss this man off," added Venables.

"You cops, you ain't doing nothing to me 'less you want to get your ass sued off."

Cove stared at the man for a moment and then said, "Right now, T, you better be real nice to me. I'm not feeling good about things, and I don't give a shit if somebody sues me or not."

"Fuck off."

"Sonny, take the next right. Head to the GW Parkway. Lot of quiet places there," he added ominously.

"You got it."

In a few minutes, they were on the George Washington, or GW, Parkway, heading north.

"Take the next turnoff," Cove said.

They pulled into a sightseeing lot that provided a beautiful view of Georgetown and, far below, the Potomac River. A stone wall served as a buffer from the steep drop. Day had turned to dusk and there were no other cars parked in the lot. Cove looked around, opened the door and pulled T out with him.

"If you dudes arresting me, I want my lawyer."

Venables got out too and looked around. He eyed the drop, glanced back at Cove and shrugged.

Cove grabbed the smallish T around the waist and lifted him up.

"What the hell you doing, man?"

Cove climbed over the stone wall and down on the other side while T struggled in vain. There was a narrow strip of ground and then a drop of about a hundred feet into the river, which was filled with rocks. Down the river and on the opposite bank were a number of buildings housing local boating clubs. They were painted bright colors and their members rowed the waters in canoes, sculls, kayaks and other assorted watercraft that required muscle rather than combustion engines to make them move. There were several of them on the water right now and T was given an inverted view of that picturesque scene because Cove was holding him upside down, by the legs, over the drop.

"Holy shit," screamed out the flailing T as he looked down to oblivion.

"Now, we can do this the easy way or the hard way, and you're gonna have to decide real quick, because I'm out of time and patience," said Cove.

Venables squatted on top of the wall and kept a lookout for other cars. "Better listen to him, T, the man doesn't lie."

"But you guys are cops," wailed T. "You can't do this shit. It's fucking unconstitutional."

"I never said I was a cop," said Cove.

T stiffened and then glanced over at Venables. "But, damn it, *he* is."

"Hey, I'm not my brother's keeper," said Venables. "And I'm getting ready to retire anyway. I don't give a shit."

"Oxy," said Cove calmly. "I want to know who's buying it in D.C."

"Are you one crazy-ass mother or what?" screamed T.

"Yes, I am." Cove let his grip slip a bit and T went down about six inches. Now Cove had hold of only the man's ankles.

"Oh, God, oh, sweet Jesus, help me," whimpered T.

"Don't be talking to Jesus, T, not after the life you've led," answered Venables. "He might just send a lightning bolt, and I'm standing way too close."

"Talk to me," said Cove in his calm voice. "Oxy."

"I can't tell you nothing. Then folks come after my ass."

Cove let his grip slip again. Now he was holding on only to the man's feet. "You're wearing loafers, T," he said. "Loafers slip right off."

"Go to hell."

Cove let go of one of the feet and now was holding T by one foot with both hands. He looked back at Venables. "Sonny, I think we better drop this one and go get us somebody else who's a little smarter."

"I got just the person. Let's go."

Cove started to let go of the foot.

"No!" screamed T. "I'll talk. I'll tell you."

Cove remained motionless.

"No, I mean put me down and I'll tell you."

"Sonny, go start the car while I throw this piece of crap in the Potomac."

"*No!* I'll talk, right here. I swear."

"Oxy," prompted Cove again.

"Oxy," repeated T, and he started talking fast, telling Cove all he needed to know.

Claire pulled her Volvo into her driveway and cut the engine. It was a nice neighborhood, not too far away from her office and she had been fortunate enough to buy into it before housing prices soared. She made a good enough income, but the cost of living in northern Virginia had become ridiculous. Builders were cramming places on any scrap of land they could find and yet there were more than enough people willing to buy them

Her house was a three-bedroom Cape Cod with a nice patch of lawn in front, flowers in window boxes, a cedar shake roof and a two-car garage attached to the house by a breezeway. The street was tree-lined and the neighborhood contained a nice mixture of young and old as well as professional and working-class people.

After being divorced for so long, Claire was close to accepting that she would forever remain single. There were few eligible men in the social circles where she mingled and none of them had captured her interest. She had girlfriends always on the lookout to fix her up with yet another tech mini-mogul or lawyer, but she found them to be so egotistical and self-centered that she figured marrying one of them wouldn't be all that different from remaining single. As a rebuke, she had asked one very self-involved high-tech chap at a party if he had ever heard of Narcissus. He had wanted to know if it was a new type of Internet software and then gone right on talking about how fabulous he was.

She pulled her briefcase out of the car and headed up to the front steps. She hadn't pulled the car into the garage because she intended to go out again. The man coming out of her backyard startled Claire. He was black and large, with a head that appeared shaven, though he wore a cap. Claire focused on his gas company uniform and the electronic gas gauge he held in his hand. He passed her, smiled and went across the street. She felt embarrassed for her automatic suspicion of a black man, though she had to admit, also with some embarrassment, that there were few people of color in her neighborhood. Yet who could blame her for being paranoid, after spending time with Web London and men like him?

She unlocked the door and went inside, her mind on her session with Web. It had been shocking in many ways but at least more revealing than shocking. She put her briefcase down and headed to her bedroom to change. It was still light out and she thought she would take advantage of the nice weather and go for a walk. She remembered the pills in her pocket, pulled them out and examined them. The unfamiliar one intrigued her greatly. She had a friend who worked in the pharmacy department at Fairfax Hospital. He could run it through some tests and tell her what this was. It didn't look like any sleep medication she had ever seen, but she could be mistaken. She also hoped she was mistaken about a drug interaction having made Web freeze up in that alley. That might be something he could never recover from. As crazy as Web's theory on voodoo was, she would take a curse over something Web had inadvertently put into his body that caused his friends to die without him. No, the answer had to lie in his past, she was convinced of that.

She sat on the bed and took off her shoes, went into her small walk-in closet, disrobed and pulled on a T-shirt and shorts because the heat had returned. Barefoot, she came back out and looked at the phone. Maybe she should call Web and talk to him. At some point she had to tell him what she had learned about Stockton's death. The timing of it, though, was critical. Too early or too late a disclosure and the consequences could be disastrous. She decided to take the chicken's way out and figure it out later. Maybe the walk would help her decide. She went over to her drawer and pulled out a baseball cap. She was about to put it on when a hand went around her mouth. She dropped the cap and instinctively began to struggle until she felt the gun barrel against her cheek and she stopped, her eyes wide with fear, breaths suddenly coming in heaves. She remembered she hadn't locked the door on the way in. It was such a safe neighborhood, or at least it had been. Her racing mind wondered if the gas man was an impostor and he had come back and was now about to rape her and then kill her.

"What do you want?" she asked in a voice that was so muffled by the hand over her mouth that it didn't sound like her own. She could tell it was a man, though his hand was gloved, because of the strength in it. The hand left her mouth and encircled her neck.

The man didn't answer and Claire saw the blindfold coming toward her, and the next moment she was in total darkness. She felt herself being led over to the bed and she was terrified the rape was about to happen. Should she scream or fight? And yet the gun was still pressed to her right cheek. And the silence of her attacker was more unnerving than hearing his voice.

"Just be cool," the man said, "all we want is information. Nothing else from you." His words seemed clear enough to her. Her body was safe. At least she could hope that.

He guided her down so that she was sitting on the edge of the bed. She told herself that if he pushed her back and climbed on her, she would fight, gun or not.

And yet she sensed him moving away from her. And at the same time she sensed the entrance of another person. She tensed as this person sat next to her on the bed. A heavy man, she deduced, for the bed went down quite a bit with his weight. But he didn't touch her, though even through the blindfold she could feel his gaze upon her.

"You seeing Web London?"

She jerked a bit at this question, for it hadn't occurred to her that this was about Web, though she wondered why it hadn't. Her life was fairly ordinary, routine, no guns and men killed. That was Web's life. Like it or not, she was now part of that life.

"What do you mean?" she managed to say.

She heard the man let out a grunt, one of annoyance, she thought.

"You're a psychiatrist and he's your patient, isn't that true?"

Claire wanted to say that ethically she couldn't reveal that information, but she felt certain that if she did, this man would kill her. As though he would care about her ethical constraints. To add credence to her belief, she heard what clearly sounded like the hammer of a gun being cocked. She had been around guns as a consulting forensic psychiatrist and knew that sound pretty well. A large cold mass formed in her stomach and her limbs became rigid, and she wondered how Web could deal with people like this every day of his life.

"I'm seeing him, yes."

"Now we getting somewhere. Did he mention a boy to you, a boy named Kevin?"

She nodded because her mouth had dried up so much she didn't think she could speak.

"He happen to know where that boy is now?"

Claire shook her head and tensed as he lightly squeezed her shoulder.

"Relax, lady, ain't nobody gonna hurt you long as you cooperate.

If you don't cooperate, then we have quite a problem," he added ominously.

Claire heard him snap his fingers and about a minute passed in silence, and then she felt something touch her lips. She drew back.

"Water," the man said. "You got dry mouth. People scared shitless get that all the time. Drink."

The last word was an order and Claire immediately obeyed it.

"Now talk, no more nods or shakes, you understand me?"

She started to nod and then caught herself. "Yes."

"What'd he say about Kevin? Everything, I have to know it all."

"Why?" She wasn't exactly sure where that bold question had come from.

"I got my reasons."

"Do you want to hurt the boy?"

"No," the man said quietly. "I just want him back nice and safe."

He sounded sincere, but then criminals often did, she reminded herself. Ted Bundy had been the king of smooth talkers while he methodically killed scores of women, smiling all the way.

"I have no reason to believe you, you know."

"Kevin, he my son."

She tensed at this and then relaxed. Could this be the Big F person Web had told her about? But he had said the man was Kevin's brother, not father. The man *sounded* like a concerned parent, yet there was something not quite right. Claire would just have to go with her professional gut on this one. What she sensed very clearly was that these men would kill her. "Web said he saw Kevin in the alley. He said Kevin said something to him and it affected him in a weird way. He saw him later, while the guns were firing. He gave him a note and sent him off. He didn't see him after that. But he's been looking for him."

"Is that all?"

She nodded and then caught herself. She could feel him move closer, and even though she wore the blindfold, she closed her eyes. She could feel tears forming there.

"Ground rules are no more nods or shakes, I need to hear words, last time I'm telling you, you got me?"

"Yes." She fought back the tears.

"Now, did he say anything else, about anything peculiar happening when he saw Kevin the second time?"

She said, "No," but she had hesitated a second too long. She could clearly feel it, as though the pause had been a day long in duration. And she thought that he had noticed it, as well. She was correct in that assumption, for she instantly felt the cold muzzle of a pistol against her cheek.

"We having a serious misunderstanding here, like maybe I ain't making myself clear. Just so we are clear, let me lay this out for you, bitch. To get my boy back, I'll blow your brains out and everybody you ever cared about in your whole life. I see pictures all over the place of this cute-looking girl. Bet that's your daughter, ain't it?" Claire didn't answer and she felt his hand wrap around her neck. His hand was gloved, which surprised her until she thought of fingerprints and DNA that machines could detect off of corpses. Her corpse! This thought made her feel faint.

"Ain't it?"

"Yes!"

He kept his hand on her neck. "See, you got you your little girl nice and safe. Perfect little house in a perfect little place. But see, I don't got me my boy and he's all I have. Why you get your girl and I ain't get my boy? You think that's fair? Do you?" He squeezed her neck a little and Claire felt herself start to gag.

"No."

"No, what?"

"No, I don't think that's fair," she managed to say in a garbled voice.

"Yeah? Well, it's a little late for that, baby."

The next thing she felt was being pushed back on the bed. Her earlier promise to fight if they attempted to rape her seemed ridiculous now. She was so frightened she could barely breathe. She felt a pillow being placed over her face and then something hard jammed into the center of the pillow. It took her a few seconds to realize that the hard object was the pistol and the pillow would serve as a crude silencer.

She thought of her daughter, Maggie, and she thought of how

her body would be found. The tears streamed down her cheeks. And then for one miraculous second her wits came back to her.

"He said that somebody had switched the kids in the alley."

The pillow did not move for some seconds and Claire thought she had lost after all.

Then it was slowly removed and she was jerked up so hard she thought her arm had been dislocated.

"Say again?"

"He said that Kevin had been switched in the alley for another boy. The boy who went to the police wasn't Kevin. He was taken in the alley before he got to the police."

"Does he know why?"

"No. And he doesn't know who did it. Only that it happened."

She felt the pistol against her cheek again. For some reason it wasn't as frightening the second time around.

"You lying, you ain't gonna like what I'm gonna do to you."

"That's what he said." She felt like she had betrayed Web to save herself and she wondered if he would have rather died than done such a thing. He probably would have. The tears started coming again, and not out of fear this time but from her own weakness.

"He thinks that Kevin being in that alley was planned by whoever was behind what happened. He thinks Kevin was somehow involved." She quickly added, "But unwittingly. He's only a child."

The pistol was removed from her cheek and her interrogator's large presence also moved away.

"That it?"

"That's all I know."

"You tell anybody we here, you know what I'll do to you. And I can find your daughter. We been through your house, we know all there is to know about you and her. Do we understand each other?"

"Yes," she managed to get out.

"I'm just doing this to get my son back, that's all. I ain't like busting in people's homes and roughing 'em up, that ain't my style, especially women, but what I got to do to get my boy back, I'll do."

She felt herself nodding at this and then stopped.

She never heard them go, although her hearing could not have been any more acute.

She waited a few minutes to make sure, then she said, "Hello?" And then she said it again. She reached up slowly to undo the blindfold. She was waiting for hands to stop her, but none came. She finally pulled off the blindfold and she quickly looked around the room, half expecting someone to leap out at her. She would have liked to collapse on the bed and cry for the rest of the day and night, but she couldn't stay here. They said they had been everywhere in her house. She threw some clothes in an overnight bag, grabbed her purse and a pair of tennis shoes and went to the front door. She looked out but saw no one. She quickly went to her car and got in. As she drove off, she kept her gaze on the rearview mirror to see if anyone was following her. She was no expert in that, but there didn't seem to be anyone there. Claire entered the Capital Beltway and sped up, unsure of exactly where she would go.

40

Antoine Peebles pulled off the gloves and sat back, a broad smile on his intelligent features. He looked over at Macy, who was driving. The man's face was inscrutable, as always.

"Damn good performance, if I do say so myself," said Peebles. "I think I got the man's voice and diction just right. I haven't said 'ain't' that many times in my whole life. So what do you think?"

"You sounded like the boss," agreed Macy.

"And the lady gets all pissed off and she goes to Web London and the cops and they go looking for Francis."

"And maybe us."

"No, I explained all that to you. You have to think at the macro and micro level, Mace," said Peebles as though lecturing a student. "We've already distanced ourselves from him. And on top of that he's got no product and half his crew is already gone because of that. His cash flow is down to almost nothing. In this business you have two-day inventory levels, tops. He had some stuff hidden, I'll give him credit for that, but that's gone. And when he shot Toona he lost four more guys just from that." Peebles shook his head. "And with all that happening, what does he do? He spends every second thinking about the kid. Every night he's looking for him, roughing people up, burning bridges, not trusting anybody."

"Guess he's smart not to trust anybody," said Macy, glancing at Peebles. "Especially you and me."

Peebles ignored this. "He could write a book on stupid management techniques, killing one of your own guys like that in front of everybody. In front of an FBI agent! He's got a death wish."

"You have to keep your guys in line," said Macy evenly. "You have to lead from strength." He looked over at Peebles with an expression that clearly showed he thought his companion lacked that attribute, but Peebles didn't notice because he was still obviously reveling in his triumph. "And you can't blame the guy for trying to find his son."

Peebles said, "You can't mix business and personal. He's screwed himself already, burning political capital, over what? Something that is never going to happen. That kid is never coming back. Whoever took him, that boy is six feet under if there was anything left of him. Now I've already got new supply lines set up and his defectors have joined me." He looked at Macy. "You probably don't know this, but my maneuver is classic Machiavelli. And I've been skimming the best crew members from other gangs over the last six months. We're just about ready to go and this time we do it all my way. We run it like a real business. Accountability, pay and promotion for merit, bonuses for exemplary performance and rewards for innovation that go right to the corporate bottom line. We're going to take over our own money-laundering efforts and cut costs where they need to be cut. Not every crew has to have jewelry and five-hundred-dollar-a-night hookers. I'm even envisioning a retirement plan instead of the brothers throwing their money after cars and carats and having nothing when they're too old to do this anymore. And I'm implementing a dress code for management level, no more of this looking like crap. A professional has to have a professional image. Look at you, you look slick, that's what I want."

Macy released a rare smile. "Some of the boys aren't going to like that."

"They have to grow up sometime." He looked over at Macy. "I gotta tell you, it was an awesome feeling having that gun in my hand."

"Would you have shot her?"

"Are you nuts? I was just scaring her."

"Well, you pull a gun, some point you may have to use it," said Macy.

"That's your job. You're head of security, Mace. My right-hand guy. You showed your stuff when you came up with the plan to nab Kevin. And you did the down-and-dirty work rounding up the other crews to join forces. Now we're going to go places, my man; a lot farther than Francis was taking us, and a lot faster. He's old school, the new ways are the best ways. That's why the dinosaurs died."

They pulled down an alley and Peebles checked his watch. "Okay, you got the meeting place all set up?"

"They're all there, just like you wanted."

"Mood?"

"Good, but suspicious. You got them worried but definitely interested."

"That's what I wanted to hear. This is where we stake out our territory, Mace, and where we let the others know that Francis is no longer the force. This is *our* time. Let's do it." He paused as a sudden thought hit him.

"What the hell was that woman talking about, somebody switching Kevin for another kid in that alley?"

Macy shrugged. "No clue."

"You got the kid, right?"

"Safe and sound. For now. You want to see him?"

"I don't want to go anywhere near that kid. He knows me, something goes wrong and he gets to Francis . . ." The fear was palpable on Peebles's features.

The car stopped and Macy got out and scanned the alley in both directions and then looked up to the rooftops. He finally signaled the all-clear to his new boss. Peebles climbed out, adjusted his tie and buttoned up his double-breasted suit. Macy held the building's door open for him and Peebles walked briskly through. They climbed the steps and with each one Peebles seemed to transform into a larger and larger presence. This was his moment and he had been waiting for it for years. Out with the old and in with the new.

He reached the top and waited for Macy to open the door for him. There would be seven men waiting for him in here, each representing a slice of the District's illegal drug distribution. They had never worked together; instead, each had grabbed his little share and overseen his own little fiefdom. They shared neither information nor resources. When disagreements came up, they resolved them by shooting each other. They fed information to the police about other crews when it suited them and the cops came in and cherry-picked them. Francis had done the same thing, and while it was a short-term fix that seemed to have merit, Peebles knew it could not have been more of a management disaster from a long-term perspective. And it was time for Antoine Peebles to step in and take charge.

He opened the door and walked into the room where he would start his own legend.

Peebles looked around. And saw no one there.

Peebles didn't even have a chance to turn before the pistol was at his head and the shot was fired into his brain. He dropped to the floor, blood running down his fine tie and over his very professional attire.

Macy put the pistol away and bent over the dead man. "I read Machiavelli, Twan," he said without a trace of conceit. He turned out the light and walked back down the stairs. He had a plane to catch because things were really going to start rocking now.

Web guided Boo up the small hill and reined up next to Gwen, who was on Baron.

Romano was covering Billy down at the equestrian center; actually, Web had left the two admiring Romano's Corvette. With most of the farm's men gone to the horse sale, Web had felt particularly vulnerable and had gotten Canfield to okay some more agents coming on the farm to patrol the grounds and keep watch, at least until the men returned.

"It's so beautiful this time of year," said Gwen. She looked over at Web. "I guess you think we have a pretty easy life here. Big house, lots of help, just ride around all day admiring the view."

She smiled, yet Web sensed she was being serious. He wondered why a woman like Gwen Canfield, with all she'd been through, would have the need to seek approval from anyone, especially a stranger like him. "I think you've both been through a lot, you've worked hard and now you're enjoying the fruits of that labor. That's supposed to be the American dream, isn't it?"

"I suppose so," she answered without conviction. She looked

at the sun overhead. "It's hot today." Web could tell the woman wanted to talk to him about something but didn't quite know how to broach it.

"I've been an FBI agent for so long, Gwen, I've heard just about everything and I tend to be a very good listener."

She shot him a glance. "I don't spill my heart even to people I know *well*, Web, at least not anymore."

"I'm not asking you to. But if you want to talk, I'm here."

They rode some more and then she stopped. "I've been thinking about the trial in Richmond. Those awful people even sued the FBI, didn't they?"

"Tried to, but it got thrown out. The lawyer, Scott Wingo, the one who was recently killed, he tried to make some hay out of that during Ernest Free's trial, but the judge saw right through it and put a stop to it. But it probably caused enough doubt in the jury's eyes that the prosecutor got scared and did a plea bargain." He paused and then added, "Of course he's dead too now, and the judge."

Gwen stared over at him with her large, sad eyes. "And yet Ernest Free is alive and free, after everything he did."

"Life makes no sense sometimes, Gwen."

"Billy and I had a wonderful life before all that happened. I love him very much. But ever since David was killed, it hasn't been the same. The fault probably lies more with me than him. It was my idea to put David in that school. I wanted him to get a first-rate education and I wanted him to be exposed to lots of different types of people—translation, people of color and ethnicity. Billy is a good man, but he was born and raised in Richmond, not with any sort of wealth or privilege but in a neighborhood where you'd never see anyone but those of your own kind." She added quickly, "He's not a racist or anything like that. Half the drivers and dockworkers at his trucking company were black and he treated them all the same. If you worked hard, you had a job at fair wages. I've even gone with him to drivers' homes when they'd fallen off the wagon. He would bring food and money to the families, counsel the men, get them professional help and pay for it, or AA meetings, get them back on their feet. And even though he could have fired them, even under union rules, he didn't. He told me once his lot on earth was to be the King of Second Chances, because he'd had enough of his. I know some people might look at him and me and not see the attraction, but I know there's nothing he wouldn't do for me and he's stood right next to me through good and bad times and we've both had our share of those."

"Hey, Gwen, you don't have to convince me. But if you're having problems, have you sought counseling? I actually know someone."

She gave Web a hopeless look, gazed up at the hot sun again and said, "I'm going for a swim."

They rode back to the stables and Web drove Gwen back to the house in one of the farm trucks. She changed into her swimsuit and met Web at the pool area. He wasn't swimming, he told her, because his gun would get wet. She smiled at this remark and went over and turned a key that was set in a device built into a stone wall next to the pool. The gray automatic pool cover slid back on its tracks.

"We put this in because we kept finding turtles, frogs and even the occasional black snake in the pool," she explained.

As the cover slid into its holding trench at the far end of the pool, Web squatted down and examined the current-machine built into the deep end of the pool. He looked up in time to see Gwen step out of her sandals and slip out of her robe. She had on a one-piece suit that was cut a little low at the bosom and a little high at the hips and buttocks. Her body had a nice tan, and the muscles in her thighs and calves matched those he had already seen in her arms and shoulders. Forget the butt-burners and thigh-masters, women should just go horseback riding.

"How's this thing work?" asked Web.

Gwen tucked her long hair under a swim cap and walked over to him. "Water's pumped from the pool and through the cannon that you see there. It shoots out the water at a certain rate providing a resistance that you can increase or decrease, as you want. We had a portable machine for a while that was very cumbersome. And then I was using it so much that it made sense to have it built in. The pool's heated, so I use it pretty much year-round."

"I guess that's why you're in such great shape."

"Thank you, kind sir. Sure you don't want to swim with me?"

"I'd probably just slow you down."

"Right. There's not an ounce of fat on you." She went over to a control panel that was bolted to the stone wall that was set against the side of the pool nearest the house, opened the box and pushed some buttons.

Web heard water pressure building up and then he looked into the pool and saw white frothing water pouring out of the underwater cannon, creating the current Gwen was going to swim against.

She put on a pair of swim goggles and dove in. Web watched as she came to the surface and started her strokes. He watched for about ten minutes. The woman never varied her pace or stroke. She was like a machine herself and Web was actually glad he had declined the woman's offer to join her in the pool. Every HRT man had to be able to swim and know how to use diving equipment, and Web was a strong swimmer, but he wasn't sure he could have kept up with Gwen Canfield.

After about twenty minutes the frothing water stopped and Gwen came over to the side of the pool.

"Done?" asked Web.

"No, I had it set for forty-five minutes. The circuit might have tripped."

"Where's the power box?"

She pointed to the double doors set in a stone wall that was built up against a small slope. "In the pool equipment room."

With the grade of land the way it was here, Web figured the room was partly underground. He headed over and turned the knob. "It's locked."

"That's odd, we never lock it."

"You know where the key is?"

"No. Like I said, we never lock it, I just assumed there wasn't a key. I guess I'll have to cut my swim short."

"No, you won't." He smiled. "The FBI is a full-service agency and a happy client is our best customer." He pulled out his key ring, on which he always carried a very slim piece of metal that could pick ninety-nine percent of the world's locks in about thirty seconds. He opened the pool equipment room in half that time.

He went in, found the light switch and turned on the lights, which was a good thing, because even with the lights, he almost took a tumble down a short flight of steps just inside the doorway. Well, he thought, that was a lawyer's dream case. The place was noisy, with water running and machinery clanking and pumping. He went down the stairs. There were shelves filled with pool stuff, big canisters of powdered chlorine, skimmers, scrubbers, an aquatic robot to clean the pool and assorted junk that probably no one had used in years. It was cool down here and Web calculated that he was about ten feet underground at this point because the floor had continued to gently slope downward once he had gone down the stairs.

Web found the power box and sure enough the circuit had tripped. Since the current machine was a new addition, unless they had upgraded their wiring, it might be throwing too much electrical strain on the system. They should probably have that looked at before it blew and started a fire. He made a mental note to tell Gwen this. As he threw the breaker back on, he heard the machine start up again. There was really quite a racket down here. As he turned to go back outside, Web didn't notice another door down a short hallway. He turned and walked back out, turning off the light.

On the other side of that door and down another short hallway was another door, for there was quite the little maze down here. Inside that room Kevin Westbrook held his breath. First he had heard footsteps and then he hadn't. He had heard the damn machine go on and then off and then on again. And the chlorine smell, for he had long ago deduced what it was and grown used to it. But the footsteps going away had surprised him. Whenever people had come down here before, they had come to see him. He wondered why they hadn't this time.

41

While Gwen showered, Web waited in the library. One wall of the room consisted of built-in cabinetry with a large-screen TV. There were also five shelves filled with videocassettes and Web idly ran his gaze along them until the handwritten numbers on one of them made him freeze. He reached out and took it off the shelf. The numbers he had seen were only a date, yet the date was one that Web would never forget. He looked around, but there was no one about.

Web popped the tape in the VCR. The scene was one he had played over and over in his head. The Richmond school was filled with smart, willing children from all types of socioeconomic backgrounds. It was quite symbolic, the newspapers had said at the time, that the former capital of the Confederacy was trying a bold program to reintegrate its schools after most federal courts and most states had thrown up their hands and said what was there was the best that could be done. Well, Richmond had tried to do more and was succeeding, drawing national attention to its programs. Then Ernest B. Free and several of his homicidal gang had walked in the front doors with body armor and enough automatic weaponry to defeat the Union in the Civil War.

Chaos had followed as the two teachers were gunned down and over forty hostages, including thirty children, ages six to sixteen, were forced to take part in an event not one of them wanted anything to do with. The negotiators had worked the phones nonstop with the men inside, trying to keep them calm, to see what they wanted and whether it could be gotten for them. And all the time Web and his Charlie Team were standing by along with Zulu Team sniper guns trained on every available point of attack. Then there were sounds of gunfire inside and Web and his men were called up to the front lines. Each man had the battle plan firmly in mind, though it had been concocted on the fly on the way down from Quantico. Web remembered that they had gotten so close to getting the call to hit the target that he had even rubbed his .45s for luck.

What little Web knew about the Frees had not made him feel any better. They were violent but disciplined and well armed. And they were entrenched and had lots of innocent lives in their control.

The Frees had contacted the negotiators through a phone system that they had jerry-rigged. The shots were merely a misfire, they had said. Right away Web hadn't liked that. He could sense something bad coming, for the very simple fact that men like the Frees didn't operate under good faith. Yet Charlie Team had been called off. After Waco, the FBI's position on hostage rescue had changed. Basically it was a sit-and-wait game and the Bureau had shown that it was willing to wait until a new year had dawned before forcing the issue, so deeply ingrained was the starkly brutal image of lost children burning in Texas. But after the Frees had broken off negotiations, HRT had been called up again and this time Web knew they were going in.

With the TV cameras out front letting the whole world watch this drama unfold frame by frame, Web and Charlie Team had inched toward a little-used entrance at the rear of the building. To maximize surprise, since the precise location of the hostages and the Frees was not known, they had decided against using a breach charge to blow the exterior door and had opted for stealth. They had gotten inside quietly and made their way down the corridor and toward the gymnasium, where the best intelligence available said the hostages probably were.

HRT had crept to the double door, where Web had peered through the glass on the door and methodically counted hostages and hostage takers. They all appeared to be there. Just before ducking down, Web had made eye contact with the boy; he tried to keep him calm so he wouldn't give Web and company away, even giving him a thumbs-up. At the time Web didn't know that the young man was David Canfield.

HRT had begun its countdown. Each operator knew exactly where to shoot and they were confident that they could take out each of the Frees without losing any more hostages, though each of them also knew that things could go to hell quickly through the unexpected.

And they did.

Right before they burst into the room, there came a loud, high-pitched sound. It could not have come at a more inopportune time. And to this day Web didn't know its source.

HRT came in firing, but the Frees, now forewarned, instantly returned it.

And the shots were carefully placed. David Canfield had been shot through his left lung, the round exiting out of his chest. He dropped to the floor. With every breath the boy was jettisoning his blood through the large hole in his body. Though it couldn't have been more than a couple of seconds, David Canfield had stared at Web with an expression the man would never forget. It was as though the boy had put his entire faith in Web, his touchstone against all the madness, and Web had let him down. Thumbs-up.

That's when the real fighting started, and Web had to forget about David Canfield and concentrate on the other hostages and the men trying to kill him. He had taken the flamer after saving Lou Patterson, then eaten the rounds in his neck and torso. After that he had been a one-man wrecking crew and none of the Frees were left standing. Web couldn't believe that Ernest Free had managed to survive.

Reliving this was sickening, yet Web hunched forward as the cameras captured him once more. He was being brought out on a stretcher, paramedics surrounding him. To his left was Lou Patterson. On his right was a sheet over a body. David Canfield was the only hostage to have died with HRT on the case. Web continued to watch himself on the TV as the cameras alternated between him fighting for his life and David Canfield's still body. A light from one of the TV cameras continued to shine on the boy until somebody actually shot it out. Web often wondered who had done it. And then the tape went dark.

"I was the one who shot out that camera light."

Web whirled around and saw Dilly Canfield standing there, staring at the TV and seemingly having been privy to Web's thoughts. He moved forward, his steps halting, his finger pointing at the screen.

Web rose from the couch. "God, Billy, I'm sorry, I shouldn't have—"

"See," Billy continued, "that damn light was shining right on my boy. They didn't have to do that." He finally focused on Web. "They didn't have to do that, it wasn't right. My little Davy was always sensitive to bright lights."

It was then that Gwen came in, dressed in jeans and a pink blouse, her feet bare and her hair still wet. Web shot her an apologetic look and she quickly deduced what had happened. She took her husband by the arm, but he immediately pulled away from her. Web read something close to hate for her in his eyes.

"Why don't you two sit in here and watch it?" he shouted at Gwen. "Damn you. I know, Gwen. Don't think I don't."

He stalked out of the room, while Gwen, without even looking at Web, fled in the other direction.

Feeling tremendous guilt, Web popped the tape out and started to put it on the shelf; and then he stopped. He glanced toward the door, slid the tape in his jacket pocket and went back to the carriage house. He put the tape in the VCR there and turned on the TV. He watched the tape five more times and something was there that he just couldn't quite get, a sound in the background. He turned up the volume and got very close to the screen, yet that didn't work. Finally he called Bates and explained what he was thinking. "I've got the tape here," he said.

Bates said, "I know the one you're talking about. It was shot by a network affiliate in Richmond. We've got one in archives. I'll have our guys give it a close look."

Web clicked the TV off and took the tape out of the VCR. It had also been discovered later that two black teenage females had been raped by the Frees; apparently their hatred for those of color did not prevent them from having forcible sex with them.

But what had Billy meant when he told Gwen that he knew? Knew what?

His ringing cell phone interrupted Web's thoughts. He answered it. The woman was nearly hysterical.

"Claire, what's wrong?"

He listened to her frightened tones and then said, "Stay right where you are. I'll be there as fast as I can." He hung up, called Romano, filled him in and was on the road in a few minutes.

42

Claire had gone to a very safe and public place, a police sub-station at a suburban mall. She hadn't filed a report with the police, she told Web when he showed up.

"Why the hell not?"

"I wanted to talk to you first."

"Look, Claire, from how you described it, it sounds like my buddy Francis Westbrook and one of his sidekicks, probably Clyde Macy. The last time I saw them, somebody died. You don't realize how lucky you are."

"But I can't tell for sure it was them, I was blindfolded."

"But you would recognize their voices?"

"Probably." She paused and looked puzzled.

"What is it, Claire, what's bugging you?"

"This Francis, how educated would you say he is?"

"In street smarts, he's a Ph.D. In book learning, nil. Why?"

"The man who threatened me had an odd way of talking. He would alternate between slang and ghetto talk, and the diction and vocabulary of an educated man. I could sense he was uncomfortable with what he was saying, because it felt forced sometimes, as though he were trying to think of appropriate words as he went along, suppressing his natural choices but occasionally erring, and using words that, you know—"

"Would be more along the lines of the person he was trying to impersonate?"

"Impersonate, exactly."

Web took a deep breath. Well, this was getting interesting. He was thinking about a second-in-command trying to pull a coup on his boss or push the knife in a little deeper, depending on how one looked at it. Antoine Peebles, the wannabe drug king with a sheepskin. He looked at her with new admiration. "You've got a good pair of ears, Claire, always waiting for those cues from us poor screwed-up head cases."

"I'm scared, Web. I'm really scared. I've counseled people for years about facing what frightens them, being proactive instead of reactive, and this happens to me and I feel paralyzed."

He found his arm going protectively around her as he led her to his car. "Well, you have a right to be scared. What happened to you would scare most people."

"But not you." She said this, he noted, almost enviously.

As they climbed in his Mach, Web told her, "It's not that I don't ever get scared, Claire, because I do."

"Well, you certainly don't show it."

"Yes, I do, just in a different way." He closed the car door and thought for a moment before glancing at her and actually gripping her hand. "You can deal with your fear in two different ways. Close up like a clam and hide from the world or do something about it."

"Now you sound like the psychiatrist," she said wearily.

"Well, I learned from the best." He squeezed her hand. "What do you say, want to help me crack this thing?"

"I trust you, Web."

This surprised him, chiefly because that wasn't what he had asked her.

He put the car in gear. "Well, let's go see if we can find a little boy named Kevin."

Web parked in the alley behind the duplex where Kevin had lived, and he and Claire went to the rear door just in case somebody was watching the front, like Bates's men. He definitely didn't want to run afoul of the Bureau right now. Web knocked.

"Yeah, who is it?" The voice was a man's, not Grandma's, and it definitely wasn't friendly.

"Jerome, is that you?"

Web could sense a presence just on the other side of the door.

"Who the hell wants to know?"

"Web London, FBI. And how are you today, Jerome?"

Web and Claire heard the word "Shit" muttered loudly, but the door did not open.

"Jerome, I'm still here and I'll stay here until you open the door. And don't try running out the front like you did last time. We've got that covered."

He heard chains sliding back and locks popping open and he was eye to eye with Jerome. Web was very surprised to see that he had on a white shirt, nice slacks and a tie to go with his sullen look.

"Got a date?"

"Damn, you real funny for a Fed. What do you want?"

"Just talk. You alone?"

Jerome stepped back. "Not anymore. Look, we told you all we know. Man, can't you stop bugging us?"

Web ushered Claire inside, followed her and then closed the door behind them. They looked around the small kitchen. "Just trying to find Kevin. You want that, don't you?" Web asked.

"What's that supposed to mean?"

"It means I don't tend to trust anyone. I just want to talk, that's all."

"Look, I'm busy. You want to talk to somebody, you can talk to my lawyer." Jerome looked at Claire. "What is she, *your* date?"

"No, she's my shrink."

"Yeah, that's a good one."

"No, really, Jerome, I am," said Claire as she stepped forward. "And I'm afraid that Mr. London has some issues."

"What does his issues have to do with me?"

"Well, he's been devoting so much time to this case that I believe he's becoming almost obsessed with it. That sort of obsession can reach dangerous, sometimes violent levels if not dealt with in a reasonable period of time."

Jerome looked over at Web and took as step back. "If this man is crazy, I had nothing to do with it. He was crazy the first time he came here."

"But you don't want anything to happen to someone, like yourself or others. Mr. London is only trying to find the truth, and in my professional opinion finding the truth, for someone with his particular set of issues, is very important. And to those who help him find it, he would, psychologically speaking, be very grateful. The flip side of that is somewhere you really don't want to go." She looked at Web with an expression of sorrow mixed with just the right touch of fear. "I've seen the results of that before with Mr. London; that's one reason why I'm here. To prevent another tragedy."

Web just had to admire the woman's work.

Jerome stared back and forth at Claire and Web. Then he said in a far more calm tone, "Look, I told you all I know. I really have."

Web spoke very firmly. "No, Jerome, you haven't. I want to know stuff about Kevin maybe you've never even thought about. Now let's cut the shit and get down to it."

Jerome motioned them to follow and turned and walked down the hallway into the small living room where Web had first spoken to them. Before he left the kitchen, Web noted that it was very clean, the sinks spotless, the floor scrubbed. As he and Claire followed Jerome down the hallway and into the living room, he saw that the trash had been picked up, the floors mopped, the walls scrubbed. Web could smell disinfectant everywhere. A door was leaning against the wall next to the bathroom, and the sheet had been taken down. The openings in the ceiling had been shored up and braced. Grandma's doing, he thought, at least he did until Jerome picked up a broom and started sweeping a pile of trash into a large garbage bag.

Web looked around at the "new" home. "Your doing?"

"We don't have to be living in no pigsty."

"Where's your grandma?"

"At work. Over at the hospital. In the cafeteria."

"How come you're not at work?"

"I will be in an hour, hope you ain't plan on keeping me long."

"You look too nice to be planning to knock over a bank."

"Man, you are a riot."

"So where's work?" *You don't have a job, Jerome, just admit it.*

Jerome finished filling the bag, tied it closed and tossed it to Web. "You mind throwing that out the front door?"

Claire opened the door and Web did so, setting the bag on the front stoop along with quite a few others. When he closed the door, Jerome had pulled a toolbox out of a closet. He took out a screwdriver, Vise-Grips and a hammer. He laid the tools next to the bathroom opening and gripped the door.

"Give me a hand, here, will you?"

Web helped him lift the door closer to the opening and then held on to it and watched as Jerome tightened the sagging hinges and used the Vise-Grips to pop out the door pins. They lifted the door up, worked it into place and Jerome tapped the hinges in with the hammer. He closed and opened the door several times to see that it was aligned properly.

"A handy guy. But that's not your job, unless carpenters wear ties to work."

Jerome put his tools away before answering. "I work nights at a company servicing their computer system. Just got the position a few months ago."

"So you know computers?" asked Claire.

"Got my AS in computer science at the community college. Yeah, I know my way around 'em."

Web was unimpressed. "Uh-huh. You know computers?"

"You got a hearing problem? That's what I said."

"Last time I was here, you didn't look gainfully employed."

"Like I said, I work nights."

"Right."

Jerome stared at Web and then went over and slid a computer case out from under the couch. He flipped it open and fired it up.

"You on-line, man?" asked Jerome.

"We talking skates or what?"

"Ha-ha. Computers. Internet. You know what that is, don't you?"

"Nah, I've been traveling around the galaxy the last ten years, I'm so behind."

Jerome punched a few keys and they listened as it was announced to Jerome that "You've got mail" on AOL.

"Wait a minute, how can you access the Internet without a phone?" said Web.

"My computer has wireless technology, a card that lets me do that. It's like having a built-in cell phone." He smiled at Web and shook his head in obvious amazement. "Man, I hope most Feds aren't as ignorant as you are about computers."

"Don't push it, Jerome."

"You know what a cookie is?"

"Sugary thing that gives you love handles."

"You just never quit, do you? A cookie is a simple piece of text. An HTTP header with a text-only string. The string has the domain, the path, value variable that a website sets and a lifetime. Lots of companies use cookies to personalize information, track popular links or for demographics. It keeps site content fresh and of interest to users. For example." He hit a few keys and the screen changed. "I've been on this site a lot recently and it knows that. So it doesn't show me the same stuff unless I specifically request it. And they're starting to use cookies in back-end interactions, like storing personal data a user has given to the site, like passwords and such."

"Storing personal data. That sounds sort of Big Brotherish," said Claire.

"Well, it can be, but cookies are just text, no program, they're not virus-susceptible. It can't even access your hard drive, although your browser can save cookie values there if necessary, but that's about it. Some people think cookies will fill up their hard drive, but that's pretty much impossible. Most ISPs put limits on cookies. Netscape limits them to three hundred, so you get up to that number and it automatically discards the older ones. Microsoft puts them in your TIF folder with a max default setting of two percent of your hard drive. And cookies are usually so small that you'd need about ten million cookies to fill up a gig hard drive. In fact, I'm writing a few million lines of code that will take cookies to a new level, taking out the bad stuff and making them a lot more useful. And maybe I'll make myself a few million bucks in the process." He grinned. "The ultimate cookie."

He shut down his computer and looked at Web. "Any more questions?"

The admiration was clear on Web's features. "Okay, you convinced me, you know computers."

"Yeah, I bust my ass in school, finally get a job that doesn't require me to wear a hair net and the fine folks at Social Services tell us we make too much damn money and we got to leave our home we been at for the last five years."

"System sucks."

"No, people who have never been on it think the system sucks. For people on it, we wouldn't have had anyplace to live without it. But it still ticks me off that I'm making a little more than damn Burger King pays and we get kicked out. It's not like my employer dropped any stock options on somebody like me."

"Look, it's still a start, Jerome. And better than the alternative around here, you know that."

"I'm gonna keep moving up. Work my ass off and then we are out of here and we're never looking back."

"You and your grandmother?"

"She took me in when my mama died. Brain tumor and no health insurance, that ain't a real good combo. My daddy bit it on a .45 he stuck in his own mouth when he was high on something. You damn right I'll take care of her, just like she took care of me."

"And Kevin?"

"I take care of Kevin too." He glowered at Web. "If you people can find him."

"We're trying. I know a little about his family. His relation to Big—I mean, Francis."

"He's Kevin's father. So what?"

"A little more than that. I've met Francis up close. Too close, actually." Web pointed out the remnants of his assorted facial injuries inflicted by the man.

Jerome looked at him curiously. "You lucky that's all he done to you."

"Yeah, I'm getting that feeling. He told me how Kevin came into this world. With his mother and all."

"Stepmother."

"What?"

"She was Francis's stepmother. Strung out most of the time. Don't know what happened to his real mama."

Web let out a relieved breath. It wasn't incest. He glanced at Claire, who said, "So they're actually not brothers. They're father and son. Does Kevin know that?"

"I never told him."

"But he thinks Francis is his brother? Is that how Francis wanted it?" asked Claire, while Web watched her closely.

"What Francis wants, he gets, that answer enough for you?"

"Why would Francis want Kevin to believe they were brothers?"

"Maybe he didn't want Kevin to know he was screwing his step-mom and Kevin's mom. Her name was Roxy. She was into drugs and all that, but she was good to Kevin before she died."

"How did Kevin get shot?" asked Web.

"He was with Francis, got caught in some gang shootout. Francis brought him here, only time I ever seen that man cry. I took him to the hospital myself 'cause cops just arrest his ass if Francis took him. Kevin never cried, not one time, and bleeding like a son of a bitch. But he's never been the same since. Other kids tease him, call him a retard."

"Kids can be cruel, and then they grow up and get even more cruel, they're just a lot more subtle about it," commented Claire.

"Kevin ain't stupid. Smart as a whip. And he can draw, man, draw like you can't believe."

Claire looked interested. "Care to show me?"

Jerome checked his watch. "I can't be late for work. And I got to take the bus."

"To your big cookie shop?" asked Web.

For the very first time Jerome and Web exchanged a smile. "I tell you what, Jerome, you show us Kevin's stuff and talk to us a little bit more and I'll personally drive you to work in one bitching machine that'll have all your friends envious as hell. How about that?"

Jerome led them upstairs and down a short hallway that ended with a very small room. When Jerome turned on the light, Web and Claire looked around in amazement. Every inch of the walls and even the ceiling was covered with drawings on paper, some in charcoal, others in colored pencil and still others in pen and ink. And on a small table next to a mattress on the floor were stacks of sketchbooks. Claire picked up one and started going through it, while Web continued to gaze at the drawings on the wall. Some of them were things Web could recognize, landscapes and people; Jerome and his grandmother were reproduced in amazing detail.

Other drawings were abstract in content and Web couldn't make sense of them.

Claire looked up from the sketchbook and her gaze swept around the room before focusing on Jerome. "I know a little something about art, Jerome, because my daughter is majoring in art history. Kevin has serious talent."

Jerome looked to Web like the proud father. "Kevin says that how he sees things sometimes. 'Just drawing what I'm seeing,' he tells me."

Web looked at the art supplies and sketchbooks piled on the table. There was also a small easel in the corner with a blank canvas on it.

"All this stuff costs money. Francis contributing?"

"I buy Kevin his art stuff. He gets Kevin other stuff, clothes, shoes, basic things."

"He offer to ever help you and your grandmother?"

"He offered. But we ain't taking that money. We know where it comes from. Kevin's another matter. It's his daddy. Father's got a right to provide for his son."

"Daddy come around much?"

Jerome shrugged. "When he wants to."

"You think he might be the one who has Kevin? Give it to me straight."

Jerome shook his head. "As much as I don't like Francis, if you ask me, he'd cut off his own head before he'd let anything happen to that boy. I mean, he'll kill you so much as look at you. But around Kevin he was gentle. A gentle giant, I guess you could say. He didn't want Kevin living with him because he knew it'd be too dangerous."

"I imagine that was a big sacrifice for Francis, giving up something that he loved so much. But that's the true test of love, really: sacrifice," said Web.

"Well, man changes where he sleeps all the time 'cause people looking to kill him. Hell of a way to live. But he had people watching Kevin, making sure nobody got to Francis by going after him. It ain't like everybody knew of the connection, but he wasn't taking any chances."

"You seen him since Kevin disappeared?" asked Web.

Jerome stepped back on that one and put his hands in his pockets, and Web instantly sensed the wall going back up.

"I'm not looking to get you in trouble, Jerome. Just tell me straight and I promise you it won't go any further. You're doing really well, keep your string going."

Jerome seemed to think about this, one hand playing with his tie, as though wondering what the thing was doing around his neck.

"The night Kevin didn't come home. It was late, maybe three in the morning. I had just got home from work and Granny was up and all a mess. She told me Kevin was missing. I was upstairs changing and getting ready to go looking for Kevin and wondering whether we should call the cops. I hear my granny downstairs talking to somebody, or *he* was talking—yelling, that is—at her. It was Francis. He was mad like I ain't heard him mad ever before." He paused and looked for a moment like he might bolt again. "He was looking for Kevin too. Was sure Granny had him hid somewhere, at least maybe he was hoping that was it. The way he was talking, I thought he be going after Granny. I almost come down the stairs. Now, I ain't no coward, and I ain't stupid either; hell, that man probably take only a second to kill me, but it ain't like I'm letting him or anybody come in here and hurt her without trying to do something about it. You understand me?"

"I do, Jerome."

"Francis, he finally calmed down, he was getting it that Kevin wasn't here. So he left. Last time we've seen him. That's the truth."

"I appreciate you telling me. I guess it's probably hard to trust people right now."

Jerome looked Web up and down. "You saved Kevin's life. That's worth something."

Web looked at him warily.

"I read the papers, Mr. Web London, Hostage Rescue Team. Kevin be dead, wasn't for you. Maybe that's why Francis didn't bust your skull."

"Hadn't really thought about it that way."

Web looked at the stack of sketchbooks again. "The other agents who came here, did you tell them any of this?"

"They didn't really ask."

"How about Kevin's room? They search up here?"

"Couple of them looked around, didn't take very long."

Web looked at Claire. They seemed to read each other's thoughts. She said, "Do you mind if I borrow those sketchbooks? I'd like to show them to my daughter."

Jerome looked at the books and then at Web. "You gotta promise to bring them back. That's Kevin whole life, right there," he said.

"I promise. I promise I'll do everything I can to bring Kevin back too." He gathered up the sketchbooks and then put a hand on Jerome's shoulder. "Now it's time to get you to work. You'll find my chauffeuring fees are very reasonable."

As they walked downstairs, Web had one more question. "Kevin was in that alley alone in the middle of the night. Did he do that a lot?"

Jerome looked away and said nothing.

"Come on, Jerome, don't get tongue-tied on me now."

"Hell, Kevin wanted to help us out, you know, make some money and we get out of this place. It bothered him that he never could do much like that. He was just a kid, but he thought like a grown-up on some things."

"I guess a particular environment might do that for you."

"Well, Kevin, he be out on the streets sometimes. Granny too old to keep up with him. I don't know who he was hanging with, and whenever I caught him out there, I brought his butt home. But maybe he might be trying to make a little cash on the side. And around here you can get that money, no matter how young you are, you hear me?"

They dropped Jerome off at work and headed back to Claire's house.

"By the way, you handled yourself like a pro back there," he said.

"I guess it's more mental than physical, and that's my jurisdiction." She glanced at Web. "You know, you were pretty rough on Jerome."

"It's probably because I've seen a million guys just like him in my life."

"Stereotyping is dangerous, Web, not to mention unfair to the person being categorized. The fact is, you can only know one Jerome at a time. And I could tell this Jerome busted your preconception all apart."

"He did," admitted Web. "I guess when you've been doing my kind of work for so long, it's easier to lump folks together."

"Like fathers?"

Web didn't answer that one.

Claire said, "It is sad about Francis and Kevin. From what Jerome said, he must love his son very much. And to have to lead such a life."

"I don't doubt the big guy loves Kevin either, but I've seen that same big guy kill a man in cold blood right in front of him, and he's also cleaned my clock twice, so my sympathy has its limits," said Web very firmly.

"One's environment does tend to dictate one's choices, Web."

"I can accept a little of that argument, but I've seen too many guys from even worse backgrounds make it just fine."

"Including maybe yourself?"

He ignored her question and instead said, "I figure you pack some things and we find you a safe house with some agents there to make sure those folks don't come back."

"I'm not so sure that's a good idea."

"I want you to be safe."

"I want to be safe too, trust me, I have no death wish. But if you're right and that person was just pretending to be Francis to scare me and throw suspicion on him, I'm probably not in any real danger."

"*Probably* is right. That's only one theory, Claire, and it might be the wrong one."

"I think if my routine remains the same, they have no reason to think I'm a threat. And I have something I really need to work on."

"What?"

She glanced over at him and Web had never seen her look so troubled. "I'm thinking about a very brave man going into an alley, listening to a little boy say something quite extraordinary and then being unable to do his job."

He shot her a look. "You can't be sure there's a connection."

She held up a page of the sketchbook for him to see. "Oh, I'm pretty sure there's a connection."

The drawing was stark, exacting, possessing a powerful clarity that seemed beyond a young boy. A figure that looked so like Kevin it could have been a self-portrait was standing in what looked to be a high-walled alley. A man who could have been Web in complete combat gear was in full running stride next to Kevin. The boy's hand was extended. What was in the boy's hand had Web fixated. The device was small, easily secreted in a trouser pocket. The stream of light that shot out from it reached across the page and ended at the margin. It was as though the boy held some sort of futuristic weapon that shot light beams, à la *Star Wars* or *Star Trek*. Actually, it was a device that all people, especially kids, would be familiar with these days. It was a remote control, and this one was sending out a beam of light. It could have been to a TV, stereo or some other electronic equipment. But Web knew that it wasn't. He hadn't even seen a TV in Kevin's house and there was certainly not one in his room. This remote control, Web felt sure, had activated the laser in the courtyard that, in turn, had triggered the mini-guns when Web and Charlie Team had come thundering into the space. The kid had kick-started it all. And somebody had prepared the boy for exactly what he would see that night, namely men in body armor with guns, for it wasn't like Kevin Westbrook had come back to his house to make this drawing after the fact.

Who was that someone?

Two cars behind Web's Mach, Francis Westbrook drove the Lincoln Navigator himself. Without product to sell, a large part of his crew had already jumped ship. Folks didn't let the grass grow under their feet in the drug trade, and the grass always seemed to be greener someplace else. Of course, when you got to the new place, it was just the same old crap. You lived and died by your wits and the stupid did not survive for very long, yet for every dealer that was killed, a dozen were ready to take his place; the lure of the drug business was strong despite its high mortality rate, because people in Francis Westbrook's world weren't exactly loaded down with options. Forget the social scientists with their little charts and graphs, Westbrook could vividly teach the mother of all courses on that subject.

He shook his head as his thoughts returned to his dilemma. Peebles was nowhere to be found, and even the once-loyal Macy had disappeared. The men he had left were not ones Westbrook really trusted, thus he had gone it alone on this mission. He had been watching Jerome's place in the hopes that Kevin might come wandering up. Instead he had gotten a nice prize in the interim. HRT London and the woman. She was the shrink, he at least had learned that before his men deserted him. He steered with his fingertip, his right hand on the grip of the pistol lying on the front seat. He had watched London and the woman go in and then come out with Jerome. The lady had been carrying Kevin's sketchbooks, and Francis wondered why. Did the books have a clue to the boy's whereabouts? He had personally searched this city high and low looking for his son, threatened people, broken bones and overinflated egos in the process, shelled out thousands in cash for snitch work, and with all that, nothing. The Feds sure as hell didn't have him; they weren't playing games with him, perhaps trying to get Kevin to testify against the father, of that he was sure. Francis had been real careful on that; Kevin knew nothing about what his old man did, at least not the sort of details that were required on the witness stand. But if he did, Francis would just bite the bullet and take the fall. Above all, he had to do what was best for Kevin. In many ways he had already led a full, rich life, about as much as someone like him could reasonably expect. But Kevin had a lot more living to do. London was a smart guy. Francis's plan was to follow him and see where that took him. Where he hoped it took him, of course, was to Kevin.

43

Web drove Claire home, where she packed some clothes and other things, and then he took her to her car and followed her to a hotel, where she checked in. After they'd promised each other to keep in touch with fresh developments, Web rushed back to East Winds.

Romano was at the carriage house. "The Canfields are in the house. I don't know what happened, but something's shook them up. White as sheets, both of them."

"I know what did it, Paulie," and Web explained about the videotape.

"You know there was nothing you could do, Web. I'm just pissed I was overseas at the time, I would've loved to hit those guys." He snapped his fingers. "Oh, before I forget, Ann Lyle called and said she really needed to talk to you."

"How come she didn't call me directly?"

"I talked to her a couple of days ago. Just checking in. I gave her the phone number here, just in case we needed a hard-line contact."

Web pulled out his phone, and while he was dialing Ann he asked Romano, "So, how'd Billy like your 'Vette?"

"Sweet, man, sweet. Said he had an opportunity to buy one a couple of years ago for—are you ready for this?—for fifty thousand dollars. Fifty big ones."

"Better not let Angie find out about that. I see four wheels and a ragtop becoming new furniture and college accounts."

Romano paled. "Shit, I never thought of that. You gotta swear you won't tell her, Web. You gotta swear."

"Hold on, Paulie." Web spoke into the phone. "Ann, it's Web, what's up?"

Ann's voice was very low. "There's something going down here. That's why I'm here so late."

Web tensed. He knew what that meant. "An op?"

"The guys built a new target in the practice area two days ago and have been going over it like crazy. The assaulters have been going through their equipment today seven ways from Sunday and the commander's doors been closed all morning, and some of the snipers have already been deployed. You know how it is, Web."

"Yeah, I know. You have any idea what the target might be?"

Ann's voice dropped even lower. "A tape from a surveillance camera came in a few days ago. It shows that a truck was parked at the loading dock of an abandoned building near where the shooting occurred. The tape wasn't at the best angle, I understand, but I believe it shows the guns being unloaded from the truck."

Web nearly tore the phone in half. Bates had kept this from him. "Who was the truck registered to, Ann?"

"Silas Free. He's one of the founders of the Free Society, Web. Pretty stupid of him to use his real name."

Son of a bitch. They were hitting the Frees. "How are they getting there?"

"Military aircraft from Andrews to an old Marine Corps airfield near Danville. They're heading out at O-twelve-hundred. The trucks have already been sent down via semi."

"What's the assault force?"

"Hotel, Gulf, X-Ray and Whiskey."

"That's it? That's not full strength."

"Echo, Yankee and Zulu are out of the country on VIP protection detail. There's no Charlie Team. And on top of that, one of the Hotel assaulters broke his leg during a training exercise and Romano's with you on special assignment. We're a little thin right now."

"I'm on my way. Don't let the train leave without me."

He looked at Romano. "Get the guys at the gates to collapse around the house and take over protection detail."

"Where are we going?"

"It's time to bang 'em and hang 'em, Paulie."

While Romano called the perimeter guards, Web ran outside,

popped the trunk of his Mach and checked what he had. The answer was he had plenty. The life of an HRT operator required that he keep several days' worth of clothes in his trunk along with a variety of other items essential for when you were called out of the country for a week or a month with virtually no notice. Web had supplemented this "normal" allotment with lots of goodies he had taken from the HRT equipment cage and the stash he kept at home, which included a formidable arsenal. Even with his FBI creds, he'd have a tough time explaining this cache to a state trooper on a routine traffic stop.

When Romano came back, Web said, "Bates kept it from me, the little shit. They found direct evidence tying the Frees to the hit on Charlie, using the damn tip *I* gave him. And he wasn't even going to invite us to the party. Probably thinks we'll freak and pop people unnecessarily."

"You know," said Romano, "that really offends my sense of professionalism."

"Well, tell your sense of professionalism to shake a leg, we don't have much time."

"Well, why didn't you say so?" He grabbed Web's arm. "If speed is what we need, we ain't taking that hunk of junk."

"What the hell are you talking about?"

Five minutes later the big-block 'Vette loaded down with weaponry blew through the open gates at East Winds and hit the main strip.

It was mostly back roads down to Quantico, but Romano kept the 'Vette on seventy pretty much the whole way, going around curves so fast Web felt himself grabbing the edge of his seat and hoping Romano didn't notice. When they got to Interstate 95, Romano smoothly shifted gears and popped the clutch. Web watched the speedometer swiftly move to triple digits. Romano slid in an eight-track tape, of all things, and revved up the music. The best of Bachman-Turner Overdrive was soon shattering the night air, because they were driving with the top down. While Romano drove, Web checked their guns. Even with the highway lights, it was very dark, but his fingers knew every inch of the things.

He looked over at Romano, who was smiling and singing along with BTO as they were "taking care of business." The guy was bobbing his head like he was back in high school and banging at a Springsteen concert.

"You gotta strange way of preparing yourself for combat, Paulie."

"What, like you and the rubbing you give your pistols for luck?" Web looked at him in surprise. "Riner told me. He thought it was a hoot."

"I guess nothing's sacred," muttered Web.

They cruised into Quantico in record time. They both knew the sentry posted at the east entrance off the Bureau Parkway, and Romano didn't bother to slow down.

"Triple eight, Jimbo," he yelled out as he roared by, referring to the crisis page of three eights that told HRT members to get the hell to Quantico.

"Go get 'em, guys!" yelled back Jimbo.

Romano parked the car; they pulled their gear and hauled it to the admin building. Romano used his security card to open the gate, and they headed to the front door, where a video surveillance camera was watching them. In front of the entrance, six trees had been planted in memory of the fallen members of Charlie Team. Inside, they passed Ann Lyle's office. She came to the door, and she and Web exchanged a glance but not more than that. Strictly from the rule book, Ann shouldn't have called and told Web about the assault. And he would never do anything to get her in trouble. But they both knew that what she had done was the right thing to do, rule book be damned.

Web met his commander, Jack Pritchard, in the hallway. The man looked in astonishment at Web and Romano with all their gear.

"Reporting for duty, sir," said Web.

"How the hell did you even know about it?" demanded Pritchard.

"I'm still a member of HRT. I can smell these things a mile away."

Pritchard didn't push it, though he did glance in the direction of Ann Lyle's office.

"I want in," said Web.

"That's impossible," said Pritchard. "You're still on SRB leave, and he"—he pointed at Romano—"got his ass taken off on special assignment that I wasn't even made privy to. Now shove off."

The commander turned on his heel and headed back to the equipment room. Web and Romano shoved off, right after the man. The assaulters and snipers who hadn't already been deployed on the mission were gathered here, going over last-minute details. The

snipers were checking to make sure they each had restocked a num-
bered lot of match-grade ammo. They were updating logbooks,
tightening trigger assemblies and cleaning scopes and barrels. The
assaulters were inspecting their own weapons and breaking out
their breaching gear, tactical bags and body armor. The personnel in
the logistics cell of HRT were running around loading gear into the
trucks and trying to remember everything the mini-invasion would
need to succeed. They all stopped doing what they were doing when
Pritchard and then Web and Romano barged into their space.

"Come on, Jack," said Web, "you got teams all over the damned
place, and not even counting Paulie, you're short a guy on Hotel,
you can use the extra hands."

Pritchard whirled around. "How the hell did you know we were
short a guy?" The HRT chief obviously had had enough of leaks.

Web looked around the room. "I can count. And I count five assaulters on Hotel. Add me and Paulie and you're at full strength."

"You haven't been briefed, you haven't worked the mock target
and you haven't even been training for a while. You're *not* going."

Web moved in front of the man and blocked his way. Jack
Pritchard was about five-ten and Web had him by at least thirty
pounds and about five years, but Web knew if it came to a fight
that he would be in for one. But he didn't want to fight, not his
own man anyway.

"Brief us on the way over. Show us the attack points. We've got
our own equipment and all we need are Kevlar, a flight suit and a
helmet. How many of these have Paulie and me done, Jack? Don't
treat us like some clueless bastard right out of NOTS. We don't deserve that."

Pritchard stepped back and stared at Web for a very long minute.
The longer it went on the more Web thought Pritchard might actually throw him out of the place. HRT, like other quasi-military
units, frowned on such insubordination.

"I tell you what, Web, I'll leave it up to them." He pointed at the
assaulters.

Web hadn't been expecting that sort of decision. But he stepped
forward and looked at each of the Hotel and Gulf guys one by one.
He had fought side-by-side with most of them, first as a sniper and
then as one of their own, an assaulter. His gaze finally settled on

Romano. The men would accept Paulie back without question. But Web was damaged goods, the guy who had frozen at the worst possible moment, and every man in this room was wondering if he would do it again and cost them their lives.

Web had saved Romano's life during a raid on a Montana militiamen site. Romano had returned the favor a year later during a VIP protection detail in the Middle East when a foot soldier from a fringe rebel group had tried to run their party down with an empty bus he had stolen. The rebel would have succeeded in getting at least Web, but Romano had pushed Web out of the way and popped the driver between the eyes with a round from his .45. Yet despite all that, and their recent time together, Web had never really been able to read the man. As he looked around the room, it seemed that the men were looking to Romano to settle the issue, and despite the guy having driven Web here to take part in the assault, Web had no clue what he would say now.

He watched as Romano put a hand on Web's shoulder. Looking at his teammates, Romano said, "Web London can cover my back anytime, anyplace."

And in the alpha male society of HRT, a man like Paul Romano—who was feared even by some of his teammates—saying that was all it took. After they finished suiting up, Pritchard called all the men into the small meeting room. He stood at the front staring at them, and they stared back. It seemed to Web that the commander spent more time gazing at him than at any of the others.

"It goes without saying," began Pritchard, "that this mission is critical. All our missions are critical. I know that each man here will conduct himself in the utmost professional manner while still doing his job to the best of his ability." Pritchard's tone was stilted, the man looked nervous, and he had done enough dangerous things in his life that Web had long assumed the man had no nerves.

Web and Romano exchanged glances. This sort of pep talk was a little out of the ordinary. They weren't a bunch of high school kids getting ready to play football.

Pritchard's stern demeanor collapsed. "Okay, let me cut the official crap. The folks we're going after tonight are suspected of doing in Charlie Team. You all know that. We hope we're going to hit them by surprise. Short and sweet and no shots fired." He paused and looked up and down the ranks once more. "You know the orders of engagement. This Free Society has come our way before, down in Richmond. That was Charlie Team too, and some think that what happened in that courtyard was an act of revenge by the Frees.

"There are no known hostages. The ground logistics are a little tricky, but we've handled far worse. We fly in, the trucks will be waiting and we execute." Pritchard was pacing now, and then he stopped. "If you have to take a shot tonight, you do it. If they fire back, I don't have to tell any of you what to do. But don't be stupid about this. The last thing we need is for the media to be screaming tomorrow morning about HRT wiping out guys who don't need to be wiped out. If they were involved in Charlie's getting ripped, let's bag them and let the legal process work its course. Don't, and I repeat don't, fire because you're thinking about what these guys might have done to six men who belonged to us. You're better than that. You deserve better than that. And I know you'll come through." He paused once more and seemed to search each of his men's faces, once again lingering the longest, it seemed, on Web.

Pritchard finished with, "Let's hit it."

As the men filed out, Web walked up next to Pritchard.

"Jack, I hear where you're coming from, but if you're that concerned about somebody going off the deep end, why have HRT do this hit at all? You said there aren't any hostages, so an FBI SWAT team could handle this with backup from the locals. Why us?"

"We're still part of the FBI, Web, although you wouldn't know it from the way some people act around here."

"Meaning orders from uptown for HRT to do this gig?"

"That's the procedure, and you know that as well as I do."

"Because of the circumstances, did you request a pass on this one?"

"Actually, I did, because I personally don't think we should be doing it. Not this soon after losing our guys. And I agree with you, a SWAT team could go easy enough."

"And they turned you down?"

"Like I said, we're part of the FBI and I do what I'm told. Now you wanted in on this, are you backing out now?"

"See you at the O.K. Corral."

A few minutes later they were on their way to Andrews Air Force Base, ready to go to war.

The Bureau, Web had learned from one of his HRT colleagues, had contemplated executing a search warrant on the Frees' compound but had decided that they would let HRT secure the place first and then execute the search. The last thing the Bureau wanted was a couple of agents getting killed while trying to serve the search warrant. Besides, video of machine guns used to kill federal agents being unloaded from a truck rented by Silas Free was pretty damning.

On the short bumpy flight down in a military transport jet, Web went over the five-paragraph operations order and he and Romano were filled in on specific details. There would be no negotiation with the Frees and no warnings to come out with their hands up. The memories of the school incident in Richmond and the massacre of Charlie Team had precluded those options. Fewer people would die tonight if HRT just hit them without warning, at least that's what the powers-that-be had decided, and Web was perfectly fine with that decision. The fact that there were no known hostages made things easier and also more complicated. Complicated in that Web was still wondering why an FBI SWAT team hadn't been called in to handle this. He hoped it was a combination of the reputation the Frees had for being extremely dangerous and well armed, and the fact that even the good guys were entitled to exact sweet justice some of the time. But something just didn't feel right about this.

Intelligence gathered by WFO over the last several months put the Frees at a compound they had created a decade earlier about forty miles west of Danville, Virginia, in a very remote part of the state with woods on three sides. Snipers from Whiskey and X-Ray had set up surveillance twenty-four hours before with WFO agents and had been feeding valuable intelligence back ever since. The plans for the target had actually been in the HRT database for a while now. HRT had rebuilt the interior of the school on its back lot and practiced with something more than the unit's usual vigor and determination. While there wasn't an HRT member who would consciously open fire unless he, another team member or an innocent person was in danger, there wasn't a single HRT operator who wasn't at least partly wishing that the Frees would try and fight back. Maybe, Web thought, that group would include Commander Jack Pritchard too, despite his passionate speech to the contrary.

They landed, climbed in their trucks, which had just been off-loaded from a special truck transport, and drove to the preliminary staging area and interfaced with the local police and folks from WFO who were spearheading the effort. Web turned his back and fiddled with some of his gear when he saw Percy Bates appear from one of the Bucars and talk to Pritchard. Web didn't really need a run-in with Bates right now for a lot of reasons, the main one being he didn't know if he could trust himself not to punch the guy's lights out for not telling him about the assault. Bates was probably just trying to protect Web, maybe from himself, but Web would have preferred to make that decision on his own.

They drove to the last staging point and received a final set of orders. Now it was time to hit the road to the target. They moved quickly through the darkened rural roads. Hotel Team was in one Suburban and was approaching the Frees' compound from the rear, while Gulf was going in the left side. The topography would require the assault teams to navigate through the dark, dense woods. That wasn't really a problem, since they had night-vision optics. Just before the truck doors popped open, Romano crossed himself. Web almost said what he had always said to Danny Garcia, that God didn't come around here and that they were on their own, but he didn't. Yet he wished Romano hadn't done the sign of the cross. This was all beginning to seem way too familiar, and for the first time Web started to wonder if he was in any shape to participate in the assault. The doors popped open before he could think any more on this and they poured into the woods and then came to a stop, crouching and surveying the terrain ahead.

Through his bone mic Web listened as the snipers filled them in on what lay ahead. Web recognized Ken McCarthy's voice from X-Ray. McCarthy's call sign was Sierra One, meaning he held the snipers' highest observation post. He was probably straddling a thick branch of one of the big oaks that ringed the perimeter around the compound, Web figured. That would allow him to see

the entire area, get a good firing lane and provide maximum de-
filade, or position of cover and concealment. The Frees were definitely inside the compound. Most of them lived there, in fact. The
snipers had counted at least ten of them inside. There were four
buildings constituting the fenced compound. Three were living
quarters and one was a large warehouse-style building where the
men held their meetings and did whatever work they did while
there, such as making bombs and plotting how to kill innocent people, no doubt, thought Web. There were often dogs at outposts like
this. Canines were always a problem—not so much a personal danger to HRT members, since even the fiercest dog couldn't bite
through Kevlar or withstand a bullet, but they were terrific early
warning sentries. Fortunately—thus far, at least—there were no
dogs here; maybe some of the Frees were allergic. The weaponry
they'd seen were mostly pistols and shotguns, although one young
lad of about seventeen, McCarthy said, was carrying an MP-5.

There were two sentries outside, one in the front and one in the
rear, armed with pistols only and bored expressions, McCarthy
wryly noted. As was customary with HRT, the sentries were given
identification names by the sniper that had first spotted them. The
guard in front was named Pale Shaq, because he bore a passing resemblance to the big basketball center but, of course, was white,
since the Frees were definitely not going to have persons of another
color around. The one in the rear was christened Gameboy, because
McCarthy had noted a Gameboy player sticking out of his front
pocket. The snipers had also observed that both sentries carried cell
phones that had a walkie-talkie feature. That posed a problem,
since they could quickly signal trouble to their confederates inside

Hotel Team spread out and moved through the woods with great
caution. Over their flight suits they wore IR camouflage, green
smocks with visual patterns that broke up each man's night profile. Thus, even if the Frees had night-vision optics, they wouldn't
get a clean visual. Though the compound was not yet in sight, in
the dense foliage the Frees might have posted either additional
pickets or even booby traps that had escaped the eyes of the
snipers, unlikely as that might be. Web's NV goggles made night
into day, but he kept one eye closed still and assumed all the oth-

ers were doing the same thing to avoid the orange burn later. They hit another stop spot and Web pulled the goggles up and blinked quickly to reduce the effects of the high-tech optics. His head was already starting to hurt. On the actual assault Romano would be point man and Web would bring up the rear. Though Romano hadn't practiced this hit with the team, he was still the best assaulter they had. Web slid his hand down the short barrel of the MP-5 subgun he was carrying. He wasn't toting his usual SR75 rifle because, after using it in that courtyard, he had found he couldn't pick the damn thing up again. He first touched the .45 pistol in his tactical holster and next the twin gun riding in his cross-draw shoulder rig that hung across his trauma plate, and he smiled tightly when he saw Romano watching him do this and giving him a thumbs-up.

"Now we're bulletproof, big guy," said Romano. The man was probably still doing BTO turns in his head, thought Web.

Web's heartbeat was not yet at sixty-four and he was striving mightily to get it there. He rubbed his fingers against his palm and was surprised to feel sweat, for it was a chilly night. Yet sixty pounds of gear and body armor made for a nice little personal sauna. He had pistol mags hanging from his gun belt and spare MP-5 ammo in his thigh pads, along with flash bangs, slap charges and other goodies that he might or might not need tonight, you just never knew. Still, he hoped the sweat didn't signal nerves that could cause him to screw up right at the moment he needed to be perfect.

They moved forward again and neared the edge of the woods. Through his goggles Web could clearly make out the Frees' compound. To ensure that communications were short and that everyone was working off the same page, the first floor of a target, in HRT parlance, was always designated Alpha, the second, Bravo. The front of the building was white; the right, red; the left, green; and the rear, black. All the doors, windows and other openings was given sequential numbers beginning with the farthest port to the left. Thus Gameboy was stationed on the outside of the fence at roughly Alpha level black port three, while Pale Shaq was at Alpha level white port four. Web checked out Gameboy through his goggles and quickly summed the guy up as untrained as well as downright careless. The accuracy of this opinion was reinforced when the guy pulled the Gameboy from his pocket and actually started playing it.

There were lights on in the main building of the compound. The lights must have been powered by portable generators, because there were no overhead electrical lines evident. If there had been, HRT would have found the transformer supplying the power and shut it off just before the assault. Going from light to dark was disorienting and would have given HRT the slight edge it needed to prevail without loss of life.

Since there were only two assault teams, snipers were standing by to jump into their blacks, or Nomex flight suits, and help in the attack. Each sniper carried, in addition to his sniper rifle, a CAR-16 auto assault rifle with a three-power Litton night scope. The plan was to hit from the front and the side in blitzkrieg style and contain the Frees in the main building. At that point the regular FBI would come in, read rights, execute search warrants and the next stop for the Frees would be court and then prison.

There was just enough to make this interesting, thought Web. The Frees had to know that the FBI was watching them. This was a very rural area and word of strangers got around, and the Bureau had had them under surveillance for a while now. HRT had to assume that their chief weapon, the element of surprise, would at least be diminished in this case.

Having learned something from the Charlie Team debacle, they had brought along two very bulky but very powerful thermal imagers. Romano fired one up and performed a sweep of each building on their side of the compound. Gulf was doing the same from the front. This thermal imager could look through darkened glass and even walls and nail the heat-filled image of any person lurking there with a slingshot or a mini-gun. Romano completed his surveillance and gave the all-clear. No automated sniper nest this time. All buildings except the main one were empty. It might go very clean.

Through his NV goggles Web looked around and noted the lights winking through the jumble of trees. These light pulses represented snipers who were wearing fireflies, infrared glow plugs the size of a cigarette lighter. The flies would blink every two seconds in a light spectrum visible only with night optics. This way the snipers could keep in touch with one another without giving away their position. If a target was suspected of having night optics as well, the flies weren't used, for obvious reasons. Assaulters never used them. Each wink of light represented a friendly body with a .308 suppressed rifle backing him up. It was comforting when you weren't sure whether you were walking into an ice-cream parlor or a hornet's nest. Web assumed tonight that it would be the latter.

With a flick of his thumb, Web put the fire selector on his MP-5 to multiple-round bursts and then worked on getting his pulse rate down to the proper zone. There were the sounds of wildlife all around—squirrels, mostly—and birds flitting from tree limb to tree limb, disturbed by the men crouched in their space with all this fancy gear. The padding of animal paws and the flapping of bird wings was somehow comforting, if only to reassure Web that he was still on planet earth, still connected to living, breathing things, though he had potential killing on his mind.

The plan here was a little dicey. The snipers were not going to open fire on the sentries. Gunning down folks in cold blood who had yet to be convicted of anything was not something law enforcement types got to do very often; Web certainly never had. It would take a very high-stakes hostage situation to justify that sort of approval from Washington. The director and probably the attorney general would have to bless that sort of operation. Here they were going to flank the guards, jump them and make sure they had no time or opportunity to warn their comrades inside of the coming attack. The assaulters could have employed a diversionary explosive, or perhaps drawn the guards into the woods somehow to be met by assaulters in Ghillies waiting to jump them, but the flanking plan had been devised based on prior intelligence gathered on the Frees. That intel had proved correct in the careless nature of the sentries. It might just work, thought Web.

If the exterior breach points were locked, they would be blown, of course. That would warn the rest of the Frees, but by then HRT would be inside and the battle would pretty much be over, barring something extraordinary occurring, which Web could no longer rule out, ever again. Hotel was going to hit from the rear, Gulf from the side, in a very explosive way. Assault teams always tried to hit from angles, never front-back or side-side, to avoid friendly fire casualties.

Web tensed as Romano asked TOC for compromise authority and

quickly got it. Now Web took one last cleansing breath and assumed the total focus of an assaulter with one of the most elite law enforcement teams ever put together. Pulse at sixty-four, Web really did just know his body's inner workings.

Romano gave the high sign and he and Web went to the left and the other two operators slid to the right. A minute later they were on both flanks of Gameboy, who was still intent on his video screen, apparently having a great time whipping the computer's ass. By the time he looked up, there were .45 pistols stuck in both of his ears. Before he even had a chance to say, "Shit," he was down on the ground, Peerless cuffs around his hands and ankles, and a plastic chain strap tied the cuffs together so that he was fully immobilized like a tethered calf during a roping contest. At the same time a strip of adhesive was placed over his mouth. They took his pistol, cell phone and a knife they found in a sheath tied to his ankle. Web did leave the man his precious Gameboy.

They passed the living quarters of the group and moved to the crisis site, the exterior rear door of the main building, and crouched low. Romano touched the door gingerly, then grasped the door handle and tried it. Through his mask, Web could see him grimace. It was locked. Romano called up the breacher, who quickly moved forward, laid his four-hundred-grain flex linear charge, rolled out his cable and readied the detonator, while the rest of the team watched his back even as they took cover.

At that point Romano informed TOC that they were at phase line green and Web listened to TOC's confirmatory response. Thirty seconds later, members of Gulf did the same thing, so Web knew they had successfully bagged Pale Shaq out front and then gone to the side of the building for their very special assault. TOC stated that it had control, and the line rankled Web even more now than it had before. *Yeah, that's what you said to Charlie, wasn't it?*

Three snipers joined the Gulf boys on the side and Ken McCarthy had come down from his Sierra One position and become an instant assaulter, along with two other Whiskey snipers who joined Web and Hotel Team. When Ken saw Web, Web couldn't see the man's expression, but Web was sure it was a surprised one. They all took off their NV goggles, since muzzle flashes and explosives made them useless anyway and would actually leave you blind and defenseless in such a light-filled environment. From here on, everyone had to simply use their ordinary five senses, and that was okay by Web.

The countdown began. Web's heartbeat seemed to slow even more with each number. When TOC reached three, Web was fully in the zone. At the count of two, every HRT operator looked away from the crisis site so that the blast wouldn't blind them. At the same moment each man's fingers also slipped off his weapon's safety once more; and then index fingers slid to triggers. *Here we go, boys,* Web thought.

The charge blew and the doors fell inward and Web and company roared through.

"Banging," called out Romano as he drew a flash bang from his stretch cordura holder, pulled the pin and lobbed. Three seconds later a hundred-and-eighty-decibel explosion screamed through the hallway with a million-candlepower flash in its wake.

Web was to the right of Romano, looking for threats from any source, his gaze going first to distant corners, then pulling back. There was a small interior room with a hallway heading left off that. Their intelligence, confirmed by their thermal imagery, had told them that the Frees were gathered in the main room in the left rear of the building. It was a large space, maybe forty-by-forty, and mostly open, so they didn't have to worry about lots of nooks and crannies for resistance to hole up in, but it was still a large space to secure, and there would no doubt be furniture and other equipment to hide behind. They dropped off one guy to hold the room they had first entered. The rules of engagement were that you never gave back ground you had taken, and you never allowed yourself to be rear-flanked. The rest of the strike force raced on.

So far, they had seen no one, although there were shouts up ahead. Web and the rest of Hotel flew down the hallway. One more turn and they'd hit the double doors to the target space.

"Banging," yelled Web. He pulled the pin, lobbed the flash bang around this last turn. Now anybody looking to ambush them from up there would have to do so while blind and deaf.

When they reached the double doors, no one bothered to check whether they were locked. Romano quickly placed a slap charge on the doorjamb. The explosive consisted of a length of tire rubber one inch wide and six inches long with a strip of C4 explosive called a Detasheet. At the bottom of the device were a shock tube and a blasting cap. The men stood back, and Romano whispered into his mic. A few seconds went by and the slap charge blew and the doors collapsed inward.

At the exact same moment the side wall of the main room exploded inward and Gulf Team charged through the opening. They had placed a flex-linear charge—a V-shaped strip of lead and foam, loaded with explosives—around the wall. It had completely taken out the wall, throwing debris into the room. One of the Frees was already on the floor, holding his bloodied head and screaming.

Hotel charged in from the main doors and blitzed the danger zones that were basically any space where somebody with a gun could take cover and do HRT harm.

"Banging," called out Romano as he raced down the right side of the room. The flash bang explosion sounded seconds later. The room was filled with smoke and blinding light and the shouts and screams were deafening as the Frees fell over each other trying to escape. However, there were no shots and Web began to think that this might just end peacefully, at least by HRT standards. Web followed Romano, his gaze sweeping the area, looking to the farthest corners for threats and then reeling back. He saw both young and old men hiding under overturned chairs, prone on the floor or pushed against the walls, all covering their eyes and holding their ears, all of them stunned by the carefully crafted assault. The overhead lights had been shot out by HRT as soon as they entered the room. They were all operating in darkness now except for the occasional flash bang.

"FBI! On the floor. Hands behind your head. Fingers interlocked. Do it! *Now!* Or you're fucking dead!" Romano screamed all this out in a Brooklyn-accented, staccato roar.

That mouthful even got Web's attention.

Most of the Frees in Web's line of sight began to obey the instruction, semi-incapacitated as they were. That's when he heard the first shot. And that was followed by another shot that hit the wall right next to Web's head. From the corner of his eye Web saw a Free coming up from the floor holding an MP-5 and pointing it his way. Romano must have seen the same thing. They fired together, both their MP-5s on multiple-round bursts. All eight shots hit the man either in the head or torso and he and his gun went back down to the floor and stayed there.

The other Frees, blinded and disoriented but also angered by the death of one of their members, pulled their weapons and opened fire from behind whatever bulwarks they could find. HRT did the same. However, it was pistols, shotguns, flesh and overmatched men playing soldier against body armor, subguns and men trained for battle and killing. The gunfight did not last very long. The Frees foolishly looked at the eyes of their opponents. Web and his men calmly keyed on the hands and the weapons held there as they fired round after round, moving forward, staying on their marks. Aim-point red laser dots from the finders bolted to their subguns were directly on their targets. They maintained their fields of fire, shooting around and over each other as though they were performing a superbly choreographed dance. The frantic Frees shot wildly and with no discipline and missed badly. HRT aimed with precision and scored hit after hit. Twice HRT operators were shot, more out of luck than skill, but they were torso hits, ordinary pistol ammo running right into the latest-generation Kevlar; and while the impacts of the bullets stung like a bitch, the only result was a deep bruise. HRT aimed for the head and chest and each time a round impacted, another Free died.

With the rout clearly on, Web had had enough of this carnage and he flipped his MP-5 to full auto and raked the tops of the cheap tables and chairs, blowing chips of particle board and wood veneer and strips of metal into the air and filling the opposite walls with lead as his weapon threw out slugs at the rate of almost nine hundred a minute. HRT did not fire warning shots, but there was nothing in the manuals or in any other training Web had done that said you had to slaughter an outclassed enemy for no reason. The remaining Frees were no danger to anyone anymore; they just needed some extra persuasion to officially give up. Romano did likewise with spray from his gun. The resulting blizzard of destruction had the opposition flat on their bellies, hands over their heads, their thoughts of fighting and perhaps winning obviously gone. In unison Web and Romano slapped in fresh ten-millimeter ammo stacks with machinelike movements and speed.

They opened fire again, once more aiming just over the heads of the cowering enemy, and poured it on until the last of the Frees still alive finally made the only sensible choice. Two crawled out from the debris of dead bodies and destroyed chairs and tables, their hands in the air, their weapons on the floor. They looked shell-shocked and were sobbing. Another Free just sat there staring at his hands, bloody from touching a large, seeping wound on his leg, and there was vomit on his shirt. An operator went over to him, cuffed him and then laid him gently back, slapped on surgical gloves and mask and started ministering to the wound; a gunman suddenly turned lifesaver of his enemy. Paramedics were called up from the medic truck that accompanied every HRT assault to tend to the wounded. The guy would probably live, Web concluded, after checking out the bloody leg, if only to spend the rest of his life in prison.

As Romano and another assaulter cuffed the first two Frees to surrender, several other operators went quickly around the room making sure that the dead actually were. The men on the floor were just bodies now, Web felt certain. Humans were not built to withstand one shot to the head, much less half a dozen.

Web finally lowered his gun and took a deep breath. He surveyed the battlefield, looked over the survivors. Some didn't even appear old enough to drive, dressed in oversized farm jeans, T-shirts and dirty boots. One of them had a peach-fuzz goatee; another even had acne. Two of the dead men looked old enough to be grandfathers and maybe had recruited their grandsons to join the Frees; and die as one. They hardly qualified as worthy opponents. They were just a bunch of stupid people with guns and screwed-up lives who had run into the realization of their worst nightmares and foolishly chosen the wrong course of action. Web counted eight dead bodies, the blood flowing thick and absorbing fast into the cheap carpet. And, though the Frees would contest it, all blood, regardless of ethnic or racial background, flowed red out of the body. At that level, everybody was the same.

He leaned against the wall even as he heard the sirens coming. It hadn't been a fair fight. Yet it had not been a fair fight last time either. A part of him should have at least felt some level of satisfaction. However, the only thing Web London felt was sick to his stomach. Killing was never an easy business and maybe that's what separated him from men like the Ernest B. Frees of the world.

Romano came up to him. "Where the hell did those shots come from?"

Web just shook his head.

"Well, shit," said Romano, "it ain't exactly how I figured this going down."

Web noted the large bullet hole in Romano's cammie smock that revealed the Kevlar underneath. The hole was near his belly button. Romano followed Web's gaze and shrugged it off like it was a mosquito bite.

"Another inch lower and Angie'd have to get her kicks somewhere else," said Romano.

Web struggled to recall exactly what he had seen and what he had heard and exactly when. Web knew one thing for certain: they were all in for a lot of questions and none of those questions held easy answers. Pritchard's warning came hurtling back to him. They had just annihilated numerous members of the Frees, the group suspected of wiping out a team of HRT. What Web and the others had really done was open fire and wasted a bunch of young boys and old men because shots had come from a source they weren't sure of and because Web had seen one of them lifting up his gun and pointing it his way. Web was completely justified in doing what he did, but it wouldn't take a master spin doctor to whip that set of facts into something that smelled to high heaven. And in Washington, D.C., they had more spinmeisters per capita than anywhere else on the planet.

Web could hear feet pounding toward them. The regulars would be showing up soon, the Bates's of the world. They would take over the task of figuring out what the hell had happened. Like Ro-

mano had said, HRT was just in the business of banging and
hanging. Well, they just might have hung themselves this time.
Web started to feel something he never had when the bullets were
flying: fear.

There was movement over a thousand yards away in the woods to
the rear of the compound and behind the perimeter set up by HRT.
The ground seemed to rise up and a man crouched there, his sniper
rifle with attached scope held in his right hand. It was the same rifle he had used to kill Chris Miller outside Randall Cove's house in
Fredericksburg. The FBI probably thought that Web London had
been the target, but they would be wrong. Miller's death was just
another way to bring further misery to Web London. And what the
man had just done, instigating the fight between the hapless Frees
and HRT, was simply another method of adding to London's
mounting troubles. The man laid aside the cloth that was covered
with dirt, mud, animal feces, leaves and other things designed to
help him blend in with the surroundings, his very own Ghillie suit.
He had long ago concluded that one should only copy from the
best. And, at least for now, HRT was the best. And Web London
was supposed to be the best of this elite group. That distinction put
him squarely in the man's sights. This was personal to him. Very
personal. He folded the material and hooked it to his backpack,
and Clyde Macy quietly made his escape. Despite his normally
stoic nature, the man just had to smile. Mission accomplished.

44

Since he hadn't been able to get a handle on the origin of the group supplying Oxy and other prescription drugs to the D.C. area, Randall Cove had changed strategies and decided to hit it from the receiving instead of the supply end. He had used what the informant T had told him to latch on to a drug crew, who T had told him had lately been dealing these narcotics. It was amazing the results you could get from a snitch when you held him upside down over a hundred-foot drop. Cove figured at some point they would have to pick up more of the product. This new tactic had brought him here tonight, and he hoped it would produce some huge dividends.

The woods were thick and Cove moved through them as quietly as a human being was equipped to do. He stopped near the tree line, squatted low and surveyed the terrain. The vehicles were parked on a dirt road that snaked through these woods near the Kentucky–West Virginia border. If Cove had had any backup to call, he would have. He had thought about bringing Venables, but Sonny had done enough and he also had a wife and kids and was getting ready to retire. Cove was not going to mess with that. Cove was a brave man, well used to being in dangerous situations, but still there was a fine line between courage and idiocy and Cove had always kept on the right side of that flimsy divider.

Cove ducked down as several men gathered around one of the vehicles. He slipped out his NV monocular for a closer look. The plastic-wrapped items the men were carrying confirmed Cove's suspicions. Not coke bricks but what looked to be tens of thousands of pills. He pulled his flashless camera and took some pictures, and then Cove debated what to do next. There were at least five men that he could see, and all of them were armed. He couldn't really execute an arrest without putting himself in serious jeopardy. While he was contemplating his next act, Cove didn't notice, but the wind changed slightly. He didn't realize it, in fact, until the dog that had been lying on the other side of the truck, and out of Cove's line of sight, came tearing around the vehicle and directly at his position.

Cove swore under his breath, turned and fled through the woods. The dog was gaining, though, with each step, and Cove's battered knees just weren't up to this anymore. And he heard something else that didn't provide him with much hope either. There were two-legged animals coming his way.

They cornered him in a swampy section of earth. The dog came at Cove, fangs bared, and Cove aimed his pistol and shot it dead. That was the last time he would fire, as an array of pistols were leveled at him. He put his gun up in the air in surrender.

"Drop it," said one of the pursuers, and Cove dropped it.

The men came forward and one of them frisked Cove and found the other gun he kept stashed in his coat sleeve and also took his camera.

Nemo Strait knelt next to the dog and touched it gently. Then he looked up at Cove like the man had just slit his mother's throat. Strait raised his pistol and stepped forward.

"I had Old Cuss for six years. Damn good dog."

Cove said nothing. Another man punched him in the back with his gun but only got a grunt from Cove.

Strait drew closer and spit in Cove's face. "Damn me for not making sure you were dead when we shoved your car down that slope. You should've just called that your luckiest day on earth and got yourself out of town."

Cove said nothing, but he took one tiny step closer to Strait. He glanced at some of the other men. The buyers of those prescription drugs were from the city and all were black. Cove didn't look to his own race for help here. Money trumped everything else in the criminal world.

Strait looked over his shoulder, toward where the horse trailer with Bobby Lee was, and then looked back at his prisoner and smiled.

"Man, you always got to be in other people's business? Huh?" He tapped his gun against Cove's cheek and then slapped it hard with the metal. "Answer me when I ask you a question."

Cove's response was to spit in the man's face.

Strait wiped off his face and put his gun against Cove's temple.

"You can just kiss your ass good-bye."

The knife came out of the same sleeve that Cove's second gun had. He had never had anyone check for weapons in the same spot where one had already been found. He aimed for the heart, but Cove's foot slipped in the mud, and Strait was a bit quicker than Cove had anticipated, and the knife plunged deeply into Strait's shoulder. Strait fell back into the swampy water, the knife still in his shoulder.

Cove stood there staring at the men surrounding him.

For a split second every sound in the world seemed to stop for Cove. In his mind he could see his wife and children running to him from across a field of nothing but beautiful flowers, and their smiles and anticipated hugs carried away every foul thing that had ever happened to him in his whole life. And there was a great deal to wash away.

And then the guns opened fire. Cove was struck several times and went down. At the same instant all the men looked to the sky because they could hear the drone of a chopper. Seconds later, lights appeared over the treetops.

Strait jumped up. "Let's get the hell out of here."

Even with his injury, the powerful Strait was able to cradle his dead dog and carry it off. In less than a minute the place was empty. The chopper soared on, its crew apparently unaware of what had happened down below. Strait had been wrong—the chopper was merely ferrying a group of businessmen back from a very late meeting.

As the sounds of the night resumed, there came a groan out of the darkness. Randall Cove tried to get up, but as strong as he was, he couldn't make it. The body armor he was wearing had absorbed three of the five shots. The two shots that had hit him directly had taken their toll though. He dropped back to the ground as his blood turned the water red.

Claire Daniels was in her office, working very late. The outer door was locked and the building had security, so she actually felt safer here than at the hotel where she was staying. Her pharmacist friend had gotten back to her on the odd-looking pill that she had taken from Web. Claire had assumed it was some powerful barbiturate because she still thought it possible that a bad drug interaction with a delayed effect had incapacitated Web in that alley. At some level it might seem far-fetched, but it did cover the facts as she knew them, and right now nothing else came close. The phone call had changed all that.

"It's a placebo," her friend had told her. "Like they use for control groups in drug tests."

A placebo? Claire was stunned. All the other pills were what they had appeared to be.

As she sat in her office now, Claire tried to figure it all out. If it wasn't a drug interaction, what could it be? She refused to believe that Kevin Westbrook had placed a curse on Web with the words "damn to hell." And yet, clearly, the words had had an effect on him. Had he just cracked?

Claire looked at some of Kevin's sketchbooks that Web had allowed her to keep. The one with Kevin pointing the remote control had gone right to the FBI, and there were no other drawings like that in any of the other sketchbooks. Claire studied the drawings she had, many of them quite expertly done. The boy had considerable artistic talent.

Nowhere in the sketchbooks were the words "damn to hell" written. It couldn't be that easy, Claire supposed. She wondered again about the words. Old-sounding—Civil War, maybe before. "Damn the torpedoes, full steam ahead," or something like that Admiral Farragut had reportedly said during a naval battle in the War Between the States.

Claire wrote the words on a piece of paper. Civil War–era, Web had thought. Slavery. Black and white. White supremacists. Her brow wrinkled as she thought about it, but then it dawned upon her. Yet Claire's next thought was that it couldn't be.

The Free Society? Damn to hell. She looked at her computer. It was just possible. A few clicks of the mouse and a few minutes gave her the answer. The Free Society had a website. A disgusting, hate-filled propaganda tool that they presumably used to recruit the ignorant and demonic into their ranks. When she saw it, the breath froze in her throat.

At that very moment her office went completely dark. The timing of the blackout coupled with what she had just learned caused her to cry out. She immediately picked up the phone and called the front security desk.

The reassuring voice of the guard came on the line and she explained what had happened. "It's not the building, Dr. Daniels. We've got lights down here. Probably a tripped circuit breaker. You want me to come up?"

She looked out her window and saw that surrounding buildings were also lit. "No, that's all right. I think I've got a flashlight. If it's just that, I can turn it back on."

She hung up, rummaged through her desk and finally found a flashlight, then felt here way out of her office and into the darkened reception area. She made her way to the closet where the power box was and turned the handle. It was locked. That was a little strange, she thought, but then she remembered that the closet also housed the phone and security system lines for the office, and those lines needed to be protected from interference. But how was she supposed to trip the breaker back, then? She contemplated packing up and going to the hotel, but all of her notes were here and she didn't have a laptop computer on which she could access the Internet from the hotel.

She shone the light on the lock. It looked pretty simple. She went into the small kitchen and found a screwdriver. She went back to the door, held the light under her armpit and worked on the lock. It took about five minutes, and resulting from more luck than skill, the lock finally gave and she opened the door. She shone the light inside and looked around. She quickly found the power

box, and the main circuit had indeed tripped. She popped it back
and the lights came on. She was about to close the door when
something caught her attention. A small device was wired into the
power lines that ran up the wall. Claire didn't know much about
such things, but it still looked out of place to her, almost like a bug.

Perhaps it was because of what she had just discovered, or that
she had suddenly become unduly paranoid, but in a flash it hit her.
She raced from the room, never noticing the tiny wireless trip button on the doorjamb that was activated whenever someone opened
the door to the power closet.

She ran to her office and looked around. Her gaze went from
floor to walls and finally to the ceiling and stopped. She grabbed
her desk chair, slipped off her shoes and stood on the chair to reach
the smoke detector. She had been working with law enforcement
folks for enough years to know that smoke detectors were favorite
places to house listening devices. She pulled the piece off the ceiling, and there appeared to be wiring there that shouldn't have
been. Was it only her office, or were others bugged as well?

She left the detector dangling from the ceiling, jumped off the
chair and ran to the office next to hers, which was O'Bannon's. It
was locked; however, it was the same lock as on the power closet.
Using the screwdriver, she was able once again to pop it. She went
in, flicked on the light and looked up. There was another smoke detector. She ripped it down and found the same suspicious wiring.
She was about to race to another office when she saw the open file
on the desk.

It went against all of her professional instincts to examine a colleague's files, but the circumstances were particularly extenuating,
she told herself.

She picked up the file. The name on it was Deborah Riner. Web
had mentioned her, the widow of one of the men from his team.
She ran her gaze through the many pages. Riner had been coming
to see O'Bannon for quite some time and at frequent intervals.
What surprised Claire was the number of notations for hypnosis
sessions that they had engaged in. O'Bannon had hypnotized the
woman almost every time she had come to see him.

Something truly awful dawned on Claire as she noted some of

the dates that Riner had come in. Three days before the slaughter of Web's team in the courtyard had occurred was one date that popped out at Claire.

She put the papers down and went over to the filing cabinet. It was locked too, yet cheaply constructed, and she quickly levered it open with the screwdriver, no longer caring about professional etiquette. She started pulling out files. There were many agents and spouses of FBI agents represented in here from many parts of the Bureau. She scanned some of the files. Like Riner's, they involved an inordinate number of hypnosis sessions.

Claire's thoughts raced. Hypnosis was a funny thing. You could, in very rare circumstances, use it to get someone to do something he or she ordinarily wouldn't do. But what you also could do was put a person under, get him or her relaxed and comfortable and trusting and then subtly pry information on what this person as agent was doing—or, in the cases of a spouse of the agent, what the husband or wife was doing. Claire could envision O'Bannon coaxing out from a hypnotized and vulnerable and perhaps distressed Debbie Riner whatever details she knew of her husband's work. Including what target was going to be visited by HRT and exactly when, if Teddy Riner shared that with his wife. And some men would, despite professional rules that prohibited it. Many marriages, Claire knew, trumped all such policies, if just to keep domestic peace. Or it could be as simple as a slip of the tongue by one of the HRT men, which a hypnotized wife would then unwittingly pass on.

It would all be fairly simple for someone as experienced as Ed O'Bannon. And, as she had done with Web, O'Bannon could always give a carefully crafted posthypnotic suggestion that would swab away from the person's memory anything suspicious that might have occurred during hypnosis—even the fact that they had been hypnotized at all. *My God,* Claire thought, *Debbie Riner might have unwittingly aided in her husband's murder.*

And on top of that, the listening devices recorded all of the confidential information that was given by the patients who came here. Valuable information that could later be used to blackmail them or set others up, as Web's team had been. Without going into detail, Web had mentioned that things were going wrong at the Bureau. If Claire was right about what O'Bannon was doing the psychiatrist could be behind many of these problems.

As she stared at the file cabinet, Claire's gaze settled on something that wasn't there. Under the letter *L* there were several files for people with a last name that started with that letter. But there was a large and empty hanging file. Claire wondered if that was where Web's file had been. Yet the one O'Bannon had given her wasn't nearly as large as the space she was looking at, unless he had not given her the whole file. Would the man have kept part of the file away from her? O'Bannon was a supremely confident, even arrogant man, she knew. In his mind no one was smarter or more experienced. It was just possible he was withholding information to keep her in the dark. Perhaps he had had an even more powerful reason, beyond professional vanity, to keep Web as a patient.

She immediately started scouring the office. She worked through the man's desk and any other space where the missing information could be hidden and found nothing. Then she looked up once more. The ceiling was a drop-down. She climbed on the chair again, holding her flashlight, and popped up one of the ceiling panels. On her tiptoes she could see above the ceiling. She shone her light around and almost immediately saw a small box that had been placed on the metal framework holding up the ceiling. She moved her chair over there and quickly pulled the box down. Inside was the rest of Web's file, and as she sat down to examine it she discovered it was a treasure trove. Claire kept shaking her head as each new page held a stunning revelation.

O'Bannon, she knew, was organized to the point of obsession, something the two had laughed about before. And he kept meticulous notes. Those notes, though cryptic and indecipherable to a layperson, revealed to Claire that he had hypnotized Web numerous times, even more than Debbie Riner, when Web had come to him after his mother's death. Each time O'Bannon had employed a posthypnotic suggestion, much as Claire had done, to suppress the session from Web's consciousness. Claire jolted upright as she discovered that during one of the hypnotic sessions, Web had revealed to O'Bannon the entire episode about his stepfather's death. The notes were almost in code, but Claire saw references to "Stockton," "attic" and "DADDY DEAREST" written in all caps, enough to convince her that O'Bannon had gotten the same story she had from Web. Now Web's shouting at her during the hypnotic session, "You already know this!" made complete sense. His subconscious *had* revealed it all once, only to O'Bannon and not to her. The use of the placebos was also discussed in the notes. Claire figured they were probably to gauge how firmly O'Bannon had insinuated his commands into Web's subconscious. And in fact, as she read further, O'Bannon had noted that the placebo had been coupled with his hypnotic suggestion to Web that these were the most powerful sleeping pills on the market, and Web had duly reported that the pills were working. Web had also told O'Bannon about the contest among HRT members with the Taser guns.

The truth of what had happened to Web in that alley finally hit her. It was ingenious, she thought, because it didn't have the problematic issue of making Web do something he didn't want to do, like kill someone in cold blood, which Claire did not believe was possible, but rather commanded Web *not* to do something.

She contemplated calling Web to tell him what she had figured out and to enlist his help, but she couldn't from here, not with all the listening devices around. She would have to leave the office and call him.

She continued leafing through the material. The cruelest aspect of this doctor-patient relationship was revealed on the very last page, and showed that O'Bannon had built in a level of certainty that Web would perform as instructed. O'Bannon had written in his cryptic manner that he had established an excellent rapport of trust with Web. And O'Bannon had noted that a psychiatrist (O'Bannon wisely was not claiming to have done so himself) could build into his hypnotic suggestion that he was a father figure to a patient such as Web and would protect him against his stepfather. And that if Web failed to carry out the psychiatrist's commands, then the stepfather would come back and kill Web; in effect, his only safety lay in doing exactly as he was instructed. O'Bannon had concluded that Web would make an excellent candidate for posthypnotic suggestion, and thus posed a security risk. It was only Claire's special knowledge and her familiarity with Web's case that allowed her to read between the lines of O'Bannon's report. Claire, with her clear understanding of Web's psychological makeup, knew it would have been impossible for Web to counteract that command. And yet, with all that, Web had still managed to temporarily overcome the posthypnotic suggestion, go into that courtyard and fire at those guns, despite a potent mental barrage telling him not to. That had to have been Web's most remarkable performance of the night.

Claire had to concede that O'Bannon had written his report very craftily and was obviously covering his tracks, another reason for her to be careful. O'Bannon had foreseen just about every contingency, except for Claire's treating Web, finding out for herself what O'Bannon already had from plumbing the depths of Web's subconscious, and now her discovering both the bugs and this file. No wonder O'Bannon had tried so hard to keep Web as his patient.

It was time to call in the people who knew how to handle these things. She was way out of her league.

Claire turned to go back to her office, to grab her things and leave. The man was standing there watching her. She held up her screwdriver, but he pointed a gun at her.

And Ed O'Bannon looked as though he would have no problem using it.

45

Back at Quantico, Web put away his gear and gave his debriefing along with the rest of the crew. They couldn't explain much. Web believed the shots could have come from outside the building. If so, those bullets would have to be in the room somewhere, though there were lots of slugs embedded in the walls that would have to be sorted through and matched to their respective weapons. The snipers were being debriefed as well, but Web didn't know what they had seen or heard. If the shots had come from outside, then the snipers must have noticed something; they had the place pretty much surrounded. No one had come out of the building, so far as Web knew. Yet if the shots had originated from outside, the shooter was already there when HRT had shown up—and that, once more, meant a probable leak of HRT's assault. None of it was good news.

WFO was combing though the compound looking for additional clues further linking the Frees to the hit on Charlie Team. Web hoped they could find enough to explain it all, though he doubted they could. How could you explain young kids and old men with that much hate in their hearts?

Showered and changed, Web and Romano were walking down the hallway of the admin building to leave when Bates appeared in front of them, motioned them to follow him into an empty office.

"I guess I'm bad luck, Perce," said Web, only half jokingly. He really was wondering if he was suddenly jinxed somehow.

Romano piped up. "No, really bad luck would've had us losing guys, not them. I'm never going to apologize for walking out of a place alive. Like flying a plane, man, any landing is a good landing."

"Both of you shut up," said Bates, and they did. "The press will rip us on this, but we can handle it," the man said. "What I can't handle are two guys disobeying orders."

"They were short-handed, Perce," said Web, "and I can't believe you never told me. I was the one who put you on to that camera."

Bates got right in his face. "I didn't tell you, Web, precisely to prevent what did happen from happening."

Web didn't back down an inch. "Whether I was there or not, the result would've been the same. If you get shot at, you shoot back. And I wasn't going to let my guys go in weak. You can run me out of the Bureau if you want, but I'd do the same damn thing again."

Both men stared at each other until their features grew calmer.

Bates sat down and shook his head. He looked up at the men and motioned them to sit too. "What the hell," said Bates, "it can't get any worse, so why should I worry?"

"If you were so concerned about something like this happening, why didn't you send a SWAT team instead?" asked Web.

"It wasn't my call. Orders came from higher up."

"How high up?"

"That's not your concern."

"It is if my ass is going to be in the ringer over this."

Bates just stubbornly shook his head

"If the shots came from outside, somebody knew we were hitting the place," said Romano.

"That's brilliant, Romano, remind me to put you in for a promotion," snapped Bates.

"Leaks can come from anywhere," said Web, "from the bottom up or the top down, right, Perce?"

"Stow it, Web."

"Is there anything you can tell us, then?"

"Actually, the night wasn't a total waste." He turned and opened a file on the desk behind him. "Found some interesting stuff on the Frees. Silas Free was among the dead. And with him were several gents in their sixties and four men who weren't old enough to vote yet. I guess the Frees had really fallen out of favor after the school shooting—recruiting problems."

"But no Ernest B. Free," said Web. "I checked."

"No. No Ernie." Bates pulled some papers out of the file. "But hidden in a space in the floor of one of the houses we did find a quantity of bomb-making materials and three intelligence files on Judge Leadbetter, Scott Wingo and Fred Watkins."

"Pretty clean trail," said Romano.

"And that's not all. We also found Oxycontin, Percocet and Percodan with a street value of about ten thousand dollars."

Web looked surprised. "The Frees working the black market for prescription drugs?"

"Membership down, probably funds running low. Oxy is a big-time moneymaker in rural areas. It makes sense," said Bates.

"Damn, do you think that's the tie-in to what Cove was investigating? Frees set up a bogus drug op center in D.C., snooker Cove and HRT gets called in and then wiped out."

Bates was already nodding. "And maybe they're the ones putting the muscle on Westbrook and the other drug crews to get them to combine," added Bates.

Though Web also nodded his head in agreement at this, something just didn't feel right.

"We also found this," continued Bates. "A roster of past and present members of the Free Society." He looked at Web. "Want to take a guess who was once a Free?"

Web shook his head. "I'm too tired to think. Tell me."

"Clyde Macy."

Web forgot all about Oxycontin. "You're kidding me."

"From ten years ago, until about two months after the shooting in Richmond. The Frees kept good records; maybe to use as blackmail on ex-members later when their cash flow ran low. KKK probably does something like that."

"Macy a Free, and then he jumps to being muscle for a black guy in ghetto D.C. Epiphany, or the man just looking for work where he can get it?"

"Don't know. And we've now lost track of him. And of course there's the other body."

"What other body?"

"Antoine Peebles. Gunshot wound to the head. We found him last night."

"You think Westbrook was behind it?"

"It makes sense, though nothing in this case has made sense so far."

Web debated whether to tell Bates about Claire's run-in with someone impersonating Big F but then finally decided against it. Web didn't think the giant had been behind Peebles's death. But he had no reason to help Big F, and he might just confuse things by telling Bates.

Web held out his hand for the file. "Mind if I take a look?"

Bates stared at him for a long moment. "Sure. But if you see anything that hits you funny, I'd appreciate knowing about it before you walk out of this office."

While Romano stepped out of the room to speak to another Hotel Team member who passed by, Web turned through the pages. There was a posed photo of a younger Clyde Macy in combat garb holding a machine gun in one hand and a shotgun in the other and with a scowl that would probably scare off bears. As he read through the file, Web saw the speeding tickets Macy had gotten and that Bates had mentioned earlier. He glanced at the tickets and looked up. "A guy like this, and all he's got are speeding tickets?"

"Hey, such is life. He's one lucky or careful bastard or both," said Bates.

"How about the rental truck that the machine guns came off?"

"Silas Free *did* rent it. We checked with the rental agency. They remembered him. But about a week after he rented it, he filed a stolen vehicle report."

"Pretty convenient," said Web.

"No, it's SOP for people plotting some serious stuff. Rent the vehicle and then say it was stolen. And you hide it somewhere and fill it full of explosives or, in this case, machine guns."

"The rental truck is direct evidence of the Frees' connection to what happened to Charlie Team," said Web.

"And after last night, we are going to need it," commented Bates ominously.

The next thing Web turned to made his mouth go dry. He looked up at Bates and showed him the pages. "What's this?"

"Oh, that's real cute. That's the Frees' newsletter. I guess they want to keep members informed on their various murders and mayhem. It's a fairly recent thing, because I'd never heard of it before. They even have a website now, if you can believe it."

Web didn't hear Bates's remark. He just stared at the name of the newsletter emblazoned across the top of the front page.

Damn to Hell. That was the name of the Free Society's newsletter. And they were also the exact words Kevin Westbrook had spoken to him in the alley.

Web and Romano walked over to the 'Vette. Web was still deep in thought over what he had learned. It was all so murky, though, like the edges of a nightmare. You knew something formidable was lurking nearby, yet you couldn't get a comfortable handle on it.

Web stowed his gear in the 'Vette and started to climb in the passenger side.

Romano was looking at him with an expression that was probably as close to sympathy as the man ever got. "Hey, Web, you know, all the years we've been working together I've never once let you drive this thing."

Web looked confused. "What?"

"How about you drive us back to the farm? Trust me, when you're feeling shitty, there's nothing like a ride in this machine to get you back."

"Thanks, Paulie, but I don't think so."

In response, Romano tossed the keys to Web, who caught them. "It's like a bottle of great wine, Web, you have to sit back and just let the experience happen." Romano climbed in the passenger side and looked at him. "You don't keep a beautiful woman waiting, Web."

"Don't tell me you gave this thing a name too, like your guns."

"Just get in." He winked at Web and added, "If you think you're man enough."

They drove out to the main road. Before they hit the highway,

Romano said, "Okay, rule number one, you get one scratch on her and your ass is mine."

"You'd think after eight years of jumping out of choppers with me in the middle of the night with explosives tied to our butts that you'd trust me to drive your stupid car."

"Rule number two, you call her a stupid car again and I'll break your face. Her name is Destiny."

"Destiny?"

"Destiny."

When they reached Interstate 95, Web headed south and passed a state trooper writing a ticket. The hour was still early enough and they were heading against traffic, so they were pretty much alone.

"Okay, we got some breathing space now and a long straight-away. So punch it now or forever hold your gonads," said Romano.

Web glanced at him and then hit the accelerator. The car roared to a hundred so fast Web could feel himself being held against the seat by the force of the acceleration. They flew past the only other car on the road as if it had been parked. "Not bad, Paulie, and I've only got it halfway to the floor. Let's see what it really can do."

Web punched the gas again and the car rocketed even faster. They were now coming up to a curve in the highway. From the corner of his eye Web watched Romano. The guy looked calmly ahead, as though he drove this fast every day. Hell, maybe he did. Web cranked the car to a hundred and thirty and then a hundred and forty. The trees on either side were one green blur and the curve was directly ahead. There was no way Web could navigate it at this speed. Web glanced at Romano again and he saw a small bead of sweat appear on the man's forehead. That alone was worth about ten million bucks.

They were two seconds from kissing a wall of pines.

"Okay, okay," said Romano, "slow the damn thing down."

"You mean slow Destiny down?"

"Just do it!"

Web hit the brakes and they soared around the long curve at a mere eighty miles an hour.

"Slow it down some more, I just changed the oil."

"I'll bet Destiny loved you being inside her. Was it good for you too?" Web cut it to seventy, found an exit and they pulled in front of a diner. Inside, they ordered coffee.

As the waitress walked off, Web leaned forward. "I hope you're prepared for the heat we're going to take about the Frees." Romano shrugged but said nothing. "It's going to come, you know."

"Let it. Those pricks had it coming. Wasting Charlie."

"They haven't been convicted yet, Paulie."

"The brass at the Bureau wouldn't have authorized the hit unless they were damn sure they knew those punks had done it." He added in a less confident tone, "At least I sure as hell hope so."

Web leaned back. "What's bothering me about this whole scenario is the fact that we're expected to believe that the guys we just wiped out were sophisticated enough to put together an automated sniper nest using mini-guns stolen from the Army and they did it so well that nobody saw it coming. And on top of that, they murdered a judge, prosecutor and attorney using cutting-edge bomb materials and came within a whisker of taking out Billy Canfield and you and me as well? And now they're supposed to be orchestrating a large-scale drug operation that's reached into the District? And this is supposed to be revenge for something that happened years ago? Hell, most of the guys we just shot were still in sixth grade back when Ernie and his buddies hit that school. Their stupid sentries were playing video games and they had one subgun in the whole group. This shit does not compute, Paulie, or am I missing something?"

"No, it doesn't add up," he agreed. "But you got direct evidence, Web, enough to go to court with and win. And who gives a shit about the Frees? They're scum."

"That's right. Who cares about the Frees? They make a perfect patsy. And everybody's figuring they busted Ernest Free out of a maximum-security prison two thousand miles from here, but he wasn't in that compound. And I'm thinking those losers would have as much chance of knocking over the White House as they would getting Ernie out of jail."

Romano stared at Web. "Okay, you've got my attention. What are you thinking?"

"I'm thinking why a real tough street-drug dealer would bother to tell me about those tunnels. And I'm also wondering why a truck registered to Silas B. Free and later reported stolen is videotaped at the exact spot where we think the guns are going in once we know about the tunnels. You didn't hear Bates say that because you had stepped out of the room. Maybe Silas was telling the truth. Maybe the truck *was* stolen. But you're right, it's connect-the-dots time, everything seems to fit. That may be nice and clean from a prosecutor's point of view, but I don't think even old Silas was that stupid, and I don't think my good buddy Francis Westbrook is that charitable." Web looked out the dirty window of the diner as sunlight started to stream in. Wouldn't it be nice if things could clear up so pristinely in his head? He looked back at Romano. "Were you born with a silver spoon in your mouth, Paulie?"

"Yeah, right, one of ten kids in tenement housing in Brooklyn? Hell, I had my own butler."

"Well, I wasn't born with one either, but my gut tells me we were just spoonfed the sweetest damn concoction you ever saw and we swallowed every drop. I think somebody wanted the Frees wiped out, and we just did it for them."

46

When they got back to East Winds, Web called Claire on her cell phone, but she didn't answer. He tried her at work and got no answer. Web called the hotel where she was staying. No luck there either. He put the phone down, not liking any of that one bit. He mulled whether to go to the hotel or not. She might simply be in the shower. He decided to try later.

The next thing he and Romano did was something neither of them could avoid: They grabbed a few hours of sleep. After that they drove up to the main house and relieved the agents patrolling there. Gwen met them at the door, her face pale.

"We've seen the news," she said. She led them inside to a sitting room off the main hallway.

"Where's Billy?" asked Web.

"Upstairs. He's just been lying in the bed. He hadn't seen that tape in years. I didn't even know it was on the damn shelf." Web could see that her face was damp with tears.

"It was my fault, Gwen, I don't know what the hell I was thinking, playing that tape in your house."

"It didn't matter, Web, it was bound to happen sometime."

"Is there anything we can do?"

"You've damn well done enough."

They all turned and looked at the doorway, where Billy stood in old jeans, bare feet, with his shirttail hanging out. His hair was in disarray and he basically looked like hell, observed Web. Billy lit up a cigarette and cupped his hand for an ashtray as he came forward. Web noted that Gwen made no move to stop him from smoking.

He sat down across from the two men, his piercing eyes watching them from behind the drifts of smoke. Web could smell the alcohol from where he stood and assumed Gwen could too. She rose from her chair to go to her husband, but he motioned her back down.

"We saw the TV," said Billy.

"That's what Gwen said," replied Web.

Billy squinted at him, as though he were having trouble seeing over the one foot that separated them. "You killed them all?"

"Not all. Most." Web kept his gaze on the man. Part of him thought Billy might toast the demise of the Frees, and part of him thought the man might throw him and Romano out for leaving any of them alive.

"How'd it feel?"

"Billy!" said Gwen. "You have no right to ask that. We're talking about people being killed."

"I know all about people being killed, honey," said Billy as he shot her a smile that had nothing in it. He looked back at Web, awaiting an answer.

"It felt like shit. It always feels like shit. Most of them were high school age or grandfathers."

"My son was ten." He said this without emotion, just stating it as a clear, indisputable fact.

"I know that."

"But I hear what you're saying. It ain't easy killing somebody, unless you're way screwed up to begin with. It's only hard for the good guys." He pointed at Web and then at Romano. "For men like you."

Gwen swiftly went to her husband before he could stop her again. She put an arm around his shoulders. "Let's go back upstairs."

Billy ignored her. "TV says old Ernest B. Free wasn't among the dead. That right?"

Web nodded and Billy smiled. "Sumbitch's luck just keeps holding, doesn't it?"

"Looks that way. But if he was planning to come home to his little group, he'll have to find somewhere else to live."

Billy considered this. "Well, that's something." He looked at Gwen. "Where's Strait?"

Gwen seemed very relieved by the change in subject. "On his

way back from the sale. He'll be here tonight. He called from the road. It went really well. Every yearling sold and we got the price we wanted on every one."

"Well, damn, that's something to celebrate." He eyed Web and Romano. "You fellows want to celebrate? I tell you what, we'll wait until old Nemo gets back tonight and then we'll have us a little party right here. What do you say?"

"I doubt that they feel much like celebrating, Billy," said Gwen.

"Well, I sure as hell do. We got yearlings sold, Frees dead and we got to give Web and Paul here a going-away party, 'cause with those boys dead, we don't need protection anymore, do we? Y'all can pack up and get out right now," he said in a loud voice.

"Billy, please," said Gwen.

Web was about to say that the jury was still out on Gwen and Billy being safe, but he stopped himself. "I tell you what, Billy, you let us stay on a couple more days and we'll come to your party tonight."

Gwen looked at him in astonishment while Billy merely nodded and grinned, sucking down the rest of his cigarette with a long pull. He put it out in his leathery palm without even wincing. Web noted the man's hands for the first time. They were large, muscular and stained with what looked to be acid or something like it. Then he recalled the taxidermy workshop. Killing and stuffing.

"See you tonight, gents," said Billy.

Gwen led them out and told Web in a low voice that he didn't have to do this.

"I'll see you tonight, Gwen," was all he said in response, and she closed the door slowly after them.

What the hell was all that about?" said Romano. "I mean, talk about your freaky shit."

Before Web could answer, his phone rang. He whipped it out, hoping it was Claire, but it was Bates.

"I guess it's time to pull the pole on the East Winds tent," Bates said.

"You can call your guys off, but the Canfields have asked Romano and me to stay."

"Are you kidding me?"

"No, and I think it's a good idea, actually. The Frees who were at that compound are gone, but who's to say they don't have more members out there? And Ernie's still at large."

"That's true. Okay, look, you hang there, but let me know if anything goes down, and I mean the second it happens, not Web London time."

"You got it. Anything from Cove?"

"Nothing. It's like he's disappeared from the face of the earth."

Web thought about Claire. "Yeah, I got one of those too."

About the time that Web was wiping out the Free Society in southern Virginia, Claire Daniels sat blindfolded with a gag stuffed painfully in her mouth. She could hear men in the background discussing, or rather arguing, presumably about her. She recognized Ed O'Bannon's voice and she bristled each time she heard it. The bastard had kept the gun on her all the way down to the parking garage and then duct-taped her arms and legs and thrown her in his trunk. She had no idea where she was. As she blinked back tears, she still couldn't believe she had worked next to the man all this time and never suspected what was going on.

The voices stopped and she felt people moving toward her. All she could think was that another pistol was going to be placed against her head, and this time the person would surely fire and kill her. Claire was suddenly pulled up so roughly she thought they had popped her arm out of place. She felt herself being lifted up and put over a shoulder. Whoever was carrying her was strong; the man wasn't even breathing hard, and where her stomach was pressing against him, he felt hard as iron.

A few minutes went by and she was laid down and then she felt the plink of metal against metal. Another car trunk. Blindfolded and shuttled from place to place, Claire had lost her sense of balance and also felt nauseous. The car started and they were soon on the move. She tried listening for sounds that would provide some clue as to where they were, but she soon gave up, there were just too many confusing noises, and they were all muffled. She judged they had been driving for about an hour when the movement of the car seemed to indicate that they had gone from straight, level roads to winding, rolling ones. Had they gone into the country? Were they driving her to some isolated wooded area to kill her and leave her body for the animals, insects and elements to slowly destroy? In her work with law enforcement, Claire had seen the remains of a woman who had been raped and murdered and left in the forest for two weeks. Other than bone, there was virtually nothing left of her. She had become sick at the sight of it. Was that how she would be found?

The car slowed and then she felt a sharp turn and then it decreased its speed again. Now they were going over rough dirt roads and she was pitched around in the trunk, hitting her head twice, once hard enough to bring tears. The car stopped again and then she heard the engine cut off and the doors open. She braced herself. She heard footsteps moving to the rear. She tensed even more, the feeling of despair and helplessness far worse than she had ever endured before. What did it feel like to die? A bullet to the head, would there be any sensation of pain? Web had been shot, twice. He knew what it was like to think he was dying. He had survived, though, because he was a survivor. He had it much tougher in life than she had. She counseled folks over their troubles, and except for a divorce that was fairly amicable, Claire had had no significant disruptions in her own life. For the first time ever, she wondered what gave her the right, other than her fancy degrees, to tell people how to get through their *issues*. Yes, Web had survived much; Claire didn't think she was that strong. She took a deep breath as the trunk was opened and strong hands closed around her and lifted her up. It wasn't O'Bannon. Claire knew he was a man of very little physical strength. From all around she heard the sounds of the forest and animals that lived there, predators that might soon be visiting her remains. She initially fought back the tears and then just decided to let them go. These people wouldn't care.

She felt the man moving over uneven ground, stumbling a few times but then righting himself. His feet went from dirt to something else, wood, brick, or perhaps stone, she wasn't sure, but she had heard the change in sounds, and then a door was unlocked and opened. This surprised her because she had assumed they were in the middle of nowhere. Perhaps it was a cabin, but then she heard noises of machinery going and what she thought was the flow of water. Were they near a stream or river? Was there a dam nearby or a water treatment plant? Was that where her body was going to end up? Then she had a sense of either going up or down, she wasn't sure about that either, for with her ruined sense of balance she had also lost her sense of direction. In fact, she thought she might be sick, and her stomach pushing into the man's hard, bony shoulder didn't help much. And there was also a strong chemical odor that seemed familiar but that she couldn't quite identify, so out of whack were all her senses. For an instant she thought that vomiting on him would give her some small sense of pleasure, of triumph, but it also might prompt him to accelerate the timing of her death.

Another door opened and they passed through, presumably into another room. He squatted and laid her down on something soft, perhaps a bed. Her skirt had risen up embarrassingly high while she'd been riding on the man's shoulders, and with her hands bound she had no way to pull it down. She tensed when she felt his hands go up her legs to a point where she thought he was going to pull down her underpants and add rape to his list of felonies. However, all he did was tug her skirt down to its normal position.

The next thing he did was pull her bound hands over her head and the clink of metal made her think that he had handcuffed her hands to something, perhaps the bed or a ring bolted to the wall. As soon as he moved away, she tried to pull her hands down, but couldn't budge them. Whatever she was handcuffed to, she wouldn't be able to escape it.

"You'll get some food and water later. For now, just try to relax." She didn't recognize the voice. The man didn't laugh at his insane words, but Claire could easily sense the mirth behind them.

The door closed and she was once again alone. Alone, that is, until she sensed movement from across the room.

"You okay, lady?" asked Kevin Westbrook.

47

Web was now getting worried. Claire had not called back, and he had phoned the hotel but gotten no answer. He called her house and there was no answer there either. Her office hadn't seen her; she had no patients scheduled because it was her normal day off. Maybe she had just gone out for a drive along the Blue Ridge or something, he thought. She hadn't mentioned a trip to him, and even if she had gone, why didn't she answer her cell phone? Every professional instinct he had was telling him something was wrong.

He left Romano at East Winds and drove to the hotel. It was not the sort of place where anyone would necessarily note the coming and going of guests, but Web figured he'd try. However, the staff that possibly would have seen her come in the previous evening was not on duty yet. And no one he talked to remembered anyone resembling Claire coming through the lobby the day before. Her car wasn't in the parking lot either. He drove to her house, found a back window open and crawled through. Web went through her house thoroughly but found nothing that could tell him where she might have gone. He did find a book with her daughter's phone number and address in it. She went to school in California, so it wasn't like Claire could have popped in to see her for the day. Web contemplated calling the daughter, but a call from the FBI might throw the girl into needless hysterics if it turned out nothing was wrong. He left and went to Claire's office. O'Bannon was not in, but another person who worked there was. She hadn't talked to Claire and didn't know where she might be.

"Three strikes and you're out," muttered Web.

He went downstairs to the security desk, flashed his badge and asked if anything unusual had happened the previous night. The rental cop snapped to attention at the sight of the FBI shield and flipped through the notes left by the night shift. Web had gone through the security check before when he had come to see Claire because guests had to sign in, but he didn't recognize this guard. They probably rotated them throughout lots of buildings.

"Yeah, the log shows a call from Dr. Daniels at twelve-thirty A.M. She said the lights had gone out in her office and the guard informed her that all electrical systems were a go and that it might be her circuit breaker and asked if she needed assistance." The young man read this all in a stilted yet quavering voice probably not all that far removed from puberty. "She replied in the negative and that was all." He looked up from the paper. "You want me to do anything?"

The kid's big eyes were just begging Web to send him into action. The guy was armed and probably shouldn't have been, Web noted.

"I know you keep a record of visitors entering and leaving the building. I just signed in on my way in."

"That's right."

Web waited patiently for a few seconds, but the kid just wasn't getting it.

"Can I *see* the register?" Web finally said.

The fellow almost jumped out of his chair. Web had noted that the kid had checked out his face and might have recognized him from all the TV stuff lately. He was probably thinking that Web was half insane and needed to be humored at all costs if one wanted to avoid a violent death. And right now Web was perfectly fine with that perception.

"Yes, sir."

He pulled the book out and Web quickly searched through the pages. There had been lots of guests during business hours the day before, but they ended at six o'clock. He looked at the guard.

"What about after hours? What's the sign-in procedure?"

"Well, it's a keycard system and the doors automatically lock at six. If you want to get in after six, a tenant has to call down and let security know, and when the guest gets here we call up and the tenant has to come down and get the person when they show up. Or the guest may use the exterior phone, identify themselves and who they're here to see. We call up, and the tenant comes down. If the tenant doesn't answer or isn't expecting the visitor, they don't come in, that's the rule. There are some government offices in here and such. I think maybe something to do with the Pentagon, even," he added, with a small measure of pride. "It's a very secure facility."

"I'm sure," said Web absently as he continued to study the pages. "This place have an underground garage?" Web had always parked out front.

"Yes, sir, but it's on a keycard system twenty-four hours a day, tenants only."

Web made a mental note to check and see if Claire's Volvo was there. "So tenants can come and go through the garage elevator and bypass security?"

"That's right, but tenants only."

"Regular lift gate on the garage?"

The guard nodded.

"How about someone slipping into the garage without a car? Can they take the elevator up without a keycard?"

"Not after hours."

"But how about during business hours?" persisted Web.

"Um, that might be possible," said the guard in a small voice, as though Web's observation had just blown his whole professional life.

"Right. Look, is there any way I can talk to the guy who was on duty last night, the one who spoke with Claire?"

"Tommy Gaines. He's a friend of mine; we actually joined up at the same time, right out of high school. He's working the ten-to-six shift." He grinned. "Tommy's probably home dead asleep."

"Call him," said Web in a tone that made the kid grab the phone and start dialing.

Tommy was reached and Web took the phone and identified himself. He could hear the sleepy Gaines become instantly alert. "How can I help you?"

Web explained what he was looking for. "I take it you didn't see Claire Daniels leave?"

"No, I figured she just went out through the garage like she always does. I worked the day shift there for a year and so I knew who she was. She was a real nice lady."

"She's not dead yet, son," said Web.

"No, sir, I didn't mean that."

"It says she called you at twelve-thirty last night. Did she often work that late?"

"Well, I wouldn't necessarily know that, since she didn't have to come and go through the front lobby."

"I understand that; I was trying to find out if you had ever seen her here that late before."

"No, I hadn't."

"Did she sound strange when she called?"

"She sounded scared, but I guess if the lights went out on me I would be too, and she was a woman by herself and all."

"Right." Web knew female FBI, Secret Service and DEA agents who could bite young Mr. Gaines in half and never break a sweat. "Did she *say* that she was all by herself?"

"What? Well, actually, come to think of it, no, she didn't. But I sort of got that impression because she called down and all."

"And the lights down here were fine?"

"Yep. And I could see some of the other buildings out the front. The lights were all right there too. That's why I told her the breaker might have popped. See, this building is set up that each unit has control boxes for their space. That way if one office is doing renovation or has to cut the power for some reason, it doesn't affect the rest of the building. There is a main power switch for the whole building, but that's locked up and the building engineer has the key."

"And you told her you'd come up, but she said that was all right and she said she'd check the circuit breaker box herself."

"That's right."

"And you didn't hear anything else from her?"

"That's right."

Web thought for a moment. The lights were working in Claire's office now. But it might be worth another check.

"Oh, Agent London," Gaines said. "Now that I think about it, about twenty minutes after Claire called I did notice something."

Web tensed. "What? And give it to me exactly as you remember it, Tommy."

"Well, an elevator started up. That can only happen after hours if somebody has a keycard and activates it."

"Where did the elevator originate?"

"From the garage, heading up. I could see it on the floor indicator. It was on P2 and then was coming back up. I was doing rounds and got a clear view of it."

The other guard piped up to Web, "Maybe that was Claire Daniels leaving."

Web shook his head. "Most elevators, especially after hours, are programmed to return to the lobby level. If Claire had hit the button for the elevator, it would have originated from the lobby, not the garage level."

"Oh, that's right," said the crestfallen kid.

Tommy Gaines obviously had heard this exchange and said, "I guess I was thinking it was Ms. Daniels too, because she had called so recently, and I was thinking the lights going out had freaked her out and she had decided to go on home. But you're right about the elevators. The car must have been called from someone on the P2 level and I happened to pass by it when it was heading back up and got it in my head that Ms. Daniels had called it up."

Web said, "But did you see where it stopped at? If I remember correctly, the office where she works takes up most of that floor."

"No, I just kept making my rounds. So I didn't see that or when it came back down either. But whoever it was didn't come out the lobby, I would have seen them." He added, "Sorry, that's all I know."

"No, that's okay, Tommy, you've helped me a lot." He looked at the kid at the desk. "And you too."

As Web hit the elevator button and headed back up, he had a lot to think about. Either it was coincidental that somebody had gone up about twenty minutes after Claire called down, perhaps just another tenant burning the midnight oil, or something else was going on. Under the circumstances, Web just had to assume it was the latter.

When Web got to Claire's offices, he asked the same woman who had helped him before if he could see the electrical closet.

"It's over there, I think," she said uncertainly.

"Thanks."

"Do you think something's happened to Claire?" the woman asked nervously.

"I'm sure she's fine."

Web went to the closet and found it locked. He looked around, but the woman had gone back into her office. He pulled out his little picklock kit and soon had the closet open. He looked around. The first thing that struck him was that something had been pulled out of the wall. There was a clear gap on the power board and wire insulation and other bits of debris were on the floor. Web had no idea whether it had been done recently or long ago. He hoped it hadn't happened last night. As he swung his head around, his experienced eyes picked up what Claire's had missed: the wireless button trip on the inside of the doorjamb, similar to those installed in homes that would trigger an alarm if the door was opened and the contacts broken. Web had seen lots of these devices but never on an electrical closet in an office building. He walked to the front door of the office and opened it. There was no trip button there; in fact, he saw no security panel at all. Why have a security system on your electrical closet and not your office? A cold sense of dread hit Web as he looked at all the closed doors of this space. Claire had told him that a great number of FBI agents, spouses and other law enforcement types sought professional help here. A lot of intimate, confidential information was being revealed behind those portals.

"Shit!" Web ran to Claire's office. The door was locked. He picked it and went in. He saw the flashlight on the floor and was about to search her desk when he happened to look up and saw the smoke detector dangling there. He reached for it and drew back as his FBI training took over. Potential crime scene, fingerprints; don't contaminate the evidence. He called Bates, explained the situation to him and the FBI put out an APB on Claire; and Bates and a tech team showed up thirty minutes later.

Within three hours the entire office had been meticulously gone over and the people questioned. Web was sitting out in the waiting room the whole time. Bates came out, looking pale.

"I don't believe this, Web, I really don't."

"The smoke detectors were listening devices, weren't they?"

Bates nodded. "And video. Pinhole cameras."

"PLC technology?"

Bates nodded again. "Like the spooks use. Sophisticated stuff."

"Well, I guess we just found our leak."

Bates looked down at a list he held. "I guess, you look at it singly, and it's like an agent here, a spouse there, no big deal. But we checked uptown, where they keep records on this because the Bureau's insurance foots the bill. Can you believe that almost two hundred agents, spouses and other personnel connected with the Bureau are patients here? I'm talking people at the bottom all the way to people at the top. And who knows how many at other agencies like DEA, Secret Service, Capitol Police?"

"Well, going to shrinks wasn't real popular with agents before this. Now I guess you can just kiss it good-bye."

"O'Bannon had high-level clearances. Ex-Army, worked in-house at the Bureau as a counselor, solid as a rock. Or so we thought."

"An ocean of intelligence." Web just shook his head. "Debbie Riner, Angie Romano and others. Guys aren't supposed to really talk to their wives about work, but it happens. I mean, everybody's human."

"That must be how they knew you guys were hitting the place that night and even which team was going to be where. It was a planned assault, lots of lead time. One of the guys could have told the missus and she lets it slip to O'Bannon and, *bam*, the bugs pick it up." Bates covered his face with his hand. "Damn, how do I tell Debbie Riner she might have helped kill her husband?"

"You don't, Perce. You don't," Web said firmly.

"But if I don't, she'll find out from some source. And, God, think of the blackmail potential. How do we know *that* hasn't happened already?"

"Face it, Perce, this is an octopus with tentacles that never stops growing." Web looked around the office. "All personnel accounted for here?"

"All except Claire Daniels."

"And O'Bannon?"

Bates sat down. "It looks like he was definitely involved. His files have been cleared out. We checked his house. That's been cleared out too. We've got APBs out, but if this all went down last night, he's got a big head start. By private plane he could already be out of the country." Bates rubbed his head. "This is a nightmare. Do you know what will happen when the media gets hold of this? The Bureau's credibility will be wrecked."

"Well, if we can nail the people behind this, we might be able to get some of it back."

"O'Bannon's not sticking around for us to come and arrest him, Web."

"I'm not talking about O'Bannon."

"Who, then?"

"First of all, let me ask you a question that'll probably make you wanta take a swing at me, but I need a straight answer if I'm going to be able to help you."

"Ask it, Web."

"Is there any possibility that O'Bannon was working with the Bureau to bug the offices so management would know what the foot soldiers' problems were?"

"That crossed my mind, actually. And the answer is no. Thing is, there are some real higher-ups who come her too, it's not just rank-and-filers. And I'm talking the kind of heavyweights—and their wives, by the way—who could bring down just about everybody at the Bureau if that sort of crap was going on."

"Okay, then let's assume that O'Bannon orchestrated this whole intelligence-gathering scheme. Why? Not for kicks. For profit. It always comes down to the bucks. He sells information to lots of different people and law enforcement operations everywhere get blown as a result. And maybe somebody bought info from O'Bannon to execute the hit on Charlie. Like you said, he could have gotten details from one of the wives he was seeing as a patient. Whoever's behind *that*, I want them."

"Well, I thought we *did* know. The Frees. We already nailed them."

"Oh, you really think so?"

"Don't you?"

"It seems to fit, almost too perfectly. Do we have any more information about what might have happened to Claire?"

"Yeah, and it's not good. Less than half an hour after the lights went out in Claire's office, O'Bannon arrived at the garage. He used his keycard to get in and that gave us both his identity and the time of entry."

Web nodded and his spirits fell even more. "She trips the alarm, O'Bannon probably had a remote unit at his house and got the signal. He hightails it over here."

"And finds Claire."

"Yeah."

"I'm sorry, Web."

Web drove back to East Winds, as depressed as he'd ever been in his life. As bad as things looked for the Bureau right now, he didn't even care. All he cared about was finding Claire alive.

Romano was cleaning one of his pistols and looked over when Web came up the stairs of the carriage house. "Man, you look bummed."

Web sat down across from him.

"I screwed up, Paulie."

"Hell, it's not the first time." Romano smiled, but Web obviously wasn't in the mood. Romano put down the gun and looked at his friend. "So talk to me."

"Claire Daniels."

"Your shrink."

"My *psychiatrist*." He paused and then added, "And my friend. Some guys threatened her but then let her go. They're connected with my case, so she was put in danger because of me. She comes to me for help, and what do I do? I don't help."

"Did you offer her protection?"

"Yes, but she didn't want to take it. She thought the threat wasn't real; she made it sound very logical. Now it turns out this O'Bannon guy she worked with was bugging all the psychiatrists' offices and getting information from patients during sessions. Lots of those patients were people who worked at the Bureau. And folks connected to them," he added. He didn't know if Romano was aware that Angie was seeing O'Bannon. And if he didn't know, Web did not want to be the one to tell him. "Then he's probably been selling the info to the highest bidder to use in knocking out law enforcement operations all over the place."

"Holy shit! Do you think Claire was in on it?"

"No! It looks like she stumbled on the truth and now she's disappeared."

"Maybe she's hiding out."

"She would've called." Web's hands balled to fists. "Damn, I'm an idiot for not putting her on around-the-clock protection. Now it's too late."

"Don't be so sure. From the little I saw of her, she can take care of herself. On the drive to the farm, I was talking to her some, and the lady is sharp."

"You mean you were trying to get some free psychiatric advice."

"I wasn't looking for any, but hey, everybody's got problems, okay? Talking to Claire, she made me see some things. Take me and Angie."

Web stared at him with great interest, if only to get his mind off Claire's plight for a few moments. "Okay, what about you and Angie?"

Romano looked vastly uncomfortable now that he had raised the subject. "She doesn't want me to do HRT anymore. She's tired of me being gone all the time. I guess no big surprise there." He added quietly, "And the boys are getting older and they deserve a father who's around more than a month out of every year."

"Is that what she said?"

Romano looked away, "No, that's what *I* said."

"So you really thinking of hanging up your .45s?"

Romano shot him a glance. "Don't you ever think about it?"

Web sat back. "I talked to Debbie Riner recently and she said more or less the same thing about Teddy. But it's different for me, I don't have a wife or kids, Paulie."

Romano hunched forward. "See, the things is, in the last eight years I've missed four Christmases, both my boys' First Communions, every damn Halloween, a couple of Thanksgivings and my son Robbie being born! And on top of that I can't tell you how many birthdays, baseball games and soccer matches, special stuff like that. Hell, it's like my boys are surprised when I'm home, Web, not when I'm gone, because me gone is like normal to them."

He touched the spot near his belly button. "And that hit I took last night? Got a nasty bruise and it hurt like hell for a while, but what if it *had* been an inch lower, or two feet higher and through my head? I'm gone. But you know what? It wouldn't have been that much different than when I was alive, at least for Angie and the boys. And then what happens? Angie's gonna get remarried, you know that, and the boys will maybe get a real dad and forget all about Paul Romano even being their old man. I'd take a damn Barrett round in the head over that, Web, I really would. Every time I think about it—shit!"

Web could actually see wetness in Romano's eyes, and the sight of one of the toughest men he had ever known being brought to his knees over love for his family hit Web harder than even Francis Westbrook ever could. Romano quickly looked away and swiped at his face.

Web gripped Romano's shoulder. "That's not going to happen, Paulie; you're a good dad. Your kids would never forget you." As soon as he said this, it struck Web. He had forgotten his father, totally and completely. A birthday party, six years old. Claire had said Web and his old man were having a really good time. Until the cops showed up. "And you're doing good for your country too, don't forget that," he added. "Nobody gives a damn about serving their country anymore. Everybody just complains about how rotten it is without doing anything to make it better. But man, the second they need you, you better be there."

"Yeah, serving my country. And wiping out a bunch of hick kids and old farts who couldn't hit the Statue of Liberty from three feet away with a bazooka."

Web sat back and said nothing because he had nothing more to say on that subject.

Romano looked up at him. "Claire will turn up, Web, and who knows, maybe you and her can be more than friends. Get a real life."

"You don't think it's too late?" It all sounded impossible to achieve.

"Hell, if it ain't too late for me, it sure ain't too late for you," said Romano.

Web didn't think he sounded too confident and the men looked miserably at each other.

Web stood. "You know, Paulie, both of us are in sorry-ass shape. And you know what else?"

"What?"

"Now I'm really looking forward to this party tonight."

48

Percy Bates was sitting in the strategic ops center at WFO when the man walked in. Buck Winters wasn't alone. He had his usual twin escorts and also several others with him. Bates recognized one as a young Bureau lawyer and another as an investigator from the Bureau's Office of Professional Responsibility, which looked into any wrongdoing by members of the FBI. With exaggerated solemnity, they all sat down across from Bates.

Winters tapped the tabletop with one of his long fingers. "How's the investigation coming, Perce?"

"It's coming real well," answered Bates. He looked at the other people. "So what's all this? Are you starting an investigation of your own?"

"Heard from Randall Cove lately?" asked Winters.

Bates once more glanced at the others. "You know, Buck, with all due respect, is it okay for these people to be hearing that name?"

"They're all cleared for it, Perce. Trust me. They've been cleared for a lot." Winters stared directly at him now. "This is a total disaster, you know."

"Look, HRT got sent in and they were fired upon and they fired back. Those rules of engagement are about as clean as you can get. Nothing in the Constitution says our guys have to stand there and get gunned down."

"I wasn't specifically talking about the Free Society massacre."

"Damn it, Buck, it wasn't a massacre. The Frees had guns too, and they were using them."

"Eight dead, old men and young boys, and not one loss on HRT's side. Now, how do you think the press will play out that one?"

Bates dropped the file he was holding along with any shred of patience he had left. "Well, if the Bureau does its usual head-in-the-sand and lets everybody else control the facts and the spin, I guess not real well. What do we have to do to make our 'image' look okay, lose a few guys on every mission?"

"Another Waco," said the fresh-faced lawyer, shaking her head.

"Like hell it is," yelled Bates. "You don't know what you're talking about. You were still in law school with your thumb up your ass when Waco went down."

"Like I was saying," said Winters calmly, "I wasn't specifically talking about the Frees."

"What, then?" asked Bates.

"Oh, I don't know, maybe the fact that the entire security of the FBI has been compromised."

Bates took a long breath. "Because of the psychiatrist's office?"

Winters exploded. "Yeah, Perce, that's right, because for God knows how long, agents and secretaries and technicians and who the hell knows who else, but apparently everybody who has a head problem in the Bureau, has spilled their guts in that place. And somebody's been vacuuming it up and using it for God knows what. I'd call that a compromise of security."

"We're out looking for O'Bannon right now."

"The damage has already been done."

"It's better than us never having found out about it."

"Not by a wide margin it's not. I guess you know that I was on record a long time ago against using outside psychiatrists and psychologists, for this very security reason."

Bates studied the man warily. *And so you're going to use this disaster to move your career a few pegs higher, right, Buck? Like maybe the director's office?*

"No, Buck, actually, I wasn't aware of that."

"It's all in the paper trail," Winters said confidently. "Check it."

"I'm sure it is, Buck. You were always the best of the best with the old paper trail." *And not much else having to do with being a real FBI agent.*

"Well, heads are going to roll on this one."

But not yours.

"So what's this I read about London participating in the assault? Please tell me that's just an enormous typo."

"He was there," admitted Bates.

Winters looked like he was ready to erupt again. Then Bates sensed a very small indication of satisfaction on the man's features, and he finally understood where this conversation was going.

"Well, the press can just go ahead and crucify us now," said Winters. "HRT takes out its revenge on old men and young boys. That'll be the lead headline on the wires tomorrow. Now hear this, Bates and hear it good, London is through, effective immediately." For effect, Winters picked up a pencil off the table and snapped it in half.

"Buck, you can't do that. It's still under review."

"Yes, I can do that. He was on official leave of absence pending an SRB inquiry." Winters motioned to one of his aides, who handed him a file. Winters took his time slipping on a pair of reading glasses and then glanced over the file. "And now I've also discovered that while on paid leave he was assigned to protection duty regarding one William Canfield who operates a horse farm in Fauquier County. Who authorized that?"

"I did. Canfield's son was killed by the Frees in Richmond. Three people connected with that incident have been murdered, we believe by the Frees. You know all that. We didn't want Canfield to become number four. Web was available and Canfield trusts him. In fact, Web saved his life. And mine. So it seemed a good fit."

"Can't say much for Canfield's judgment, then."

"And we had direct evidence connecting a truck, rented by Silas Free, to the machine guns that were used to ambush HRT. We had every right to hit them. And the assault was okayed by all appropriate parties. Check the paper trail."

"I realize that. I actually signed off on it myself."

"You did?" Bates asked, with a curious expression. "I actually wanted a SWAT team, Buck. You didn't insist on HRT going in, did you?" Winters didn't answer, and right then and Bates realized exactly why HRT had been sent in. Winters had wanted something like this to happen to fuel his crusade against Hostage Rescue. And

Bates also knew that, as wily as Winters was, he'd never be able to prove it.

"I was not made aware that Web London was part of the assault," Winters continued.

"Well, that came later," Bates said slowly. He was defenseless on that one and he knew it.

"Oh, thanks for the explanation, that really clears it all up. And who authorized London being in on the assault?"

"His commander, Jack Pritchard, would've had to give the okay."

"Then he's gone. Effective now."

Bates stood. "My God, Buck, you can't do that. Pritchard's pulled twenty-three years at the Bureau. He's one of the best we've ever had."

"Not anymore he's not. As of now, he's one of the worst. And it will be duly noted for the official record. And I'm going to recommend that he be stripped of everything, including his pension, for insubordination, action detrimental to the Bureau and about a half dozen other things. Believe me, it'll be an easy sell once all this breaks. There will be an enormous need for scapegoats."

"Buck, please don't do this. Okay, maybe he stepped out of bounds a little on this one, but he's got a list of commendations taller than I am. He's risked his life more times than I can count. And he's got a wife and five kids, two of them in college. This'll ruin him. This will kill him."

Winters put the file down. "I tell you what, Perce, I'll make a deal with you, because I like you and I respect you."

Bates sat down, instantly suspicious as the cobra moved in for the kill. "What sort of deal?"

"If Pritchard stays, London goes. No questions asked. No fight, no defenses. He just goes. What's it going to be?"

Percy Bates just sat there while Buck Winters watched him, waiting for his answer.

For years Claire had been a tooth grinder, to such an extent, in fact, that her dentist had made her a mouth guard that she wore at night to save her teeth from being worn down to the gums. She had wondered where this symptom of anxiety came from, perhaps from listening to her patients' problems. Now she was thankful for her grinding because she had worn the gag down such that it had finally ripped apart and she spit it out. The way her hands were bound over her head, however, made removing the blindfold impossible. She had tried to rub her head against the wall to pry it off that way, until it felt like she had worn off most of her hair. Exhausted, she slumped over.

"It's okay, lady, I'll be your eyes," said Kevin. "They got me locked up too, but I'm working on that."

With her gag off, they had started talking and Claire had learned who Kevin was.

"Web London told me about you," she said. "And I've been to your house. We spoke to Jerome."

Kevin looked anxious. "I bet they worried. I bet Granny about to die from worry."

"They're okay, Kevin. But they *are* worried. Jerome loves you very much."

"He always good to me. He and Granny."

"Do you know where we are?"

"Nope."

Claire took a deep breath. "It smells like chemicals. Like we're near a dry cleaner's shop or some type of manufacturing plant." She struggled to recall the details of how she had gotten here. The roads and the terrain the man had carried her over seemed more reminiscent of the country than the city.

"How long have you been here?"

"Ain't know. Days sort of run together."

"Has anyone been in to see you?"

"Same man. Ain't know who he is. He treats me nice. But he gonna kill me, I can see that in his eyes. It's the nice ones you got to watch out for. Folks who scream and shake their fist, I'll take them any day over the quiet ones."

If she hadn't been so unnerved at the thought of being murdered, Claire might have smiled at the boy's mature insight into human nature.

"How did you get hooked up with all this?"

"Money," Kevin said plainly.

"We saw the sketch you did, with the remote control."

"I ain't know what was gonna happen. Nobody told me that. They just give me it and told me what to say"

"Damn to hell?"

"Yep. Then I was supposed to trail 'em going down that alley and then, when I got close enough to the courtyard, hit the remote button. I seen that man, Web, he all froze up, and the rest of his buddies went running into that courtyard. Web, he ain't never see me behind him. He got up and followed his buddies, but he was walking like he was drunk or something. I hit the button and then hung back."

"Because you wanted to see what happened?"

"Those people ain't never tell me about no guns. I swear that on my mama's grave, I swear!"

"I believe you, Kevin."

"I was supposed to go back to where I was, but I couldn't. Seeing all them folks die like that. And then Web, he yelled at me. About give me a heart attack. He saved my butt. I would've run out there if it ain't for him and then I be dead too."

"Web said that somebody switched you for another boy."

"That's right. I ain't know why."

Claire took a deep breath and the strong chemical smell invaded her lungs again. Now she too was able to identify it as chlorine, but she had no idea what its source was. She felt totally helpless.

49

Web and Romano met Nemo Strait on their way up to the mansion to attend the party.

"What happened to you?" asked Romano. Strait's arm was in a sling.

"Let a damn horse get the drop on me. Thing kicked me. Felt like my collarbone was in my throat."

"Anything broken?" asked Web.

"They x-rayed it up at the hospital in Kentucky and they didn't see anything, but they put me in this thing for the time being. Now I'm a one-armed farm manager and Billy's probably going to be pissed at that."

They were welcomed at the house by Billy. Web was surprised at how he was dressed. He had on nice, pressed slacks and a blue blazer, his hair was neatly combed and he had even shaved. Yet as they passed through, Web could smell on the man's breath that he had begun the party a while back.

Billy led them down to the lower level.

Next to the bar were two men Web didn't know. They were dressed expensively if casually in Armani, Bruno Magli with no socks, Tag Heuer watches, and gold necklaces that were visible because the men's shirts were open about two buttons too many. They were deeply tanned, fit and trim, nails professionally manicured and hair perfectly coifed, and for many reasons Web's initial impression was that they were gay.

Billy led Romano and Web over to them. "Wanta introduce y'all to a couple new friends of mine. Giles and Harvey Ransome, they're brothers, now, they ain't married." Billy was the only one to laugh at that remark. "They're my neighbors from next door. Finally got them to come over for a drink."

Web and Romano exchanged a quick glance.

"This is Web London and Paul—no, make that Paulie," Billy added with a wink. "From the Federal Bureau of Investigation."

The Ransome brothers both looked ready to run at that. Harvey Ransome, Web thought, appeared as though he might faint.

Web put out his hand. "We're off duty tonight."

The Ransome brothers cautiously extended their hands, as though they feared that there was a real threat of handcuffs being placed on them.

"Billy didn't tell us the FBI would be here tonight," Giles said, giving his host an unfriendly stare.

"I love surprises," said Billy. "Ever since I was a kid." He looked over at Strait. "What in the hell happened to you?"

"Horse got the better of me."

"This is my farm manager, Nemo Strait," said Billy to the Ransome brothers. "He just made me a small fortune up in Kentucky selling a bunch of horse meat to some new suckers."

"We did real well," said Strait quietly.

"Where the hell are my manners?" said Billy. "You boys need some drinks." He pointed at Web and Romano. "I know you boys are beer drinkers. How 'bout you, Nemo?"

"Whiskey and water, best kind of painkiller there is."

Billy went behind the bar. "I'll join you in that one." He looked toward the stairs. "Well, come on down and join the party."

Web looked toward the stairs, expecting to see Gwen. Instead there was Percy Bates.

"Billy was nice enough to give me an invite," he explained as he joined them. He smiled at Web, but in that smile Web could see something that he didn't particularly like.

Once they all had drinks in hand, they broke up into small groups. Web went over to the Ransome brothers and began subtly probing them as to what was going on at the Southern Belle, but the men were being exceptionally guarded, which made Web even more suspicious. Nemo and Romano were looking over Canfield's collection of shotguns, while Billy was standing all alone and scowling back at the grizzly bear in the corner.

One by one all their heads turned when she came down the stairs. If Billy was more overdressed than usual, his wife looked ready to attend a Hollywood premiere; she was as far removed from her normal boots-and-jeans horse-rider persona as it was possible to be. The red gown was long, body-hugging and ran down to her ankles; the slit came to midthigh, right at the precise point where decency was still maintained but where male fantasy was compelled to sprint. The shoes were open-toed, with ankle straps that, to Web, at least, suggested the concept of bondage if one hadn't already been thinking about it. The gown was strapless, her bare shoulders tanned and muscular but retaining much feminine allure despite the ripples. The gown's bodice was cut low enough to make maneuvering difficult without revealing too much, and perhaps that was the intent. Her hair was piled high on her head, her jewelry tasteful and the woman required very little makeup.

There was complete silence as she descended to them until Web heard Romano whisper, "*Amore,*" and then he took a gulp of beer.

"Now the party can really get started," said Billy. "What you having, Gwen?"

"Ginger ale."

Billy filled this order. He looked over at the Ransome brothers.

"She's stunning," said Harvey.

"A goddess," echoed Giles.

"She's also my wife." He brought the drink over to her. "Nemo got himself all banged up with a horse."

Web noted that she barely glanced in the man's direction. "So I see." She nodded toward the Ransomes. "I don't believe we've met," she said coolly.

Harvey and Giles fell over themselves to see which of them she would meet first.

Web just stood back and watched all this happen. The woman was, without doubt, exceptionally beautiful, yet the way she was dressed, the magisterial way that she was acting, seemed totally out of sync with Gwen Canfield, at least as he had pegged her. Perhaps he had been wrong.

He didn't notice Bates at his elbow until the man spoke.

"A going-away party, I understand."

"Yeah, case closed. Good guys win again," Web added dryly. "Time to get drunk and pat ourselves on the back, at least until all the shit comes back tomorrow."

"We need to talk later. It's important."

Web glanced at him. To someone who didn't know the man well, Bates looked like he didn't have a care in the world. To Web, who did know him about as well as anybody, the man seemed ready to implode with whatever he was carrying around inside.

"Don't tell me I won the lottery?"

"I guess it's all in how you look at it. I'll let you decide. You want to slip outside and discuss it now?"

Web eyed the man steadily. So it *was* pretty bad. "No, Perce, right now I just want to enjoy my drink and go over and talk to a very beautiful woman."

He left Bates and managed to extract Gwen from the fawning Ransome brothers. They settled in twin club leather chairs, and Gwen cradled her drink in her lap and looked over at her husband.

"He's already been partying hard for about six hours."

"So I see." He looked her over without seeming to. At least he thought so until she shot him a glance.

"A little different attire than you're used to, I know," she said. Her cheeks reddened slightly at this remark.

"Hey, you got it, flaunt it. I'm just glad there aren't any other women here, because they'd really be out of their league. They wouldn't just be wallflowers, they'd be part of the wall, as far as the men here are concerned."

She patted his hand. "You're sweet. The fact is, I'm about as uncomfortable in this dress as I can be; worried that I'm going to fall out any second and embarrass myself, and my feet are already killing me. These Italian shoes are pretty to look at and absolutely impossible to wear if your feet are over a size four."

"So why the getup, then?"

"Billy picked it out for me. He's not the sort of man who tells his wife what to do or wear," she added quickly. "Quite the contrary. I usually pick his clothes out. But he wanted me to look really knock-'em-dead, he said."

Web raised his glass. "Consider your mission accomplished. But why?"

"I don't know, Web, I really don't know what's going through his head right now."

"Maybe it has something to do with that damn tape. Again, I'm sorry."

Gwen just shook her head. "It's not just that. This has been brewing for some time. Billy's been changing over the last few months or so, and I'm not sure why."

To Web it seemed like the woman did know why but wasn't to the point where she was going to reveal it to a semi-stranger like him.

"His behavior has been becoming more and more bizarre."

He looked at her curiously. "How so?"

"Well, he's become obsessed with his stuffed animals, always down there messing around. My God, that is the most repulsive thing."

"It is pretty gruesome."

"And he's been drinking hard, even for him." She looked at Web and spoke in a lower voice. "Do you know what he told me while we were getting dressed?" She took a sip of her ginger ale. "He said that they should put all the heads of the Free Society members up on poles and parade them around, like they used to do hundred of years ago."

"Why? To send a message?"

"No."

They both looked up and saw Billy standing there.

He downed the rest of his whiskey. "No, you do it because the best place to put your enemies is right in front of you, so you know exactly where they are all the time."

"That's not always easy to do," commented Web.

Billy smiled through his drink glass. "That's right. And that's why folks' enemies get the drop on 'em more often than not." It was just a quick glance, but Web was almost certain that Billy looked at Nemo Strait when he said this.

Billy held up his glass. "Ready for a fresh one?"

"I'm still working on this one."

"Well, let me know. Gwen, you ready for a real libation?"

"Dressed this way in a room full of men, I think I need to keep my wits about me tonight," she said with a coy smile.

For the record, Web noted, her husband didn't return the smile.

Right before they went up to dinner, Web heard a scream and looked over to its source. The gun cabinet was swung open, revealing the secret room. And Harvey and Giles were both holding their chests after having been surprised by Billy's slave mannequin. And the man himself was leaning against the wall laughing so hard he was gagging. Web just had to smile.

After dinner, coffee and snifters of brandy that Billy insisted everybody try, they all took their leave. Gwen gave Web a hug and he felt her soft breasts push into his own hard chest. Her fingers seemed to cling to him a beat too long. He didn't know exactly how to take that and so all he managed to say was good-bye.

They went outside and Strait climbed in his truck and one-armed it back to his house. A limo pulled up in the front circle and Harvey and Giles Ransome piled inside. They had both made fools of themselves over Gwen, Web had thought, but she had taken it with good graces. She was no doubt upstairs right this minute slipping out of the painful shoes and the uncomfortable dress. In fact, she was probably naked right now, and Web felt himself glancing toward the upstairs windows—in hopes of what? he asked himself. A glimpse? It didn't happen.

Bates came up to him and Romano.

"Romano, Web and I need to talk."

The man said it in such a tone that all Romano did was turn and walk toward the carriage house.

Web and Bates faced off. "Okay," Web said, "what's the deal?"

Bates told him and Web took it silently until the man finished.

"What about Romano?" asked Web.

"Buck didn't mention him, so I'm assuming he's okay."

"Let's keep it that way."

"I don't know what to do, Web. I'm caught between a rock and a hard place."

"No, you're not. I'll make it easy for you. I'll resign."

"Are you shitting me?"

"It's time for me to move on, Perce, do something else. I'm not getting any younger, and to tell you the truth, I'd like to find out what it's like having a job where people aren't shooting at you."

"We can fight this, Web. Winters doesn't have the final say on this."

"I'm tired of fighting, Perce."

Bates just looked at the man helplessly. "I didn't want it to end this way."

"Me and Romano will finish up here and then I'll be moving on."

"You know the heat this is going to generate, with what happened with the Frees. And with you leaving HRT, the timing of that will make everyone assume you're the scapegoat. It's going to get dicey. The media will come after you. In fact, it's already starting."

"There was a time when that would've bothered me. But not now."

The men stood there quietly for a few seconds as many years of fighting the good fight together suddenly had abruptly come to an end for them and it seemed neither of them was prepared for it. Web finally turned and walked away.

50

It was around two o'clock in the morning. The only movements at East Winds were the horses in the pastures and the wildlife in the encroaching forest. Then came footsteps that crept along the path leading through the trees.

There was one light on in the house and a man's silhouette was stark in the outline of the window. Nemo Strait held a cold beer can against his injured shoulder, grimacing as the frosty metal hit the damaged skin. He wore a T-shirt and boxer shorts; his thick, muscular legs had split the fabric at the thigh. He lay on his bed, picked up the semiautomatic pistol there and deftly loaded the gun's magazine, but with only one hand he had trouble sliding the bolt back to chamber a round. Frustrated, he finally put the gun on the nightstand, lay back on the bed and sipped his beer.

Nemo Strait, by nature, was a worrier. And right now he had a lot to concern him. He was still thinking about the chopper that had come out of nowhere in the dark woods. Strait had watched the flight of the aircraft. It had not landed in the woods, and it did not appear to be the police. Strait had thought about going back to where they had shot Cove to make certain the guy was dead. Yet he had to be. They had fired five shots into him, no one could shake that, and even if the man somehow managed to live, he'd be a vegetable, incapable of telling anyone what had happened. Still, Strait didn't like it and he had scanned every news program he could find in the hopes of learning that an FBI undercover agent had been found dead. And he also wanted to hear that there were no clues to the killers. He rubbed his shoulder. Strait's blood was out there, of course, but they had to have something to match his DNA to, and his was not on file anywhere that he could remember. Except the Army! But after more than twenty-five years, would they still have it? Would the stuff be any good? He doubted it. Still, he could feel it was getting close to the time he would be moving on. He had accomplished everything he had set out to do, and last night's transaction had left him with enough money to retire to just about anywhere he wanted. At first he had thought about buying a place up in the Ozarks and passing the rest of his life doing nothing more than fishing and spending his money in increments that would arouse no suspicions. Now he was rethinking that strategy. Now he was thinking that another country might be a far better retirement venue. Well, he had heard the fishing was terrific in Greece.

If Strait heard the back door open, he made no indication. It had been a long day and his painkiller was wearing off. He took another slug of it and wiped his lips.

The door to his bedroom slowly opened. Again, Strait seemed not to notice. The person moved into the room. Strait turned on some music on the radio next to his bed. The figure moved closer to the bed. Finally Strait stopped what he was doing and slowly looked around.

"I didn't think you were going to come tonight," he said. "Thinking with one arm I wasn't good enough anymore." He took a drink of his beer and then put it down.

Gwen stood looking down at him. She wore the red dress she had had on at the party, but her high heels had been replaced with flats; her gold anklet glittered a bit in the wash of light.

She moved closer to him, her gaze drifting to his shoulder. "Does it hurt much?"

"Just every time I breathe."

"Which horse did it?"

"Bobby Lee."

"He's not known as a kicker."

"Every horse can be a kicker."

"I forgot, you're the expert." She smiled demurely, but there was something behind the look that was not nearly so playful.

"No, but I grew up with the damn things. I mean, you don't learn this stuff in a year or even in ten years. Look at Billy, he's a fast learner, but he still basically knows shit about running a horse farm."

"You're right. That's why we hired you and your good old boys." She paused. "You're our white knight, Nemo."

Strait lit up a cigarette. "Yeah, that's a good one." She surprised him by reaching over and taking a drink of his beer.

"Don't you have anything stronger than this?" she asked.

"Bourbon."

"Get it."

While he pulled out the bottle and glasses, she perched on the bed and rubbed her calf. She touched the anklet, a gift from Billy. It had both their names engraved on it. Strait handed her a full glass and she downed it in one pass and handed it back to him for a refill.

"Take it easy on that stuff, Gwen. It's not candy."

"It is to me. Besides, I didn't drink at the party. I was a good girl."

Strait's gaze ran down her long body, took in her bare legs, her ample bosom. "Every man in the place wanted to jump your bones."

Gwen did not smile at this compliment. "Not every man."

"Hey, Billy's getting up there, can't do it on demand anymore. Hell, I'm getting to that point myself faster than I'd like."

"It has nothing to do with age." She reached over and took a puff of the cigarette and then handed it back. "And when your husband hasn't touched you in years, it tends to drive a woman to other sources." She glanced at him. "I hope you recognize your limited role here."

He shrugged. "A man has to take what he can get. But it ain't right that he still blames you for what happened to your son."

"He has every right. I was the reason David was at that school."

"You didn't order them crazy Frees in there to shoot up the place, now, did you?"

"No, and I didn't ask the FBI to send down a bunch of men who were too cowardly or incompetent to save my son either."

"Kind of strange, having the FBI right here on the farm."

"We knew that was a very real possibility."

Strait smiled. "Come here to protect you."

Gwen said dryly, "From ourselves."

"Well, the little bomb in Billy's phone that I detonated when Web tossed it out the car, that threw them off the scent for good. They're not looking in our direction."

"Web London is a lot smarter than you probably think."

"Oh, I know he's real smart. I ain't going around underestimating anybody on this one."

Gwen took a sip of her second bourbon, slipped off her flats and slid back on the bed.

He caressed her hair. "I been missing you, lady."

"Billy could care less, but it's a little difficult to move around with the FBI patrolling your property."

"Well," said Strait, "now it's just Web and Romano. He's another one to watch. Ex-SWAT and Delta, that dude can be bad news. See it in his eyes."

Gwen rolled over on her stomach, propped up on her elbows and stared at him. His eyes were locked on her cleavage, which was now spilling out of her dress. She noted his gaze, but apparently his attention did not interest her.

"I wanted to ask you about the horse trailers."

Gwen's question caused his gaze to lift from her breasts to her face.

"What about 'em?"

"I grew up on a horse farm too, Nemo. You had some of those rigs customized in a very special way, and I want you to tell me why."

He grinned. "Can't a man have any secrets?"

She got up on her knees and slid closer to him. She started kissing his neck, and his hand went first to her chest and then moved to her bottom. He hiked her dress up to her waist and discovered she had on no underwear.

"Good thinking. With me as horny as I am, you would've just gotten those panties ripped off anyway."

She moaned into his ear as his fingers moved over her. One of her hands went to his face and then down to the neckline of his T-shirt. And then with a flash she had ripped the shirt down the front and sat back.

Her movement surprised Strait so much that he almost fell off the bed.

He followed her gaze to the bloodstained bandage on his shoulder.

"Mighty odd bruise from a horse kick," said Gwen.

The two stared at each other. And before he could stop her, Gwen picked up Strait's pistol, chambered a round and drew aims at various points in the room. She looked at the gun.

"The balance on this is off. And you really should get some lithium sights, Nemo. They do make a difference with night fire."

A bead of sweat appeared on Strait's forehead. "You handle that thing real good."

"Horses weren't the only thing I grew up with in Kentucky. My father and brothers were very active members of the NRA. I would've joined too, only it wasn't deemed ladylike by my parents."

"Hey, that's real good to know. I'm a member too." He breathed a sigh of relief when she set the safety, yet she still didn't put the gun down.

"So what is it?" she asked. "Drugs?"

"Look, baby, why don't we just have a drink and get to—"

The pistol came up and the safety went off. "I came here to screw you, Nemo, not to be screwed *with*. It's late and I'm starting to get tired. If you want any candy tonight, you better cut the bullshit."

"Okay, okay. Damn, you are something." He took a quick belt of his drink and wiped his mouth with his hand. "It's drugs, but not the kind you think. Prescription stuff with a kick twice that of morphine. No lab, no border problem. Just steal 'em or work a deal with a pharmacy assistant making eight bills an hour. This Oxy-contin stuff started rural. But I'm taking it to the big cities. About damn time us country folks got a piece of the pie. It's sweet."

"And you're using East Winds as your base and our trailers to move your product."

"Well, we've been distributing the drugs, mostly in pickup trucks, prearranged drop spots and even through the mail. Then I got the idea to use the horse trailers. We move horses across state lines all the time. And if the cops stop us for permits and papers on the trailers or the horses, the smell's gonna keep them away from where the stuff is, and I don't know of many dogs trained to sniff out prescription drugs. I've been shuffling men and trailers around so you and Billy wouldn't notice. The run we made to Kentucky was our biggest yet."

He raised his beer in salute, apparently to himself.

Gwen eyed his wound. "But not a complete success."

"Well, you do something illegal, you got to be prepared to face some risk."

"Did this risk come from your demand chain or maybe the cops?"

"Come on, now, honey, what does it matter?"

"You're right. I guess either way it means you've put us at risk. You were supposed to be working for us, Nemo, full-time."

"Well, a person's got to look out for himself. And it was too good a deal to pass up. And I ain't breaking my back on horse farms the rest of my life, okay?"

"I hired you for a specific purpose, because of your unique qualities and experience."

"Right, the fact that I got a damn good head on my shoulders, know folks who don't mind killing people and I can put together some pretty slick explosives. Well, I done that, baby." He ticked the points off his fingers. "A federal judge, a U.S. attorney, a defense counsel."

"Leadbetter, Watkins and Wingo. A judge with no backbone, a prosecutor with no guts and a defense counsel who would gladly defend his own mother's killer if the guy had enough money. I consider that we did society a service by ending their pathetic lives."

"Right, and we took out HRT and then suckered them into wiping out the damn Frees. Man, we tricked a veteran undercover into thinking that he'd come upon the drug operation to end all drug operations. We set that place up like something straight out of the movie *The Sting*." He looked at her and his features grew grim. "So I delivered for you, lady. So what I do on my time is *my* business. I ain't your damn slave, Gwen."

She kept the pistol pointed at him. "Web London is still standing."

"Well, hell, you said to keep him that way. Make him look like a coward. We got lucky when I found out the shrink he was seeing was an old acquaintance of mine from Vietnam. So everybody thinks Web's rotten to the core. This whole thing took a lot of planning, had a lot of risk, and let me tell you we executed it to damn near perfection, and you got it for pennies on the dollar 'cause I think what happened to your son stinks." He looked at her with a hurt expression. "And I don't even remember you saying thank you."

Her tone was businesslike, her expression unreadable. "Thank you. How much money have you made off the drugs?"

Surprised, he lowered his drink. "Why?"

"After what I've paid you and what we've sunk into this place, Billy and I are in the hole. They'll be coming to take his antique car collection pretty soon because we borrowed against that too. We could use some free cash flow, because we're going to be selling out and moving on too, especially since however you got that injury tells me that one day somebody's going to come knocking on our door with questions I don't have answers for. And frankly, I've had enough of Virginia hunt country. I'm thinking our next stop is a small island where it never gets cold and there are no damn phones."

"You want me to give you a share of *my* drug money?" he asked incredulously.

"Actually, demand would be more accurate."

Nemo spread his hands. "Well, I wasn't kidding, darlin', we got some good prices for those fine yearlings," he said in a very sincere tone.

She laughed at him. "This place never made any money before we bought it and it's not going to make any money now. Fine yearlings or not."

"Well, what do you want from me?"

"It's very simple. I want you to tell me how much you have made from the drugs."

He hesitated for a moment before answering. "Not that much, actually."

She raised the pistol and pointed it in his direction. "How much?"

"Okay, 'bout a million. There, you satisfied?"

She gripped the pistol with both hands and took very careful aim at his head. "Last chance. How *much*, Nemo?"

"Okay, okay, don't get your panties all twisted." He let out a deep breath. "Tens of millions."

"Then I want twenty percent. And then we go our separate ways."

"Twenty damn percent!"

"Wired to an offshore account. I'm assuming that a great businessman like yourself has set up some secret accounts somewhere to hide your millions. Excuse me, *tens* of millions."

"But look, I got expenses."

"Right, you probably paid your help off in pills, since most of them are too stupid to know better. And since running prescription drugs means low cost, lower risk, I imagine your profit margins are pretty nice, and I don't think you've been paying taxes on the income. And on top of that, you use our equipment that we paid for to move your product and also the manpower we're paying to work the farm to do it for you. So there was very little capital out of your pocket, and that makes for an even greater return on investment. And so, yes, I want my share. We'll call it rental fees for equipment and labor. And you're lucky it's only twenty percent." She slid a hand enticingly down her front. "In fact, you're fortunate that I'm in a generous mood right now."

Strait just shook his head. "What, was your dad a damn MBA too?"

"Billy and I have gotten the wrong end of the deal for long enough. At least we're still alive. My son only had ten years. Does that sound fair to you?"

"And if I say no?"

"I'll shoot you."

"In cold blood. A religious woman like yourself?"

"I pray for my son every day, but I can't say that my faith in God is absolute anymore. And I can always call the cops."

Nemo smiled and shook his head. "And tell them what? I'm dealing drugs? And oh, yeah, I killed a bunch of people for you? What's your leverage?"

"My leverage, Nemo, is that I don't give a damn anymore what happens to me. That's the best leverage of all. I have nothing more to lose because I've already lost everything."

"What about Billy?"

"He knows nothing about this. And now it's twenty-five percent."

"Well, hell."

Keeping the gun trained on him, she stood, unzipped her dress and let it fall to the floor, then stepped out of it completely naked.

"And here's the sweetener," she said. "Going once, going twice . . ."

"Deal!" said Nemo Strait as he held his arms out for her.

The sex was hard and left them both breathless. Strait collapsed on his back nursing his aching arm, while Gwen let her legs down and stretched them out. Strait had almost driven her right through the box springs and twisted her legs back into positions they were never meant to go. She would be hurting for a couple days, but it was a wonderful pain, something her husband had withheld from her for so long. And not just the sex, but also the love, which was far worse. In public he made a pretense of affection; in private he bothered not at all. He had never been abusive to her—on the contrary it was extreme diffidence coupled with irreversible melancholy; being ignored had never been so painful.

Gwen sat back against the headboard, lit a cigarette and blew fat rings to the ceiling. She lay there for about an hour and then reached over and put a hand on Strait's hairy chest, slowly rousing him.

"That was wonderful, Nemo."

"Uh-huh," he grunted back.

"Think you can do it again before sunrise?"

He opened one eye. "Damn it, woman, I ain't nineteen, and I got a bad wing. You get me some of that Viagra crap, maybe I can."

"In your line of work I'd think you'd be tired of pills."

He raised his head slightly and looked at her. "Hey, you wouldn't entertain the notion of moving to Greece with me, would you? It'd be a hell of a lot of fun. Guaranteed."

"I have no doubt, but my place is with my husband whether he knows it or not."

He slumped back down. "Yeah, I thought you'd say that."

"And you're really just looking to cut me out of my twenty-five percent."

"Okay, I give up."

"Nemo?"

"Yeah?"

"What do you think happened to Ernest B. Free?"

He sat up, used her cigarette to light his, then sat back next to her and put an arm around her.

"Hell if I know. That one's really got me stumped. I thought he'd be at the compound HRT hit, but he wasn't. Unless the Feds are lying, but why would they? They bag him, they'd be screaming that to the world. And the guy I used to set up the Frees also planted the drugs and other stuff down there, including some made-up files on the judge and two lawyers. He actually knows old Ernie, so he would've seen and recognized him if he was down there. Even if they had him real well hidden."

She ran her fingers through his hair. "Web and Romano are leaving soon."

"Yeah, I know. Good riddance. They're cramping my style, although it was pretty sweet driving fifty thousand stolen pills right out under the Feds' noses. But to tell you the truth, I kind of like those guys. If they found out what we've done, they'd try and put us on death row, but except for that, I wouldn't mind popping back a few brews with them from time to time."

Strait glanced over at Gwen, and the look on her face startled him.

"I loathe Web London," she said.

"Look, Gwen, I know what happened with your son and all—"

She exploded and beat the mattress with her fists. "It makes me sick to see his face. They're worse than the Frees. They come rushing in to save the world and innocent people start dying. Those people swore to me that once HRT was called in, no one else would die. And then they paraded around Web London as this big hero while my son lies dead in his grave. I'd love to shoot them all down myself."

Strait swallowed nervously at her wild tone and words as she knelt there on the bed, her hair in her face. Her lean, naked body, every muscle tensed, made her look like a panther about to spring. He eyed the gun where she'd put it on the nightstand and was ready to make a lunge for it, but she was quicker. She pointed the gun all around the room as Strait looked on nervously. Finally the barrel ended up pointed at Gwen herself. She looked down at it, as though she wasn't sure what it was. Her finger eased closer to the trigger.

"Then why don't you do it yourself?" he said, eyeing the gun. "Kill Web, I mean. Like you said, accidents happen. Especially on horse farms."

Gwen thought about this and finally dropped her angry look and smiled at him, putting down the gun.

"Maybe I will."

"Just don't blow it, though, 'cause we're in the home stretch."

She got under the covers, snuggled against him, kissed his cheek and put her hand under the sheet, rubbed him down there. "Just one more time," she said in a low, throaty voice, her gaze holding his. She slid the sheet off them both and looked down and smiled.

"My goodness, who needs Viagra, Nemo?"

"Woman, you are playing me like Charlie Daniels plays the fiddle."

Even without the potency drug, Strait managed to satisfy her one more time though it about killed him.

Later, as Gwen dressed, he watched her.

"Damn, you are a hellcat."

She zipped up her dress and held her shoes in one hand. Strait got up and started gingerly pulling his shirt over his bad arm. She looked at him. "Early morning plans?"

"Aw, you know how the life on a horse farm is, there's always something to do."

She turned to leave.

"You know, nothing personal or anything, Gwen, but it ain't good for a person to carry that much hate around. You just got to let it go at some point or else it'll ruin you. I was like that when my ex took the kids. At some point you just got to let it go."

She slowly turned and looked at him. "When you've seen your only child lying dead right in front of you with a bloody hole in his chest, Nemo, and then you lose the only other person you love because of it; when you've reached the lowest point of despair a person can reach and then watch yourself drop even lower—*then* you can come and talk to me about letting go of the hate."

51

Claire jerked up from a deep sleep that she had fallen into from exhaustion and despite her terror. She felt the fingers against her skin and she was about to strike out at her attacker when the voice made her stop.

"It's just me, Claire," said Kevin as he lifted off her blindfold.

There was no light, so Claire had to let her eyes adjust to the darkness. She looked down at Kevin, who was sitting next to her, his hands around the cuffs that held her to the wall.

"I thought you were tied up too."

He smiled and held up a small bit of metal. "I was. But I took this off one of the markers they give me to draw with. Picked the lock. I'm good with my hands."

"I can see that."

"Give me just one more minute and I get you loose too."

In less time than that, Kevin had her free. She rubbed her wrists and sat up, looked around and eyed the door. "I take it the door's locked?"

"Always has been. Maybe not now, if they think we chained up."

"Good point." She stood, taking a moment to get her balance after being off her feet for so long, a condition that was compounded by the darkness. She looked around again. "Anything we can use for a weapon, in case someone's on the other side of that door?" she whispered.

Kevin went over to the cot, turned it over on its side and unscrewed two of the metal legs. He kept one and handed the other to Claire.

"You hit 'em high and I hit 'em low," he said.

Claire nodded, without a lot of confidence, though. She wasn't sure she could hit anybody.

Kevin seemed to sense her trepidation, because he added, "We only hit 'em if they trying to hurt us, right?"

"Right," said Claire a lot more firmly.

They inched over to the door and tried it. It was locked. They listened intently for a bit yet could hear no one on the other side, even though the machinelike sounds were not as loud now. "I guess we're not getting out of here until they want us to," said Claire.

Kevin eyed the door and stepped back. "I ain't never noticed that before."

"What?"

"That the door hinges are on the inside."

Claire looked hopeful, but only for an instant. "But we'd need a screwdriver and hammer to get them out."

"Well, we got the hammer." He held up the metal table leg. "And right here is the screwdriver."

He went over to where the cuffs that had held Claire were attached to a bolt in the wall. With Claire's help, they finally managed to unscrew the bolt from the wall and Kevin slid off the cuffs. He held up one of the cuffs. "It got an nice edge to it, like a screwdriver."

"Good thinking again, Kevin," said Claire with considerable admiration. Here she was, feeling totally helpless, and Kevin was pulling one miracle after another out of his hat.

It took them some time and they kept stopping and listening for anyone coming, but the hinge pins finally came out. They were able to pry open the door and step through. It was dark here too, and they stumbled along, touching the walls of the narrow corridor for guidance. The smell of chlorine was very strong now. They were confronted with another locked door that Kevin was able to pick with his pen clasp. They encountered yet another door that, thankfully, was unlocked.

Claire took in a long breath, as did Kevin. He smiled at her. "Feels good to finally be outside."

"Well, let's get going before they come and lock us back up."

They moved past the covered pool, crept through the bushes and then down a winding grass path. As they neared the end of the path, Claire could see a building far up ahead. It was the mansion. She had glimpsed it on her visit. They were at East Winds Farm!

"Omigod," she exclaimed.

"Shhh," said Kevin.

She whispered into his ear, "I know where we are. I have friends who are here, we just have to get to them." The problem was that, in the darkness, it was hard to tell in which direction was the house that Web and Romano were using, even with the mansion as a marker.

"If they at the place where we been locked up, how you know they really your friends?"

"I just know. Come on." She took his hand and they made their way in what Claire thought was the direction of the carriage house. Long before they could reach it, however, both stiffened when they heard a vehicle coming. They ran back into the bushes and peered out. Claire's spirits plummeted. It was a truck, not the Mach or Romano's Corvette. She gasped when the truck pulled to a stop and several men with guns climbed out. Their escape had apparently been detected. She and Kevin ran deeper into the woods, such that Claire totally lost her bearings.

They finally stopped, caught their breath. Kevin looked around. "I ain't never seen so many trees in one place. Can't tell which way's out."

Claire breathed deeply, attempting to get her lungs and her nerves under control. She nodded. "I know." She studied the lay of the unfamiliar land and was attempting to make a decision on which direction they should go when they heard footsteps. Claire pulled Kevin to her and they squatted low in the underbrush.

The person was on the path and walked right past them, obviously unaware of Claire's and Kevin's presence. Claire peeked out. She didn't know Gwen Canfield and thus had no idea why a woman in a long red dress was walking barefoot through thick woods at this hour. Claire thought about calling out to her but finally decided against it. She had no idea who their captors were. This woman could be part of that group.

Once Gwen was out of sight, Claire and Kevin started moving again. They came to a darkened house, but that had a truck parked out front. Claire was debating whether to try and slip inside the place and use the phone to call the police when a man charged out of the house, jumped in his truck and roared off.

"I think that person just found out we got loose," she whispered to Kevin. "Come on."

They ran to the house. Claire had noted that in his haste the man had left the door open. They were about to go inside when they heard a sound that made Claire's stomach lurch.

"He's coming back," cried out Kevin. They raced back into the woods even as the truck bore down on them.

Pushing their way through the thick undergrowth, Claire quickly lost her shoes, and her and Kevin's clothes were being shredded by thorny vines and hard branches. They reached an open bit of ground, paused to catch their breath but took off running again when they heard the sounds of feet crashing through the underbrush.

They raced through to an open space and Claire saw a building loom up out of the darkness.

"Quick," she said to Kevin, "in there."

They climbed up on a loading dock and entered the Monkey House through a hole in the wall. Claire and Kevin looked around at the ruined insides of the place. Claire shivered when she observed the rusted cages. Kevin held his nose.

"Damn, it stinks in here," he said.

The sounds of men, and now the baying of dogs, were growing closer. "Over there," Claire said frantically. She climbed onto a box, boosted Kevin up and into a hole in the wall that probably once housed a ventilator fan. "Stay down and keep quiet," she told him.

"Where you going?"

"Not far," she said. "But if they find me, don't come out; whatever they say they'll do to me, don't come out. Do you understand?"

Kevin nodded slowly. "Claire," he said. She turned back. "Please be careful."

She smiled weakly, squeezed his hand and climbed back down. She looked around for a moment and then crept out through a gash in the rear wall. Once she was outside, the sounds of the dogs was even more terrifying. They must have given the animals something with her and Kevin's scent on it. She tore off a bit of her dress, grabbed a small rock, tied it inside the strip of material and threw it as far away from the Monkey House as she could. Then she ran off in the opposite direction. She reached the woods again, slid down an embankment and halted at the bottom. She looked around, trying to gauge the direction the sounds of men and dogs were coming from. Unfortunately, because of the topography, the noises were echoing all around. She forded a small creek, falling down halfway across and soaking herself. She struggled up and managed to scale a small embankment on the other side, then found herself on flat land. She was so tired now, part of her just wanted to lie here and wait for them to find her. Yet Claire pushed herself up and ran. When she reached another steep climb, she gripped a sapling and used it to thrust herself up. At the top she surveyed the land. Off in the distance she saw a light, and then another and another, all in pairs. A road. She took several deep breaths and took off at a steady jog. Her feet were torn and bleeding, but she didn't allow the pain to slow her down. She had to get help. She had to get help for Kevin.

The sounds of the men and dogs were gone now and she allowed herself the small hope that she might actually manage to succeed in escaping. She crawled the last few feet to the road and sat in the ditch for a moment, the tears spilling from her, partly from exhaustion, fear and having gained her freedom. She heard a car coming, stood and ran into the road, waving her arms and screaming for help.

At first it didn't appear the vehicle was going to stop at all. And Claire realized that she must look like some lunatic. But the vehicle finally slowed and then stopped. She ran to the passenger door and pulled it open. Her first sight was of Kevin sitting in the front seat, his mouth gagged, his arms and legs bound. The second sight was of Nemo Strait pointing a gun at her.

"Hey, Doc," he said. "You need a ride?"

He stretched his long body and then involuntarily shivered. The night had been a little cool and the dampness seemed to have settled into him. He wrapped the blanket tighter around him.

Francis Westbrook was not accustomed to camping out. What he was doing was about as close to camping as he was probably ever going to get, and he was not enjoying it. He drank some water and then edged his head out from his hiding place. The sun would be rising soon, he gauged. He hadn't slept particularly well; hell, he hadn't really slept since Kevin had disappeared. One lousy phone call, that was all he had been given. He had met with London, like they had told him to, and filled him in on the tunnels, again like they had told him to. He had undertaken a little unfinished business along the way with Toona, sure. Contrary to what Westbrook had told Web, he could abide skimmers and even those who used the product because if you didn't you wouldn't have anyone willing to come to work for you in the drug trade, it was as simple as that. But what he would never tolerate was a snitch. Macy had tipped him off to what Toona was doing and he had checked it out himself and found out Macy had been correct. So Toona was, appropriately enough, fish food. Sometimes life *was* fair, he thought.

Through the street grapevine he had learned that Peebles had been killed. The boy just didn't have what it took. But Westbrook had also learned, albeit too late, that Peebles had been orchestrating a takeover of his crew and consolidation of other crews in the area. That one had caught him off guard. He hadn't thought that old Twan had that in him. Macy had simply disappeared. That disloyalty had really ticked him off. Westbrook shrugged. Served him right for putting any trust in a white boy.

Now whoever had killed Twan might be gunning for him. Westbrook would just have to lie low and rely only upon himself until things worked out. Relying only on himself—it was just like old times. He had a couple of pistols, a few mags of ammo, about a thousand dollars in his pocket. He had abandoned the Navigator when he had come here, and the cops were still looking for him. Well, let them look. He had seen the Feds patrolling the place, but he had spent enough time dodging the cops to know how to hide even his very large carcass so that he blended right in with where he was. He had seen some strange things going on here. And he had heard the sounds of dogs barking off in the distance. The dogs were bad news. He had hunkered down farther into his hiding place and pulled over him a blanket he had covered with branches and leaves until the sounds had receded. As best as he could figure, London was still close by, and if London thought this place was important, then Westbrook did too. He checked his gun and settled back, took another drink of water, listened to the crickets and wondered what the new day would bring. Maybe it would bring Kevin.

Ed O'Bannon paced around the small, bare space. He hadn't smoked in years, yet he had gone through almost a pack in the last two hours. Discovery was something that he had always contemplated, but as time went on and things went smoothly, his fears had receded, even as his bank account had swollen. He heard someone coming and turned to the door. It was locked, and thus he was surprised when he heard the knob turning. O'Bannon backed away. When the man came in, he breathed a sigh of relief.

"Long time no see, Doc."

O'Bannon put out his hand and Nemo Strait shook it.

"I wasn't sure you were going to make it, Nemo."

"When have I ever let you down?"

"I've got to get going. The Feds are bottling the country up."

"Don't get yourself all bent out of shape. We got lots of ways for you to go and the planes, papers and the people to get you there." Strait held up a packet of documents. "Through Mexico to Rio and then on to Johannesburg. From there you got your option of Australia, New Zealand, lots of fugitives go there. Or maybe hit our old stomping grounds in Southeast Asia."

O'Bannon eyed the packet and breathed another sigh of relief. He smiled and lit another cigarette. "That seems like a hundred years ago."

"Hey, I'll never forget. You saved my ass after the Viet Cong screwed with my mind."

"Deprogramming, not so difficult for someone who knows what he's doing."

"Lucky for me you did," said Strait. He paused and grinned.

"And catching a little drug action on the side. That was a nice little side benefit for your practice."

O'Bannon shrugged. "Everyone was doing that back then."

"Hell, yes, they were, myself included, though it was just for my personal use."

"I have to hand it to you, when you looked me up with your idea of bugging my offices and selling the information on the streets, that was pure genius."

Strait grinned. "Well, the Feds got all these resources, we had to level the playing field a little bit. But it was a win-win. You got the info, I got folks who need that stuff to conduct their business, myself included. You make money, I make money and the Feds get the short end of the stick. What could be better?"

When Gwen had brought Strait in on her plan to exact revenge on the people involved with her son's death, he had started investigating both Hostage Rescue and Web London. Growing up on a horse farm just made a person methodical like that, Strait had long ago realized. You got all the information you could, formed a plan and executed that plan. Until he had been captured by the Viet Cong, Strait had been an excellent soldier, leading his company in and out of many hellish situations, and he had a chest full of medals to prove it, not that that had ever mattered to him. Then he discovered that the Ed O'Bannon he had known in Vietnam was the same O'Bannon treating Web London. That had given him the idea to both set up London and HRT because he knew firsthand what Ed O'Bannon could do with someone's mind. Initially, however, O'Bannon wanted no part of it. But when Strait had learned how many law enforcement people he had as patients, he had approached O'Bannon again and repeated his offer to bug the premises, sell the information to criminals and split the proceeds fifty-fifty with the good doctor. With that inducement O'Bannon had signed on immediately. The passage of years had not lessened the man's greed. Some of the bugged psychiatrist sessions had also provided Strait with all the information he needed to set up HRT. He had never told O'Bannon about his Oxycontin drug trade because the man no doubt would've wanted a cut of that too. And now Strait already had a partner in Gwen Canfield. Twenty-five percent, damn! But he had to admit, last night had been worth it.

Nemo said, "I was one surprised pup when you brought Claire Daniels to us. Although I guess I shouldn't have been. When you told me London was seeing her, I knew it'd be a problem down the road."

"I tried to get him to stay with me. But like I said, I couldn't push too hard without raising suspicions. I kept most of his file from her, of course. And you were the only ones I could turn to."

"You did the right thing. I can guarantee you this: She'll never testify against you in court."

O'Bannon shook his head. "It's hard to believe it's over."

"Well, we had us one sweet operation going."

"'Had' is right," O'Bannon said mournfully.

"I guess you got no love for our federal government either."

"After what I saw in Vietnam? No. And working for the Bureau in-house didn't do much to change that opinion."

"Well, I'm betting you got you a nice little nest egg to last you the rest of your days."

O'Bannon nodded. "I've been smart about it. Now I just hope I get to enjoy it."

"I want to thank you, Doc, for all your help. You did London perfect."

"With his background, believe me, he was an easy case. Didn't even need any drugs." He smiled. "The man trusted me. What does that say for the mighty FBI?"

Strait yawned and rubbed at his eyes.

"Late night?" asked O'Bannon.

"You could say that. Sort of burning the candle at both ends and in the middle too."

There was a quiet knock at the door.

Strait said, "Come on in." He looked at O'Bannon. "Here's your ride. This is my best guy. He'll take care of everything."

Clyde Macy walked in and stared first at O'Bannon and then at Strait.

"I go way back with this boy. Showed him the error of his ways, I guess, ain't that right?"

Macy said, "The old man I never had."

Strait laughed. "You got that right. If you can believe it, this boy infiltrated a black drug crew in D.C. Set 'em up to take the heat for what we did. One of 'em, dude named Antoine Peebles, was trying to take over this fellow Westbrook's turf. So Mace played along with this little plan, Peebles helped us when we needed it, and then Mace killed Peebles."

O'Bannon looked puzzled. "Why'd you do that?"

"Because I wanted to," said Macy, his remorseless eyes dead on O'Bannon. "It was a mission I put together for myself. And I successfully completed it."

Strait chuckled. "Then he made sure HRT and the Free Society shot it out. The man is invaluable. Okay, Mace, this is Ed O'Bannon, the friend I told you about." He handed O'Bannon the documents and slapped him on the shoulder and shook his hand.

"I meant what I said, Doc, you did right by us. Thanks again, and you make yourself one fun-loving fugitive from justice."

Strait turned and left. As he closed the door behind him, he heard the first muffled shot and then one more. Damn, that Macy was efficient. He'd taught the boy real well. He did have some faults, though. Macy's competition thing with the FBI was sometimes inconvenient. One of the concessions he had made to keep the boy happy had been pretty risky, but all in all Strait could not have pulled this off without Clyde Macy.

Strait had nothing against Ed O'Bannon, but loose ends were loose ends. And Nemo Strait didn't trust Ed O'Bannon or anyone else. Okay, one problem down, now just two more to go: Kevin Westbrook and Claire Daniels. They had escaped once, but they wouldn't have a chance to do it again. And then it was time to call it a career. The Greek islands were sounding better and better. Not bad for a boy who had grown up dirt poor and who had lived by his wits ever since. America was the land of opportunity indeed.

As he got in his truck, Nemo Strait wondered if there were any horse farms in Greece. He hoped not.

In the carriage house Web opened his eyes and looked around. He didn't hear Romano stirring, and when he glanced at his watch he knew why. It was not yet six. He got up, opened the window and inhaled an early morning breeze. He had slept unusually heavily.

He would be gone from here soon and part of him was glad about that and part of him wasn't.

What he was thinking about mostly, though, was Claire. His experience told him that there was very little chance that the woman was still alive. It was numbing, the thought of never seeing her again.

As he continued to gaze outside, he saw Gwen driving down the road from the mansion in a Jeep with its top off. She pulled into the cobblestone courtyard in front of the carriage house and got out. She was dressed to ride in jeans, boots and a sweater; her long hair gracefully framed her face. She wore no hat.

As she walked to the door, he called out. "Rent check's in the mail, call off the eviction."

She looked up, smiled and waved. "I thought we might go for one last ride." She looked at the lightening sky. "By the time we saddle up, it'll be the best time of the day to cruise the trails. You with me, Mr. London?" She flashed a smile that seemed to push away just about every concern Web had.

They saddled their mounts, Gwen on Baron and Web on a smaller roan horse named Comet. Gwen explained that Boo had an infected leg.

"Hope the big fellow will be all right."

"Not to worry, horses are very resilient," answered Gwen.

They covered a good deal of ground over about an hour and a half, and as they rode along all Gwen could think was that she had never killed anyone before. Yes, she had bluffed Nemo Strait the night before, but when it came down to it, could she do it? She looked at Web riding next to her and tried her best to cast him in the form of her worst enemy, her most terrifying nightmare. Yet it was difficult to do. For years she had dreamed about killing each and every member of this so-called heroic band of federal agents whom everyone had assured here were the best there was. That they would get her son and all the other hostages out alive; that was what they had drilled into her, until Gwen's fears had receded and her expectations had soared. It was like being told you had cancer but that it was absolutely curable, and you believed this until they closed your coffin and put you in the ground. Well, they had almost accomplished their goal of rescuing every hostage, allowing only her son to perish. And then she had watched, seething, as Web London's face graced newspaper, magazines, TV shows, his heroic deeds outlined in nauseating detail, ending with a medal given to him personally by the President himself. She could not think of his horrible injuries. She did not know of the grueling ordeals he had endured as he fought his way back on to HRT. Not that any of that would have mattered to her. All she could think of was that Web was alive and her son was dead. Some hero.

Yes, the sight of her son lying dead next to Web London had popped something in her brain. She could actually remember the crackle that seemed to go through every nerve in her body, like lightning had struck; and she had never been the same since. She had never had a day since when she did not see the bloody body of her son lying there on the ground. Nor could she ever forget the image of men in battle gear going in to rescue her son and somehow managing to bring everyone out alive except him. She looked back at Web and he slowly took on hues of black, of evil. He was the last man. Yes, she could kill him. And maybe her nightmare would finally be over.

"I suppose you and Romano will be leaving today?"

"Looks that way."

Gwen smiled and flicked at her hair. She kept a tight grip on her reins, for she felt her hand might start shaking. "Your good work done?"

"Something like that. How's Billy?"

"All right. He goes through moods, like we all do."

"You don't strike me as moody. You seem the type to roll with the punches."

"You'd be surprised sometimes."

"That was some party last night."

"Billy can really throw them. The Ransome brothers were not exactly what I expected."

"You don't believe that's their real name, do you?"

"Not for a second."

"When I first met them I thought they were gay. That is, until you walked into the room, and then their sexual orientation became pretty clear."

Gwen laughed. "I'll take that as a compliment."

They rode past the opening to the small glen where Gwen's chapel was.

"Aren't you going to the chapel today?"

"Not today." Gwen looked away from the opening in the trees. Today was not a day for prayer. While Web wasn't looking, though, she crossed herself. *Forgive me, God, for what I am about to do.* Even as she silently mouthed the words, she never really expected that prayer to be answered.

They reached a steep slope of earth that at the top was covered with trees. She had never taken Web this way before. Perhaps in the back of her mind she had known this day would come.

Gwen whipped up Baron and charged toward the slope, Web and Comet right on their heels. They galloped up the slope, Web almost nosing ahead of Gwen. When they got to the top, they stopped their mounts and gazed out over the countryside while the horses sucked in huge amounts of air.

Gwen looked at Web with genuine admiration. "I'm impressed."

"Hey, I had a great teacher."

"The watchtower is close by. The view's even better from there."

Web didn't tell her he'd already been up there with Romano when they had checked out the Ransomes' spread. "Sounds good."

They rode to the tower, tethered the horses to a wooden post and let them graze. Gwen led Web up to the top of the tower and they watched the sun rising and the woods coming to life down below.

"I guess it doesn't get much better than this," said Web.

"You'd think not," said Gwen.

He leaned against the belly-high wall and looked at her.

"Problems with you and Billy?"

"It's that obvious?"

"I've seen worse."

"Have you? What if I told you that you have no damn idea what you're talking about?" she said with sudden anger.

Web's tone remained calm. "You know, we've never really done that. Talked."

She avoided his gaze. "Actually, I've talked to you more than I do to most people. And I barely know *you*."

"Chitchat, maybe. And I'm not that hard to get to know."

"I'm not totally comfortable with you yet, Web."

"Well, we're running out of time. I don't think our worlds will come together again. But I guess that's a good thing."

"I suppose," she said. "I'm not sure Billy and I will be at East Winds much longer."

Web looked surprised. "I thought this was it for you two. Why go anywhere else? You may have your problems, but you're happy here. Aren't you? This is the life you wanted, right?"

She spoke slowly. "There's a lot of factors that go into the equation of happiness. Some are more apparent than others."

"I guess I can't help you there. I'm not an expert on happiness, Gwen."

She shot him a curious glance. "Neither am I." They stared at each other awkwardly for a long moment.

"Well, you deserve to be happy, Gwen."

"Why?" she asked quickly. For some reason, she actually wanted to hear his reasoning.

"Because you've suffered so much. It's only fair—that is, if anything in this life is fair."

"Have *you* suffered?" There was a harsh bite to her words, but she covered it quickly with a sympathetic expression. She wanted to hear that he had. But it couldn't come close to what she had endured.

"I've had my share of bad times. My childhood wasn't exactly the American dream. And my adulthood hasn't really made up for that."

"I always wondered why people do what you do. The good guys." She said this with a completely straight face.

"I do the things I do because they need doing and most people can't or won't do them. I'd much prefer that my occupation become obsolete, but I just don't see that happening." He looked down. "I never had a chance to tell you this, but I might not get another one." He drew in a long breath. "What happened in Richmond, that was about my first time as an assaulter, the guys who go in and get the hostages." He paused again. "After Waco the FBI was really spooked and got ultraconservative in those situations. I'm not saying that that was right or wrong, just that it was different. We wait around for the negotiators listening to all the lies on the phone. It seemed like it always took someone dying before they let us do what we do, and by then we were always playing catch-up. But those were the new rules and we had to play by them." He shook his head. "I knew something was up when the Frees broke off negotiations. I could feel it. I'd been a sniper for a lot of years, and watching things unfold all that time, you get a sixth sense for what's coming. You just do." He looked at Gwen. "I've never told you about this. Do you want to hear it?"

"Yes." Gwen said this so fast, she had no time to even think about it.

"Billy knows some of it. When he came to see me in the hospital."

"I'm sorry I never was able to."

"I didn't expect you to. I was stunned to see Billy, actually." Web seemed to take a few moments to compose his thoughts. While he did so, Gwen stared out at the foothills of the Blue Ridge in the distance. Now that she thought about it, she really didn't want to hear this, but she couldn't tell him no.

Web said, "We got to the gymnasium entrance clean. I looked through the window. Your son saw me. We made eye contact."

This clearly surprised her. "I didn't know that."

"Well, I never told anyone before, not even Billy. The time never seemed right."

"What did he look like?" she said slowly. Her pulse was pounding in her ears as she waited for his answer.

"He looked scared, Gwen. But he also looked stubborn, defiant. Not an easy thing when you're ten years old and facing a bunch of psychos with guns. I guess now I see where David got that spirit."

"Go on," she said in a small voice.

"I motioned to him to keep calm. I gave him the thumbs-up because I wanted him to stay cool. If he got spooked and reacted or something, they probably would have shot him instantly."

"Did he?"

Web nodded. "He was smart. He knew what I was trying to do. He was right with me, Gwen. With all that stuff going down, he was as brave as anyone could be."

Gwen could see that there were tears in his eyes. She tried to say something but found she couldn't speak. The terrible years of her life started to seem erased by his words.

"We were about to go in. Quiet, no explosive. We'd seen through the window where each of the Frees was positioned. We were just going to pop them all at once. We got our countdown and then it happened."

"What? What happened?"

"A sound from inside. It was like a damn bird or whistle, or alarm or something. It was loud, high-pitched and it couldn't have come at a worse time. The Frees were instantly on alert and when we came through the door, they opened fire. I don't know why they shot David, but he was the first to go down."

Gwen wasn't looking at Web now. Her gaze seemed frozen on the hills. *A whistle?*

"I saw the shot hit him." Web's voice was now very shaky. "I saw his face. His eyes." Web closed his and the tears dribbled out from under the lids. "They were still looking at me."

Gwen's eyes were filled with tears now too, yet she still wasn't looking at Web. "What did he look like then?"

He turned and stared at her. "He looked betrayed," Web said. He touched his damaged face. "My face, and the two bullet holes I have in my body, none of it hurt me more than the look on your son's face." He said again, "Betrayed."

Gwen was trembling so badly now that she had to support herself against the railing as the tears poured from her. Still, she couldn't look at him. *A whistle.*

"Maybe that's why I disobeyed orders when I joined the attack on the Frees." He stared at her. "It cost me my career, Gwen, I've been kicked out of the Bureau for it. But I'd do it again. Maybe it was my way of atoning for things. See, your son deserved better than I could give him. I live with that every day. And I'm sorry that I let him and you down. I don't expect forgiveness, but I just wanted you to know."

She said quietly, "We probably should get back."

Gwen went down first and walked over to Comet instead of Baron. She lifted the horse's foreleg. Every nerve in Gwen's body was now on fire, her pulse still banging in her ears. She could barely stand, but she had to do this, despite all that had just been revealed, she had to do this. She had waited long enough. She closed her eyes and then reopened them.

"Is there a problem?" asked Web.

She couldn't look at the man. "It seemed like he was a bit off in front. But it looks all right. I'll have to keep an eye on it."

She reached up and patted Comet's neck, and while Web wasn't looking she slipped the object she held in her hand under the saddle.

"Okay, now this is your big test," she said. "We're going to gallop hard down that slope toward those trees, but then you have to rein in the horse quickly because the path through the trees is too narrow to do much more than a walk. Understand?"

"I'm game." Web patted Comet's neck.

"I'm sure you are. Let's ride," she said with finality.

They both swung into the saddle and started toward the trees.

"You want to lead?" asked Web as he settled into the saddle.

"You go ahead. I want to watch Comet's leg—"

The horse bolted and Web wasn't ready for it. Comet accelerated and headed at full gallop down the slope and straight for the thick trees.

"Web!" screamed Gwen, and she rode after him, but she was subtly reining Baron in and was falling behind. As she watched, Web lost a stirrup and then almost fell off. The reins dropped from his hands and he clutched the saddle horn in desperation even as the ground between him and trees was closing fast. He didn't know it, but every bounce in the saddle was driving the small tack Gwen had placed under the saddle further into the horse's body.

Web never looked back. But if he had, he would have seen a woman suddenly in terrible conflict. Gwen Canfield wanted so desperately to see horse and rider slam into those trees. She wanted to see Web London die right in front of her, to be vanquished forever. She wanted to be released from the pain that had tormented her for so long. She just couldn't endure it anymore. She was beyond her limit. Something had to give. All she had to do was sit back. Instead she whipped up Baron and thundered after Web. Fifty feet separated Web from those trees, and Comet was living up to his name. At forty feet, Gwen slipped a little to the side of her horse. At thirty feet she started reaching out, poising her hand at just the right angle. They were twenty feet from the trees and now Gwen had thrown her fate in with Web's, for if she couldn't stop Comet, she and Baron would be hitting those trees too.

At ten feet she managed to lean far enough over to grab the reins. And she pulled with a strength that came from all the agony bottled up inside her for all those years, for she almost single-handedly pulled down a thousand-pound horse going at break-neck speed barely five feet from the tree line.

Breathless, she looked over at Web, who just sat there, slumped over. He finally glanced at her but still said nothing. And yet Gwen felt like the load of the collective misery of the world had been lifted from her shoulders. She had long envisioned it as akin to barnacles against her soul, impossible to remove; and yet now it had disappeared like sand in a breeze. And she marveled that finally letting go of all the hate could actually feel this wonderful. Yet the cruelty of life had not finished with her, because now Gwen's hate had been replaced with something even more corrosive: guilt.

52

When Gwen dropped Web off at the carriage house, she was strangely silent. He tried to thank her for saving his life, but she had cut him off and driven away. A very curious woman was Gwen Canfield. Maybe she blamed herself somehow for what had happened with Comet.

Yet at least Web had accomplished his goal of finally telling the woman what he had been holding in all these years. He thought about going up and telling Billy too, but maybe it would be better coming from Gwen—that is, if she bothered to tell her husband at all.

He went inside and Romano was eating breakfast. "You look a little whipped," commented Romano.

"Hard ride."

"So we are officially done here, aren't we? See, Angie's back and she is one ticked-off lady. I'm going to need to head home sometime and face the music."

"Yeah, I guess we're done here."

"Hey, Web, I'll race you back to Quantico, we'll find out what your Mach is really made of."

"Look, Paulie, the last thing I need is a speeding " He froze and Romano looked at him curiously.

"What? It's not the end of the world getting stopped for speeding. You flash your creds and they let you go. Professional courtesy."

Web pulled out his cell phone and punched in the numbers. He asked for Percy Bates, but he wasn't in.

"Where is he? This is Web London."

Web knew Bates's secretary, June, and she recognized his voice. "I know it's you, Web. I'm so sorry what happened."

"So Perce isn't around?"

"The truth is, he took a couple days off. The media relations people are going nuts. They wanted to bring you in to get some quotes, but Perce said no. Have you seen the TV or the papers?"

"No."

"Well, someone would've thought we killed the Pope by mistake, for the fuss people are making over what happened."

"Well, a lot of people did die, June."

"People with guns shooting at other people take that risk, Web," she said, steadfastly toeing the Bureau line. "Anyway, Perce said he had to get away for a couple of days. I know he felt horrible about what happened with you."

"I know, June, but maybe there's a silver lining in there for me."

"I hope so, I really do. Now, can I help you with anything?"

"Clyde Macy, he worked as a foot soldier for one of the local drug crews. I saw some speeding tickets in his file. I just wanted to find out exactly where he had gotten them and when."

"I'll have to call somebody for that, but it should only take a few minutes."

Web gave her his number to call back. As promised, she did shortly. She gave him the information and Web thanked her and clicked off. He looked over at Romano with a dumbfounded expression.

"What?" asked Romano as he swallowed the last bite of his pastrami-on-rye breakfast.

"Clyde Macy got three speeding tickets over a six-month period. Almost lost his license."

"Big whoop. So he drives too fast."

"Guess where he got all three?"

"Where?"

"All within one mile of the Southern Belle farm, and one of them less than a hundred yards from the entrance. The entrance was actually noted as a landmark on the Fauquier County police officer's report. That's why I picked up on it."

"Okay, so I guess I'm not going home to Angie today?"

"Sure you are. But tonight we're hitting the Southern Belle."

They packed their gear and got in their cars.

"You tell them we're heading out?" He motioned toward the mansion.

"They know." Web glanced back at the stone house and said quietly, "Good luck, Gwen."

As they were driving out, they saw Nemo heading toward them in his truck. He slowed and stopped. He looked, Web noted, very surprised to see him.

"Hey, you boys wanta have a beer?" Nemo asked.

The 'Vette's top was down, and Romano was seated up on the top of the seat back. "Give me a rain check on that."

Strait pointed at him and grinned. "You got it, Delta."

"Thanks for your help, Nemo," said Web.

"I guess you guys are closing up shop."

"Looks that way, but keep an eye out on the Canfields. Old Ernie is still at large."

"That I will."

As Web and Romano drove off, Nemo looked thoughtfully after them and then stared up ahead at the mansion. Apparently the hellcat had lost her nerve.

Angie Romano was not in a good mood. She'd had her sons by herself all this time and the trip to Bayou Country apparently had not been all that pleasant. Web tried to give her a friendly hug when he came to pick up Romano but stopped when she glared at him like she might break his arms if he tried.

And so the toughest member of Hotel Team and the sole survivor of Charlie Team fled the Romano household late at night and climbed in the Mach for what might well be their final gig together. Web had not told Romano about him resigning from the Bureau, but the word had gotten around and Romano had found out when he got back home. He had been really upset at Web for not telling him, but now he was more upset at the Bureau.

"You give 'em everything you got, and this . . . this is how they thank you. Man, it almost makes me want to go and work for a cartel in Colombia. At least you know where you stand with those guys."

"Forget it, Paulie. Hell, if things work out right, I'll start my own protection company and you can come and work for me."

"Yeah, and I'm wearing a bra under my Kevlar."

The men were prepared to go to war, with their .45s and MP-5s and body armor and even their .308 sniper rifles, because they weren't exactly sure what they would find at the Southern Belle. They couldn't call the Bureau in because they had nothing to tell them except some speeding tickets and a few conspiracy theories. But the bright side to Web's not being officially with the Bureau anymore was that sometimes an honest citizen could get into places and do things a cop never could. Web had had second thoughts about taking Romano, but when he voiced those concerns with Romano, the man had told him that if he didn't go, neither would Web, because Romano said he'd shoot Web in a place no man would want to be shot. And Web chose not to test Romano's resolve.

Web parked the Mach on a dirt road that ran along the property line between East Winds and the Southern Belle. As they were making their way through the dense forest, Romano was complaining. "These damn NV goggles are already giving me a headache. I hate the sons of bitches. They weigh a ton. And you can't even shoot anyone when you're wearing 'em. So what the hell good is that?"

"Then take the damn things off, Paulie, or stop complaining, before *you* give *me* a headache." However, Web slid his off too and rubbed his neck.

As forest sounds came at them from all directions, Romano said, "No snipers to cover our butt. I'm feeling kind of nervous and lonely, Web."

The man was just kidding, Web knew. There was nothing on this earth that really scared Paul Romano, at least that Web knew of. Well, except for Angie.

"You'll get over it."

"Hey, Web, you still haven't told me what you expect to find tonight."

"Whatever it is, it'll be more than we know right now." Without Bureau resources behind him, Web had not been able to send the FBI's fact-digging machine into gear to discover what it could about Harvey and Giles Ransome. He could have called Ann Lyle, but he just didn't want to talk to the woman right now. With him out of HRT, it would've been too hard because she would no doubt break down and then so would he.

The two men made their way forward through the trees until they could make out the buildings they had seen from the watchtower. Web signaled for Romano to hold up while Web crept forward. Web smiled when he reached the edge of the tree line. There was a lot of activity at the old Southern Belle tonight. A large truck was parked at one of the warehouse-style buildings, its ramp down. Men were carrying equipment out of the truck and Web's gaze went over each of them looking for weaponry, yet he saw none. A large crate on a forklift was being driven to the warehouse. When the door slid open, Web tried to make out what was going on inside, but he couldn't. All he could see were blinding lights before the door closed. Off to one side Web did see a horse trailer with a man working around it. From his angle Web couldn't see if there was actually a horse in it or not.

He spoke into his walkie-talkie and called Romano up to his position. Romano joined him a minute later and squatted next to him. He surveyed what Web had been looking at and whispered to him, "So, what's your take?"

"Could be anything from drugs to a chop shop, I don't know."

At that moment the door to the building opened and the forklift came back out. And that's when they heard the woman's scream. It rose higher and higher. Web and Romano looked at each other.

"Or maybe a slavery ring," hissed Romano.

They put their MP-5s on automatic fire and slid out from the woods. Each held the butt of his weapon against his right pec, the muzzle gripped with the index and forefinger.

They made it to the side of the warehouse without being seen. Web spotted a side door and pointed it out to Romano, who nodded. Web made more hand signals, telling Romano with his fingers in the special language of the assaulter what he was planning. In a way it was like the communication between a baseball pitcher and his catcher. However, the big difference was they would be facing something a lot more ominous than a Louisville Slugger.

Web tried the door. Surprisingly, it was unlocked. He opened it a notch farther. Then they heard the woman scream again in a garbled manner, like someone was driving something right down her throat.

Web and Romano burst in, guns ready, took in the scene in seconds. From the corner of his eye Web could see Giles Ransome sitting in a chair.

Web bellowed out, "FBI, on the floor, fingers interlocked behind your head. Do it or you're fucking dead." Romano would be proud, thought Web.

There were more screams from all corners as people hit the floor. Web caught a glimpse of somebody flying by to his left and he pointed his gun that way. Romano was charging straight ahead and then stopped.

Harvey Ransome was standing in the middle of what looked like a bedroom, a bunch of papers in one hand. On the bed were three beautiful, surgically enhanced and totally naked women and one young man, fully aroused.

"What in the hell is going on here?" yelled Harvey. When he saw that it was Web, he paled.

Web and Romano were looking around now and they both noted the film cameras, banks of lights, generators, grips, gaffers, cameramen, props and the mock bedroom suite, which was one of four different sets, the others resembling an office, the inside of a limo and, Web noted with surprise, a church. That's what this was? The Southern Belle was the cover for a porno studio? The screams had been ones of false ecstasy?

Web lowered his weapon as Harvey advanced toward him, script in hand.

"What the hell is going on, Web?"

Web shook his head clear and stared fiercely at the man. "You tell me."

"This is a perfectly legit business. You can look it up. We have all the permits and approvals." He motioned toward the naked people in the large bed. "And all of these people are professional actors, of legal age. You can check them out."

Romano went over to the bed, where Web joined him.

The young women looked at the two men with defiant expressions, while the man tried to hide under the sheet, his most prominent feature now long since deflated.

The women didn't make a move to cover themselves up in the presence of strange men with guns.

"All you people here voluntarily?" asked Romano.

"You bet, sugar," said one whose bosom was so large it almost covered her stomach. "Hey, you want a part in the movie? I'd like to show you how *voluntarily* I can be." When Romano blushed, the women all started laughing.

"You got a gun that big in your pants?" said another woman.

"Web?" Romano asked helplessly. "What do you want to do here?"

Giles joined his brother. "This is First Amendment territory, Web. You don't want to go there. We'll have you and the Bureau in court for years and we'll win."

"Well, if it's so legit, why the farm cover?"

"We have to think of the neighbors. If they knew what we were really doing, they could make trouble for us. They're wealthy and they know powerful people in public office who could make our lives miserable."

"All we want," said Harvey, "is to be left alone to create our art."

"Art?" said Web. He waved his hand at the naked bodies. "Is that what you call screwing on a two-bit set with inflated Barbie dolls? Art?"

One of the women stood up in all her naked and pumped-up glory. She barely looked twenty. "Who the hell do you think you are?"

"No offense, lady, but I'm just calling it like I see it."

"You don't know what the hell you're talking about."

"Yeah, you're right, and I bet your mommy's real proud of you too, isn't she?" said Web.

Harvey put a hand on Web's shoulder. "Listen, Web, we *are* legit. We pay our taxes, we do things by the book. Check it out; we're not going anywhere. My brother and I have been doing this for thirty years out in California."

"So why'd you move here?"

"We got tired of the LA scene," answered Giles. "And this is such pretty country."

Romano looked at the naked actors. "Well, I doubt they ever see it."

"We don't want trouble, Web," said Harvey. "Like I said, we'll win in court, but we don't want it to go to court. We're not hurting anybody here. And lots of people, whether they admit it or not, use our product. And not just flakes on the fringes, but moms and dads smack in the middle of mainstream USA. You know what they say, sex is good for the soul, and watching professional sex can be even better."

"It's fantasy, man, all fantasy," added Giles. "We just give people what they want."

"Okay, okay, I get your point." No wonder the two brothers had been all over Gwen Canfield. They probably wanted to hire her for their next production.

"Listen, is there anything we can do for you? You know, to say thank you for keeping this on the QT?" asked Harvey anxiously.

"Just so we understand each other, Harv, I *will* check you out. And if you're lying to me, or any of these 'actors' are underage, I'll be back. And if you're thinking of sneaking out in the meantime, don't try, because we'll have people posted."

"All right. I guess that's fair."

"Oh, and there is something you can do for me."

"Just name it."

"Stop flying your aircraft over East Winds. It's bothering some friends of mine."

Harvey put out his hand. "You have my word."

Web didn't shake his hand. Instead he looked at the young women. "And you ladies have my sympathy."

Romano and Web made their way out, laughter following in their wake.

"Gee," said Romano, "I'd call that mission a sterling success."

"Shut up, Paulie."

As they were heading back to the woods, Web saw the same man standing by the horse trailer that he had observed earlier. Web walked over. The fellow was dressed like a farmhand. He looked alarmed when he saw their guns until Romano flashed his badge.

"Look, I don't want any trouble," said the man, who looked to be about fifty. "Serves me right, though, for hiring on to this outfit."

"I guess you help provide the legitimate cover."

The man looked toward the warehouse—or, as Web now knew, film soundstage. "Lots of things need covering up around here. If my poor wife were still with us, she'd skin me alive, but they're paying twice the going rate."

"That should've told you something," said Web.

"I know, I know, but I guess everybody gets greedy and I been doing this work a long time. Too long, I suppose."

Web looked over at the trailer. There was a horse in it. Web could see the top of its head.

"You going somewhere?"

"Yep. Got a long ride. Taking that horse up for sale. Got to put on a pretense that we know what we're doing here. And that yearling is actually pretty nice."

Web went over to the trailer. "Really? He looks kind of small to me."

The man looked at Web like he was crazy. "Small? He's fifteen hands. That ain't small for a yearling."

Web looked inside the trailer. The top of it was a good eighteen inches above the horse's head. He looked at the man. "Is this a special trailer?"

"Special . . . what do you mean?"

"Sizewise. Is it particularly big?"

"Nope, it's your standard seven-foot Townsmand bumper pull."

"*This* is a standard Townsmand? And that yearling is fifteen hands high? You're sure?"

"As sure as I'm standing here."

Web shone his light around the interior.

"If this is a standard trailer, how come you don't have your tack boxes down there?" He looked at the man suspiciously and shone his light at the sides of the trailer's interior.

The man looked at where the light was shining. "Well, the first point, son, is you don't never put anything like that where a horse can nick its leg on 'em. A nicked leg can blow a sale."

"You can pad them," Web shot back.

"And the second point is . . ." He pointed up to the front of the trailer, where Web could see a large compartment filled with tack, medicine bottles, ropes, blankets and the like. "And the second point is, you got all that tack room right there, so why do you need to put something special in that might just tear up your horse's legs?" The man looked at Web like he really was insane.

Web wasn't paying attention because something was starting to seep into his brain that, if true, would put a whole new face on everything that had been happening. He fumbled in his pocket and pulled out some photos he had kept in an envelope, photos Bates had given him. Web picked one out and held it in front of Romano as he shone his light on it. "The guy who you gave the kid to that night?" he said. "Is this him? Think of him with a blond crew cut, not bald. I know it's hard because he was wearing shades. But try."

Romano studied the photo and then gaped at Web. "I think that's him."

Web immediately took off running for the tree line, Romano right behind him.

"What the hell's got into you, Web?"

Web didn't answer. He just kept running.

53

The door to the underground room opened and Nemo Strait walked in. Claire and Kevin were each cuffed to a large iron bolt in the wall, and their arms and legs were also bound with thick rope. Strait had ordered them gagged but not blindfolded. "You've already seen way too much, Doc," he had explained to Claire, "but it won't matter none." His chilling meaning had been absolutely clear.

His men poured in behind Strait and came at her and Kevin with blankets and more ropes.

"Help us, help us," Claire tried to scream out, but her words were barely audible because of the gag. She struggled vainly against the men. Kevin just stared silently at his captors, as though his expectation of death had finally been realized.

"Let's move it," said Nemo Strait. "We don't have all night, and we got a lot to do."

As they carried Kevin out, Strait affectionately patted the boy on the head.

Web looked in each of the back windows of Nemo Strait's house. The man's truck wasn't parked out front, but Web was taking no chances. Romano was checking the sides and the front. They hooked up and Romano shook his head. "Nothing. Place is empty."

"Not for long," said Web.

It took all of twenty seconds to pick the back door lock and they were inside. They methodically searched the place until they came to the man's bedroom.

"What exactly are we looking for, Web?"

Web was in the bedroom closet and didn't answer right away. He finally backed out with an old shoebox. "This might be a start."

He sat on a chair next to the bed and started going through the old photos. He held one up. "Here we go. Remember Strait said he was a guard at a juvenile detention center when he got back from Nam?"

"So?"

"So, guess who was an inmate at that same juvie center for putting a meat cleaver in his grandma's head? I saw the file when I met with Bates at WFO."

"Who are you talking about?"

"Clyde Macy. He's the guy in the photo I showed you, the guy who impersonated an FBI agent. Damn, I wish I'd shown you his photo before. Now I'm betting if we looked at the dates it'll show Macy and Strait were there at the same time."

"But Macy was with the Frees after that."

"And maybe Strait finds him and convinces him to come and work for him."

"But you said Macy was muscle for Westbrook."

"What Macy is, is a cop wannabe. I'm thinking he was undercover and was infiltrating Westbrook's organization as part of Strait's drug ring."

"Strait's drug ring!"

"Oxycontin. Horse trailers, the perfect way to move the stuff. The trailer at the Southern Belle was how a Townsmand is really set up. Strait had the one at East Winds put in with a false bottom that raised the floor so much a fifteen-hands-high yearling's head almost touched the roof. And he had storage boxes put in to carry even more drugs. And the speeding tickets? Macy wasn't going to the Southern Belle, he was coming here. And I bet he was the one who found out Toona was snitching for Cove. He used that information to set up Cove and us and then told Westbrook, who eliminated Toona."

"You think maybe Macy was the one who fired the shots at the Free compound and started the slaughter?"

"And planted the drugs there and all the other 'evidence' for us to conveniently find. And he probably stole Silas's truck. I'm betting he was also the one who shot Chris Miller outside of Cove's house. And Strait is ex-Army and maybe that's how he got hold of those machine guns, and he probably knows something about making bombs."

"But that means they were both tied in somehow to the hit on HRT. Why?"

All this time Web had been going through the photos until he stopped and pulled another one out. "Son of a bitch."

"What?"

Web turned the photo around. It was a picture of Strait in uniform in Vietnam. Next to him was a man that Romano didn't recognize, but Web certainly did. Even though the guy was much younger in the photo, he really hadn't changed all that much.

"Ed O'Bannon. He was the army shrink who helped Strait after he escaped from the Viet Cong."

"Jesus."

"And that means that they may have Claire, and even Kevin, around here somewhere. The farm would be a perfect place to hide them."

"But I still don't get it, Web, why would Strait and O'Bannon and Macy want to take out Charlie Team? It makes no sense."

Web thought hard, but that answer wasn't coming to him. At least it didn't until he glanced down and saw it. He put the shoebox aside and slowly reached down and plucked the object up from where it had fallen partially under the bed.

He held the anklet up and shone his light on it. Yet Web already knew to whom it belonged. He ripped the bedspread off and examined the pillows with his flashlight. It only took him a few moments to find the long blond hairs.

He looked at Romano in disbelief. "Gwen."

The trailer was backed up to the pool equipment room. The horse ramp was down and one of Strait's men had slid out the long piece of metal revealing the false bottom space that was easily big enough for a large shipment of pills . . . or the bodies of a woman and a little boy.

Strait was overseeing the transfer of Claire and Kevin to this compartment. They were struggling mightily and making noise—too much noise.

"Open the pool," he ordered. "Be easier if we drown 'em first. And cleaner than shooting them here."

The cover over the pool cranked back and then the men partially slipped the ropes and blankets off Claire and Kevin and started dragging them over to the water.

That's when the voice called out.

"What the hell are you doing?"

Strait and his men whirled around. Gwen was standing there, holding a pistol.

"Hey, Gwen, what are you doing up?" asked Strait innocently.

She looked at Claire and Kevin.

"Who are they, Nemo?"

"Just a couple of issues I got to deal with and then we can all ride off into the sunset."

"You're going to kill them?"

"No, I'm going to let them testify and put me on death row."

Several of Strait's men laughed at this. Strait drew closer to Gwen, never taking his eyes off her.

"Let me ask you a question, Gwen. You said you were going to take care of London. But I saw him ride off today and the man was breathing just fine."

"I changed my mind."

"Oh, that's good, you changed your mind. You mean you got cold feet. I figured. When you get right down to it, Gwen, you ain't got the stuff to do this. The killing. That's why you need men like me to do it for you."

"I want you to leave now. You and all your people."

"Well, I'm planning to do that."

"No, I mean without your *issues*."

Strait smiled and drew still closer to the woman. "Now sweetie, you know I can't do that."

"I'll let you have a head start of twelve hours before I release them."

"And then what? That's a lot of explaining to do. And you'll take the heat for it?"

"I'm not going to let you kill them, Nemo. Enough people have died already. And it's my fault. You were right, I should have let go of the hate a long time ago, but whenever I tried all I could see was my son, dead."

"See, the problem is, if I leave them here and they talk, the cops will never stop looking for me. But if I kill them, then when I exit stage left, nobody gives a crap. And that's a big difference, because once I settle down in a place, I like to stay there, and I'm not spending my retirement running from the FBI."

He glanced toward one of his men; he was circling around behind Gwen.

Gwen gripped her pistol and aimed it at Strait's head. "I'm telling you for the last time, leave!"

"And what about your cut of the drug money?"

"That was all your doing. And I don't want it. I'll take the heat for everything. Just go!"

"Damn, woman, what got into you, you see God or something?"

"Get the hell off my land, Strait, now!"

"Look out, Gwen!" screamed Web.

The voice caught all of them off guard, but the man circling behind Gwen still fired his gun, which missed because she had ducked down at Web's warning. The shot hit behind her.

Web's sniper rifle barked and the man fell dead into the pool, the chlorinated water instantly turning red.

Nemo and his men took cover behind the horse trailer and opened fire, while Gwen disappeared into the bushes

After they had left Strait's place, Web and Romano had gone to the equestrian center because Web wanted to check something; sure enough, he found the small wound on Comet's back. Gwen had plotted to kill him and then had a change of heart. Because of their talk? If so, Web wished he had had it years ago with the woman. He didn't have proof of it all, but it seemed clear to him that Gwen had enlisted Nemo and his men to exact her revenge for her son's death. Whether it was Billy Canfield's neglect that had driven her to Strait's bed, he didn't know.

They were headed to the mansion next when they had heard the noise at the pool area and come running in time to hear the exchange between Gwen and Strait, in time to hear Gwen admit that the people killed had been her fault, her revenge. Now they were in a full-fledged firefight with no way to call in reinforce-ments. And the big problem was that Claire and Kevin were caught in the middle.

It seemed that Strait realized this because he called out, "Hey, Web, why don't you come on out now? 'Cause if you don't, I'm gonna put a bullet into the woman and the kid."

Web and Romano looked at each other. Strait didn't know Romano was there. Romano turned and headed to the left. Web headed right and then stopped.

"Come on, Nemo, you've got no chance, and the cavalry's on the way."

"That's right, I'm a desperate man with not a damn thing to lose." He fired a shot very close to Claire's head where she and Kevin lay on the pool deck.

"Look, Nemo," said Web, "two more killings aren't going to help you any."

Strait laughed. "Hell, Web, they ain't gonna *hurt* me none either."

"Okay, Nemo, tell me the one thing I haven't been able to figure out," Web called out. "Why the kid switch in the alley?"

"What? You want me to incriminate myself?" Strait yelled back and laughed again.

"Look around, Nemo—I got all the evidence I need."

"So if I do like you say, you'll put in a good word for me with the judge, right?" Strait laughed again.

"Couldn't hurt."

"Well, Web, in my line of work you tend to congregate with some interesting folks. And one particular fellow had some right definite demands, and he's the sort of fellow you got to accommodate. This is definitely a fellow you got to keep happy, you know what I'm saying?"

"Clyde Macy?"

"Now, I ain't naming no names, Web. I ain't no squealer."

"Let me help you then. Macy is a wannabe cop. He's just itching to prove he's better. He was dying to dress like an FBI agent, waltz in and take the kid right out of our hands. Just to show himself that he could pull it off."

"Damn, Web, you'd make a good detective."

"But maybe you weren't as confident. You needed Kevin, and

you couldn't risk Macy not pulling it off and getting Kevin back. You had to use Kevin in the first place in that alley to throw suspicion on Big F, and you needed Kevin later as leverage over him. So you substituted the other kid for Kevin. That way, Macy gets to have his fun at the Bureau's expense, and if he fails you still have Kevin. Am I right?"

"Hell, I guess we'll never know."

"So where's the other kid?"

"Like I said, I guess we'll never know."

Web's walkie-talkie crackled. Romano was in position.

"Okay, one more chance, Nemo, you got five seconds to surrender."

Web didn't bother counting to five. He slipped his MP-5 to full auto and opened fire, strafing the horse trailer behind which Nemo and his men had taken cover.

Strait and his men dropped flat to the ground at the same time Romano came up behind them.

One of the men saw him and turned to fire and took two MP-5 rounds between his eyes for his trouble.

"Guns on the ground. Now!" ordered Romano.

Web saw it, but Romano didn't because his back was to it: a small bit of condensation that was rising into the air off in the woods. Condensation caused by the cold coming up from a gun barrel. It was a classic mistake by someone who knew something about fieldcraft and sniping, but not the small, critical details that really made the difference. As a sniper Web would use his breath to heat his barrel and eliminate the condensation.

"Six o'clock, Romano," he screamed.

But it was too late. The shot hit Romano at the base of his spine and the impact from the high-speed round knocked him down.

"Paulie!" yelled Web.

Another man rolled out and took aim at the fallen HRT, but Web dropped him with his .308. He wedged the MP-5 against his pec with one hand and pulled out one of his .45s with the other.

"Romano!"

He breathed a sigh of relief as Romano started to rise. While it had penetrated his armor, the slug could not get through Link, the third .45 he kept back there in a special holster.

Another shot hit near Web and he dropped to the ground even as

Romano threw himself into the bushes. Strait took this opportunity to race out and grab Claire and half carry, half drag her to the truck hooked to the trailer.

Web looked up and saw what Strait was trying to do. Web shot out the truck tires. Cursing loudly, Strait dragged Claire off into the darkness.

Web snagged his walkie-talkie. "Paulie, Paulie, you okay?" Several anxious seconds went by and then Romano answered. His voice was a little shaky, but he was the same old Romano.

"Whoever shot me doesn't know jack-shit about bullet drop over distance. Fired too low."

"Lucky for you. I didn't see the barrel condensation until it was too late. I'm betting it's Macy out there somewhere. Strait's got Claire. I'm going after them. Kevin Westbrook is still by the pool."

"I got things covered here, Web."

"You sure?"

"Hell, it's only four against one. Go!"

Web turned and raced after Claire and Strait.

Romano had lost his MP-5 and his sniper rifle was not going to be very efficient at such close quarters. He pulled out his .45s and, taking a page from Web's book, actually rubbed one of them for luck. Despite his bravado, four against one were not good odds. He could get three of them and still be undone by number four. And there was still the shooter who had nailed him to worry about. He squatted low and edged along the bushes that surrounded the pool area. Shots were fired, but he didn't fire back, because they were way off, and muzzle flashes told him where his adversaries were. He kept moving and watching. Each time a shot was fired, he duly noted it. These guys were amateurs, but even amateurs got lucky, especially with superior numbers. He crouched low and saw the kid by the pool. He wasn't moving and Romano was thinking that maybe one of the shots had found its mark. But then the kid raised his head slightly. Romano slipped on his NV goggles and now he could see what the boy's problem was. His legs were still tightly bound.

Romano kept moving, putting distance between himself and the enemy. He wanted to get some range so that he could use his rifle. He had his night scope on and all he would need was a sliver of head to work with. Reduce the enemy to three or maybe even one and then he would move in with his pistols. One on one, Romano would win every time.

His plan was textbook. Read their muzzle signatures. Keep moving. Outflank them. Then move in, pop one or two, the others would lose their nerve and give themselves away, maybe start running and he would use his sniper rifle, wait for them to enter the kill zone and then it would all be over.

A voice called out, "Hey, Romano, come on out now, and without the gun."

Romano said nothing. He was spending his time getting a fix on the exact location of that voice so he could silence it. He thought it was the farmhand he had dropped on his first day at the farm, but he wasn't sure.

"Romano, I hope you're listening to me. Because you got five seconds to come out or I'm going to put a bullet into the kid's head."

Romano muttered under his breath as he drew closer to the source of the voice. He had no desire to let the boy die, but if he came out of cover, the reality was that both he and Kevin Westbrook would die. Romano never played that game and his only course of action was to try and kill them all before they got to the boy, which was going to be pretty much impossible.

"I'm sorry, kid," he muttered under his breath as he moved forward and took up his firing position.

The man who had spoken was indeed the fellow Romano had knocked down at the equestrian center. He was crawling forward on his belly, holding his pistol. He stopped, silently counted to five and called out once more. "Last chance, HRT." He waited a moment, shrugged, stood and took direct aim at Kevin Westbrook's head from the cover of the bushes. The man was not a great shot, but this execution would not require a high level of skill.

All of the air left the man's body as the enormous man burst from cover and hit him so hard he landed about seven feet away and on the pool deck. The big man raced to the boy and swooped him up in one massive arm. Then Francis Westbrook turned and ran off into the night with his son, even as he fired his pistol back over his shoulder.

Another man jumped out from cover and took aim at Westbrook's broad back. He was about to fire when Romano came out from cover and shot him down. He didn't know that the large man was Francis Westbrook, but Romano wasn't going to sit back and let anyone take it in the back. The only problem was that he revealed his position and he took a round in the leg for being such a nice guy. Romano tried to drag himself off but soon found an array of guns pointed at him. He was hauled down to the pool deck and three men stood over him.

"Well, shit, HRTs ain't so hot after all," said one. That one started getting Romano worked up.

"Just shoot his ass," said another. Romano's face turned red and his hands turned to fists.

"I say we stick his head in the water and drown the mother, nice and slow."

Romano looked up and saw that this came from the gent whom Westbrook had drop-kicked on to the pool deck, the same guy Romano had floored his first day at East Winds. His big gut was still sucking in huge amounts of air and there was blood around his nose where he had skidded across the stone.

"What do you say to that, Romano?" the man asked, even as he prodded Romano in the side with his boot.

"Sounds good to me," Romano said. He exploded forward and laid his shoulder into the man's quivering gut and they both went into the water. Romano took a huge breath and then dragged the man under. The two men on the pool deck did what Romano thought they would. They fired into the water. But Romano and the other man were too deep for the bullets to do any damage.

One of the guys had a seemingly brilliant idea. He raced over and hit the button to close the pool cover. As it settled over Romano and the man he was still struggling with, Romano, far from being concerned, knew that now he had the means to actually survive this. He slipped out his knife and cut the man's throat. Blood filled the water. Romano then grabbed the body around the legs and pushed it up until he could feel the man's head slam against the cover, as though he were bursting to the surface for air. Then he heard what he expected to hear, the guns firing into the head. He lowered the body, moved his position and then lifted the body up again. Again the guns fired, sending little jets of propelled water by him on either side. Now, they no doubt thought both of them were dead. At least Romano hoped they did; in fact, he was counting on it to survive.

He lowered the body again and then let go of it. It slowly sank to the bottom of the pool to join the one already there, the man Web had shot earlier. Now Romano had to undertake the riskiest part of this plan. He let out most of his remaining air, floated to the top and hooked his arm into the filter opening as though he had been caught there after getting his head blown off. As the cover opened, he was really hoping these guys did not understand the physics of freshly killed bodies in water, namely that they sank rather than floated on the surface. If they opened fire on him now, he was dead. But they didn't. The cover dragged his body some and Romano didn't move a muscle. It wasn't time yet. When the hands reached down and pulled him out, he still didn't move. They laid him on the pool deck facedown. He could sense them on either side. And then he heard it. They all did. Sirens. Somebody had called the cops.

One of the men said, "Let's get the hell out of here."

That was the last thing he would ever say. Romano erupted to his feet and hit both men dead center of their chests with backward thrusts of the two knives he had hidden in both of his hands. The blades went in up to their hilts, piercing each of their hearts.

They stared at him even as they dropped into the water. Romano stood up straight, surveyed the battlefield, ripped off his shirt and used a small tree branch to put a tourniquet on his leg, fished Link, the pistol that had blocked the bullet from hitting his back, out of the water and held up the ruined gun

"Well, hell," he said.

54

Web was trailing Strait and Claire as best as he could. He was alternating with his NV goggles and his own eyes, but it was very dark here and even NVs needed some ambient light to work properly. He was relying more on his hearing than his eyes, actually, but he couldn't fire at anything based on that, because he could as easily hit Claire as Strait.

He approached the Monkey House, slowed his pace and finally stopped. The ruined building looked ominous during the day; now it was completely unnerving. The problem was, if Strait was inside and Web moved past without clearing the building first, Strait could rear-flank him.

Web kept a tight grip on his MP-5 and quietly moved forward. He entered the place from the south end and stepped over the debris that littered the former animal prison. Shafts of moonlight came through the holes in the roof as the clouds overhead moved past. The light eerily washed over the wrecked cages and the sight was a test even for Web's hardened nerves.

Moving through the space without making a sound was impossible and Web's gaze kept darting in all directions in hope that he would see something that would give him the instant he needed to save his and Claire's lives and end Strait's in the bargain. There was the issue of Macy being out there too, and that was troublesome because the man did have some tactical skill.

Web immediately sank to the floor as he heard a creak to his left. He slipped on his NV goggles and scanned the space grid by grid.

He looked overhead too because there was a catwalk up there. That's when the garbled scream rang out.

He rolled and the shot hit right where he had been lying. He came up, his gun ready to fire. That had sounded like Claire's voice warning him. He heard shuffling at the far end of the building and then feet running away. He was about to race after them when he saw the same thing he had seen before, gun barrel condensation. He dropped just before the gun fired, and the bullet hit one of the cages and ricocheted harmlessly into a wall.

Well, that was good to know—Macy, if that's who it really was, wasn't smart enough to realize his earlier error.

Web did a sweep of the space in the direction where the shot had come from with his MP-5, blowing junk in the air and rattling empty cages. When he stopped and put in a fresh clip he heard another pair of feet running away. He slipped out and took up the chase again grateful to be leaving the Monkey House behind.

He felt like he was closing in when Web sensed something to his left and hit the ground again. The shot smacked into a tree directly behind where he'd been standing.

Rifle shot, not pistol, he judged. It was Macy again, then, not Strait. He had probably dropped back again and was covering for his boss. "The wannabe against the real thing," Web said softly. "Well, bring it on."

As a sniper, Web would remain totally motionless when he was on duty. The rule was that in a standoff, the first man to move and give himself away died. Thus he could lie completely still while waiting to kill someone. He was able to slow down his pulse and even regulate the efficiency of his bladder so that he could go long intervals without having to urinate. He was like an anaconda lying in wait in the grass for a jaguar. When it came, the snake exploded, and no more jaguar.

As he lay there, Web wondered how Macy was able to track him as effectively as he had. That made Web start thinking about the equipment the guy might be carrying. Bates had given him an additional piece of information about the attack on the Frees' compound. Two .308 slugs had been dug out of the walls. If Macy was carrying the same ordnance that HRT used, maybe he was carrying other equipment similar to what Web was using. Web recalled the photo of Macy in his paramilitary regalia. All those elements definitely fit the profile of a wannabe.

Web slithered forward on his belly, making only minimal noise. He wanted to test something, and giving away his position seemed to be the best way to do it.

A shot hit close to him.

Okay, that confirmed that, thought Web. The guy had night optics too.

He slipped on his NV goggles and did a sweep of the area. That's when he saw it; only for an instant, but it was enough. It was just enough.

Clyde Macy was feeling good about his strategy. He knew that HRT members were very skilled, but he had always suspected they were also overrated. He had, after all, breached their perimeter at the Frees' compound. And he had shot one of them down at the pool area. He hadn't stuck around long enough to see Romano get back up. When Strait had grabbed Claire and run, Macy, ever the loyal lieutenant, had left to cover his boss's back. Strait had been good to him, taking him under his wing at the detention center. And when Macy had gotten out and strayed into the world of the Frees, Strait had tracked him down and made him see the light. The Frees were amateurs. The debacle in Richmond showed him that. And, Strait had pointed out, they don't pay you a dime, yet they expect you to help support them. And for what? Strait had pointedly asked him. For the privilege of associating with stupid people.

He had taken the sound advice and had worked with Strait for several years. The current gig had been the most lucrative. They had made a fortune with the drug running, and Macy had even gotten to set up the Free Society in the bargain. That and gunning down old Twan—it was all worth it. Now that the plan was disappearing as quickly as the sirens were heading their way, Macy had one more goal left. To kill London. That would prove his ultimate superiority. In a way, Macy had been training his entire adult life for this very moment.

He slipped on his NV goggles, fired them up and scanned the area where he had last seen London. The man was obviously losing it, moving around like that. He was overconfident and had suddenly found himself matched against a foe who was actually better than he was. And now it was time to finish it. Just as he thought this, he locked onto the green beacon blaring at him. For a second Macy was stunned, for he didn't know what it was. And then he realized it must be a reflection from London's night optics. He aimed, exhaled all his breath; muscle on muscle his finger slid to the trigger. He became absolutely motionless. And then he fired. The shot hit the beacon dead center and the light went out. It was only then that Macy realized his own night optics, turned on full power as they were, were probably giving off the same beacon. But one had to be looking through his own night optics to see the light, and he had just finished off London. He was just a split second quicker, and because of that he was alive and London wasn't. That's what it often came down to.

Before Macy could draw another breath, the bullet hit him squarely in the forehead. For a millisecond his mind didn't react to the fact that half of his head was now missing. Then the gun fell from his hands and Clyde Macy slumped to the dirt.

Web rose from behind a small berm about three ticks on the clock away from where he had propped up his goggles on a stump and turned them on full power. He hadn't had to rely on the green beacon coming from Macy's night optics. As soon as Macy fired at what he thought was Web's head, his muzzle flash had revealed his position. A second later, it was over. Final score: professional, one; wannabe, dead.

He didn't have time to reflect further on his victory because the crash of feet rushing through the underbrush made Web hit the ground and aim his .308. When the pair cleared the tree line and stepped into his kill zone, Web hesitated and then rose on his knees, his rifle pointed directly at the man's enormous chest.

"Put down the gun, Francis!"

Westbrook jerked and looked around in the darkness. Through his rifle scope Web could clearly see the giant push Kevin behind him, shielding the boy from this new threat.

"It's Web London, Francis. Put the weapon down. Now!"

"Stay behind me, Kev," said Westbrook as he edged away from the sound of Web's voice.

"Last time, Francis; gun down and then you. Or you'll be going down another way."

"I getting Kevin out of here, little man. That all I want to do. No problems, no problems."

Web aimed his shot at a tree branch ten feet above Westbrook's head. The limb was cleanly cut in two and fell behind them. That was the first warning shot Web had ever fired in his career, and he wondered why he had even bothered. Kevin yelled out, but Westbrook said nothing. He just kept backing up. Then he did something that surprised even Web. He dropped his gun, knelt down and pulled Kevin up on his back. At first Web thought he was going to use Kevin as a shield, but Westbrook kept his body between Web and the boy. And he kept retreating.

"No problems, HRT. Just heading on out. Got things to do."

Web put another shot in the dirt to the left of him. A second warning. Shit. What the hell was wrong with him? Take the guy. He's a criminal. A murderer.

"No problems," said Westbrook again. "Just heading out, me and the kid."

Web aimed the next shot at the man's head. Then he realized that, with the ammo he was chambering he couldn't shoot Westbrook, because the bullet might pass through even the big man's thick body and hit Kevin. He could aim for the legs and drop the giant. He contemplated this and was aiming for the best possible location when he heard Kevin.

"Web, please, don't shoot my brother. Please. He just helping me."

Through his scope Web could see the boy's face next to his father's. He was holding on to the thick neck with both hands, his face filled with fear, tears running down his cheeks. Francis Westbrook looked calm, as though he were ready to face his death. Web recalled all the scars on the man's belly. He had obviously faced down death many times. He was 120 in whitey years. Web's finger slid to the trigger. If Web shot him in the leg, at least Kevin would be able to visit him in prison. It was the right thing to do. He was a cop. The man was a criminal. That's how things worked. No exceptions. No involved internal deliberations. Just shoot.

And yet Web allowed the pair to slide off into the woods and disappear. Web's finger moved away from the trigger. He screamed out, "Take him back to his home, Francis. And then you better run like hell, because I'll be coming for you, you son of a bitch."

55

Strait had heard the sirens too and he couldn't believe how quickly everything had gone to hell. Story of his life. He put his gun against Claire's head and pulled out her gag. He had already untied her so he wouldn't have to carry her.

"Afraid you're my ticket out of here, lady. And even that might not be enough. But just so you don't get your hopes up, if it looks like they're going to take me, I'm gonna shoot you."

"Why?" wailed Claire helplessly.

"'Cause I'm pissed off, that's why. 'Cause I worked my ass off for nothing, that's why. Now come on." He jerked her along as they made their way toward the equestrian center. There were trucks there that maybe, just maybe he could use to get out of here. They were approaching the center from the east and when he saw the peak of the big hay barn, Strait actually smiled. The farm was vast and its topography complex, and the cops would come in the front, no doubt, while Strait left from the rear. By the time they realized what was going on, he would have ditched the truck, gotten to the little safe house he had set up just for this contingency and then quietly disappeared, not with all his money, but with some of it.

They cleared a rise in the land and started down toward the horse stalls. The man came at them from out of the darkness. At first Strait thought it was Macy, but then the clouds moved past and the moonlight revealed Billy Canfield standing there, shotgun in hand. Strait instantly held Claire in front of him, the gun to her temple.

"Get out the way, old man, I ain't got no time for you."

"Why, because the cops are coming? You damn right they are, 'cause I called 'em."

Strait shook his head, a vicious look on his features. "And why'd you do that?"

"I don't know what the hell you been doing on my farm, but I do know you been sleeping with my wife. You must think I'm stupid or something."

"Well, somebody had to be screwing her, Billy, 'cause you sure as hell weren't."

"That's my business," roared Canfield, "not yours."

"Oh, it's my business, all right, and let me tell you it was some damn fine business. You didn't know what you were missing, old man."

Canfield raised his shotgun.

"Yeah, go on and fire, Billy, and with that scattergun you'll kill this nice lady too."

The men silently stared at each other until Strait completely realized his advantage.

Still using Claire as a shield, he pointed his pistol at Billy and prepared to fire.

"Billy!"

Strait looked over in time to see Gwen and Baron charging straight at him. He yelled, pushed Claire away and got off two quick shots. And then a bullet hit him in the head, instantly crumpling him.

Web had rushed out of the woods, quickly taken in what was happening and fired, killing Strait. Baron reared up and his front hooves came down on Strait's body.

Web quickly ran to Claire's side. He didn't have to check Strait. He knew the man was dead.

"Are you okay?" he asked Claire.

She nodded, then sat up and started crying. Web hugged her and then looked over and saw that Billy Canfield had shuffled over to a dark mass and then dropped to his knees. Web rose, and went over to him and looked at where Gwen lay on the ground, her chest covered by a pool of blood where at least one of Strait's shots had hit its mark. She looked up at them both, her breath coming in painful gasps. Web dropped to his knees, ripped open her shirt and saw the wound. He slowly covered her chest back up and looked at her. His expression obviously told her the truth.

She gripped his hand. "I'm so scared, Web."

Web knelt down closer as Billy just squatted there, staring at his dying wife.

"You're not alone, Gwen." That was all he could think to say. He wanted to hate this woman for what she had done to him, to Teddy Riner and all the rest. But he couldn't. And it wasn't just because she had saved his life, and Claire's and Kevin's. It was because Web didn't know what he would have done had he been in the woman's shoes, with all that rage and hatred building up over the years. Maybe he would have done the same; he just hoped not.

"I'm not scared of dying, Web. I'm scared I won't see David." Blood dribbled from her mouth and her words were a little garbled, but Web understood her.

Heaven and hell; that was it? With maybe purgatory not even an option.

Her eyes were starting to lose focus and Web could feel her grip loosening.

"David," she said weakly. "David." She looked to the sky. "Forgive me, Father, for I have sinned . . ." Her voice trailed off and she started sobbing.

Web assumed the woman would have crawled to her little chapel if she'd had the strength. He looked around for something, anything. And then it appeared in the form of Paul Romano walking stiffly over to them. He had driven off in the truck that had been hooked to the trailer by the pool, flat tires and all, thanks to Web.

Web rushed over to him, looked at his bloody leg. "You okay?"

"Just a scratch. Thanks for asking."

"Paulie, can you take Gwen's Last Confession?"

"What?"

Web pointed to where Gwen lay in the grass. "Gwen's dying. I want you to hear her Last Confession."

Romano took a step back. "Are you nuts? Do I look like a priest?"

"She's dying, Paulie, she won't know. She believes she's going to hell and she won't see her son."

"This is the same woman who masterminded wiping out Charlie Team and you want me to forgive her too for all the stuff she's done?"

"Yes, it's important."

"No way am I doing that."

"Come on, Romano, it won't kill you."

Romano looked to the sky for an instant. "How do you know?"

"Paulie, please, I know I have no right to ask you, but please, there's not much time. It's the right thing to do." He added in desperation, "God will understand."

The men stared at each other for a long moment and then Romano shook his head, limped over and knelt down beside Gwen. He took her hand in his, made the sign of the cross over her and asked her if she wanted to make her Last Confession. In weakening tones she said she did.

Finished, Romano rose and stepped away.

Web again knelt down beside Gwen. Her eyes were starting to glaze over, but for a brief moment she was able to focus on him and even gave him a weak smile as though to thank him, as with each breath she pumped more blood out of her body. The resemblance to the wound that had claimed her son was striking.

She clutched Web's hand with renewed strength and mouthed the words, "I'm so sorry, Web, can you forgive me?"

Web looked at the beautiful eyes that were growing dimmer by the second. In those eyes and the woman's features he saw a different image, that of a young boy who had trusted Web and who had then been failed by him.

"I forgive you," he said to the dying woman, and he hoped that somewhere, somehow, David Canfield was doing the same for him.

With that, Web stepped back and passed her hand over to Billy, who took it and knelt down beside his wife. Web watched as the chest rose and fell with greater and greater speed, and then, finally, it just stopped and the hand went limp. As Billy quietly sobbed over the body of his wife, Web helped Claire stand, put his arm under Romano to assist him, and the three started to walk off together.

The shotgun blast made them all jump. When they turned around, Billy was just then walking away from Strait's body, a curl of smoke rising from his shotgun.

56

For the next few days, the police and the FBI had poured all over East Winds, collecting evidence, wrapping up bodies and generally trying to figure everything out, although that, under even the best circumstances, would take some time. On a very somber note, the body of the boy who had been substituted for Kevin in the alley had been found in a grave deep in the woods at East Winds. They boy had been identified as a runaway from Ohio who had somehow had the great misfortune to run into Nemo Strait and Clyde Macy, no doubt with promises of some fast money.

As Web walked over the grounds, he could only shake his head at how quickly the pastoral setting of the farm had turned into a battlefield. Bates had cut short his vacation and was now here overseeing things. Romano was in the hospital getting his leg wound treated, but the bullet had hit neither bone nor major artery and the doctors predicted a quick and full recovery for someone as fit as Paul Romano. However, Web was certain that Angie was giving her husband a really hard time about almost getting killed. No doubt if someone was going to do Romano in, she wanted the honors.

As Web was walking up the drive to the mansion, he saw Bates coming out the front door. Billy Canfield stood on the porch and stared at seemingly nothing. The man had nothing left, Web thought. Bates saw Web and came over.

"Damn, what a mess," Bates said.

"Well, it's pretty clear now that it was a mess for a long time before this."

"Actually, you're right. We discovered records at Strait's house

and chased down his suppliers. The shot that killed Antoine Peebles was traced to a gun we found on Macy. Ed O'Bannon's turned
up too, in a Dumpster. Same gun killed him. And the rifle Macy
was carrying when you shot him, we matched that to the hits on
Judge Leadbetter and Chris Miller."

"A ballistics hat trick. Don't you just love it when the pieces start
falling into place?"

"Oh, and we also checked the tape of the shooting in Richmond
like you asked us to."

Web shot him a glance. "What'd you find?"

"You were right, there was something there. A phone ringing."

"It wasn't a ringing sound. It was more like a—"

"A whistle? That's right. It was a cellular phone. You know, you
can do just about any ringing sound you want. This one was a bird
whistle. Nobody ever thought much about it before. It's not like we
needed it as evidence to nail Ernie Free."

"Whose phone was it?"

"David Canfield's. A cell phone his mother had given him in case
of emergency."

Web looked stunned, even as Bates nodded sadly.

"It was Gwen calling him. He never answered. Probably the only
way she thought she could talk to him at that point. She just
picked the worst time to do it. She didn't know when HRT was going in, of course."

"So you think that's why the phones were the theme with the
killings?"

"Well, we'll never know for sure, but it looks that way. Maybe
she felt since she couldn't talk to her son, she wanted the phones
to be the last things those three guys ever saw. She also left a written statement that exonerated Billy. I guess Gwen was thinking
she wouldn't survive this, and she turned out to be right. We've
confirmed Billy's innocence from other sources. And we were also
able to nab a few of Strait's men who weren't at the farm that
night. They spilled their guts."

"Good. The man's suffered enough."

Bates shook his head. "Those guys confirmed that Gwen wasn't
in on the drug stuff. But I guess she found out later and wanted a
cut of it. God, and she looked so normal."

"She was normal," snapped Web. "But what happened to her son just took over her life." He sighed deeply. "You know, I have every reason to hate the woman, and the only thing I feel is sorry for her. Sorry that she couldn't have gone on. And part of me is thinking that if I had saved her son, none of this would have happened. That maybe I do a lot more harm than good."

"You can't carry that burden, Web. That's not fair to you."

"Well, life wasn't very fair to Gwen Canfield, now, was it?"

The two men walked along.

"Well, if you want some good news, you're reinstated with the Bureau, and if you so request, Buck Winters will give you a personal apology. And I'm counting on you so requesting."

Web shook his head. "I need some time to think about it, Perce."

"Buck's apology?"

"Coming back to the Bureau."

Bates gaped at him. "You're kidding. Come on, Web, you got your whole life tied up in it."

"I know, that's the problem."

"Well, take all the time that you want. After all this, the official word at the Bureau is that anything you want, you got."

"Gee, that's really nice of them."

"How's Romano?"

"Bitching and complaining, so he's just fine."

They stopped and looked back at the mansion, where Billy Canfield was just now turning and going into the house.

Bates pointed at him. "Now, there's the guy I really feel sorry for. He's lost it all."

Web nodded in agreement.

"You remember he said at the party, you keep your enemies out in the open, right where you can see them all the time?" Bates shook his head and looked around. "Well, his enemies were all around him and the poor guy never knew it.'

"Yeah."

"You need a ride back?"

"I'm gonna hang here awhile longer."

Bates and Web shook hands. "Thanks, Web, for everything."

Bates turned and walked off, while Web ambled along. And then he stopped, turned and looked in Bates's direction and then at the mansion. Web suddenly took off at a dead run to the stone house. He raced through the front door and down the stairs to the lower level, where he made a beeline for Billy's taxidermy room. It was locked. Web easily broke open the lock, went inside and quickly found what he was searching for. He carried the small jar in one hand and ran over to the gun cabinet. He found and hit the hidden latch and the door swung open. He pulled the flashlight off the wall and went inside. The mannequin peered back at him. Web hung the light on a peg on the wall so that the beam shone on the dummy. He took off the mannequin's hairpiece and carefully peeled off the whiskers. Next he opened the jar and carefully applied the paint remover to the face. It came off quickly. Web kept working away until the dark skin became white. With the hair and whiskers gone and the original skin color, Web stood back. He had seen the face so many times he would have recognized it in his sleep, and yet the few devices Canfield had used to disguise the face had worked to perfection. The man *had* been true to his word: He had kept his real enemy right where he could always find him.

Web knew he was looking upon Ernest B. Free for the first time since the shootout in Richmond.

"You know those I-talians I told you about?"

Web whipped around and there was Billy Canfield.

"Those I-talians," Billy continued, "who'd offer me all that money to move their stolen property? Remember I was telling you about them?"

"I remember."

Canfield seemed to be in a fog. He wasn't even looking at Web; he was staring at Ernie, maybe admiring his handiwork, Web thought.

"Well, contrary to what I told you, I accepted one of those offers and did a real good job for them. Then, after what happened to my son and all, they came to me one day about four months ago and offered to do me a favor in appreciation for all my years of loyalty to the family."

"Break Ernest Free out of prison and deliver him to you?"

"See, them I-talians are strong on family, and after what that man did to my son . . ." Billy stopped and rubbed at his eyes. "Anyway, Gwen probably showed you the little building what used to be a Civil War hospital at the farm."

"She did."

"Well, that's where I did him. I sent Strait and his men off to pick up some horses and put Gwen on a plane to see her family in Kentucky, so I could work uninterrupted. I used some of the same surgical instruments the folks back in the Civil War did." He went over and touched Free's shoulder. "Cut his tongue out first 'cause he was making such a ruckus. I expected that from a little worm like him. Love to make others suffer but can't take a drop of pain themselves. And then you know what I did?"

"Tell me."

Billy smiled proudly. "I gutted him just the way you would a deer. Cut his balls off first. See, I figured somebody what done something like that to a little boy, he can't call himself no man, so why would he need any balls? You see my reasoning?"

Web said nothing, but though Billy did not appear to be armed, Web's hand slipped to the grip of his pistol. Canfield did not seem to notice, or if he did, he didn't seem to care.

He cocked his head and surveyed his work from different angles. "Now, I'm not an educated man or anything, ain't read many books and such, but it seemed sort of poetic justice, I guess you'd say, that old Ernie B. Free would sit locked in a little room where slaves came through hunting for their freedom. But he ain't never gonna get his. Freedom, that is. And I'd know right where the son of a bitch was every minute of every day and show people to frighten them, like he was some little carnival freak." He looked at Web with the expression of a man no longer part of the sane world. "Don't that seem right to you?"

Again Web said nothing.

Billy stared at him and nodded. "I'd do it again, you know. In a minute I would."

"Tell me, Billy, what did it feel like, killing a man?"

Canfield studied him for a very long moment. "It felt like shit."

"Did it take any of the hurt away?"

"Not a damn drop. And now I got nothing left." He paused, his lips trembling. "I shut her out of my life, you know. My own wife.

Drove her to Strait's bed, ignored her. She knew I knew and I didn't say nothing about it, and that probably hurt more than if I'd beaten her for it. Right when she needed me most I wasn't there. Maybe if I had been, she could've got herself through this."

Web stared at him. "Maybe she could have, Billy. But now we'll never know."

They heard footsteps coming down the stairs and both men walked outside the room. It was Bates. He looked surprised to see Web.

"I forgot I needed to ask you a few more things, Billy." Bates looked at Web's pale face. "Are you okay?" He glanced at the stricken Billy and then back at Web. "What's going on here?"

Web looked at Billy and then said to Bates, "Everything's just fine. Why don't you ask Billy the questions later? I think he needs some time to himself." Web looked once more at Canfield, and then he put his arm around Bates and led him up the stairs.

They had just reached the main floor when they heard the blast. It was the fancy Churchill shotgun.

Web just knew.

57

Web dropped in on Kevin Westbrook two days after Billy Canfield killed himself. The boy was back with Jerome and his granny, thanks to his father. Part of Web hoped Francis "Big F" Westbrook made it to his retirement. At least he had left his son out of it. The grandmother, whose name Web learned was Rosa, was in wonderful spirits and had made them all lunch. As promised, Web had brought back the photo of Kevin and given it to Rosa, returned the sketchbooks Claire had taken previously to Kevin and also had a long talk with Jerome.

"Never saw the man," said Jerome of Big F. "One minute Kevin wasn't here, and now he is."

"How's the big cookie coming?" asked Web.

Jerome smiled and said, "It's in the oven and I'm about to turn on the heat."

Before Web left, Kevin gave him a sketch he had done. It showed a little boy and a large man side by side.

"Is that you and your brother?" Web asked.

"Nope, that's me and you," Kevin answered, and then gave Web a hug.

When he went back to his car, Web got quite a shock. On his windshield was a piece of paper. What was written on the paper made Web look in all directions, one hand on his pistol grip. Yet the man was long gone. He looked at the paper again. It simply read, "I owe you. Big F."

Some other good news was that Randall Cove had been found.

Some kids playing in the woods had come across him. He had been admitted into a local hospital as a John Doe, since he was carrying no identification. He had been unconscious for several days but had finally come to, and the Bureau had been notified. He was also expected to fully recover from his wounds.

Web went to see him after Cove was flown back to Washington. The man was covered in bandages, had lost a lot of weight and wasn't in the best of moods, but he was alive. That was something to feel good about, Web told him, and got a growl in return.

"I've been right where you are," Web told him, "except I was missing half my face. You got off easy."

"None of it feels easy. Not a damn bit."

"They say bullet wounds give you character."

"I got enough character to last the rest of my life, then."

Web had glanced around the room. "So how long you in for?"

"Hell if I know. I'm just the patient. But if they stick me with one more needle, somebody around here besides me is gonna be hurting."

"I don't like hospitals much either."

"Well, if I hadn't been wearing my Kevlar, I'd be at the morgue. Got two bruises on my chest I think are with me permanently."

"First rule of engagement, always place one in the head."

"I'm glad they didn't read your rules of engagement. So you broke the Oxy ring?"

"I'd say *we* did it."

"And you popped Strait?"

Web nodded. "And then Billy Canfield added a layer of buckshot. I don't think it was necessary, but it probably made him feel better. But then again, not that much better."

Cove nodded. "I guess I can see that." Web got up to leave. "Hey, Web, I owe you. I mean, I really owe you a lot."

"No, you don't. Nobody owes me a damn thing."

"Hey, HRT, you brought the whole house of cards down."

"What I did was my job. And to tell you the truth, I'm getting a little tired of doing it." The men shook hands.

"Take it easy, Cove. And when they cut you loose from here, let the Bureau give you a nice, safe desk job where the only nasty things people are shooting at you are memos."

"Memos? Sounds pretty boring."

"Yeah, it does, doesn't it?"

Web parked the Mach at the curb and walked up the sidewalk. Claire Daniels was not dressed in work clothes on this warm evening but rather a pretty sundress and sandals. The dinner was tasty, the wine a nice companion to the meal and the lights low and inviting, and Web had no idea why he was here as Claire sat across from him on the couch by the empty fireplace and tucked her legs under her.

"Fully recovered?" he asked.

"Not that I ever will be. Business-wise, I'm great. I thought this thing with O'Bannon would've wrecked my practice, but the phone hasn't stopped ringing."

"Hey, lots of people are in need of a good shrink—excuse me, psychiatrist."

"Actually, I've been taking a fair amount of time off."

"Different priorities?"

"Something like that. I did see Romano."

"He's out of the hospital now. Did you go to his house?"

"No. At my office. He came with Angie. I guess she told him about her seeing a psychiatrist. I'm helping them work through some issues together. They said they didn't mind you knowing."

Web took a sip of wine. "Well, everybody sure as hell has issues, don't they?"

"I wouldn't be surprised if Romano left HRT."

"We'll see."

She eyed him. "So, are you leaving HRT?"

"We'll see."

She put down the wineglass she'd been holding. "I wanted to thank you for saving my life, Web. That's one of the reasons I invited you for dinner tonight."

He tried to keep it light. "Hey, that's what I do, rescue hostages." But then his jovial look faded. "You're welcome, Claire. I'm just glad I was there." He looked at her curiously. "One of the reasons. So, what are the others?"

"Cueing on my body language? Reading between the lines?" She refused to catch his gaze, and Web could sense the nervousness underneath the joking manner.

"What is it, Claire?"

"I'm filing my report with the FBI soon. The report detailing what I believe happened to you in the alley when you froze. I wanted to discuss it with you first."

Web sat forward. "Okay, let me have it."

"I think O'Bannon gave you a posthypnotic suggestion. A command, an instruction of sorts to stop you from doing your job."

"But you said that you can't make someone do something they don't want to do, or wouldn't do normally, while under hypnosis."

"That's right, but there are always exceptions to such rules. If the person being hypnotized has a very strong relationship with the person doing the hypnotizing or that person is a powerful authority figure, the person may do something outside his normal range of action, even hurting someone else. The rationale may be that he feels this authority figure would not make anyone do something really wrong. It really comes down to issues of trust. And according to his notes, O'Bannon had established a trusting relationship with you."

"How do you get from trust to me freezing? Did he brainwash me? Like the *Manchurian Candidate*?"

"Brainwashing is something very different from hypnotizing. It takes time and is more of an indoctrination in which, through sleep deprivation, physical torture and mental manipulation, you change the personality of someone, make him wholly different, you break his will, his spirit and then you recast it as you wish. What O'Bannon did was build an order into your unconscious. When you heard the phrase 'Damn to hell' the reaction would start.

"The phrase was coupled with a safety valve of some sort, in case you heard the phrase or something similar to it elsewhere. In your case I think that safety valve was hearing communications over your wireless receiver when you were in the alley. Remember, that's when you said you actually froze. In O'Bannon's notes was a record of the Taser gun story you also told me. So the physical reaction he programmed in was one he knew would paralyze you. 'Damn to hell' plus communications over the radio would cause you to freeze, like you had been hit with a Taser dart."

Web shook his head. "And O'Bannon could do all that to my mind?"

Claire said, "I believe you to be a somnabule, Web, a person very susceptible to hypnotic suggestion. But you were almost able to override that suggestion. I'm certain you weren't supposed to be able to rise and walk in that courtyard. That was your pure will coming through, if that makes you feel any better. It was probably your most remarkable feat of the night, machine guns notwithstanding."

"And they used the phrase 'Damn to hell' to further incriminate the Free Society because it was the name of their newsletter."

"Yes. When I saw that on their website lots of things started making sense."

"That's a lot to take in, Claire."

She sat forward, her hands in her lap. Suddenly Web felt like he was back in her office, enduring another session. "Web, I have something else to tell you, something even more disconcerting. I should have told you before, but I wasn't sure you were ready to deal with it, and with everything that happened, well, I was just afraid to, I guess. Compared to you, I'm not very brave. Compared to you, nobody's brave, actually."

He ignored the compliment and simply stared at her. "Tell me what?"

She looked directly at him. "When I hypnotized you, I learned a lot more than that your father was arrested at your sixth-year birthday party." She added quickly, "But I couldn't tell you about it then. It would have been too traumatic."

"Tell me what? I don't remember a damn thing happening other than the party, and even that was a little fuzzy."

"Web, please listen very carefully to me."

He rose in his distress. "I thought you said I was in complete control. That it was a heightened state of awareness. Damn it, that's what you said, Claire. Did you lie to me?"

"It's usually that way, Web, but I had to do it differently. For a very good reason."

"The only *reason* I let you play around in my mind, lady, was because you said I'd be there running the show." Web sat down and clenched his hands together so they'd stop shaking. *What the hell had he told her while he was under other than the birthday fiasco?*

"There are times, Web, when I have to make the decision not to allow the patient under hypnosis to remember what occurred. I don't take that step lightly, and I certainly didn't do it lightly with you."

He had to admire her. In voice and manner, she was in control. He didn't know whether to lean across and kiss her or slap her face.

"What, exactly, Claire, did you do to me?"

"I gave you a posthypnotic suggestion." She looked down. "The same technique O'Bannon used on you to make you freeze in the alley, so you wouldn't remember some things from our hypnosis session."

"Great, Claire, I'm easy, I'm a frigging somnabule so it's easy to screw with my mind, right?"

"Web, I did what I thought was best—"

"Claire, just tell me!" snapped Web impatiently.

"It has to do with your mother and your stepfather. How he died, actually."

His face flushed for an instant. Web was suddenly fearful. He suddenly hated her guts. "I already told you how he died. He fell. It's in your precious little file. Go read it again."

"You're right. He did fall. But he wasn't alone. You told me about a pile of clothes near the attic entrance?"

He stared at her. "They're gone, they've been gone a long time."

"They were a great hiding place for a terrified and abused young man to hide."

"What? Meaning me?"

"A great hiding place at the behest of your mother. She knew that Stockton went up there to get his drugs."

"So what? I knew that too. I told you that when I *wasn't* hypnotized."

"You also told me about some rolls of old carpet." She added very quietly, "That they were as hard as iron."

Web stood and backed away from her like a frightened child. "Okay, Claire, this is officially nuts."

"She got you to do it, Web. That was her way of taking care of the abusive father."

Web sat down on the floor and put his head in his hands. "I'm not understanding any of this, Claire. None of it!"

Claire took a deep breath. "You didn't kill him, Web. You struck him with the carpet and he fell. But your mother—"

"Stop it!" he shouted. "Just stop it! This is the biggest bunch of bullshit I've ever heard."

"Web, I'm telling you the truth. Otherwise how would I know these things?"

"I don't know!" he shouted. "I don't know anything!"

Claire knelt down in front of him, reached out and took his hand. "After all you've done for me, I feel terrible about all of it. But please believe me that I only did it to help you. This was so hard for me too. Can you understand that? Can you believe that? Can you trust me?"

He stood so abruptly she almost fell backward in surprise. Web headed for the door.

She called after him. "Web, please."

He walked outside and she followed him, the tears falling freely from her now.

Web climbed in the car and fired up the Mach. Claire walked unsteadily down the sidewalk toward him.

"Web, we can't leave it like this."

He rolled down the window and looked at her even as Claire's eyes searched his.

"I'm going away for a while, Claire."

She looked bewildered. "Going away? Where?"

"I'm going to see my father. Why don't you analyze that one while I'm gone."

He gunned the car and drove off under a sky dominated by a gathering storm, the black Mach quickly vanishing into the darkness. Web glanced back once, his gaze catching Claire Daniels standing there, illuminated by the wash of light from her cozy house. And then Web looked ahead and kept going.

Acknowledgments

To my good friends Philip Edney and Neal Schiff at the FBI for all their help and counsel. Thanks for always being there for me.

Thanks to Special Agent W. K. Walker for his help and advice.

To Dr. Steve Sobelman for his invaluable assistance with the psychological aspects of the novel and for being a great guy and dear friend. Steve, we'd love you anyway, even if you weren't married to your fabulous wife, Sloane Brown.

To my wonderful friends Kelly and Scott Adams for all their help and advice with the equestrian and horse farm aspects of the novel, and for tramping through the snow with me over a couple thousand acres. Kelly, thanks also for teaching me to ride Boo. I'll be back for more!

To my new friend Dr. Stephen P. Long for help on the Oxycontin portion of the book. Steve, your comments were insightful and right on the mark.

To Lisa Vance and Lucy Childs for keeping my literary life straight.

To Art and Lynette for all they do for us.

To Steve Jennings for again reading every page with his eagle eye.

To Dr. Catherine Broome for patiently explaining complicated medical matters to me in a way even I could understand.

To Aaron Priest for all your great advice on this one. I owe you.

To Frances Jalet-Miller for another superb editing job. You outdid yourself this time, Francie. And to Rob McMahon for his very thoughtful comments.

To Deborah Hocutt for making my life so much better. And to her husband, Daniel, for designing an incredible website.

To Michelle for keeping our crazy world straight on course.

To all those wonderful souls at the Warner Books family, including Larry, Maureen, Jamie, Tina, Emi, Martha, Karen, Jackie Joiner and Jackie Meyer, Bob Castillo, Susanna Einstein, Kelly Leonard and Maja Thomas: You're the best.

And, finally, to my friend Chris Whitcomb, Hostage Rescue Team operator, who also happens to be a wonderful writer and one of the most extraordinary individuals I've ever met. Chris, I couldn't have done this novel without you. You went far beyond the call of duty in helping me and I will never forget it. I wish you every success in your writing career, you deserve it.

split second

David Baldacci
Published December 2003

DON'T BLINK your life might depend on it . . .

'He was the only one in the room who could see it. His attention stayed there for one beat, two beats, three beats, far too long. Yet who could blame him for not being able to pull his gaze away from *that*?'

When something distracts Secret Agent Sean King for a split second, it costs him his career and presidential candidate Clyde Ritter his life. What stole his attention? Why was Ritter shot? Where were the other detail leaders?

Eight years later Michelle Maxwell is on the fast track through the ranks of the Secret Service when her career is stopped short: presidential candidate John Bruno is abducted from a funeral home while under her protection.

The similarity between the two cases drives Michelle to re-open investigations into the Ritter fiasco and join forces with attractive ex-agent, King. The pair are determined to get to the bottom of what happened in those critical moments.

Meanwhile, high-ranking members of the legal system and key witnesses from both cases are going missing. King is losing friends, colleagues and clients fast and his ex-lover, Joan Dillinger, is playing curious games – she wants Sean back, but she also owes him for something . . .

AN EXTRACT FROM THIS STUNNING THRILLER FOLLOWS . . .

PROLOGUE

September, 1996

It only took a split second. Although, it seemed like the longest split second ever.

They were on the campaign trail at a nondescript hotel meet-and-greet in a place so far out you had to use long distance to reach the boonies. Standing behind his protectee, he had scanned the crowd, while his ear mike buzzed sporadically with unremarkable information. It had been muggy in the large room filled with excited people waving "Elect Clyde Ritter" pennants. There were more than a few infants being thrust toward the smiling candidate. He hated this because the babies could so easily shield a gun until it was too late. Yet the little ones just kept coming and Clyde kissed them all, and ulcers seemed to form in his belly as he observed this potentially dangerous spectacle.

The crowd drew closer, right up to the velvet rope on stanchions that had been placed as a line in the sand. In response, he had moved closer to Ritter. The palm of his outstretched hand rested lightly on the candidate's sweaty, coatless back, so that he could pull him down in an instant if something happened. He couldn't very well stand in front of the man, for the candidate belonged to the *people*. His catechism was set in stone: shake hands, wave, smile, nail a sound bite in time for the six o'clock news, then pucker up and kiss a fat baby. And all the time he silently watched the crowd, keeping his hand on Ritter's soaked shirt and looked for threats, he hoped in all the right places.

Someone called out from the rear of the space. Ritter answered the jibe back with his own bit of humor and the crowd laughed good-naturedly, or at least most of them did. There were people here who hated Ritter and all he stood for. Faces didn't lie, not for those trained to read them, and he could read a face, as well as he could shoot a gun. That's what he spent all his working life doing: reading the hearts and souls of men and women through their eyes, their physical tics.

He keyed on two men in particular, ten feet away, on the right. They looked like potential trouble although each wore a short sleeve shirt and tight pants with no place to house a weapon, which dropped them several pegs on the danger meter. Assassins tended to favor bulky clothing and small handguns. Still, he mumbled a few words into his mic, telling others of his concern. Then his gaze flitted to the clock on the back of the wall. It was 10:32 in the morning. Five more minutes and then they were on to the next town where the handshakes, the sound bites, the baby kisses and the face reading would continue.

His gaze had turned in the direction of the new sound, and then the new sight, something totally unexpected. Standing facing the crowd and behind the hard-politicking Ritter, he was the only one in the room who could see it. His attention stayed there for one beat, two beats, three beats, far too long. Yet who could blame him for not being able to pull his gaze away from *that*? Everyone, as it turned out, including himself.

He heard the bang, like the sound of a dropped book. He could feel the moisture on his hand where it had touched Ritter's back. And now the moisture wasn't just sweat. His hand stung, where the slug had come out the body and taken a chunk off his middle finger before hitting the wall behind him. As Ritter dropped, the split second moved into maximum overdrive akin to a comet going hell-bent and still taking a billion light years to get where it was actually going.

Shrieks from the crowd poured out and then seemed to dissolve into one long, soulless moan. Faces stretched into images one only saw in carnival fun houses. Then the blur hit him like the force of an exploding grenade as feet moved and bodies gyrated and the screams came at him from all directions. People pushed, pulled and ducked to get out of the way. He remembered thinking that there was no greater chaos than when swift, violent death knocks on the door of an unsuspecting crowd.

And the now ex-presidential candidate Clyde Ritter was lying by his feet on the hardwood floor shot right through the heart. His gaze left the newly deceased and was now on the shooter, a tall, handsome man in a tweed jacket and wearing glasses. The killer's Smith & Wesson .44 was still pointing at the spot where Ritter had been standing, as though waiting for the target to get back up so he could be shot all over again. The mass of panicked people held back the guards who were fighting to get through, so that he and the killer were the only ones at the party.

He pointed his pistol at the chest of the assassin. He gave no warning, called out not one constitutional right accorded the assassin under American jurisprudence. His duty now clear, he fired once, and then again, though the first time was enough. It dropped the man right where he stood. He never said a word, as though he had expected to die for what he'd done, and accepted the terms stoically like a good martyr should. And all martyrs left behind people like him, the ones who were blamed for letting it happen in the first place. Three men had actually died that day, and he had been one of them.

Sean Ignatius King, Born August 1, 1960 – Died September 21, 1996 in a place he had never even heard of until the final day of his life. And yet he had it far worse than the other fallen. They went tidily into their coffins and were forever mourned by those who loved them or at least loved what they stood for. The soon to be ex-Secret Service agent King had no such luck. After his death, his unlikely burden was to keep right on living.